Tim Haydock is the author of
lives in Devon, on the edge o

THE MAMMOTH BOOK OF
CLASSIC CHILLERS

THE MAMMOTH BOOK OF
CLASSIC CHILLERS

Edited by Tim Haydock

R

ROBINSON PUBLISHING
LONDON

First published in 1986 by
Robinson Publishing
11 Shepherd House
5 Shepherd Street
London W1Y 7LD

British Library Cataloguing in Publication Data
The Mammoth book of classic chillers.
  1. Horror tales, English
  I. Haydock, Tim
  823'.01'0816[FS] PR1309.H6

  ISBN 0-948164-25-5

Printed by Richard Clay (The Chaucer Press) Ltd

CONTENTS

ACKNOWLEDGEMENTS

The publishers are grateful to the following for permission to reprint the material in this volume: A. D. Peters & Co. Ltd. for *The Pipe-Smoker* by Martin Armstrong and *The Man Who Liked Dickens* by Evelyn Waugh; Curtis Brown Ltd. and Alfred A. Knopf Inc. for *Telling* by Elizabeth Bowen; The Society of Authors for *The Monkey's Paw* by W. W. Jacobs. Every effort has been made to trace copyright holders, but the publishers would be interested to hear from anyone not here acknowledged.

THE MAN WHO LIKED DICKENS
Evelyn Waugh

ALTHOUGH Mr. McMaster had lived in Amazonas for nearly sixty years, no one except a few families of Shiriana Indians was aware of his existence. His house stood in a small savannah, one of those little patches of sand and grass that crop up occasionally in that neighbourhood, three miles or so across, bounded on all sides by forest.

The stream which watered it was not marked on any map; it ran through rapids, always dangerous and at most seasons of the year impassable, to join the upper waters of the River Uraricuera, whose course, though boldly delineated in every school atlas, is still largely conjectural. None of the inhabitants of the district, except Mr. McMaster, had ever heard of the republic of Colombia, Venezuela, Brazil or Bolivia, each of whom had at one time or another claimed its possession.

Mr. McMaster's house was larger than those of his neighbours, but similar in character—a palm-thatch roof, breast-high walls of mud and wattle, and a mud floor. He owned a dozen or so head of puny cattle which grazed in the savannah, a plantation of cassava, some banana and mango trees, a dog, and, unique in the neighbourhood, a single-barrelled, breech-loading shotgun. The few commodities which he employed from the outside world came to him through a long succession of traders, passed from hand to hand, bartered for in a dozen languages at the extreme end of one of the longest threads in the web of commerce that spreads from Manáos into the remote fastness of the forest.

One day, while Mr. McMaster was engaged in filling some cartridges, a Shiriana came to him with the news that a white man was approaching through the forest, alone and very sick. He closed the cartridge and loaded his gun with it, put those that were finished into his pocket and set out in the direction indicated.

The man was already clear of the bush when Mr. McMaster

reached him, sitting on the ground, clearly in a bad way. He was without hat or boots, and his clothes were so torn that it was only by the dampness of his body that they adhered to it; his feet were cut and grossly swollen, every exposed surface of skin was scarred by insect and bat bites; his eyes were wild with fever. He was talking to himself in delirium, but stopped when Mr. McMaster approached and addressed him in English.

"I'm tired," the man said; then: "Can't go on any farther. My name is Henty and I'm tired. Anderson died. That was a long time ago. I expect you think I'm very odd."

"I think you are ill, my friend."

"Just tired. It must be several months since I had anything to eat."

Mr. McMaster hoisted him to his feet and, supporting him by the arm, led him across the hummocks of grass towards the farm.

"It is a very short way. When we get there I will give you something to make you better."

"Jolly kind of you." Presently he said: "I say, you speak English. I'm English, too. My name is Henty."

"Well, Mr. Henty, you aren't to bother about anything more. You're ill and you've had a rough journey. I'll take care of you."

They went very slowly, but at length reached the house.

"Lie there in the hammock. I will fetch something for you."

Mr. McMaster went into the back room of the house and dragged a tin canister from under a heap of skins. It was full of a mixture of dried leaf and bark. He took a handful and went outside to the fire. When he returned he put one hand behind Henty's head and held up the concoction of herbs in a calabash for him to drink. He sipped, shuddering slightly at the bitterness. At last he finished it. Mr. McMaster threw out the dregs on the floor. Henty lay back in the hammock sobbing quietly. Soon he fell into a deep sleep.

"Ill-fated" was the epithet applied by the Press to the Anderson expedition to the Parima and upper Uraricuera region of Brazil. Every stage of the enterprise from the preliminary arrangements in London to its tragic dissolution in Amazonas was attacked by misfortune. It was due to one of the early setbacks that Paul Henty became connected with it.

He was not by nature an explorer; an even-tempered, good-looking young man of fastidious tastes and enviable possessions, unintellectual, but appreciative of fine architecture and the ballet, well travelled in the more accessible parts of the world, a collector though not a connoisseur, popular among hostesses, revered by his aunts. He was married to a lady of exceptional charm and beauty, and it was she who upset the good order of his life by confessing her affection for another man for the second time in the eight years of their marriage. The first occasion had been a short-lived infatuation with a tennis professional, the second was a captain in the Coldstream Guards, and more serious.

Henty's first thought under the shock of this revelation was to go out and dine alone. He was a member of four clubs, but at three of them he was liable to meet his wife's lover. Accordingly he chose one which he rarely frequented, a semi-intellectual company composed of publishers, barristers, and men of scholarship awaiting election to the Athenæum.

Here, after dinner, he fell into conversation with Professor Anderson and first heard of the proposed expedition to Brazil. The particular misfortune that was retarding arrangements at the moment was defalcation of the secretary with two-thirds of the expedition's capital. The principals were ready—Professor Anderson, Dr. Simmons the anthropologist, Mr. Necher the biologist, Mr. Brough the surveyor, wireless operator and mechanic—the scientific and sporting apparatus was packed up in crates ready to be embarked, the necessary facilities had been stamped and signed by the proper authorities but unless twelve hundred pounds was forthcoming the whole thing would have to be abandoned.

Henty, as has been suggested, was a man of comfortable means; the expedition would last from nine months to a year; he could shut his country house—his wife, he reflected, would want to remain in London near her young man—and cover more than the sum required. There was a glamour about the whole journey which might, he felt, move even his wife's sympathies. There and then, over the club fire he decided to accompany Professor Anderson.

When he went home that evening he announced to his wife: "I have decided what I shall do."

"Yes, darling?"

"You are certain that you no longer love me?"

"*Darling*, you *know*, I *adore* you."

"But you are certain you love this guardsman, Tony whatever-his-name-is, more ?"

"Oh, yes, *ever* so much more. Quite a different thing altogether."

"Very well, then. I do not propose to do anything about a divorce for a year. You shall have time to think it over. I am leaving next week for the Uraricuera."

"Golly, where's that ?"

"I am not perfectly sure. Somewhere in Brazil, I think. It is unexplored. I shall be away a year."

"But darling, how ordinary ! Like people in books—big game, I mean, and all that."

"You have obviously already discovered that I am a very ordinary person."

"Now, Paul, don't be disagreeable—oh, there's the telephone. It's probably Tony. If it is, d'you mind terribly if I talk to him alone for a bit ?"

But in the ten days of preparation that followed she showed greater tenderness, putting off her soldier twice in order to accompany Henty to the shops where he was choosing his equipment and insisting on his purchasing a worsted cummerbund. On his last evening she gave a supper-party for him at the Embassy to which she allowed him to ask any of his friends he liked ; he could think of no one except Professor Anderson, who looked oddly dressed, danced tirelessly and was something of a failure with everyone. Next day Mrs. Henty came with her husband to the boat train and presented him with a pale blue, extravagantly soft blanket, in a suède case of the same colour furnished with a zip fastener and monogram. She kissed him good-bye and said, "Take care of yourself in wherever it is."

Had she gone as far as Southampton she might have witnessed two dramatic passages. Mr. Brough got no farther than the gangway before he was arrested for debt—a matter of £32 ; the publicity given to the dangers of the expedition was responsible for the action. Henty settled the account.

The second difficulty was not to be overcome so easily. Mr. Necher's mother was on the ship before them ; she carried a missionary journal in which she had just read an account of the Brazilian forests. Nothing would induce her to permit her son's departure; she would remain on board until he came ashore with her. If necessary, she would sail with him, but go into those forests alone he should not. All argument was unavailing with the resolute old lady who eventually, five minutes before the time of embarkation, bore her son off in triumph, leaving the company without a biologist.

Nor was Mr. Brough's adherence long maintained. The ship in which they were travelling was a cruising liner taking passengers on a round voyage. Mr. Brough had not been on board a week and had scarcely accustomed himself to the motion of the ship before he was engaged to be married; he was still engaged, although to a different lady, when they reached Manáos and refused all inducements to proceed farther, borrowing his return fare from Henty and arriving back in Southampton engaged to the lady of his first choice, whom he immediately married.

In Brazil the officials to whom their credentials were addressed, were all out of power. While Henty and Professor Anderson negotiated with the new administrators, Dr. Simmons proceeded up river to Boa Vista where he established a base camp with the greater part of the stores. These were instantly commandeered by the revolutionary garrison, and he himself imprisoned for some days and subjected to various humiliations which so enraged him that, when released, he made promptly for the coast, stopping at Manáos only long enough to inform his colleagues that he insisted on leaving his case personally before the central authorities at Rio.

Thus while they were still a month's journey from the start of their labours, Henty and Professor Anderson found themselves alone and deprived of the greater part of their supplies. The ignominy of immediate return was not to be borne. For a short time they considered the advisability of going into hiding for six months in Madeira or Teneriffe, but even there detection seemed probable, there had been too many photographs in the illustrated papers before they left London. Accordingly, in low spirits, the two explorers at last set out alone for the Uraricuera with little hope of accomplishing anything of any value to anyone.

For seven weeks they paddled through green, humid tunnels of forest. They took a few snapshots of naked, misanthropic Indians, bottled some snakes and later lost them when their canoe capsized in the rapids; they overtaxed their digestions, imbibing nauseous intoxicants at native galas, they were robbed of the last of their sugar by a Guianese prospector. Finally, Professor Anderson fell ill with malignant malaria, chattered feebly for some days in his hammock, lapsed into coma and died, leaving Henty alone with a dozen Maku oarsmen, none of whom spoke a word of any language known to him. They reversed their course and drifted down stream with a minimum of provisions and no mutual confidence.

One day, a week or so after Professor Anderson's death, Henty awoke to find that his boys and his canoe had disappeared during the night, leaving him with only his hammock and pyjamas some two or three hundred miles from the nearest Brazilian habitation. Nature forbade him to remain where he was although there seemed little purpose in moving. He set himself to follow the course of the stream, at first in the hope of meeting a canoe. But presently the whole forest became peopled for him with frantic apparitions, for no conscious reason at all. He plodded on, now wading in the water, now scrambling through the bush.

Vaguely at the back of his mind he had always believed that the jungle was a place full of food, that there was danger of snakes and savages and wild beasts, but not of starvation. But now he observed that this was far from being the case. The jungle consisted solely of immense tree trunks, embedded in a tangle of thorn and vine rope, all far from nutritious. On the first day he suffered hideously. Later he seemed anæsthetized and was chiefly embarrassed by the behaviour of the inhabitants who came out to meet him in footmen's livery, carrying his dinner, and then irresponsibly disappeared or raised the covers of their dishes and revealed live tortoises. Many people who knew him in London appeared and ran round him with derisive cries, asking him questions to which he could not possibly know the answer. His wife came, too, and he was pleased to see her, assuming that she had got tired of her guardsman and was there to fetch him back, but she soon disappeared, like all the others.

It was then that he remembered that it was imperative for him to reach Manáos, he redoubled his energy, stumbling against boulders in the stream and getting caught up among the vines. "But I mustn't waste my breath," he reflected. Then he forgot that, too, and was conscious of nothing more until he found himself lying in a hammock in Mr. McMaster's house.

His recovery was slow. At first, days of lucidity alternated with delirium, then his temperature dropped and he was conscious even when most ill. The days of fever grew less frequent, finally occurring in the normal system of the tropics between long periods of comparative health. Mr. McMaster dosed him regularly with herbal remedies.

"It's very nasty," said Henty, "but it does do good."

"There is medicine for everything in the forest," said Mr. McMaster; "to make you well and to make you ill. My mother was an Indian and she taught me many of them. I have learned others from time to time from my wives. There are plants to cure you and give you fever, to kill you and send you mad, to keep away snakes, to intoxicate fish so that you can pick them out of the water with your hands like fruit from a tree. There are medicines even I do not know. They say that it is possible to bring dead people to life after they have begun to stink, but I have not seen it done."

"But surely you are English?"

"My father was—at least a Barbadian. He came to British Guiana as a missionary. He was married to a white woman but he left her in Guiana to look for gold. Then he took my mother. The Shiriana women are ugly but very devoted. I have had many. Most of the men and women living in this savannah are my children. That is why they obey—for that reason and because I have the gun. My father lived to a great age. It is not twenty years since he died. He was a man of education. Can you read?"

"Yes, of course."

"It is not everyone who is so fortunate. I cannot."

Henty laughed apologetically. "But I suppose you haven't much opportunity here."

"Oh, yes, that is just it. I have a great many books. I will show you when you are better. Until five years ago there was an Englishman—at least a black man, but he was well educated in Georgetown. He died. He used to read to me every day until he died. You shall read to me when you are better."

"I shall be delighted to."

"Yes, you shall read to me," Mr.· McMaster repeated, nodding over the calabash.

During the early days of his convalescence Henty had little conversation with his host; he lay in the hammock staring up at the thatched roof and thinking about his wife, rehearsing over and over again different incidents in their life together, including her affairs with the tennis professional and the soldier. The days, exactly twelve hours each, passed without distinction. Mr. McMaster retired to sleep at sundown, leaving a little lamp burning—a hand-wove wick drooping from a pot of beef fat—to keep away vampire bats.

The first time that Henty left the house Mr. McMaster took him for a little stroll around the farm.

"I will show you the black man's grave," he said, leading him to a mound between the mango trees. "He was very kind to me. Every afternoon until he died, for two hours, he used to read to me. I think I will put up a cross—to commemorate his death and your arrival—a pretty idea. Do you believe in God?"

"I've never really thought about it much."

"You are perfectly right. I have thought about it a *great* deal and I still do not know . . . Dickens did."

"I suppose so."

"Oh yes, it is apparent in all his books. You will see."

That afternoon Mr. McMaster began the construction of a headpiece for the negro's grave. He worked with a large spokeshave in a wood so hard that it grated and rang like metal.

At last when Henty had passed six or seven consecutive days without fever, Mr. McMaster said, "Now I think you are well enough to see the books."

At one end of the hut there was a kind of loft formed by a rough platform erected up in the eaves of the roof. Mr. McMaster propped a ladder against it and mounted. Henty followed, still unsteady after his illness. Mr. McMaster sat on the platform and Henty stood at the top of the ladder looking over. There was a heap of small bundles there, tied up with rag, palm leaf and raw hide.

"It has been hard to keep out the worms and ants. Two are practically destroyed. But there is an oil the Indians know how to make that is useful."

He unwrapped the nearest parcel and handed down a calf-bound book. It was an early American edition of *Bleak House*.

"It does not matter which we take first."

"You are fond of Dickens ?"

"Why, yes, of course. More than fond, far more. You see, they are the only books I have ever heard. My father used to read them and then later the black man . . . and now you. I have heard them all several times by now but I never get tired ; there is always more to be learned and noticed, so many characters, so many changes of scene, so many words. . . . I have all Dickens's books except those that the ants devoured. It takes a long time to read them all—more than two years."

"Well," said Henty lightly, "they will well last out my visit."

"Oh, I hope not. It is delightful to start again. Each time I think I find more to enjoy and admire."

They took down the first volume of *Bleak House* and that afternoon Henty had his first reading.

He had always rather enjoyed reading aloud and in the first year of marriage had shared several books in this way with his wife, until one day, in one of her rare moments of confidence, she remarked that it was torture to her. Sometimes after that he had thought it might be agreeable to have children to read to. But Mr. McMaster was a unique audience.

The old man sat astride his hammock opposite Henty, fixing him throughout with his eyes, and following the words, soundlessly, with his lips. Often when a new character was introduced he would say, "Repeat the name, I have forgotten him," or, "Yes, yes, I remember her well. She dies, poor woman." He would frequently interrupt with questions ; not as Henty would have imagined about the circumstances of the story—such things as the procedure of the Lord Chancellor's Court or the social conventions of the time, though they must have been unintelligible, did not concern him— but always about the characters. "Now, why does she say that ? Does she really mean it ? Did she feel faint because of the heat of the fire or of something in that paper ?" He laughed loudly at all the jokes and at some passages which did not seem humorous to Henty, asking him to repeat them two or three times ; and later at the description of the sufferings of the outcasts in "Tom-all-alone" tears ran down his cheeks into his beard. His comments on the story were usually simple. "I think that Dedlock is a very proud man," or, "Mrs. Jellyby does not take enough care of her children." Henty enjoyed the readings almost as much as he did.

At the end of the first day the old man said, "You read beautifully, with a far better accent than the black man. And you explain better. It is almost as though my father were here again." And always at the end of a session he thanked his guest courteously. "I enjoyed that very much. It was an extremely distressing chapter. But, if I remember rightly, it will all turn out well."

By the time that they were well into the second volume, however, the novelty of the old man's delight had begun to wane, and Henty was feeling strong enough to be restless. He touched more than once on the subject of his departure, asking about canoes and rains and the possibility of finding guides. But Mr. McMaster seemed obtuse and paid no attention to these hints.

One day, running his thumb through the pages of *Bleak House* that remained to be read, Henty said, "We still have a lot to get through. I hope I shall be able to finish it before I go."

"Oh, yes," said Mr. McMaster. "Do not disturb yourself about that. You will have time to finish it, my friend."

For the first time Henty noticed something slightly menacing in his host's manner. That evening at supper, a brief meal of farine and dried beef eaten just before sundown, Henty renewed the subject.

"You know, Mr. McMaster, the time has come when I must be thinking about getting back to civilization. I have already imposed myself on your hospitality for too long."

Mr. McMaster bent over his plate, crunching mouthfuls of farine, but made no reply.

"How soon do you think I shall be able to get a boat ? . . . I said how soon do you think I shall be able to get a boat ? I appreciate all your kindness to me more than I can say, but . . ."

"My friend, any kindness I may have shown is amply repaid by your reading of Dickens. Do not let us mention the subject again."

"Well, I'm very glad you have enjoyed it. I have,

too. But I really must be thinking of getting back . . ."

"Yes," said Mr. McMaster. "The black man was like that. He thought of it all the time. But he died here . . ."

Twice during the next day Henty opened the subject but his host was evasive. Finally he said, "Forgive me, Mr. McMaster, but I really must press the point. When can I get a boat?"

"There is no boat."

"Well, the Indians can build one."

"You must wait for the rains. There is not enough water in the river now."

"How long will that be?"

"A month . . . two months . . ."

They had finished *Bleak House* and were nearing the end of *Dombey and Son* when the rain came.

"Now it is time to make preparations to go."

"Oh, that is impossible. The Indians will not make a boat during the rainy season—it is one of their superstitions."

"You might have told me."

"Did I not mention it? I forgot."

Next morning Henty went out alone while his host was busy, and, looking as aimless as he could, strolled across the savannah to the group of Indian houses. There were four or five Shirianas sitting in one of the doorways. They did not look up as he approached them. He addressed them in the few words of Maku he had acquired during the journey but they made no sign whether they understood him or not. Then he drew a sketch of a canoe in the sand, he went through some vague motions of carpentry, pointed from them to him, then made motions of giving something to them and scratched out the outlines of a gun and a hat and a few other recognizable articles of trade. One of the women giggled, but no one gave any sign of comprehension, and he went away unsatisfied.

At their midday meal Mr. McMaster said: "Mr. Henty, the Indians tell me that you have been trying to speak with them. It is easier that you say anything you wish through me. You realize, do you not, that they would do nothing without my authority. They regard themselves, quite rightly in most cases, as my children."

"Well, as a matter of fact, I was asking them about a canoe."

"So they gave me to understand . . . and now if you have

finished your meal perhaps we might have another chapter. I am quite absorbed in the book."

They finished *Dombey and Son*; nearly a year had passed since Henty had left England, and his gloomy foreboding of permanent exile became suddenly acute when, between the pages of *Martin Chuzzlewit*, he found a document written in pencil in irregular characters.

Year 1919.

I James McMaster of Brazil do swear to Barnabas Washington of Georgetown that if he finish this book in fact Martin Chuzzlewit I will let him go away back as soon as finished.

There followed a heavy pencil X, and after it : *Mr. McMaster made this mark signed Barnabas Washington.*

"Mr. McMaster," said Henty, "I must speak frankly. You saved my life, and when I get back to civilization I will reward you to the best of my ability. I will give you anything within reason. But at present you are keeping me here against my will. I demand to be released."

"But, my friend, what is keeping you ? You are under no restraint. Go when you like."

"You know very well that I can't get away without your help."

"In that case you must humour an old man. Read me another chapter."

"Mr. McMaster, I swear by anything you like that when I get to Manáos I will find someone to take my place. I will pay a man to read to you all day."

"But I have no need of another man. You read so well."

"I have read for the last time."

"I hope not," said Mr. McMaster politely.

That evening at supper only one plate of dried meat and farine was brought in and Mr. McMaster ate alone. Henty lay without speaking, staring at the thatch.

Next day at noon a single plate was put before Mr. McMaster, but with it lay his gun, cocked, on his knee, as he ate. Henty resumed the reading of *Martin Chuzzlewit* where it had been interrupted.

Weeks passed hopelessly. They read *Nicholas Nickleby* and *Little Dorrit* and *Oliver Twist*. Then a stranger arrived in the savannah, a half-caste prospector, one of that lonely order of men who wander for a lifetime through the forests, tracing the little streams, sifting the gravel and, ounce by ounce, filling the little leather sack of gold dust, more often than not dying of exposure and starvation with five hundred dollars' worth of gold hung round their necks. Mr. McMaster was vexed at his arrival, gave him farine and *passo* and sent him on his journey within an hour of his arrival, but in that hour Henty had time to scribble his name on a slip of paper and put it into the man's hand.

From now on there was hope. The days followed their unvarying routine ; coffee at sunrise, a morning of inaction while Mr. McMaster pottered about on the business of the farm, farine and *passo* at noon, Dickens in the afternoon, farine and *passo* and sometimes some fruit for supper, silence from sunset to dawn with the small wick glowing in the beef fat and the palm thatch overhead dimly discernible ; but Henty lived in quiet confidence and expectation.

Some time, this year or the next, the prospector would arrive at a Brazilian village with news of his discovery. The disasters to the Anderson expedition would not have passed unnoticed. Henty could imagine the headlines that must have appeared in the popular Press ; even now probably there were search parties working over the country he had crossed ; any day English voices might sound over the savannah and a dozen friendly adventurers come crashing through the bush. Even as he was reading, while his lips mechanically followed the printed pages, his mind wandered away from his eager, crazy host opposite, and he began to narrate to himself incidents of his home-coming—the gradual re-encounters with civilization ; he shaved and bought new clothes at Manáos, telegraphed for money, received wires of congratulation ; he enjoyed the leisurely river journey to Belem, the big liner to Europe ; savoured good claret and fresh meat and spring vegetables ; he was shy at meeting his wife and uncertain how to address . . . "*Darling*, you've been much longer than you said. I quite thought you were lost. . . ."

And then Mr. McMaster interrupted. "May I trouble you to read that passage again ? It is one I particularly enjoy."

The weeks passed ; there was no sign of rescue, but Henty endured the day for hope of what might happen on the morrow; he even felt a slight stirring of cordiality towards his gaoler and was therefore quite willing to join him when, one evening after a long conference with an Indian neighbour, he proposed a celebration.

"It is one of the local feast days," he explained, "and they have been making *piwari*. You may not like it, but you should try some. We will go across to this man's home to-night."

Accordingly after supper they joined a party of Indians that were assembled round the fire in one of the huts at the other side of the savannah. They were singing in an apathetic, monotonous manner and passing a large calabash of liquid from mouth to mouth. Separate bowls were brought for Henty and Mr. McMaster, and they were given hammocks to sit in.

"You must drink it all without lowering the cup. That is the etiquette."

Henty gulped the dark liquid, trying not to taste it. But it was not unpleasant, hard and muddy on the palate like most of the beverages he had been offered in Brazil, but with a flavour of honey and brown bread. He leant back in the hammock feeling unusually contented. Perhaps at that very moment the search party was in camp a few hours' journey from them. Meanwhile he was warm and drowsy. The cadence of song rose and fell interminably, liturgically. Another calabash of *piwari* was offered him and he handed it back empty. He lay full length watching the play of shadows on the thatch as the Shirianas began to dance. Then he shut his eyes and thought of England and his wife and fell asleep.

He awoke, still in the Indian hut, with the impression that he had outslept his usual hour. By the position of the sun he knew it was late afternoon. No one else was about. He looked for his watch and found to his surprise that it was not on his wrist. He had left it in the house, he supposed, before coming to the party.

"I must have been tight last night," he reflected. "Treacherous drink, that." He had a headache and feared a recurrence of fever. He found when he set his feet to the ground that he stood with difficulty; his walk was unsteady and his mind confused as it had been during the first weeks of his convalescence. On the way across the savannah he was obliged to stop more than once, shutting his eyes and breathing deeply. When he reached the house he found Mr. McMaster sitting there.

"Ah, my friend, you are late for the reading this afternoon. There is scarcely another half-hour of light. How do you feel ?"

"Rotten. That drink doesn't seem to agree with me."

"I will give you something to make you better. The forest has remedies for everything ; to make you awake and to make you sleep."

"You haven't seen my watch anywhere ?"

"You have missed it ?"

"Yes. I thought I was wearing it. I say, I've never slept so long."

"Not since you were a baby. Do you know how long ? Two days."

"Nonsense. I can't have."

"Yes, indeed. It is a long time. It is a pity because you missed our guests."

"Guests ?"

"Why, yes. I have been quite gay while you were asleep. Three men from outside. Englishmen. It is a pity you missed them. A pity for them, too, as they particularly wished to see you. But what could I do ? You were so sound asleep. They had come all the way to find you, so— I thought you would not mind—as you could not greet them yourself I gave them a little souvenir, your watch. They wanted something to take home to your wife who is offering a great reward for news of you. They were very pleased with it. And they took some photographs of the little cross I put up to commemorate your coming. They were pleased with that, too. They were very easily pleased. But I do not suppose they will visit us again, our life here is so retired . . . no pleasures except reading . . . I do not suppose we shall ever have visitors again . . . well, well, I will get you some medicine to make you feel better. Your head aches, does it not. . . . We will not have any Dickens to-day . . . but to-morrow, and the day after that, and the day after that. Let us read *Little Dorrit* again. There are passages in that book I can never hear without the temptation to weep."

THE CASE OF M. VALDEMAR
Edgar Allan Poe

OF course I shall not pretend to consider it any matter for wonder, that the extraordinary case of M. Valdemar has excited discussion. It would have been a miracle had it not —especially under the circumstances. Through the desire of all parties concerned, to keep the affair from the public, at least for the present, or until we had further opportunities for investigation—through our endeavours to effect this—a garbled or exaggerated account made its way into society, and became the source of many unpleasant misrepresentations, and, very naturally, of a great deal of disbelief.

It is now rendered necessary that I give the *facts*—as far as I comprehend them myself. They are, succinctly, these :

My attention, for the last three years, had been repeatedly drawn to the subject of Mesmerism ; and, about nine months ago, it occurred to me, quite suddenly, that in the series of experiments made hitherto, there had been a very remarkable and most unaccountable omission :—no person had as yet been mesmerized *in articulo mortis.* It remained to be seen, first, whether, in such condition, there existed in the patient any susceptibility to the magnetic influence ; secondly, whether, if any existed, it was impaired or increased by the condition ; thirdly, to what extent, or for how long a period, the encroachments of Death might be arrested by the process. There were other points to be ascertained, but these most excited my curiosity—the last one especially, from the immensely important character of its consequences.

In looking around me for some subject by whose means I might test these particulars, I was brought to think of my friend, M. Ernest Valdemar, the well-known compiler of the *Bibliotheca Forensica,* and author (under the *nom de plume* of Issachar Marx) of the Polish versions of *Wallenstein* and *Gargantua.* M. Valdemar, who has resided principally at Haarlem, N.Y., since the year 1839, is (or was) particularly noticeable for the extreme spareness of his person—his lower limbs much resembling those of John Randolph; and, also, for the whiteness of his whiskers, in violent contrast to the blackness of his hair—the latter, in consequence, being very generally mistaken for a wig. His temperament was markedly nervous, and rendered him a good subject for mesmeric experiment. On two or three occasions I had put him to sleep with little difficulty, but was disappointed in other results which his peculiar constitution had naturally led me to anticipate. His will was at no period positively, or thoroughly, under my control, and in regard to *clairvoyance*, I could accomplish with him nothing to be relied upon. I always attributed my failure at these points to the disordered state of his health. For some months previous to my becoming acquainted with him, his physicians had declared him in a confirmed phthisis. It was his custom, indeed, to speak calmly of his approaching dissolution, as of a matter neither to be avoided nor regretted.

When the ideas to which I have alluded first occurred to me, it was of course very natural that I should think of M. Valdemar. I knew the steady philosophy of the man too well to apprehend any scruples from *him*; and he had no relatives in America who would be likely to interfere. I spoke to him frankly upon the subject; and, to my surprise, his interest seemed vividly excited. I say to my surprise; for, although he had always yielded his person freely to my experiments, he had never before given me any tokens of sympathy with what I did. His disease was of that character which would admit of exact calculation in respect to the epoch of its termination in death; and it was finally arranged between us that he would send for me about twenty-four hours before the period announced by his physicians as that of his decease.

It is now rather more than seven months since I received, from M. Valdemar himself, the subjoined note:

My Dear P——,
  You may as well come now. D—— and F—— are agreed that I cannot hold out beyond to-morrow midnight; and I think they have hit the time very nearly.

                                                      Valdemar.

I received this note within half an hour after it was written, and in fifteen minutes more I was in the dying man's chamber. I had not seen him for ten days, and was appalled by the fearful alteration which the brief interval had wrought in him. His face wore a leaden hue ; the eyes were utterly lustreless ; and the emaciation was so extreme that the skin had been broken through by the cheek-bones. His expectoration was excessive. The pulse was barely perceptible. He retained, nevertheless, in a very remarkable manner, both his mental power and a certain degree of physical strength. He spoke with distinctness —took some palliative medicines without aid—and, when I entered the room was occupied in pencilling memoranda in a pocket-book. He was propped up in the bed by pillows. Doctors D—— and F—— were in attendance.

After pressing Valdemar's hand, I took these gentlemen aside, and obtained from them a minute account of the patient's condition. The left lung had been for eighteen months in a semi-osseous or cartilaginous state, and was, of course, entirely useless for all purposes of vitality. The right, in its upper portion, was also partially, if not thoroughly, ossified, while the lower region was merely a mass of purulent tubercles, running one into another. Several extensive perforations existed ; and, at one point, permanent adhesion to the ribs had taken place. These appearances in the right lobe were of comparatively recent date. The ossification had proceeded with very unusual rapidity ; no sign of it had been discovered a month before, and the adhesion had only been observed during the three previous days. Independently of the phthisis, the patient was suspected of aneurism of the aorta ; but on this point the osseous symptoms rendered an exact diagnosis impossible. It was the opinion of both physicians that M. Valdemar would die about midnight on the morrow (Sunday). It was then seven o'clock on Saturday evening.

On quitting the invalid's bedside to hold conversation with myself, Doctors D—— and F—— had bidden him a final farewell. It had not been their intention to return ; but, at my request, they agreed to look in upon the patient about ten the next night.

When they had gone, I spoke freely with M. Valdemar on the subject of his approaching dissolution, as well as, more particularly, of the experiment proposed. He still professed himself quite willing and even anxious to have it made, and urged me to commence it at once. A male and a female nurse were in attendance ; but I did not feel myself altogether at liberty to engage in a task of this character with no more reliable witnesses than these people, in case of sudden accident, might prove. I therefore postponed operations until about eight the next night, when the arrival of a medical student with whom I had some acquaintance (Mr. Theodore L——l), relieved me from further embarrassment. It had been my design, originally, to wait for the physicians; but I was induced to proceed, first by the urgent entreaties of M. Valdemar, and secondly, by my conviction that I had not a moment to lose, as he was evidently sinking fast.

Mr. L——l was so kind as to accede to my desire that he would take notes of all that occurred; and it is from his memoranda that what I now have to relate is, for the most part, either condensed or copied *verbatim*.

It wanted about five minutes to eight when, taking the patient's hand, I begged him to state, as distinctly as he could, to Mr. L——l, whether he (M. Valdemar) was entirely willing that I should make the experiment of mesmerizing him in his then condition.

He replied feebly, yet quite audibly, "Yes, I wish to be mesmerized"—adding immediately afterwards, "I fear you have deferred it too long."

While he spoke thus, I commenced the passes which I had already found most effectual in subduing him. He was evidently influenced with the first lateral stroke of my hand across his forehead; but although I exerted all my powers, no further perceptible effect was induced until some minutes after ten o'clock, when Doctors D—— and F—— called, according to appointment. I explained to them, in a few words, what I designed, and as they opposed no objection, saying that the patient was already in the death agony, I proceeded without hesitation—exchanging, however, the lateral passes for downward ones, and directing my gaze entirely into the right eye of the sufferer.

By this time his pulse was imperceptible and his breathing was stertorous, and at intervals of half a minute.

This condition was nearly unaltered for a quarter of an hour. At the expiration of this period, however, a natural although a very deep sigh escaped the bosom of the dying man, and the stertorous breathing ceased—that is to say, its stertorousness was no longer apparent; the intervals were undiminished. The patient's extremities were of an icy coldness.

At five minutes before eleven I perceived unequivocal signs of the mesmeric influence. The glassy roll of the eye was changed for that expression of uneasy *inward* examination which is never seen except in cases of sleep-waking, and which it is quite impossible to mistake. With a few rapid lateral passes I made the lids quiver, as in incipient sleep, and with a few more I closed them altogether. I was not satisfied, however, with this, but continued the manipulations vigorously, and with the fullest exertion of the will, until I had completely stiffened the limbs of the slumberer, after placing them in a seemingly easy position. The legs were at full length; the arms were nearly so, and reposed on the bed at a moderate distance from the loins. The head was very slightly elevated.

When I had accomplished this, it was fully midnight, and I requested the gentlemen present to examine M. Valdemar's condition. After a few experiments, they admitted him to be in an unusually perfect state of mesmeric trance. The curiosity of both the physicians was greatly excited. Dr. D—— resolved at once to remain with the patient all night, while Dr. F—— took leave with a promise to return at daybreak. Mr. L——l and the nurses remained.

We left M. Valdemar entirely undisturbed until about three o'clock in the morning, when I approached him and found him in precisely the same condition as when Dr. F—— went away—that is to say, he lay in the same position; the pulse was imperceptible; the breathing was gentle (scarcely noticeable, unless through the application of a mirror to the lips); the eyes were closed naturally; and the limbs were as rigid and as cold as marble. Still, the general appearance was certainly not that of death.

As I approached M. Valdemar I made a kind of half effort to influence his right arm into pursuit of my own, as I passed the latter gently to and fro above his person. In such experiments with this patient I had never perfectly succeeded before, and assuredly I had little thought of succeeding now; but to my astonishment, his arm very readily, although feebly, followed every direction I assigned it with mine. I determined to hazard a few words of conversation.

"M. Valdemar," I said, "are you asleep?" He made no answer, but I perceived a tremor about the lips, and was thus induced to repeat the question, again and again. At its third repetition, his whole frame was agitated by a very slight shivering ; the eyelids unclosed themselves so far as to display a white line of the bell ; the lips moved sluggishly, and from between them, in a barely audible whisper, issued the words :

"Yes ; asleep now. Do not wake me—let me die so !"

I here felt the limbs and found them as rigid as ever. The right arm, as before, obeyed the direction of my hand. I questioned the sleep-waker again :

"Do you still feel pain in the breast, M. Valdemar ?"

The answer now was immediate, but even less audible than before :

"No pain—I am dying."

I did not think it advisable to disturb him further just then, and nothing more was said or done until the arrival of Dr. F——, who came a little before sunrise, and expressed unbounded astonishment at finding the patient still alive. After feeling the pulse and applying a mirror to the lips, he requested me to speak to the sleep-waker again. I did so, saying :

"M. Valdemar, do you still sleep ?"

As before, some minutes elapsed ere a reply was made ; and during the interval the dying man seemed to be collecting his energies to speak. At my fourth repetition of the question, he said very faintly, almost inaudibly :

"Yes ; still asleep—dying."

It was now the opinion, or rather the wish, of the physicians that M. Valdemar should be suffered to remain undisturbed in his present apparently tranquil condition, until death should supervene—and this, it was generally agreed, must now take place within a few minutes. I concluded, however, to speak to him once more, and merely repeated my previous question.

While I spoke, there came a marked change over the countenance of the sleep-waker. The eyes rolled themselves slowly open, the pupils disappearing upwardly ; the skin generally assumed a cadaverous hue, resembling not so much parchment as white paper ; and the circular hectic spots which, hitherto, had been strongly defined in the centre of each cheek, *went out* at once. I use this expression, because the suddenness of their departure put me in mind of nothing so much as the extinguishment of a candle by a puff of the breath. The upper lip, at the same time, writhed itself away from the teeth, which it had previously covered completely ; while the lower jaw fell with an audible jerk, leaving the mouth widely extended, and disclosing in full view the swollen and blackened tongue. I presume that no member of the party then present had been unaccustomed to death-bed horrors ; but so hideous beyond conception was the appearance of M. Valdemar at this moment that there was a general shrinking back from the region of the bed.

I now feel that I have reached a point of this narrative at which every reader will be startled into positive disbelief. It is my business, however, simply to proceed.

There was no longer the faintest sign of vitality in M. Valdemar ; and concluding him to be dead, we were consigning him to the charge of the nurses, when a strong vibratory motion was observable in the tongue. This continued for perhaps a minute. At the expiration of this period, there issued from the distended and motionless jaws a voice—such as it would be madness in me to attempt describing. There are, indeed, two or three epithets which might be considered as applicable to it in parts ; I might say, for example, that the sound was harsh, and broken, and hollow ; but the hideous whole is indescribable, for the simple reason that no similar sounds have ever jarred upon the ear of humanity. There were two particulars, nevertheless, which I thought then, and still think, might fairly be stated as characteristic of the intonation—as well adapted to convey some idea of its unearthly peculiarity. In the first place, the voice seemed to reach our ears—at least mine—from a vast distance, or from some deep cavern within the earth. In the second place, it impressed me (I fear, indeed, that it will be impossible to make myself comprehended) as gelatinous or glutinous matters impress the sense of touch.

I have spoken both of "sound" and of "voice." I mean to say that the sound was one of distinct—of even wonderfully, thrillingly distinct—syllabification. M. Valdemar *spoke*—obviously in reply to the question I had propounded to him a few minutes before. I had asked him, it will be remembered, if he slept. He now said :

"Yes ; no ; I *have been* sleeping—and now—now—*I am dead*."

No person present even affected to deny, or attempted to repress, the unutterable shuddering horror which these few words, thus uttered, were so calculated to convey. Mr. L——l (the student) swooned. The nurses immediately left the chamber, and could not be induced to return. My own impressions I would not pretend to render intelligible to the reader. For nearly an hour we busied ourselves, silently—without the utterance of a word—in endeavours to revive Mr. L——l. When he came to himself, we addressed ourselves again to an investigation of M. Valdemar's condition.

It remained in all respects as I have last described it, with the exception that the mirror no longer afforded evidence of respiration. An attempt to draw blood from the arm failed. I should mention, too, that this limb was no further subject to my will. I endeavoured in vain to make it follow the direction of my hand. The only real indication, indeed, of the mesmeric influence was now found in the vibratory movement of the tongue whenever I addressed M. Valdemar a question. He seemed to be making an effort to reply, but had no longer sufficient volition. To queries put to him by any other person than myself he seemed utterly insensible—although I endeavoured to place each member of the company in mesmeric *rapport* with him. I believe that I have now related all that is necessary to an understanding of the sleep-waker's state at this epoch. Other nurses were procured, and at ten o'clock I left the house in company with the two physicians and Mr. L——l.

In the afternoon we all called again to see the patient. His condition remained precisely the same. We had now some discussion as the propriety and feasibility of awakening him ; but we had little difficulty in agreeing that no good purpose would be served by so doing. It was evident that, so far, death (or what is usually termed death) had been arrested by the mesmeric process. It seemed clear to us all that to awaken M. Valdemar would be merely to insure his instant, or at least his speedy dissolution.

From this period until the close of last week—*an interval of nearly seven months*—we continued to make daily calls at M. Valdemar's house, accompanied now and then by medical and other friends. All this time the sleep-waker remained *exactly* as I have last described him. The nurses' attentions were continual.

It was on Friday last that we finally resolved to make the experiment of awakening, or attempting to awaken him ; and it is the (perhaps) unfortunate result of this latter experiment which has given rise to so much discussion in private circles—

to so much of what I cannot help thinking unwarranted popular feeling.

For the purpose of relieving M. Valdemar from the mesmeric trance, I made use of the customary passes. These, for a time, were unsuccessful. The first indication of revival was afforded by a partial descent of the iris. It was observed, as especially remarkable, that this lowering of the pupil was accompanied by the profuse outflowing of a yellowish ichor (from beneath the lids) of a pungent and highly offensive odour.

It was now suggested that I should attempt to influence the patient's arm, as heretofore. I made the attempt and failed. Dr. F—— then intimated a desire to have me put a question. I did so, as follows :

"M. Valdemar, can you explain to us what are your feelings or wishes now ?"

There was an instant return of the hectic circles on the cheeks ; the tongue quivered, or rather rolled violently in the mouth (although the jaws and lips remained rigid as before) ; and at length the same hideous voice which I have already described broke forth :

"For God's sake !—quick !—quick !—put me to sleep— or, quick !—waken me !—quick ! *I say to you that I am dead* !"

I was thoroughly unnerved, and for an instant remained undecided what to do. At first I made an endeavour to re-compose the patient ; but, failing in this through total abeyance of the will, I retraced my steps and as earnestly struggled to awaken him. In this attempt I soon saw that I should be successful—or at least I soon fancied that my success would be complete—and I am sure that all in the room were prepared to see the patient awaken.

For what really occurred, however, it is quite impossible that any human being could have been prepared.

As I rapidly made the mesmeric passes, amid ejaculations of "dead ! dead !" absolutely *bursting* from the tongue and not from the lips of the sufferer, his whole frame at once—within the space of a single minute, or even less, shrunk—crumbled —absolutely *rotted* away beneath my hands. Upon the bed, before that whole company, there lay a nearly liquid mass of loathsome—of detestable putridity.

THE PIPE-SMOKER
Martin Armstrong

I DON'T usually mind walking in rain, but on this occasion the rain was coming down in torrents and I still had ten miles to go. That was why I stopped at the first house, a house about a mile from the village ahead of me, and looked over the garden gate. The house didn't look promising, for I saw at once that it was empty. All the windows were shut, and not one of them had a blind or a curtain. Through one on the ground floor I saw bare walls, a bare mantelpiece, and an empty grate. The garden, too, was wild, the beds full of weeds : you would hardly have known it for a garden but for the fence, the vestiges of straight paths and the lilac-bushes which were in full bloom and sent showers of water to the grass every time the wind tossed them.

You can imagine, then, that I was surprised when a man strolled out from the lilacs and came slowly towards me down the path. What was surprising was not merely that he was there, but that he was strolling aimlessly about, bare-headed and without a mackintosh, in the drenching rain. He was rather a fat man and dressed as a clergyman, grey-haired, bald, clean-shaven, with that swollen-headed and over-intense look which one sees in portraits of William Blake. I noticed at once how his arms hung limply at his sides. His clothes and —what made him still stranger—his face, were streaming with water ! He didn't seem to be in the least aware of the rain. But I was. It was beginning to trickle through my hair and down my neck, and I said :

"Excuse me, sir, but may I come in and shelter ?"

He started and raised puzzled eyes to mine. "Shelter ?" he said.

"Yes," I replied, "from the rain."

"Ah, from the rain. Yes, sir, by all means. Pray come in."

I opened the garden gate and followed him down a path

towards the front door, where he stood aside with a slight bow to let me pass in first. "I fear you won't find it very comfortable," he said when we were in the hall. "However, come in, sir ; in here, first door on the left."

The room, which was a large one with a bow-window divided into five lights, was empty, except for a deal table and bench and a smaller table in a corner near the door with an unlighted lamp on it.

"Pray sit down, sir," he said, pointing to the bench with another slight bow. There was an old-fashioned politeness in his manner and language. He himself did not sit down, but walked to the window and stood looking out at the streaming garden, his arms still hanging idly at his sides.

"Apparently you don't mind rain as much as I do, sir," I said, in an attempt to be amiable.

He turned round, and I had the impression that he could not turn his head and so had to turn his whole body in order to look at me.

"No, oh, no !" he replied. "Not at all. In point of fact, I hadn't observed it till you pointed it out."

"But you must be very wet," I said. "Wouldn't it be wiser to change ?"

"To change ?" His gaze became searching and suspicious at the question.

"To change your wet clothes."

"Change my clothes ?" he said. "Oh, no ! Oh, dear me, no, sir ! If they're wet, doubtless they'll dry in course of time. It isn't raining in here, I take it ?"

I looked at his face. He really was asking for information. "No," I replied, "it isn't raining in here, thank goodness."

"I fear I can't offer you anything," he said politely. "A woman comes from the village in the morning and evening, but meanwhile I'm quite helpless." He opened and closed his hanging hands. "Unless," he added, "you would care to go to the kitchen and make yourself a cup of tea, if you understand such things."

I refused, but asked leave to smoke a cigarette.

"Pray do," he said. "I fear I have none to offer you. The other, my predecessor, used to smoke cigarettes, but I'm a pipe-smoker." He brought a pipe and pouch from his pocket ; it was a relief to see him use his arms and hands.

When we had both lit up, I spoke again ; I was conscious

all the while that the responsibility for conversation was mine; that, if I had not spoken, my strange host would have made no attempt to break the silence, but would simply have stood with his arms at his sides looking straight in front of him either at the garden or at me.

I glanced round the bare room. "You're just moving in, I suppose?" I said.

"Moving in?" He shifted slightly and turned his intense, uncomfortable gaze on me again.

"Moving into this house, I mean."

"Oh, no," he said. "Oh, dear me, no, sir. I've been here for several years; or, rather, I myself have been here for nearly a year, and the other, my predecessor, was here for five years before that. Yes, it must be seven months now since he passed away. No doubt, sir"—a melancholy, wistful smile unexpectedly transformed his face—"no doubt you won't believe me—Mrs. Bellows wouldn't—when I tell you I've been here only seven months, there or thereabouts."

"If you say so, sir," I replied, "why should I disbelieve you?"

He took a few steps towards me and lifted his right hand. Reluctantly I took it, a thick, limp, cold hand that gave me an unpleasant thrill. "Thank you, sir," he said; "thank you. You're the first, absolutely the first . . . !"

I dropped the hand and he did not finish the phrase. He had fallen, apparently, into a reverie. Then he began again. "No doubt all would have been well if only my . . . that is, my predecessor's old cousin, had not left him this house. He was better off where he was. He was a clergyman, you know." He opened his hands, exhibiting himself. "These are his clothes."

Again he absented himself, fell into a reverie, while his body in its clergyman's clothes stood before me. Suddenly he asked me: "Do you believe in confession?"

"In confession?" I said. "You mean in the religious sense of the term?"

He took a step closer. He was almost touching me now. "What I mean is," he said, lowering his voice and looking at me intensely, "do you believe that to confess, to confess a sin or a . . . crime, brings relief?"

What was he going to tell me? I should have liked to say "No," to discourage any confession from the poor old creature, but he had put his question so appealingly that I could not find it in my heart to repulse him. "Yes," I said, "I think that by speaking of it one can often rid oneself of a weight on the mind."

"You have been so sympathetic, sir," he said with one of his polite bows, "that I feel tempted to trespass. . . .!" He lifted one of his heavy hands in a perfunctory gesture and dropped it again. "Would you have the patience to listen ?"

He stood beside me as if he had been a tailor's dummy that had been placed there. His leg touched my knee. I felt strongly repelled by his closeness. "Won't you sit down there ?" I said, pointing to the other end of the bench on which I was sitting. "I should find it easier to listen."

He turned his body and gazed earnestly at the bench, then sat down on it, facing me, a leg on either side of it, leaning towards me. He was about to speak, but he checked himself and glanced at the window and the door. Then he took his pipe from his mouth and laid it on the table, and his eyes returned to me. "My secret, my terrible secret," he said, "is that I'm a murderer."

His statement horrified me, as well it might ; and yet, I think, it hardly surprised me. His extreme strangeness had prepared me, to some extent, for something rather grim. I caught my breath and stared at him, and he, with horror in his eyes, stared back at me. He seemed to be waiting for me to speak, but at first I could not speak. What, in the name of sanity, could I say ? What I did say at last was something fantastically inadequate. "And this," I said, "weighs on your mind ?"

"It haunts me," he said, suddenly clenching his heavy, limp hands that lay on the bench in front of him. "Would you have the patience . . . ?"

I nodded. "Tell me about it," I said.

"If it hadn't been for the legacy of this house," he began, "nothing would have happened. The other, my predecessor, would have stayed in his Rectory, and I . . . I should never have come on the scene at all. Although it must be confessed that he, my predecessor, was not happy in his Rectory. He met with unfriendliness, suspicion. That was why he first came to this house—just as a trial, you see. It was bequeathed to him empty : simply the house—no furniture, no money— and he came and put in one or two things—this table, this bench, a few kitchen things, a folding bed upstairs. He wanted, you see, to try it, first. Its remoteness appealed to him, but he wanted to be sure about it in other ways. Some houses, you see, are safe, and some are not, and he wanted to make sure that this was a safe house before moving into it." He paused and then said very earnestly : "Let me advise you, my friend, always to do that when you contemplate moving into a strange house, because some houses are very unsafe."

I nodded. "Quite so !" I said. "Damp walls, bad drainage, and so on."

He shook his head. "No," he said, "not that. Something much more serious than that. I mean the spirit of the house. Don't you feel"—his gaze grew more piercing than ever—"that this is a dangerous house ?"

I shrugged my shoulders. "Empty houses are always a little queer," I said.

He reflected on this statement. "And you have noticed," he inquired at last, "the queerness of this one ?"

I did, as he asked me the question, feel that the house was queer ; but it was *his* queerness, I knew well enough, and the grim suggestiveness of his talk, that made it so, and I replied : "Not queerer than other empty houses, sir."

He gazed at me incredulously. "Strange !" he said. "Strange that you shouldn't feel it. Though it's true that . . . that the other, my predecessor, didn't feel it at first. Even this room—for this room, sir, is the dangerous room— didn't seem strange to him at first ; no, even in spite of a very peculiar thing about it."

If it had been fine, I should have ended the conversation and left him, for the old man's talk and manner were making me feel more and more uncomfortable. But it was not fine : it was raining as hard as ever and was becoming very dark. Evidently we were in for a thunderstorm.

The old man got up from the bench. "I think I can show you, now," he said, "the peculiar thing about the room. It is visible only after dark, but I think it is dark enough now."

He went to the little table in the corner and began to light the lamp. When it was alight and he had replaced the frosted-glass globe, he brought it to the larger table and set it down on my left. "Now," he said to me, "sit square to the table."

I did so. Before me across the bare room was the curtain-less five-lighted bow-window.

"You are sitting now," he said, laying a heavy hand on my shoulder, "where the other, my predecessor, used to sit and take his meals."

I could not restrain a start, nor resist the impulse to turn and face him. It made me uneasy to have him standing over me, behind me, out of sight. He appeared surprised. "Pray don't be alarmed, sir," he said, "but turn back and tell me what you see."

I obeyed. "I see the window," I said.

"Is that all ?" he asked.

I stared at the window. "No," I said. "I also see five reflections of myself, one in each light of the window."

"Just so," said the old man; "just so ! That is what the other saw when he took his meals alone. He saw the five other selves each eating its lonely meal. When he poured out some water, each of them poured out water ; when he lit a cigarette, each of them lit a cigarette."

"Of course," I said. "And that alarmed your friend, the clergyman ?"

"The Reverend James Baxter," said the old man ; "that was his name. Be sure not to forget it, my friend ; and if people ask you who lives here, remember to say the Reverend James Baxter. Nobody knows, you see, that . . . that . . . !"

"Nobody knows what you told me. I understand."

"Exactly !" he said, suddenly dropping his voice. "Nobody knows. Not a soul. You're the first person I've mentioned it to."

"And you've had no inquiries ?" I asked. "This Mr. Baxter was not missed ?"

He shook his head. "No," he said. "Even Mrs. Bellows, who looked after him from the start, is not aware of what happened."

I turned round and faced him incredulously. "Not aware, you mean to say . . . ?"

"Not aware that I'm not he. You see," he explained, "we were very much alike. Quite remarkably so ! I can show you a photograph of him before you go and you'll see for yourself."

I now decided that, rain or no rain, I would go ; there did not seem much reason, beyond the rain, for my staying. I stood up. "Well, sir," I said, "I can only hope that you will benefit of having relieved your mind of your . . . secret."

The old gentleman became very much agitated. He clasped and unclasped his two limp hands. "Oh, but you must not go yet. You haven't heard half of it. You haven't heard how it happened. I had hoped, sir—you have been so kind—that you'd have the patience and the kindness to . . . !"

I sat down again on the bench. "By all means," I said, "if you have more to say."

"I had just told you, hadn't I," the old gentleman went on, "that I . . . that the other . . . that my predecessor used to sit here at his meals and see his five other selves mimicking him ? When he lit his cigarette he saw five other cigarettes lighted simultaneously. . . !"

"Naturally," I said.

"Yes, naturally," said the old man ; "it was all perfectly natural, as you say ; perfectly natural till one night, one terrible night." He stopped and stared at me with horror in his eyes.

"And then ?" I said.

"Then a strange, a dreadful thing happened. When he, my predecessor, had lit his cigarette, watching those other selves, as he always did, he saw that one of them, the one of the extreme left, had lit, not a cigarette, but a pipe."

I burst out laughing. "Oh, come, come, sir !"

The old man wrung his hands in agitation. "It is comic, I know," he said, "but it is also terrible. What would you have thought if you had actually *seen* it yourself ? Wouldn't you have thought it terrible ? Wouldn't you have been appalled ?"

"Yes," I said, "if it had actually happened. If I had really seen such a thing, of course I should."

"Well," said the old man, "it *did* happen. There was no possible mistake about it. It was appalling, ghastly." There was as much horror in his voice as if he had actually seen the thing himself.

"But, my dear sir," I said to him, "you have only the word of this Mr. . . . Mr. Baxter for it."

He stared at me, his eyes blazing with conviction. "I *know* it happened," he said ; "I know it much more certainly that if I had seen it. Listen. The thing went on for five days : on five successive evenings my predecessor watched in horror for the thing to right itself."

"But why didn't he go—leave the house ?" I asked.

"He daren't," said the old man in a strained whisper. "He daren't go : he *had* to stay and see for certain that the thing had righted itself."

"And it didn't ?"

"On the sixth night," said the old man with bated breath, "the fifth reflection, the one that had broken away from obedience, had gone."

"Gone ?"

"Yes, gone from the window. My predecessor sat gazing in terror at the blank pane and the other four stared back in terror into this room. He glanced from the empty pane to them and they stared back at him, or at something behind him, with horror in their eyes. Then he began to choke . . . to choke," gasped the old man, himself almost choking, "to choke, because hands were round his throat, clutching, throttling him."

"You mean that the hands were the hands of the fifth ?" I asked, and it was only my horror at the old man's horror that prevented my smiling cynically.

"Yes," he hissed, and he held out his thick, heavy hands, gazing at me with staring eyes. "Yes. *My* hands !"

For the first time I was really terrified. We stared speechless at one another, he still gasping and wheezing. Then, hoping to soothe him, I said as calmly as I could : "I see : so you were the fifth reflection ?"

He pointed to his pipe on the table. "Yes," he gasped ; "I, the pipe-smoker."

I stood up ; my impulse was to hurry to the door. But some scruple held me there still, a feeling that it would be inhuman to leave him alone, a prey to his horrible fantasy ; and, with a vague idea of bringing him to his senses, of easing his tortured mind, I asked : "And what did you do with the body ?"

He caught his breath, a shudder distorted his face, and, clenching his two extended hands, he began to beat his breast convulsively. "*This*," he shouted in a voice of agony, "*this* is the body."

THE RED ROOM
H. G. Wells

"I CAN assure you," said I, "that it will take a very tangible ghost to frighten me." And I stood up before the fire with my glass in my hand.

"It is your own choosing," said the man with the withered arm, and glanced at me askance.

"Eight-and-twenty years," said I, "I have lived, and never a ghost have I seen as yet."

The old woman sat staring hard into the fire, her pale eyes wide open. "Ay," she broke in; "and eight-and-twenty years you have lived and never seen the likes of this house, I reckon. There's a many things to see, when one's still but eight-and-twenty." She swayed her head slowly from side to side. "A many things to see and sorrow for."

I half suspected the old people were trying to enhance the spiritual terrors of their house by their droning insistence. I put down my empty glass on the table and looked about the room, and caught a glimpse of myself, abbreviated and broadened to an impossible sturdiness, in the queer old mirror at the end of the room. "Well," I said, "if I see anything to-night, I shall be so much the wiser. For I come to the business with an open mind."

"It's your own choosing," said the man with the withered arm once more.

I heard the sound of a stick and a shambling step on the flags in the passage outside, and the door creaked on its hinges as a second old man entered, more bent, more wrinkled, more aged even than the first. He supported himself by a single crutch, his eyes were covered by a shade, and his lower lip, half-averted, hung pale and pink from his decaying yellow teeth. He made straight for an arm-chair on the opposite side of the table, sat down clumsily, and began to cough. The man with the withered arm gave this new-comer a short glance of positive dislike; the old woman took no notice of his arrival, but remained with her eyes fixed steadily on the fire.

"I said—it's your own choosing," said the man with the withered arm, when the coughing had ceased for a while.

"It's my own choosing," I answered.

The man with the shade became aware of my presence for the first time, and threw his head back and sideways for a moment, to see me. I caught a momentary glimpse of his eyes, small and bright and inflamed. Then he began to cough and splutter again.

"Why don't you drink?" said the man with the withered arm, pushing the beer towards him. The man with the shade poured out a glassful with a shaky arm that splashed half as much again on the deal table. A monstrous shadow of him crouched upon the wall and mocked his action as he poured and drank. I must confess I had scarce expected these grotesque custodians. There is to my mind something inhuman in senility, something crouching and atavistic; the human qualities seem to drop from old people insensibly day by day. The three of them made me feel uncomfortable, with their gaunt silences, their bent carriage, their evident unfriendliness to me and to one another.

"If," said I, "you will show me to this haunted room of yours, I will make myself comfortable there."

The old man with the cough jerked his head back so suddenly that it startled me, and shot another glance of his red eyes at me from under the shade; but no one answered me. I waited a minute, glancing from one to the other.

"If," I said a little louder, "if you will show me to this haunted room of yours, I will relieve you from the task of entertaining me."

"There's a candle on the slab outside the door," said the man with the withered arm, looking at my feet as he addressed me. "But if you go to the red room to-night——"

("This night of all nights!" said the old woman.)

"You go alone."

"Very well," I answered. "And which way do I go?"

"You go along the passage for a bit," said he, "until you come to a door, and through that is a spiral staircase, and half-way up that is a landing and another door covered with baize. Go through that and down the long corridor to the end, and the red room is on your left up the steps."

"Have I got that right?" I said, and repeated his directions. He corrected me in one particular.

"And are you really going?" said the man with the shade, looking at me again for the third time, with that queer, unnatural tilting of the face.

("This night of all nights!" said the old woman.)

"It is what I came for," I said, and moved towards the door. As I did so, the old man with the shade rose and staggered round the table, so as to be closer to the others and to the fire. At the door I turned and looked at them, and saw they were all close together, dark against the firelight, staring at me over their shoulders, with an intent expression on their ancient faces.

"Good night," I said, setting the door open.

"It's your own choosing," said the man with the withered arm.

I left the door wide open until the candle was well alight, and then I shut them in and walked down the chilly, echoing passage.

I must confess that the oddness of these three old pensioners in whose charge her ladyship had left the castle, and the deep-toned, old-fashioned furniture of the housekeeper's room in which they foregathered, affected me in spite of my efforts to keep myself at a matter-of-fact phase. They seemed to belong to another age, an older age, an age when things spiritual were different from this of ours, less certain; an age when omens and witches were credible, and ghosts beyond denying. Their very existence was spectral; the cut of their clothing, fashions born in dead brains. The ornaments and conveniences of the room about them were ghostly— the thoughts of vanished men, which still haunted rather than participated in the world of to-day. But with an effort I sent such thoughts to the right-about. The long, draughty subterranean passage was chilly and dusty, and my candle flared and made the shadows cower and quiver. The echoes rang up and down the spiral staircase, and a shadow came sweeping up after me, and one fled before me into the darkness overhead. I came to the landing and stopped there for a moment, listening to a rustling that I fancied I heard; then, satisfied of the absolute silence, I pushed open the baize-covered door and stood in the corridor.

The effect was scarcely what I expected, for the moonlight,

coming in by the great window on the grand staircase, picked out everything in vivid black shadow or silvery illumination. Everything was in its place : the house might have been deserted on the yesterday instead of eighteen months ago. There were candles in the sockets of the sconces, and whatever dust had gathered on the carpets or upon the polished flooring was distributed so evenly as to be invisible in the moonlight. I was about to advance, and stopped abruptly. A bronze group stood upon the landing, hidden from me by the corner of the wall, but its shadow fell with marvellous distinctness upon the white panelling, and gave me the impression of someone crouching to waylay me. I stood rigid for half a minute perhaps. Then, with my hand in the pocket that held my revolver, I advanced, only to discover a Ganymede and Eagle glistening in the moonlight. That incident for a time restored my nerve, and a porcelain China-man on a buhl table, whose head rocked silently as I passed him, scarcely startled me.

The door to the red room and the steps up to it were in a shadowy corner. I moved my candle from side to side, in order to see clearly the nature of the recess in which I stood before opening the door. Here it was, thought I, that my predecessor was found, and the memory of that story gave me a sudden twinge of apprehension. I glanced over my shoulder at the Ganymede in the moonlight, and opened the door of the red room rather hastily, with my face half-turned to the pallid silence of the landing.

I entered, closed the door behind me at once, turned the key I found in the lock within, and stood with the candle held aloft, surveying the scene of my vigil, the great red room of Lorraine Castle, in which the young duke had died. Or, rather, in which he had begun his dying, for he had opened the door and fallen headlong down the steps I had just ascended. That had been the end of his vigil, of his gallant attempt to conquer the ghostly tradition of the place ; and never, I thought, had apoplexy better served the ends of superstition. And there were other and older stories that clung to the room, back to the half-credible beginning of it all, the tale of a timid wife and the tragic end that came to her husband's jest of frightening her. And looking around that large shadowy room, with its shadowy window bays, its recesses and alcoves, one could well understand the legends that had sprouted in its black corners, its germinating darkness. My candle was a little tongue of flame in its vastness, that failed to pierce the opposite end of the room, and left an ocean of mystery and suggestion beyond its island of light.

I resolved to make a systematic examination of the place at once, and dispel the fanciful suggestions of its obscurity before they obtained a hold upon me. After satisfying myself of the fastening of the door, I began to walk about the room, peering round each article of furniture, tucking up the valances of the bed, and opening its curtains wide. I pulled up the blinds and examined the fastenings of the several windows before closing the shutters, leant forward and looked up the blackness of the wide chimney, and tapped the dark oak panelling for any secret opening. There were two big mirrors in the room, each with a pair of sconces bearing candles, and on the mantelshelf, too, were more candles in china candlesticks. All these I lit one after the other. The fire was laid—an unexpected consideration from the old housekeeper—and I lit it, to keep down any disposition to shiver, and when it was burning well, I stood round with my back to it and regarded the room again. I had pulled up a chintz-covered arm-chair and a table, to form a kind of barricade before me, and on this lay my revolver ready to hand. My precise examination had done me good, but I still found the remoter darkness of the place, and its perfect stillness, too stimulating for the imagination. The echoing of the stir and crackling of the fire was no sort of comfort to me. The shadow in the alcove, at the end in particular, had that undefinable quality of a presence, that odd suggestion of a lurking living thing, that comes so easily in silence and solitude. At last, to reassure myself, I walked with a candle into it, and satisfied myself that there was nothing tangible there. I stood that candle upon the floor of the alcove, and left it in that position.

By this time I was in a state of considerable nervous tension, although to my reason there was no adequate cause for the condition. My mind, however, was perfectly clear. I postulated quite unreservedly that nothing supernatural could happen, and to pass the time I began to string some rhymes together, Ingoldsby fashion, of the original legend of the place. A few I spoke aloud, but the echoes were not pleasant. For the same reason I also abandoned, after a time, a conversation with myself upon the impossibility of ghosts and haunting. My mind reverted to the three old and distorted people downstairs, and I tried to keep it upon that topic. The sombre reds and blacks of the room troubled me; even with seven candles the place was merely dim. The one in the alcove flared in a draught, and the fire-flickering kept the shadows and penumbra perpetually shifting and stirring. Casting about for a remedy, I recalled the candles I had seen in the passage, and, with a slight effort, walked out into the moonlight, carrying a candle and leaving the door open, and presently returned with as many as ten. These I put in various knick-knacks of china with which the room was sparsely adorned, lit and placed where the shadows had lain deepest, some on the floor, some in the window recesses, until at last my seventeen candles were so arranged that not an inch of the room but had the direct light of at least one of them. It occurred to me that when the ghost came, I could warn him not to trip over them. The room was now quite brightly illuminated. There was something very cheery and reassuring in these little streaming flames, and snuffing them gave me an occupation, and afforded a reassuring sense of the passage of time.

Even with that, however, the brooding expectation of the vigil weighed heavily upon me. It was after midnight that the candle in the alcove suddenly went out, and the black shadow sprang back to its place. I did not see the candle go out; I simply turned and saw that the darkness was there, as one might start and see the unexpected presence of a stranger. "By Jove!" said I aloud; "that draught's a strong one!" and, taking the matches from the table, I walked across the room in a leisurely manner to relight the corner again. My first match would not strike, and as I succeeded with the second, something seemed to blink on the wall before me. I turned my head involuntarily, and saw that the two candles on the little table by the fireplace were extinguished. I rose at once to my feet.

"Odd!" I said. "Did I do that myself in a flash of absent-mindedness?"

I walked back, relit one, and as I did so, I saw the candle in the right sconce of one of the mirrors wink and go right out, and almost immediately its companion followed it. There was no mistake about it. The flame vanished, as if the wicks had been suddenly nipped between a finger and a thumb, leaving the wick neither glowing nor smoking, but black. While I stood gaping, the candle at the foot of the bed went out, and the shadows seemed to take another step towards me.

"This won't do!" said I, and first one and then another candle on the mantelshelf followed.

"What's up?" I cried, with a queer high note getting into my voice somehow. At that the candle on the wardrobe went out, and the one I had relit in the alcove followed.

"Steady on!" I said. "These candles are wanted," speaking with a half-hysterical facetiousness, and scratching away at a match the while for the mantel candlesticks. My hands trembled so much that twice I missed the rough paper of the matchbox. As the mantel emerged from darkness again, two candles in the remoter end of the window were eclipsed. But with the same match I also relit the larger mirror candles, and those on the floor near the doorway, so that for the moment I seemed to gain on the extinctions. But then in a volley there vanished four lights at once in different corners of the room, and I struck another match in quivering haste, and stood hesitating whither to take it.

As I stood undecided, an invisible hand seemed to sweep out the two candles on the table. With a cry of terror, I dashed at the alcove, then into the corner, and then into the window, relighting three, as two more vanished by the fireplace; then, perceiving a better way, I dropped the matches on the iron-bound deedbox in the corner, and caught up the bedroom candlestick. With this I avoided the delay of striking matches; but for all that the steady process of extinction went on, and the shadows I feared and fought against returned, and crept in upon me, first a step gained on this side of me and then on that. It was like a ragged storm-cloud sweeping out the stars. Now and then one returned for a minute, and was lost again. I was now almost frantic with the horror of coming darkness, and my self-possession deserted me. I leaped panting and dishevelled from candle to candle, in a vain struggle against that remorseless advance.

I bruised myself on the thigh against the table, I sent a chair headlong, I stumbled and fell and whisked the cloth from the table in my fall. My candle rolled away from me, and I snatched another as I rose. Abruptly this was blown out, as I swung it off the table, by the wind of my sudden movement, and immediately the two remaining candles followed. But there was light still in the room, a red light that staved off the shadows from me. The fire! Of course, I could thrust my candle between the bars and relight it!

I turned to where the flames were dancing between the glowing coals, and splashing red reflections upon the furniture, made two steps towards the grate, and incontinently the flames dwindled and vanished, the glow vanished, the reflections rushed together and vanished, and as I thrust the candle between the bars, darkness closed upon me like the shutting of an eye, wrapped about me in a stifling embrace, sealed my vision, and crushed the last vestiges of reason from my brain. The candle fell from my hand. I flung out my arms in a vain effort to thrust that ponderous blackness away from me, and, lifting up my voice, screamed with all my might—once, twice, thrice. Then I think I must have staggered to my feet. I know I thought suddenly of the moonlit corridor, and, with my head bowed and my arms over my face, made a run for the door.

But I had forgotten the exact position of the door, and struck myself heavily against the corner of the bed. I staggered back, turned, and was either struck or struck myself against some other bulky furniture. I have a vague memory of battering myself thus, to and fro in the darkness, of a cramped struggle, and of my own wild crying as I darted to and fro, of a heavy blow at last upon my forehead, a horrible sensation of falling that lasted an age, of my last frantic effort to keep my footing, and then I remember no more.

I opened my eyes in daylight. My head was roughly bandaged, and the man with the withered arm was watching my face. I looked about me, trying to remember what had happened, and for a space I could not recollect. I turned to the corner, and saw the old woman, no longer abstracted, pouring out some drops of medicine from a little blue phial into a glass. "Where am I?" I asked. "I seem to remember you, and yet I cannot remember who you are."

They told me then, and I heard of the haunted Red Room as one who hears a tale. "We found you at dawn," said he, "and there was blood on your forehead and lips."

It was very slowly I recovered my memory of my experience. "You believe now," said the old man, "that the

room is haunted?" He spoke no longer as one who greets
an intruder, but as one who grieves for a broken friend.

"Yes," said I; "the room is haunted."

"And you have seen it. And we, who have lived here
all our lives, have never set eyes upon it. Because we have
never dared. . . . Tell us, is it truly the old earl who——"

"No," said I; "it is not."

"I told you so," said the old lady, with the glass in her
hand. "It is his poor young countess who was frightened——"

"It is not," I said. "There is neither ghost of earl nor
ghost of countess in that room, there is no ghost there at all;
but worse, far worse——"

"Well?" they said.

"The worst of all the things that haunt poor mortal man,"
said I; "and that is, in all its nakedness—*Fear*! Fear that
will not have light nor sound, that will not bear with reason,
that deafens and darkens and overwhelms. It followed me
through the corridor, it fought against me in the room——"

I stopped abruptly. There was an interval of silence. My
hand went up to my bandages.

Then the man with the shade sighed and spoke. "That
is it," said he. "I knew that was it. A Power of Darkness.
To put such a curse upon a woman! It lurks there always.
You can feel it even in the daytime, even of a bright summer's
day, in the hangings, in the curtains, keeping behind you
however you face about. In the dusk it creeps along the
corridor and follows you, so that you dare not turn. There
is Fear in that room of hers—black Fear, and there will be—
so long as this house of sin endures."

THE DERELICT
William Hope Hodgson

"It's the *Material*," said the old ship's doctor. . . . "The *Material*, plus the conditions ; and, maybe," he added slowly, "a third factor—yes, a third factor ; but there, there. . . ." He broke off his half-meditative sentence, and began to charge his pipe.

"Go on, Doctor," we said encouragingly, and with more than a little expectancy. We were in the smoke-room of the *Sand-a-lea*, running across the North Atlantic ; and the doctor was a character. He concluded the charging of his pipe, and lit it ; then settled himself, and began to express himself more fully :

"The *Material*," he said, with conviction, "is inevitably the medium of expression of the Life-Force—the fulcrum, as it were ; lacking which, it is unable to exert itself, or, indeed, to express itself in any form or fashion that would be intelligible or evident to us.

"So potent is the share of the *Material* in the production of that thing which we name Life, and so eager the Life-Force to express itself, that I am convinced it would, if given the right conditions, make itself manifest even through so hopeless-seeming a medium as a simple block of sawn wood ; for I tell you, gentlemen, the Life-Force is both as fiercely urgent and as indiscriminate as Fire—the Destructor ; yet which some are now growing to consider the very essence of Life rampant. . . . There is a quaint seeming paradox there," he concluded, nodding his old grey head.

"Yes, Doctor," I said. "In brief, your argument is that Life is a thing, state, fact, or element, call-it-what-you-like, which requires the *Material* through which to manifest itself, and that given the *Material*, plus the conditions, the result is Life. In other words, that Life is an evolved product, manifested through Matter and bred of conditions—eh ?"

"As we understand the word," said the old doctor.

"Though, mind you, there *may* be a third factor. But, in my heart, I believe that it is a matter of chemistry ; conditions and a suitable medium ; but given the conditions, the Brute is so almighty that it will seize upon anything through which to manifest itself. It is a force generated by conditions ; but nevertheless this does not bring us one iota nearer to its *explanation*, any more than to the explanation of electricity or fire. They are, all three, of the Outer Forces—Monsters of the Void. Nothing we can do will *create* any one of them ; our power is merely to be able, by providing the conditions, to make each one of them manifest to our physical senses. Am I clear ?"

"Yes, Doctor, in a way you are," I said. "But I don't agree with you ; though I think I understand you. Electricity and fire are both what I might call natural things ; but life is an abstract something—a kind of all-permeating wakefulness. Oh, I can't explain it ; who could ? But it's spiritual ; not just a thing bred out of a condition, like fire, as you say, or electricity. It's a horrible thought of yours. Life's a kind of spiritual mystery. . . ."

"Easy, my boy !" said the old doctor, laughing gently to himself ; "or else I may be asking you to demonstrate the spiritual mystery of life of the limpet, or the crab, shall we say ?"

He grinned at me, with ineffable perverseness. "Anyway," he continued, "as I suppose you've all guessed, I've a yarn to tell you in support of my impression that life is no more a mystery or a miracle than fire or electricity. But, please to remember, gentlemen, that because we've succeeded in naming and making good use of these two forces, they're just as much mysteries, fundamentally, as ever. And, anyway, the thing I'm going to tell you, won't explain the mystery of life ; but only give you one of my pegs on which I hang my feeling that life is, as I have said, a force made manifest through conditions (that is to say, natural chemistry), and that it can take for its purpose and need, the most incredible and unlikely matter ; for without matter, it cannot come into existence—it cannot become manifest. . . ."

"I don't agree with you, Doctor," I interrupted. "Your theory would destroy all belief in life after death. It would . . ."

"Hush, sonny," said the old man, with a quiet little smile of comprehension. "Hark to what I've to say first ; and, anyway, what objection have you to material life, after death ; and if you object to a material framework, I would still have you remember that I am speaking of life, as we understand the word in this our life. Now do be a quiet lad, or I'll never be done :

"It was when I was a young man, and that is a good many years ago, gentlemen. I had passed my examination ; but was so run down with overwork, that it was decided that I had better take a trip to sea. I was by no means well off, and very glad, in the end, to secure a nominal post as doctor in a sailing passenger-clipper, running out to China.

"The name of the ship was the *Bheotpte*, and soon after I had got all my gear aboard, she cast off, and we dropped down the Thames, and next day were well away out in the Channel.

"The captain's name was Gannington, a very decent man ; though quite illiterate. The first mate, Mr. Berlies, was a quiet, sternish, reserved man, very well read. The second mate, Mr. Selvern, was, perhaps, by birth and upbringing, the most socially cultured of the three ; but he lacked the stamina and indomitable pluck of the two others. He was more of a sensitive ; and emotionally and even mentally, the most alert man of the three.

"On our way out, we called at Madagascar, where we landed some of our passengers ; then we ran eastward, meaning to call at North-West Cape ; but about a hundred degrees east, we encountered very dreadful weather, which carried away all our sails and sprung the jibboom and fore t'gallant mast.

"The storm carried us northward for several hundred miles, and when it dropped us finally, we found ourselves in a very bad state. The ship had been strained, and had taken some three feet of water through her seams ; the main top-mast had been sprung, in addition to the jibboom and fore t'gallant mast ; two of our boats had gone, as also one of the pigsties (with three fine pigs), this latter having been washed overboard but some half-hour before the wind began to ease, which it did quickly ; though a very ugly sea ran for some hours after.

"The wind left us just before dark, and when morning came, it brought splendid weather ; a calm, mildly undulating sea, and a brilliant sun, with no wind. It showed us also that we were not alone ; for about two miles away to the west-ward was another vessel, which Mr. Selvern, the second mate, pointed out to me.

" 'That's a pretty rum-looking packet, Doctor,' he said, and handed me his glass. I looked through it, at the other vessel, and saw what he meant ; at least, I thought I did.

" 'Yes, Mr. Selvern,' I said, 'she's got a pretty old-fashioned look about her.'

"He laughed at me, in his pleasant way.

" 'It's easy to see you're not a sailor, Doctor,' he remarked. 'There's a dozen rum things about her. She's a derelict, and has been floating round, by the look of her, for many a score of years. Look at the shape of her counter, and the bows and cut-water. She's as old as the hills, as you might say, and ought to have gone down to Davy Jones a long time ago. Look at the growths on her, and the thickness of her standing rigging ; that's all salt encrustations, I fancy, if you notice the white colour. She's been a small barque ; but don't you see she's not a yard left aloft. They've all dropped out of the slings ; everything rotted away ; wonder the standing rigging hasn't gone too. I wish the Old Man would let us take the boat, and have a look at her ; she's be well worth it. '

"There seemed little chance, however, of this ; for all hands were turned-to and kept hard at it all day long, repairing the damage to the masts and gear, and this took a long while, as you may think. Part of the time I gave a hand, heaving on one of the deck-capstans ; for the exercise was good for my liver. Old Captain Gannington approved, and I persuaded him to come along and try some of the same medicine, which he did ; and we grew very chummy over the job.

"We got talking about the derelict, and he remarked how lucky we were not to have run full tilt on to her, in the darkness ; for she lay right away to leeward of us, according to the way that we had been drifting in the storm. He also was of the opinion that she had a strange look about her, and that she was pretty old but on this latter point, he plainly had far less knowledge than the second mate ; for he was, as I have said, an illiterate man, and he knew nothing of sea-craft beyond what experience had taught him. He lacked the book know-ledge, which the second mate had, of vessels previous to his day, which it appeared the derelict was.

" 'She's an old 'un, Doctor,' was the extent of his observations in this direction.

"Yet, when I mentioned to him that it would be interesting to go aboard, and give her a bit of an overhaul, he nodded his head, as if the idea had been already in his mind, and accorded with his own inclinations.

" 'When the work's over, Doctor,' he said. 'Can't spare the men now, ye know. Got to get all shipshape an' ready as smart as we can. But we'll take my gig, an' go off in the Second Dog Watch. The glass is steady, an' it'll be a bit of jam for us.'

"That evening, after tea, the captain gave orders to clear the gig and get overboard. The second mate was to come with us, and the skipper gave him word to see that two or three lamps were put into the boat, as it would soon fall dark. A little later, we were pulling across the calmness of the sea with a crew of six at the oars, and making very good speed of it.

"Now, gentlemen, I have detailed to you with great exactness, all the facts, both big and little, so that you can follow step by step each incident in this extraordinary affair; and I want you now to pay the closest attention.

"I was sitting in the stern-sheets, with the second mate and the captain, who was steering; and as we drew nearer and nearer to the stranger, I studied her with an ever-growing attention, as, indeed, did Captain Gannington and the second mate. She was, as you know, to the westward of us, and the sunset was making a great flame of red light to the back of her, so that she showed a little blurred and indistinct, by reason of the halation of the light, which almost defeated the eye in any attempt to see her rotting spars and standing rigging, submerged as they were in the fiery glory of the sunset.

"It was because of this effect of the sunset, that we had come quite close, comparatively, to the derelict before we saw that she was surrounded by a sort of curious scum, the colour of which was difficult to decide upon, by reason of the red light that was in the atmosphere; but which afterwards we discovered to be brown. This scum spread all about the old vessel for many hundreds of yards, in a huge, irregular patch, a great stretch of which reached out to the eastward, upon our starboard side, some score, or so, fathoms away.

" 'Queer stuff,' said Captain Gannington, leaning to the side, and looking over. 'Something in the cargo as 'as gone rotten an' worked out through 'er seams.'

" 'Look at her bows and stern,' said the second mate ; 'just look at the growth of her.'

"There were, as he said, great clumpings of strange-looking sea-fungi under the bows and the short counter astern. From the stump of her jibboom and her cutwater, great beards of rime and marine growths hung downward into the scum that held her in. Her blank starboard side was presented to us, all a dead, dirtyish white, streaked and mottled vaguely with dull masses of heavier colour.

" 'There's a steam of haze rising off her,' said the second mate, speaking again ; 'you can see it against the light. It keeps coming and going. Look !'

"I saw then what he meant—a faint haze or steam, either suspended above the old vessel, or rising from her ; and Captain Gannington saw it also :

" 'Spontaneous combustion !' he exclaimed. 'We'll 'ave to watch w'en we lift the 'atches ; 'nless it's some poor devil that's got aboard of her ; but that ain't likely.'

"We were now within a couple of hundred yards of the old derelict, and had entered into the brown scum. As it poured off the lifted oars, I heard one of the men mutter to himself—'dam treacle !' and indeed, it was something like it. As the boat continued to forge nearer and nearer to the old ship, the scum grew thicker and thicker ; so that, at last, it perceptibly slowed us.

" 'Give way, lads ! Put some beef to it !' sung out Captain Gannington ; and thereafter there was no sound, except the panting of the men, and the faint, reiterated suck, suck, of the sullen brown scum upon the oars, as the boat was forced ahead. As we went, I was conscious of a peculiar smell in the evening air, and whilst I had no doubt that the puddling of the scum, by the oars, made it rise, I felt that in some way, it was vaguely familiar ; yet I could give it no name.

"We were now very close to the old vessel, and presently she was high above us, against the dying light. The captain called out then to—'in with the bow oars, and stand-by with the boat-hook,' which was done.

" 'Aboard there ! Ahoy ! Aboard there ! Ahoy !' shouted Captain Gannington, but there came no answer, only the flat sound of his voice going lost into the open sea, each time he sang out.

" 'Ahoy ! Aboard there ! Ahoy !' he shouted, time after time ; but there was only the weary silence of the old hulk that answered us ; and, somehow as he shouted, the while that I stared up half expectantly at her, a queer little sense of oppression, that amounted almost to nervousness, came upon me. It passed, but I remember how I was suddenly aware that it was growing dark. Darkness comes fairly rapidly in the tropics, though not so quickly as many fiction-writers seem to think ; but it was not that the coming dusk had perceptibly deepened in that brief time, of only a few moments, but rather that my nerves had made me suddenly a little hyper-sensitive. I mention my state particularly ; for I am not a nervy man, normally ; and my abrupt touch of nerves is significant, in the light of what happened.

" 'There's no one aboard there !' said Captain Gannington. 'Give way, men !' For the boat's crew had instinctively rested on their oars, as the captain hailed the old craft. The men gave way again ; and then the second mate called out excitedly —'Why, look there, there's our pigsty ! See, it's got *Bheotpte* painted on the end. It's drifted down here, and the scum's caught it. What a blessed wonder !'

"It was, as he had said, our pigsty that had been washed overboard in the storm, and most extraordinary to come across it there.

" 'We'll tow it off with us, when we go,' remarked the captain, and shouted to the crew to get down to their oars ; for they were hardly moving the boat, because the scum was so thick, close in around the old ship, that it literally clogged the boat from going ahead. I remember that it struck me in a half-conscious sort of way, as curious that the pigsty, containing our three dead pigs, had managed to drift in so far, unaided, whilst we could scarcely manage to *force* the boat in now that we had come right into the scum. But the thought passed from my mind ; for so many things happened within the next few minutes.

"The men managed to bring the boat in alongside, within a couple of feet of the derelict, and the man with the boat-hook hooked on.

" ' 'Ave you got 'old there, forrard ?' asked Captain Gannington.

" 'Yessir !' said the bow man ; and as he spoke there came a queer noise of tearing.

" 'What's that ?' asked the Captain.

" 'It's tore, Sir. Tore clean away !' said the man ; and his tone showed that he had received something of a shock.

" 'Get a hold again then !' said Captain Gannington, irritably. 'You don't s'pose this packet was built yesterday ! Shove the hook into the main chains.' The man did so gingerly, as you might say ; for it seemed to me, in the growing dusk, that he put no strain on to the hook, though, of course, there was no need ; you see, the boat could not go very far, of herself, in the stuff in which she was embedded. I remember thinking this, also, as I looked up at the bulging side of the old vessel. Then I heard Captain Gannington's voice :

" 'Lord ! but she's old ! An' what a colour, Doctor ! She don't half want paint, do she ! . . . Now then, some-body—one of them oars.'

"An oar was passed to him, and he leant it up against the ancient, bulging side, then he paused, and called to the second mate to light a couple of the lamps, and stand by to pass them up ; for darkness had settled down now upon the sea.

"The second mate lit two of the lamps, and told one of the men to light a third, and keep it handy in the boat ; then he stepped across, with a lamp in each hand, to where Captain Gannington stood by the oar against the side of the ship.

" 'Now, my lad,' said the captain, to the man who had pulled stroke, 'up with you, an' we'll pass ye up the lamps.'

"The man jumped to obey ; caught the oar, and put his weight upon it, and as he did so, something seemed to give a little.

" 'Look !' cried out the second mate, and pointed, lamp in hand . . . 'It's sunk in !'

"This was true. The oar had made quite an indentation into the bulging, somewhat slimy side of the old vessel.

" 'Mould, I reckon,' said Captain Gannington, bending towards the derelict, to look. Then to the man :

" 'Up you go, my lad, and be smart . . . Don't stand there waitin' !'

"At that, the man, who had paused a moment as he felt the oar give beneath his weight, began to shin up, and in a few seconds he was aboard, and leant out over the rail for the lamps. These were passed up to him, and the captain called to him to steady the oar. Then Captain Gannington went, calling to me to follow, and after me the second mate.

"As the captain put his face over the rail, he gave a cry of astonishment :

" 'Mould, by gum! Mould . . . Tons of it! . . . Good Lord!'

"As I heard him shout that, I scrambled the more eagerly after him, and in a moment or two, I was able to see what he meant—everywhere that the light from the two lamps struck, there was nothing but smooth great masses and surfaces of a dirty-white mould.

"I climbed over the rail, with the second mate close behind, and stood upon the mould-covered decks. There might have been no planking beneath the mould, for all that our feet could feel. It gave under our tread, with a spongy, puddingy feel. It covered the deck-furniture of the old ship, so that the shape of each article and fitment was often no more than suggested through it.

"Captain Gannington snatched a lamp from the other man, and the second mate reached for the other. They held the lamps high, and we all stared. It was most extraordinary, and, somehow, most abominable. I can think of no other word, gentlemen, that so much describes the predominant feeling that effected me at the moment.

" 'Good Lord!' said Captain Gannington, several times. 'Good Lord!' But neither the second mate nor the man said anything, and for my part I just stared, and at the same time began to smell a little at the air, for there was again a vague odour of something half familiar, that somehow brought to me a sense of half-known fright.

"I turned this way and that, staring, as I have said. Here and there, the mould was so heavy as to entirely disguise what lay beneath, converting the deck-fittings into indistinguishable mounds of mould, all dirty-white, and blotched and veined with irregular, dull purplish markings.

"There was a strange thing about the mould, which Captain Gannington drew attention to—it was that our feet did not crush into it and break the surface, as might have been expected, but merely indented it.

" 'Never seen nothin' like it before! . . . Never!' said the captain, after having stooped with his lamp to examine the mould under our feet. He stamped with his heel, and the stuff gave out a dull, puddingy sound. He stooped again, with a quick movement, and stared, holding the lamp close to the deck. 'Blest if it ain't a reg'lar skin to it !' he said.

"The second mate and the man and I all stooped, and looked at it. The second mate progged it with his forefinger, and I remember I rapped it several times with my knuckles, listening to the dead sound it gave out, and noticing the close, firm texture of the mould.

" 'Dough !' said the second mate. 'It's just like blessed dough ! . . . Pouf !' He stood up with a quick movement. 'I could fancy it stinks a bit,' he said.

"As he said this, I knew suddenly what the familiar thing was, in the vague odour that hung about us—it was that the smell had something animal-like in it ; something of the same smell only *heavier*, that you will smell in any place that is infested with mice. I began to look about with a sudden very real uneasiness . . . There might be vast numbers of hungry rats board . . . They might prove exceedingly dangerous, if in a starving condition, yet, as you will understand, somehow I hesitated to put forward my idea as a reason for caution, it was too fanciful.

"Captain Gannington had begun to go aft, along the mould-covered main-deck, with the second mate ; each of them holding his lamp high up, so as to cast a good light about the vessel. I turned quickly and followed them, the man with me keeping close to my heels, and plainly uneasy. As we went, I became aware that there was a feeling of moisture in the air, and I remembered the slight mist, or smoke, above the hulk, which had made Captain ·Gannington suggest spontaneous combustion in explanation.

"And always, as we went, there was that vague animal smell ; and suddenly I found myself wishing we were well away from the old vessel.

"Abruptly, after a few paces, the captain stopped and pointed at a row of mould-hidden shapes on either side of the main-deck . . . 'Guns,' he said. 'Been a privateer in the old days, I guess ; maybe worse ! We'll 'ave a look below, doctor ; there may be something worth touchin'. She's older than I thought. Mr. Selvern thinks she's about three hundred years old ; but I scarce think it.'

"We continued our way aft, and I remember that I found myself walking as lightly and gingerly as possible ; as if I were subconsciously afraid of treading through the rotten, mould-hid decks. I think the others had a touch of the same feeling, from the way that they walked. Occasionally the soft mould would grip our heels, releasing them with a little, sullen suck.

"The captain forged somewhat ahead of the second mate, and I know that the suggestion he had made himself, that perhaps there might be something below, worth the carrying away, had stimulated his imagination. The second mate was however, beginning to feel somewhat the same way that I did ; at least, I have that impression. I think if it had not been for what I might truly describe as Captain Gannington's sturdy courage, we should all of us have just gone back over the side very soon; for there was most certainly an unwholesome feeling abroad, that made one feel queerly lacking in pluck, and you will soon perceive that this feeling was justified.

"Just as the captain reached the few, mould-covered steps, leading up on to the short half-poop, I was suddenly aware that the feeling of moisture in the air had grown very much more definite. It was perceptible now, intermittently, as a sort of thin, moist, fog-like vapour, that came and went oddly, and seemed to make the decks a little indistinct to the view, this time and that. Once, an odd puff of it beat up suddenly from somewhere, and caught me in the face, carrying a queer, sickly, heavy odour with it, that somehow frightened me strangely, with a suggestion of a waiting and half-comprehended danger.

"We had followed Captain Gannington up the three mould-covered steps, and now went slowly aft along the raised after-deck.

"By the mizzen-mast, Captain Gannington paused, and held his lantern near to it. . . .

" 'My word, Mister,' he said to the second mate, "it's fair thickened up with the mould ; why, I'll g'antee it's close on four foot thick.' He shone the light down to where it met the deck. 'Good Lord !' he said, 'look at the sea-lice on it !' I stepped up ; and it was as he had said ; the sea-lice were thick upon it, some of them huge, not less than the size of large beetles, and all a clear, colourless shade, like water, except where there were little spots of grey in them, evidently their internal organisms.

" 'I've never seen the like of them, 'cept on a live cod !' said Captain Gannington, in an extremely puzzled voice. 'My

word ! but they're whoppers !'   Then he passed on, but a few
paces farther aft, he stopped again, and held his lamp near to
the mould-hidden deck.

" 'Lord bless me, Doctor !' he called out, in a low voice,
'did ye ever see the like of that ? Why, it's a foot long, if it's a
hinch !'

"I stooped over his shoulder, and saw what he meant ;
it was a clear, colourless creature, about a foot long, and about
eight inches high, with a curved back that was extraordinary
narrow. As we stared, all in a group, it gave a queer little
flick, and was gone.

" 'Jumped !' said the captain. 'Well, if that ain't a giant
of all the sea-lice that ever I've seen ! I guess it jumped twenty-
foot clear.' He straightened his back, and scratched his head
a moment, swinging the lantern this way and that with the
other hand, and staring about us. 'Wot are *they* doin' aboard
'ere !' he said. 'You'll see 'em (little things) on fat cod, an'
such like. . . . I'm blowed, Doctor, if I understand.'

"He held his lamp towards a big mound of the mould,
that occupied part of the after portion of the low poop-deck,
a little foreside of where there came a two-foot high 'break' to
a kind of second and loftier poop, that ran away aft to the
taffrail. The mound was pretty big, several feet across, and
more than a yard high. Captain Gannington' walked up to
it :

" 'I reckon this 's the scuttle,' he remarked, and gave it a
heavy kick. The only result was a deep indentation into the
huge, whitish hump of mould, as if he had driven his foot into
a mass of some doughy substance. Yet, I am not altogether
correct in saying that this was the only result ; for a certain
other thing happened—from a place made by the captain's
foot, there came a little gush of a purplish fluid, accompanied
by a peculiar smell, that was, and was not, half familiar. Some
of the mould-like substance had stuck to the toe of the captain's
boot, and from this, likewise, there issued a sweat, as it were,
of the same colour.

" 'Well !' said Captain Gannington, in surprise, and drew
back his foot to make another kick at the hump of mould ;
but he paused, at an exclamation from the second mate :

" 'Don't, Sir !' said the second mate.

"I glanced at him, and the light from Captain Gannington's
a mp showed me that his face had a bewildered, half-frightened

look, as if it were suddenly and unexpectedly half afraid of something, and as if his tongue had given way to his sudden fright, without any intention on his part to speak.

"The captain also turned and stared at him.

" 'Why, Mister ?' he asked, in a somewhat puzzled voice, through which there sounded just the vaguest hint of annoyance. 'We've got to shift this muck, if we're to get below.'

"I looked at the second mate, and it seemed to me that, curiously enough, he was listening less to the captain, than to some other sound.

"Suddenly, he said in a queer voice—'Listen, everybody !'

"Yet we heard nothing, beyond the faint murmur of the men talking together in the boat alongside.

" 'I don't hear nothin',' said Captain Gannington, after a short pause. 'Do you, Doctor ?'

" 'No,' I said.

" 'Wot was it you thought you heard ?' asked the captain, turning again to the second mate. But the second mate shook his head, in a curious, almost irritable way ; as if the captain's question interrupted his listening. Captain Gannington stared a moment at him, then held his lantern up, and glanced about him, almost uneasily. I know I felt a queer sense of strain. But the light showed nothing, beyond the greyish-dirty-white of the mould in all directions.

" 'Mister Selvern,' said the captain at last, looking at him, 'don't get fancying things. Get hold of your bloomin' self. Ye know ye heard nothin' ?'

" 'I'm quite sure I heard something, Sir !' said the second mate. 'I seemed to hear—' He broke off sharply, and appeared to listen, with an almost painful intensity.

" 'What did it sound like ?' I asked.

" 'It's all right, Doctor,' said Captain Gannington, laughing gently. 'Ye can give him a tonic when we get back. I'm goin' to shift this stuff.'

"He drew back, and kicked for the second time at the ugly mass, which he took to hide the companion-way. The result of his kick was startling ; for the whole thing wobbled sloppily, like a mound of unhealthy-looking jelly.

"He drew his foot out of it, quickly, and took a step backwards, staring, and holding his lamp towards it :

" 'By gum !' he said, and it was plain that he was genuinely startled, 'the blessed thing's gone soft !'

"The man had run back several steps from the suddenly flaccid mound, and looked horribly frightened. Though, of what, I am sure he had not the least idea. The second mate stood where he was, and stared. For my part, I know I had a most hideous uneasiness upon me. The captain continued to hold his light towards the wobbling mound, and stare.

"'It's gone squashy all through!' he said. 'There's no scuttle there. There's no bally woodwork inside that lot! Phoo! what a rum smell!'

"He walked round to the after-side of the strange mound, to see whether there might be some signs of an opening into the hull at the back of the great heap of mould-stuff. And then:

"'*Listen* !' said the second mate, again, and in the strangest sort of voice.

"Captain Gannington straightened himself upright, and there succeeded a pause of the most intense quietness, in which there was not even the hum of talk from the men alongside in the boat. We all heard it—a kind of dull, soft Thud! Thud! Thud! Thud! somewhere in the hull under us, yet so vague that I might have been half doubtful I heard it, only that the others did so, too.

"Captain Gannington turned suddenly to where the man stood:

"'Tell them—' he began. But the fellow cried out something, and pointed. There had come a strange intensity into his somewhat unemotional face; so that the captain's glance followed his action instantly. I stared, also, as you may think. It was the great mound, at which the man was pointing. I saw what he meant.

"From the two gaps made in the mould-like stuff by Captain Gannington's boot, the purple fluid was jetting out in a queerly regular fashion, almost as if it were being forced out by a pump. My word! but I stared. And even as I stared, a larger jet squirted out, and splashed as far as the man, spattering his boots and trouser-legs.

"The fellow had been pretty nervous before, in a stolid, ignorant sort of way, and his funk had been growing steadily; but, at this, he simply let out a yell, and turned about to run. He paused an instant, as if a sudden fear of the darkness that held the decks between him and the boat had taken him. He snatched at the second mate's lantern, tore it out of his hand, and plunged heavily away over the vile stretch of mould.

"Mr. Selvern, the second mate, said not a word; he was just standing , staring at the strange-smelling twin streams of dull purple, that were jetting out from the wobbling mound. Captain Gannington, however, roared an order to the man to come back ; but the man plunged on and on across the mould, his feet seeming to be clogged by the stuff, as if it had grown suddenly soft. He zigzagged as he ran, the lantern swaying in wild circles as he wrenched his feet free, with a constant plop, plop ; and I could hear his frightened gasps, even from where I stood.

" 'Come back with that lamp !' roared the captain again ; but still the man took no notice, and Captain Gannington was silent an instant, his lips working in a queer, inarticulate fashion ; as if he were stunned momentarily by the very violence of his anger at the man's insubordination. And in the silence, I heard the sounds again :—Thud ! Thud ! Thud ! Thud ! Quite distinctly now, beating, it seemed suddenly to me, right down under my feet, but deep.

"I stared down at the mould on which I was standing, with a quick, disgusting sense of the terrible all about me ; then I looked at the captain, and tried to say something, without appearing frightened. I saw that he had turned again to the mound, and all the anger had gone out of his face. He had his lamp out towards the mound, and was listening. There was a further moment of absolute silence ; at least, I know that I was not conscious of any sound at all, in all the world, except that extraordinary Thud ! Thud ! Thud ! Thud ! down somewhere in the huge bulk under us.

"The captain shifted his feet, with a sudden, nervous movement ; and as he lifted them, the mould went plop ! plop ! He looked quickly at me, trying to smile, as if he were not thinking anything very much about it :—'What do you make of it, Doctor ?' he said.

" 'I think——' I began. But the second mate interrupted with a single word ; his voice pitched a little high, in a tone that made both stare instantly at him :—

" 'Look !' he said, and pointed at the mound. The thing was all of a slow quiver. A strange ripple ran outward from it, along the deck, like you will see a ripple run inshore out of a calm sea. It reached a mound a little fore-side of us, which I had supposed to be the cabin-skylight ; and in a moment the second mound sank nearly level with the surrounding decks, quivering floppily in a most extraordinary fashion. A sudden quick tremor took the mould right under the second·mate, and he gave out a hoarse little cry, and held his arms out on each side of him, to keep his balance. The tremor in the mould spread, and Captain Gannington swayed, and spread his feet with a sudden curse of fright. The second mate jumped across to him, and caught him by the wrist :

"'The boat, Sir !' he said, saying the very thing that I had lacked the pluck to say. 'For God's sake——'

"But he never finished ; for a tremendous hoarse scream cut off his words. They hove themselves round, and looked. I could see without turning. The man who had run from us, was standing in the waist of the ship, about a fathom from the starboard bulwarks. He was swaying from side to side and screaming in a dreadful fashion. He appeared to be trying to lift his feet, and the light from his swaying lantern showed an almost incredible sight. All about him the mould was in active movement. His feet had sunk out of sight. The stuff appeared to be *lapping* at his legs ; and abruptly his bare flesh showed. The hideous stuff had rent his trouser-legs away, as if they were paper. He gave out a simply sickening scream, and, with a vast effort, wretched one leg free. It was partly destroyed. The next instant he pitched face downward, and the stuff heaped itself upon him, as if it were actually alive, with a dreadful savage life. It was simply infernal. The man had gone from sight. Where he had fallen was now a writhing, elongated mound, in constant and horrible increase, as the mould appeared to move towards it in strange ripples from all sides.

"Captain Gannington and the second mate were stone silent, in amazed and incredulous horror ; but I had begun to reach towards a grotesque and terrific conclusion, both helped and hindered by my professional training.

"From the men in the boat alongside, there was a loud shouting, and I saw two of their faces appear suddenly above the rail. They showed clearly a moment in the light from the lamp which the man had snatched from Mr. Selvern ; for strangely enough, this lamp was standing upright and un-harmed on the deck, a little way fore-side of that dreadful, elongated, growing mound, that still swayed and writhed with an incredible horror.   The lamp rose and fell on the passing ripples of the mould just—for all the world—as you will see a boat rise and fall on little swells.   Is is of some interest to me now, psychologically, to remember how that rising and falling lantern brought home to me, more than anything, the incomprehensible, dreadful strangeness of it all.

"The men's faces disappeared, with sudden yells, as if they had slipped or been suddenly hurt; and there was a fresh uproar of shouting from the boat.   The men were calling to us to come away; to come away.   In the same instant, I felt my left boot drawn suddenly and forcibly downward, with a horrible painful grip.   I wrenched it free, with a yell of angry fear.   Forrard of us, I saw that the vile surface was all a-move, and abruptly I found myself shouting in a queer frightened voice :

" 'The boat, Captain ! The boat, Captain !'

"Captain Gannington stared round at me, over his right shoulder, in a peculiar, dull way, that told me he was utterly dazed with bewilderment and the incomprehensibleness of it all.   I took a quick, clogged, nervous step towards him, and gripped his arm and shook it fiercely.

" 'The boat !' I shouted at him.   'The boat ! For God's sake, tell the men to bring the boat aft !'

"Then the mould must have drawn his feet down ; for, abruptly, he bellowed fiercely with terror, his momentary apathy giving place to furious energy.   His thick-set, vastly muscular body doubled and writhed with his enormous effort, and he struck out madly, dropping the lantern.   He tore his feet free, something ripped as he did so.   The *reality* and necessity of the situation had come upon him, brutishly real, and he was roaring to the men in the boat :

" 'Bring the boat aft ! Bring 'er aft ! Bring 'er aft !'

"The second mate and I were shouting the same thing, madly.

" 'For God's sake be smart, lads !' roared the captain, and stooped quickly for his lamp, which still burned.   His feet were gripped again, and he hove them out, blaspheming breathlessly, and leaping a yard high with his effort.   Then he made a run for the side, wrenching his feet free at each step.   In the same instant, the second mate cried out something, and grabbed at the captain :

" 'It's got hold of my feet ! It's got hold of my feet !' he screamed. His feet had disappeared up to his boot-tops, and Captain Gannington caught him round the waist with his powerful left arm, gave a mighty heave, and the next instant had him free ; but both his boot-soles had almost gone.

"For my part, I jumped madly from foot to foot, to avoid the plucking of the mould ; and suddenly I made a run for the ship's side. But before I got there, a queer gap came in the mould, between us and the side, at least a couple of feet wide, and how deep I don't know. It closed up in an instant, and all the mould, where the gap had been, went into a sort of flurry of horrible ripplings, so that I ran back from it ; for I did not dare to put my foot upon it. Then the captain was shouting at me :

" 'Aft, Doctor ! Aft, Doctor ! This way, Doctor ! Run !' I saw then that he had passed me, and was up on the after raised portion of the poop. He had the second mate thrown like a sack, all loose and quiet, over his left shoulder ; for Mr. Selvern had fainted, and his long legs flopped, limp and helpless, against the captain's massive knees as the captain ran. I saw, with a queer unconscious noting of minor details, how the torn soles of the second mate's boots flapped and jigged, as the captain staggered aft.

" 'Boat ahoy ! Boat ahoy ! Boat ahoy !' shouted the captain ; and then I was beside him, shouting also. The men were answering with loud yells of encouragement, and it was plain they were working desperately to force the boat aft, through the thick scum about the ship.

"We reached the ancient, mould-hid taffrail, and slewed about, breathlessly, in the half darkness, to see what was happening. Captain Gannington had left his lantern by the big mound, when he picked up the second mate ; and as we stood gasping, we discovered suddenly that all the mould between us and the light was full of movement. Yes, the part on which we stood, for about six or eight feet forrard of us, was still firm.

"Every couple of seconds, we shouted to the men to hasten, and they kept on calling to us that they would be with us in an instant. And all the time, we watched the deck of that dreadful hulk, feeling, for my part, literally sick with mad suspense, and ready to jump overboard into that filthy scum all about us.

"Down somewhere in the huge bulk of the ship, there was all the time that extraordinary, dull, ponderous Thud ! Thud !

Thud! Thud! growing ever louder. I seemed to feel the whole hull of the derelict beginning to quiver and thrill with each dull beat. And to me, with the grotesque and monstrous suspicion of what made that noise, it was, at once, the most dreadful and incredible sound I have ever heard.

"As we waited desperately for the boat, I scanned incessantly so much of the grey-white bulk as the lamp showed. The whole of the decks seemed to be in strange movement. Forrard of the lamp I could see, indistinctly, the moundings of the mould swaying and nodding hideously, beyond the circle of the brightest rays. Nearer, and full in the glow of the lamp, the mound which should have indicated the skylight, was swelling steadily. There were ugly purple veinings on it, and as it swelled, it seemed to me that the veinings and mottling on it were becoming plainer—rising, as though embossed upon it, like you will see the veins stand out on the body of a powerful full-blooded horse. It was most extraordinary. The mound that we had supposed to cover the companion-way had sunk flat with the surrounding mould, and I could not see that it jetted out any more of the purplish fluid.

"A quaking movement of the mould began, away forrard of the lamp, and came flurrying away aft towards us; and at the sight of that, I climbed up on to the spongy-feeling taffrail, and yelled afresh for the boat. The men answered with a shout, which told me they were nearer, but the beastly scum was so thick that it was evidently a fight to move the boat at all. Beside me, Captain Gannington was shaking the second mate furiously, and the man stirred and began to moan. The captain shook him awake.

" 'Wake up! Wake up, Mister!' he shouted.

"The second mate staggered out of the captain's arms, and collapsed suddenly, shrieking:—'My feet! Oh, God! My feet!' The captain and I lugged him off the mould, and got him into a sitting position upon the taffrail, where he kept up a continual moaning.

" 'Hold 'im, Doctor,' said the captain, and whilst I did so, he ran forrard a few yards, and peered down over the starboard quarter rail. 'For God's sake, be smart, lads! Be smart! Be smart!' he shouted down to the men; and they answered him, breathless, from close at hand; yet still too far away for the boat to be any use to us on the instant.

"I was holding the moaning, half-unconscious officer, and

staring forrard along the poop decks. The flurrying of the mould was coming aft, slowly and noiselessly. And then, suddenly, I saw something closer :

" 'Look out, Captain !' I shouted ; and even as I shouted, the mould near to him gave a sudden peculiar slobber. I had seen a ripple stealing towards him through the horrible stuff. He gave an enormous, clumsy leap, and landed near to us on the sound part of the mould, but the movement followed him. He turned and faced it, swearing fiercely. All about his feet there came abruptly little gapings, which made horrid sucking noises.

" 'Come *back*, Captain !' I yelled. 'Come back, *quick* !'

"As I shouted, a ripple came at his feet—lipping at them ; and he stamped insanely at it, and leaped back, his boot torn half off his foot. He swore madly with pain and anger, and jumped swiftly for the taffrail.

" 'Come on, Doctor ! Over we go !' he called. Then he remembered the filthy scum, and hesitated, roaring out desperately to the men to hurry. I stared down, also.

" 'The second mate ?' I said.

" 'I'll take charge, doctor,' said Captain Gannington, and caught hold of Mr. Selvern. As he spoke, I though I saw something beneath us, outlined against the scum. I leaned out over the stern, and peered. There was something under the port quarter.

" 'There's something down there, Captain !' I called, and pointed in the darkness.

"He stooped far over, and stared.

" 'A boat, by Gum ! *A boat !*' he yelled, and began to wriggle swiftly along the taffrail, dragging the second mate after him. I followed.

" 'A boat it is, sure !' he exclaimed, a few moments later, and, picking up the second mate clear of the rail, he hove him down into the boat, where he fell with a crash into the bottom.

" 'Over ye go, Doctor !' he yelled at me, and pulled me bodily off the rail, and dropped me after the officer. As he did so, I felt the whole of the ancient, spongy rail give a peculiar sickening quiver, and began to wobble. I fell on to the second mate, and the captain came after, almost in the same instant ; but fortunately he landed clear of us, on to the fore thwart, which broke under his weight, with a loud crack and splinter-ing of wood.

" 'Thank God!' I heard him mutter. 'Thank God! . . . I guess that was a mighty near thing to goin' to hell.'

"He struck a match, just as I got to my feet, and between us we got the second mate straightened out on one of the after thwarts. We shouted to the men in the boat, telling them where we were, and saw the light of their lantern shining round the starboard counter of the derelict. They called back to us, to tell us they were doing their best, and then, while we waited, Captain Gannington struck another match, and began to overhaul the boat we had dropped into. She was a modern, two-oared boat, and on the stern there was painted *Cyclone Glasgow*. She was in pretty fair condition, and had evidently drifted into the scum and been held by it.

"Captain Gannington struck several matches, and went forrard towards the derelict. Suddenly he called to me, and I jumped over the thwarts to him.

" 'Look, Doctor,' he said; and I saw what he meant—a mass of bones, up in the bows of the boat. I stooped over them and looked. They were the bones of at least three people, all mixed together, in an extraordinary fashion, and quite clean and dry. I had a sudden thought concerning the bones; but I said nothing; for my thought was vague, in some ways, and concerned the grotesque and incredible suggestion that had come to me, as to the cause of that ponderous, dull Thud! Thud! Thud! Thud! that beat on so infernally within the hull, and was plain to hear even now that we had got off the vessel herself. And all the while, you know, I had a sick, horrible, mental picture of that frightful wriggling mound aboard the hulk.

"As Captain Gannington struck a final match I saw something that sickened me, and the captain saw it in the same instant. The match went out, and he fumbled clumsily for another, and struck it. We saw the thing again. We had not been mistaken. . . . A great lip of grey-white was protruding in over the edge of the boat—a great lappet of the mould was coming stealthily towards us; a live mass of *the very hull itself*. And suddenly Captain Gannington yelled out, in so many words, the grotesque and incredible thing I was thinking:

" '*She's Alive!*'

"I never heard such a sound of *comprehension* and terror in a man's voice. The very horrified assurance of it, made actual to me the thing that, before, had only lurked in my sub-conscious mind. I knew he was right; I knew that the explanation, my reason and my training, both repelled and reached towards, was the true one . . . I wonder whether anyone can possibly understand our feelings in that moment . . . The unmitigable horror of it, and the *incredibleness*.

"As the light of the match burned up fully, I saw that the mass of living matter, coming towards us, was streaked and veined with purple, the veins standing out, enormously distended. The whole thing quivered continuously to each ponderous Thud! Thud! Thud! Thud! of that gargantuan organ that pulsed within the huge grey-white bulk. The flame of the match reached the captain's fingers, and there came to me a little sickly whiff of burned flesh; but he seemed unconscious of any pain. Then the flame went out, in a brief sizzle, yet at the last moment, I had seen an extraordinary raw look, become visible upon the end of that monstrous, pro-truding lappet. It had become dewed with a hideous, purplish sweat. And with the darkness, there came a sudden charnel-like stench.

"I heard the match-box split in Captain Gannington's hands, as he wrenched it open. Then he swore, in a queer frightened voice; for he had come to the end of his matches. He turned clumsily in the darkness, and tumbled over the nearest thwart, in his eagerness to get to the stern of the boat, and I after him; for he knew that thing was coming towards us through the darkness, reaching over that piteous mingled heap of human bones, all jumbled together in the bows. We shouted madly to the men, and for answer saw the bows of the boat emerge dimly into view, round the starboard counter of the derelict.

" 'Thank God!' I gasped out; but Captain Gannington yelled to them to show a light. Yet this they could not do, for the lamp had just been stepped on, in their desperate efforts to force the boat round to us.

" 'Quick! Quick!' I shouted.

" 'For God's sake be smart, men!' roared the captain; and both of us faced the darkness under the port counter, out of which we knew (but could not see) the thing was coming towards us.

" 'An oar! Smart now; pass me an oar!' shouted the captain; and reached out his hands through the gloom toward the oncoming boat. I saw a figure stand up in the bows, and hold something out to us, across the intervening yards of scum. Captain Gannington swept his hands through the darkness, and encountered it.

" 'I've got it. Let go there !' he said, in a quick, tense voice.

"In the same instant, the boat we were in, was pressed over suddenly to starboard by some tremendous weight. Then I heard the captain shout :—'Duck y'r head, Doctor, and directly afterwards he swung the heavy, fourteen-foot ash oar round his head, and struck into the darkness. There came a sudden squelch, and he struck again, with a savage grunt of fierce energy. At the second blow, the boat righted, with a slow movement, and directly afterwards the other boat bumped gently into ours.

"Captain Gannington dropped the oar, and springing across to the second mate, hove him up off the thwart, and pitched him with knee and arms clear in over the bows among the men ; then he shouted to me to follow, which I did, and he came after me, bringing the oar with him. We carried the second mate aft, and the captain shouted to the men to back the boat a little ; then they got her bows clear of the boat we had just left, and so headed out through the scum for the open sea.

" 'Where's Tom 'Arrison ?' gasped one of the men, in the midst of his exertions. He happened to be Tom Harrison's particular chum ; and Captain Gannington answered him briefly enough :

" 'Dead ! Pull ! Don't talk !'

" Now, difficult as it had been to force the boat through the scum to our rescue, the difficulty to get clear seemed tenfold. After some five minutes pulling, the boat seemed hardly to have moved a fathom, if so much ; and a quite dreadful fear took me afresh ; which one of the panting men put suddenly into words :

" 'It's got us !' he gasped out ; 'same as poor Tom !' It was the man who had inquired where Harrison was.

" 'Shut y'r mouth an' *pull* !'' roared the captain. And so another few minutes passed. Abruptly, it seemed to me that the dull, ponderous Thud ! Thud ! Thud ! Thud ! came more plainly through the dark, and I stared intently over the stern. I sickened a little ; for I could almost swear that the dark mass of the monster was actually *nearer* . . . that it was coming nearer to us through the darkness. Captain Gannington must have had the same thought; for after a brief look into the darkness, he made one jump to the stroke-oar, and began to double-bank it.

" 'Get forrid under the thwarts, Doctor !' he said to me, rather breathlessly. 'Get in the bows, an' see if you can't free the stuff a bit round the bows.'

"I did as he told me, and a minute later I was in the bows of the boat, puddling the scum from side to side with the boat-hook, and trying to break up the viscid, clinging muck. A heavy, almost animal-like odour rose off it, and all the air seemed full of the deadening smell. I shall never find words to tell any one the whole horror of it all—the threat that seemed to hang in the very air around us ; and, but a little astern, that incredible thing, coming, as I firmly believe, nearer, and the scum holding us like half-melted glue.

"The minutes passed in a deadly, eternal fashion, and I kept staring back astern into the darkness ; ; but never ceased to puddle that filthy scum, striking at it and switching it from side to side, until I sweated.

"Abruptly, Captain Gannington sang out :

" 'We're gaining, lads. Pull !' And I felt the boat forge ahead perceptibly, as they gave way, with renewed hope and energy. There was soon no doubt of it ; for presently that hideous Thud ! Thud ! Thud ! Thud ! had grown quite dim and vague somewhat astern, and I could no longer see the derelict ! for the night had come down tremendously dark, and all the sky was thick overset with heavy clouds. As we drew nearer and nearer to the edge of the scum, the boat moved more and more freely, until suddenly we emerged with a clean, sweet, fresh sound, into the open sea.

" 'Thank God !' I said aloud, and drew in the boat-hook, and made my way aft again to where Captain Gannington now sat once more at the tiller. I saw him looking anxiously up at the sky, and across to where the lights of our vessel burned, and again he would seem to listen intently ; so that I found myself listening also.

" 'What's that, Captain ?' I said sharply ; for it seemed to me that I heard a sound far astern, something between a queer whine and a low whistling. 'What's that ?'

" 'It's wind, Doctor,' he said, in a low voice. 'I wish to God we were aboard.'

"Then, to the men : 'Pull ! Put y'r backs into it, or ye'll never put y'r teeth through good bread again !'

"The men obeyed nobly, and we reached the vessel safely, and had the boat safely stowed, before the storm came, which it did in a furious white smother out of the west. I could see it for some minutes beforehand, tearing the sea, in the gloom, into a wall of phosphorescent foam ; and as it came nearer, that peculiar whining, piping sound grew louder and louder, until it was like a vast steam-whistle, rushing towards us across the sea.

"And when it did come, we got it very heavy indeed ; so that the morning showed us nothing but a welter of white seas ; and that grim derelict was many a score of miles away in the smother, lost as utterly as our hearts could wish to lose her.

When I came to examine the second mate's feet, I found them in a very extraordinary condition. The soles of them had the appearance of having been partly digested. I know of no other word that so exactly describes their condition ; and the agony the man suffered, must have been dreadful.

"Now," concluded the doctor, "that is what I call a case in point. If we could know exactly what that old vessel had originally been loaded with, and the juxtaposition of the various articles of her cargo, plus the heat and time she had endured, plus one or two other only guessable quantities, we should have solved the chemistry of the Life-Force, gentlemen. Not necessarily the *origin*, mind you ; but, at least, we should have taken a big step on the way. I've often regretted that gale, you know—in a way, that is, in a way ! It was a most amazing discovery ; but, at the time, I had nothing but thankfulness to be rid of it. . . . A most amazing chance. I often think of the way the monster woke out of its torpor. And that scum. . . . The dead pigs caught in it. . . . I fancy that was a grim kind of net, gentlemen. . . . It caught many things. . . . It . . ."

The old doctor sighed and nodded.

"If I could have had her bill of lading," he said, his eyes full of regret. "If— It might have told me something to help. But, anyway . . ." He began to fill his pipe again. . . . "I suppose," he ended, looking round at us gravely, "I s'pose we humans are an ungrateful lot of beggars, at the best ! . . . But . . . but what a chance ! What a chance— eh ?"

THE JUDGE'S HOUSE
Bram Stoker

WHEN the time for his examination drew near Malcolm
Malcolmson made up his mind to go somewhere to read by
himself. He feared the attractions of the seaside, and also he
feared completely rural isolation, for of old he knew its
charms, and so he determined to find some unpretentious
little town where there would be nothing to distract him.
He refrained from asking suggestions from any of his friends,
for he argued that each would recommend some place of
which he had knowledge, and where he had already acquaint-
ances. As Malcolmson wished to avoid friends he had no
wish to encumber himself with the attention of friends' friends
and so he determined to look out for a place for himself.
He packed a portmanteau with some clothes and all the books
he required, and then took ticket for the first name on the
local time-table which he did not know.

When at the end of three hours' journey he alighted at
Benchurch, he felt satisfied that he had so far obliterated his
tracks as to be sure of having a peaceful opportunity of
pursuing his studies. He went straight to the one inn which
the sleepy little place contained, and put up for the night.
Benchurch was a market town, and once in three weeks was
crowded to excess, but for the remainder of the twenty-one
days it was as attractive as a desert. Malcolmson looked
around the day after his arrival to try to find quarters more
isolated than even so quiet an inn as "The Good Traveller"
afforded. There was only one place which took his fancy,
and it certainly satisfied his wildest ideas regarding quiet; in
fact, quiet was not the proper word to apply to it—desolation
was the only term conveying any suitable idea of its isolation.
It was an old, rambling, heavy-built house of the Jacobean
style, with heavy gables and windows, unusually small, and
set higher than was customary in such houses, and was surrounded with a high brick wall massively built. Indeed, on

examination, it looked more like a fortified house than an ordinary dwelling. But all these things pleased Malcolmson. "Here," he thought, "is the very spot I have been looking for, and if I can only get opportunity of using it I shall be happy." His joy was increased when he realized beyond doubt that it was not at present inhabited.

From the post-office he got the name of the agent, who was rarely surprised at the application to rent a part of the old house. Mr. Carnford, the local lawyer and agent, was a genial old gentleman, and frankly confessed his delight at anyone being willing to live in the house.

"To tell you the truth," said he, "I should be only too happy, on behalf of the owners, to let anyone have the house rent free, for a term of years if only to accustom the people here to see it inhabited. It has been so long empty that some kind of absurd prejudice has grown up about it, and this can be best put down by its occupation—if only," he added with a sly glance at Malcolmson, "by a scholar like yourself, who wants its quiet for a time."

Malcolmson thought it needless to ask the agent about the "absurd prejudice"; he knew he would get more information, if he should require it, on that subject from other quarters. He paid his three months' rent, got a receipt, and the name of an old woman who would probably undertake to "do" for him, and came away with the keys in his pocket. He then went to the landlady of the inn, who was a cheerful and most kindly person, and asked her advice as to such stores and provisions as he would be likely to require. She threw up her hands in amazement when he told her where he was going to settle himself.

"Not in the Judge's House!" she said, and grew pale as she spoke. He explained the locality of the house, saying that he did not know its name. When he had finished she answered:

"Aye, sure enough—sure enough the very place! It is the Judge's House sure enough." He asked her to tell him about the place, why so called, and what there was against it. She told him that it was so called locally because it had been many years before—how long she could not say, as she was herself from another part of the country, but she thought it must have been a hundred years or more—the abode of a judge who was held in great terror on account of his harsh sentences and his hostility to prisoners at Assizes. As to what there was against the house itself she could not tell. She had often asked, but no one could inform her, but there was a general feeling that there was *something*, and for her own part she would not take all the money in Drinkwater's Bank and stay in the house an hour by herself. Then she apologized to Malcolmson for her disturbing talk.

"It is too bad of me, sir, and you—and a young gentleman, too—if you will pardon me saying it, going to live there all alone. If you were my boy—and you'll excuse me for saying it—you wouldn't sleep there a night, not if I had to go there myself and pull the big alarm bell that's on the roof!" The good creature was so manifestly in earnest, and was so kindly in her intentions, that Malcolmson, although amused, was touched. He told her kindly how much he appreciated her interest in him, and added :

"But, my dear Mrs. Witham, indeed you need not be concerned about me ! A man who is reading for the Mathematical Tripos has too much to think of to be disturbed by any of these mysterious 'somethings,' and his work is of too exact and prosaic a kind to allow of his having any order in his mind for mysteries of any kind. Harmonical Progression, Permutations and Combinations, and Elliptic Functions have sufficient mysteries for me !" Mrs. Witham kindly undertook to see after his commissions, and he went himself to look for the old woman who had been recommended to him. When he turned to the Judge's House with her, after an interval of a couple of hours, he found Mrs. Witham herself waiting with several men and boys carrying parcels, and an upholsterer's man with a bed in a cart, for she said, though table and chairs might be all very well, a bed that hadn't been aired for maybe fifty years was not proper for young ones to lie on. She was evidently curious to see the inside of the house, and though manifestly so afraid of the 'somethings' that at the slightest sound she clutched on to Malcolmson, whom she never left for a moment, went over the whole place.

After his examination of the house, Malcolmson decided to take up his abode in the great dining-room, which was big enough to serve for all his requirements, and Mrs. Witham, with the aid of the charwoman, Mrs. Dempster, proceeded to arrange matters. When the hampers were brought in and unpacked, Malcolmson saw that with much kind forethought she had sent from her own kitchen sufficient provisions to last for a few days. Before going she expressed all sorts of kind wishes, and at the door turned and said :

"And perhaps, sir, as the room is big and draughty it might be well to have one of those big screens put round your bed at night—though, truth to tell, I would die myself if I were to be so shut in with all kinds of—of 'things,' that put their heads round the sides, or over the top, and look on me !" The image which she had called up was too much for her nerves and she fled incontinently.

Mrs. Dempster sniffed in a superior manner as the landlady disappeared, and remarked that for her own part she wasn't afraid of all the bogies in the kingdom.

"I'll tell you what it is, sir," she said, "bogies is all kinds and sorts of things—except bogies ! Rats and mice, and beetles and creaky doors, and loose slates, and broken panes, and stiff drawer handles, that stay out when you pull them and then fall down in the middle of the night. Look at the wainscot of the room ! It is old—hundreds of years old ! Do you think there's no rats and beetles there ? And do you imagine, sir, that you won't see none of them ? Rats is bogies, I tell you, and bogies is rats, and don't you get to think anything else !"

"Mrs. Dempster," said Malcolmson gravely, making her a polite bow, "you know more than a Senior Wrangler ! And let me say that, as a mark of esteem for your indubitable soundness of head and heart, I shall, when I go, give you possession of this house, and let you stay here by yourself for the last two months of my tenancy, for four weeks will serve my purpose."

"Thank you kindly, sir !" she answered, "but I couldn't sleep away from home a night. I am in Greenhow's Charity, and if I slept a night away from my rooms I should lose all I have got to live on. The rules is very strict, and there's too many watching for a vacancy for me to run any risks in the matter. Only for that, sir, I'd gladly come here and attend on you altogether during your stay."

"My good woman," said Malcolmson hastily, "I have come here on a purpose to obtain solitude, and believe me that I am grateful to the late Greenhow for having so organized his admirable charity—whatever it is—that I am perforce denied the opportunity of suffering from such a form of temptation ! Saint Anthony himself could not be more rigid on the point !"

The old woman laughed harshly. "Ah, you young gentlemen," she said, "you don't fear for nought, and belike you'll get all the solitude you want here." She set to work with her cleaning, and by nightfall, when Malcolmson returned from his walk—he always had one of his books to study as he walked—he found the room swept and tidied, a fire burning on the old hearth, the lamp lit, and the table spread for supper with Mrs. Witham's excellent fare. "This is comfort indeed," he said, and rubbed his hands.

When he had finished his supper, and lifted the tray to the other end of the great oak dining-table, he got out his books again, put fresh wood on the fire, trimmed his lamp, and set himself down to a spell of real hard work. He went on without a pause till about eleven o'clock, when he knocked off for a bit to fix his fire and lamp, and to make himself a cup of tea. He had always been a tea-drinker, and during his college life had sat late at work and had taken tea late. The rest was a great luxury to him, and he enjoyed it with a sense of delicious voluptuous ease. The renewed fire leaped and sparkled, and threw quaint shadows through the great old room, and as he sipped his hot tea he revelled in the sense of isolation from his kind. Then it was that he began to notice for the first time what a noise the rats were making.

"Surely," he thought, "they cannot have been at it all the time I was reading. Had they been, I must have noticed it!" Presently, when the noise increased, he satisfied himself that it was really new. It was evident that at first the rats had been frightened at the presence of a stranger, and the light of fire and lamp, but that as the time went on they had grown bolder and were now disporting themselves as was their wont.

How busy they were—and hark to the strange noises! Up and down the old wainscot, over the ceiling and under the floor they raced, and gnawed, and scratched! Malcolmson smiled to himself as he recalled to mind the saying of Mrs. Dempster, "Bogies is rats, and rats is bogies!" The tea began to have its effect of intellectual and nervous stimulus, he saw with joy another long spell of work to be done before the night was past, and in the sense of security which it gave him, he allowed himself the luxury of a good look round the room. He took his lamp in one hand, and went all round, wondering that so quaint and beautiful an old house had been so long neglected. The carving of the oak on the panels of the wainscot was fine, and on and round the doors and windows it was beautiful and of rare merit. There were some old pictures on the walls, but they were coated so thick with dust and dirt that he could not distinguish any detail of them, though he held his lamp as high as he could over his head. Here and there as he went round he saw some crack or hole blocked for a moment by the face of a rat with its bright eyes glittering in the light, but in an instant it was gone, and a squeak and a scamper followed. The thing that most struck him, however, was the rope of the great alarm bell on the roof, which hung down in a corner of the room on the right-hand side of the fireplace. He pulled up close to the hearth a great high-backed carved oak chair, and sat down to his last cup of tea. When this was done he made up the fire, and went back to his work, sitting at the corner of the table, having the fire to his left. For a little while the rats disturbed him somewhat with their perpetual scampering, but he got accustomed to the noise as one does to the ticking of the clock or to the roar of moving water, and he became so immersed in his work that everything in the world, except the problem which he was trying to solve, passed away from him.

He suddenly looked up, his problem was still unsolved, and there was in the air that sense of the hour before the dawn, which is so dread to doubtful life. The noise of the rats had ceased. Indeed it seemed to him that it must have ceased but lately and that it was the sudden cessation which had disturbed him. The fire had fallen low, but still it threw out a deep red glow. As he looked he started in spite of his *sang froid*.

There, on the great high-backed carved oak chair by the right side of the fire-place sat an enormous rat, steadily glaring at him with baleful eyes. He made a motion to it as though to hunt it away, but it did not stir. Then he made the motion of throwing something. Still it did not stir, but showed its great white teeth angrily, and its cruel eyes shone in the lamplight with an added vindictiveness.

Malcolmson felt amazed, and seizing the poker from the hearth ran at it to kill it. Before, however, he could strike it the rat, with a squeak that sounded like the concentration of hate, jumped upon the floor, and, running up the rope of the alarm bell, disappeared in the darkness beyond the range of the green-shaded lamp. Instantly, strange to say, the noisy scampering of the rats in the wainscot began again.

By this time Malcolmson's mind was quite off the problem, and as a shrill cock-crow outside told him of the approach of morning, he went to bed and to sleep.

He slept so sound that he was not even waked by Mrs. Dempster coming in to make up his room. It was only when she had tidied up the place and got his breakfast ready and tapped on the screen which closed in his bed that he woke. He was a little tired still after his night's hard work, but a strong cup of tea soon freshened him up and, taking his book, he went out for his morning walk, bringing with him a few sandwiches lest he should not care to return till dinner-time. He found a quiet walk between high elms some way outside the town, and here he spent the greater part of the day studying his Laplace. On his return he looked in to see Mrs. Witham and to thank her for her kindness. When she saw him coming through the diamond-paned bay window of her sanctum she came out to meet him and asked him in. She looked at him searchingly and shook her head as she said :

"You must not overdo it, sir. You are paler this morning than you should be. Too late hours and too hard work on the brain's isn't good for any man ! But tell me, sir, how did you pass the night ? Well, I hope ? But, my heart ! sir, I was glad when Mrs. Dempster told me this morning that you were all right and sleeping sound when she went in."

"Oh, I was all right," he answered smiling, "the 'some-things' didn't worry me, as yet. Only the rats, and they had a circus, I tell you, all over the place. There was one wicked-looking old devil that sat up on my own chair by the fire, and wouldn't go till I took the poker to him, and then he ran up the rope of the alarm bell and got to somewhere up the wall or the ceiling—I couldn't see where, it was so dark."

"Mercy on us," said Mrs. Witham, "an old devil, and sitting on a chair by the fireside ! Take care, sir ! take care ! There's many a true word spoken in jest."

"How do you mean ? 'Pon my word, I don't understand."

"An old devil ! The old devil, perhaps. There ! sir, you needn't laugh," for Malcolmson had broken into a hearty peal. "You young folks think it easy to laugh at things that makes older ones shudder. Never mind, sir ! never mind ! Please God, you'll laugh all the time. It's what I wish you myself !" and the good lady beamed all over in sympathy with his enjoyment, her fears gone for a moment.

"Oh, forgive me !" said Malcolmson presently. "Don't think me rude, but the idea was too much for me—that the old devil himself was on the chair last night !" And at the thought he laughed again. Then he went home to dinner.

This evening the scampering of the rats began earlier, indeed it had been going on before his arrival, and only ceased whilst his presence by its freshness disturbed them. After dinner he sat by the fire for a while and had a smoke, and then, having cleared his table, began to work as before. To-night the rats disturbed him more than they had done on the previous night. How they scampered up and down and under and over ! How they squeaked and scratched and gnawed ! How they, getting bolder by degrees, came to the mouths of their holes and to the chinks and cracks and crannies in the wainscoting till their eyes shone like tiny lamps as the firelight rose and fell. But to him, now doubtless accustomed to them, their eyes were not wicked, only their playfulness touched him. Some-times the boldest of them made sallies out on the floor or along the mouldings of the wainscot. Now and again as they disturbed him Malcolmson made a sound to frighten them, smiting the table with his hand or giving a fierce "Hsh, hsh," so that they fled straightway to their holes.

And so the early part of the night wore on, and despite the noise Malcolmson got more and more immersed in his work.

All at once he stopped, as on the previous night, being overcome by a sudden sense of silence. There was not the faintest sound of gnaw, or scratch, or squeak. The silence was as of the grave. He remembered the odd occurrence of the previous night, and instinctively he looked at the chair standing close by the fireside. And then a very odd sensation thrilled through him.

There, on the great old high-backed carved oak chair beside the fireplace sat the same enormous rat, steadily glaring at him with baleful eyes.

Instinctively he took the nearest thing to his hand, a book of logarithims, and flung it at it. The book was badly aimed and the rat did not stir, so again the poker performance of the previous night was repeated, and again the rat, being closely pursued, fled up the rope of the alarm bell. Strangely, too, the departure of this rat was instantly followed by the renewal of the noise made by the general rat community. On this occasion, as on the previous one, Malcolmson could not see at what part of the room the rat disappeared, for the green shade of his lamp left the upper part of the room in darkness and the fire had burned low.

On looking at his watch he found it was close on midnight, and, not sorry for the *divertissement*, he made up his fire and made himself his nightly pot of tea. He had got through a good spell of work, and thought himself entitled to a cigarette, and so he sat on the great carved oak chair before the fire and enjoyed it. Whilst smoking he began to think that he would like to know where the rat disappeared to, for he had certain ideas for the morrow not entirely disconnected with a rat-trap. Accordingly he lit another lamp and placed it so that it would shine well into the right-hand corner of the wall by the fireplace. Then he got all the books he had with him, and placed them handy to throw at the vermin. Finally he lifted the rope of the alarm bell and placed the end of it on the table, fixing the extreme end under the lamp. As he handled it he could not help noticing how pliable it was, especially for so strong a rope and one not in use. "You could hang a man with it," he thought to himself. When his preparations were made he looked around, and said complacently:

"There now, my friend, I think we shall learn something of you this time!" He began his work again, and though, as before, somewhat disturbed at first by the noise of the rats, soon lost himself in his propositions and problems.

Again he was called to his immediate surroundings suddenly. This time it might not have been the sudden silence only which took his attention; there was a slight movement of the rope, and the lamp moved. Without stirring, he looked to see if his pile of books was within range, and then cast his eye along the rope. As he looked he saw the great rat drop from the rope on the oak arm-chair and sit there glaring at him. He raised a book in his right hand, and taking careful aim, flung it at the rat. The latter, with a quick movement, sprang aside and dodged the missile. He then took another book, and a third, and flung them one after another at the rat, but each time unsuccessfully. At last, as he stood with a book poised in his hand to throw, the rat squeaked and seemed afraid. This made Malcolmson more than ever eager to strike, and the book flew and struck the rat a resounding blow. It gave a terrified squeak, and turning on his pursuer a look of terrible malevolence, ran up the chair-back and made a great jump to the rope of the alarm bell and ran up it like lightning. The lamp rocked under the sudden strain, but it was a heavy one and did not topple over. Malcolmson kept his eyes on the rat, and saw it by the light of the second lamp leap to a moulding of the wainscot and disappear through a hole in one of the great pictures which hung on the wall, obscured and invisible through its coating of dirt and dust.

"I shall look up my friend's habitation in the morning," said the student, as he went over to collect his books. "The third picture from the fireplace, I shall not forget." He picked up the books one by one, commenting on them as he lifted them. "*Conic Sections* he does not mind, nor *Cyloidal Oscillations*, nor the *Principia*, nor *Quaternions*, nor *Thermodynamics*. Now for the book that fetched him!" Malcolmson took it up and looked at it. As he did so he started, and a sudden pallor overspread his face. He looked round uneasily and shivered slightly, as he murmured to himself:

"The Bible my mother gave me! What an odd coincidence. He sat down to work again, and the rats in the wainscot renewed their gambols. They did not disturb him, however; somehow their presence gave him a sense of companionship. But he could not attend to his work, and after striving to master the subject on which he was engaged gave it up in despair, and went to bed as the first streak of dawn stole in through the eastern window.

He slept heavily but uneasily, and dreamed much, and when Mrs. Dempster woke him late in the morning he seemed ill at ease, and for a few minutes did not seem to realize exactly where he was. His first request rather surprised the servant.

"Mrs. Dempster, when I am out to-day I wish you would get the steps and dust or wash those pictures—specially that one the third from the fireplace—I want to see what they are."

Late in the afternoon Malcolmson worked at his books in the shaded walk, and the cheerfulness of the previous day came back to him as the day wore on, and he found that his reading was progressing well. He had worked out to a satisfactory conclusion all the problems which had as yet baffled him, and it was in a state of jubilation that he paid a visit to Mrs. Witham at "The Good Traveller." He found a stranger in the cosy sitting-room with the landlady, who was introduced to him as Dr. Thornhill. She was not quite at ease, and this, combined with the doctor's plunging at once into a series of questions, made Malcolmson come to the conclusion that his presence was not an accident, so without preliminary he said :

"Dr. Thornhill, I shall with pleasure answer you any question you may choose to ask me if you will answer me one question first."

The doctor seemed surprised, but he smiled and answered at once, "Done! What is it ?"

"Did Mrs. Witham ask you to come here and see me and advise me ?"

Dr. Thornhill for a moment was taken aback, and Mrs. Witham got fiery red and turned away, but the doctor was a frank and ready man, and he answered at once and openly :

"She did, but she didn't intend you to know it. I suppose it was my clumsy haste that made you suspect. She told me that she did not like the idea of your being in that house all by yourself, and that she thought you took too much strong tea. In fact, she wants me to advise you, if possible, to give up the tea and the very late hours. I was a keen student in my time, so I suppose I may take the liberty of a college man, and without offence, advise you not quite as a stranger."

Malcolmson with a bright smile held out his hand. "Shake— as they say in America," he said. "I must thank you for your kindness, and Mrs. Witham too, and your kindness deserves a return on my part. I promise to take no more strong tea— no tea at all till you let me—and I shall go to bed to-night at one o'clock at latest. Will that do ?"

"Capital," said the doctor. "Now tell us all that you noticed in the old house," and so Malcolmson then and there told in minute detail all that had happened in the last two nights. He was interrupted every now and then by some exclamation from Mrs. Witham, till finally when he told of the episode of the Bible the landlady's pent-up emotions found vent in a shriek, and it was not till a stiff glass of brandy and water had been administered that she grew composed again. Dr. Thornhill listened with a face of growing gravity, and when the narrative was complete and Mrs. Witham had been restored he asked :

"The rat always went up the rope of the alarm bell ?"

"Always."

"I suppose you know," said the Doctor after a pause, "what the rope is?"

"No?"

"It is," said the Doctor slowly, "the very rope which the hangman used for all the victims of the Judge's judicial rancour!" Here he was interrupted by another scream from Mrs. Witham, and steps had to be taken for her recovery. Malcolmson having looked at his watch, and found that it was close to his dinner-hour, had gone home before her complete recovery.

When Mrs. Witham was herself again she almost assailed the Doctor with angry questions as to what he meant by putting such horrible ideas into the poor young man's mind. "He has quite enough there already to upset him," she added.

Dr. Thornhill replied:

"My dear madam, I had a distinct purpose in it! I wanted to draw his attention to the bell-rope, and to fix it there. It may be that he is in a highly over-wrought state, and has been studying too much, although I am bound to say that he seems as sound and healthy a young man, mentally and bodily, as ever I saw—but then the rats—and that suggestion of the devil." The doctor shook his head and went on. "I would have offered to go and stay the first night with him but that I felt sure it would have been a cause of offence. He may get in the night some strange fright or hallucination, and if he does I want him to pull that rope. All alone as he is it will give us warning, and we may reach him in time to be of service. I shall be sitting up pretty late to-night and shall keep my ears open. Do not be alarmed if Benchurch gets a surprise before morning."

"Oh, Doctor, what do you mean? What do you mean?"

"I mean this, that possibly—nay, more probably—we shall hear the great alarm-bell from the Judge's House to-night," and the Doctor made about as effective an exit as could be thought of.

When Malcolmson arrived home he found that it was a little after his usual time, and Mrs. Dempster had gone away—the rules of Greenhow's Charity were not to be neglected. He was glad to see that the place was bright and tidy with a cheerful fire and a well-trimmed lamp. The evening was colder than might have been expected in April, and a heavy wind was blowing with such rapidly-increasing strength that there was every promise of a storm during the night. For a few minutes after his entrance the noise of the rats ceased, but so soon as they became accustomed to his presence they began again. He was glad to hear them, for he felt once more the feeling of companionship in their noise, and his mind ran back to the strange fact that they only ceased to manifest themselves when the other—the great rat with the baleful eyes—came upon the scene. The reading-lamp only was lit and its green shade kept the ceiling and the upper part of the room in darkness so that the cheerful light from the hearth spreading over the floor and shining on the white cloth laid over the end of the table was warm and cheery. Malcolmson sat down to his dinner with a good appetite and a bouyant spirit. After his dinner and a cigarette he sat steadily down to work, determined not to let anything disturb him, for he remembered his promise to the doctor, and made up his mind to make the best of the time at his disposal.

For an hour or so he worked all right, and then his thoughts began to wander from his books. The actual circumstances around him, the calls on his physical attention, and his nervous susceptibility were not to be denied. By this time the wind had become a gale, and the gale a storm. The old house, solid though it was, seemed to shake to its foundations, and the storm roared and raged through its many chimneys and its queer old gables, producing strange, unearthly sounds in the empty rooms and corridors. Even the great alarm-bell on the roof must have felt the force of the wind, for the rope rose and fell slightly, as though the bell were moved a little from time to time, and the limber rope fell on the oak floor with a hard and hollow sound.

As Malcolmson listened to it he bethought himself of the doctor's words, "It is the rope which the hangman used for the victims of the Judge's judicial rancour," and he went over to the corner of the fireplace and took it in his hand to look at it. There seemed a sort of deadly interest in it, and as he stood there he lost himself for a moment in speculation as to who these victims were, and the grim wish of the Judge to have such a ghastly relic ever under his eyes. As he stood there the swaying of the bell on the roof still lifted the rope now and again, but presently there came a new sensation—a sort of tremor in the rope, as though something was moving along it.

Looking up instinctively Malcolmson saw the great rat coming slowly down towards him, glaring at him steadily. He dropped the rope and started back with a muttered curse, and the rat turning ran up the slope again and disappeared, and at the same instant Malcolmson became conscious that the noise of the other rats, which had ceased for a while, began again.

All this set him thinking, and it occurred to him that he had not investigated the lair of the rat or looked at the pictures, as he had intended. He lit the other lamp without the shade, and, holding it up went and stood opposite the third picture from the fireplace on the right-hand side where he had seen the rat disappear on the previous night.

At the first glance he started back so suddenly that he almost dropped the lamp, and a deadly pallor overspread his face. His knees shook, and heavy drops of sweat came on his forehead, and he trembled like an aspen. But he was young and plucky, and pulled himself together, and after the pause of a few seconds stepped forward again, raised the lamp, and examined the picture which had been dusted and washed, and now stood out clearly.

It was of a judge dressed in his robes of scarlet and ermine. His face was strong and merciless, evil, crafty, and vindictive, with a sensual mouth, hooked nose of ruddy colour, and shaped like the beak of a bird of prey. The rest of the face was of a cadaverous colour. The eyes were of peculiar brilliance and with a terribly malignant expression. As he looked at them, Malcolmson grew cold, for he saw there the very counterpart of the eyes of the great rat. The lamp almost fell from his hand, he saw the rat with its baleful eyes peering out through the hole in the corner of the picture, and noted the sudden cessation of the noise of the other rats. However, he pulled himself together, and went on with his examination of the picture.

The Judge was seated in a great high-backed carved oak chair, on the right-hand side of a great stone fireplace where, in the corner, a rope hung down from the ceiling, its end lying coiled on the floor. With a feeling of something like horror, Malcolmson recognized the scene of the room as it stood, and gazed around him in an awestruck manner as though he expected to find some strange presence behind him. Then he looked over to the corner of the fireplace—and with a loud cry he let the lamp fall from his hand.

There, in the judge's arm-chair, with the rope hanging behind, sat the rat with the Judge's baleful eyes, now intensified and with a fiendish leer. Save for the howling of the storm without there was silence.

The fallen lamp recalled Malcolmson to himself. Fortunately it was of metal, and so the oil was not spilt. However, the practical need of attending to it settled at once his nervous apprehensions. When he had turned it out, he wiped his brow and thought for a moment.

"This will not do," he said to himself. "If I go on like this I shall become a crazy fool. This must stop! I promised the doctor I would not take tea. Faith, he was pretty right! My nerves must have been getting into a queer state. Funny I did not notice it. I never felt better in my life. However, it is all right now, and I shall not be such a fool again."

Then he mixed himself a good stiff glass of brandy and water and resolutely sat down to his work.

It was nearly an hour when he looked up from his book, disturbed by the sudden stillness. Without, the wind howled and roared louder than ever, and the rain drove in sheets against the windows, beating like hail on the glass, but within there was no sound whatever save the echo of the wind as it roared in the great chimney, and now and then a hiss as a few raindrops found their way down the chimney in a lull of the storm. The fire had fallen low and had ceased to flame, though it threw out a red glow. Malcolmson listened attentively, and presently heard a thin, squeaking noise, very faint. It came from the corner of the room where the rope hung down, and he thought it was the creaking of the rope on the floor as the swaying of the bell raised and lowered it. Looking up, however, he saw in the dim light the great rat clinging to the rope and gnawing it. The rope was already nearly gnawed through—he could see the lighter colour where the strands were laid bare. As he looked the job was completed, and the severed end of the rope fell clattering on the oaken floor, whilst for an instant the great rat remained like a knob or tassel at the end of the rope, which now began to sway to and fro. Malcolmson felt for a moment another pang of terror as he thought that now the possibility of calling the outer world to his assistance was cut off, but an intense anger took its place, and seizing the book he was reading he hurled it at the rat. The blow was well-aimed, but before the missile could reach him the rat dropped off and struck the floor with a soft thud. Malcolmson instantly rushed over towards him, but it darted away and disappeared in the darkness of the shadows of the room. Malcolmson felt that his work was over for the night, and determined then and there to vary the monotony of the proceedings by a hunt for the rat, and took off the green shade of the lamp so as to insure a wider spreading light. As he did so the gloom of the upper part of the room was relieved, and in the new flood of light, great by comparison with the previous darkness, the pictures on the wall stood out boldly. From where he stood, Malcolmson saw right opposite to him the third picture on the wall from the right of the fireplace. He rubbed his eyes in surprise, and then a great fear began to come upon him.

In the centre of the picture was a great irregular patch of brown canvas, as fresh as when it was stretched on the frame. The background was as before, with chair and chimney-corner and rope, but the figure of the Judge had disappeared.

Malcolmson, almost in a chill of horror, turned slowly round, and then he began to shake and tremble like a man in a palsy. His strength seemed to have left him, and he was incapable of action or movement, hardly even of thought. He could only see and hear.

There, on the great high-backed carved oak chair sat the judge in his robes of scarlet and ermine, with his baleful eyes glaring vindictively, and a smile of triumph on the resolute cruel mouth, as he lifted with his hands a *black cap*. Malcolmson felt as if the blood was running from his heart, as one does in moments of prolonged suspense. There was a singing in his ears. Without, he could hear the roar and howl of the tempest, and through it, swept on the storm, came the striking of midnight by the great chimes in the market-place. He stood for a space of time that seemed to him endless still as a statue, and with wide-open, horror-struck eyes, breathless. As the clock struck, so the smile of triumph on the Judge's face intensified, and at the last stroke of midnight he placed the black cap on his head.

Slowly and deliberately the Judge rose from his chair and picked up the piece of rope of the alarm bell which lay on the floor, drew it through his hands as if he enjoyed its touch and then deliberately began to knot one end of it, fashioning it into a noose. This he tightened and tested with his foot, pulling hard at it till he was satisfied and then making a running noose of it, which he held in his hand. Then he began to move along the table on the opposite side of Malcolmson keeping his eyes on him until he had passed him, when with a quick movement he stood in front of the door. Malcolmson then began to feel that he was trapped, and tried to think of what he should do. There was some fascination in the Judge's eyes, which he never took off him, and he had, perforce, to look. He saw the Judge approach—still keeping between him and the door—and raise the noose and throw it towards him as if to entangle him. With a great effort he made a quick movement to one side, and saw the rope fall beside him, and heard it strike the oaken floor. Again the Judge raised the noose and tried to ensnare him, ever keeping his baleful eyes fixed on him, and each time by a mighty effort the student just managed to evade it. So this went on for many times, the Judge seeming never discouraged nor discomposed at failure, but playing as a cat does with a mouse. At last in despair, which had reached its climax, Malcolmson cast a quick glance round him. The lamp seemed to have blazed up, and there was a fairly good light in the room. At the many rat-holes and in the chinks and crannies of the wainscot he saw the rat's eyes, and this aspect, that was purely physical, gave him a gleam of comfort. He looked round and saw that the rope of the great alarm bell was laden with rats. Every inch of it was covered with them, and more and more were pouring through the small circular hole in the ceiling whence it emerged, so that with their weight the bell was beginning to sway.

Hark! it had swayed till the clapper had touched the bell. The sound was but a tiny one, but the bell was only beginning to sway, and it would increase.

At the sound the Judge, who had been keeping his eyes fixed on Malcolmson, looked up, and a scowl of diabolical anger overspread his face. His eyes fairly glowed like hot coals, and he stamped his foot with a sound that seemed to make the house shake. A dreadful peal of thunder broke overhead as he raised the rope again, whilst the rats kept running up and down the rope as though working against time. This time, instead of throwing it, he drew close to his victim, and held open the noose as he approached. As he came closer there seemed something paralyzing in his very presence, and Malcolmson stood rigid as a corpse. He felt the Judge's icy fingers touch his throat as he adjusted the rope. The noose tightened—tightened. Then the Judge, taking the rigid form of the student in his arms, carried him over and placed him standing in the oak chair, and stepping up beside him, put his hand up and caught the end of the swaying rope of the alarm-bell. As he raised his hand the rats fled squeaking and disappeared through the hole in the ceiling. Taking the end of the noose which was round Malcolmson's neck he tied it to the hanging bell-rope, and then descending, pulled away the chair.

.   .   .   .   .

When the alarm-bell of the Judge's House began to sound a crowd soon assembled. Lights and torches of various kinds appeared, and soon a silent crowd was hurrying to the spot. They knocked loudly at the door, but there was no reply. Then they burst in the door, and poured into the great dining-room, the doctor at the head.

There at the end of the rope of the great alarm-bell hung the body of the student, and on the face of the Judge in the picture was a malignant smile.

FROM WHAT STRANGE LAND
Blanche Bane Kuder

I HAD seen her the first night out, at dinner, but it was twenty-four hours before I could recall when and how we had met. That first night, stretched in a chair on the deck, watching the quiet stars and lulled by the rhythm of sea and sky, I gave myself to speculation. I tried to fit her face, remote, unstartled, into some familiar scene. Where had I met her? Or did she merely bear a resemblance to someone I knew? No, that was wrong. And I slept upon it.

The next morning, passing through the salon, I saw her again, this time with a little boy of five or six sitting on the lounge beside her. I looked at her with, perhaps, too prolonged a gaze for good breeding. But she gave me no sign. I strolled out to the smoking-room—and as I reached the door a lovely soprano voice began singing. A record had been put on the Victrola—"O Gentle Lady!" And with kaleidoscopic precision the woman on the lounge dropped into her environment.

We had been fellow guests at a house party—four, six, no, it had been seven years back. A house party at a charming old country place. And, because it was the eve of La Toussaint, and because spirits walked, and chiefly because we were young and free and life was all ahead, we had peered into the future in all of the customary ways. Finally, as midnight drew on, someone suggested inviting the Guest.

You know how it is done. A girl goes, alone, into a room, where a table is spread for two. She seats herself at one place, and, as the clock strikes twelve, her future husband appears, occupies the vacant seat, and joins her in the meal. Of course, none of us had an atom of faith in any such mystic introduction to fate. Equally, of course, we all professed to be true believers, and there was so much holding back and coyness among the girls that the midnight clock was in a fair way to strike before anyone could be persuaded.

At last Ellen consented. (I was even remembering her name!) And with much gaiety two places were hastily set at a small table in a little room opening from the main drawing-room, and with another door leading into the hall. Ellen was escorted to the destiny, both doors were shut, and we gathered in a giggling group in the drawing-room. I could see Ellen as we closed the door, sitting facing the empty chair, her light gown spreading around her on the floor, the candles gleaming on her fair hair and quiet eyes. She smiled at us as we shut her in.

Midnight, and we waited. But Ellen did not come out. And, in a few minutes, hearing no sound, exchanging uneasy looks, we opened the door. The room was empty.

"She has gone out by the hall door," one of the men said.

We rushed to the hall, and then upstairs. Ellen was in her room, and to our knocking and questioning gave one answer, "Please go away—I'm tired." She left the house the next day, and to all of our eager queries—"What happened, Ellen, what happened?"—said only, "Nothing." Later, I had heard that she had married, had borne a son, had been left a widow.

Perhaps, after the years, this all would not have been so clear had not one quality of Ellen's impressed me so deeply. That quality was her exceeding gentleness. She could not bear to see anything hurt. She spent hours nursing sparrows that had fallen from the nest, and gave up an afternoon's riding to poultice the infected paw of the Gordon setter. The girls who knew her said that at school no one could discuss accident or suffering before Ellen—she actually seemed to experience the pain. The richness of sympathy was a part of herself, like her blonde hair and her fair skin. She could no more help one than the other.

And that was seven years ago. She was changed, of course, and yet in appearance not so much older as different. There was in her face a brooding, a watchfulness, almost an expectancy touched by dread. I thought of her long that night. She had given me no glance of recognition. After all, I had been one of a dozen. She easily might have forgotten me.

The next day was rough. Many passengers stayed below, and I tramped the deck almost alone. A high wind was blowing. I walked with head down, chin buried in turned-up coat collar. And, as I made the corner, above the noise of ship and wind I thought I heard a faint cry. It was very indistinct. I stopped for a moment, cocked an ear toward a deck chair covered with a steamer rug—the general direction of the sound—decided I had been mistaken, and passed on. But on the second lap I heard again the same wail.

The chair, with the rug, made an effectual shelter for a secluded angle of the rail. I went close, the sound of my approach muffled by the wind and the creaking of the ship. And I peered over the screening chair.

Crouched in the corner, his back to me, was the small boy whom I had seen with Ellen the night before. Between his knees he held a tiny black kitten. And even now I shudder when I think of what he was doing to the helpless, squirming animal. I could not see his face. But the attitude was absorbed, intense—he was wholly wrapt in his work. And he was doing it with a thoroughness that left me for a moment appalled and speechless. Only for a moment. Then I knocked over the chair and hauled him to his feet. The kitten, whimpering, fell to the floor.

"You young devil——!"

I literally had no words, but I shook the child until his head rolled on his shoulders. He did not resist. But when I released him, he clutched the chair for support, and smiled. He said something to me, but in a jargoned way that was indescribably repulsive. I had known, once, a man with a cleft palate. The boy's speech was not unlike that. Then he turned and sidled down the deck, looking back over his shoulder, and smiling at me. I picked up the kitten. I could not bear to look at the poor mutilated thing, and with a swift toss I threw it into the green and white churning far beneath.

The day was long and monotonous. I filled it in as best I could—walked the deck, smoked far too much, tried to read. A barren day. I welcomed the dinner hour, with its lights and music and the diverting ritual that accompanies civilized eating, and I hoped that my mind might be drawn from the sickening moment of the morning. In a measure, it was. Only when I saw the two again seated in the dining saloon did the wave of revulsion sweep over me. I looked at Ellen, at her son—of course he was her son—dining quietly and every now and then raising questioning eyes to his mother's face. The scene of a few hours ago seemed incredible.

It was about nine o'clock, and finishing a tramp around the deck, I thought of turning in. The wind had died, the air was mild, and a pale moon rode high in the heavens. The brightly lighted rooms held most of the passengers who had not succumbed to the rough day. I was alone on deck. No —in a sheltered corner the moonlight showed two figures grouped so closely as to be almost a unit. Impulse made me turn in that direction. And as I drew near I saw that they were Ellen and the boy.

I made a sudden resolve. I would go and speak to her— surely, if I called up old memories, she would know me. And I bravely approached. Ellen's arm was around the boy's shoulder, a light shawl enveloping them both. The moon shone directly on their faces—Ellen's pale and watchful, the boy with an absorbed, dreamy look.

She did not move when I paused, nor withdraw her arm, but she spoke.

"I knew you the first time I saw you," she said, without preamble.

"And I you, the second day," I admitted. "But I hesitated."

Ellen smiled, gravely.

"Perhaps you will sit with us for a while."

I turned to draw up a chair. When I faced the two again I was shocked at the change in Ellen's face. In the pallid light she was ghastly, her forehead furrowed, her lips a bitten straight line.

"Ellen!" I cried, "Ellen! What is wrong?"

Slowly her features relaxed. She gave a long sigh. The child, immobile, continued his dreamy gaze out over the water.

"Nothing," she said. But even as her lips framed the words the tortured change came again. I bent over her. And as I did so, I noticed a slight, almost imperceptible twitching of the arm under the shawl.

Like a flash the morning's scene came to me. With a swiftness that gave him no opportunity I snatched away the garment. The white arm lay, as I have said, over the boy's shoulder, Ellen's hand resting on his sleeve.

With his free hand he was pinching her bare arm.

This time he gave me no chance to vent my anger. Slipping from his chair, he bowed to me, formally. Then, speaking to his mother, he walked unhurriedly away, turning, as he vanished in an open doorway, to give me that curiously triumphant smile.

I sank down in the chair by Ellen. What could I say, or do ? He was her son. But the outrage of it ! For minutes we sat in silence. Then, drawing her shawl closer, Ellen spoke.

"No one has seen him do that before," she said.

"You mean——?"

"Yes, frequently."

Silence again. Then she turned her face to me.

"You knew, of course, that I married. An officer—a man I met at my aunt's house in Edinburgh. It was my cousin's coming-out party. Love at first sight, they said. Ah, it was not first sight. But it was love !"

Again we sat in silence. Now, I thought, she will speak. Now that unexplained October night will be made clear. Nor was I wrong.

"You remember," she went on, in a low thoughtful tone, almost as though she spoke to herself alone, "That night at the house party, so many years ago. And you remember my going into the little room and waiting for the guest ? It was all rather foolish, I thought. But none of the others would do it. I felt silly and self-conscious when you closed the door and left me facing the vacant chair. And when the door leading into the hall slowly opened I looked up smiling, expecting to see one of the men I knew. It was not anyone I knew. Will you believe me—but that does not matter. You do not need to believe me. It is the truth that through the open door came a young man in uniform, a sword at his side. He did not look at me. Unfastening the sword from its belt, he placed it by his chair, and sat down. Then he began to eat.

"I was frozen. I could hear all of you laughing outside the door, but I could not speak. I could only stay there, motionless, cold with incredulous fear. My eyes unwillingly took in the details of his lean, dark face: On the little finger of his right hand he wore a ring, with a carved green stone, and, fascinated, I watched the play of the candle-light on that ring.

"When he had eaten, he rose. He had once looked at me. He laid down his napkin, pushed back his chair, and left the room. But he did not take his sword. Then I came to life. You were calling to me 'Ellen, Ellen!' I picked up the sword, opened the door very softly, and hastened up the stairs. I had hardly reached my room before I heard you bursting into the hall. As you know, I went away the next day. And the sword went in my luggage with me.

"Six months later my cousin made her debut. For six months there had been no waking moment that I had not seen that strange guest. And, when my aunt brought to me across the ball-room floor a young officer, it seemed quite natural that his should be the well-remembered face. I felt that I had come to the end of a long journey, and had reached at last a friendly inn."

Her voice trailed off, almost inaudibly. But when she spoke again, it was almost with passion.

"Never once did he show that he had seen me before! Not even when he put his ring on my finger in token of betrothal, nor in these unspeakably rapturous intimacies of our wedded life, did he give a sign. And I, too, was silent. We were together—that was enough. When I found I was to have a child I knew there had never been a bliss like mine since time began.

"But with the advent of the following autumn, I grew strangely restless. Some desperate urging impelled me. 'Tell him,' it pressed me, 'Tell him!' And one day I spoke.

" 'This is an anniversary,' I said.

"He did not answer.

" 'A year ago we first met,' I persisted. Still silence. Then, driven, I went to the secret place where I had put the sword, brought it forth, and showed it to him.

"He sighed.

" 'You have sent me back, my dear,' he said. And then he was not in the room."

I had no word for her.

"I waited," she said with difficulty, "And he did not return. His son was born, and he did not come. He has never come."

"Must you tell me?" The words were rung from me. That Ellen, so gentle, should suffer like this!

"Let me finish. The boy was strong and well, and resembled his father. Only one thing about him troubled me. He did not talk until he was nearly four years old.

I tried to teach him, fearing my grief had made him without speech. Oh, that it had!"

I looked at her in wonder. She went on rapidly.

"One day he began to talk. Not detached words, as most children do, but whole sentences, clear, intelligible, with scarcely a trace of baby speech. I was astonished, almost frightened. And a few weeks later came a terrible day when, in defiance over some whim denied, he stood before me and poured forth a string of vileness such as I had never heard. One obscenity after another came from his baby mouth. I was stunned with the frightfulness of it. There was no possible place he could have heard the words. When he had made an end, he smiled at me, a wise, unchildlike smile, and left the room.

"From that time on I lived in dread. I could never tell when the horror would begin. You cannot know the awfulness of it, to see him stand, eyes fixed on my face, softly calling me unnameable things. I did not try to reason it out, for it was beyond reason and understanding. The thing was a mystery, of the same unreal world as the mystery of his father. I spent my days trying to avert the storms.

"One day I was sewing. He came to me, clutching at my work, and thoughtlessly I pushed him aside. Another outburst, and he ended by drawing close and putting out his tongue at me. I was a little mad, I know. I hardly knew what I had done until the blood spurted from his mouth and the stained scissors fell to the floor."

I was mute. I felt I could endure no more. But there was little more to come.

"Now you know," the tired voice almost whispered. "The reason for his speech. I must keep him with me—I cannot endanger others. And I cannot see the end."

She rose, folded her shawl about her, and left me alone. There was no farewell. Nor was there sleep for me that night.

EL VERDUGO
Honoré de Balzac

MIDNIGHT had just sounded from the belfry tower of the little town of Menda. A young French officer leaning over the parapet of the long terrace at the further end of the castle gardens, seemed to be unusually absorbed in deep thought for one who led the reckless life of a soldier, but it must be admitted that never was the hour, the scene, and the night more favourable to meditation.

The blue dome of the cloudless sky of Spain was overhead, he was looking out over the coy windings of a lovely valley lit by the uncertain starlight and the soft radiance of the moon. The officer, leaning against an orange-tree in blossom, could also see, a hundred feet below him, the town of Menda, which seemed to nestle for shelter from the north wind at the foot of the crags on which the castle itself was built. He turned his head and caught sight of the sea, the moonlit waves made a broad frame of silver for the landscape.

There were lights in the castle windows. The mirth and movement of a ball, the sounds of the violins, the laughter of the officers and their partners in the dance was borne towards him, and blended with the far-off murmur of the waves. The cool night had a certain bracing effect upon his frame, wearied as he had been by the heat of the day. He seemed to bathe in the air, made fragrant by the strong, sweet scent of flowers and of aromatic trees in the gardens.

The castle of Menda belonged to a Spanish grandee, who was living in it at that time with his family. All through the evening the oldest daughter of the house had watched the officer with such a wistful interest that the Spanish lady's compassionate eyes might well have set the young Frenchman dreaming. Clara was beautiful, and although she had three brothers and a sister, the broad lands of the Marqués de Léganès appeared to be sufficient warrant for Victor Marchand's belief that the young lady would have a splendid dowry.

But how could he dare to imagine that the most fanatical believer in blue blood in all Spain would give his daughter to the son of a grocer in Paris ? Morever, the French were hated. It was because the Marqués had been suspected of an attempt to raise the country in favour of Ferdinand VII that General G——, who governed the province, had stationed Victor Marchand's battalion in the little town of Menda to overawe the neighbouring districts which received the Marqués de Légañès' word as law. A recent despatch from Marshal Ney had given ground for fear that the English might ere long effect a landing on the coast and had indicated the Marqués as being in correspondence with the Cabinet in London.

In spite, therefore, of the welcome with which the Spaniards had received Victor Marchand and his soldiers, that officer was always on his guard. As he went towards the terrace, where he had just surveyed the town and the districts confided to his charge, he had been asking himself what construction he ought to put upon the friendliness which the Marqués had invariably shown him, and how to reconcile the apparent tranquillity of the country with his General's uneasiness. But a moment later these thoughts were driven from his mind by the instinct of caution and very legitimate curiosity. It had just struck him that there was a very fair number of lights in the town below. Although it was the feast of Saint James, he himself had issued orders that very morning that all lights must be put out in the town at the hour prescribed by military regulations. The castle alone had been excepted in this order. Plainly here and there he saw the gleam of bayonets, where his own men were at their accustomed jobs, but in the town there was a solemn silence, and not a sign that the Spaniards had given themselves up to the intoxication of a festival. He tried vainly for a while to explain this breach of the regulations on the part of the inhabitants, the mystery seemed but so much the more obscure because he had left instructions with some of his officers to do police duty that night, and make the rounds of the town.

With the impetuosity of youth, he was about to spring through a gap in the wall preparatory to a rapid scramble down the rocks, thinking to reach a small guard-house at the nearest entrance into the town more quickly than by the beaten track, when a faint sound stopped him. He fancied that he could hear the light footstep of a woman along the gravelled garden walk. He turned his head and saw no one, for one moment his eyes were dazzled by the wonderful brightness of the sea, the next he saw a sight so ominous that he stood stock-still with amazement, thinking that his senses must be deceiving him. The white moonbeams lighted the horizon, so that he could distinguish the sails of ships still a considerable distance out at sea. A shudder ran through him, he tried to persuade himself that this was some optical delusion brought about by chance effects of moonlight on the waves, and even as he made the attempt, a hoarse voice called to him by name. The officer glanced at the gap in the wall, saw a soldier's head slowly emerge from it, and knew the grenadier whom he had ordered to accompany him to the castle.

"Is that you, Commandant ?"

"Yes. What is it ?" returned the young officer in a low voice. A kind of presentiment warned him to act cautiously.

"Those beggars down there are creeping about like worms, and, by your leave, I came as quickly as I could to report my little reconnoitring expedition."

"Go on," answered Victor Marchand.

"I have just been following a man from the castle who came round this way with a lantern in his hand. A lantern is a suspicious matter with a vengeance ! I don't imagine that there was any need for that good Christian to be lighting tapers at this time of night. Says I to myself, 'They mean to gobble us up !' and I set myself to dogging his heels, and that is how I found out that there is a pile of faggots, sir, two or three steps away from here."

Suddenly a dreadful shriek rang through the town below, and cut the man short. A light flashed in the Commandant's face, and the poor grenadier dropped down with a bullet through his head. Ten paces away a bonfire flared up like a conflagration. The sounds of music and laughter ceased all at once in the ball-room, the silence of death, broken only by groans, succeeded to the rhythmical murmur of the festival. Then the roar of cannon sounded from across the white plain of the sea.

A cold sweat broke out on the young officer's forehead. He had left his sword behind. He knew that his men had been murdered, and that the English were about to land.

He knew that if he lived he would be dishonoured, he saw himself summoned before a court-martial. For a moment his eyes measured the depth of the valley, the next, just as he was about to spring down, Clara's hand caught his.

"Fly!" she cried. "My brothers are coming after me to kill you. Down yonder at the foot of the cliff you will find Juanito's Andalusian. Go!"

She thrust him away. The young man gazed at her in dull bewilderment, but obeying the instinct of self-preservation, which never deserts even the bravest, he rushed across the park in the direction pointed out to him, springing from rock to rock in places unknown to any save the goats. He heard Clara calling to her brothers to pursue him, he heard the footsteps of the murderers, again and again he heard their balls whistling about his ears, but he reached the foot of the cliff, found the horse, mounted, and fled with lightning speed.

A few hours later the young officer reached General G——'s quarters, and found him at dinner with the staff.

"I put my life in your hands!" cried the haggard and exhausted Commandant of Menda.

He sank into a seat, and told his horrible story. It was received with an appalling silence.

"It seems to me that you are more to be pitied than to blame," the terrible General said at last. "You are not answerable for the Spaniard's crimes, and unless the Marshal decides otherwise, I acquit you."

These words brought but cold comfort to the unfortunate officer.

"When the Emperor comes to hear about it!" he cried.

"Oh, he will be for having you shot," said the General, "but we shall see. Now we will say no more about this," he added severely, "except to plan a revenge that shall strike a salutary terror in this country, where they carry on war like savages."

An hour later a whole regiment, a detachment of cavalry, and a convoy of artillery were upon the road. The General and Victor marched at the head of the column. The soldiers had been told of the fate of their comrades, and their rage knew no bounds. The distance between headquarters and the town of Menda was crossed at a wellnigh miraculous speed. Whole villages by the way were found to be under arms, and every one of the wretched hamlets was surrounded, and their inhabitants decimated.

It so chanced that the English vessels still lay out at sea, and were no nearer the shore, a fact inexplicable until it was known afterwards that they were artillery transports which had outsailed the rest of the fleet. So the townsmen of Menda, left without the assistance on which they had reckoned when the sails of the English appeared, were surrounded by French troops almost before they had had time to strike a blow. This struck such terror into them that they offered to surrender at discretion. An impulse of devotion, no isolated instance in the history of the Peninsula, led the actual slayers of the French to offer to give themselves up, seeking in this way to save the town, for from the General's reputation for cruelty it was feared that he would give Menda over to the flames, and put the whole population to the sword. General G—took their offer, stipulating that every soul in the castle from the lowest servant to the Marqués should likewise be given up to him. These terms being accepted, the General promised to spare the lives of the rest of the townsmen, and to prohibit his soldiers from pillaging or setting fire to the town. A heavy contribution was levied, and the wealthiest inhabitants were taken as hostages to guarantee payment within twenty-four hours.

The General took every necessary precaution for the safety of his troops, provided for the defence of the place, and refused to billet his men in the houses of the town. After they had bivouacked, he went up to the castle and entered it as a conqueror. The whole family of Légañès and their household were gagged, shut up in the great ball-room, and closely watched. From the windows it was easy to see the whole length of the terrace above the town.

The staff was established in an adjoining gallery, where the General forthwith held a council as to the best means of preventing the landing of the English. An aide-de-camp was despatched to Marshal Ney, orders were issued to plant batteries along the coast, and then the General and his staff turned their attention to their prisoners. The two hundred Spaniards given up by the townsfolk were shot down then and there upon the terrace. And after this military execution, the General gave orders to erect gibbets to the number of the prisoners in the ball-room in the same place, and to send for the hangman out of the town. Victor took advantage of the interval before dinner to pay a visit to the prisoners. He soon came back to the General.

"I am come in haste," he faltered out, "to ask a favour."

"*You*!" exclaimed the General, with bitter irony in his tones.

"Alas!" answered Victor, "it is a sorry favour. The Marqués has seen them erecting the gallows, and hopes that you will commute the punishment for his family; he entreats you to have the nobles beheaded."

"Granted," said the General.

"He further asks that they may be allowed the consolations of religion, and that they may be unbound; they give you their word that they will not attempt to escape."

"That I permit," said the General, "but you are answerable for them."

"The old noble offers you all that he has if you will pardon his youngest son."

"Really!" cried the Commander. "His property is forfeit already to King Joseph." He paused; a contemptuous thought set wrinkles in his forehead, as he added, "I will do better than they ask. I understand what he means by that last request of his. Very good. Let him hand down his name to posterity; but whenever it is mentioned, all Spain shall remember his treason and its punishment! I will give the fortune and his life to any one of the sons who will do the executioner's office. . . . There, don't talk any more about them to me."

Dinner was ready. The officers sat down to satisfy an appetite whetted by hunger. Only one among them was absent from the table—that one was Victor Marchand. After long hesitation, he went to the ball-room, and heard the last sighs of the proud house of Léganès. He looked sadly at the scene before him. Only last night, in this very room, he had seen their faces whirled past him in the waltz, and he shuddered to think that those girlish heads with those of the three young brothers must fall in a brief space by the executioner's sword. There sat the father and mother, their three sons and two daughters, perfectly motionless, bound to their gilded chairs. Eight serving men stood with their hands tied behind them. These fifteen prisoners, under sentence of death, exchanged grave glances! it was difficult to read the thoughts that filled them from their eyes, but profound resignation and regret that their enterprise should have failed so completely was written on more than one brow.

The impassive soldiers who guarded them respected the grief of their bitter enemies. A gleam of curiosity lighted up all faces when Victor came in. He gave orders that the condemned prisoners should be unbound, and himself unfastened the cords that held Clara a prisoner. She smiled mournfully at him. The officer could not refrain from lightly touching the young girl's arm ; he could not help admiring her dark hair, her slender waist. She was a true daughter of Spain, with a Spanish complexion, a Spaniard's eyes, blacker than the raven's wing beneath their long curving lashes.

"Did you succeed ?" she asked, with a mournful smile, in which a certain girlish charm still lingered.

Victor could not repress a groan. He looked from the faces of the three brothers to Clara, and again at the three young Spaniards. The first, the oldest of the family, was a man of thirty. He was short, and somewhat ill made ; he looked haughty and proud, but a certain distinction was not lacking in his bearing, and he was apparently no stranger to the delicacy of feeling for which in olden times the chivalry of Spain was famous. His name was Juanito. The second son, Felipe, was about twenty years of age ; he was like his sister Clara ; and the youngest was a child of eight. In the features of the little Manuel a painter would have discerned something of that Roman steadfastness which David has given to the children's faces in his Republican *genre* pictures. The old Marqués, with his white hair, might have come down from some canvas of Murillo's. Victor threw back his head in despair after this survey ; how should one of these accept the General's offer ? Nevertheless he ventured to intrust it to Clara. A shudder ran through the Spanish girl, but she recovered herself almost instantly, and knelt before her father.

"Father," she said, "bid Juanito swear to obey the commands that you shall give him, and we shall be content."

The Marquésa trembled with hope, but as she leant towards her husband and learned Clara's hideous secret, the mother fainted away. Juanito understood it all, and leapt up like a caged lion. Victor took it upon himself to dismiss the soldiers, after receiving an assurance of entire submission from the Marqués. The servants were led away and given over to the hangman and their fate. When only Victor remained on guard in the room, the old Marqués de Légañès rose to his feet.

"Juanito," he said. For answer Juanito bowed his head in a way that meant refusal; he sank down into his chair, and fixed tearless eyes upon his father and mother in an intolerable gaze. Clara went over to him and sat on his knee; she put her arms about him, and pressed kisses on his eyelids, saying gaily—

"Dear Juanito, if you but knew how sweet death at your hands will be to me! I shall not be compelled to submit to the hateful touch of the hangman's fingers. You will snatch me away from the evils to come and . . . Dear, kind Juanito, you could not bear the thought of my belonging to anyone —well, then?"

The velvet eyes gave Victor a burning glance; she seemed to try to awaken in Juanito's heart his hatred for the French.

"Take courage," said his brother Felipe, "or our well-nigh royal line will be extinct."

Suddenly Clara sprang to her feet. The group round Juanito fell back, and the son who had rebelled with such good reason was confronted with his aged father.

"Juanito, I command you!" said the Marqués solemnly.

The young Count gave no sign, and his father fell on his knees; Clara, Manuel, and Felipe unconsciously followed his example, stretching out suppliant hands to him who must save their family from oblivion, and seeming to echo their father's words.

"Can it be that you lack the fortitude of a Spaniard and true sensibility, my son? Do you mean to keep me on my knees? What right have you to think of your own life and of your own sufferings?—Is this my son, madam?" the old Marqués added, turning to his wife.

"He will consent to it," cried the mother in agony of soul. She had seen a slight contraction of Juanito's brows which she, his mother, alone understood.

Mariquita, the second daughter, knelt, with her slender clinging arms about her mother; the hot tears fell from her eyes, and her little brother Manuel upbraided her for weeping. Just at that moment the castle chaplain came in; the whole family surrounded him and led him up to Juanito. Victor felt that he could endure the sight no longer, and with a sign to Clara he hurried from the room to make one last effort for them. He found the General in boisterous spirits ; the officers were still sitting over their dinner and drinking together ; the wine had loosened their tongues.

An hour later, a hundred of the principal citizens of Menda were summoned to the terrace by the General's orders to witness the execution of the family of Légañès. A detachment had been told off to keep order among the Spanish townsfolk, who were marshalled beneath the gallows whereon the Marqués's servants hung ; the feet of those martyrs of their cause all but touched the citizens' heads. Thirty paces away stood the block ; the blade of a scimitar glittered upon it, and the executioner stood by in case Juanito should refuse at the last.

The deepest silence prevailed, but before long it was broken by the sound of many footsteps, the measured tramp of a picket of soldiers, and the jingling of their weapons. Mingled with these came other noises—loud talk and laughter from the dinner-table where the officers were sitting ; just as the music and the sound of the dancers' feet had drowned the preparations for last night's treacherous butchery.

All eyes turned to the castle, and beheld the family of nobles coming forth with incredible composure to their death. Every brow was serene and calm. One alone among them, haggard and overcome, leant on the arm of the priest, who poured forth all the consolations of religion for the one man who was condemned to live. Then the executioner, like the spectators, knew that Juanito had consented to perform his office for a day. The old Marqués and his wife, Clara and Mariquita, and their two brothers knelt a few paces from the fatal spot. Juanito reached it, guided by the priest. As he stood at the block the executioner plucked him by the sleeve, and took him aside, probably to give him certain instructions. The confessor so placed the victims that they could not witness the executions, but one and all stood upright and fearless, like Spaniards, as they were.

Clara sprang to her brother's side before the others.

"Juanito," she said to him, "be merciful to my lack of courage. Take me first !"

As she spoke, the footsteps of a man running at full speed echoed from the walls, and Victor appeared upon the scene.

Clara was kneeling before the block; her white neck seemed to appeal to the blade to fall. The officer turned faint, but he found strength to rush to her side.

"The General grants you your life if you will consent to marry me," he murmured.

The Spanish girl gave the officer a glance full of proud disdain.

"Now, Juanito!" she said in her deep-toned voice.

Her head fell at Victor's feet. A shudder ran through the Marquésa de Légañès, a convulsive tremor that she could not control, but she gave no other sign of her anguish.

"Is this where I ought to be, dear Juanito? Is it all right?" little Manuel asked his brother.

"Oh, Mariquita, you are weeping!" Juanito said when his sister came.

"Yes," said the girl; "I am thinking of you, poor Juanito; how unhappy you will be when we are gone."

Then the Marqués's tall figure approached. He looked at the block where his children's blood had been shed, turned to the mute and motionless crowd, and said in a loud voice as he stretched out his hands to Juanito—

"Spaniards! I give my son a father's blessing.—Now, *Marqués*, strike 'without fear'; thou art 'without reproach.'"

But when his mother came near, leaning on the confessor's arm—"She fed me from her breast!" Juanito cried, in tones that drew a cry of horror from the crowd. The uproarious mirth of the officers over their wine died away before that terrible cry. The Marquésa knew that Juanito's courage was exhausted; at one bound she sprang to the balustrade, leapt forth, and was dashed to pieces on the rocks below. A cry of admiration broke from the spectators. Juanito swooned.

"General," said an officer, half drunk by this time, "Marchand has just been telling me something about this execution; I will wager that it was not by your orders——"

"Are you forgetting, gentlemen, that in a month's time five hundred families in France will be in mourning, and that we are still in Spain?" cried General G——. "Do you want us to leave our bones here?"

But not a man at the table, not even a subaltern, dared to empty his glass after that speech.

In spite of the respect in which all men hold the Marqués de Légañès, in spite of the title of *El Verdugo* (the executioner) conferred upon him as a patent of nobility by the King of Spain, the great noble is consumed by a gnawing grief. He lives a retired life, and seldom appears in public. The burden of his heroic crime weighs heavily upon him, and he seems to wait impatiently till the birth of a second son shall release him, and he may go to join the Shades that never cease to haunt him.

TELLING
Elizabeth Bowen

TERRY looked up ; Josephine lay still. He felt shy, embarrassed all at once at the idea of anyone coming here. His
brain was ticking like a watch : he looked up warily.

But there was nobody. Outside the high, cold walls,
beyond the ragged arch of the chapel, delphiniums crowded
in sunshine—straining with brightness, burning each other
up—bars of colour that, while one watched them, seemed to
turn round slowly. But there was nobody there.

The chapel was a ruin, roofed by daylight, floored with
lawn. In a corner the gardener had tipped out a heap of cut
grass from the lawn-mower. The daisy-heads wilted, the cut
grass smelt stuffy and sweet. Everywhere, cigarette ends,
scattered last night by the couples who'd come here to kiss.
"First the dance," thought Terry, "then this : the servants will
never get straight." The cigarette ends would lie here for
days, till after the rain, and go brown and rotten.

Then he noticed a charred cigarette stump in Josephine's
hair. The short wavy ends of her hair fell back—still in lines
of perfection—from temples and ears ; by her left ear the
charred stump showed through. For that, he thought, she
would never forgive him ; fastidiousness was her sensibility,
always tormented. ("If you must know," she had said,
"well, you've got dirty nails, haven't you ? Look.") He
bent down and picked the cigarette end out of her hair ; the
fine ends fluttered under his breath. As he threw it away,
he noticed his nails were still dirty. His hands were stained
now—naturally—but his nails must have been dirty before.
Had she noticed again ?

But had she, perhaps, for a moment been proud of him ?
Had she had just a glimpse of the something he'd told her
about ? He wanted to ask her : "What do you feel now ?
Do you believe in me ?" He felt sure of himself, certain,
justified. For nobody else would have done this to Josephine.

126

Himself they had all—always—deprecated. He felt a shrug in this attitude, a thinly disguised kind of hopelessness. "Oh, *Terry* . . ." they'd say, and break off. He was no good : he couldn't even put up a tennis-net. He never could see properly (whisky helped that at first, then it didn't), his hands wouldn't serve him, things he wanted them to hold slipped away from them. He was no good ; the younger ones laughed at him till they, like their brothers and sisters, grew up and were schooled into bitter kindliness. Again and again he'd been sent back to them all (and repetition never blunted the bleak edge of these home-comings) from school, from Cambridge, now—a month ago—from Ceylon. "The bad penny !" he would remark, very jocular. "If I could just think things out," he had tried to explain to his father, "I know I could do *something*." And once he had said to Josephine : "I know there is Something I could do."

"And they will know now," he said, looking round (for the strange new pleasure of clearly and sharply seeing) from Josephine's face to her stained breast (her heavy blue beads slipped sideways over her shoulder and coiled on the grass— touched, surrounded now by the unhesitant trickle) ; from her breast up the walls to their top, the top crumbling, the tufts of valerian trembling against the sky. It was as though the dark-paned window through which he had so long looked out had swung open suddenly. He saw (clear as the walls and the sky) Right and Wrong, the old childish fixities. "I have done right," he thought (but his brain was still ticking). "*She ought not to live* with this flaw in her. Josephine ought not to live, had to die."

All night he had thought this out, walking alone in the shrubberies, helped by the dance-music, dodging the others. His mind had been kindled, like a dull coal suddenly blazing. He was not angry ; he kept saying : "I must not be angry, I must be just." He was in a blaze (it seemed to himself) of justice. The couples who came face to face with him down the paths started away. Someone spoke of a minor prophet, someone breathed, "Caliban." . . . He kept saying : "That flaw right through her. She damages truth. She kills souls ; she's killed mine." So he had come to see, before morning,. his purpose as God's purpose.

She had laughed, you see. She had been pretending. There was a tender and lovely thing he kept hidden, a spark in him ; she had touched it and made it the whole of him, made him a man. She had said : "Yes, *I* believe, Terry. I understand." That had been everything. He had thrown off the old dull armour. . . . Then she had laughed.

Then he had understood what other men meant when they spoke of her. He had seen at once what he was meant to do. "This is for me," he said. "No one but I can do it."

All night he walked alone in the garden. Then he watched the french windows and when they were open again stepped in quickly and took down the African knife from the dining-room wall. He had always wanted that African knife. Then he had gone upstairs (remembering, on the way, all those meetings with Josephine, shaving, tying of ties), shaved, changed into flannels, put the knife into his blazer pocket (it was too long, more than an inch of the blade came out through the inside lining) and sat on his window-sill, watching sunlight brighten and broaden from a yellow agitation behind the trees into swathes of colour across the lawn. He did not think ; his mind was like somebody singing, somebody able to sing.

And, later, it had all been arranged for him. He fell into, had his part in, some kind of design. Josephine had come down in her pleated white dress (when she turned the pleats whirled). He had said, "Come out !" and she gave that light, distant look, still with a laugh at the back of it, and said, "Oh—right-o, little Terry." And she had walked down the garden ahead of him, past the delphiniums into the chapel. Here, to make justice perfect, he had asked once more : "*Do* you believe in me ?" She had laughed again.

She lay now with her feet and body in sunshine (the sun was just high enough), her arms flung out wide at him, desperately, generously : her head rolling sideways in shadow on the enclosed, silky grass. On her face was a dazzled look (eyes half closed, lips drawn back), and expression almost of diffidence. Her blood quietly soaked through the grass, sinking through to the roots of it.

He crouched a moment and, touching her eyelids—still warm—tried to shut her eyes. But he didn't know how. Then he got up and wiped the blade of the African knife with a handful of grass, then scattered the handful away. All the time he was listening ; he felt shy, embarrassed at the thought of anyone finding him here. And his brain, like a watch, was still ticking.

On his way to the house he stooped down and dipped his hands in the garden tank. Someone might scream; he felt embarrassed at the thought of somebody screaming. The red curled away through the water and melted.

He stepped in at the morning-room window. The blinds were half down—he stooped his head to avoid them —and the room were in dark-yellow shadow. (He had waited here for them all to come in, that afternoon he arrived back from Ceylon.) The smell of pinks came in, and two or three bluebottles bumbled and bounced on the ceiling. His sister Catherine sat with her back to him, playing the piano. (He had heard her as he came up the path.) He looked at her pink pointed elbows—she was playing a waltz and the music ran through them in jerky ripples.

"Hullo, Catherine," he said, and listened in admiration. So his new voice sounded like this!

"Hullo, Terry." She went on playing, worrying at the waltz. She had an anxious, methodical mind, but loved gossip. He thought: "Here is a bit of gossip for you— Josephine's down in the chapel, covered with blood. Her dress is spoilt, but I think her blue beads are all right. I should go and see.

"I say, Catherine——"

"Oh, Terry, they're putting the furniture back in the drawing-room. I wish you'd go and help. It's getting those big sofas through the door . . . and the cabinets." She laughed: "I'm just putting the music away," and went on playing.

He thought: "I don't suppose she'll be able to marry now. No one will marry her." He said: "Do you know where Josephine is?"

"No, I haven't"—rum-tum-tum, rum-tum-*tum*—"the slightest idea. Go on, Terry."

He thought: "She never liked Josephine." He went away.

He stood in the door of the drawing-room. His brothers and Beatrice were punting the big arm-chairs, chintz-skirted, over the waxy floor. They all felt him there, for as long as possible didn't notice him. Charles—fifteen, with his pink scrubbed ears—considered a moment, shoving against the cabinet, thought it was rather a shame, turned with an honest, kindly look of distaste, said, "Come on, Terry." "He can't go back to school now," thought Terry, "can't go anywhere, really : wonder what they'll do with him—send him out to the Colonies ?" Charles had perfect manners : square, bluff, perfect. He never thought about anybody, never felt anybody —just classified them. Josephine was "a girl staying in the house", "a friend of my sisters". He would think at once (in a moment when Terry had told him), "A girl staying in the house . . . it's . . . well, I mean, if it hadn't been *a girl staying in the house* . . ."

Terry went over to him ; they pushed the cabinet. But Terry pushed too hard, crooked ; the further corner grated against the wall. "Oh, I say, we've scratched the paint," said Charles. And indeed they had ; on the wall was a grey scar. Charles went scarlet : he hated things to be done badly. It was nice of him to say : "*We've* scratched the paint." Would he say later : "We've killed Josephine" ?

"I think perhaps you'd better help with the sofas," said Charles civilly.

"You should have seen the blood on my hands just now," said Terry.

"Bad luck !" Charles said quickly and went away.

Beatrice, Josephine's friend, stood with her elbows on the mantelpiece looking at herself in the glass above. Last night a man had kissed her down in the chapel (Terry had watched them). This must seem to Beatrice to be written all over her face—what else could she be looking at ? Her eyes in the looking-glass were dark, beseeching. As she saw Terry come up behind her she frowned angrily and turned away.

"I say, Beatrice, do you know what happened down in the chapel ?"

"Does it interest you ?" She stooped quickly and pulled down the sofa loose-cover where it had "runkled" up, as though the sofa legs were indecent.

"Beatrice, what would you do if I'd killed somebody ?"

"Laugh," said she wearily.

"If I'd killed a woman ?"

"Laugh harder. Do you know any women ?"

She was a lovely thing, really : he'd ruined her, he supposed. He was all in a panic. "Beatrice, swear you won't go down to the chapel." Because she might, well

—of course she'd go down : as soon as she was alone and they didn't notice, she'd go creeping down to the chapel. It had been *that* kind of kiss.

"Oh, be quiet about that old chapel !" Already he'd spoilt last night for her. How she hated him ! He looked round for John. John had gone away.

On the hall table were two letters, come by the second post, waiting for Josephine. No one, he thought, ought to read them—he must protect Josephine ; he took them up and slipped them into his pocket.

"I say," called John from the stairs, "what are you doing with those letters ?" John didn't mean to be sharp, but they had taken each other unawares. They none of them wanted Terry to *feel* how his movements were sneaking movements ; when they met him creeping about by himself they would either ignore him or say : "Where are *you* off to ?" jocosely and loudly, to hide the fact of their knowing he didn't know. John was Terry's elder brother, but hated to sound like one. But he couldn't help knowing those letters were for Josephine, and Josephine was "staying in the house".

"I'm taking them for Josephine."

"Know where she is ?"

"Yes, in the chapel. . . . I killed her there."

But John—hating this business with Terry—had turned away. Terry followed him upstairs, repeating : "I killed her there, John. . . . John, I've killed Josephine in the chapel." John hurried ahead, not listening, not turning round. "Oh yes," he called over his shoulder. "Right you are, take them along." He disappeared into the smoking-room, banging the door. It had been John's idea that, from the day after Terry's return from Ceylon, the sideboard cupboard in the dining-room should be kept locked up. But he'd never said anything ; oh no. What interest could the sideboard cupboard have for a brother of his ? he pretended to think.

"Oh yes," thought Terry, "you're a fine man with a muscular back, but you couldn't have done what I've done." There had, after all, been Something in Terry. He *was* abler than John (they'd soon know). John had never kissed Josephine.

Terry sat down on the stairs, saying : "Josephine,

Josephine !'' He sat there gripping a baluster, shaking with exaltation.

The study door-panels had always looked solemn ; they bulged with solemnity. Terry had to get past to his father ; he chose the top left-hand panel to tap on. The patient voice said : "Come in !"

"Here and now," thought Terry. He had a great audience ; he looked at the books round the dark walls and thought of all those thinkers. His father jerked up a contracted, strained look at him. Terry felt that hacking with his news into this silence was like hacking into a great, grave chest. The desk was a havoc of papers.

"What exactly do you want ?" said his father, rubbing the edge of the desk.

Terry stood there silently : everything ebbed. "I want," he said at last, "to talk about my future."

His father sighed and slid a hand forward, rumpling the papers. "I suppose, Terry," he said as gently as possible, "you really *have* got a future ?" Then he reproached himself. "Well, sit down a minute. . . . I'll just . . ."

Terry sat down. The clock on the mantelpiece echoed the ticking in his brain. He waited.

"Yes ?" said his father.

"Well, there must be some kind of future for me, mustn't there ?"

"Oh, certainly. . . ."

"Look here, Father, I have something to show you. That African knife——"

"What about it ?"

"That African knife. It's here. I've got it to show you."

"What about it ?"

"Wait just a minute." He put a hand into either pocket : his father waited.

"It *was* here—I did have it. I brought it to show you. I must have it somewhere—that African knife."

But it wasn't there, he hadn't got it ; he had lost it ; left it, dropped it—on the grass, by the tank, anywhere. He remembered wiping it. . . . Then ?

Now his support was all gone ; he was terrified now ; he wept.

"I've lost it," he quavered, "I've lost it."

"What do you mean?" said his father, sitting blankly there like a tombstone, with his white, square face. "What are you trying to tell me?"

"Nothing," said Terry, weeping and shaking. "Nothing, nothing, nothing."

THE TREASURE OF ABBOT THOMAS
M. R. James

"Verum usque in præsentem diem multa garriunt inter se Canonici de abscondito quodam istius Abbatis Thomæ thesauro, quem sæpe, quanquam adhuc incassum, quæsiverunt Steinfeldenses. Ipsum enim Thomam adhuc florida in ætate existentem ingentem auri massam circa monasterium defodisse perhibent ; de quo multoties interrogatus ubi esset, cum risu respondere solitus erat : 'Job, Johannes, et Zacharias vel vobis vel posteris indicabunt! ; idemque aliquando adiicere se inventuris minime invisurum. Inter alia huius Abbatis opera, hoc memoria præcipue dignum iudico quod fenestram magnam in orientali parte alæ australis in ecclesia sua imaginibus optime in vitro depictis impleverit : id quod et ipsius effigies et insignia ibidem posita demonstrant. Domum quoque Abbatialem fere totam restauravit : puteo in atrio ipsius effosso et lapidibus marmoreis pulchre cælatis exornato. Decessit autem, morte aliquantulum subitanea perculsus, ætatis suæ anno lxxii^do, incarnationis vero Dominicæ mdxxix°."

"I suppose I shall have to translate this," said the antiquary to himself, as he finished copying the above lines from that rather rare and exceedingly diffuse book, the *"Sertum Stein-feldense Norbertinum."*[1] "Well, it may as well be done first as last," and accordingly the following rendering was very quickly produced :

"Up to the present day there is much gossip among the Canons about a certain hidden treasure of this Abbot Thomas, for which those of Steinfeld have often made search, though

[1] An account of the Premonstratensian Abbey of Steinfeld, in the Eiffel, with lives of the Abbots, published at Cologne in 1712 by Christian Albert Erhard, a resident in the district. The epithet *Norbertinum* is due to the fact that St. Norbert was founder of the Premonstratensian Order.

hitherto in vain. The story is that Thomas, while yet in the vigour of life, concealed a very large quantity of gold somewhere in the monastery. He was often asked where it was, and always answered, with a laugh : 'Job, John, and Zachariah will tell either you or your successors.' He sometimes added that he should feel no grudge against those who might find it. Among other works carried out by this Abbot I may specially mention his filling the great window at the east end of the south aisle of the church with figures admirably painted on glass, as his effigy and arms in the window attest. He also restored almost the whole of the Abbot's lodging, and dug a well in the court of it, which he adorned with beautiful carvings in marble. He died rather suddenly in the seventy-second year of his age, A.D. 1529."

The object which the antiquary had before him at the moment was that of tracing the whereabouts of the painted windows of the Abbey Church of Steinfeld. Shortly after the Revolution, a very large quantity of painted glass made its way from the dissolved abbeys of Germany and Belgium to this country, and may now be seen adorning various of our parish churches, cathedrals, and private chapels. Steinfeld Abbey was among the most considerable of these involuntary contributors to our artistic possessions (I am quoting the somewhat ponderous preamble of the book which the antiquary wrote), and the greater part of the glass from that institution can be identified without much difficulty by the help, either of the numerous inscriptions in which the place is mentioned, or of the subjects of the windows, in which several well-defined cycles or narratives were represented.

The passage with which I began my story had set the antiquary on the track of another identification. In a private chapel—no matter where—he had seen three large figures, each occupying a whole light in a window, and evidently the work of one artist. Their style made it plain that that artist had been a German of the sixteenth century ; but hitherto the more exact localizing of them had been a puzzle. They represented—will you be surprised to hear it ?—JOB PATRIARCHA, JOHANNES EVANGELISTA, ZACHARIAS PROPHETA, and each of them held a book or scroll, inscribed with a sentence from his writings. These, as a matter of course, the antiquary had noted, and had been struck by the curious way in which they differed from any text of the Vulgate that he had been able to examine. Thus the scroll in Job's hand was inscribed : "Auro est locus in quo absconditur" (for "conflatur") ;* on the book of John was : "Habent in vestimentis suis scripturam quam nemo novit"† (for "investimento scriptum," the following words being taken from another verse) ; and Zacharias had : "Super lapidem unum septem oculi sunt"‡ (which alone of the three presents an unaltered text).

A sad perplexity it had been to our investigator to think why these three personages should have been placed together in one window. There was no bond of connection between them, either historic, symbolic, or doctrinal, and he could only suppose that they must have formed part of a very large series of Prophets and Apostles, which might have filled, say, all the clerestory windows of some capacious church. But the passage from the *"Sertum"* had altered the situation by showing that the names of the actual personages represented in the glass now in Lord D——'s chapel had been constantly on the lips of Abbot Thomas von Eschenhausen of Steinfeld, and that this Abbot had put up a painted window, probably about the year 1520, in the south aisle of his abbey church. It was no very wild conjecture that the three figures might have formed part of Abbot Thomas's offering ; it was one which, moreover, could probably be confirmed or set aside by another careful examination of the glass. And, as Mr. Somerton was a man of leisure, he set out on pilgrimage to the private chapel with very little delay. His conjecture was confirmed to the full. Not only did the style and technique of the glass suit perfectly with the date and place required, but in another window of the chapel he found some glass, known to have been bought along with the figures, which contained the arms of Abbot Thomas von Eschenhausen.

At intervals during his researches Mr. Somerton had been haunted by the recollection of the gossip about the hidden treasure, and, as he thought the matter over, it became more and more obvious to him that if the Abbot meant anything by the enigmatical answer which he gave to his questioners, he must have meant that the secret was to be found somewhere

* There is a place for gold where it is hidden.
† They have on their raiment a writing which no man knoweth.
‡ Upon one stone are seven eyes.

in the window he had placed in the abbey church. It was undeniable, furthermore, that the first of the curiously-selected texts on the scrolls in the window might be taken to have a reference to hidden treasure.

Every feature, therefore, or mark which could possibly assist in elucidating the riddle which, he felt sure, the Abbot had set posterity, he noted with scrupulous care, and, returning to his Berkshire manor-house, consumed many a pint of the midnight oil over his tracings and sketches. After two or three weeks, a day came when Mr. Somerton announced to his man that he must pack his own and his master's things for a short journey abroad, whither for the moment we will not follow him.

II

Mr. Gregory, the Rector of Parsbury, had strolled out before breakfast, it being a fine autumn morning, as far as the gate of his carriage-drive, with intent to meet the postman and sniff the cool air. Nor was he disappointed of either purpose. Before he had had time to answer more than ten or eleven of the miscellaneous questions propounded to him in the lightness of their hearts by his young offspring, who had accompanied him, the postman was seen approaching ; and among the morning's budget was one letter bearing a foreign postmark and stamp (which became at once the objects of an eager competition among the youthful Gregorys), and was addressed in an uneducated but plainly an English hand.

When the Rector opened it, and turned to the signature, he realized that it came from the confidential valet of his friend and squire, Mr. Somerton. Thus it ran :

Honourd Sir,—

Has I am in great anxiety about Master I write at is Wish to Beg you Sir if you could be so good as Step over. Master Has add a Nastey Shock and keeps His Bedd. I never Have known Him like this but No wonder and Nothing will serve but you Sir. Master says would I mintion the Short Way Here is Drive to Cobblince and take a Trap. Hopeing I Have maid all Plain, but am much Confused in Myself what with Anxiatey and Weakfulness at Night.

*If I might be so Bold Sir it will be a Pleasure to see a Honnes
British Face among all These Forig ones.*

I am Sir

Your obed^t Servt

William Brown.'

P.S.—*The Villiage for Town I will not Turm It is name
Steenfeld.*

The reader must be left to picture to himself in detail the
surprise, confusion, and hurry of preparation into which the
receipt of such a letter would be likely to plunge a quiet
Berkshire parsonage in the year of grace 1859. It is enough
for me to say that a train to town was caught in the course of
the day, and that Mr. Gregory was able to secure a cabin in
the Antwerp boat and a place in the Coblentz train. Nor was
it difficult to manage the transit from that centre to Steinfeld.

I labour under a grave disadvantage as narrator of this
story in that I have never visited Steinfeld myself, and that
neither of the principal actors in the episode (from whom I
derive my information) was able to give me anything but a
vague and rather dismal idea of its appearance. I gather that
it is a small place, with a large church despoiled of its ancient
fittings; a number of rather ruinous great buildings, mostly
of the seventeenth century, surround this church; for the
abbey, in common with most of those on the Continent, was
rebuilt in a luxurious fashion by its inhabitants at that period.
It has not seemed to me worth while to lavish money on a
visit to the place, for though it is probably far more attractive
than either Mr. Somerton or Mr. Gregory thought it, there
is evidently little, if anything, of first-rate interest to be seen
—except, perhaps, one thing, which I should not care to see.

The inn where the English gentleman and his servant
were lodged is, or was, the only "possible" one in the village.
Mr. Gregory was taken to it at once by his driver, and found
Mr. Brown waiting at the door. Mr. Brown, a model when
in his Berkshire home of the impassive whiskered race who
are known as confidential valets, was now egregiously out of
his element, in a light tweed suit, anxious, almost irritable,
and plainly anything but master of the situation. His relief
at the sight of the "honest British face" of his Rector was
unmeasured, but words to describe it were denied him. He
could only say :

"Well, I ham pleased, I'm sure, sir, to see you. And so I'm sure, sir, will master."

"How *is* your master, Brown?" Mr. Gregory eagerly put in.

"I think he's better, sir, thank you; but he's had a dreadful time of it. I 'ope he's gettin' some sleep now, but——"

"What has been the matter—I couldn't make out from your letter? Was it an accident of any kind?"

"Well, sir, I 'ardly know whether I'd better speak about it. Master was very partickler he should be the one to tell you. But there's no bones broke—that's one thing I'm sure we ought to be thankful——"

"What does the doctor say?" asked Mr. Gregory.

They were by this time outside Mr. Somerton's bedroom door, and speaking in low tones. Mr. Gregory, who happened to be in front, was feeling for the handle, and chanced to run his fingers over the panels. Before Brown could answer, there was a terrible cry from within the room.

"In God's name, who is that?" were the first words they heard. "Brown, is it?"

"Yes, sir—me, sir, and Mr. Gregory," Brown hastened to answer, and there was an audible groan of relief in reply.

They entered the room, which was darkened against the afternoon sun, and Mr. Gregory saw, with a shock of pity, how drawn, how damp with drops of fear, was the usually calm face of his friend, who, sitting up in the curtained bed, stretched out a shaking hand to welcome him.

"Better for seeing you, my dear Gregory," was the reply to the Rector's first question, and it was palpably true.

After five minutes of conversation Mr. Somerton was more his own man, Brown afterwards reported, than he had been for days. He was able to eat a more than respectable dinner, and talked confidently of being fit to stand a journey to Coblentz within twenty-four hours.

"But there's one thing," he said, with a return of agitation which Mr. Gregory did not like to see, "which I must beg you to do for me, my dear Gregory. Don't," he went on, laying his hand on Gregory's to forestall any interruption—"don't ask me what it is, or why I want it done. I'm not up to explaining it yet; it would throw me back—undo all the good you have done me by coming. The only word I will say about it is that you run no risk whatever by doing it, and that Brown can and will show you to-morrow what it is. It's merely to put back—to keep—something— No; I can't speak of it yet. Do you mind calling Brown?"

"Well, Somerton," said Mr. Gregory, as he crossed the room to the door, "I won't ask for any explanations till you see fit to give them. And if this bit of business is as easy as you represent it to be, I will very gladly undertake it for you the first thing in the morning."

"Ah, I was sure you would, my dear Gregory; I was certain I could rely on you. I shall owe you more thanks than I can tell. Now, here is Brown. Brown, one word with you."

"Shall I go?" interjected Mr. Gregory.

"Not at all. Dear me, no. Brown, the first thing to-morrow morning—(you don't mind early hours, I know, Gregory)—you must take the Rector to—*there*, you know" (a nod from Brown, who looked grave and anxious), "and he and you will put that back. You needn't be in the least alarmed; it's *perfectly* safe in the daytime. You know what I mean. It lies on the step, you know, where—where we put it." (Brown swallowed dryly once or twice, and, failing to speak, bowed.) "And—yes, that's all. Only this one other word, my dear Gregory. If you *can* manage to keep from questioning Brown about this matter, I shall be still more bound to you. To-morrow evening, at latest, if all goes well, I shall be able, I believe, to tell you the whole story from start to finish. And now I'll wish you good night. Brown will be with me —he sleeps here—and if I were you, I should lock my door. Yes, be particular to do that. They—they like it, the people here, and it's better. Good night, good night."

They parted upon this, and if Mr. Gregory woke once or twice in the small hours and fancied he heard a fumbling about the lower part of his locked door, it was, perhaps, no more than what a quiet man, suddenly plunged into a strange bed and the heart of a mystery, might reasonably expect. Certainly he thought, to the end of his days, that he had heard such a sound two or three times between midnight and dawn.

He was up with the sun, and out in company with Brown soon after. Perplexing as was the service he had been asked to perform for Mr. Somerton, it was not a difficult or an alarming one, and within half an hour from his leaving the inn it was over. What it was I shall not as yet divulge.

Later in the morning Mr. Somerton, now almost himself again, was able to make a start from Steinfeld; and that same evening, whether at Coblentz or at some intermediate stage on the journey I am not certain, he settled down to the promised explanation. Brown was present, but how much of the matter was ever really made plain to his comprehension he would never say, and I am unable to conjecture.

III

This was Mr. Somerton's story:

"You know roughly, both of you, that this expedition of mine was undertaken with the object of tracing something in connection with some old painted glass in Lord D——'s private chapel. Well, the starting-point of the whole matter lies in this passage from an old printed book, to which I will ask your attention."

And at this point Mr. Somerton went carefully over some ground with which we are already familiar.

"On my second visit to the chapel," he went on, "my purpose was to take every note I could of figures, lettering, diamond-scratchings on the glass, and even apparently accidental markings. The first point which I tackled was that of the inscribed scrolls. I could not doubt that the first of these, that of Job—'There is a place for the gold where it is hidden'—with its intentional alteration, must refer to the treasure; so I applied myself with some confidence to the next, that of St. John—'They have on their vestures a writing which no man knoweth.' The natural question will have occurred to you: Was there an inscription on the robes of the figures? I could see none; each of the three had a broad black border to his mantle, which made a conspicuous and rather ugly feature in the window. I was nonplussed, I will own, and but for a curious bit of luck I think I should have left the search where the Canons of Steinfeld had left it before me. But it so happened that there was a good deal of dust on the surface of the glass, and Lord D——, happening to come in, noticed my blackened hands, and kindly insisted on sending for a Turk's head broom to clean down the window. There must, I suppose, have been a rough piece in the broom;

anyhow, as it passed over the border of one of the mantles, I noticed that it left a long scratch, and that some yellow stain instantly showed up. I asked the man to stop his work for a moment, and ran up the ladder to examine the place. The yellow stain was there, sure enough, and what had come away was a thick black pigment, which had evidently been laid on with the brush after the glass had been burnt, and could therefore be easily scraped off without doing any harm. I scraped, accordingly, and you will hardly believe—no, I do you an injustice ; you will have guessed already—that I found under this black pigment two or three clearly-formed capital letters in yellow stain on a clear ground. Of course, I could hardly contain my delight.

"I told Lord D——— that I had detected an inscription which I thought might be very interesting, and begged to be allowed to uncover the whole of it. He made no difficulty about it whatever, told me to do exactly as I pleased, and then, having an engagement, was obliged—rather to my relief, I must say—to leave me. I set to work at once, and found the task a fairly easy one. The pigment, disintegrated, of course, by time, came off almost at a touch, and I don't think that it took me a couple of hours, all told, to clean the whole of the black borders in all three lights. Each of the figures had, as the inscription said, 'a writing on their vestures which nobody knew.'

"This discovery, of course, made it absolutely certain to my mind that I was on the right track. And, now, what was the inscription ? While I was cleaning the glass I almost took pains not to read the lettering, saving up the treat until I had got the whole thing clear. And when that *was* done, my dear Gregory, I assure you I could almost have cried from sheer disappointment. What I read was only the most hopeless jumble of letters that was ever shaken up in a hat. Here it is :

Job.　　　DREVICIOPEDMOOMSMVIVLISLCAVI
　　　　　BASBATAOVT

St. John.　RDIIEAMRLESIPVSPODSEEIRSETTA A
　　　　　ESGIAVNNR

Zachariah.　FTEEAILNQDPVAIVMTLEEATTOHIO
　　　　　ONVMCAAT.H.Q.E.

"Blank as I felt and must have looked for the first few minutes, my disappointment didn't last long. I realized almost at once that I was dealing with a cipher or cryptogram; and I reflected that it was likely to be of a pretty simple kind, considering its early date. So I copied the letters with the most anxious care. Another little point, I may tell you, turned up in the process which confirmed my belief in the cipher. After copying the letters on Job's robe I counted them, to make sure that I had them right. There were thirty-eight; and, just as I finished going through them, my eye fell on a scratching made with a sharp point on the edge of the border. It was simply the number xxxviii in Roman numerals. To cut the matter short, there was a similar note, as I may call it, in each of the other lights; and that made it plain to me that the glass-painter had had very strict orders from Abbot Thomas about the inscription, and had taken pains to get it correct.

"Well, after that discovery you may imagine how minutely I went over the whole surface of the glass in search of further light. Of course, I did not neglect the inscription on the scroll of Zachariah—'Upon one stone are seven eyes,' but I very quickly concluded that this must refer to some mark on a stone which could only be found *in situ*, where the treasure was concealed. To be short, I made all possible notes and sketches and tracings, and then came back to Parsbury to work out the cipher at leisure. Oh, the agonies I went through! I thought myself very clear at first, for I made sure that the key would be found in some of the old books on secret writing. The '*Steganographia*' of Joachim Trithemius, who was an earlier contemporary of Abbot Thomas, seemed particularly promising; so I got that, and Selenius's '*Cryptographia*' and Bacon's '*de Augmentis Scientiarum*,' and some more. But I could hit upon nothing. Then I tried the principle of the 'most frequent letter,' taking first Latin and then German as a basis. That didn't help, either; whether it ought to have done so, I am not clear. And then I came back to the window itself, and read over my notes, hoping almost against hope that the Abbot might himself have somewhere supplied the key I wanted. I could make nothing out of the colour or pattern of the robes. There were no landscape backgrounds with subsidiary objects; there was nothing in the canopies. The only resource possible seemed to be in the attitude of the figures. 'Job,' I read : 'scroll in left hand, forefinger of right hand extended upwards. John : holds inscribed book in left hand ; with right hand blesses, with two fingers. Zachariah : scroll in left hand ; right hand extended upwards, as Job, but with three fingers pointing up.' In other words, I reflected, Job has *one* finger extended, John has *two*, Zachariah has *three*. May not there be a numeral key concealed in that ? My dear Gregory," said Mr. Somerton, laying his hand on his friend's knee, "that *was* the key. I didn't get it to fit at first, but after two or three trials I saw what was meant. After the first letter of the inscription you skip *one* letter, after the next you skip *two*, and after that skip *three*. Now look at the result I got. I've underlined the letters which form words :

DREVICIOPEDMOOMSMVIVLISLCAVIBASBA
TAOVT

RDIIEAMRLESIPVSPODSEEIRSETTAAESGIA
VNNR

FTEEAILNQDPVAIVMTLEEATTOHIOONVMC
AAT.H.Q.E.

"Do you see it ? *'Decem millia auri reposita sunt in puteo in at . . .'* (Ten thousand [pieces] of gold are laid up in a well in . . .), followed by an incomplete word beginning *at*. So far so good. I tried the same plan with the remaining letters ; but it wouldn't work, and I fancied that perhaps the placing of dots after the three last letters might indicate some difference of procedure. Then I thought to myself, 'Wasn't there some allusion to a well in the account of Abbot Thomas in that book the *Sertum* ?' Yes, there was : he built a *puteus in atrio* (well in the court). There, of course, was my word *atrio*. The next step was to copy out the remaining letters of the inscription, omitting those I had already used. That gave what you will see on this slip :

RVIIOPDOOSMVVISCAVBSBTAOTDIEAMLSIV
SPDEERSETAEGIANRFEEALQDVAIMLEATTH
OOVMCA.H.Q.E.

"Now, I knew what the three first letters I wanted were,—namely, *rio*—to complete the word *atrio* ; and, as you will see, these are all to be found in the first five letters. I was a little confused at first by the occurrence of two *i*'s, but very soon I saw that every alternate letter must be taken in the remainder of the inscription. You can work it out for yourself, the results, continuing where the first 'round' left off, is this :

'rio domus abbatialis de Steinfeld a me, Thoma, qui posui custodem super ea. Gare aqui la touche.'

"So the whole secret was out :

'Ten thousand pieces of gold are laid up in the well in the court of the Abbot's house of Steinfeld by me, Thomas, who have set a guardian over them. *Gara à qui la touche.*'

"The last words, I ought to say, are a device which Abbot Thomas had adopted. I found it with his arms in another piece of glass at Lord D——'s, and he drafted it bodily into his cipher, though it doesn't quite fit in point of grammar.

"Well, what would any human being have been tempted to do, my dear Gregory, in my place ? Could he have helped setting off, as I did, to Steinfeld, and tracing the secret literally to the fountain-head ? I don't believe he could. Anyhow, I couldn't, and, as I needn't tell you, I found myself at Steinfeld as soon as the resources of civilization could put me there, and installed myself in the inn, you saw. I must tell you that I was not altogether free from forebodings—on one hand of disappointment, on the other of danger. There was always the possibility that Abbot Thomas's well might have been wholly obliterated, or else that someone, ignorant of cryptograms, and guided only by luck, might have stumbled on the treasure before me. And then"—there was a very perceptible shaking of the voice here—"I was not entirely easy, I need not mind confessing, as to the meaning of the words about the guardian of the treasure. But, if you don't mind, I'll say no more about that until—until it becomes necessary.

"At the first possible opportunity Brown and I began exploring the place. I had naturally represented myself as being interested in the remains of the abbey, and we could not avoid paying a visit to the church, impatient as I was to be elsewhere. Still, it did interest me to see the windows where the glass had been, and especially that at the east end of the south aisle. In the tracery lights of that I was startled to see some fragments and coats-of-arms remaining—Abbot Thomas's shield was there, and a small figure with a scroll inscribed 'Oculos habent, et non videbunt' (They have eyes, and shall not see,) which, I take it, was a hit of the Abbot at his Canons.

"But, of course, the principal object was to find the Abbot's house. There is no prescribed place for this, so far as I know, in the plan of a monastery, you can't predict of it, as you can of the chapter-house, that it will be on the eastern side of the cloister, or, as of the dormitory, that it will communicate with a transept of the church. I felt that if I asked many questions I might awaken lingering memories of the treasure, and I thought it best to try first to discover it for myself. It was not a very long or difficult search. That three-sided court south-east of the church, with deserted piles of building round it, and grass-grown pavement, which you saw this morning, was the place. And glad enough I was to see that it was put to no use, and was neither very far from our inn nor overlooked by any inhabited building ; there were only orchards and paddocks on the slopes east of the church. I can tell you that fine stone glowed wonderfully in the rather watery yellow sunset that we had on the Tuesday afternoon.

"Next, what about the well ? There was not much doubt about that, as you can testify. It is really a very remarkable thing. That curb is, I think, of Italian marble, and the carving I thought must be Italian also. There were reliefs, you will perhaps remember, of Eliezer and Rebekah, and of Jacob opening the well for Rachel, and similar subjects, but, by way of disarming suspicion, I suppose, the Abbot had carefully abstained from any of his cynical and allusive inscriptions.

"I examined the whole structure with the keenest interest, of course—a square well-head with an opening in one side, an arch over it, with a wheel for the rope to pass over, evidently in very good condition still, for it had been used within sixty years, or perhaps even later, though not quite recently. Then there was the question of depth and access to the interior. I suppose the depth was about sixty to seventy feet, and as to the other point, it really seemed as if the Abbot had wished to lead searchers up to the very door of his treasure-house, for, as you tested for yourself, there were big blocks of stone bonded into the masonry, and leading down in a regular staircase round and round the inside of the well.

"It seemed almost too good to be true. I wondered if there was a trap—if the stones were so contrived as to tip over when a weight was placed on them, but I tried, a good many with my own weight and with my stick, and all seemed, and actually were, perfectly firm. Of course, I resolved that Brown and I would make an experiment that very night.

"I was well prepared. Knowing the sort of place I should have to explore, I had brought a sufficiency of good rope and bands of webbing to surround my body, and cross-bars to hold to, as well as lanterns and candles and crowbars, all of which would go into a single carpet-bag and excite no suspicion. I satisfied myself that my rope would be long enough, and that the wheel for the bucket was in good working order, and then we went home to dinner.

"I had a little cautious conversation with the landlord, and made out that he would not be over-much surprised if I went out for a stroll with my man about nine o'clock, to make (Heaven forgive me!) a sketch of the abbey by moonlight. I asked no questions about the well, and am not likely to do so now. I fancy I know as much about it as anyone in Steinfeld, at least"—with a strong shudder—"I don't want to know any more.

"Now we come to the crisis, and, though I hate to think of it, I feel sure, Gregory, that it will be better for me in all ways to recall it just as it happened. We started, Brown and I, at about nine with our bag, and attracted no attention, for we managed to slip out at the hinder end of the inn-yard into an alley which brought us quite to the edge of the village. In five minutes we were at the well, and for some little time we sat on the edge of the well-head to make sure that no one was stirring or spying on us. All we heard was some horses cropping grass out of sight farther down the eastern slope. We were perfectly unobserved, and had plenty of light from the gorgeous full moon to allow us to get the rope properly fitted over the wheel. Then I secured the band round my body beneath the arms. We attached the end of the rope very securely to a ring in the stonework. Brown took the lighted lantern and followed me; I had a crowbar. And so we began to descend cautiously, feeling every step before we set foot on it, and scanning the walls in search of any marked stone.

"Half aloud I counted the steps as we went down, and we got as far as the thirty-eighth before I noted anything at all irregular in the surface of the masonry. Even here there was no mark, and I began to feel very blank, and to wonder if the Abbot's cryptogram could possibly be an elaborate hoax. At the forty-ninth step the staircase ceased. It was with a very sinking heart that I began retracing my steps, and when I was back on the thirty-eighth—Brown, with the lantern, being a step or two above me—I scrutinized the little bit of irregularity in the stonework with all my might, but there was no vestige of a mark.

"Then it struck me that the texture of the surface looked just a little smoother than the rest, or, at least, in some way different. It might possibly be cement and not stone. I gave it a good blow with my iron bar. There was a decidedly hollow sound, though that might be the result of our being in a well. But there was more. A great flake of cement dropped on to my feet, and I saw marks on the stone underneath. I had tracked the Abbot down, my dear Gregory ; even now I think of it with a certain pride. . It took but a very few more taps to clear the whole of the cement away, and I saw a slab of stone about two feet square, upon which was engraven a cross. Disappointment again, but only for a moment. It was you, Brown, who reassured me by a casual remark. You said, if I remember right :

"It's a funny cross, looks like a lot of eyes."

"I snatched the lantern out of your hand, and saw with inexpressible pleasure that the cross *was* composed of seven eyes, four in a vertical line, three horizontal. The last of the scrolls in the window was explained in the way I had anticipated. Here was my 'stone with the seven eyes.' So far the Abbot's data had been exact, and, as I thought of this, the anxiety about the 'guardian' returned upon me with increased force. Still, I wasn't going to retreat now.

"Without giving myself time to think, I knocked away the cement all round the marked stone, and then gave it a prise on the right side with my crowbar. It moved at once, and I saw that it was but a thin slab, such as I could easily lift out myself, and that it stopped the entrance to a cavity. I did lift it out unbroken, and set it on the step, for it might be very important to us to be able to replace it. Then I waited for several minutes on the step just above. I don't know why, but I think to see if any dreadful thing would rush out. Nothing happened. Next I lit a candle, and very cautiously I placed it inside the cavity, with some idea of seeing whether there were foul air, and of getting a glimpse of what was inside. There *was* some foulness of air which nearly extinguished the flame, but in no long time it burned quite steadily. The hole went some little way back, and also on the right and left of the entrance, and I could see some rounded light-coloured objects within which might be bags. There was no use in waiting. I faced the cavity, and looked in. There was nothing immediately in the front of the hole. I put my arm in and felt to the right, very gingerly. . . .

"Just give me a glass of cognac, Brown. I'll go on in a moment, Gregory. . . .

"Well, I felt to the right, and my fingers touched something curved, that felt—yes—more or less like leather ; dampish it was, and evidently part of a heavy full thing. There was nothing, I must say, to alarm one. I grew bolder, and putting both hands in as well as I could, I pulled it to me, and it came. It was heavy, but moved more easily than I had expected. As I pulled it towards the entrance, my left elbow knocked over and extinguished the candle. I got the thing fairly in front of the mouth and began drawing it out. Just then Brown gave a sharp ejaculation and ran quickly up the steps with the lantern. He will tell you why in a moment. Startled as I was, I looked round after him, and saw him stand for a minute at the top and then walk away a few yards. Then I heard him call softly, 'All right, sir,' and went on pulling out the great bag, in complete darkness. It hung for an instant on the edge of the hole, then slipped forward on to my chest, and *put its arms round my neck*.

"My dear Gregory, I am telling you the exact truth. I believe I am now acquainted with the extremity of terror and repulsion which a man can endure without losing his mind. I can only just manage to tell you now the bare outline of the experience. I was conscious of a most horrible smell of mould, and of a cold kind of face pressed against my own, and moving slowly over it, and of several—I don't know how many— legs or arms or tentacles or something clinging to my body. I screamed out, Brown says, like a beast, and fell away backward from the step on which I stood, and the creature slipped downwards, I suppose, on to that same step. Providentially the band round me held firm. Brown did not lose his head, and was strong enough to pull me up to the top and get me over the edge quite promptly. How he managed it exactly I don't know, and I think he would find it hard to tell you. I believe he contrived to hide our implements in the deserted building near by, and with very great difficulty he got me back to the inn. I was in no state to make explanations, and Brown knows no German, but next morning I told the people some tale of having had a bad fall in the abbey ruins, which, I suppose, they believed. And now, before I go further, I should just like you to hear what Brown's experiences during those few minutes were. Tell the Rector, Brown, what you told me."

"Well, sir," said Brown, speaking low and nervously, "it was just this way. Master was busy down in front of the 'ole and I was 'olding the lantern and looking on, when I 'eard somethink drop in the water from the top, as I thought. So I looked up, and I see someone's 'ead lookin' over at us. I s'pose I must ha' said somethink, and I 'eld the light up and run up the steps, and my light shone right on the face. That was a bad un, sir, if ever I see one! A holdish man, and the face very much fell in, and larfin, as I thought. And I got up the steps as quick pretty nigh as I'm tellin' you, and when I was out on the ground there warn't a sign of any person. There 'adn't been the time for anyone to get away, let alone a hold chap, and I made sure he warn't crouching down by the well, nor nothink. Next thing I hear master cry out somethink 'orrible, and hall I see was him hanging out by the rope, and, as master says, 'owever I got him up I couldn't tell you."

"You hear that, Gregory?" said Mr. Somerton. "Now, does any explanation of that incident strike you?"

"The whole thing is so ghastly and abnormal that I must own it puts me quite off my balance, but the thought did occur to me that possibly the—well, the person who set the trap might have come to see the success of his plan."

"Just so, Gregory, just so. I can think of nothing else so—*likely*, I should say, if such a word had a place anywhere in my story. I think it must have been the Abbot . . . Well, I haven't much more to tell you. I spent a miserable night, Brown sitting up with me. Next day I was no better, unable to get up, no doctor to be had, and, if one had been available, I doubt if he could have done much for me. I made Brown write off to you, and spent a second terrible night. And, Gregory, of this I am sure, and I think it affected me more than the first shock, for it lasted longer, there was someone or something on the watch outside my door the whole night. I almost fancy there were two. It wasn't only the faint noises I heard from time to time all through the dark hours, but there was the smell—the hideous smell of mould. Every rag I had had on me on that first evening I had stripped off and made Brown take it away. I believe he stuffed the things into the stove in his room, and yet the smell was there, as intense as it had been in the well; and, what is more, it came from outside the door. But with the first glimmer of dawn it faded out, and the sounds ceased, too; and that convinced me that the thing or things were creatures of darkness, and could not stand the daylight, and so I was sure that if anyone could put back the stone, it or they would be powerless until someone else took it away again. I had to wait until you came to get that done. Of course, I couldn't send Brown to do it by himself, and still less could I tell anyone who belonged to the place.

"Well, there is my story, and if you don't believe it, I can't help it. But I think you do."

"Indeed," said Mr. Gregory, "I can find no alternative. I *must* believe it! I saw the well and the stone myself, and had a glimpse, I thought, of the bags or something else in the hole. And, to be plain with you, Somerton, I believe my door was watched last night, too."

"I dare say it was, Gregory, but, thank goodness, that is over. Have you, by the way, anything to tell about your visit to that dreadful place?"

"Very little," was the answer. "Brown and I managed easily enough to get the slab into its place, and he fixed it very firmly with the irons and wedges you had desired him to get, and we contrived to smear the surface with mud so that it looks like the rest of the wall. One thing I did notice in the carving on the well-head, which I think must have escaped you. It was a horrid grotesque shape—perhaps more like a toad than anything else, and there was a label by it inscribed with the two words, 'Depositum custodi.'"

THE BIRTHRIGHT
Hilda Hughes

MARTIN DRAKE was considered to be clairvoyant from a little child. At the age of ten he had dreamed of a drowning fatality in the brook on his uncle's farm, and the very next morning they had found his grandfather lying face downwards in the ditch. His clothes were sodden with water, and he was dead, as Martin had seen him in his dream.

Two years later Martin, in the cold grey dawn in his waking hours, had seen, as clearly as if it had happened before him, the horse on which Lord Karney was riding stumble and fall, with its rider thrown under it. And when they picked him up Lord Karney's neck was found to be broken.

Martin's mother, susceptible to her boy's gifts, which were looked upon with disfavour by his father, who gave all his affection to his firstborn Michael, took the vision as an evil omen. She had not been through the tragedy of her father's suicide for nothing. She rushed down to the Manor, asked to see Lord Karney himself, and begged him not to ride to hounds that morning. He scoffed at the superstition of his steward's wife who listened to the precocious prattling of her younger boy, and rode to the meet in the market-place. Three hours later his horse fell clumsily and rolled over upon its master. They carried Lord Karney home upon a hurdle—Karney with his broken neck and his mouth gaping. And Martin had felt a strange thrill of pleasure when he had been told. It was as he had predicted.

He became a person of some importance in the village after that. The schoolmaster, who dabbled in Spiritualism, suggested that Martin was mediumistic. The vision was, in his opinion, not due to the boy's clairvoyance, but to some spirit control. The child should be watched. Eminent research students who were investigating psychic phenomena should have an opportunity of talking with him. Mr. Drake, however, was indignant, and refused to consider "such an

infamous piece of humbug". His wife's pleading left him
adamant. The boy was a prig, and should be thrashed until
he dropped his posing. And, when old women from the
village tried to encourage Martin to have premonitions about
themselves and their own concerns, Mr. Drake let it be understood that there was to be no more nonsensical talk of the
kind. Perhaps his anger merely veiled his fear. Nothing
Martin ever did could please his father, but any suggestion
of the boy's supernatural powers merely infuriated him.

And so during the next few years Martin's clairvoyance
—call it what you will—was discouraged, although his
mother, convinced of her boy's uncanny powers, secretly
regaled the ladies' sewing meeting with talk that brought a
gleam to the eyes of the least susceptible and made the superstitious experience a curdling of the blood.

When he was twenty-four Martin's father died. Mrs.
Drake, a sensitive woman who had experienced a good deal
of sorrow, lived on in the old house, because Michael had
followed in his father's footsteps and been made steward of
the present Lord Karney's estate.

A will, made several years before his death, left the entire
estate to the elder son, since the widow had money of her
own. In due course the will was proved, and Mrs. Drake
grieved secretly because the bitterness of her husband for her
younger son had lived on in his heart throughout his life,
had outlived his body. It was as if the father's evil, bitter
spirit towards her boy—their boy—brooded about the house,
even stronger in death than it had been in life. Once she
spoke to Martin about it.

"I couldn't understand your father as he got older,"
she said. "When I married him I saw only the gentle side
of his nature. He was loving and kind. But he faced all
kinds of trouble, and he couldn't weather the storms. He
was a bitter man—a cruel man. He did you a grievous
wrong, my boy. He hated you in his lifetime, and his hate
lives on. If he has any consciousness in that place where
the dead go he may come to be sorry. Perhaps it will
trouble him. I can't rest at night in the room where we
used to sleep. Perhaps you wouldn't mind changing bed-
rooms with me, my boy. It's silly, I know."

"Your nerves are going to pieces, Mother," he said.
"I'll change rooms with you."

He did as she bade him, and he too had many sleepless nights.

He gave them the shock of their lives at breakfast-time on the anniversary of his father's death.

"I couldn't sleep last night," he told them. "I knew there was something strange about the place. I knew, too, what I should see. It was that old power working in me. I dreaded to see my father."

His mother shuddered, her lips trembling, a strange sound whistling through her teeth. It was what she, too, had feared. But she dreaded still more that anyone should ever learn her secret, should know that her love for her man had slowly turned to hate and dread. She had trembled before him in his lifetime. She feared him still in death. It was terrible that, having hated him so much, she had been forced to give him her body. The horror of it had seared her mind. But what was her boy saying now?

She looked at him, drawing his hand through his long, straight brown hair. His face looked distorted, as she watched him through narrowing eyes.

"I dreaded seeing him," Martin said in strange, thick tones. "He hated me so. I could feel his hate wrapping round me. The air seemed to be full of it. I couldn't breathe. I thought I should choke where I lay."

"You must have had nightmare," his brother interjected, but his mother hung upon every word, and then she turned her face aside and put her hand over her eyes so that they should not look into her soul.

"It was awful," he went on. "It was like a poisoned gas in the air, physical as well as spiritual, if you see what I mean. I tried to sit up and then fell back exhausted. I was sick to the heart and horribly afraid. And I can remember those trivial things which do stand out on days like this. I heard the cuckoo-clock in the hall, just as I heard it a few minutes before he died. I can remember noticing the awful ticking of my own watch, which lay on the dressing-table beside me and ticked with a terrifying insistence, seeming to get louder and louder.

"I could hear the leaves tapping on the window, and the head of Abraham Lincoln on the table looked strange in the moonlight. Even the knobs on the bedstead, with my dressing-gown thrown over the rail, were unnerving. I shall never forget it—the insistence upon my consciousness of all these things ; and yet I knew that something terrifying was going to happen, that I was a prisoner, numb with cold, yet suffocating slowly."

"Go on !" his mother screamed, and they were both shocked by her voice, hollow and toneless. But Martin's voice was deep, and what he said seemed inevitable. People might cry, might batter themselves against Fate ; these things were true, unalterable.

"I noticed the Thing near the window at first. Then it moved sickeningly towards the cupboard as though it could not see, but must feel its way. And then it swung round and faced me. And I saw my father's face with hollows where the eyes used to be—like a skull."

"A skull ! Oh, my God !"

"The face was white as he never was even in death. I can't remember what clothes he had, or if he had any, but he wrung his hands, and a terrible dry sobbing came from his lips. I tried to scream out, but I couldn't make a sound. I sat up in bed and clutched the sheets. And slowly I could understand what he meant. It was a voice all right, but the words were strange—like someone trying to speak who has been dumb for years."

"Oh, God !"

"And he shot out one hand towards me, and although it didn't touch me I had the sensation of something icy-cold. 'I've done you a wrong, my boy,' he said. 'Look in my old coat . . . open the family Bible. You'll find it in Genesis.' And then he turned aside and wailed and wrung his hands.

"I watched him as he went ; he seemed to merge into the dusk. He was like light—thin, white, transparent—but he seemed to fade away into the darkness, or else became lost in the moonbeam. I got out of bed when I could. I wanted to say something, but I couldn't find him. I got back into bed, and cold sweat poured off me."

"I don't wonder," said Michael, shocked to the depths but trying to make a pretence of calm.

"What do you think he meant ?" cried the mother.

Martin's long fingers played nervously with his lips.

"How should I know ?"

"You say he mentioned his old coat ?"

He nodded.

"I wanted to give it to Johnson two days before he died," said the widow. "It was so shabby, but he would cling to it. There was a scene."

"Where is it now?" asked Michael. "Couldn't you, with your powers, tell us that, Martin, old boy?"

Mrs. Drake spoke quickly before her elder son could notice that his brother was not prepared to reply.

"In the cupboard with all his other old clothes. I left them untouched after he died."

"*He* went towards the *cupboard* first," said Martin.

They looked at each other significantly, as people do when they think they have found a clue.

"We must go up at once," said Mrs. Drake.

Michael took her arm. Martin followed them.

They entered the bedroom where she had known so many unhappy nights. She knocked against the dressing-table and bruised one hip in her hurry. Then she crossed to the built-in cupboard beside the fireplace and flung open the doors. Some old clothes of her own, three or four pairs of shoes, an old hat or two met her gaze. She took them out, threw them upon the floor, took down her husband's frock-coat which had done duty at funerals, and, though very old, was not to be despised even now. Then she produced a dressing-gown, and lastly, from among a number of old garments, the coat in question. The outside pockets gave no clue. Then as Michael, sitting on the floor, ran his fingers over it, he heard a crackling and felt something in a breast-pocket. He took out a thin sheet of notepaper.

Kneeling on the floor together among the debris of the wardrobe, they read it.

I was unjust. I want to make amends before I die, and I have a premonition of death. For my last will and testament look in the family Bible—Genesis.

"Just as he said," put in Martin.

"You didn't say anything about a will," said his brother.

"He didn't exactly mention the word. But I remember him saying look in Genesis."

"Where is it, Mother?"

"It's such a heavy book," said Mrs. Drake. "We never

use it now. It's got all your ages written upon the flyleaf. I remember your father's Cousin Jane would do it."

"Silly old girl!" said Michael.

"What does it matter?" sighed Martin.

Mrs. Drake went carefully through a pile of books in the cupboard, but could find no trace of the family Bible. They found it at last in the bottom drawer of the chiffonier in the dining-room. And between the pages of Genesis they found the will. It had been drawn up three years before and witnessed by Cousin Jane and Henry Deane. The premonition of death had evidently come to the strong man not a few days before he actually died, as they had at first supposed, but during a severe attack of influenza three years earlier.

"I remember now he was very nervous about himself," said the widow.

"Strong men always are when they're ill," said Martin.

In the will the property was to be divided equally between the two brothers.

"I'm glad your father didn't forget you, after all," went on Mrs. Drake.

"But the will's already been proved," said Michael.

"The last will must stand," his mother interposed. "You'll share and share alike now. It's only just. Your father regretted his bitterness—and to think I never knew!"

Her eyes strayed to the printed page of the Bible.

"And Esau said unto his father, Hast thou but one blessing, my father? Bless me, even me also, O my father. And Esau lifted up his voice, and wept."

It was the poignant story of Jacob and Esau. Her husband must have read that when he was ill. It had brought him to a new state of mind.

.   .   .   .   .

The finding of the second will brought calm to Mary Drake's troubled spirit. Her boy—her baby—had not been forgotten. Perhaps her husband's heart had changed before he died. Perhaps he had become more like the man she once had loved passionately—not the fiend she had known in later life.

The proving of the second will took time. The technicalities of the Law always do. But the inheritance of the two brothers was shared equally at last. It was only Martin, benefiting by several thousands, who took it so calmly. His mother sometimes wondered if his father's change of spirit meant much to him. It was nice, of course, to have the money, but surely the justice of the thing must appeal to him. He must be sensitive. Was he not clairvoyant—perhaps a medium ?

Martin and his brother talked for a long time about investments one night beside the fire in the old-fashioned dining-room with its horsehair furniture and its copper kettles on the mantelpiece, and its willow-pattern china upon the dresser, and its sporting prints to decorate the walls. They had taken advice upon the subject that very afternoon, and were viewing themselves and each other as men of property. With the money well invested there was no knowing what they might do in the future. Neither of them had any responsibilities, any ties. Each had himself to consider, and money meant much to both of them, not merely because of the things it would bring them, but because it spelt power.

When Martin went to bed that night in the old four-poster, which his mother and father had once used, he went to sleep as soon as his head touched the pillow.

It was a large room with low beams and only one door. Rain fell outside and leaves rattled against the window-pane, but they had no power to disturb Martin. He had his fortune. He had power. His dreams as the night passed were fantastic. He could see himself as Master of the Hunt, living in the fine old Manor; he could see more money coming from his mother later, and a wife and children sitting beside him at a table spread with silver and crystal. Yet he had never really loved in his life. But the woman in the dream was beautiful, and she was looking across the table with a smile. He could see himself lifting his glass and draining it . . . it was a funny thing to experience the sensation of good old wine in a dream. He could feel it nice to his palate, soothing to his stomach. His legs were tingling. He saw himself stand up and propose a toast. Then the scene changed. They were all at the Hunt Ball, he and his friends, and they were drinking at the bar, and then later dancing madly in a gallop. There seemed to be a fever in his blood. He danced the gallop, which had returned to fashion in order to round off a Hunt Ball programme, as he had never danced it before. A girl was looking up into his eyes—he bent over her—wanted to snatch a kiss—then he awoke.

There was something in the room. He could not see it, but he could feel. It was not the blind either, which was flapping at the open window, nor the curtain which was blown about and then seemed to bulge into the room. And how the wind howled! It was on him before he knew. He could feel something scorching him—was it this fiend's breath, or the heat from the wood fire, crackling in the grate?

He tried to get up, to escape. But small, greenish eyes looked into his. His father stood over him, brooding over him, with intense hate and loathing on his face and in his eyes. There were no hollows, as in a skull. It was the face of a madman who acted with disconcerting logicality.

The Thing was trying to speak now.

"What was that nonsense you told them . . . the face of a skull?"

The voice made him cower in his bed.

"You lied! You never saw me! I did not come!"

Martin put his hand before his eyes to shut out the sight. The feeling of heat was terrible.

"You lied! You lied!" The voice screamed out the truth in a crescendo.

Sweat poured off Martin's face, his tongue was cloven. He lay trembling, as if in an ague. Words failed. Screams would not come, yet every nerve in his body cried aloud in pain, in horror for the peril that was to come.

And the Thing was drawing nearer . . . leaning over the bed.

"You forged my name—and the witnesses' names—upon that false will. You wrote letters in my handwriting about my premonitions, and I never so much as thought of death in all my life. Would to God I had! You were a forger!"

The voice died away and then rose again in a scream. His father's great red hands with sandy hairs upon them reached out towards his throat.

Martin made a last effort to cry out. And then the Thing was upon him. His blood-curdling scream was his swan song.

.   .   .   .   .

His brother and a fireman forced their way into the room. The smoke was thick, but the fire had not done much damage.

Martin, however, lay white and still upon the bed. They lifted him before they realized.

The doctor came.

"It was not the fire that killed him," he said; "it didn't even touch him. But these things are easily explained. Death was undoubtedly due to shock."

LAZARUS RETURNS
Guy Endore

I'm innocent !   I swear I'm innocent !
Oh, why will no one believe me ?

LET me begin my confession with that first day when I went out to visit my Uncle Jacob in New Jersey.

We went together, Julia and I.   Oh, lovely Julia, whose cheeks were like the petals of a dark tea-rose, whose hair was like jet, whose eyes were like black cherries, whose mouth was a flame.   You must know that Julia and I first met as students in the chemistry laboratory of Columbia University.   Julia and I fell deeply in love and we would have been married long before, had we been in a position to do so, but I was, practically speaking, without a cent and Julia was not much better off.

It was natural, then, that my thoughts should turn now and then to my wealthy uncle, Jacob Lazarus, despite the ill-repute that had always clung to him and his money.   When Father and Mother were still alive they used to speak now and then of my only other living relative in the United States, namely, Uncle Jacob, but they spoke of him in terms that were far from complimentary, for they felt proud of their honourable poverty when they thought of Uncle Jacob and his tainted money.

It seems that Uncle Jacob had earned his wealth in a most shameful way.   I can well recall how, when I was young, if this matter came up for discussion, I used to be sent on a fictitious errand, or, if I remained present, then the language in which the subject was discussed was so veiled that I could not make head or tail of it.   Uncle Jacob therefore took on a certain glamour in my mind, a glamour to which he was not entitled and which my parents would not have wanted to foster in me.

But it was only much later that I gathered that Uncle Jacob's sudden accession to large sums of money was due to the fact that he had gone into the loathsome business of providing young peasant girls from Central Europe for the brothels of South America. But by the time I heard this, Uncle Jacob's glamour was so fixed in my mind that I could scarcely credit this story as being much above gossip or resting on any more secure base than the fact that Uncle Jacob had got rich rather quickly and that poor people, being envious, suspected at once that his wealth could not have been come by honestly.

Well, enough of that. In short, in our penury I thought of Uncle Jacob, whom I hadn't seen for several years ; in fact, since the death of my father, when he had generously come forward to assume all the expenses of the funeral. I remembered this trait of generosity with a pang when, in answer to a letter from me, he sent a most pathetic note about "a very old man who has been waiting for years in the solitude of his study to hear from his only nephew."

And thus it happened that one afternoon, just as the sun was setting, we stood before Uncle Jacob's grey old house in New Jersey and rang the bell. Far inside one could hear the faint tinkle, and then after a long pause the shuffle of slow footsteps. A moment later the door opened to admit us to a dark hall decorated in that lugubrious style current in the period of General Grant, a hall of heavy mahogany woodwork illuminated by a tragic ruby light.

Uncle Jacob, dressed as I have always remembered him, in a black alpaca frock-coat, bade us enter, with a honeyed smile on his round face. He was a dumpy sort of fellow, quite fat and rather bald and with but a bit of a beard such as those have who clip their face-hair instead of shaving it.

He shook hands with me, a flabby sort of handshake, and then he turned inquiringly toward Julia, and I said, "Uncle Jacob, I want you to meet Julia Levine." And I felt very proud because Julia's beauty was of that striking Oriental type that painters reserve for depicting Judith or Esther or Ruth of the Bible.

In his throaty vibrant voice that always made one want to clear one's own throat as if the frog were there, Uncle Jacob said, "I'm very pleased to meet you, Julia." He lingered on the words.

Then he preceded us towards the dining-room, limping a bit. It was now that I first noticed the strange sort of limp he had. Picture to yourself a leg which takes one perfect step forward but which, when comes its turn to bear the whole weight of the body, while the other leg advances, collapses just the least fraction of an inch and at once recovers to move into another step. Thus Uncle Jacob walked with only this gentle halt in his gait, that is to say, every time the right leg had to support the entire weight of his fat body.

We followed him down the dark passage-way. Julia put her hands into mine suddenly and said, "I'm so cold, David." Indeed, her fingers were icy.

Before he entered the dining-room, Uncle Jacob paused to raise his hand and touch the mazuza, that bit of the holy scroll which orthodox Jews attach to the posts of their doors, and he brought his fingers to his mouth. I could see out of the corner of my eye that Julia was displeased. Religion to her was a very private affair; she was convinced that a show of piety could not be anything else but hypocrisy.

The table was already set and we took places at once. The meal progressed most uncomfortably. To begin with, we were served by Uncle Jacob's housekeeper, an ancient Jewish woman who wore a brown wig. It was most annoying, when this creature bent before one with her platter, to be able to see the stitches down the centre of that wig.

As if he had noticed our aversion to this sight, Uncle Jacob, when the old servant happened to be out in the kitchen, whispered across to us, "I would not for the world have a shikse in the house." A shikse, I must explain, is a Gentile girl, and this housekeeper of Uncle Jacob's was, it was plain, a good Jewish woman from Central Europe, who followed the tradition of shaving her hair and never allowing it to grow again after her bridal night.

"But now, children," Uncle Jacob went on in his husky voice, "please tell me about yourselves. You cannot realize how glad I am to see you. David, why do you visit me so rarely?"

"Well, you know how busy I have been. Julia will tell you how hard I work in the laboratory. Julia and I are to be married, Uncle Jacob, that is to say, just as soon as we can scrape up enough money to pay for a couple of months' rent and furnish ourselves a little place to live in."

"Why, my dear children," exclaimed Uncle Jacob, "why don't you come out here and live with me? I have plenty

of room. Why, there are all kinds of rooms in this house."
He paused to gulp down all the well-done chicken that
parted easily from the drumstick, and with his mouth full,
exclaimed, "You should have pity on an old man. I live
here so alone."

Involuntarily I shuddered at the thought of living with
him, and beneath the table I felt Julia's hand reach across to
mine and squeeze it tightly.

"Why don't you eat anything, David? And you, Julia?
Why, you eat like birds! Julia, why do you have nothing
but vegetables? Would you rival our Queen Esther who,
on her vegetarian diet, was still the most beautiful woman in
the realm at the age of seventy-five?" He smiled, and then
added, "But she was never as beautiful as you, Julia.

"Oh, how I envy you, David!" he said. "You have, in
truth, the vessel of gold of which the daughter of Rabbi
Gamliel spoke. Do you know the story? Rabbi Gamliel
tried to convert the emperor, and the emperor studied the
Bible under his tutelage. But the emperor said one day to
the Rabbi, 'Your God is a thief, for is it not written that
. . . *the Lord God caused a deep sleep to fall upon Adam and
he slept. And God took a rib from Adam. Is not that theft?*'

"Now Rabbi Gamliel had a beautiful daughter and she
broke into this discussion. 'Let me answer that aspersion,'
she cried. 'Last night the robbers broke into my room and
stole therefrom a silver vessel; but they left a golden one in
its stead.'

"The emperor understood. 'God took a rib, and what
is a rib compared to a woman, the golden vessel that God,
as thief, left in its place?'"

All the while he spoke, Uncle Jacob kept his slits of
beady eyes fixed on Julia, who was boiling within as I could
sense. If we bore up under this, it was only because we
promised ourselves a great reward. For my part, I had
made up my mind to be very bold about it; I would come
right out with a request for money, and if he did not accede
to my desires, then I certainly had no intention of ever
exposing myself to an evening like this again.

When the meal was at last over, for with Uncle Jacob
filling his plate again and again it seemed as if it would never
come to an end, then a new torture was prepared for us,
and particularly for Julia, who detested smoking of any

kind. Uncle Jacob smoked a vile stogie, a most evil-smelling weed, yet he relished it so hugely that he must ever and anon bring the burning end of it to his nostrils as if he had to inhale the fragrance direct from the heart of it.

Meanwhile he kept up his heavy-handed compliments to Julia's Biblical beauty, and interspersed them with repeated requests that we accept his hospitality and go to live with him.

We thought that with the finishing of his cigar he would rise and give us a chance to recuperate, but no, he continued to talk of this and that, in his husky unclear voice that made me say *mmmm* again and again, as if I could get rid of the frog in his voice by clearing my own throat.

To top it all, he had the nastiest habit of chewing his finger-nails, talking all the while he bit down on them. And, of course, inasmuch as he was an habitual biter of his finger-nails, there wasn't much left to bite, and so he would go hunting around for a choice spot into which he could dig his teeth.

It should not have been surprising, then, that he should find himself biting down into the quick now and then; nevertheless it revolted us to see a tiny gout of blood well up on one mistreated finger. Uncle Jacob held the member up before him, watched the drop swell, and then brought the finger to his mouth again.

Thereupon, Julia could no longer stand it and rose, and said, "Is there any place I can fix myself up a bit?"

"Sure," said Uncle Jacob, "the room right at the head of the staircase."

When Julia had left, Uncle Jacob took me into his library and began to show me his vast collection of Hebrew books, but I cut him short.

"Uncle Jacob," I pleaded, "you know that we need money. Why don't you help us out a little?"

"You?" said Uncle Jacob, as if surprised. "Why, you, with your Julia, have more than all the treasures of the earth."

"Uncle Jacob," I said rather wearily, thinking that he was going to side-track me in order to escape.

"Come now, David, which would you rather have—my money or your Julia?"

"Oh, but Uncle Jacob!" I said, with surprise and annoyance,

"But, David, my lad, you cannot expect to have everything." He paused for a moment, and then said slowly, "I see . . . I see how you would choose. David, you are a wise lad. Yes, the price of a woman is, after all, not above diamonds and rubies. . . ."

I followed Uncle Jacob's mysterious words with mingled feelings of anger and annoyance, but when he ended his speech with the words, "When I die, all I own will all be yours, David . . ." then my heart gave a great bound! All my money troubles were over. I was so moved that I seized Uncle Jacob's flabby nail-less hand and wrung it.

And Uncle Jacob went on, "I have about half a million dollars and this house and some other property. . . ."

I did not listen to him further. I had let myself sink back in one of Uncle Jacob's comfortably upholstered chairs and was floating away on dreams of prosperity. I saw myself buying a car; I saw myself travelling on fine ships; putting up at expensive hotels. I saw myself studying at foreign universities. . . .

But suddenly I sat up. Why was I leaving Julia out of my dreams of wealth?

It was then that I noticed with a start that Uncle Jacob had left me alone, and ill at ease at being alone in this room, I went out into the hall. From upstairs the confused murmur of voices reached me—the voice of Uncle Jacob, then that of Julia. What could they be discussing up there in that room where Julia had gone to fix her hair?

I mounted the stairs rapidly and paused before the closed door and would have entered if I had not heard words that rooted me to the spot.

"But my little dove, my sweet dove," Uncle Jacob was saying in his husky voice, "you are mine now."

And Julia answered, "If you weren't David's uncle, I'd scream out loud and let the whole neighbourhood know what kind of a man you are. Get away from that door and let me out!"

"Very well, my sweet, since you insist," said Uncle Jacob, "but let me tell you, my rose of Sharon, that I have bought you, and what I buy is mine. Do you understand? Mine! Paid for with all my fortune! Mine! Mine to all eternity! Do you hear? Why, if I were dead in my grave, I'd rise to claim you! Yes, your David sold you to me!"

"It's a lie!" I shouted, pushing open the door. "Why, you damned scoundrel! You damned white slaver!"

Julia rushed into my arms. "David," she pleaded, "take me away quick!"

Uncle Jacob cried out, "She's mine, David! A bargain is a bargain!"

But we ran down the stairs and out of that house, paying no attention to him, though my heart was full of things I wanted to say, and though I heard him snicker as we left the front door, "Why, didn't I pay a good price for her?"

. . . . .

Only when we were on the train and well on our way to New York did Julia recover sufficiently to exclaim, "Oh, isn't he loathsome!" Then she shuddered. "Oh, David, he tried to kiss me!"

"Well, how did all this begin?" I asked.

Whereupon she told me he had come into the room and talked to her for a moment, and then suddenly he had come out with: "You do not know how much I love you!"

"I was so taken by surprise," Julia explained, "that I did not know what to do. Only when he pushed his face, reeking with that horrible stogie breath, up to mine, did I realize how serious he was.

"Then I ran away from him and made for the door, but he blocked my way and began to apologize, saying he was sure I could get used to him.

"It was then I threatened to raise my voice, and I ordered him to let me out. But he still insisted and told me that he had bought me, that you had sold me to him for all his fortune."

"So that's it," I said, and I related for my part how Uncle Jacob had spoken so mysteriously of my making a choice between his money and my Julia. "I really could not make head or tail of what he was driving at, but suddenly he concluded, 'All my money will be yours when I am dead,' and we shook hands on that. Oh, the dirty old vulture! No wonder my father and my mother hated him," I said. "His head is still full of buying and selling women. God only knows how many lives he's ruined!"

"David, David," said Julia, very quietly, and looked up into my eyes. "You would not sell me? You would not sell me ? Not to him!" And she buried her face in her hands.

"How ridiculous," I said, and gathered her into my arms.

．　　．　　．　　．　　．

Now since I am really laying bare here all my soul, let me confess that I did have a little heart-pang to see all my beautiful dreams of wealth shattered so suddenly. Unwittingly, I began to argue to myself that if Julia had been a really clever woman she could have humoured the old bird along, instead of taking him seriously. She could have just laughed it off.

After all, Uncle Jacob could not live for ever, and eventually we'd have his money and be none the worse for having played along with him for a while.

Such thoughts kept recurring to me during the next few days while I spent long hours drilling the elementary facts of chemistry into the dunderheads of students. Really I was heartily sick of that old job that netted me only a few dollars a week, whereas a half of a million dollars . . . let me see . . . why, invested at four per cent—and one could really safely count on much more than that—that would be ten, no, fifteen times what I was earning. . . .

Oh, with what pleasure, I thought, I'd kiss all this good-bye! Now, if only Julia had played her cards better. . . . And thus I would go on thinking. . . .

Then about four days later I received a telegram from Uncle Jacob, conceived in this fashion : *"Won't you please come to see me to-night? I have something for you. Bring Julia."*

"Why, you're not thinking of going, are you ?" Julia asked in great surprise.

"Well," I said, hesitatingly, and feeling rather uncomfortable, "of course I'd be crazy if I let *you* go. But I don't see how I can very well refuse to acknowledge his invitation in some way. Possibly he wants to apologize. I guess he's just a little bit cracked. But if he thinks that I'm going to bring you along, he's sadly mistaken. Though I imagine that he'll be on his good behaviour this time."

I would have gone on talking thus endlessly, I suppose, in my desire to hide from Julia my very real anxiety to visit

173

Uncle Jacob again and have once more a chance at his fortune, but Julia herself cut me short.

"I see you're determined to go. Very well, then, but be very careful, David dear, because I'll be worried silly until I see you again. Call me up just as soon as you leave his house, will you ?"

Grateful for having got off so cheaply, I promised faithfully and left.

.   .   .   .   .

As soon as I came within sight of the old grey house, whose bleak shingles glistened in the gentle rain that was coming down, I was overcome with a feeling that something was amiss. I was not long in finding out what the trouble was ; the undertakers were in possession of the house.

Uncle Jacob had died.

There was present in the house a certain Mr. Simcoff, an ancient bearded man who was known to me vaguely as a very distant relative of the family, and he gave me the details.

Uncle Jacob had been in his study at his favourite work, the perusing of the Talmud, that many-volumed repository of Jewish logic and legend that is a kind of second Bible expanded and commented upon by all the sages of Judaism, and while thus at work, Uncle Jacob had felt the need of a glass of hot tea and lemon, and he had rung for his old crone to bring it to him.

When she returned with the drink, she found her master sitting bolt upright in his chair and staring straight ahead. He was quite dead.

As I listened to Mr. Simcoff, my heart shrank within me. It was not enough that I was afraid that my chances of inheriting my uncle's fortune were wiped out, I must sustain, too, that insupportable close feeling in the chest that comes upon us when death brushes so near to us that we can feel the wind of his wings.

If I die, I thought to myself, let it at least be like this, sudden ! So that I may have the comfort of getting over with it as fast as possible. And I mused out loud to Mr. Simcoff, "Uncle Jacob was a fortunate man. His health was fair all his life, I believe, and he was certainly rich. And now he is dead, true enough, but without any of the torments of dying. Such a sudden exit," I added, "was called by the Greeks the greatest gift of the Gods."

With his gnarled and trembling hands, Mr. Simcoff rolled himself a cigarette, fumbling the paper and the tobacco between his knobby finger-tips, and having licked it, he paused to scold me.

"Greeks?" he asked, in his heavily accented English, and I suddenly recalled that to a good Jew of the old school the Greeks and their philosophies were a hated race of sinners. "Greeks," said Mr. Simcoff, "epicureans then, eh? You mean people who want nothing but pleasure out of life? The Talmud,"—and here Mr. Simcoff waved a monitory finger at me, "doesn't say that man is fortunate or to be envied who dies suddenly.

"The Talmud"—and Mr. Simcoff's voice took on that peculiar singsong oratorical tone adopted by those who conceive that they are speaking the direct words of God— "the Talmud says that when God loves a man He gives him three days in which to die, warning him on the first day so that he may have one day to close up his business affairs and send messengers to his distant friends, giving him a second day to do good deeds so that he may earn the respect even of his enemies, and granting him still a final day in which he càn take leave of his closest friends and relatives and have time left to counsel his sons and daughters. . . . Yes, thus dies the good man, beloved of God, who is not afraid of death."

I must confess that Mr. Simcoff's description of slow death and all this leave-taking before the grave struck me with chill. For to me death is never impersonal, it always calls to mind my own inevitable decease, and that is a subject I had rather not dwell upon.

"I'd prefer to die suddenly," I insisted, "and get it over with."

"Epicurean!" snorted Mr. Simcoff, and that, in the eyes of a Talmudist, is a heavy reproach. "My friend," he went on, and then paused to light his cigarette, "my friend, you should know that your uncle, Mr. Jacob Lazarus, as much as he studied the Talmud, was not a good man; he was not beloved of God."

He puffed his weed for a moment, and then continued. "I say this not only from what I know regarding the manner in which he made his money ; I say this not only because he died suddenly. . . . Do you know that in the Talmud it stands written that : 'Man is born with his hands clenched, sign of his desire to grasp whatever life can offer. But man dies with his hands wide open, sign that he willingly returns to the world all that life ever gave him ? ' "

Mr. Simcoff cleared his throat noisily. "Mr. Jacob Lazarus died with his hands clenched ! Now, what can a dead man want of life ?" He paused. "What can a dead man want of life ?" he repeated.

As I was leaving, the old housekeeper came up to me and handed me an envelope. "I believe your uncle left this for you," she said in a very low voice.

The envelope was indeed marked "David." I opened it and read on a slip of paper the single sentence, "I stick to my bargain." I was filled with sudden joy. "Then I shall inherit his money," I exulted.

. . . . .

Let me pass over rapidly the exciting days that followed while I was in constant fever of wondering if Uncle Jacob had in truth left me his fortune. The will finally came up for reading and proved to contain some rather maudlin statements about an old man who wanted his nephew and his nephew's wife to think well of him. All his fortune, except a bit that was to keep his old housekeeper from indigence for the rest of her days, he left to his "dear nephew David," provided only that I and Julia were married and lived in his house, sleeping and eating there for at least three whole months.

"Julia !" I cried, when I heard this. "Julia, think of it !"

She was not so happy as I was. Very soberly she answered, "I really wish that I could say no. But I see that you intend to have your uncle's money. And it would be a lot of money to turn down. Very well then ! We'll live in his gloomy old house, but not a day longer than three months !"

So, immediately after we were married, we went to live there, thinking that we had best get it over with as quickly as possible. The old house was certainly a gloomy abode. The feel of Uncle Jacob's death lingered in it and gave its very silence a sinister portent. The dust that lay on the ancient walnut furniture looked too undisturbed.

In the evening, particularly, the place took on a menacing aspect. There were not enough lights to properly illuminate the place. The shadows seemed only to retreat a bit before the old-fashioned lustres with their coloured bulbs, seemed only to gather themselves together in the corners of the immense rooms and to lie in ambush there in every bay and alcove, as if waiting to spring out suddenly and destroy our puny lights.

At night I woke up and felt that Julia was lying awake too.

As silent as the house had been during the day, now it was loud with noises. There was an unending succession of mysterious creakings and snappings.

"It's just the woodwork that expanded during the heat of the day," I explained, "and that is now contracting in the cold."

"Yes," said Julia, curtly. I could sense that my explanation did not satisfy her, though she recognized its justness. Nor could I, either, rid myself of a feeling of discomfort.

"I wish it would stop contracting, then," said Julia; "it can't keep on contracting for ever. And now what is that?"

I listened, and heard as if a knocking at the door downstairs.

"It's just the wind," I said.

We both sat there and listened. "It's just the wind," I repeated, as if I needed repetition to convince myself. "I'll fix that front door in the morning. It's a little loose in the latch."

"It's not the front door, it's the back door, or else that garden door," Julia whispered.

"For God's sake, don't whisper," I cried angrily. "What's there to whisper about? It's just a draughty old house and the doors rattle." But still I could not get rid of the feeling that it was not the wind that was rattling the doors, but someone, something, that was going silently from door to door and trying them gently.

Trying them gently, and if they did not give, then knocking gently at their panels. . . .

"Hell!" I said. "We're like two babies. I'm going down to see what it is."

"No, no," cried Julia, "don't leave me! Don't leave me. Oh, I'm so scared."

She clung to me and we remained thus, listening to the doors and windows rattling, following the noise from one place to another, and trying in vain to pierce the mystery of it.

"It's stopped," I said, but just then I thought I could detect it, hollow and distant, coming up from the depths of the cellar. It's got into the cellar, I thought, but already my mind was hazy with sleep.

On the following morning Mr. Simcoff came to see us and asked us how everything was getting along.

"Fine," I said, "only the house is full of draughts and all the doors and windows rattle at night."

Mr. Simcoff looked at me sharply. "The doors and windows rattle?" he asked, but then he spoke of other matters.

Later a representative from the title and trust company came to see if I was carrying out the provisions of the will, and I went to accompany Mr. Simcoff to the door. He put his hand up to touch the mazuza on the door-post, and then, as if taken by a sudden thought, he reached up and removed the lightly attached brass case which usually harbours the bit of holy scroll.

"Just as I thought," he said, when he had unrolled the blank piece of parchment, "not a letter from the Holy Torah.

"Look, David," he said to me, "I don't like what I hear about the doors and windows rattling at night. If I were you, I'd be careful not to say 'Come in' when you hear them.

"And," he added, "I'd have these replaced with the real article," and he contemptuously cast aside the blank mazuza.

That night—yes, it was that night—the wind's insistence at the doors seemed more noisy than before, and I woke up and found myself on the point of crying out, "Come in." I caught myself up with the words burning on the tip of my tongue, and then at once, because I was amused, began to laugh, but a little hysterically because I felt as if I had just saved myself from a vast danger.

Julia woke up with a cry. "David! What are you laughing about? David! You frighten me." And then she heard the noise at the doors. "There it goes again," she said wearily.

"Listen, this is funny," I said. "You know what Mr. Simcoff told me? He said, 'Be sure and don't say *Come in* when the doors rattle.' Ha-ha!"

"Oh, don't laugh!" Julia cried. "That's not funny!"

We sat there in silence for a moment. *Bang* went a window in the garret. *Rat-tat-tat* said a door in the cellar. I laughed again. "You know, if only that darned fool, Simcoff, hadn't suggested it to me, I would never have thought of it. Ha-ha-ha, the idea of saying 'Come in' to the wind at two o'clock in the morning. But now I can't get it out of my mind. I simply must say it. I must!"

"Don't, David!" Julia cried out in great alarm, and swung her arms around me.

Again I laughed. Really, it was irresistible. Finally, I felt that I had myself under control. "Why, it's like that story about the king and the alchemist," I said. "Do you remember how the king put him in prison and tortured him until he would consent to teach the king how to make gold? And the alchemist said that he would gladly do so, only he knew that the king could not possibly learn. 'However, we'll try a small sample,' he said. So he showed the king how to mix the lead and the salt and the other ingredients and how to heat them in a retort, and so forth, and in the end the king had made a small lump of gold. 'Why, I did it!' the king exclaimed, in triumph. 'Marvellous!' applauded the alchemist, 'and do you know why you succeeded? It was because you never once thought of a hippopotamus while you were making it.' Of course the king never once succeeded in making gold again, for he couldn't possibly drive the thought of a hippopotamus out of his mind any more.

"And now," I concluded, "all I can think of is saying, 'Come in.'"

Julia didn't say anything. Silence followed in the wake of my story, a silence all the deeper because it followed my voice. I wanted desperately to think of some other anecdote to recount, but my mind refused to function. At a door below there was a gentle knocking as if a beggar were pleading for shelter. Then the knocking grew stormy as if an officer were commanding that the doors be flung open.

"I can't stand it," Julia breathed.

"Nor can I," I cried. All my being ached to yell out,

"Come in !" But I bit down on my own lips. And then, suddenly, I could no longer contain myself. I pushed Julia aside, and calmly, but distinctly, I spoke out into the darkness straight ahead :

"Come in !"

Silence.

"Come in, damn you !" I shouted.

Silence.

"COME IN !"

"David !" Julia shouted, and began to weep. I lay back, all undone. The house seemed suddenly steeped in quietness.

. . . . .

I remember the following morning very well, because it was then that I first experienced that strange sore throat. . . .

"No, it doesn't hurt much," I said to Julia, in a deep, strained voice.

"Well, I don't think you ought to go out to-day. Particularly since it looks like rain. Stay home and get well. Gargle it with some salt water ; that helps."

So I remained at home.

Time hung heavy on my hands. I stood at the garden door and watched the rain pelting the thin shoots of spring. The recently sprouted flowers nodded, drooped, buried their heads in the mud that was lashed up by the rain.

I sighed and looked around for something to amuse me. There was Uncle Jacob's library, that would be interesting to look through. I browsed around a while, looking for bits of Latin letters here and there on title-pages, and so forth, and not making very much sense out of this collection of Hebrew books.

Then I stumbled upon a Hebrew-English grammar and opened it up. Lesson I, so the first page bore on the head of it. So I sat down in a comfortable chair and began to study it.

Time passed quickly that way. Before I knew it, the afternoon was far advanced, and pretty soon Julia came home.

"Why, you know," I said to Julia, as we prepared ourselves a simple meal, "I find Hebrew a very easy language. I must have a natural unsuspected aptitude for languages. Do you think that's possible ?"

"I'm glad you like it," said Julia, drily. "Personally, I think it's a lot of dry rot in this day and age. Your sore throat doesn't seem any better. Have you been gargling it?"

"No, I forgot all about it. That's because it doesn't hurt so very much. It's just a kind of thickness."

That night we slept in peace. In the morning, as I did not seem to be getting ready to leave, Julia remarked, "I think you had better come with me this morning; it won't do for you to be missing too many classes. You'll lose your laboratory assistantship."

For some reason, the very thought of chemistry bored me. "Oh," I said, "I don't need that silly job any more. I don't have to work for a living now. Why don't you stay home, too?"

"What would I do around here all day long?" Julia wanted to know. "I'd rather be at the lab. But if you're staying home, please do something in the house; clean up a bit and get supper ready for me."

Thus it was that I spent another pleasant day poring over my Hebrew books, finding the subject not only enthralling, but so readily grasped that I took the resolution of mastering it. In the afternoon, I actually took down a tome and spelled my way through the first chapter. With the help of a dictionary, I managed to go through a very fascinating discussion of dybbuks (spirits) and black magic and other mysterious subjects that the Jews of the Middle Ages were so fond of.

In the evening, when Julia came home, she scolded me for not having prepared a meal for her as I had promised. "Really, now," she said, "this is going too far. Why, you haven't even shaved. You look a mess."

I laughed and shrugged my shoulders. As a matter of fact, I was anxious to get back to my studies, and if I had not thought it too impolite, I would really have gone back to them after dinner, but Julia wanted to talk.

But you can be sure that I was down in the study very early on the following morning, long before Julia got up. She found me there when she was going off to the laboratory.

"It would be useless, I suppose," she said, "to ask you to prepare supper to-night?"

"No, it wouldn't," I replied. "To-night, I promise you supper will be ready for you."

"Your throat must be terrible," Julia exclaimed. "Your voice is like a bass viol."

"Why, I hardly notice it any more," I said.

"You ought to go to a doctor about it, perhaps," Julia suggested.

"Oh, it will clear up," I said, and returned to my books, while Julia went off to the city.

Perhaps I was trying to go too fast in Hebrew. After all, I had scarcely spent three days with it, and here I was trying to read a heavy book on esoteric lore, all about ghosts and spirits of evil, and what not. Some of the passages were damned difficult. I would wrack my brain, thumb through my grammar, chew on my nails, and get into an actual sweat before the answer would suddenly pop into my mind. "Why, of course, the subjunctive," I would say to myself.

Suddenly I noticed that it was late. By Jove! I thought, and I haven't washed the dishes, and as for preparing a meal, I simply haven't thought of it.

Just then I heard the bell at the door. "That can't be Julia!" I exclaimed. "Of course not; she wouldn't ring the bell."

It turned out to be the old housekeeper, she of the brown wig.

What did she want?

She had nothing to do, she explained, in broken English. The money Uncle Jacob had left her was enough for herself, but then she had a poor sister and two nieces she was helping to support. Besides, she wasn't so old that she couldn't work.

Well, here's luck for you, I said to myself. "Come in. My wife will be home soon. Do you suppose you can fix up a quick supper?"

That settled that, and I could go back to my Hebrew with an easy conscience.

Julia, of course, was extremely displeased, but I argued that she was scarcely home during the day and wouldn't see much of her. Besides, I didn't intend to cook. And then we could fire her whenever we wanted to. . . .

A few days passed thus, and one afternoon I had the pleasure of receiving a visit from Mr. Simcoff.

"Ah, come right in," I said. "How have you been?"

"Fine," he said, curtly, sitting on the edge of his chair and obviously ill at ease.

"What's the matter?" I asked.

He hemmed and hawed, and then he asked suddenly, "You haven't replaced the mazuza on the door-post?"

"Oh, I forgot about it," I said lightly. "Will you have a stogie?" I asked.

"A stogie?" he said, with some surprise. "Since when do you smoke stogies?"

"Why, just since this morning. That old housekeeper of Uncle Jacob's recommended them for my sore throat. I always hated them, but they seem to be doing me good."

"Tell me, David," said Mr. Simcoff, with great seriousness, "how is the rattling at the windows and doors?"

"Oh, we aren't bothered by it any more. As a matter of fact," I laughed, "those very words you said I shouldn't say were precisely the ones that stopped it!"

He didn't laugh and he didn't smile. And as I saw him look at me with staring eyes of fright, my own smile froze on my face. Holding his gaze riveted upon me, he rose slowly from his chair.

"No more knockings?" he faltered, moving backwards away from me.

"No," I said, in my husky voice.

He raised his hands above his head. "Imbecile!" he shouted, and being at the door to the hall, he turned and fled to the entrance. "Imbecile!" I could hear him shouting, and then: "Who continues to knock once he has been bidden to enter?" The door crashed behind him.

I stood there, where I was overcome with a strange, chilly shivering of my skin.

     ·   ·   ·   ·   ·

"Julia," I said, "you're becoming entirely too critical. If I'm hungry, let me eat. I know I'm getting fat, but then you wouldn't want me to starve myself just for the sake of a pretty figure. What am I? A motion-picture actress? And why should I shave?

"And as for these stogies, well, it's just a plain fact that they help my throat. Perhaps I smoke too many of them but then I don't count them. I get so interested in those books that I forget everything else, and just light one after another.

"And . . . and," I smiled in embarrassment, "I don't know how I got into this habit of chewing my finger-nails." I giggled. "It just got me." I spoke between compressed lips, for I was actually chewing away at them that very moment.

As a matter of fact, I had chewed them down pretty low, so that I had a rim of pink where I had gnawed them down to the quick. And still I chewed at them so that, as I sat there talking to Julia, I bit just a little too far, and I held up my finger and watched a gout of blood swell up. And then I brought my finger to my mouth to lick. . . . I suddenly noticed that Julia was watching me with a face stiff with horror, and I paused.

Then I put the drop of blood to my lips.

Julia looked around wildly as if she were searching for someone. "Where are you, David?" she cried. And then she screamed, "David!" again and again. "Where are you, David? David! Save me, David!"

The little fool, she had turned her face away from me and was screaming out toward emptiness. I went up to her and clapped my hand over her mouth.

She made no resistance, and I took my hand off her mouth after a little while.

She sat just there, and I went back to my chair and watched her. I could see what she was planning to do. She was going to dash out of the door.

Well, she wasn't! I would see to that. Why, if she went out of that door, then she would never come back, and that would mean, in turn, that the provision of the will, namely, that we should spend three months eating and sleeping in this house, would have been violated. And I wouldn't inherit that money.

"Oh, no, you don't!" I yelled, and caught her just as she was making a dash for the door, even as I had suspected she would.

The old housekeeper helped me tie her up and put a gag in her mouth, and then I hoisted her on my shoulder to take her up to a certain store-room, where she would be safe.

"Come, my little dove," I said. "Come, my rose of Sharon, come with me." And I walked with her to the staircase, limping a bit under the load.

If she hadn't tried to escape, it would never have happened. But she always struggled so, my little dove did, when I went to visit her. It was thus that, one day, weeks later, she managed to get loose from her bonds, and somehow ducked past me and whisked out of that store-room.

Despite my little limp, I ran after her. My alpaca frock-coat caught in my legs and almost tripped me up, but I caught her all right.

"So you were going to run away from me, my sweet darling. Oh, no, but you shan't."

But she struggled so hard in my embrace that both of us fell to the floor. And then she lay quiet, her eyes closed. I saw then that she had struck herself on the head, and given herself an ugly gash. I carried her over to a couch, my heart suddenly bleeding with remorse.

She never opened her eyes again. But she did regain consciousness for a minute. "David," she said, and moved her hands vaguely. I took them into mine.

"Julia, forgive me," I cried wildly, and for the first time in weeks my voice was free of huskiness. "I do not know what came over me!"

"You sold me to him," she said wearily, "and he's here to take me."

"No," I sobbed, "no!"

.   .   .   .   .

I'm innocent! I swear I'm innocent! Will no one believe?

Ah, but I do not mind dying. For if it was not I who killed her, it was I who committed the great crime of selling her for gold.

So let me die, for she will need me there where she has gone.

THE ISLAND OF THE UD
William Hope Hodgson

PIBBY TAWLES, cabin-boy and deck-hand, stood to leeward of the half-poop, and stared silently at the island, incredibly lonely against the translucence of the early dawn—a place of lonesome and mysterious silence, with strange birds of the sea wheeling and crying over it, and making the silence but the more apparent.

Away to wind'ard, Captain Jat, his Master, stood stiff.and erect against the growing light, all his leathery length of six feet five inches set into a kind of grim attention as he stared at that black shadow upon the sea that lay off his weather bow.

The minutes passed slowly, and the dawn seemed to dream, stirred to reality only by the far and chill sound of the birds crying so dreely. The small barque crept on, gathering the slight morning airs to her aid, whilst the dawn-shine grew subtly and strengthened up, so that the island darkened the more against it for a little while, and grew stealthily more real. And all the time, above it, the sea birds swung about in noiseless circling against the gold of light that hung now in all the lower sky.

Presently there came the hoarse hail of the look-out man, who must have waked suddenly :

"Land on weather bow, sir !"

But the lean grim-looking figure to wind'ard vouchsafed no reply, beyond a low-growled "grrrrr !" of contempt.

And all the time Pibby Tawles, the boy, stared, overwhelmed with strange imaginings—treasure, monsters, lovely women, weirdness unutterable, terror brooding beyond all powers of his imagination to comprehend ! He had listened to some marvellously strange things, when Captain Jat had been in drink ; for it was often then the Captain's whim to make the boy sit at table with him, and dip his cup likewise in the toddy-bowl.

And presently, when Captain Jat had drunk his toddy steadily out of a big pewter mug, he would begin to talk ; rambling on in garrulous fashion from tale to tale ; and, at last, as like as not, mixing them quite inextricably. And as he talked, the long, lean man would throw his glance back over his shoulder suspiciously every minute or so, and perhaps bid the boy go up on to the little half-poop, and discover the whereabouts of the officer of the watch, and then into the cabin of the officer whose watch it might chance to be below, and so to make sure that neither of his Mates were attending listening ears on the sly.

"Don't never tell the Mates, boy!" he would say to Pibby Tawles, "or I'll sure maul you! They'd be wantin' profits."

For that was, in the main, the substance of all his talks—treasure, that is to say. To be exact, treasure and women.

"Never a word, boy. I trusts you, but not no one else in this packet."

And, truly, Captain Jat did seem to have a trust in the boy; for, in his cups, he told him everything that came up in his fuddled mind; and always the boy would listen with a vast interest, putting in an odd question this time and that to keep the talk running. And, indeed it suited him very well; for though he could never tell how much to believe, or how little, he was very pleased to be sitting drinking his one cup of toddy slowly in the cabin, instead of being out on deck, doing shipwork.

It is true that the Captain appeared both to like the boy in his own queer fashion and to trust him; but, for all that, he had with perfect calmness and remorseless intent, shown him the knife with which he would cut his throat, if ever he told a word of anything that his Master might say to him during his drinking bouts.

Captain Jat's treatment of the lad was curious in many ways. He had him to sleep in a little cabin abaft the Mate's, where, through the open door, he could see the boy in his bunk. When he ran out of toddy, he would heave his pewter mug at the lad's head, as he lay asleep, and roar to him to turn-out and brew him fresh and stronger; but this trick of the Captain's was no trouble to Pibby; for he rigged a dummy oakum-head to that end of his bunk which showed through the open doorway, and slept then the other way about.

And so, with this little that I have told, you may know something of the life aft in the cabin of the little barque *Gallat*, which vessel belonged, stick-and-keel, to Captain Jat; and some pretty rum doings there were aboard her first and last, as you may now have chance to judge.

At times, another side of Captain Jat would break out, and he would spend the whole of a watch, having a gorgeous pistol-shooting match against Pibby; and a wonderfully good shot the boy was, both by natural eye, and by the training he had this way. In the end, the boy became a better shot than Captain Jat himself, who was an extraordinarily fine marksman, though somewhat unequal. Yet, for all that Pibby beat him time after time, this peculiar man showed no annoyance; but persisted in the matches, as if his primary intention were to make the boy an expert with the weapon; and indeed, I have little doubt but that this was his real desire.

Now, although Pibby Tawles had tremendously confused and vague ideas as to what strangeness or mystery was concerned with the island, yet he knew perfectly that it was no chance that had brought them that way; for all the Captain's talks over his toddy had gone to show that the *true* aim of the voyage was to bring-up near the island for some purpose that the lad could only guess at in a mystified way, owing to the muddling fashion in which Captain Jat had run his yarns one into another, treasure, women, monsters and odd times a queer habit of muttering to himself about his little priestess—his little priestess! And once he had broken out into a kind of hazy ramble about the Ud, rolling his eyes at the boy strangely, and gesticulating so impressively with his pewter mug that he had managed to spread his toddy in an un-prejudiced manner over Pibby, the table and the floor generally.

Therefore, having, as I have said, a sure knowledge that the island they approached was the real goal of the voyage, though there was an honest enough cargo below hatches, you may imagine something of Pibby's blank astonishment when Captain Jat allowed the barque to sail quietly past, touching neither brace, sheet nor tack; so that, by the time morning was full come, the island lay upon the weather quarter, and presently far away astern.

Yes, as he had gone past, the lad had studied it very eagerly, and had seen in the light of the coming day that it was wooded almost everywhere, even close down to the shores, with a long, bold reef of stark rock running out in a great sweep upon the south side, so that it was plain a boat could be landed there very safely and easily under its lee. The island, Pibby had noticed, rose towards the centre, into a low, seeming flat-topped hill, with the forests of great trees very heavy on its slopes.

All the morning the *Gallat* stood to the southward, until they had sunk the island below the horizon. They hove-to then, and drifted until near evening, when they filled once more on her, and stood back to the northward. By four bells that night they sighted the island, looking like a doleful smudge in the darkness away to the north-east.

Presently, the barque was put in irons, and orders given to lower the dinghy. When she was in the water, Captain Jat flipped Pibby on the ear, and growled to him to jump down into the boat. The boy climbed over, and Captain Jat followed, after having first directed the second mate, whose watch it was, to reach out into the open, and run in again about midnight.

The Captain took the after oar, and rowed standing up, with his face to the bows, whilst Pibby, the boy, took the bow oar and rowed sitting down.

"Easy with that oar, boy!" said Captain Jat presently, after he had pulled awhile. "Put your shirt round it." And this, Pibby had to do, and row naked to the waist, whilst his shirt muffled the sound of his oar between the thole-pins. But, after all, the night was pretty warm.

Meanwhile, the Captain had pulled off his own coat and ripped out one of the sleeves, which he reeved on to his oar, and so made it as silent as the lad's. And this way, almost as quietly as a shadow boat in the darkness, they came in presently under the shelter of the great barrier reef, and very soon then to the uncomfortable silence of the shore under the date-trees that came down so near to the sea.

Here, before Captain Jat landed, he bid the boy lay on his oar, while he listened. But they could hear nothing, except the far dull booming of the sea upon the exposed beach beyond the great reef—the solemn noise of the sea coming very hushed and distant to them, and blending with the dree little sounds that came out of the near forest, as the night's airs went wandering on into its gloom.

"Keep her afloat till I come, boy," said Captain Jat, as he stepped ashore. He walked a few paces up the beach, settling a brace of great double-barrelled pistols in his belt. Then he turned sharply and came back:

"Not a sound, boy, or you're as good as dead," he said grimly, in a low tone. "Not a sound, so what you hears! Keep off there in the shadow of the reef. You'll hear me squark like a catched molley-hawk, when I come. Keep your eyes wide open, boy!" And with that, he slewed round on his heel, and went up pretty quick across the sand into the darkness of the black trees.

Pibby Tawles, the boy, stood in the bows of the boat, and stared after him, listening to the vague sounds of his passage growing ever distant and more distant, but odd-whiles sounding out clear through the dark forests, as some dried kindling snapped under his weight. Then, as Captain Jat went farther and farther, the silence of the island fell again about Pibby, save for the odd whispering of the leaves in the little airs that came off the sea, and the constant solemn booming of the ocean on the far beach that lay exposed upon the outward arc of the great reef.

And so listening there, and full of the mystery of all the vague and muddled tales that Captain Jat had maundered through so often, over the toddy, is it any matter for surprise that the lad Pibby grew suddenly frightened of the loneliness and the silence, and began to think there were pale ovals among the dark tree-trunks that peered at him?

He thrust his hand down, inside of his trousers, and eased a small double-barrelled pistol out of a canvas pocket he had stitched in there with a palm and needle, and sail-twine for thread. The feel of the small weapon gave him a degree of comfort, and abruptly he remembered that Captain Jat had told him to keep the boat off in the shadows of the reef. He jumped out over the bows, holding his pistol in his right hand, and found to his dismay that the boat was aground. He put his bare shoulder to her stem, and hove madly awhile, sweating, for he felt that Captain Jat was quite capable of knifing him on his return, if he found the boat hard ashore. With a determination, vague but dogged, to protect himself with his pistol if necessary, he made one vast, final effort, and the boat slid afloat.

He jumped in over the bows, ran aft and put his pistol on the stern thwart; then with the boat-hook he pushed out, and so came in a minute under the gloom of the reef, which rose up just there into a chaos of great rocks, weed-hidden at their bases. He thrust the boat-hook into a mass of weed, and anchored the boat temporarily.

Then, with a sudden shiver, he remembered his shirt, and, having freed it, he covered his damp back.

Pibby Tawles had been sitting quietly in the boat for, maybe, half an hour, when he heard something that made him lean forward on the thwart and listen tensely. There was something moving, in among the great rocks and boulders where the reef thrust into the shore ; and the sounds were exceedingly curious : Slither! slither! click, click, and then a loud squelch and a great splashing, as if some huge thing, scrambling over the rocks, had slipped and fallen into one of the pools left by the sea.

There was a little time of silence, and then again came the sharp click, click, followed by a loud grating noise over the rocks. The noise frightened the boy extraordinarily, and he freed the boat-hook silently from the weed, and began nervously to punt the boat out further from the shore ; but keeping very carefully in the gloom that the shadow of the reef cast.

He held the boat again, some dozen fathoms farther out, and waited. He could hear the strange noises continuing, oddly broken by pauses of profound quiet ; then again the slithering and clicking sounds. Abruptly, there was a loud crash—a huge boulder had been moved bodily and sent rolling down from the higher parts of the reef on to the shore. The boulder was a big one, for Pibby could see it vaguely through the darkness, where it had bounded out into the soft sand. He thought vividly and horridly of Captain Jut's muddled yarns of grim things, and he began again silently to push the boat farther out.

Even as he loosed the hook of the boat-hook out from the weed, there came a tremendous scrambling noise among the rocks in-shore, and something moved out silently on to the vague white sand of the beach. It passed over a darker patch of pebbles, and the lad heard the rounded stones grinding against each other, as if under a vast weight. The pistol seemed only a foolish toy in his hands, and he got down suddenly on to the bottom-boards of the boat and lay flat.

A long while seemed to pass, during which he heard further sounds that told him the thing was moving along the beach. He kept very still, and presently there was only the silence of the quiet sea and the island about him again, with the seas booming far and hollowly on the unprotected shore beyond the reef, and the faint stirrings of the forest trees whispering oddly to him across the quiet strip of sea that held the boat off the sand.

He sat up cautiously, and found that the boat still rose and fell on the gentle heaves of the sea close in under the gloom of the reef. He took the boat-hook and anchored her again, and all the time his gaze searched the vague shore; but he saw nothing and heard nothing, and gradually he grew easier.

A long time passed, while he sat, pistol in hand, watching and listening. Everything remained quiet, and slowly he began to nod, drowsing and waking through the minutes, so that he could not be said to be either awake or asleep. And then, in a moment he was wide awake, for there was a sound breaking the utter stillness. He sat up, gripping his pistol, and staring nervously; and as he stared, the sound came again, a far, faint, inhuman howling away up through the dark forests to the north of him. He stood up in the boat, and, abruptly a great way off in the night, there came the sound of a shot, and once more the howling, only that now there was a strange screaming as well. There was another shot, and one single shrill scream that came to him far and attenuated out of the night air; and then, for the best part of an hour, an absolute silence.

Suddenly, far off among the trees, Pibby saw a faint gleam of light, moving here and there, and growing bigger as the minutes passed. Presently, he saw that there were four of these gleams, and then six, all moving and dancing about strangely; but no sound; at least, not for a time.

All at once he heard the snapping of a twig, apparently a long way off in the wood, the sound echoing strangely in the quietness. And then, very abrupt and dreadful, the inhuman howling began again, mingled with a wild screaming, seeming to be but a few hundred paces deep in the woods. To the boy, it seemed as though something that was half a woman and half something else, howled and shrieked there among the trees; and he chilled with a very literal fright.

The six lights danced and blended and again separated, and all the time the abominable howling and screaming continued through the grim woods. Then very sharp and sudden, the noise of one of Captain Jat's double-barrelled pistols—bang! bang! And, almost immediately, Captain Jat's voice shouting, at some distance, to bring the boat in, to bring the boat in.

The lad freed the boat-hook, and started the dinghy into the shore, and as he did so, he heard the crashing of Captain Jat's footsteps through the rotten wood and leaves; and it was plain to him that the Captain had started to make an undisguised run for the boat.

As Pibby thrust the boat in-shore, he realized a number of things : the Captain was being followed, and those lights and the strange howling had something to do with whatever followed him. The nose of the boat grounded, and Pibby picked up his weapon, and ran forrard and stood on the forethwart, waiting.

The strange lights came nearer, moving swiftly among the trees, and suddenly the lad saw something that was plainly monstrous. He had a clear view up a long vista of dark trees, which the light had made visible, and he saw the figure of a man, black and immensely tall against the light, running and staggering down towards the beach. He knew it was Captain Jat. The dancing lights, beyond, entered the vista, and came dancing and flaring down through the wood ; and abruptly the boy got a clear view of the things that carried them. The lights were great torches, and were carried by a number of wild-looking women who were nearly naked, with great manes of hair all loose and wild about them.

But the monstrous and horrid thing that caught the boy's eye was something he saw as the women came nearer, running. They had faces so flat as to be almost featureless. At first, if he thought at all, he supposed that they were wearing some kind of mask ; but as they ran, the nearest woman opened her mouth and howled, the same disgusting sound that he had heard earlier that night. As she howled, she brandished both the hand that held the torch, and the other hand, above her head. But she had no hands ; her arms ended in enormous claws, like the claws of a great crab. The other women began to howl, and to wave their torches and arms as they ran, and Pibby saw that some of them were like the foremost woman. He stared, with the wide-eyed acceptance of youth of the horrific and the monstrous.

Captain Jat came blundering and reeling out of the wood. He stubbed his toe against something, and fell headlong on to the sand, and those extraordinary and brutish things close astern of him. Pibby saw suddenly that three of the women had knives, and somehow the sight of the knives made him feel better—it was more human. In the same moment, he loosed off his right barrel and immediately his left, and with each shot there fell a woman, screaming, their torches flying along the sand, and throwing showers of great sparks. Captain Jat staggered up, and came on at a heavy run to the boat. He reached it, and fell all his great length in over the bows.

"Put off, boy!" he gasped. "Put off!" And even as he spoke, the boat was away from the shore with the push he had given it as he came aboard. He scrambled to his feet, seized an oar, and thrust down hard, so that the water boiled under the stern, with the way that he gave the boat. In a moment, they had the oars between the tholes, and were backing the boat madly out into the darkness of the sea; so that in a few minutes they were a good way off the shore, with the quiet and hush of the water about them.

But they danced on the beach, at the edge of the sea, those monstrous-faced and monstrous-armed women, and howled at them across the sea, and a dreadful enough noise to hear. They waved their great torches, and jigged crazily, so that the light splashed redly across the swells; and all the time as they danced, their black manes flew about them, and always they howled.

"Pull, boy!" said Captain Jat, still very hoarse with breathlessness. "Pull, boy!" But indeed, the lad was pulling fit to break his youthful back. There passed a further time of labour and gasping silence, and presently they were out in the open water, where the quiet swells moved big and free under them in the darkness, and the reef lay between them and the shore. But they could still see the mad dancing of the lights at the edge of the sea.

Awhile later, Captain Jat eased, and they put the boat round, after which he lay on his oar, and the boy the same, for he could scarcely breathe. The lights were gone now from the shore, and there was no sound, except the far hollow noise of the breaking seas upon the exposed beaches of the island, to the eastward.

Now, never a word of thanks said Captain Jat for the way the boy had saved him with a pistol; but presently he pulled his oar in across the boat, and lit his pipe, after which he hove the plug of his tobacco at the lad. That was his way.

"Boy," he said, after smoking a little, "I'm wondering if they knew I was whistlin' to her."

"Who, sir?" asked Pibby.

But Captain Jat made no answer to this. After smoking a long time, he said, suddenly: "Them was the Ud-women, boy . . . devil-women . . . Priestesses of the Ud, that's Devil in their talk. I was here a matter of four years gone for water, and I found out somethin' then, boy, about them an' their pearl-fishin' and devil-worshipping, an' how they've kep' it quiet from all the world. I found one of the Priestesses alone one-time, a little woman, an' pretty, not like *them*!" He jerked his thumb shorewards. "I was a week lyin' off here, an' there mightn't have been anyone on the island, the way they kep' hid, boy; not till I found the little priestess down near by the spring. I knew her lingo, a bit, and we got talking. I saw her all that week, every night, secret like. She liked me. I liked her. I had her aboard once, an' she told me a heap. When I put her ashore, I took the Mate with me, Jeremiah Stimple, he was, an' we went prospecting for them pearls I'd learned about; but she'd never told me proper about the Ud an' the Ud-women. She'd never say much that way. That's how we got into trouble. We'd near got to the top of the hill, an' then come some of them devil-women. I was all cut about, an' I guessed they likely sacrificed the Mate. I never saw him again.

"There must be hundreds of them devil-women ashore there in them forests. But I always meant to come back, boy. I've seen the pearls this very night. They're down in the bottom of the crater that's inside of yon hill in the middle of the island, all strung round a great carved post, an' I'm goin' to to get 'em too, boy. You sh'd see the pearls them hag-women was dressed with. You mustn't be feared of their claws, boy. They'm only cast off claw-shells, or somethin' of that sort. Mind you, the little priestess, she said some of 'em was *real*—growed that way; but I can't think, it, scarcely. But you never know what you may find in them sorts of places. What their pet Devil is, I don't know. . . ."

"I saw somethin', sir, after you was gone," began Pibby, interrupting. "It were a 'orrible thing. . . ."

"I saw the little Priestess to-night, down in the crater," went on Captain Jat, without taking the least apparent notice of what the boy had begun to tell him. "I was at the top; it's not all of twenty fathom deep. I whistled soft an' gentle to her. She saw me, an' near did a faint, boy, by the look of her, an' waved me to go away pretty quick. By the look of things down there, they're in for one of their Devil-Festas. They'd big torches burning—you can see the light of 'em now." And Captain Jat nodded towards the island.

The lad, Pibby, stared away through the darkness, and surely enough there was a faint loom of light in the night above the island.

"I reck'n the Festa'll be pretty soon now, boy, at the dark of the moon, an' like there'll be chiefs from the islands round for a thousand miles, and a sprinklin' of rotten whites, I guess, and devil-work uncounted. I'm hopin' them devil-priestesses didn't see the little woman wavin' me away, or maybe she'll be into bad trouble. They come on me, just after she signed to me to clear out, an' near finished me before I'd time to slew round. They've butcher's knives, some on 'em, as long as your leg, boy, an' one of em near ripped me up." He opened his coat, and the lad saw dimly in the gloom that his shirt was all stained dark.

"I settled four of the brutes," Captain Jat continued, "and you outed two. That's six gone to hell, where they come from. . . ." He broke off, and puffed meditatively at his pipe for a time, leaning on his oar, which rested on the gunnels. Pibby had never heard him talk so much before when sober.

"The native name for yon island means The Island of the Devil, boy," said Captain Jat, presently. "I heard that years gone from more than one; but none of 'em could tell me anythin', or wouldn't, 'cept it was an almighty unhealthy place for a white man . . . or a native either, for that matter, except, maybe, as I'm thinking, when there's one of their big secret, damn Ud-festas on. . . ." He broke off short, and slipped his pipe into his pocket.

"Pull, boy, an' break your damn back. There's the ship !" he said.

Ten minutes later they were safe aboard.

All next day, Captain Jat kept the barque away to the southward of the island, but he sent Pibby aloft, time and again, with his own telescope ; and when that youth came down finally in the late afternoon, to report numbers of small craft on the horizon, steering north, he nodded his head, as if the news were what he had expected.

"Native boats, boy," he said. "Keep your mouth shut, an' tell nothin' to no one. They'll hold that festa to-night, an' they'll have all their pearls strung up, an' we'll be there. You clean up all them big double-barr'lled pistols, an' load 'em nice and careful, like I've showed you. Get a move on you now !"

That night, with all lights dowsed, the barque stood again to the northward, and dropped Captain Jat and the lad in the dinghy, off the island. Captain Jat had four great pistols in his belt, and he had spent the dog-watches in mounting an old duck-gun on its swivel, in the bows of the boat. Pibby, the boy, had also two big heavy pistols tucked into his belt, not to mention his own small weapon which reposed snugly in its canvas pocket inside his trousers. They were quite heavily armed. Moreover, he had seen to it, this time, that the oars were properly muffled.

In addition to these preparations, Captain Jat had been very particular concerning the depositing in the boat of a considerable length of chain, with two stout padlocks in the ends.

Captain Jat took the boat round to the north of the island, and, presently, after pulling cautiously for an hour, he bid the lad ease up and lay on his oar a bit, and keep his eyes well skinned. For his part, the Captain lay down on his stomach on the thwarts, and spied along the surface of the quietly heaving sea, with his night-glass. And suddenly, he reached out and caught Pibby a clip with the glass.

"Down under the gunnel, boy, or they'll see you!" he muttered, and Pibby ducked and slid down under his oar, and stared away breathlessly through the darkness to the northward.

Now that he had his eyes nearer to the surface of the sea, he discovered the thing that Captain Jat had seen with the night-glass. There was a prodigious string of native boats, within two hundred fathoms of them, paddling through the night to the island. Pibby counted them, and numbered eighty; but probably missed some in the darkness.

Captain Jat allowed these craft to get well in-shore; then, taking his oar, he shoved it out through a steering-grommet, which he had fixed up in the stern, and began to scull steadily after them; but allowing nothing more than his hand and forearm to rise above the gunnel of the boat. As the dinghy crept into the wake of all those silent craft ahead, the boy noticed suddenly that there had come again above the island the strange loom of light that he had seen the night before.

Presently, the heave of the sea had almost died from under the boat, and it was plain that they had come under the lee of some out-jutting "lie" of rocks. The last of the craft ahead vanished into the shadow of the island; but Captain Jat had marked the place, and followed dead on. A minute later, they saw the shore directly ahead, not a score of fathoms away; but there was no beach; only the dark trees and bushes coming right down, apparently to the water's edge. There was no heave at all now under the boat, so that they had evidently been piloted into a perfectly sheltered cove.

Captain Jat kept the boat going straight ahead. He made no attempt to slacken her way, despite the fact that they seemed to be heading straight ashore into the middle of the heavy underwood. The bows of the dinghy reached the dank bushes, where they hung out over the water, and Captain Jat took both hands to his oar, and forced her in among them.

For a few moments the overgrowth seemed to smother the boat, all wet and slimy and rank. Then the boat had passed clean through, into open water beyond. Pibby, the lad, stared in front into the darkness ; but could see nothing. He looked upward, and saw a narrow, winding ribbon of night-sky far above them, which told him that Captain Jat had discovered the way into a deep-set tidal passage, the mouth of which was completely masked by the undergrowth and overhanging trees. It was, obviously, a huge crack through the side of the low crater, which the sea had turned into a creek.

Very cautiously, Captain Jat sculled ahead. It was like sculling into a pitch black night, so black that the far upward ribbon of night-sky seemed almost to shine, by comparison. As they went, little hollow sobbing sounds, of the water in the crannies of the unseen rocky sides, came to them, dankly and somehow drearily. But Captain Jat handled the sculling oar so softly that not once did the clinker-built entry of the boat "mutter" on the water. And this way quite half an hour passed ; though it seemed much longer, going utterly slow and silent and cautious in that grim dark, and steering by the winding pattern of the night-sky above, and by the odd vague sense which told the Captain when they were come over-near to one side or the other, in the darkness.

Once, as they went so quiet and stealthily, there came to them indefinitely out of the night, a far howling, once and then again ; and, later, an attenuated, incredibly shrill screaming, that died away and left the boy frightened and holding the stocks of his heavy pistols. But Captain Jat sculled steadily on.

Abruptly Captain Jat ceased sculling, and stood silent. It was plain to the lad that he was either listening or staring intently ; and the boy peered round, every way, nervously. Suddenly, he saw an indefinite glow of light ahead, evidently beyond a bend in the narrow creek. The glow grew rapidly into a bright light, that danced and flickered, and, in the space of a' minute, there came round the bend of the creek, upon the left side, two of those brutish things that had followed the Captain the night before. They were running through the stunted trees and bushes, parallel with the course of the creek, but about twenty feet above the level of the water, winding in and out, as they went, among the trees and great bushes that grew up in the steep lower slope of the creek-side. Their agility was incredible; here and there they leaped like goats from rock to rock, their torches dripping and flaring, as they ran, one behind the other.

Captain Jat stood motionless in the stern of the dinghy, with his oar in one hand, and one of his pistols in the other. He watched the two beastly creatures run by, and the boy —glancing at him swiftly in his fright—saw that his face was perfectly calm; but the lights from the torches seemed to glow in his eyes, so that they shone, almost like the eyes of a wild animal.

The lad's gaze jumped back to the two running brutes. He could not see their hideous flat faces; for their great manes, all loose and wild, hung over them, damp and black and matted, as if they were fresh come up out of the sea; and indeed there was rank wet weed all entangled in their hair; for he saw it glisten in the blaze of the torches. Yet, though he could not see their faces, he saw their arms from their naked shoulders downward. The arms of the foremost woman ended in two monstrous claws; but the boy saw plainly that they were no more than the cast-off shells of some huge sea reptile, if I may so-describe it. He saw where they ended, rough and rude, just below her elbows, and that her right hand came through a hole between the mandibles of the claw, to hold her great torch.

But the second woman gave him a horrible feeling; he could not see where her arms ended and the claws began. He remembered what the little priestess had told Captain Jat. And even as he stared, frightened and horrified, the two creatures were gone past. He saw then that the foremost one had an ugly great knife, stuck naked into the back of a kind of broad belt; and the belt was all stitched with what at first he took to be big shining beads. Then, he realized that perhaps they were not beads, but pearls, as the Captain had told him. Yet it was less of that possible fortune in pearls that Pibby Tawles, the boy, thought in that tense moment, than of the fact that he could not see where the arms of the second woman ended and the claws began.

Then the two running, leaping, bestial things were gone away down the creek; and a minute after, they were out of sight round one of the rocky bends, and all was dark again about the boat.

The dinghy began to move ahead once more in the darkness, as Captain Jat took up work again with the sculling-oar. A matter of some ten minutes of silence passed, with the water of the creek making odd gurglings and echoes on either hand among the crannies and holes in the rocks, when Pibby realized that the enormous, steep sides of the creek had joined overhead, and that they were moving forward through complete blackness of an invisible cavern.

And then, even as he realized the fact uneasily, there showed far ahead a small, bright spot of light. The boat began to sway, and a little murmur broke out under her bows, as Captain Jat increased the speed; but he eased it at once, for the faint noise of the water under her entrance, made a strangely loud sound in that silence. But still they moved ahead steadily, and that speck of light grew, until the lad saw that it was an inner mouth to the cavern, and beyond it some bright flaring light.

The boat approached, unseen in the darkness of the cavern to within a dozen fathoms of this newly discovered entrance, and for the last minute, Pibby had been staring with a fixed and astounded interest at what he saw. The arch of the cave mouth must have been fully thirty feet high, and the width of it a little less. And through this great opening, Pibby was looking into a big circular space, apparently several hundred feet across, the walls of which went up out of his sight into the darkness above.

But what fixed both his and Captain Jat's attention was the centre portion of this extraordinary natural amphitheatre; for in the centre was a small lake of sea-water, maybe about sixty feet across, and out of the centre of the lake there rose a weed-hung hump of rock, and from the centre of the hump of rock there rose a great pole, maybe fifty feet in height, black through all its length, and polished so highly that it reflected brilliantly the light of six enormous torches that burned on the tops of six great piles that stood up out of the rock all round the central pool or lake. And this pole, from its grotesquely carved head, flat-faced and repulsive, to its base, where it had been cut into the shape of a bunch of huge claws, was banded every few feet with strings of countless beads, that glimmered in a semi-luminous fashion in the flare of the torch-lights. *And every bead was a pearl.*

The water from the cavern in which the dinghy floated, ran in a perfectly straight channel into the central pool or lake, and the weeded floor of the ancient crater rose a foot or so on each side, spreading away then in one level, brown, weed-covered reach to the great walls of the inside of the low mountain.

The torches showed that the bottom parts of the mountain walls were all grown with weed, to a height of about six feet above the bottom of the crater, so that it was plain that the sea, entering through the creek and the cavern, rose at high tide to at least that height, in which case there would be only the six great torches and the lofty polished black pole in the centre, with its profusion of strings of pearls, visible when the tide was up. It must have been a strange sight then, even stranger than when Captain Jat and Pibby looked out at it from the cavern.

And now, but not very distinctly in that light, Pibby saw where all that great line of boats had gone to ; for there, so far as he could see all around the bottom of the great natural amphitheatre, were the boats, where they had been drawn up, head to stern upon the weed, and scarcely seen above the weed, out of which they rose only a little, except for their lofty head and stern timbers, which, however, had been so draped with weed as to blend with the weed-grown walls behind.

Over the sides of all these boats, and there were vastly more than the flotilla that they had followed in (for they lay side by side, apparently three or four deep), Captain Jat and the lad saw the heads of hundreds and hundreds of natives ; but all vague and indistinct ; both because of the uncertain flarings of the great torches, and because each native had dressed his head with a mass of the weed. Indeed, it would have been easy to have entered the crater, under the impression that there was no more life in it than the blaze of the huge torches.

As Pibby strained his eyes to make out the boats, wondering whether it had been hard to drag them up out of the creek, and across the weed, he felt the dinghy beginning to move silently back into the cavern; and, turning, he saw that Captain Jat was using his oar noiselessly, as an Indian uses his paddle, and so fetching the boat gently astern.

In this way they progressed for about a hundred yards, and then Captain Jat set the dinghy in to the side, and began to grope along. Presently, he gave out a little grunt of satisfaction, and pushed the boat across to the other side; but was evidently unable to find what he wanted; for he continued to punt the boat astern with his hands, until the great opening of the cave appeared no more than a distant speck of light. Then he grunted again, and immediately sent the boat across once more to the other side. A minute later, he gave out a further note of satisfaction, and suddenly Pibby heard his voice muttering to him to pass up one end of the chain, and one of the padlocks.

He heard the Captain fumbling for a time, and the odd, slight chinking of the chain; then the dinghy was thrust out again, and Captain Jat was bidding him pay out the chain gently without a sound, whilst he paddled the boat once more across. They reached the other; and Pibby grasped his Master's idea, which was obviously to put a chain boom across, slackly, so that if they had to retreat in a hurry, they could pass over it; then tauten it up, and padlock it in position, and so get away easily, whilst all the boats of the pursuers ran foul of the boom.

The boy ran his hands in along the chain, where the Captain was working, and found that he was "anchoring" it round a huge boulder. Pibby had no doubt but that the other end was quite as efficiently secured, and he began to feel comfortable again in his mind; it was such an efficient retreat. Then, as he sat in the darkness, he fell to wondering just what those natives were waiting for, all hid with weed like they were . . . and the great torches . . . and the huge, carved and polished pole with the fortune of splendid pearls strung about it.

And then, as he worried the thought over nervously in his mind, he thrilled suddenly; for Captain Jat was once more sculling the boat ahead towards the brightly shining arch of the cavern's entrance into the arena.

Abruptly, as the boat forged ahead, there came a queer swirl deep down in the dark water, somewhere astern of the boat, that sent little waves into the sides of the gloomy cavern, breaking in the darkness with a multitudinous chattering of liquid sounds. Something huge passed under the boat, which was now approaching the entrance at a fair speed. They felt the great thing pass under them, deep below the surface, but drawing after it a wave that humped the boat up, stern first, and then the bows.

"My God!" said Captain Jat huskily, aloud. . . . "The UD!" His voice came back, husky and dreadful, from a thousand places in the darkness: "My God! . . . The UD! My God! . . . The UD!" And in the same moment Pibby felt the dinghy begin to sway heavily, and heard Captain Jat gasp, as he began sculling with a kind of mad violence, whispering: "The Little Priestess! The Little Priestess! My God! They saw her waving! My . . ."

Pibby never heard any more; for they had come sufficiently near the arch now for him to be able to see again into the crater with some clearness. He stared in complete and dreadful amazement; for though the whole of the great amphitheatre was as silent as when they left it, there was now a little, naked, brown woman, lashed by her neck, her waist, and her ankles to the great, pearl-stringed, central pole that came up out of the hump of rock in the pool. She had been brought there and made fast during the time in which they had been fixing up the chain boom. That was why the weed-hidden boats waited. . . . She was the sacrifice. . . . The thing that had passed under the boat . . . ! She had been seen waving to the Captain. . . . She . . .

The chaos of his thoughts stilled abruptly into a fearful attention. He bent forward from the forethwart, and stared, almost petrified. Something was coming up out of the water, climbing up on to the hump of rock. . . . Enormous legs were coming up out of the pool, scrambling at the rock, slipping, slipping, and tearing away great chunks of the weed, and finally effecting a hold. A moment afterwards, a thing like a vast, brown, shell-encrusted dish-cover, as big as an ordinary old-fashioned, oval, mahogany table, began to rise up out of the pool.

The boy shook as he stared; he did not know that such things existed. . . . A crab . . . ! That was no word for it. It was a monster, capable of destroying an elephant. . . . He remembered the great thing that had slipped and slithered

among the big rocks at the in-shore end of the reef. The
thing was rising higher and higher. Nothing could save the
woman . . . nothing on earth! They had better get away at
once, before it discovered them. The thing was reaching out
three of its great, pincer-armed legs towards the little brown
woman, who began now to scream in a peculiar, breathless
voice. Then Pibby was suddenly caught by the shoulder from
behind, and Captain Jat dashed him aft into the stern-sheets
of the dinghy, out of his way. As he fell, he saw Captain Jat
against the light; he had the great duck-gun in his hand.
Pibby remembered that it was loaded with the thick end of
a broken marlin-spike. There was a rip of fire, that coincided
with the flashes of light he saw as his head met the stern-
thwart; there was a crashing thump of sound that added to
the muddle of his fall, and Captain Jat pitched bodily backward on to the top of him, literally felled by the recoil of the
big weapon. The boy screamed, and everything went grey
for a moment; then Captain Jat rolled free of him, and in
the same moment there was a vast thrashing of water, and
the boat was cast up a yard into the air by a wave that came
travelling down the cavern from the crater. The dinghy slewed
half round, rolled heavily, and shipped several gallons; then
steadied.

Pibby staggered to his feet, shaken and sick. He stared
towards the pool; the water appeared to be boiling all about
the hump of rock; but there was no sign of the thing that
had come out of the water. The boiling motion of the water
began to ease, and Pibby saw that the little brown woman
sagged in her lashings against the carved black pole; but
there was no mark on her to show that she had been hurt;
she had become unconscious.

The next thing he knew, he had an oar in his hand, and
Captain Jat had another, and they were out of the great
cavern, and pulling madly up the channel that cut across the
floor of the crater to the pool. He noticed, with a curious
inconsequence, that he could now see trees far up at the top
of the walls of the crater, shaking a little in the night-wind
against the stars.

The boat bumped into the masses of weed about the
hump of rock, and Captain Jat gave one great spring upward,
and was on to the rock, having used his oar against the
bottom-boards, as a kind of vaulting-pole. His effort forced

the boat away; but Pibby grabbed the boat-hook, jabbed it into a mass of the weed, and pulled her back. He saw Captain Jat sawing savagely at the lashings; and was conscious for the first time that the crater was full of a wild yelling. He saw his Master pluck the little brown woman loose, and the next moment she was hove down into the boat, with a crash. He did not look at her, but at Captain Jat. . . . Captain Jat was reaching up, and slashing at the lowest string of great pearls. The string gave, and the pearls went spraying and bounding all over the hump of rock, into the water; but Captain Jat had secured a handful.

A spear struck the polished pole, chipping it, and flew off to the side, passing through Captain Jat's sleeve. The boy glanced once now round at the arena, and saw, suddenly, that there were literally hundreds and hundreds of natives scrambling and slipping and leaping over the weed-covered floor towards them. He saw also another thing; two of the horrible, claw-armed women were slashing at a native with their great knives; it may have been the man who had thrown the spear and chipped the post. . . . The post was obviously an incredibly sacred thing.

He heard his own voice shouting strangely to Captain Jat to come; but that indomitable length of man had swarmed a fathom up the polished pole, and was cutting loose another string of the pearls. There came a shower of them bounding on to the rock, and into the weed and water; but again Captain Jat had secured a share. He gave one leap to the rock, and another into the boat; then, stern-foremost, they rowed grimly for the opening into the cavern.

One of the savages, a huge fat man, had out-distanced the others, in spite of his fat. Perhaps his fat accounted for it; for he had come across the slippery weed, creeping on hands and feet, and had therefore lost no time in falling. He rose up at the edge of the channel; but as he made to spring at the boat, he slipped and fell squelching on his back, and Captain Jat pistolled him calmly as he lay.

Yet, now the danger was appalling; for scores of the natives were getting near, and a shower of spears came over the boat, four of them striking her starboard quarter, and making it look literally rather like a gigantic pin-cushion; but no one was hurt, though the Captain's clothing was cut in two places. They replied with their heavy pistols, and left a dozen of the natives dead, and so managed to ram the dinghy stern first into the cavern.

Captain Jat put the boat round, as soon as they were well out of sight, and they both settled down to pull. Yet when they had gone about a hundred fathoms they heard a splash, and saw that one of the smaller native boats had already been hauled across the weed, and was now in the water of the channel. They knew that in another few minutes there would be scores of boats after them.

Half a minute later, Pibby's oar stubbed against the slack chain of the boom, and they pulled in oars, and hauled the boat along to the side of the cavern, being now on the seaward side of the boom. Captain Jat worked desperately, and Pibby lighted the chain up to him, so as to get it as taut as possible; yet it took time; for they were in utter darkness; but the chain must be taut, if it were to act as a boom; otherwise the natives would manage either to shove their boats under or over it.

And all the time, as they worked, boats were entering the mouth of the great cavern, with torches held high over their bows to show them the way; while the boat that had been first launched into the creek was now scarcely a hundred and fifty feet away; and still Captain Jat growled to Pibby to "Light up the slack! Light up the slack!"

The small boat came on steadily, until she was not more than seventy or eighty feet away, and suddenly a great shout told Captain Jat and the boy that the light of the distant torches must have picked them out in the blackness. Immediately afterwards, all around them in the water there was, plunk, plunk, the noise of thrown spears. There came a sharp, chinking sound, as a single spear struck the rocky side. It glanced, gashed along the Captain's face, and took away a part of his ear. He swore grimly, and gave one more pull on the chain; then closed the big padlock and locked it with a swift deliberation.

Immediately afterwards, he fetched a spare pistol out of his side pocket, and loosed off into the approaching boat, with such good aim that one of his bullets punched a hole in two of the men, who happened to be in a line. Then, dropping his pistol into the bottom of the boat, he sprang to his oar, and a minute later they were away round the bend, bumping heavily in the darkness against the rocky side of the cavern, and listening to the fierce outcry that came echoing along the cavern, as the boom opposed all progress for the time being.

"Done 'em, boy !" said Captain Jat. "Now pull easy ! We don't want the boat stove. Back water when I sings out." And therewith the two settled down to work with the oars.

Some forty minutes later, they passed through the screen of overhanging bushes and trees that masked the mouth of the creek, and were presently out into the wholesome sweetness of the sea, with the island no more than a shape of darkness astern. Yet, when they came to look for the little brown woman, she had gone. It was evident that she had come-to, and slipped overboard in the darkness, preferring, it appears, to face any risk that the island might contain for her, to the facing of the unknown.

"The ship, boy ! Pull !" said Captain Jat, a little while afterwards. And, indeed, the ship it was ; and soon they were safely aboard, steering northward, away from the island, for good this time.

Down in his cabin, with the door safely closed, yet not without more than one suspicious glance towards it, Captain Jat was presently conning over, and exhibiting to Pibby, his spoils. On the table was a jug of very special toddy, and Captain Jat was investigating it with the aid of his big pewter mug. Pibby also, it must be confessed, had adopted a fairish-sized drinking cup for the same purpose ; for Captain Jat allowed him only the one, and no more.

It may be that the unusual richness of the toddy developed a latent generosity in the lean Captain ; for after a lot of fingering and weighing and examining, he presented to Pibby, as his share, one of the smallest of the pearls, which had been somewhat badly chipped.

Pibby Tawles, cabin-boy-deck-hand, call him what you will, took the little, damaged pearl with sufficient evidences of gratitude. He could afford to ; for inside his shirt there reposed a number of pearls as fine as any that Captain Jat had brought away with him. The boy had picked them off the bottom-boards of the dinghy, where they had fallen when his Master cut the strings of pearls about the Sacred Pole.

In short, we may conclude, I think, that whatever else he might be, Pibby Tawles was one who had a very sound eye to the main chance ; a conclusion which a further adventure of Captain Jat's has rather impressed upon me.

FEAR
Guy de Maupassant

AFTER dinner we gathered on deck. The Mediterranean lay without a ripple, its surface shot with the silver radiance of the full moon. The great ship glided along, sending up to the star-strewn sky a snaky column of black smoke. In our wake foamed and whirled a white streak of water, ploughed up by the swift passage of the vessel, churned by the screw, and emitting such brilliant flashes of brightness that it seemed like liquid moonlight, all bubbling and boiling.

Six or seven of us stood there in silent admiration, our eyes turned towards the distant shores of Africa, whither we were bound. The Captain, who had joined us and was smoking a cigar, resumed a conversation begun at the dinner-table.

" Yes, I knew what fear was that day. My ship lay for six hours spiked on a rock with the seas breaking over her. Luckily towards evening we were sighted and picked up by an English collier."

A man who had not yet spoken now broke the silence. He was tall, of tanned complexion and grave aspect, the type of man whom one instinctively assumes to have travelled through vast tracts of unexplored countries amid ever-threatening dangers ; whose steady eyes retain in their depths something of the strange lands through which he has wandered, and who is courageous through and through.

" You say, Captain, that you knew what fear was, I don't believe it. You are mistaken both as to the term you used and the sensation you experienced. A brave man has never any fear in the presence of imminent danger. He may be excited, agitated and anxious, but as for fear, that is quite another thing."

The Captain laughed.

" Stuff and nonsense ! I tell you I was in a blue funk."

The bronze-faced man replied in deliberate tones :

" Allow me to explain. Fear—and the bravest of men can experience fear—is a dreadful thing ; it is an appalling sensation, as if one's soul were disintegrating ; it is a torturing pang, convulsing mind and heart ; a horror, of which the mere remembrance evokes a shudder of anguish. But a brave man is not subject to it at the prospect of a hostile attack, or confronted with certain death, or any familiar form of danger. It comes upon him in certain abnormal conditions, when certain mysterious influences are at work, in the face of perils which he does not understand. True fear has in it something of the memory of fantastic terrors of long ago. Now a man who believes in ghosts, and thinks he sees a spectre in the night, is bound to experience fear in all its devastating horror.

" About ten years ago I myself had this feeling in broad daylight, and last winter it came upon me again, one December night. Yet I have often run risks and had death hanging over me, and I have seen a lot of fighting. I have been left for dead by brigands. I have been sentenced to be hanged as a rebel in America, and flung into the sea from the deck of a ship off the coast of China. Each time I gave myself up for lost, and accepted the situation without emotion, even without regret.

" But fear is a very different thing. I felt a first hint of it in Africa. And yet the North is its real home ; the sun disperses it like a fog. This is an interesting point. With Orientals, life is of no account ; they are fatalists, one and all. The clear Eastern nights foster none of those sinister forebodings which haunt the minds of those who dwell in cold countries. In the East there is such a thing as panic, but fear is unknown.

" Well, this is what happened to me over there in Africa. I was crossing the vast sandhills south of Ouargla, one of the strangest tracts of country in the world. You all know what the smooth level sands of a sea-beach are like, running on and on interminably. Now picture in your minds the ocean itself turned to sand in the middle of a hurricane. Imagine a tempest without sound and with billows of yellow sand that never move. To the height of mountains they rise, these irregular waves of all shapes and sizes, surging like the ungovernable waters of ocean, but vaster and streaked like watered silk. And the pitiless rays of the devastating southern

sun beat straight down upon that raging sea, lying there
without sound or motion. A journey across these steeps of
golden dust is one continual ascent and descent, without a
moment of respite, or a vestige of shade. The horses pant
and sink in up to their knees, and flounder down the slopes
of these extraordinary hills.

" Our party consisted of my friend and myself, with an
escort of eight spahis, four camels and their drivers. Overcome with heat and fatigue, parched with thirst as the burning
desert itself, we rode in silence. Suddenly one of our men
uttered a cry ; everyone halted ; and we remained rooted to
the spot, surprised by a phenomenon, which, though familiar
to travellers in those God-forsaken parts, has never been
explained. From somewhere near at hand, but in a direction
difficult to determine, came the roll of a drum, the mysterious
drum of the sandhills. Its beating was distinct, now loud,
now soft, now dying away, now resuming its weird tattoo.

" The Arabs looked at one another in horror, and one of
them said in his own tongue :

" ' Death is upon us.'

" And as he spoke, my comrade, my friend, who was
almost like a brother to me, fell headlong from his horse, struck
down by sunstroke.

" For two hours, while I laboured in vain to save his life,
that phantom drum filled my ears with its monotonous, inter-
mittent and baffling throbbing. And I felt fear, real fear,
ghastly fear, glide into my bones, as I gazed at the body of
the man I loved, there in that sun-baked hollow, between four
sandhills, six hundred miles from the nearest French settlement,
with that rapid, mysterious drumming echoing in our ears.

" That day I knew what fear was. I realised it even more
profoundly on another occasion."

The Captain interrupted him :

" Excuse me, sir, but what was that drum ? "

" I don't know," the traveller replied, " Nobody knows.
Military officers, who have often been startled at this singular
sound, are generally of opinion that it is caused by sand
scudding before the wind and brushing against tufts of dry
grass, the echo being intensified and multiplied to prodigious
volume by the valley formation of that desert region. It has
been observed that the phenomenon always occurs near small
plants burnt up by the sun and as hard as parchment. According

to this theory, the drum was simply a sort of sound mirage, nothing more. But I did not learn this till later.

" I come to my second experience.

" It was last winter in a forest in the north-east of France. The sky was so overcast that night fell two hours before its time. My guide was a peasant, who walked beside me along a narrow path beneath over-arching fir trees, through which the wind howled. Through the tree-tops I saw the clouds scurrying past in wild confusion, as if fleeing in dismay and terror. Now and then, struck by a furious blast, the whole forest groaned as if in pain and swayed in one direction. In spite of my rapid pace and my thick clothes, I was perishing with cold. We were to sup and sleep at the house of a forest-guard, who lived not far away. I had come for some shooting.

" Now and then my guide looked up and muttered :

" ' Miserable weather ! '

" Then he talked about the people to whose house we were going. The master of the house had killed a poacher two years before, and ever since he had seemed depressed as if haunted by the memory. His two married sons lived with him. The darkness was intense. I could see nothing before me or around me, and the boughs of the trees, clashing together, filled the night with a ceaseless uproar. At last I saw a light and my companion was soon knocking at a door. Shrill cries of women answered us. Then a man, speaking in a strangled voice, asked :

" ' Who goes there ? '

" My guide gave his name and we entered. It was a scene I shall never forget. A white-haired old man with wild eyes, stood waiting for us in the middle of the kitchen with a loaded gun in his hand, while two stout lads, armed with axes, guarded the door. I could make out two women kneeling in the dark corners of the room with their faces hidden against the wall.

" We explained our business. The old man replaced his weapon against the wall, and ordered my room to be made ready. As the women did not stir, he said to me abruptly :

" ' You see, sir, two years ago to-night I killed a man. Last year he appeared and called me. I expect him again this evening.'

" And he added in a tone which made me smile :

" ' So we are rather uneasy.'

" I did what I could to soothe him and felt glad that I had come that evening, just in the nick of time to witness this exhibition of superstitious terror. I told stories and almost succeeded in calming down the whole family.

" By the fire lay an old dog, asleep with his head on his paws. He was nearly blind, and with his moustached muzzle he was the sort of dog who reminds one of some acquaintance.

" Outside the tempest beat fiercely on the little house, and through a small square opening, a sort of peep-hole near the door, I suddenly saw, by the glare of vivid lightning, a confused mass of trees, tossed about by the wind.

" I realised that, in spite of my efforts, these people were under the sway of some deep-seated terror. When ever I stopped talking, every ear was straining into the distance. Tired of the spectacle of these foolish fears, I was about to retire to bed when the old forest-guard suddenly jumped up from his chair, seized his gun again and gasped in frenzied tones :

" ' There he is. There he is. I can hear him.'

" The two women fell on their knees again and hid their faces ; the sons picked up their axes. I was preparing to make another attempt to calm them when the sleeping dog suddenly raised his head and stretched his neck and, looking into the fire with his dim eyes, uttered one of those melancholy howls which startle the benighted traveller. All eyes turned towards him. He stood there perfectly rigid, as if he had seen a ghost. And again he howled at something invisible, something unknown, and, to judge from his bristling coat, something that frightened him.

" Livid with terror, the forest-guard cried out :

" ' He scents him. He scents him. He was with me when I killed him.'

" The two distracted women began to mingle their howls with those of the dog. In spite of myself, a cold shudder ran down my spine. The dog's clairvoyance, in that place, at that hour of the night, in the midst of those terror-stricken people, was an uncanny thing to see.

" For a whole hour that dog went on howling without stirring from the spot. He howled as if in the agony of a nightmare, and fear, appalling fear, came upon me. Fear of what ? I have no idea. All I can say is that it was fear.

" We remained there pale and motionless, awaiting some

dreadful sequel, with ears intent and beating hearts, convulsed by the slightest sound. Then the dog began to roam about the room, sniffing the walls, and whining incessantly. The brute was driving us mad. At last the peasant, my guide, seized him in a sort of paroxysm of angry terror and, throwing open a door, flung him out into a small courtyard.

" Immediately the dog was still, and we remained plunged in a silence, which was even more nerve racking. Suddenly we all gave a simultaneous bound. Something was gliding along the outer wall on the side nearest the forest. It brushed against the door and seemed to fumble there with hesitating touch. Then followed two minutes of a silence that maddened us. Then the thing returned, brushing against the wall as before, and scratching on it lightly, like a child scratching with its fingernail. Suddenly a head appeared at the peephole, a white face with gleaming eyes, like those of a wild beast. And from its mouth came a vague sound like a plaintive moan.

" There was a noise of a tremendous explosion in the kitchen. The old forest-guard had fired his gun. At the same time the two sons rushed to block up the peephole with the big table, which they reinforced with the dresser.

" And I solemnly assure you that at that unexpected report of the gun, such an agonising pang shot through me, heart and soul and body, that I was ready to faint, ready to die of fear.

" We stayed there till dawn, unable to stir or utter a word, in the grip of a horror I cannot describe.

" No one ventured to move the barricade till we saw, through a chink in the pent-roof, a slender ray of daylight.

" At the foot of the wall, close against the door, lay the old dog with a bullet in his throat. He had got out of the courtyard by digging a hole under the fence."

The man with the bronzed face ceased speaking. Then he added :

" That night I was in no danger whatever. But I would rather go through again all the worst perils I have encountered than that single moment when the gun was fired at that hairy face at the window."

TWELVE O'CLOCK
Charles Whibley

IN 1779, the year of his mysterious death, Thomas, Lord Lyttelton had climbed the pinnacle of fame. Though he was but six and thirty, he was already known as "the wicked Lord Lyttelton." In what his wickedness consisted is not clear. Such reputations are seldom deserved, and are commonly founded upon flattery and vainglory. He is said to have had a great love of gambling, and was so unlucky in his youth that more than once he was compelled to leave his companions "abruptly" in far-off countries. But he presently became more artful and turned his sad experience to good account. "The pigeon turned into a hawk," we are told, and at his death he had gained by play some £30,000. For the rest, he had practised with much success those vices in which Whiggish ministers in his day had full licence to excel. There is no evidence that he was a genuine rival in dissipation to Charles James Fox, for instance, of whom a partisan has confessed that when he returned to Eton from the Continent his "Parisian experiences . . . produced a visible and durable change for the worse in the morals and habits of the place." In brains there was not much to choose between the two men. Dr. Barnard, the Head Master of Eton, who had had them both under his care, thought that the abilities of Lyttelton were vastly superior.

Whatever shape his legendary wickedness took, there is no doubt that he was shaped for nobler purposes. Fatigue is for rakes a better cure than repentance, and the years as they passed fashioned Thomas Lyttelton into a gravely ambitious statesman. Though he owned himself that his amendment was slow and progressive, it might be said of him, as was said of the great Rochester, whom he somewhat resembled, that "he seem'd to study nothing more than which way to make that great understanding God had given him most useful to his country." Like Rochester too, he spoke in the House of Peers with general approbation. Men of all parties are agreed in his praise. Even his enemies were generous in extolling his gifts of eloquence and statesmanship. Sandwich, for instance, was no friend of Lyttelton. Lyttelton had attacked Sandwich with a bitter ferocity, and this is what Sandwich found to say about Lyttelton in 1775 : " I think that so far from reprehension, the noble lord deserves commendation and thanks for so ably defending and asserting the rights of the British Parliament and the supreme legislative authority of the Mother Country. I think I never before heard such a speech delivered by anybody, and I am proud to testify my perfect approbation by affirming that it was the finest ever delivered within these walls."

The praise, if excessive, was disinterested, and that Sandwich was not alone in approbation is proved by Lyttelton's early promotion. At the age of thirty-two he was sworn of His Majesty's Privy Council, and made one of the Chief Justices in Eyre. As a politician he was energetically and consistently opposed to the rebels in America. His speeches breathe the true spirit of patriotism, and had he been able to carry the administration with him, England would not have been forced to endure an unjust, unmerited disgrace. And by a freakish accident we remember less clearly how he lived than how he died. His once famous dissipations are but a rumour ; the speeches, which were heard with a reluctant enthusiasm in the House of Peers, are a vague echo from the past ; the ghostly apparition, which heralded his death, still holds the wonder of the world, and is an incitement to controversy after a century and a half.

I have said so much about the man and his character, because without some understanding of them the story of his death might fail of its effect. He would not seem to be of those who stand in awe of the invisible world. His hard, practical sense, his determination to snatch from life whatever of pleasure it held, are not the qualities which we expect in those to whom beckonings come from beyond the boundaries of the world. Yet he had always been a dreamer of dreams and a seer of visions. Not long before his death " I dreamt," said he, " that I was dead, and was hurried away to the infernal regions, which appeared as a large dark room, at the end of which was seated Mrs. Brownrigg,[1] who told me it was

---

[1] Mrs. Brownrigg is the woman made immortal in *The Anti-Jacobin:*
        " Dost thou ask her crime ?
    She whipped two female prentices to death,
    And hid them in the coal-hole.
    . . . For this act
    Did Brownrigg swing. Harsh laws ! "

appointed for her to pour red-hot bullets down my throat for a thousand years. The resistance I endeavoured to make to her awakened me, but the agitation of my mind when I awoke is not to be described, nor can I get the better of it." So ugly a visitation as that of Mrs. Brownrigg visited him but seldom. It was but the shadow cast by a disordered fancy. Far more benign and amiable in aspect was the apparition which foretold his death. The legend, repeated by many and divers tongues, may be shaped into this : On Wednesday, 24th November, 1779, Lyttelton, at his house in Hill Street, saw, or dreamed that he saw, a bird fly into his bedroom. He tried to clutch it, and found it, like Macbeth's dagger, " of the mind, a false creation." Presently it turned into a woman, draped in white, and recalling by her ghostly features one whom Lyttelton had treated none too well. In a solemn voice, as from the grave, the voice with which spirits are said to intensify their effect, the disembodied woman told Lyttelton that he must die. " I hope not soon," he murmured, " not in two months." " In three days," said she. In vain he attempted to speak to her. She vanished from his sight, echoing as she went, " Three days, three days ! "

Lyttelton was profoundly affected by this message from the other world. Like most men of a doubting temper, he was superstitious. He told those who lodged in his house what he had seen, and the vision lost nothing of terror and persuasiveness in the telling. His allotted span must come to an end, if the ghost spoke true, at midnight on Saturday. But even though he were credulous, Lyttelton would not allow meanwhile the fateful message to turn him from the paths of duty and pleasure. He went about his business with zeal and address. Before the House of Lords he delivered the best speech that ever he made. It was his swan-song. For the first time he seceded openly from the Government, whose cowardly conduct in America and in Ireland he attacked with pitiless contempt and unrelenting logic. And all the while the visions of the dove and the white lady were before his eyes. When he said, in the solemn language which befitted the time and place, and which gained in solemnity after the event, " It is true I hold a place, but perhaps I shall not hold it long," the ministers laughed. From them the irony was concealed. " The noble lords smile at what I say," he retorted ; " let them turn their eyes on their own pusillanimity . . . and then let them declare in their consciences which is most fitly the object of contempt, my thus openly and unreservedly speaking my sentiments in Parliament . . . or their consenting, in a moment of difficulty and danger like the present, to pocket the wages of prostitution." While they thought of·the place which he would not hold long, he remembered that, of the three days given him by the ghost, one was all but at an end.

On Friday morning George Fortescue called upon him, and presently the two of them took the air together. Lyttelton was still reflecting upon an early death, when they crossed the churchyard of St. James's Church. "Now look at all the vulgar fellows," said he, pointing to the tombstones ; "they die in their youth, at five and thirty. But you and I, who are gentlemen, shall live to a good old age." A few hours later he went down to his house at Epsom, where he entertained a party, not such a party as the gossip of Walpole invented "a caravan of nymphs," nor "four virgins, whom he had picked up in the Strand "—but a party of ladies and gentleman, whom he counted among his intimate friends. There was upon them all a certain foreboding, and when Saturday evening came, they thought of nothing but the ghost. Meanwhile, his friends all did their best to avert the depression, which settled upon Lyttelton, who, amid the shouting and the laughter of the others, exclaimed, "We shall jockey the ghost after all." A musician, named Russell, who had been summoned to entertain the company, noticed that despite the efforts of his friends, Lyttelton's melancholy still clung about him. So midnight drew on, the hour at which Lyttelton had been doomed to die by the ghost, and in spite of himself he kept an anxious eye upon the time. His valet, by an artful foresight, had put on the clock a quarter of an hour, in the hope that his master should not know when the foreordained minute came, and should not aid his death by a just fear. Slowly the seconds moved, and when Lyttelton saw that the clock marked the approach of midnight, he got up abruptly and bade good night to his guests. He had bilked the ghost, as he thought, and went upstairs to his bedroom with the light foot of a man reprieved. His thoughts were all of the morrow. He spoke to his servant with a cheerful voice, and "particularly enquired of him what care had been taken to provide good rolls for breakfast the next morning." He then bade the man prepare him a dose of medicine, and when he began to stir the medicine with a toothpick (or, according to another account, with a key), Lyttelton told him he was a dirty fellow, and bade him go downstairs and fetch a spoon. When the servant returned he found his master speechless upon his pillow and in the last agony of death. The attempt to cheat the clock had failed, for Russell, the musician, records that at the moment when the servant came down to do his master's bidding, the clock of the parish church, which had not been tampered with, began slowly to strike the midnight hour.

Thus died Thomas, the second Lord Lyttelton, eminent alike in vice and virtue, renowned for eloquence in his life, most highly renowned for the manner of his death, which provided gossip for the malicious, and thought for the philosopher. Horace Walpole cut a new pen that he might share his contempt for the dead man with his friends. Samuel Johnson, the Commentator-General of his age, who heard the story with his own ears from Lyttelton's uncle, Lord Westcote, expressed at once his interest in it, and his faith. " It is the most extraordinary thing," said he, " that has happened in my day. . . I am so glad to have every evidence of the spiritual world, that I am willing to believe it."

A DESCENT INTO THE MAELSTROM
Edgar Allan Poe

WE had now reached the summit of the loftiest crag. For some minutes the old man seemed too much exhausted to speak.

"Not long ago," he said at length, "and I could have guided you on this route as well as the youngest of my sons ; but, about three years past, there happened to me an event such as never happened before to mortal man—or at least such as no man ever survived to tell of—and the six hours of deadly terror which I then endured have broken me up body and soul. You suppose me a *very* old man—but I am not. It took less than a single day to change these hairs from a jetty black to white, to weaken my limbs, and to unstring my nerves, so that I tremble at the least exertion, and am frightened at a shadow. Do you know I can scarcely look over this little cliff without getting giddy ? "

The " little cliff," upon whose edge he had so carelessly thrown himself to rest that the weightier portion of his body hung over it, while he was only kept from falling by the tenure of his elbow on its extreme and slippery edge—this " little cliff " arose, a sheer unobstructed precipice of black shining rock, some fifteen or sixteen hundred feet from the world of crags beneath us. Nothing would have tempted me to within half a dozen yards of its brink. In truth, so deeply was I excited by the perilous position of my companion, that I fell at full length upon the ground, clung to the shrubs around me, and dared not even glance upwards at the sky— while I struggled in vain to divest myself of the idea that the very foundations of the mountain were in danger from the fury of the winds. It was long before I could reason myself into sufficient courage to sit up and look out into the distance.

"You must get over these fancies," said the guide, " for I have brought you here that you might have the best possible view of the scene of that event I mentioned—and to tell you the whole story with the spot just under your eye.

"We are now," he continued, in that particularizing manner

" This," said I at length to the old man, " this *can* be nothing else than the great whirlpool of the Maelström."

" So it is sometimes termed," said he. " We Norwegians call it the Moskoe-ström, from the island of Moskoe in the midway."

The ordinary accounts of this vortex had by no means prepared me for what I saw. That of Jonas Ramus, which is perhaps the most circumstantial of any, cannot impart the faintest conception either of the magnificence, or of the horror of the scene—or of the wild bewildering sense of *the novel* which confounds the beholder. I am not sure from what point of view the writer in question surveyed it, nor at what time ; but it could neither have been from the summit of Helseggen, nor during a storm. There are some passages of his description, nevertheless, which may be quoted for their details, although their effect is exceedingly feeble in conveying an impression of the spectacle.

" Between Lofoden and Moskoe," he says, " the depth of the water is between thirty-six and forty fathoms ; but on the other side, towards Ver (Vurrgh), this depth decreases so as not to afford a convenient passage for a vessel, without the risk of splitting on the rocks, which happens even in the calmest weather. When it is flood, the stream runs up the country between Lofoden and Moskoe with a boisterous rapidity ; but the roar of its impetuous ebb to the sea is scarce equalled by the loudest and most dreadful cataracts ; the noise being heard several leagues off, and the vortices or pits are of such an extent and depth, that if a ship comes within its attraction, it is inevitably absorbed and carried down to the bottom, and there beat to pieces against the rocks ; and when the water relaxes, the fragments thereof are thrown up again. But these intervals of tranquillity are only at the turn of the ebb and flood, and in calm weather, and last but a quarter of an hour, its violence gradually returning. When the stream is most boisterous, and its fury heightened by a storm, it is dangerous to come within a Norway mile of it. Boats, yachts, and ships have been carried away by not guarding against it before they were within its reach. It likewise happens frequently that whales come too near the stream, and are overpowered by its violence ; and then it is impossible to describe their howlings and bellowings in their fruitless struggles to disengage themselves. A bear, once, attempting to swim from Lofoden to Moskoe, was caught by the stream and borne down, while he roared terribly, so as to be heard on shore. Large stocks of firs and pine trees, after being absorbed by the current, rise again broken and torn to such a degree as if bristles grew upon them. This plainly shows the bottom to consist of craggy rocks, among which they are whirled to and fro. This stream is regulated by the flux and reflux of the sea—it being constantly high and low water every six hours. In the year 1645, early in the morning of Sexagesima Sunday, it raged with such noise and impetuosity that the very stones of the houses on the coast fell to the ground.".

In regard to the depth of the water, I could not see how this could have been ascertained at all in the immediate vicinity of the vortex. The "forty fathoms" must have reference only to portions of the channel close upon the shore either of Moskoe or Lofoden. The depth in the centre of the Moskoe-ström must be immeasurably greater ; and no better proof of this fact is necessary than can be obtained from even the sidelong glance into the abyss of the whirl which may be had from the highest crag of Helseggen. Looking down from this pinnacle upon the howling Phlegethon below, I could not help smiling at the simplicity with which the honest Jonas Ramus records, as a matter difficult of belief, the anecdotes of the whales and the bears ; for it appeared to me, in fact, a self-evident thing, that the largest ships of the line in existence, coming within the influence of that deadly attraction, could resist it as little as a feather the hurricane, and must disappear bodily and at once.

The attempts to account for the phenomenon—some of which, I remember, seemed to me sufficiently plausible in perusal—now wore a very different and unsatisfactory aspect. The idea generally received is that this, as well as three smaller vortices among the Ferroe islands, " have no other cause than the collision of waves rising and falling, at flux and reflux, against a ridge of rocks and shelves, which confines the water so that it precipitates itself like a cataract, and thus the higher the flood rises, the deeper must the fall be ; and the natural result of all is a whirlpool or vortex, the prodigious suction of which is sufficiently known by lesser experiments." These are the words of the *Encyclopædia Britannica*. Kircher and others imagine that in the centre of the channel of the Maelström is an abyss penetrating the globe, and issuing in some very remote part—the gulf of Bothnia being somewhat decidedly named in one instance. This opinion, idle in itself, was the one to which, as I gazed, my imagination most readily assented; and, mentioning it to the guide, I was rather surprised to hear him say that, although it was the view almost universally entertained of the subject by the Norwegians, it nevertheless was not his own. As to the former notion, he confessed his inability to comprehend it; and here I agreed with him—for, however conclusive on paper, it becomes altogether unintelligible, and even absurd, amid the thunder of the abyss.

"You have had a good look at the whirl now," said the old man; "and if you will creep round this crag, so as to get in its lee, and deaden the roar of the water, I will tell you a story that will convince you I ought to know something of the Moskoe-ström."

I placed myself as desired, and he proceeded:

"Myself and my two brothers once owned a schooner-rigged smack of about seventy tons burthen, with which we were in the habit of fishing among the islands beyond Moskoe, nearly to Vurrgh. In all violent eddies at sea there is good fishing, at proper opportunities, if one has only the courage to attempt it; but among the whole of the Lofoden coastmen, we three were the only ones who made a regular business of going out to the islands, as I tell you. The usual grounds are a great way lower down to the southward. There fish can be got at all hours, without much risk, and therefore these places are preferred. The choice spots over here among the rocks, however, not only yield the finest variety, but in far greater abundance; so that we often got in a single day what the more timid of the craft could not scrape together in a week. In fact, we made it a matter of desperate speculation —the risk of life standing instead of labour, and courage answering for capital.

"We kept the smack in a cove about five miles higher up the coast than this; and it was our practice, in fine weather, to take advantage of the fifteen minutes' slack to push across the main channel of the Moskoe-ström, far above the pool, and then drop down upon anchorage somewhere near Otterholm, or Sandflesen, where the eddies are not so violent as elsewhere. Here we used to remain until nearly time for slack-water again, when we weighed and made for home. We never set out upon this expedition without a steady side wind for going and coming—one that we felt sure would not fail us before our return—and we seldom made a miscalculation upon this point. Twice, during six years, we were forced to stay all night at anchor, on account of a dead calm, which is a rare thing indeed just about here ; and once we had to remain on the grounds nearly a week, starving to death, owing to a gale which blew up shortly after our arrival, and made the channel too boisterous to be thought of. Upon this occasion we should have been driven out to sea in spite of everything (for the whirlpools threw us round and round so violently that at length we fouled our anchor and dragged it) if it had not been that we drifted into one of the innumerable cross-currents—here to-day and gone to-morrow—which drove us under the lee of Flimen, where, by good luck, we brought up.

"I could not tell you the twentieth part of the difficulties we encountered ' on the ground '—it is a bad spot to be in, even in good weather—but we make shift always to run the gauntlet of the Moskoe-ström itself without accident; although at times my heart has been in my mouth when we happened to be a minute or so behind or before the slack. The wind sometimes was not as strong as we thought it at starting, and then we made rather less way than we could wish, while the current rendered the smack unmanageable. My eldest brother had a son eighteen years old, and I had two stout boys of my own. These would have been of great assistance at such times in using the sweeps, as well as afterward in fishing—but, somehow, although we ran the risk ourselves, we had not the heart to let the young ones get into the danger—for, after all said and done, it *was* a horrible danger, and that is the truth.

"It is now within a few days of three years since what I am going to tell you occurred. It was on the 10th of July, 18—, a day which the people of this part of the world will never forget—for it was one in which blew the most terrible hurricane that ever came out of the heavens. And yet all the morning, and indeed until late in afternoon, there was a gentle and steady breeze from the south-west, while the sun shone brightly, so that the oldest seaman amongst us could not have foreseen what was to follow.

"The three of us—my two brothers and myself—had

crossed over to the islands about two o'clock p.m., and soon nearly loaded the smack with fine fish, which, we all remarked, were more plentiful that day than we had ever known them. It was just seven *by my watch* when we weighed and started for home, so as to make the worst of the Ström at slack water, which we knew would be at eight.

" We set out with a fresh wind on our starboard quarter, and for some time spanked along at a great rate, never dreaming of danger, for indeed we saw not the slightest reason to apprehend it. All at once we were taken aback by a breeze from over Helseggen. This was most unusual—something that had never happened to us before—and I began to feel a little uneasy, without exactly knowing why. We put the boat on the wind, but could make no headway at all for the eddies, and I was upon the point of proposing to return to the anchorage when, looking astern, we saw the whole horizon covered with a singular copper-coloured cloud that rose with the most amazing velocity.

" In the meantime the breeze that had headed us off fell away, and we were dead becalmed, drifting about in every direction. This state of things, however, did not last long enough to give us time to think about it. In less than a minute the storm was upon us—in less than two the sky was entirely overcast—and what with this and the driving spray, it became suddenly so dark that we could not see each other in the smack.

" Such a hurricane as then blew it is folly to attempt describing. The oldest seaman in Norway never experienced anything like it. We had let our sails go by the run before it cleverly took us ; but, at the first puff, both our masts went by the board as if they had been sawed off—the mainmast taking with it my youngest brother, who had lashed himself to it for safety.

" Our boat was the lightest feather of a thing that had ever sat upon water. It had a complete flush deck, with only a small hatch near the bow, and this hatch it had always been our custom to batten down when about to cross the Ström, by way of precaution against the chopping seas. But for this circumstance we should have foundered at once—for we lay entirely buried for some moments. How my elder brother escaped destruction I cannot say, for I never had an opportunity of ascertaining. For my part, as soon as I had let the foresail run, I threw myself flat on deck, with my feet against the narrow gunwale of the bow, and with my hands grasping a ring-bolt near the foot of the foremast. It was mere instinct that prompted me to do this—which was undoubtedly the very best thing I could have done—for I was too much flurried to think.

"For some moments we were completely deluged, as I say, and all this time I held my breath and clung to the bolt. When I could stand it no longer I raised myself upon my knees, still keeping hold with my hands, and thus got my head clear. Presently our little boat gave herself a shake, just as a dog does in coming out of the water, and thus rid herself, in some measure, of the seas. I was now trying to get the better of the stupor that had come over me, and to collect my senses so as to see what was to be done, when I felt somebody grasp my arm. It was my elder brother, and my heart leaped for joy, for I had made sure that he was overboard—but the next moment all this joy was turned into horror—for he put his mouth close to my ear, and screamed out the word ' *Moskoe-ström !* '

"No one ever will know what my feelings were at that moment. I shook from head to foot as if I had had the most violent fit of ague. I knew what he meant by that one word well enough—I knew what he wished to make me understand. With the wind that now drove us on, we were bound for the whirl of the Ström, and nothing could save us !

"You perceive that in crossing the Ström *channel* we always went a long way up above the whirl, even in the calmest weather, and then had to wait and watch carefully for the slack—but now we were driving right upon the pool itself, and in such a hurricane as this ! ' To be sure,' I thought, ' we shall get there just about the slack—there is some little hope in that '—but in the next moment I cursed myself for being so great a fool as to dream of hope at all. I knew very well that we were doomed, had we been ten times a ninety-gun ship.

"By this time the first fury of the tempest had spent itself, or perhaps we did not feel it so much, as we scudded before it, but at all events the seas, which at first had been kept down by the wind, and lay flat and frothing, now got up into absolute mountains. A singular change, too, had come over the heavens. Around in every direction it was still as black as pitch, but nearly overhead there burst out, all at once, a circular rift of clear sky—as clear as I ever saw—and of a deep bright blue—and through it there blazed forth the full moon with a lustre that I never before knew her to wear. She lit up everything about us with the greatest distinctness—but, oh God, what a scene it was to light up !

" I now made one or two attempts to speak to my brother —but in some manner which I could not understand, the din had so increased that I could not make him hear a single word, although I screamed out at the top of my voice in his ear. Presently he shook his head, looking as pale as death, and held up one of his fingers, as if to say ' *listen.*'

" At first I could not make out what he meant—but soon a hideous thought flashed upon me. I dragged my watch from its fob. It was not going. I glanced at its face by the moonlight, and then burst into tears as I flung it far away into the ocean. *It had run down at seven o'clock ? We were behind the time of the slack, and the whirl of the Ström was in full fury ?*

" When a boat is well built, properly trimmed, and not deep laden, the waves in a strong gale, when she is going large, seem always to slip from beneath her—which appears very strange to a landsman—and this is called *riding*, in sea phrase.

" Well, so far we had ridden the swells very cleverly ! but presently a gigantic sea happened to take us right under the counter, and bore us with it as it rose—up—up—as if into the sky. I would not have believed that any wave could rise so high. And then down we came with a sweep, a slide, and a plunge, that made me feel sick and dizzy, as if I was falling from some lofty mountain-top in a dream. But while we were up I had thrown a quick glance around—and that one glance was sufficient. I saw our exact position in an instant. The Moskoe-ström whirlpool was about a quarter of a mile dead ahead, but no more like the everyday Moskoe-ström than the whirl as you now see it is like a mill-race. If I had not known where we were, and what we had to expect, I should not have recognized the place at all. As it was, I involuntarily closed my eyes in horror. The lids clenched themselves together as if in a spasm.

" It could not have been two minutes afterwards when we suddenly felt the waves subside, and were suddenly enveloped in foam. The boat made a short half-turn to larboard, and then shot off in its new direction like a thunderbolt. At the same moment the roaring noise of the waters was completely drowned in a shrill shriek—such a sound as you might imagine given out by the water-pipes of many thousand steam-vessels, letting off their steam all together. We were now in the belt of surf that always surrounds the whirl! and I thought, of course, that another moment would plunge us into the abyss —down which we could only see indistinctly on account of the amazing velocity with which we were borne along. The boat did not seem to sink into the water at all, but to skim like an air-bubble on the surface of the surge. Her starboard side was next the whirl, and on the larboard arose the world of ocean we had left. It stood like a huge, writhing wall between us and the horizon.

"It may appear strange, but now, when we were in the very jaws of the gulf, I felt more composed than when we were only approaching it. Having made up my mind to hope no more, I got rid of a great deal of that terror which unmanned me at first. I supposed it was despair that strung my nerves.

"It may look like boasting—but what I tell you is truth— I began to reflect how magnificent a thing it was to die in such a manner, and how foolish it was in me to think of so paltry a consideration as my own individual life, in view of so wonderful a manifestation of God's power. I do believe that I blushed with shame when this idea crossed my mind. After a little while I became possessed with the keenest curiosity about the whirl itself. I positively felt a *wish* to explore its depths, even at the sacrifice I was going to make! and my principal grief was that I should never be able to tell my old companions on shore about the mysteries I should see. These, no doubt, were singular fancies to occupy a man's mind in such extremity—and I have often thought since that the revolutions of the boat around the pool might have rendered me a little light-headed.

"There was another circumstance which tended to restore my self-possession; and this was the cessation of the wind, which could not reach us in our present situation—for, as you saw yourself, the belt of surf is considerably lower than the general bed of the ocean, and this latter now towered above us, a high, black, mountainous ridge. If you have never been at sea in a heavy gale, you can form no idea of the

confusion of mind occasioned by the wind and spray together.
They blind, deafen, and strangle you, and take away all power
of action or reflection. But we were now, in a great measure,
rid of these annoyances—just as death-condemned felons in
prison are allowed petty indulgences, forbidden them while
their doom is yet uncertain.

" How often we made the circuit of the belt it is impossible
to say. We careered round and round for perhaps an hour,
flying rather than floating, getting gradually more and more
into the middle of the surge, and then nearer and nearer to
its horrible inner edge. All this time I had never let go of the
ring-bolt. My brother was at the stern holding on to an
empty water-cask, which had been securely lashed under the
coop of the counter, and was the only thing on deck that had
not been swept overboard when the gale first took us. As
we approached the brink of the pit he let go his hold upon
this, and made for the ring, from which, in the agony of his
terror, he endeavoured to force my hands, as it was not large
enough to afford us both a secure grasp. I never felt deeper
grief than when I saw him attempt this act—although I knew
he was a madman when he did it—a raving maniac through
sheer fright. I did not care, however, to contest the point
with him. I knew it could make no difference whether either
of us held on at all ; so I let him have the bolt and went astern
to the cask. This there was no great difficulty in doing ; for
the smack went round steadily enough, and upon an even keel
—only swaying to and fro with the immense swelters of the
whirl. Scarcely had I secured myself in my new position,
when we gave a wild lurch to starboard, and rushed headlong
into the abyss. I muttered a hurried prayer to God, and
thought all was over.

" As I felt the sickening sweep of the descent, I had
instinctively tightened my hold upon the barrel, and closed
my eyes. For some seconds I dared not open them—while
I expected instant destruction, and wondered that I was not
already in my death-struggles with the water. But moment
after moment elapsed. I still lived. The sense of the falling
had ceased ; and the motion of the vessel seemed much as
it had been before, while in the belt of the foam, with the
exception that she now lay more along. I took courage and
looked once again upon the scene.

" Never shall I forget the sensation of awe, horror, and

admiration with which I gazed about me. The boat appeared to be hanging, as if by magic, midway down, upon the interior surface of a funnel, vast in circumference, prodigious in depth, and whose perfectly smooth sides might have been mistaken for ebony, but for the bewildering rapidity with which they spun around, and for the gleaming and ghastly radiance they shot forth, as the rays of the full moon, from that circular rift amid the clouds which I have already described, streamed in a flood of golden glory along the black walls and far away down into the inmost recess of the abyss.

"At first I was too much confused to observe anything accurately. The general burst of terrific grandeur was all that I beheld. When I recovered myself a little, however, my gaze fell instinctively downward. In this direction I was able to obtain an unobstructed view, from the manner in which the smack hung on the inclined surface of the pool. She was quite upon an even keel—that is to say, her deck lay in a plain parallel with that of the water—but this latter sloped at an angle of more than forty-five degrees, so that we seemed to be lying upon our beam ends. I could not help observing, nevertheless, that I had scarcely more difficulty in maintaining my hold and footing in this situation than if we had been upon a dead level; and this, I suppose, was owing to the speed at which we revolved.

"The rays of the moon seemed to search the very bottom of the profound gulf; but still I could make out nothing distinctly, on account of a thick mist in which everything there was enveloped, and over which there hung a magnificent rainbow, like that narrow and tottering bridge which Mussulmen say is the only pathway between Time and Eternity. This mist, or spray, was no doubt occasioned by the clashing of the great walls of the funnel, as they all met together at the bottom—but the yell that went up to the heavens from out of that mist, I dare not attempt to describe.

"Our first slide into the abyss itself, from the belt of foam above, had carried us a great distance down the slope; but our further descent was by no means proportionate. Round and round we swept—not in any uniform movement—but in dizzying swings and jerks that sent us sometimes only a few hundred yards—sometimes nearly the complete circuit of the whirl. Our progress downwards, at each revolution, was slow, but very perceptible.

" Looking about me upon the wide waste of liquid ebony on which we were thus borne, I perceived that our boat was not the only object in the embrace of the whirl. Both above and below us were visible fragments of vessels, large masses of building timber and trunks of trees, with many smaller articles, such as pieces of house furniture, broken boxes, barrels, and staves. I have already described the unnatural curiosity which had taken the place of my original terrors. It appeared to grow upon me as I drew nearer and nearer to my dreadful doom. I now began to watch, with a strange interest, the numerous things that floated in our company. I *must* have been delirious—for I even sought *amusement* in speculating upon the relative velocities of their several descents toward the foam below. ' This fir tree,' I found myself at one time saying, ' will certainly be the next thing that takes the awful plunge and disappears '—and then I was disappointed to find that the wreck of a Dutch merchant ship overtook it and went down before. At length, after making several guesses of this nature, and being deceived in all—this fact—the fact of my invariable miscalculation, set me upon a train of reflection that made my limbs again tremble, and my heart beat heavily once more.

"It was not a new terror that thus affected me, but the dawn of a more exciting *hope*. This hope arose partly from memory, and partly from present observation. I called to mind the great variety of buoyant matter that strewed the coast of Lofoden, having been absorbed and then thrown forth by the Moskoe-ström. By far the greater number of the articles were shattered in the most extraordinary way—so chafed and roughened as to have the appearance of having been stuck full of splinters—but then I distinctly recollected that there were *some* of them which were not disfigured at all. Now I could not account for this difference except by supposing that the roughened fragments were the only ones that had been *completely absorbed*—that the others had entered the whirl at so late a period of the tide, or, from some reason, had descended so slowly after entering, that they did not reach the bottom before the turn of the flood came, or of the ebb, as the case might be. I conceived it possible in either instance that they might thus be whirled up again to the level of the ocean, without undergoing the fate of those which had been drawn in more early or absorbed more rapidly. I made, also, three important observations. The first was, that as a general rule, the larger the bodies were, the more rapid their descent—the second, that, between two masses of equal extent, the one spherical and the other *of any other shape*, the superiority in speed of descent was with the sphere—the third, that, between two masses of equal size, the one cyclindrical and the other of any other shape, the cylinder was absorbed the more slowly. Since my escape, I have had several conversations on this subject with an old schoolmaster of the district; and it was from him that I learned the use of the word ' cylinder ' and ' sphere.' He explained to me, although I have forgotten the explanation—how what I observed was, in fact, the natural consequence of the forms of the floating fragments—and showed me how it happened that a cylinder, swimming in a vortex, offered more resistance to its suction, and was drawn in with greater difficulty than an equally bulky body, of any form whatever.[1]

" There was one startling circumstance which went a great way in enforcing these observations, and rendering me anxious to turn them to account, and this was that, at every revolution, we passed something like a barrel, or else the yard or the mast of a vessel, while many of these things, which had been on our level when I first opened my eyes upon the wonders of the whirlpool, were now high up above us, and seemed to have moved but little from their original station.

" I no longer hesitated what to do. I resolved to lash myself securely to the water-cask upon which I now held, to cut it loose from the counter, and to throw myself with it into the water. I attracted my brother's attention by signs, pointed to the floating barrels that came near us, and did everything in my power to make him understand what I was about to do. I thought at length that he comprehended my design, but, whether this was the case or not, he shook his head despairingly, and refused to move from his station by the ring-bolt. It was impossible to reach him ; the emergency admitted of no delay ; and so, with a bitter struggle, I resigned him to his fate, fastened myself to the cask by means of the lashings which secured it to the counter, and precipitated myself with it into the sea, without another moment's hesitation.

" The result was precisely what I had hoped it might be.

[1] See Archimedes *De Incidentibus in Fluido*, lib. 2.

As it is myself who now tells you this tale—as you see that I *did* escape—and as you are already in possession of the mode in which this escape was effected, and must therefore anticipate all that I have further to say—I will bring my story quickly to conclusion. It might have been an hour, or thereabout, after my quitting the smack, when, having descended to a vast distance beneath me, it made three or four wild gyrations in rapid succession, and, bearing my loved brother with it, plunged headlong, at once and for ever, into the chaos of foam below. The barrel to which I was attached sunk very little farther than half the distance between the bottom of the gulf and the spot at which I leaped overboard, before a great change took place in the character of the whirlpool. The slope of the sides of the vast funnel became momentarily less and less steep. The gyrations of the whirl grew, gradually, less and less violent. By degrees, the froth and the rainbow disappeared, and the bottom of the gulf seemed slowly to uprise. The sky was clear, the winds had gone down, and the full moon was setting radiantly in the west, when I found myself on the surface of the ocean, in full view of the shores of Lofoden, and above the spot where the pool of the Moskoeström *had been*. It was the hour of the slack—but the sea still heaved in mountainous waves from the effects of the hurricane. I was borne violently into the channel of the Ström, and, in a few minutes, was hurried down the coast into the ' grounds ' of the fishermen. A boat picked me up—exhausted from fatigue—and (now that the danger was removed) speechless from the memory of its horror. Those who drew me on board were my old mates and daily companions—but they knew me no more than they would have known a traveller from the spirit-land. My hair, which had been raven-black the day before, was as white as you see it now. They say, too, that the whole expression of my countenance had changed. I told them my story—they did not believe it. I now tell it to *you* —and I can scarcely expect you to put more faith in it than did the merry fishermen of Lofoden."

THE STRANGER
Ambrose Bierce

A MAN stepped out of the darkness into the little illuminated circle about our failing camp-fire and seated himself
upon a rock.

"You are not the first to explore this region," he said
gravely.

Nobody controverted his statement; he was himself proof
of its truth, for he was not of our party and must have been
somewhere near when we camped. Moreover, he must have
companions not far away; it was not a place where one
would be living or travelling alone. For more than a week
we had seen, besides ourselves and our animals, only such
living things as rattlesnakes and horned toads. In an Arizona
desert one does not long coexist with only such creatures as
these; one must have pack animals, supplies, arms—"an
outfit." And all these imply comrades. It was, perhaps, a
doubt as to what manner of men this unceremonious stranger's
comrades might be, together with something in his words
interpretable as a challenge, that caused every man of our
half-dozen "gentlemen adventurers" to rise to a sitting
posture and lay his hand upon a weapon—an act signifying,
in that time and place, a policy of expectation. The stranger
gave the matter no attention, and began again to speak in
the same deliberate, uninflected monotone in which he had
delivered his first sentence:

"Thirty years ago Ramon Gallegos, William Shaw, George
W. Kent and Berry Davis, all of Tucson, crossed the Santa
Catalina Mountains and travelled due west, as nearly as the
configuration of the country permitted. We were prospecting
and it was our intention, if we found nothing, to push through
to the Gila river at some point near Big Bend, where we
understood there was a settlement. We had a good outfit
but no guide—just Ramon Gallegos, William Shaw, George
W. Kent and Berry Davis."

The man repeated the names slowly and distinctly, as if to
fix them in the memories of his audience, every member of

which was now attentively observing him, but with a slackened apprehension regarding his possible companions somewhere in the darkness which seemed to enclose us like a black wall, for in the manner of this volunteer historian was no suggestion of an unfriendly purpose. His act was rather that of a harmless lunatic than an enemy. We were not so new to the country as not to know that the solitary life of many a plainsman had a tendency to develop eccentricities of conduct and character not always easily distinguishable from mental aberration. A man is like a tree : in a forest of his fellows he will grow as straight as his generic and individual nature permits ; alone, in the open, he yields to the deforming stresses and tortions that environ him. Some such thoughts were in my mind as I watched the man from the shadow of my hat, pulled low to shut out the fire-light. A witless fellow, no doubt, but what could he be doing there in the heart of a desert ?

Nobody having broken the silence, the visitor went on to say :

"This country was not then what it is now. There was not a ranch between the Gila and the Gulf. There was a little game here and there in the mountains, and near the infrequent water-holes grass enough to keep our animals from starvation. If we should be so fortunate as to encounter no Indians we might get through. But within a week the purpose of the expedition had altered from discovery of wealth to preservation of life. We had gone too far to go back, for what was ahead could be no worse than what was behind ; so we pushed on, riding by night to avoid Indians and the intolerable heat, and concealing ourselves by day as best we could. Sometimes, having exhausted our supply of wild meat and emptied our casks, we were days without food and drink ; then a water-hole or a shallow pool in the bottom of an arroyo so restored our strength and sanity that we were able to shoot some of the wild animals that sought it also. Sometimes it was a bear, sometimes an antelope, a coyote, a cougar—that was as God pleased ; all were food.

"One morning as we skirted a mountain range, seeking a practicable pass, we were attacked by a band of Apaches who had followed our trail up a gulch—it is not far from here. Knowing that they outnumbered us ten to one, they took none of their usual cowardly precautions, but dashed upon us at a gallop, firing and yelling. Fighting was out of the question. We urged our feeble animals up the gulch as far as there was footing for a hoof, then threw ourselves out of our saddles and took to the chaparral on one of the slopes, abandoning our entire outfit to the enemy. But we retained our rifles, every man—Ramon Gallegos, William Shaw, George W. Kent and Berry Davis."

"Same old crowd," said the humorist of the party. A gesture of disapproval from our leader silenced him, and the stranger proceeded with his tale :

"The savages dismounted also, and some of them ran up the gulch beyond the point at which we had left it, cutting off further retreat in that direction and forcing us on up the side. Unfortunately the chaparral extended only a short distance up the slope, and as we came into the open ground above we took the fire of a dozen rifles ; but Apaches shoot badly when in a hurry, and God so willed it that none of us fell. Twenty yards up the slope, beyond the edge of the brush, were vertical cliffs, in which, directly in front of us, was a narrow opening. Into that we ran, finding ourselves in a cavern about as large as an ordinary room. Here for a time we were safe. A single man with a repeating rifle could defend the entrance against all the Apaches in the land. But against hunger and thirst we had no defence. Courage we still had, but hope was a memory.

"Not one of those Indians did we afterwards see, but by the smoke and glare of their fires in the gulch we knew that by day and by night they watched with ready rifles in the edge of the bush—knew that if we made a sortie not a man of us would live to take three steps into the open. For three days, watching in turn, we held out, before our suffering became insupportable. Then—it was the morning of the fourth day—Ramon Gallegos said :

"'Señores, I know not well of the good God and what please him. I have lived without religion, and I am not acquaint with that of you. Pardon, señores, if I shock you, but for me the time is come to beat the game of the Apache.'

"He knelt upon the rock floor of the cave and pressed his pistol against his temple. 'Madre de Dios,' he said, 'comes now the soul of Ramon Gallegos.'

"And so he left us—William Shaw, George W. Kent and Berry Davis.

"I was the leader. It was for me to speak.

" ' He was a brave man,' I said. ' He knew when to die, and how. It is foolish to go mad from thirst and fall by Apache bullets, or be skinned alive—it is in bad taste. Let us join Ramon Gallegos.'

" ' That is right,' said William Shaw.

" ' That is right,' said George W. Kent.

" I straightened the limbs of Ramon Gallegos and put a handkerchief over his face. Then William Shaw said : ' I should like to look like that a little while.'

" And George W. Kent said that he felt that way too.

" ' It shall be so,' I said. ' The red devils will wait a week. William Shaw and George W. Kent, draw and kneel.'

" They did so and I stood before them.

" ' Almighty God, our Father,' said I.

" ' Almighty God, our Father,' said William Shaw.

" ' Almighty God, our Father,' said George W. Kent.

" ' Forgive us our sins,' said I.

" ' Forgive us our sins,' said they.

" ' And receive our souls.'

" ' And receive our souls.'

" ' Amen ! '

" ' Amen ! '

" I laid them beside Ramon Gallegos and covered their faces."

There was a quick commotion on the opposite side of the camp-fire. One of our party had sprung to his feet, pistol in hand.

" And you ! " he shouted, " you dared to escape ?—you dare to be alive ? You cowardly hound, I'll send you to join them if I hang for it ! "

But with the leap of a panther the captain was upon him, grasping his wrist. " Hold it in, Sam Yountsey, hold it in ! "

We were now all upon our feet—except the stranger, who sat motionless and apparently inattentive. Someone seized Yountsey's other arm.

" Captain," I said, " there is something wrong here. This fellow is either a lunatic or merely a liar—just a plain, everyday liar that Yountsey has no call to kill. If this man was of that party it had five members, one of whom—probably himself— he has not named."

" Yes," said the captain, releasing the insurgent, who sat down, " there is something—unusual. Years ago four dead bodies of white men, scalped and shamefully mutilated, were found about the mouth of that cave. They are buried there; I have seen the graves—we shall all see them to-morrow."

The stranger rose, standing tall in the light of the expiring fire, which in our breathless attention to his story we had neglected to keep going.

"There were four," he said. "Ramon Gallegos, William Shaw, George W. Kent and Berry Davis."

With this reiterated roll-call of the dead he walked into the darkness and we saw him no more.

At that moment one of our party, who had been on guard, strode in among us, rifle in hand and somewhat excited.

"Captain," he said, "for the last half-hour three men have been standing out there on the *mesa*." He pointed in the direction taken by the stranger. "I could see them distinctly, for the moon is up, but as they had no guns and I had them covered with mine, I thought it was their move. They have made none, but, damn it! they have got on my nerves."

"Go back to your post, and stay till you see them again," said the captain. "The rest of you lie down again, or I'll kick you all into the fire."

The sentinel obediently withdrew, swearing, and did not return. As we were arranging our blankets, the fiery Yountsey said: "I beg your pardon, Captain, but who the devil do you take them to be?"

"Ramon Gallegos, William Shaw and George W. Kent."

"But how about Berry Davis? I ought to have shot him."

"Quite needless; you couldn't have made him any deader. Go to sleep."

THE PIONEERS OF PIKE'S PEAK
Basil Tozer

IT was a perfect night about the end of June, the sort of night common enough in Colorado at that time of the year. At the end of the game we rose from the card-table and strolled out into the cool, refreshing air. The stars were shining with extraordinary brilliance in a sky so clear that one seemed almost to hear them winking. The moon had not yet risen above the range of mighty peaks which tower into the heavens until their crests gradually vanish into great belts of clouds, and at night seem to touch the lowermost of the celestial bodies ; but a sort of halo, gradually spreading, served to show that presently the moon herself would shed a flood of light from the summit of the highest peaks down into the little village nestling at the feet of the mighty range. No sound broke the perfect stillness. The very houses seemed to sleep.

It was only when my friend and I re-entered the smoky bar saloon, where our companions, grown tired of card playing, were now quietly talking, that we noticed an odd-looking and apparently elderly stranger seated alone beside a little window at the farther end of the room. The window was open, and he was staring through it vacantly, interrupting his reverie only now and again in order to blow a long cloud of smoke into the air. My friend cast a glance of inquiry in his direction.

"He came in about five minutes ago," one of the card-players said.

"Who is he ? "

"Some crank, I suppose. He has not stirred since he sat down there."

"What is he staring at ? " someone asked presently.

"Pike's Peak, apparently," replied Watson, the man who had called the stranger a crank.

Though the words were spoken in an undertone, the

" crank " evidently overheard them, for he turned his head and frowned. Then he resumed his former position—his vigil. Conversation drifted from one topic to another, until the subject of the Rocky Mountains in particular engrossed our attention.

" And who really was the first to reach the top of Pike's Peak ? " Watson asked, looking round at us.

" Not Pike himself," answered a man named Norton. " They say that some man—— Look out, you fellows ! "

The stranger had left his seat and was approaching us with a slow, stealthy tread, his eyes oddly dilated. We all turned to face him. He was a man of immense proportions, well over six feet in height, and could not have been over fifty years of age, though he looked quite sixty. His hair was white and rather long. He had evidently been handsome in his day, but now the face, neck and hands were disfigured by numberless little sunken blotches not unlike the pits left by smallpox. He wore an old drab suit, a coon cap, thick boots, and leather leggings.

" Who did you say first reached the top of Pike's Peak ? " he asked in a threatening, hollow voice. He had dropped into a chair on the opposite side of the table beside me. Norton, whom he had interrupted, came to the rescue.

" I believe that—— "

" *I* was the first to reach it ! You don't know the story of our ascent ? "

" I know only what I have read and been told," Norton said.

" You yourself have been up Pike's Peak ? "

" I have—by the funicular."

" You have seen the summit, then ? "

" Yes."

" And what did you see that struck you most—there, fifteen thousand feet above the sea's level ? "

Norton had an inspiration.

" Do you mean the stone ? " he said.

Instantly the stranger's expression changed. He looked round at us all quite intelligently.

" It *is* there, then ? " he inquired eagerly, bending forward across the table.

" Of course it is there," Norton replied. " I can give you the inscription word for word."

"Do! What is it? Tell me, what is it?"

"The inscription says: '*This stone is erected in memory of William Dawkins, James Weston, and Walter Hellier, Pioneers of Pike's Peak, who were devoured by mountain rats while endeavouring to reach this summit.*'"

"Ah!" he ejaculated, greatly relieved. "I am glad it is there—I am glad it is still there. Do you know the story of my friends, the story of those pioneers?"

He had grown suddenly calm. He seemed suddenly to have regained his reason. Our interest and curiosity were now thoroughly aroused. We could see that the stranger was quite sober and though his mind seemed unhinged, he had now a lucid interval.

We noticed that he poured brandy into his tumbler until it was three parts full. Just then the moon shone over the summit of the famous peak, and from where we sat the outline of the glorious mountain could be clearly discerned. Watson drew the stranger's attention to it. An odd, bitter smile flitted across his face. It was the first time we had seen him smile. He sighed once, but did not utter a word. Then his gaze became again riveted on the gigantic peak.

"Pike never would—never could have reached it. He tried several times. Finally he stood upon a hill near the stalactite caves at the base of my mountain, and, pointing with his arm at the summit, said: 'No mortal man will ever tread that peak.'

"But we—*we* were determined to. Our friends shook us by the hands and bade us farewell.

"'But you are fools,' they said, 'You will never come back. You don't know what you may meet in those mountains. You know what Pike said when he came back. You know the tale he told. And some things he would not tell.'

"'Don't go, oh, don't go!' my wife cried in agony.

"I loved her, yet I forced her from me. She was but a unit. In the success of our enterprise lay the welfare of thousands. I told her that to comfort her. It was the last time I saw her alive.

"Early in the morning we started. We took with us arms, food and drink for many days, and the bare necessities of life. We carried everything ourselves. We knew where and how Pike had failed. We would succeed.

"A week later we were fairly in the midst of difficulties.

The work was terribly severe, but we had determination, strength and courage. We had expected to find obstacles, and we were not disappointed. Here enormous boulders which had to be circumvented, there unlooked-for waterfalls and ravines that delayed us, besides vegetation so thick that in places we had to hack our way through it. Then the unknown dangers. There might be snakes concealed among those immense boulders ; there might be death-dealing plants such as flourish in South America—indeed, we did not know what there might not be. But we did not pause to consider those things.

"Over a fortnight went by. As we mounted gradually higher and higher our spirits rose as if in sympathy. Far down in the valley we had once or twice during our progress caught glimpses of this very townlet, now called Colorado Springs, also of the village of Manitou. Tiny villages, indeed, they were in those days ; and as we saw them from those great heights they looked like little chessboards upon a vast expanse of prairie. And still we fought our way upward.

"How long our expedition had been started I cannot quite remember, when our surroundings gradually changed. In place of rock and black soil we now came upon wide tracks of sandy formation. The undergrowth was still dense, however, though here and there thousands upon thousands of slim fir trees lay rotting upon the ground, evidently swept down by terrific storms, for storms in these mountains sweep down trees as a reaping machine sweeps down standing corn. Sometimes we came upon broad, open spaces, spaces swept clear apparently in early days by giant waterfalls long since dried up. Then, as we penetrated still higher, and the vegetation decreased in density, even the boulders grew smaller. They now looked as though in prehistoric times they had been flung together by a tremendous seismic disturbance.

"'Have you noticed,' one of my comrades remarked one day, 'what a quantity of insects there are here ? And the rats are getting more plentiful. We seldom see any of those grey squirrels now.'

"As he spoke he stamped his foot upon an immense brown spider that was running away. Its body burst with a crack, and glutinous liquid spurted out all round his boot. Almost instantly several spiders ran out from beneath a large stone as if to ascertain what had happened. They stopped. For a moment they seemed for all the world as if they looked at us—looked at us with a malignant, vindictive expression. Then they scuttled away.

" 'I believe I felt several of those spiders scampering over my face last night,' he continued. 'You had better be careful ; they bite like mischief. These mountains are famous for them, and—just look at that ! '

" A couple of large rats were chasing an enormous spider across a long, flat boulder. A moment later spider and rats disappeared over the edge.

" 'They say that mountain rats will devour any living thing,' Weston said presently. ' They will eat us if we don't watch them ! ' he added in jest.

" During the early part of the afternoon we had made good progress, when suddenly we came upon a large sloping tract of bare white sand. The sun, still high in the heavens, shone down upon it, and at first sight the sand seemed to be alive with small, moving bodies.

" 'Talk of spiders ! ' Dawkins said, laughing. 'Did you ever see anything like that ? '

" We had long ago, in previous expeditions, grown accustomed to surprises. Few things astonished us now. Never in our lives, however, had we seen such an assemblage. There must have been thousands upon thousands of them running about in every direction, colliding with one another and tumbling over one another apparently for no reason. The sight made me think of a gigantic ants' nest overrun with mammoth ants, and an odd sort of smell that for several days had pervaded the air struck our nostrils with renewed strength.

" Now, as we stepped forward into the open tract, a strange thing happened, for the entire space, which a moment before had been alive, became instantly motionless. The spiders were all there, right under our eyes, but of one accord they had stopped running. Oddly enough, too, every spider was now facing us. Instinctively we felt that we had become objects of intense curiosity. And as we stood there, interested and amused, we could distinctly see the spiders' great eyes sticking out and evidently watching us. The sight would have given some people ' the creeps,' but we rather enjoyed it.

" 'Pish ! you hideous things,' Dawkins said, pitching a

pebble into their midst. In less than a minute hardly a spider was to be seen.

" ' If we describe that sight when we get back we shall be called liars,' Weston said, glancing at his watch. ' ' I've seen insects in my time, but never anything like that.'

" The offensive smell was still strong in the air, and as we progressed it increased. Once or twice it became almost unbearable. We had now a long stretch of clear going before us, so we hastened to avail ourselves of it by advancing briskly. And still we saw spiders at every turn, spiders by the thousand sunning themselves on every rock and boulder, great brown spiders with fat, oval bodies, and with thick, hairy legs bent in grotesque curves. I kicked over a stunted little tree that lay rotting—ugh! Quite two or three hundred spiders must have scuttled away from under it.

" ' This is getting beyond a joke,' Hellier, who seldom spoke, and was generally considered to be rather surly, suddenly said. ' I tell you what it is : these spiders will go for us.'

" ' Like Weston's rats ! ' Dawkins said, laughing at him, and we were still chaffing Hellier and Weston when Dawkins happened to look round.

" ' Why, Harry ! ' he exclaimed.

" There was anxiety in his tone, and I felt his hand grip my shoulder. And no wonder. Though anything but a coward, Dawkins could not help at once realising what we all realised a moment later—that Hellier's evil omen was more than likely to come true. A sickening feeling of fear had come over him.

" For there, barely fifty yards away, a reddish-brown mass gradually assuming the form of a crescent was steadily, swiftly gliding over the sand, steadily and swiftly overtaking us. And as it approached we could see thousands upon thousands of spiders hastening towards it from every direction and quickly increasing its size. The swarm when we saw it first must have covered between twelve and fifteen square feet. Before it had glided over another twenty yards of sand the entire mass was about one-third as large again. Yet a sort of horrible fascination kept us rooted to the spot where we now stood watching the swarm approach. In order to brace up our courage we told one another that the spiders could not be pursuing us at all ; that if we moved aside they would pass us by. But in our hearts we knew that we tried to think a lie. And when we moved aside in order to convince ourselves the creeping crescent immediately swayed round towards us and seemed if anything to advance more quickly.

"Suddenly the intense horror of the situation flashed across my mind and struck terror into our hearts. For what could we do to avert the terrible fate that threatened us? Savage animals we might have coped with; treacherous human beings, even, we might have bested; but now we were face to face with a peril totally unexpected, utterly loathsome and unassailable.

"'Our only chance lies in flight,' Hellier said bitterly.

"'Flight! And where shall we fly to? The top of the mountain, I suppose. Look there, Hellier.'

"It was Dawkins who spoke, and he spoke in tones of scorn. Looking around us, we now saw what we had not noticed before. We were surrounded. Everywhere we saw spiders—spiders approaching in brown, gliding crescents of varying sizes. And over a hundred yards away the largest and darkest mass of all could clearly be distinguished, also winding its way along the sand, also approaching, also closing us in. And as this great crescent surged undulatingly, unswervingly across the hillocks and irregularities in the surface of the soil and sand it resembled the great wave of a sluggish, turbid stream leaving a factory sluice.

"'Fire into them!' I exclaimed, slipping a couple of shot cartridges into my gun. The two charges cut a lane in the approaching wave, but almost instantly the lane closed up and the undulating mass advanced as if nothing had happened. Together Dawkins and Weston fired four barrels. Rather a broader lane this time; but again it closed up. I had reloaded.

"'Give them a volley,' Weston called out; 'that may turn them.'

"We did so, but by the time the smoke had cleared, the swarm had well-nigh resumed its former size and shape. Could we sweep a lane with our eight barrels and then rush through it? No, that was obviously impossible; the width of the wave was too great. And still recruits were pouring in upon every side, and as we fired volley after volley into the quickly approaching swarms in the vain hope of turning them, the distant ravines rang again and again with echoes.

" ' My God, we are done for ! ' came despairingly from Hellier, as for the twentieth time he closed his gun with a snap.

" Our barrels had now become almost too hot to hold, and still the hideous, crawling waves, which must have contained trillions of spiders, were fast approaching with a strange swaying motion, and rapidly narrowing our little circle. In a few minutes they would be upon us, overrunning us, dragging us down. Already many stragglers were running up our legs and over our bodies. Now the first swarm was so near that we could distinctly hear it rushing up us, and—ah ! the smell, how it still hangs in my nostrils. . . ."

For a moment the stranger stopped. His eyes were widely distended. His limbs trembled. He clutched the table frantically, in order to support himself.

" Suddenly I saw several spiders run up Weston's face and fix upon his eyes. With a scream he dashed them away, but as he did so his eyes began to swell, for the brutes had bitten him badly."

He stopped again. He was quivering all over with excitement. Suddenly he dashed from his seat to the farthermost corner of the room.

" Keep them from me ! Keep them off ! " he cried, glaring wildly all round the floor. " Look at them now—look at them—ah ! God help me !—help me !—help me ! . . ."

He sprang to right and left, then towards the door. Perspiration was pouring down his face. Then suddenly he snatched wildly at imaginary spiders running up his sleeves and legs, running up his body, running over his head, over his face, over his eyes, into his mouth. It was a dreadful sight.

" Stop him ! " my friend cried out, jumping from his seat and rushing towards the old man ; but as he approached a blindly directed blow from the stranger's fist almost stunned him, and the innkeeper and two rough-looking men entered the room.

" Hold him, boys," the innkeeper said calmly, as the two men pounced upon the stranger and the innkeeper sauntered towards us.

" Poor fellow," he said, " I always have to be ready for him—look at him now, yet the doctors pronounce him sane. He often is sane, of course, but when I heard him starting on the spiders and saw him drinking brandy I knew what to expect."

"Is there any truth in his spider story?" I asked.

"Any truth? It's all truth—at least, that's my belief. Though I was quite a lad at the time the expedition started, I can remember it well. Four of them there were, all strong and hearty when they set out. Two months later *he* came back."

"Did he alone escape?"

"He alone came back—came back quite done for and disfigured all over with red blotches. Afterwards they turned into pits. Some years later another expedition went up and reached the summit, but they always maintained that rats, not spiders, devoured those poor fellows, so they set a stone with an inscription on it at the top of the mountain—you have seen it, no doubt."

"What do you yourself think they were killed by?"

"I don't think anything. As sure as you are standing there they were devoured by swarms of great spiders, as Mad Harry has told you. I have heard him tell the story often enough, and he always tells the same story. These marks are not rats' bites."

"It's a horrible place, that mountain," he said, looking at its rugged peak so clearly outlined in the moonlight. "Though you can go up it now by the winding funicular, which is eight miles long, you don't know what horrors may exist in other parts of it. Many a man has gone into those mountains, but few have ever returned."

THE FOURTH MAN
John Russell

THE raft might have been taken for a swath of cut sedge or a drifting tangle of roots as it slid out of the shadowy river mouth at dawn and dipped into the first ground swell. But while the sky brightened and the breeze came fresh off shore it picked a way among shoals and swampy islets with purpose and direction, and when at last the sun leaped up and cleared his bright eye of the morning mist it had passed the wide entrance to the bay and stood to open sea.

It was a curious craft for such a venture, of a type that survives here and there in the obscure corners of the world. The coracle-maker would have scorned it. The first navigating pithecanthrope built nearly as well with his log and bush. A mat of pandanus leaves served for its sail and a pad of niaouli wood for its helm. But it had a single point of real seaworthiness. Its twin floats, paired as a catamaran, were woven of reed bundles and bamboo sticks upon triple rows of bladders. It was light as a bladder itself, elastic, fit to ride any weather. One other quality this raft possessed which recommended it beyond all comfort and all safety to its present crew. It was very nearly invisible. They had only to unstep its mast and lie flat in the cup of its soggy platform and they could not be spied half a mile away.

Four men occupied the raft. Three of them were white. Their bodies had been scored with brambles and blackened with dried blood, and on wrist and ankle they bore the dark and wrinkled stain of the gyves. The hair upon them was long and matted. They wore only the rags of blue canvas uniforms. But they were whites, members of the superior race—members of a highly superior race, according to those philosophers who rate the criminal aberration as a form of genius.

The fourth man was the man who had built the raft and was now sailing it. There was nothing superior about him.

His skin was a layer of soot. His prognathous jaw carried out the angle of a low forehead. No line of beauty redeemed his lean limbs and knobby joints. Nature had set upon him her plainest stamp of inferiority, and his only attempts to relieve it were the twist of bark about his middle and the prong of pig ivory through the cartilage of his nose. Altogether a very ordinary specimen of one of the lowest branches of the human family—the Canaques of New Caledonia.

The three whites sat together well forward, and so they had sat in silence for hours. But at sunrise, as if some spell had been raised by the clang of that great copper gong in the east they stirred and breathed deep of the salt air and looked at one another with hope in their haggard faces, and then back toward the land which was now no more than a grey-green smudge behind them . . . "Friends," said the eldest, whose temples were bound with a scrap of crimson scarf, "Friends— the thing is done."

With a gesture like conjuring he produced from the breast of his tattered blouse three cigarettes, fresh and round, and offered them round.

"Nippers!" cried the one at his right. "True nippers— name of a little good man! And here! Doctor, I always said you were a marvel. See if they be not new from the box!"

Dr. Dubosc smiled. Those who had known him in very different circumstances about the boulevards, the lobbies, the clubs, would have known him again and in spite of all disfigurement by that smile. And here, at the bottom of the earth, it had set him still apart in the prisons, the cobalt mines, the chain-gangs of a community not much given to mirth. Many a crowded lecture-hall at Montpellier had seen him touch some intellectual firework with just such a twinkle behind his bristly grey brows, with just such a thin curl of lip.

"By way of celebration," he explained. "Consider. There are seventy-five evasions from Nouméa every six months, of which not more than one succeeds. I had the figures myself from Dr. Pierre at the infirmary. He is not much of a physician, but a very honest fellow. Could anybody win on that percentage without dissipating? I ask you."

"Therefore you prepared for this?"

"It is now three weeks since I bribed the night-guard to get these same nippers."

The other regarded him with admiration. Sentiment came readily upon this beardless face, tender and languid, but overdrawn, with eyes too large and soft and oval too long. It was one of these faces familiar enough to the police which might serve as model for an angel were it not associated with some revolting piece of devilry. Fenayrou himself had been condemned "to perpetuity" as an incorrigible.

"Is not our doctor a wonder?" he inquired as he handed a cigarette along to the third white man. "He thinks of everything. You should be ashamed to grumble. See— we are free, after all. Free!"

The third was a gross, pock-marked man with hairless lids known sometimes as Niniche, Trois Huit, Le Tordeur, but chiefly among companions as Perroquet—a name derived perhaps from his beaked nose, or from some perception of his jail-bird character. He was a garrotter by profession, accustomed to rely upon his fists only for the exchange of amenities. Dubosc might indulge a fancy and Fenayrou seek to carry it as a pose, but The Parrot remained a gentleman of strictly serious turn. There is perhaps a tribute to the practical spirit of penal administration in the fact that while Dubosc was the most dangerous of these three and Fenayrou the most depraved Perroquet was the one with the official reputation, whose escape would be signalled first among the "Wanted." He accepted the cigarette because he was glad to get it, but he said nothing until Dubosc passed a tin box of matches and the first gulp of picadura filled his lungs. . . .

"Wait till you've got your two feet on a *pavé*, my boy. That will be the time to talk of freedom. What? Suppose there came a storm."

"It is not the season of storms," observed Dubosc.

But The Parrot's word had given them a check. Such spirits as these, to whom the land had been a horror, would be slow to feel the terror of the sea. Back there they had left the festering limbo of a convict colony, oblivion. Out here they had reached the rosy threshold of the big round world again. They were men raised from the dead, charged with all the furious appetites of lost years, with the savour of life strong and sweet on their lips. And yet they paused and looked about in quickened perception, with the clutch at the throat that takes the landsman on big waters. The spaces were so wide and empty. The voices in their ears were so strange and murmurous. There was a threat in each wave that came from the depths, a sinister vibration. None of them knew the sea. None knew its ways, what tricks it might play, what traps it might spread—more deadly than those of the jungle.

The raft was running now before a brisk chop with alternate spring and wallow, while the froth bubbled in over the prow and ran down among them as they sat. "Where is that cursed ship that was to meet us here?" demanded Fenayrou.

"It will meet us right enough." Dubosc spoke carelessly, though behind the blown wisp of his cigarette he had been searching the outer horizon with keen glance. "This is the day as agreed. We will be picked up from the mouth of the river."

"You say," growled Perroquet. "But where is any river now? Or any mouth? Sacred name, this wind will blow us to China if we keep on."

"We dare not lie in any closer. There is a Government launch at Torrien. Also the traders go armed hereabouts, ready for chaps like us. And don't imagine that the native trackers have given us up. They are likely to be following still in their proas."

"So far?"

Fenayrou laughed, for The Parrot's dread of their savage enemies had a morbid tinge.

"Take care, Perroquet. They will eat you yet."

"Is it true?" demanded the other, appealing to Dubosc. "I have heard it is even permitted these devils to keep all runaways they can capture—name of God!—to fatten on."

"An idle tale," smiled Dubosc. "They prefer the reward. But one hears of convicts being badly mauled. There was a forester who made a break from Baie du Sud and came back lacking an arm. Certainly these people have not lost the habit of cannibalism."

"Piecemeal," chuckled Fenayrou. "They will only sample you, Perroquet. Let them make a stew of your brains. You would miss nothing."

But The Parrot swore.

"Name of a name—what brutes!" he said, and by a gesture recalled the presence of that fourth man who was of their party and yet so completely separated from them that they had almost forgotten him.

The Canaque was steering the raft. He sat crouched at the stern, his body glistening like varnished ebony with spray. He held the steering paddle, immobile as an image, his eyes fixed upon the course ahead. There was no trace of expression on his face, no hint of what he thought or felt or whether he thought or felt anything. He seemed not even aware of their regard, and each one of them experienced somehow that twinge of uneasiness with which the white confronts his brother of colour—this enigma brown or yellow or black he is fated never wholly to understand or to fathom. . . .

"It occurs to me," said Fenayrou, in a pause, "that our friend here who looks like a shiny boot is able to steer us God knows where. Perhaps to claim the reward."

"Reassure yourself," answered Dubosc. "He steers by my order. Besides, it is a simple creature—an infant, truly, incapable of any but the most primitive reasoning."

"Is he incapable of treachery ?"

"Of any that would deceive us. Also, he is bound by his duty. I made a bargain with his chief, up the river, and this one is sent to deliver us on board our ship. It is the only interest he has in us."

"And he will do it ?"

"He will do it. Such is the nature of the native."

"I am glad you feel so," returned Fenayrou, adjusting himself indolently among the drier reeds and nursing the last of his cigarette. "For my part I wouldn't trust a figurehead like that for two sous. Mazette ! What a monkey face !"

"Brute !" repeated Perroquet, and this man, sprung from some vile river-front slum of Argenteuil, whose home had been the dock pilings, the grog shop, and the jail, even this man viewed the black Canaque from an immeasurable distance with the look of hatred and contempt. . . .

Under the heat of the day the two younger convicts lapsed presently into dozing. But Dubosc did not doze. His tormented soul peered out behind its mask as he stood to sweep the skyline again under shaded hand. His theory had been so precise, the fact was so different. He had counted absolutely on meeting the ship—some small schooner, one of those flitting, half-piratical traders of the copra islands that can be hired like cabs in a dark street for any questionable enterprise. Now there was no ship, and here was no cross-roads where one might sit and wait. Such a craft as the catamaran could not be made to lie to.

The doctor foresaw ugly complications for which he had not prepared and whereof he must bear the burden. The escape had been his own conception, directed by him from the start. He had picked his companions deliberately from the whole forced labour squad, Perroquet for his great strength, Fenayrou as a ready echo. He had made it plain since their first dash from the mine, during their skirmish with the military guards, their subsequent wanderings in the brush with bloodhounds and trackers on their trail—through every crisis —that he alone should be the leader.

For the others, they had understood well enough which of their number was the chief beneficiary. Those mysterious friends on the outside that were reaching half around the world to further their release had never heard of such individuals as Fenayrou and The Parrot. Dubosc was the man who had pulled the wires : that brilliant physician whose conviction for murder had followed so sensationally, so scandalously, upon his sweep of academic and social honours. There would be clacking tongues in many a Parisian salon, and white faces in some, when news should come of his escape. Ah, yes, for example, they knew the highflyer of the band, and they submitted—so long as he led them to victory. They submitted, while reserving a depth of jealousy, the inevitable remnant of caste persisting still in this democracy of stripes and shame.

By the middle of the afternoon the doctor had taken certain necessary measures.

"Ho !" said Fenayrou sleepily. "Behold our colours at the masthead. What is that for, comrade ?"

The sail had been lowered and in its place streamed the scrap of crimson scarf that had served Dubosc as a turban.

"To help them sight us when the ship comes."

"What wisdom !" cried Fenayrou. "Always he thinks of everything, our doctor, everything——"

He stopped with the phrase on his lips, and his hand outstretched toward the centre of the platform. Here, in a damp depression among the reeds, had lain the wicker-covered bottle of green glass in which they carried their water. It was gone.

"Where is that flask ?" he demanded. "The sun has grilled me like a bone."

"You will have to grill some more," said Dubosc grimly. "This crew is put on rations."

Fenayrou stared at him wide-eyed, and from the shadow of a folded mat The Parrot thrust his purpled face. "What do you sing me there? Where is that water?"

"I have it," said Dubosc.

They saw, in fact, that he held the flask between his knees, along with their single packet of food in its wrapping of coco-nut husk.

"I want a drink," challenged Perroquet.

"Reflect a little. We must guard our supplies like reason-able men. One does not know how long we may be floating here. . . ."

Fell a silence among them, heavy and strained, in which they heard only the squeaking of frail basketwork as their raft laboured in the wash. Slow as was their progress, they were being pushed steadily outward and onward, and the last cliffs of New Caledonia were no longer even a smudge in the west, but only a hazy line. And still they had seen no moving thing upon the great round breast of the sea that gleamed in its corselet of brass plates under a brazen sun. "So that is the way you talk now?" began The Parrot, half choking. "You do not know how long? But you were sure enough when we started."

"I am still sure," returned Dubosc. "The ship will come. Only she cannot stay for us in one spot. She will be cruising to and fro until she intercepts us. We must wait."

"Ah, good! We must wait. And in the meantime, what? Fry here in the sacred heat with our tongues hanging out while you deal us drop by drop—hein?"

"Perhaps."

"But no!" The garrotter clenched his hands. "Blood of God, there is no man big enough to feed me with a spoon!"

Fenayrou's chuckle came pat, as it had more than once, and Dubosc shrugged.

"You laugh!" cried Perroquet, turning in fury. "But how about this lascar of a captain that lets us put to sea unprovided? What? He thinks of everything, does he? He thinks of everything! . . . Sacred farceur—let me hear you laugh again!"

Somehow Fenayrou was not so minded.

"And now he bids us be reasonable," concluded the Parrot.

"Tell that to the devils in hell. You and your cigarettes, too. Bah—comedian!"

"It is true," muttered Fenayrou, frowning. "A bad piece of work for a captain of runaways."

But the doctor faced mutiny with his thin smile.

"All this alters nothing. Unless we would die very speedily, we must guard our water."

"By whose fault?"

"Mine," acknowledged the doctor. "I admit it. What then? We can't turn back. Here we are. Here we must stay. We can only do our best with what we have."

"I want a drink," repeated The Parrot, whose throat was afire since he had been denied.

"You can claim your share, of course. But take warning of one thing. After it is gone do not think to sponge on us—on Fenayrou and me."

"He would be capable of it, the pig!" exclaimed Fenayrou, to whom this thrust had been directed. "I know him. See here, my old, the doctor is right. Fair for one, fair for all."

"I want a drink."

Dubosc removed the wooden plug from the flask.

"Very well," he said quietly.

With the delicacy that lent something of legerdemain to all his gestures, he took out a small canvas wallet, the crude equivalent of the professional black bag, from which he drew a thimble. Meticulously he poured a brimming measure, and Fenayrou gave a shout at the grumbler's fallen jaw as he accepted that tiny cup between his big fingers. Dubosc served Fenayrou and himself with the same amount before he recorked the bottle.

"In this manner we should have enough to last us three days—maybe more—with equal shares among the three of us. . . ."

Such was his summing of the demonstration, and it passed without comment, as a matter of course in the premises, that he should count as he did—ignoring that other who sat alone at the stern of the raft, the black Canaque, the fourth man.

Perroquet had been out-manœuvred, but he listened sullenly while for the hundredth time Dubosc recited his easy and definite plan for their rescue, as arranged with his secret correspondents.

"That sounds very well," observed The Parrot, at last.

"But what if these jokers only mock themselves of you ? What if they have counted it good riddance to let you rot here ? And us ? Sacred name, that would be a famous jest ! To let us wait for a ship and they have no ship !"

"Perhaps the doctor knows better than we how sure a source he counts upon," suggested Fenayrou slyly.

"That is so," said Dubosc, with great good humour. "My faith, it would not be well for them to fail me. Figure to yourselves that there is a safety vault in Paris full of papers to be opened at my death. Certain friends of mine could hardly afford to have some little confessions published that would be found there . . . Such a tale as this, for instance——"

And to amuse them he told an indecent anecdote of high life, true or fictitious, it mattered nothing, so he could make Fenayrou's eyes glitter and The Parrot growl in wonder. Therein lay his means of ascendancy over such men, the knack of eloquence and vision. Harried, worn, oppressed by fears that he could sense so much more sharply than ever, he must expend himself now in vulgar marvels to distract these ruder minds. He succeeded so far that when the wind fell at sunset they were almost cheerful, ready to believe that the morning would bring relief. They dined on dry biscuit and another thimbleful of water apiece and took watch by amiable agreement. And through that long, clear night of stars whenever the one of the three who kept awake between his comrades chanced to look aft, he could see the vague blot of another figure—the naked Canaque, who slumbered there apart. . . .

It was an evil dawning. Fenayrou, on the morning trick, was aroused by a foot as hard as a hoof, and started up at Perroquet's wrathful face, with the doctor's graver glance behind.

"Idler ! Good-for-nothing ! Will you wake at least before I smash your ribs ? Name of God, here is a way to stand watch !"

"Keep off !" cried Fenayrou wildly. "Keep off. Don't touch me !"

"Eh, and why not, fool ? Do you know that the ship could have missed us ? A ship could have passed us a dozen times while you slept ?"

"Bourrique !"

"Vache !"

They spat the insults of the prison while Perroquet knotted

his great fist over the other, who crouched away cat-like, his mobile mouth twisted to a snarl. Dubosc stood aside in watchful calculation until against the angry red sunrise in which they floated there flashed the naked red gleam of steel. Then he stepped between.

"Enough. Fenayrou, put up that knife."

"The dog kicked me!"

"You were at fault," said Dubosc sternly. "Perroquet!"

"Are we all to die that he may sleep?" stormed The Parrot.

"The harm is done. Listen now, both of you. Things are bad enough already. We may need all our energies. Look about."

They looked and saw the far, round horizon and the empty desert of the sea and their own long shadows that slipped slowly before them over its smooth, slow heaving, and nothing else. The land had sunk away from them in the night—some one of the chance currents that sweep among the islands had drawn them none could say where or how far. The trap had been sprung. "Good God, how lonely it is!" breathed Fenayrou in a hush.

No more was said. They dropped their quarrel. Silently they shared their rations as before, made shift to eat something with their few drops of water, and sat down to pit themselves one against another in the vital struggle that each could feel was coming—a sort of tacit test of endurance.

A calm had fallen, as it does between trades in this flawed belt, an absolute calm. The air hung weighted. The sea showed no faintest crinkle, only the maddening, unresting heave and fall in polished undulations on which the lances of the sun broke and drove in under their eyelids as white, hot splinters; a savage sun that kindled upon them with the power of a burning glass, that sucked the moisture from poor human bits of jelly and sent them crawling to the shelter of their mats and brought them out again, gasping, to shrivel anew. The water, the world of water, seemed sleek and thick as oil. They came to loathe it and the rotting smell of it, and when the doctor made them dip themselves overside they found little comfort. It was warm, sluggish, slimed. But a curious thing resulted. . . .

While they clung along the edge of the raft they all faced inboard, and there sat the black Canaque. He did not join them. He did not glance at them. He sat hunkered on his heels in the way of the native, with arms hugging his knees. He stayed in his place at the stern, motionless under that shattering sun, gazing out into vacancy. Whenever they raised their eyes they saw him. He was the only thing to see.

"Here is one who appears to enjoy himself quite well," remarked Dubosc.

"I was thinking so myself," said Fenayrou.

"The animal!" rumbled Perroquet.

They observed him, and for the first time with direct interest, with thought of him as a fellow-being—with the beginning of envy.

"He does not seem to suffer."

"What is going on in his brain? What does he dream of there? One would say he despises us."

"The beast!"

"Perhaps he is waiting for us to die," suggested Fenayrou with a harsh chuckle. "Perhaps he is waiting for the reward. He would not starve on the way home, at least. And he could deliver us—piecemeal."

They studied him.

"How does he do it, doctor? Has he no feeling?"

"I have been wondering," said Dubosc. "It may be that his fibres are tougher—his nerves."

"Yes, we have had water and he none."

"But look at his skin, fresh and moist."

"And his belly, fat as a football!"

The Parrot hauled himself aboard.

"Don't tell me this black beast knows thirst!" he cried with a strange excitement. "Is there any way he could steal our supplies?"

"Certainly not."

"Then, name of a dog, what if he has supplies of his own hidden about?"

The same monstrous notion struck them all, and the others swarmed to help. They knocked the black aside. They searched the platform where he had set, burrowing among the rushes, seeking some secret cache, another bottle or a gourd. They found nothing.

"We are mistaken," said Dubosc.

But Perroquet had a different expression for disappointment. He turned on the Canaque and caught him by the kinky mop of the hair and proceeded to give him what is known as gruel in the cobalt mines. This was a little speciality of the Parrot's. He paused only when he himself was breathless and exhausted and threw the limp, unresisting body from him.

"There, lump of dirt! That will teach you. Maybe you're not so chipper now, my boy—hein? Not quite so satisfied with your luck. Pig! That will make you feel. . . ."

It was a ludicrous, a wanton, a witless thing. But the others said nothing. The learned Dubosc made no protest. Fenayrou had none of his usual jests at the garrotter's stupidity. They looked on as at the satisfaction of a common grudge. The white trampled the black with or without cause, and that was natural. And the black crept away into his place with his hurts and his wrongs and made no sign and struck no blow. And that was natural, too.

The sun declined into a blazing furnace whereof the gates stood wide, and they prayed to hasten it and cursed because it hung enchanted. But when it was gone their blistered bodies still held the heat like things incandescent. The night closed down over them like a purple bow, glazed and impermeable. They would have divided the watches again, though none of them thought of sleep, but Fenayrou made a discovery.

"Idiots!" he rasped. "Why should we look and look? A whole navy of ships cannot help us now. If we are becalmed, why so are they!"

The Parrot was singularly put out.

"Is this true?" he asked Dubosc.

"Yes, we must hope for a breeze first."

"Then, name of God, why didn't you tell us so? Why did you keep on playing out the farce? You are wise, eh? You are very wise. You know things we do not and you keep them to yourself." He leaned forward to peer into the doctor's face. "Very good. But if you think you're going to use that cursed smartness to get the best of us in any way—see here, my zig, I pull your gullet out like the string of an orange . . . Like that. What?"

Fenayrou gave a nervous giggle and Dubosc shrugged, but it was perhaps about this time that he began to regret his intervention in the knife play.

For there was no breeze and there was no ship.

By the third morning each had sunk within himself, away from the rest. The doctor was lost in a profound depression,

Perroquet in dark suspicion, and Fenayrou in bodily suffering which he supported ill. Only two effective ties still bound their confederacy. One was the flask which Dubosc had slung at his side by a strip of the wickerwork. Every move he made with it, every drop he poured, was followed by burning eyes. And he knew, and he had no advantage of them in knowing, that the will to live was working its relentless formula aboard that raft. Under his careful saving there still remained nearly half of their original store.

The other bond, as it had come to be by strange mutation, was the presence of the black Canaque.

There was no forgetting the fourth man now, no over-looking of him. He loomed upon their consciousness, more formidable, more mysterious, more exasperating with every hour. Their own powers were ebbing. The naked savage had yet to give the slightest sign of complaint or weakness.

During the night he had stretched himself out on the platform as before, and after a time he had slept. Through the hours of darkness and silence while each of the whites wrestled with despair, this black man had slept as placidly as a child, with easy, regular breathing. Since then he had resumed his place aft. And so he remained, unchanged, a fixed fact and a growing wonder.

The brutal rage of Perroquet, in which he had vented his distorted hate of the native, had been followed by super-stitious doubts.

"Doctor," he said at last, in awed huskiness, "is this a man or a fiend ?"

"It is a man."

"A miracle," put in Fenayrou.

But the doctor lifted a finger in a way his pupils would have remembered :

"It is a man," he repeated, "and a very poor and wretched example of a man. Yoy will find no lower type anywhere. Observe his cranial angle, the high ears, the heavy bones of his skull. He is scarcely above the ape. There are educated apes more intelligent."

"Ah ! Then what ?"

"He has a secret," said the doctor.

That was a word to transfix them.

"A secret! But we see him—every move he makes, every instant. What a chance for a secret?"

The doctor rather forgot his audience, betrayed by chagrin and bitterness.

"How pitiful!" he mused. "Here are we three—children of the century, products of civilization—I fancy none would deny that, at least. And here is this man who belongs before the Stone Age. In a set trial of fitness, of wits, or resource, is he to win! Pitiful!"

"What kind of secret!" demanded Perroquet, fuming.

"I cannot say," admitted Dubosc, with a baffled gesture. "Possibly some method of breathing, some peculiar posture that operates to cheat the sensations of the body. Such things are known among primitive peoples—known and carefully guarded—like the properties of certain drugs, the uses of hypnotism and complex natural laws. Then, again, it may be psychologic—a mental attitude persistently held. Who knows?"

"To ask him? Useless. He will not tell. Why should he? We scorn him. We give him no share with us. We abuse him. He simply remains inscrutable—as he has always been and will always be. He never tells those innermost secrets. They are the means by which he has survived from the depth of time, by which he may yet survive when all our wisdom is dust."

"I know several very excellent ways of learning secrets," said Fenayrou as he passed his dry tongue over his lips. "Shall I begin?"

Dubosc came back with a start and looked at him.

"It would be useless. He could stand any torture you could invent. No, that is not the way."

"Listen to mine," said Perroquet, with sudden violence. "Me, I am wearied of the gab. You say he is a man? Very well. If he is a man, he must have blood in his veins. That would be, anyway, good to drink."

"No," returned Dubosc. "It would be hot. Also it would be salt. For food—perhaps. But we do not need food."

"Kill the animal, then, and throw him over!"

"We gain nothing."

"Well, sacred name, what do you want?"

"To beat him!" cried the doctor, curiously agitated. "To

beat him at the game—that's what I want! For our own
sakes, for our racial pride, we must, we must. To outlast
him, to prove ourselves his masters. By better brain, by
better organization and control. Watch him, watch him,
friends—that we may ensnare him, that we may detect and
defeat him in the end!"

But the doctor was miles beyond them.

"Watch?" growled The Parrot. "I believe you, old
windbag. It is all one watch. I sleep no more and leave any
man alone with that bottle."

To this the issue finally sharpened. Such craving among
such men could not be stayed much longer by driblets. They
watched. They watched the Canaque. They watched each
other. And they watched the falling level in their flask—
until the tension gave.

Another dawn upon the same dead calm, rising like a
conflagration through the puddled air, cloudless, hopeless!
Another day of blinding, slow-drawn agony to meet. And
Dubosc announced that their allowance must be cut to half
a thimbleful.

There remained perhaps a quarter of a litre—a miserable
reprieve of bare life among the three of them, but one good
swallow for a yearning throat.

At sight of the bottle, at the tinkle of its limpid contents,
so cool and silvery green inside the glass, Fenayrou's nerve
snapped. . . .

"More!" he begged, with pleading hands. "I die. More!"

When the doctor refused him he grovelled among the
reeds, then rose suddenly to his knees and tossed his arms
abroad with a hoarse cry:

"A ship! A ship!"

The others spun about. They saw the thin unbroken ring
of this greater and more terrible prison to which they had
exchanged: and that was all they saw, though they stared
and stared. They turned back to Fenayrou and found him
in the act of tilting the bottle. A cunning slash of his knife
has loosed it from its sling at the doctor's side. . . . Even
now he was sucking at the mouth, spilling the precious
liquid—

With the one sweep Perroquet caught up their paddle and
flattened him, crushed him.

Springing across the prostrate man, Dubosc snatched the

flask upright and put the width of the raft between himself
and the big garrotter who stood wide-legged, his bloodshot
eyes alight, rumbling in his chest.

"There is no ship," said The Parrot. "There will be no
ship. We are done. Because of you and your rotten promises
that brought us here—doctor, liar, ass!"

Dubosc stood firm.

"Come a step nearer and I break bottle and all over your
head."

They stood regarding each other, and Perroquet's brows
gathered in a slow effort of thought.

"Consider," urged Dubosc with his quaint touch of
pedantry. "Why should you and I fight? We are rational
men. We can see this trouble through and win yet. Such
weather cannot last for ever. Besides, here are only two of
us to divide the water now."

"That is true," nodded The Parrot. "That is true, isn't
it? Fenayrou kindly leaves us his share. An inheritance—
what? A famous idea. I'll take mine now."

Dubosc probed him keenly.

"My share, at once, if you please," insisted Perroquet,
with heavy docility. "Afterward, we shall see. Afterward."

The doctor smiled his grim and wan little smile.

"So be it."

Without relinquishing the flask he brought out his canvas
wallet once more—that wallet which replaced the professional
black bag—and rolled out the thimble by some swift sleight
of his flexible fingers while he held Perroquet's glance with
his own.

"I will measure it for you."

He poured the thimbleful and handed it over quickly, and
when Perroquet had tossed it off he filled again and again.

"Four—five," he counted. "That is enough."

But The Parrot's big grip closed quietly around his wrist
at the last offering and pinioned him and held him helpless.

"No, it is not enough. Now I will take the rest. Ha,
wise man! Have I fooled you at last?"

There was no chance to struggle, and Dubosc did not
try, only stayed smiling up at him, waiting.

Perroquet took the bottle.

"The best man wins," he remarked. "Eh, my zig? A
bright notion—of yours. The—best——"

His lips moved, but no sound issued. A look of the most intense surprise spread upon his round face. He stood swaying a moment, and collapsed like a huge hinged toy when the string is cut.

Dubosc stooped and caught the bottle again, looking down at his big adversary, who sprawled in brief convulsion and lay still, a bluish scum oozing between his teeth. . . .

"Yes, the best man wins," repeated the doctor, and laughed as he in turn raised the flask for a draft.

"The best wins !" echoed a voice in his ear.

Fenayrou, writhing up and striking like a wounded snake, drove the knife home between his shoulders.

The bottle fell and rolled to the middle of the platform, and there, while each strove vainly to reach it, it poured out its treasure in a tiny stream that trickled away and was lost.

It may have been minutes or hours later—for time has no count in emptiness—when next a sound proceeded from that frail slip of a raft, hung like a mote between sea and sky. It was a phrase of song, a wandering strain in half tones and fluted accidentals, not unmelodious. The black Canaque was singing. He sang without emotion or effort, quite casually and softly to himself. So he might sing by his forest hut to ease some hour of idleness. Clasping his knees and gazing out into space, untroubled, unmoved, enigmatic to the end, he sang—he sang.

And after all, the ship came.

She came in a manner befitting the sauciest little tops'l schooner between Nukahiva and the Pelews—as her owner often averred and none but the envious denied—in a manner worthy, too, of that able Captain Jean Guibert, the merriest little scamp that ever cleaned a pearl bank or snapped a cargo of labour from a scowling coast. Before the first whiff out of the west came the *Petite Susanne*, curtsying and skipping along with a flash of white frill by her forefoot, and brought up startled and stood shaking her skirts and keeping herself quite daintily to windward.

"And 'ere they are sure enough, by dam' !" said the polyglot Captain Jean in the language of commerce and profanity. "Zose passengers for us, hey ? They been here all the time, not ten mile off—I bet you, Marteau. Ain't it 'ell ? What you zink, my gar ?"

The second, a tall and excessively bony individual of gloomy outlook, handed back the glasses.

"More bad luck. I never approved of this job. And now —see ?—we have had our voyage for nothing. What misfortune !"

"Marteau, if that good Saint Pierre gives you some day a gold 'arp still you would holler bad luck—bad job !" retorted Captain Jean. "Do I 'ire you to stand zere and cry about ze luck ? Get a boat over, and quicker zan zat !"

M. Marteau aroused himself sufficiently to take command of the boat's crew that presently dropped away to investigate. . . .

"It is even as I thought," he called up from the quarter when he returned with his report. "I told you how it would be, Captain Jean."

"Hey ?" cried the captain, bouncing at the rail. "Have you got zose passengers yet, *enfant de salaud* ?"

"I have not," said Marteau in the tone of lugubrious triumph. There was nothing in the world that could have pleased him quite so much as this chance to prove Captain Jean the loser on a venture. "We are too late. Bad luck, bad luck—that calm. What misfortune ! They are all dead !"

"Will you mind your business ?" shouted the skipper.

"But still, the gentlemen are dead——"

"What is zat to me ? All ze better, they will cost nozing to feed."

"But how——"

"Hogsheads, my gar," said Captain Jean paternally. "Zose hogsheads in the afterhold. Fill them nicely with brine, and zere we are !" And, having drawn all possible satisfaction from the other's amazement, he sprang the nub of his joke with a grin. "Ze gentlemen's passage is all paid, Marteau. Before we left Sydney, Marteau. I contrac' to bring back three escape' convicts, and so by 'ell I do—in pickle ! And now if you'll kindly get zose passengers aboard like I said an' bozzer less about ze goddam luck, I be much oblige'. Also, zere is no green on my eye, Marteau, and you can dam' well smoke it !"

Marteau recovered himself with difficulty in time to recall another trifling detail. "There is a fourth man on board that raft, Captain Jean. He is a Canaque—still alive. What shall we do with him ?"

"A Canaque?" snapped Captain Jean. "A Canaque! I have no word in my contrac' about any Canaque. . . . Leave him zere. . . . He is only a dam' nigger. He'll do well enough where he is."

And Captain Jean was right, perfectly right, for while the *Petite Susanne* was taking aboard her grisly cargo the wind freshened from the west, and just about the time she was shaping away for Australia the "dam' nigger" spread his own sail of pandanus leaves and twirled his own helm of niaouli wood and headed the catamaran eastward, back toward New Caledonia.

Feeling somewhat dry after his exertion, he plucked at random from the platform a hollow reed from a sharp end, and, stretching himself at full length in his accustomed place, at the stern, he thrust the reed down into one of the bladders underneath and drank his fill of sweet water. . . .

He had a dozen such storage bladders remaining, built into the floats at intervals above the water line—quite enough to last him safely home again.

DRACULA'S GUEST
Bram Stoker

WHEN we started for our drive the sun was shining brightly on Munich, and the air was full of the joyousness of early summer. Just as we were about to depart, Herr Delbrück (the maître d'hôtel of the Quatre Saisons, where I was staying) came down, bareheaded, to the carriage and, after wishing me a pleasant drive, said to the coachman, still holding his hand on the handle of the carriage door:

"Remember you are back by nightfall. The sky looks bright, but there is a shiver in the north wind that says there may be a sudden storm. But I am sure you will not be late." Here he smiled, and added, "For you know what night it is."

Johann answered with an emphatic, "Ja, mein Herr," and, touching his hat, drove off quickly. When we had cleared the town, I said, after signalling to him to stop:

"Tell me, Johann, what is tonight?"

He crossed himself, as he answered laconically: "Walpurgis nacht." Then he took out his watch, a great, old-fashioned German-silver thing as big as a turnip, and looked at it, with his eyebrows gathered together and a little impatient shrug of his shoulders. I realized that this was his way of respectfully protesting against the unnecessary delay, and sank back in the carriage, merely motioning him to proceed. He started off rapidly, as if to make up for lost time. Every now and then the horses seemed to throw up their heads and sniffed the air suspiciously. On such occasions I often looked round in alarm. The road was pretty bleak, for we were traversing a sort of high, wind-swept plateau. As we drove, I saw a road that looked but little used, and which seemed to dip through a little winding valley. It looked so inviting that, even at the risk of offending him, I called Johann to stop. And when he had pulled up I told him I would like to drive down that road. He made all sorts of excuses, and frequently crossed himself as he spoke. This somewhat piqued my curiosity, so I asked him various questions. He answered fencingly, and repeatedly looked at his watch in protest. Finally I said :

"Well, Johann, I want to go down this road. I shall not ask you to come unless you like ; but tell me why you do not like to go, that is all I ask." For answer he seemed to throw himself off the box, so quickly did he reach the ground. Then he stretched out his hands appealingly to me, and implored me not to go. There was just enough of English mixed with the German for me to understand the drift of his talk. He seemed always just about to tell me something—the very idea of which evidently frightened him ; but each time he pulled himself up, saying, as he crossed himself : "Walpurgis nacht !"

I tried to argue with him, but it was difficult to argue with a man when I did not know his language. The advantage certainly rested with him, for although he began to speak in English—of a very crude and broken kind—he always got excited and broke into his native tongue—and every time he did so he looked at his watch. Then the horses became restless and sniffed the air. At this he grew very pale, and, looking around in a frightened way, he suddenly jumped forward, took them by the bridles and led them on some twenty feet. I followed, and asked why he had done this. For answer he crossed himself, pointed to the spot we had left, and drew his carriage in the direction of the other road, indicating a cross, and said, first in German, then in English : "Buried him—him what killed themselves."

I remembered the old custom of burying suicides at crossroads : "Ah ! I see, a suicide. How interesting !" But for the life of me I could not make out why the horses were frightened.

Whilst we were talking, we heard a sort of sound between a yelp and a bark. It was far away ; but the horses got very restless, and it took Johann all his time to quiet them. He was pale, and said : "It sounds like a wolf—but yet there are no wolves here now."

"No ?" I said, questioning him ; "isn't it long since the wolves were so near the city ?"

"Long, long," he answered, "in the spring and summer ; but with the snow the wolves have been here not so long."

Whilst he was petting the horses and trying to quiet them,

dark clouds drifted rapidly across the sky. The sunshine passed away, and a breath of cold wind seemed to drift past us. It was only a breath, however, and more in the nature of a warning than a fact, for the sun came out brightly again. Johann looked under his lifted hand at the horizon and said :

"The storm of snow, he comes before long time." Then he looked at his watch again, and, straightway, holding his reins firmly—for the horses were still pawing the ground restlessly, and shaking their heads—he climbed to his box as though the time had come for proceeding on our journey.

I felt a little obstinate, and did not at once get into the carriage.

"Tell me," I said, "about this place where the road leads." And I pointed down.

Again he crossed himself and mumbled a prayer, before he answered : "It is unholy."

"What is unholy ?" I enquired.

"The village."

"Then there is a village ?"

"No, no. No one lives there hundreds of years."

My curiosity was piqued : "But you said there was a village."

"There was."

"Where is it now ?"

Whereupon he burst out into a long story in German and English, so mixed up that I could not quite understand exactly what he said, but roughly I gathered that long ago, hundreds of years, men had died there and been buried in their graves ; and sounds were heard under the clay, and when the graves were opened, men and women were found rosy with life, and their mouths red with blood. And so, in haste to save their lives (ay, and their souls !—and here he crossed himself), those who were left fled away to other places, where the living lived, and the dead were dead and not—not something. He was evidently afraid to speak the last words. As he proceeded with his narration, he grew more and more excited. It seemed as if his imagination had got hold of him, and he ended in a perfect paroxysm of fear—white-faced, perspiring, trembling and looking round him, as if expecting that some dreadful presence would manifest itself there in the bright sunshine on the open plain. Finally, in an agony of desperation, he cried :

"Walpurgis nacht !" and pointed to the carriage for me to get in. All my English blood rose at this, and, standing back, I said :

"You are afraid, Johann—you are afraid. Go home ; I shall return alone ; the walk will do me good." The carriage door was open. I took from the seat my oak walking-stick— which I always carry on my holiday excursions—and closed the door, pointing back to Munich, and said, "Go home, Johann—Walpurgis nacht doesn't concern Englishmen."

The horses were now more restive than ever, and Johann was trying to hold them in, while excitedly imploring me not to do anything so foolish. I pitied the poor fellow, he was so deeply in earnest ; but all the same I could not help laughing. His English was quite gone now. In his anxiety he had forgotten that his only means of making me understand was to talk my language, so he jabbered away in his native German. It began to be a little tedious. After giving the direction, "Home !" I turned to go down the cross-road into the valley.

With a despairing gesture, Johann turned his horses towards Munich. I leaned on my stick and looked after him. He went slowly along the road for a while : then there came over the crest of the hill a man tall and thin. I could see so much in the distance. When he drew near the horses, they began to jump and kick about, then to scream with terror. Johann could not hold them in ; they bolted down the road, running away madly. I watched them out of sight, then looked for the stranger, but I found that he, too, was gone.

With a light heart I turned down the side road through the deepening valley to which Johann had objected. There was not the slightest reason, that I could see, for his objection ; and I dare say I tramped for a couple of hours without thinking of time or distance, and certainly without seeing a person or a house. So far as the place was concerned, it was desolation itself. But I did not notice this particularly till, on turning a bend in the road, I came upon a scattered fringe of wood ; then I recognized that I had been impressed unconsciously by the desolation of the region through which I had passed.

I sat down to rest myself, and began to look around. It struck me that it was considerably colder than it had been at the commencement of my walk—a sort of sighing sound seemed to be around me, with, now and then, high overhead, a sort of muffled roar. Looking upwards, I noticed that great thick clouds were drifting rapidly across the sky from north to south at a great height. There were signs of coming storm in some lofty stratum of the air. I was a little chilly, and, thinking that it was the sitting still after the exercise of walking, I resumed my journey.

The ground I passed over was now much more picturesque. There were no striking objects that the eye might single out ; but in all there was a charm of beauty. I took little heed of time and it was only when the deepening twilight forced itself upon me that I began to think of how I should find my way home. The brightness of the day had gone. The air was cold, and the drifting of clouds high overhead was more marked. They were accompanied by a sort of far-away rushing sound, through which seemed to come at intervals that mysterious cry which the driver had said came from a wolf. For a while I hesitated. I had said I would see the deserted village, so on I went, and presently came on a wide stretch of open country shut in by hills all around. Their sides were covered with trees, which spread down to the plain, dotting, in clumps, the gentler slopes and hollows which showed here and there. I followed with my eye the winding of the road, and saw that it curved close to one of the densest of these clumps and was lost behind it.

As I looked there came a cold shiver in the air, and the snow began to fall. I thought of the miles and miles of bleak country I had passed, and then hurried on to seek the shelter of the wood in front. Darker and darker grew the sky, and faster and heavier fell the snow, till the earth before and around me was a glistening white carpet the farther edge of which was lost in misty vagueness. The road was here but crude, and, when on the level, its boundaries were not so marked as when it passed through the cuttings ; and in a little while I found that I must have strayed from it, for I missed underfoot the hard surface, and my feet sank deeper in the grass and moss. Then the wind grew stronger and blew with ever increasing force, till I was fain to run before it. The air became icy-cold, and in spite of my exercise I began to suffer. The snow was now falling so thickly and whirling around me in such rapid eddies that I could hardly keep my eyes open. Every now and then the heavens were torn asunder by vivid lightning, and in the flashes I could see ahead of me a great mass of trees, chiefly yew and cypress all heavily coated with snow.

I was soon amongst the shelter of the trees, and there, in comparative silence, I could hear the rush of the wind high overhead. Presently the blackness of the storm had become merged in the darkness of the night. By and by the storm seemed to be passing away : it now only came in fierce puffs or blasts. At such moments the weird sound of the wolf appeared to be echoed by many similar sounds around me.

Now and again, through the black mass of drifting cloud, came a straggling ray of moonlight, which lit up the expanse, and showed me that I was at the edge of a dense mass of cypress and yew trees. As the snow had ceased to fall, I walked out from the shelter and began to investigate more closely. It appeared to me that, amongst so many old founda-tions as I had passed, there might be still standing a house in which, though in ruins, I could find some sort of shelter for a while. As I skirted the edge of the copse, I found that a low wall encircled it, and following this I presently found an opening. Here the cypresses formed an alley leading up to a square mass of some kind of building. Just as I caught sight of this, however, the drifting clouds obscured the moon, and I passed up the path in darkness. The wind must have grown colder, for I felt myself shiver as I walked ; but there was hope of shelter, and I groped my way blindly on.

I stopped, for there was a sudden stillness. The storm had passed ; and, perhaps in sympathy with Nature's silence, my heart seemed to cease to beat. But this was only moment-arily ; for suddenly the moonlight broke through the clouds, showing me that I was in a graveyard, and that the square object before me was a great massive tomb of marble, as white as the snow that lay on and all around it. With the moonlight there came a fierce sigh of the storm, which appeared to resume its course with a long, low howl, as of many dogs or wolves. I was awed and shocked, and felt the cold perceptibly grow upon me till it seemed to grip me by the heart. Then, while the flood of moonlight still fell on the marble tomb, the storm gave further evidence of renewing—as though it was returning on its track. Impelled by some sort of fascination, I approached the sepulchre to see what it was, and why such a thing stood alone in such a place. I walked around it, and read, over the Doric door, in German :

COUNTESS DOLINGER OF GRATZ
IN STYRIA
SOUGHT AND FOUND DEAD
1801

On the top of the tomb, seemingly driven through the solid marble—for the structure was composed of a few vast blocks of stone—was a great iron spike or stake. On going to the back I saw, graven in great Russian letters :

The dead travel fast.

There was something so weird and uncanny about the whole thing that it gave me a turn and made me feel quite faint. I began to wish, for the first time, that I had taken Johann's advice. Here a thought struck me, which came under almost mysterious circumstances and with a terrible shock. This was Walpurgis night !

Walpurgis night, when, according to the belief of millions of people, the devil was abroad—when the graves were opened and the dead came forth and walked. When all evil things of earth and air and water held revel. This very place the driver had specially shunned. This was the depopulated village of centuries ago. This was where the suicide lay ; and this was the place where I was alone—unmanned, shivering with cold in a shroud of snow with a wild storm gathering again upon me ! It took all my philosophy, all the religion I had been taught, all my courage, not to collapse in a paroxysm of fright.

And now a perfect tornado burst upon me. The ground shook as though thousands of horses thundered across it ; and this time the storm bore on its icy wings, not snow, but great hailstones which drove with such violence that they might have come from the thongs of Balearic slingers— hailstones that beat down leaf and branch and made the shelter of the cypresses of no more avail than though their stems were standing corn. At the first I had rushed to the nearest tree ; but I was soon fain to leave it and seek the only spot that seemed to afford refuge, the deep Doric door-way of the marble tomb. There, crouching against the massive bronze door, I gained a certain amount of protection from the beating of the hailstones, for now they only drove against me as they ricochetted from the ground and the side of the marble.

As I leaned against the door it moved slightly and opened inwards. The shelter of even a tomb was welcome in that pitiless tempest, and I was about to enter it when there came a flash of forked lightning that lit up the whole expanse of the heavens. In the instant, as I am a living man, I saw, as my eyes were turned into the darkness of the tomb, a beautiful woman, with rounded cheeks and red lips, seemingly sleeping on a bier. As the thunder broke overhead, I was grasped as by the hand of a giant and hurled out into the storm. The whole thing was so sudden that, before I could realize the shock, moral as well as physical, I found the hailstones beating me down. At the same time I had a strange, dominating feeling that I was not alone. I looked towards the tomb. Just then there came another blinding flash, which seemed to strike the iron stake that surmounted the tomb and to pour through to the earth, blasting and crumbling the marble, as in a burst of flame. The dead woman rose for a moment of agony, while she was lapped in the flame, and her bitter scream of pain was drowned in the thundercrash. The last thing I heard was this mingling of dreadful sound, as again I was seized in the giant grasp and dragged away, while the hailstones beat on me, and the air around seemed reverberant with the howling of wolves. The last sight that I remembered was a vague, white, moving mass, as if all the graves around me had sent out the phantoms of their sheeted dead, and that they were closing in on me through the white cloudiness of the driving hail.

· · · · ·

Gradually there came a sort of vague beginning of consciousness ; then a sense of weariness that was dreadful. For a time I remembered nothing ; but slowly my senses returned. My feet seemed positively racked with pain, yet I could not move them. They seemed to be numbed. There was an icy feeling at the back of my neck and all down my spine, and my ears, like my feet, were dead, yet in torment ; but there was in my breast a sense of warmth which was, by comparison, delicious. It was as a nightmare—a physical nightmare, if one may use such an expression ; for some heavy weight on my chest made it difficult for me to breathe.

This period of semi-lethargy seemed to remain a long time, and as it faded away I must have slept or swooned. Then came a sort of loathing, like the first stage of sea-sickness, and a wild desire to be free from something—I knew not what. A vast stillness enveloped me, as though all the world were asleep or dead—only broken by the low panting as of some animal close to me. I felt a warm rasping at my throat, then came a consciousness of the awful truth, which chilled me to the heart and sent the blood surging up through my brain. Some great animal was lying on me and now licking my throat. I feared to stir, for some instinct of prudence bade me lie still ; but the brute seemed to realize that there was now some change in me, for it raised its head. Through my eyelashes I saw above me the two great flaming eyes of a gigantic wolf. Its sharp white teeth gleamed in the gaping red mouth, and I could feel its hot breath fierce and acrid upon me.

For another spell of time I remembered no more. Then I became conscious of a low growl, followed by a yelp, renewed again and again. Then, seemingly very far away, I heard a "Holloa ! Holloa !" as of many voices calling in unison. Cautiously I raised my head and looked in the direction whence the sound came ; but the cemetery blocked my view. The wolf still continued to yelp in a strange way, and a red glare began to move round the grove of cypresses, as though follow- ing the sound. As the voices drew closer, the wolf yelped faster and louder. I feared to make either sound or motion. Nearer came the red glow, over the white pall which stretched into the darkness around me. Then all at once from beyond the trees there came at a trot a troop of horsemen bearing torches. The wolf rose from my breast and made for the cemetery. I saw one of the horsemen (soldiers by their caps and their long military cloaks) raise his carbine and take aim. A companion knocked up his arm, and I heard the ball whizz over my head. He had evidently taken my body for that of the wolf. Another sighted the animal as it slunk away, and a shot followed. Then, at a gallop, the troop rode forward ; some towards me, others following the wolf as it disappeared amongst the snow-clad cypresses.

As they drew nearer I tried to move, but was powerless, although I could see and hear all that went on around me. Two or three of the soldiers jumped from their horses and knelt beside me. One of them raised my head, and placed his hand over my heart.

"Good news, comrades !" he cried. "His heart still beats !"

Then some brandy was poured down my throat ; it put vigour into me, and I was able to open my eyes fully and look around. Lights and shadows were moving among the trees, and I heard men call to one another. They drew together uttering frightened exclamations ; and the lights flashed as the others came pouring out of the cemetery pell-mell, like men possessed. When the farther ones came close to us, those who were around me asked them eagerly :

"Well, have you found him ?"

The reply rang out hurriedly :

"No ! No ! Come away quick—quick ! This is no place to stay, and on this of all nights !"

"What was it ?" was the question, asked in all manner of keys. The answer came variously and all indefinitely as though the men were moved by some common impulse to speak, yet were restrained by some common fear from giving their thoughts.

"It—it—indeed !" gibbered one, whose wits had plainly given out for the moment.

"A wolf—and yet not a wolf !" another put in shudderingly.

"No use trying for him without the sacred bullet," a third remarked in a more ordinary manner.

"Serve us right for coming out on this night ! Truly we have earned our thousand marks !" were the ejaculations of a fourth.

"There was blood on the broken marble," another said after a pause ; "the lightning never brought that there. And for him—is he safe ? Look at his throat ! See, comrades, the wolf has been lying on him and keeping his blood warm."

The officer looked at my throat and replied :

"He is all right; the skin is not pierced. What does it all mean ? We should never have found him but for the yelping of the wolf."

"What became of it ?" asked the man who was holding up my head, and who seemed the least panic-stricken of the party, for his hands were steady and without tremor. On his sleeve was the chevron of a petty officer.

"It went to its home," answered the man, whose long face was pallid, and who actually shook with terror as he glanced around him fearfully. "There are graves enough there in which it may lie. Come, comrades—come quickly! Let us leave this cursed spot."

The officer raised me to a sitting posture as he uttered a word of command; then several men placed me upon a horse. He sprang to the saddle behind me, took me in his arms, gave the word to advance; and, turning our faces away from the cypresses, we rode away in swift, military order.

As yet my tongue refused its office, and I was perforce silent. I must have fallen asleep; for the next thing I remembered was finding myself standing up, supported by a soldier on each side of me. It was almost broad daylight, and to the north a red streak of sunlight was reflected, like a path of blood, over the waste of snow. The officer was telling the men to say nothing of what they had seen, except that they found an English stranger, guarded by a large dog.

"Dog! That was no dog," cut in the man who had exhibited such fear. "I think I know a wolf when I see one."

The young officer answered calmly: "I said a dog."

"Dog!" reiterated the other ironically. It was evident that his courage was rising with the sun; and, pointing to me, he said, "Look at his throat. Is that the work of a dog, master?"

Instinctively I raised my hand to my throat, and as I touched it I cried out in pain. The men crowded round to look, some stooping down from their saddles; and again there came the calm voice of the young officer:

"A dog, as I said. If aught else were said we should only be laughed at."

I was then mounted behind a trooper, and we rode on into the suburbs of Munich. Here we came across a stray carriage, into which I was lifted, and it was driven off to the Quatre Saisons—the young officer accompanying me, whilst a trooper followed with his horse, and the others rode off to their barracks.

When we arrived, Herr Delbrück rushed so quickly down the steps to meet me that it was apparent he had been watching within. Taking me by both hands he solicitously led me in. The officer saluted me and was turning to withdraw, when I recognized his purpose, and insisted that he should come to my rooms. Over a glass of wine I warmly thanked him and his brave comrades for saving me. He replied simply that he was more than glad, and that Herr Delbrück had at the first taken steps to make all the searching-party pleased; at which ambiguous utterance the maître d'hôtel smiled, while the officer pleaded duty and withdrew.

"But Herr Delbrück," I inquired, "how and why was it that the soldiers searched for me?"

He shrugged his shoulders, as if in depreciation of his own deed, as he replied:

"I was so fortunate as to obtain leave, from the commander of the regiment in which I served, to ask for volunteers."

"But how did you know I was lost?" I asked.

"The driver came hither with the remains of his carriage, which had been upset when the horses ran away."

"But surely you would not send a search-party of soldiers merely on this account?"

"Oh no!" he answered; "but even before the coachman arrived, I had this telegram from the Boyar whose guest you are," and he took from his pocket a telegram, which he handed to me, and I read:

Bistrize.

Be careful of my guest—his safety is most precious to me. Should aught happen to him, or if he be missed, spare nothing to find him and ensure his safety. He is English and therefore adventurous. There are often dangers from snow and wolves and night. Lose not a moment if you suspect harm to him. I answer your zeal with my fortune.

Dracula.

As I held the telegram in my hand, the room seemed to whirl around me; and, if the attentive maître d'hôtel had not caught me, I think I should have fallen. There was something so strange in all this, something so weird and impossible to imagine, that there grew on me a sense of my being in some way the sport of opposite forces—the mere vague idea of which seemed in a way to paralyse me. I was certainly under some form of mysterious protection. From a distant country had come, in the very nick of time, a message that took me out of the danger of the snow-sleep and the jaws of the wolf.

THE FALL OF THE HOUSE OF USHER
Edgar Allan Poe

DURING the whole of a dull, dark, and soundless day in the autumn of the year, when the clouds hung oppressively low in the heavens, I had been passing alone, on horseback, through a singularly drear tract of country; and at length found myself, as the shades of the evening drew on, within view of the melancholy House of Usher. I know not how it was—but, with the first glimpse of the building, a sense of insufferable gloom pervaded my spirit. I say insufferable; for the feeling was unrelieved by any of that half-pleasurable, because poetic, sentiment, with which the mind usually receives even the sternest natural images of the desolate or terrible. I looked upon the scene before me—upon the mere house, and the simple landscape features of the domain—upon the bleak walls—upon the vacant eye-like windows—upon a few rank sedges—and upon a few white trunks of decayed trees—with an utter depression of soul which I can compare to no earthly sensation more properly than to the after-dream of the reveller upon opium—the bitter lapse into everyday life—the hideous dropping off of the veil. There was an iciness, a sinking, a sickening of the heart—an unredeemed dreariness of thought which no goading of the imagination could torture into aught of the sublime. What was it—I paused to think—what was it that so unnerved me in the contemplation of the House of Usher? It was a mystery all insoluble; nor could I grapple with the shadowy fancies that crowded upon me as I pondered. I was forced to fall back upon the unsatisfactory conclusion, that while, beyond doubt, there *are* combinations of very simple natural objects which have the power of thus affecting us, still the analysis of this power lies among considerations beyond our depth. It was possible, I reflected, that a mere different arrangement of the particulars of the scene, of the details of the picture, would be sufficient to modify, or perhaps to annihilate its capacity for sorrowful impression; and, acting upon this idea, I reined my horse to the precipitous brink of a black and lurid tarn that lay in unruffled lustre by the dwelling, and gazed down—but with a shudder even more thrilling than before—upon the remodelled and inverted images of the grey sedge, and the ghastly tree-stems, and the vacant and eye-like windows.

Nevertheless, in this mansion of gloom I now proposed to myself a sojourn of some weeks. Its proprietor, Roderick Usher, had been one of my boon companions in boyhood; but many years had elapsed since our last meeting. A letter, however, had lately reached me in a distant part of the country —a letter from him—which, in its wildly importunate nature had admitted of no other than a personal reply. The MS. gave evidence of nervous agitation. The writer spoke of acute bodily illness—of a mental disorder which oppressed him— and of an earnest desire to see me, as his best and indeed his only personal friend, with a view of attempting, by the cheerfulness of my society, some alleviation of his malady. It was the manner in which all this, and much more, was said—it was the apparent *heart* that went with his request—which allowed me no room for hesitation; and I accordingly obeyed forthwith what I still considered a very singular summons.

Although, as boys, we had been even intimate associates, yet I really knew little of my friend. His reserve had always been excessive and habitual. I was aware, however, that his very ancient family had been noted, time out of mind, for a peculiar sensibility of temperament, displaying itself, through long ages, in many works of exalted art, and manifested, of late, in repeated deeds of munificent yet unobtrusive charity, as well as a passionate devotion to the intricacies, perhaps even more than to the orthodox and easily recognisable beauties of musical science. I had learned, too, the very remarkable fact that the stem of the Usher race, all time-honoured as it was, had put forth, at no period, any enduring branch; in other words, that the entire family lay in the direct line of descent, and had always, with very trifling and very temporary variation, so lain. It was this deficiency, I considered, while running over in thought the perfect keeping of the character of the premises with the accredited character of the people, and while speculating upon the possible influence which the one, in the long lapse of centuries, might have exercised upon the other—it was this deficiency, perhaps, of collateral issue, and the consequent undeviating transmission from sire to son of the patrimony with the name, which had, at length, so identified the two, as to merge the original title of the estate in the quaint and equivocal appellation of the " House of Usher "—an appellation which seemed to include, in the minds of the peasantry who used it, both the family and the family mansion.

I have said that the sole effect of a somewhat childish experiment—that of looking down within the tarn—had been to deepen the first singular impression. There can be no doubt that the consciousness of the rapid increase of my superstition—for why should I not so term it ?—served mainly to accelerate the increase itself. Such, I have long known, is the paradoxical law of all sentiments having terror as their basis. And it might have been for this reason only that, when I again uplifted my eyes to the house itself, from its image in the pool, there grew in my mind a strange fancy—a fancy so ridiculous, indeed, that I but mention it to show the vivid force of the sensations which oppressed me. I had so worked upon my imagination as really to believe that about the whole mansion and domain there hung an atmosphere peculiar to themselves and their immediate vicinity—an atmosphere which had no affinity with the air of heaven, but which had reeked up from the decayed trees, and the grey wall, and the silent tarn—a pestilent and mystic vapour, dull, sluggish, faintly discernible, and leaden-hued.

Shaking off from my spirit what *must* have been a dream, I scanned more narrowly the real aspect of the building. Its principal feature seemed to be that of an excessive antiquity. The discoloration of ages had been great. Minute fungi overspread the whole exterior, hanging in a fine tangled web-work from the eaves. Yet all this was apart from any extraordinary dilapidation. No portion of the masonry had fallen ; and there appeared to be a wild inconsistency between its still perfect adaptation of parts and the crumbling condition of the individual stones. In this there was much that reminded me of the specious totality of old woodwork which has rotted for long years in some neglected vault, with no disturbance from the breath of the external air. Beyond this indication of excessive decay, however, the fabric gave little token of instability. Perhaps the eye of a scrutinizing observer might have discovered a barely perceptible fissure, which, extending from the roof of the building in front, made its way down the wall in a zigzag direction, until it became lost in the sullen waters of the tarn.

Noticing these things, I rode over a short causeway to the house. A servant in waiting took my horse, and I entered the Gothic archway of the hall. A valet, of stealthy step, thence conducted me, in silence, through many dark and intricate passages in my progress to the *studio* of his master. Much that I encountered on the way contributed, I know not how, to heighten the vague sentiments of which I have already spoken. While the objects around me—while the carvings of the ceilings, the sombre tapestries of the walls, the ebon blackness of the floors, and the phantasmagoric armorial trophies which rattled as I strode, were but matters to which, or to such as which, I had been accustomed from my infancy—while I hesitated not to acknowledge how familiar was all this—I still wondered to find how unfamiliar were the fancies which ordinary images were stirring up. On one of the staircases, I met the physician of the family. His countenance, I thought, wore a mingled expression of low cunning and perplexity. He accosted me with trepidation, and passed on. The valet now threw open a door, and ushered me into the presence of his master.

The room in which I found myself was very large and lofty. The windows were long, narrow, and pointed, and at so vast a distance from the black oaken floor as to be almost inaccessible from within. Feeble gleams of encrimsoned light made their way through the trellised panes, and served to render sufficiently distinct the more prominent objects around ; the eye, however, struggled in vain to reach the remoter angles of the chamber, or the recesses of the vaulted and fretted ceiling. Dark draperies hung upon the wall. The general furniture was profuse, comfortless, antique, and tattered. Many books and musical instruments lay scattered about, but failed to give any vitality to the scene. I felt that I breathed an atmosphere of sorrow. An air of stern, deep, and irredeemable gloom hung over and pervaded all.

Upon my entrance, Usher arose from a sofa on which he had been lying at full length and greeted me with a vivacious warmth which had much in it, I at first thought, of an overdone cordiality—of the constrained effort of the *ennuyé* man of the world. A glance, however, at his countenance, convinced me of his perfect sincerity. We sat down ; and for some moments, while he spoke not, I gazed upon him with a feeling half of pity, half of awe. Surely, man had never before so terribly altered, in so brief a period, as had Roderick Usher! It was with difficulty that I could bring myself to admit the identity of the wan thing before me with the companion of my early boyhood. Yet the character of his face had at all times been remarkable. A cadaverousness of complexion; an eye large, liquid, and luminous beyond comparison; lips somewhat thin and very pallid, but of a surpassingly beautiful curve; a nose of a delicate Hebrew model, but with a breadth of nostril usual in similar formations; a finely moulded chin speaking, in its want of prominence, of a want of moral energy; hair of a more than web-like softness and tenuity; these features, with an inordinate expansion above the regions of the temple, made up altogether a countenance not easily to be forgotten. And now in the mere exaggeration of the prevailing character of these features, and of the expression they were wont to convey, lay so much of change that I doubted to whom I spoke. The now ghastly pallor of the skin, and the now miraculous lustre of the eye, above all things startled and even awed me. The silken hair, too, had been suffered to grow, all unheeded, and as, in its wild gossamer texture, it floated rather than fell about the face, I could not, even with effort, connect its arabesque expression with any idea of simple humanity.

In the manner of my friend I was at once struck with an incoherence—an inconsistency; and I soon found this to arise from a series of feeble and futile struggles to overcome an habitual trepidancy—an excessive nervous agitation. For something of this nature I had indeed been prepared, no less by his letter than by reminiscences of certain boyish traits, and by conclusions deducted from his peculiar physical conformation and temperament. His action was alternately vivacious and sullen. His voice varied rapidly from a tremulous indecision (when the animal spirit seemed utterly in abeyance) to that species of energetic concision—that abrupt, weighty, unhurried and hollow-sounding enunciation—that leaden, self-balanced and perfectly modulated guttural utterance, which may be observed in the lost drunkard, or the irreclaimable eater of opium, during the periods of his most intense excitement.

It was thus that he spoke of the object of my visit, of his

earnest desire to see me, and of the solace he expected me to afford him. He entered, at some length, into what he conceived to be the nature of his malady. It was, he said, a constitutional and a family evil, and one for which he despaired to find a remedy—a mere nervous affection, he immediately added, which would undoubtedly soon pass off. It displayed itself in a host of unnatural sensations. Some of these, as he detailed them, interested and bewildered me ; although, perhaps, the terms, and the general manner of the narration, had their weight. He suffered much from a morbid acuteness of the senses ; the most insipid food alone was endurable ; he could wear only garments of a certain texture ; the odours of all flowers were oppressive ; his eyes were tortured by even a faint light ; and there were but peculiar sounds, and these from stringed instruments, which did not inspire him with horror.

To an anomalous species of terror I found him a bounden slave. " I shall perish," said he ; " I *must* perish in this deplorable folly. Thus, thus, and not otherwise, shall I be lost. I dread the events of the future, not in themselves, but in their results. I shudder at the thought of any, even the most trivial incident, which may operate upon this intolerable agitation of soul. I have, indeed, no abhorrence of danger except in its absolute effect—in terror. In this unnerved—in this pitiable condition—I feel that the period will sooner or later arrive when I must abandon life and reason altogether in some struggle with the grim phantasm, FEAR."

I learned, moreover, at intervals, and through broken and equivocal hints, another singular feature of his mental condition. He was enchained by certain superstitious impressions in regard to the dwelling which he tenanted, and whence, for many years, he had never ventured forth—in regard to an influence whose supposititious force was conveyed in terms too shadowy here to be restated—an influence which some peculiarities in the mere form and substance of his family mansion had, by dint of long suffering he said, obtained over his spirit—an effect which the *physique* of the grey walls and turrets, and of the dim tarn into which they all looked down, had, at length, brought about upon the *morale* of his existence.

He admitted, however, although with hesitation, that much of the peculiar gloom which thus afflicted him could be traced to a more natural and far more palpable origin—to the severe and long-continued illness—indeed to the evidently appoaching dissolution—of a tenderly beloved sister—his sole companion for long years—his last and only relative on earth. "Her decease," he said, with a bitterness which I can never forget, "would leave him (him the hopeless and the frail) the last of the ancient race of the Ushers." While he spoke, the lady Madeline (for so was she called) passed slowly through a remote portion of the apartment, and, without having noticed my presence, disappeared. I regarded her with an utter astonishment not unmingled with dread—and yet I found it impossible to account for such feelings. A sensation of stupor oppressed me, as my eyes followed her retreating steps. When a door at length closed upon her, my glance sought instinctively and eagerly the countenance of the brother—but he had buried his face in his hands, and I could only perceive that a far more than ordinary wanness had overspread the emaciated fingers through which trickled many passionate tears.

The disease of the lady Madeline had long baffled the skill of her physicians. A settled apathy, a gradual wasting away of the person, and frequent although transient affections of apartially cataleptical character, were the unusual diagnosis. Hitherto she had steadily borne up against the pressure of her malady, and had not betaken herself finally to bed; but on the closing in of the evening of my arrival at the house she succumbed (as her brother told me at night with inexpressible agitation) to the prostrating power of the destroyer; and I learned that the glimpse I had obtained of her person would thus probably be the last I should obtain—that the lady, at least while living, would be seen by me no more.

For several days ensuing, her name was unmentioned by either Usher or myself; and during this period I was busied in earnest endeavours to alleviate the melancholy of my friend. We painted, and read together; or I listened, as if in a dream, to the wild improvisations of his speaking guitar. And thus, as a closer intimacy admitted me more unreservedly into the recesses of his spirit, the more bitterly did I perceive the futility of all attempt at cheering a mind from which darkness, as if an inherent positive quality, poured forth upon all objects of the moral and physical universe in one unceasing radiation of gloom.

I shall ever bear about me a memory of the many solemn
hours I thus spent alone with the master of the House of
Usher. Yet I should fail in any attempt to convey an idea of
the exact character of the studies, or of the occupations, in
which he involved me, or led me the way. An excited and
highly distempered ideality threw a sulphurous lustre over all.
His long improvised dirges will ring for ever in my ears.
Among other things I hold painfully in mind a certain singular
perversion and amplification of the wild air of the last waltz of
Von Weber. From the paintings over which his elaborate
fancy brooded, and which grew, touch by touch, into vague-
nesses at which I shuddered the more thrillingly, because I
shuddered knowing not why ;—from these paintings (vivid
as their images now are before me) I would in vain endeavour
to educe more than a small portion which should lie within
the compass of merely written words. By the utter simplicity,
by the nakedness of his designs, he arrested and overawed
attention. If ever mortal painted an idea, that mortal was
Roderick Usher. For me at least—in the circumstances then
surrounding me—there arose out of the pure abstraction
which the hypochondriac contrived to throw upon his canvas,
an intensity of intolerable awe, no shadow of which felt
I ever yet in the contemplation of the certainly glowing yet
too concrete reveries of Fuseli.

One of the phantasmagoric conceptions of my friend,
partaking not so rigidly of the spirit of abstraction, may be
shadowed forth, although feebly, in words. A small picture
presented the interior of an immensely long rectangular vault
or tunnel, with low walls, smooth, white, and without interruption or device. Certain accessory points of the design
served well to convey the idea that this excavation lay at an
exceeding depth below the surface of the earth. No outlet
was observed in any portion of its vast extent, and no torch,
or other artificial source of light was discernible ; yet a flood
of intense rays rolled throughout, and bathed the whole in
a ghastly and inappropriate splendour.

I have just spoken of that morbid condition of the auditory
nerve which rendered all music intolerable to the sufferer,
with the exception of certain effects of stringed instruments.
It was, perhaps, the narrow limits to which he thus confined
himself upon the guitar, which gave birth, in great measure, to
the fantastic character of his performances. But the fervid

facility of his *impromptus* could not be so accounted for. They must have been, and were, in the notes, as well as in the words of his wild fantasias (for he not unfrequently accompanied himself with rhymed verbal improvisations), the result of that intense mental collectedness and concentration to which I have previously alluded as observable only in particular moments of the highest artificial excitement. The words of one of these rhapsodies I have easily remembered. I was, perhaps, the more forcibly impressed with it, as he gave it, because, in the under or mystic current of its meaning, I fancied that I perceived, and for the first time, a full consciousness on the part of Usher, of the tottering of his lofty reason upon her throne. The verses, which were entitled " The Haunted Palace," ran very nearly, if not accurately, thus :

I

By good angels tenanted,
Once a fair and stately palace—
    Radiant palace—reared its head.
In the monarch Thought's dominion—
In the greenest of our valleys,
    It stood there ;
Never seraph spread a pinion
    Over fabric half so fair.

II

Banners, yellow, glorious, golden,
    On its roof did float and flow ;
(This—all this—was in the olden
    Time long ago).
And every gentle air that dallied
    In that sweet day,
Along the ramparts plumed and pallied
    A winged odour went away.

III

Wanderers in that happy valley
    Through two luminous windows saw
Spirits moving musically
    To a lute's well-tunéd law,
Round about a throne, were sitting
    (Porphyrogene !)
In state his glory well befitting,
    The ruler of the realm was seen.

IV

And all with pearl and ruby glowing
 Was the fair palace door,
Through which came, flowing, flowing, flowing
 And sparkling evermore,
A troop of Echoes whose sweet duty
 Was but to sing,
In voices of surpassing beauty,
 The wit and wisdom of their king.

V

But evil things, in robes of sorrow,
 Assailed the monarch's high estate ;
(Ah, let us mourn, for never morrow
 Shall dawn upon him desolate !)
And around about his home, the glory
 That blushed and bloomed
Is but a dim-remembered story
 Of the old time entombed.

VI

And travellers now within that valley,
 Through the red-litten windows see
Vast forms that move fantastically
 To a discordant melody ;
While, like a rapid ghastly river,
 Through the pale door,
A hideous throng rush out forever,
 And laugh—but smile no more.

I well remember that suggestions arising from this ballad led us into a train of thought wherein there became manifest an opinion of Usher's which I mention not so much on account of its novelty (for other men have thought thus) as on account of the pertinacity with which he maintained it. This opinion, in its general form, was that of the sentience of all vegetable things. But, in his disordered fancy, the idea had assumed a more daring character, and trespassed, under certain conditions, upon the kingdom of inorganisation. I lack words to express the full extent, or the earnest *abandon* of his persuasion. The belief, however, was connected (as I have previously hinted) with the grey stones of the home of his forefathers. The conditions of the sentience had been here, he imagined, fulfilled in the method of collocation of these stones—in the order of their arrangement, as well as in that of the many *fungi* which overspread them, and of the decayed trees which stood around—above all, in the long-undisturbed endurance of this arrangement, and its reduplication in the still waters of the tarn. Its evidence—the evidence of the sentience—was to be seen, he said (and I here started as he spoke), in the gradual yet certain condensation of an atmosphere of their own about the waters and the walls. The result was discoverable, he added, in that silent, yet importunate and terrible influence which for centuries had moulded the destinies of his family, and which made *him* what I now saw him—what he was. Such opinions need no comment, and I will make none.

Our books (the books which, for years, had formed no small portion of the mental existence of the invalid) were, as might be supposed, in strict keeping with this character of phantasm. We pored together over such works as *The Ververt et Chartreuse* of Gresset; *The Belphegor* of Machiavelli; *The Heaven and Hell* of Swedenborg; *The Subterranean Voyage of Nicholas Klimm*, by Holberg; *The Chiromancy* of Robert Flud, of Jean d'Indaginé, and of De las Chambre; *The Journey into the Blue Distance* of Tieck; and *The City of the Sun* of Campanella. One favourite volume was a small octavo edition of *The Directorium Inquisitorium*, by the Dominican Eymeric de Gironne; and there were passages in " Pomponius Mela," about the old African Satyrs and Œgipans, over which Usher would sit dreaming for hours. His chief delight, however, was found in the perusal of an exceedingly rare and curious book in quarto Gothic— the manual of a forgotten church—*The Vigiliæ Mortuorum secundum Chorum Ecclesiæ Maguntinæ*.

I could not help thinking of the wild ritual of this work, and of its probable influence upon the hypochondriac, when, one evening, having informed me abruptly that the lady Madeline was no more, he stated his intention of preserving her corpse for a fortnight (previously to its final interment) in one of the numerous vaults within the main walls of the building. The worldly reason, however, assigned for this singular proceeding, was one which I did not feel at liberty to dispute. The brother had been led to his resolution (so he told me) by consideration of the unusual character of the malady of the deceased, of certain obtrusive and eager inquiries on the part of her medical men, and of the remote and exposed situation of the burial-ground of the family. I will

not deny that when I called to mind the sinister countenance
of the person whom I met upon the staircase, on the day of
my arrival at the house, I had no desire to oppose what I
regarded as at best but a harmless, and by no means an
unnatural, precaution.

At the request of Usher, I personally aided him in the
arrangements for the temporary entombment. The body
having been encoffined, we two alone bore it to its rest. The
vault in which we placed it (and which had been so long
unopened that our torches, half smothered in its oppressive
atmosphere, gave us little opportunity for investigation) was
small, damp, and entirely without means of admission for
light ; lying, at great depth, immediately beneath that portion
of the building in which was my own sleeping apartment. It
had been used, apparently, in remote feudal times, for the
worst purposes of a donjon-keep, and, in latter days, as a
place of deposit for powder, or some other highly combustible
substance, as a portion of its floor, and the whole interior of
a long archway through which we reached it, were carefully
sheathed with copper. The door, of massive iron, had
been, also, similarly protected. Its immense weight caused
an unusually sharp grating sound, as it moved upon its
hinges.

Having deposited our mournful burden upon tressles
within this region of horror, we partially turned aside the yet
unscrewed lid of the coffin, and looked upon the face of the
tenant. A striking similitude between the brother and sister
now first arrested my attention ; and Usher, divining, perhaps
my thoughts, murmured out some few words from which
I learned that the deceased and himself had been twins, and
that sympathies of a scarcely intelligible nature had always
existed between them. Our glances, however, rested not long
upon the dead—for we could not regard her unawed. The
disease which had thus entombed the lady in the maturity
of youth, had left, as usual, in all maladies of a strictly cataleptical character, the mockery of a faint blush upon the bosom and
the face, and that suspiciously lingering smile upon the lip
which is so terrible in death. We replaced and screwed down
the lid, and, having secured the door of iron, made our way,
with toil, into the scarcely less gloomy apartments of the upper
portion of the house.

And now, some days of bitter grief having elapsed, an

observable change came over the features of the mental disorder of my friend. His ordinary manner had vanished. His ordinary occupations were neglected or forgotten. He roamed from chamber to chamber with hurried, unequal, and objectless step. The pallor of his countenance had assumed, if possible, a more ghastly hue—but the luminousness of his eye had utterly gone out. The once occasional huskiness of his tone was heard no more ; and a tremulous quaver, as if of extreme terror, habitually characterised his utterance. There were times, indeed, when I thought his unceasingly agitated mind was labouring with some oppressive secret, to divulge which he struggled for the necessary courage. At times, again, I was obliged to resolve all into the mere inexplicable vagaries of madness, for I beheld him gazing upon vacancy for long hours, in an attitude of the profoundest attention, as if listening to some imaginary sound. It was no wonder that his condition terrified—that it infected me. I felt creeping upon me, by slow yet certain degrees, the wild influences of his own fantastic, yet impressive, superstitions.

It was, especially, upon retiring to bed late in the night of the seventh or eighth day, after the placing of the lady Madeline within the donjon, that I experienced the full power of such feelings. Sleep came not near my couch—while the hours waned and waned away. I struggled to reason off the nervousness which had dominion over me. I endeavoured to believe that much, if not all of what I felt, was due to the bewildering influence of the gloomy furniture of the room—of the dark and tattered draperies, which, tortured into motion by the breath of a rising tempest, swayed fitfully to and fro upon the walls, and rustled uneasily about the decorations of the bed. But my efforts were fruitless. An irrepressible tremor gradually pervaded my frame ; and, at length, there sat upon my very heart an incubus of utterly causeless alarm. Shaking this off with a gasp and a struggle, I uplifted myself upon the pillows, and peering earnestly within the intense darkness of the chamber, hearkened—I know not why, except that an instinctive spirit prompted me—to certain low and indefinite sounds which came, through the pauses of the storm, at long intervals, I knew not whence. Overpowered by an intense sentiment of horror, unaccountable yet unendurable, I threw on my clothes with haste (for I felt that I should sleep no more during the night), and endeavoured to arouse myself from the pitiable condition into which I had fallen, by pacing rapidly to and fro through the apartment.

I had taken but few turns in this manner, when a light step on an adjoining staircase arrested my attention. I presently recognised it as that of Usher. In an instant afterwards he rapped with a gentle touch at my door, and entered, bearing a lamp. His countenance was, as usual, cadaverously wan, but moreover there was a species of mad hilarity in his eyes —an evidently restrained *hysteria* in his whole demeanour. His air appalled me—but anything was preferable to the solitude which I had so long endured, and I even welcomed his presence as a relief.

"And you have not seen it?" he said, abruptly, after having stared about him for some moments in silence—" you have not then seen it?—but, stay! you shall." Thus speaking, and having carefully shaded his lamp, he hurried to one of the casements, and threw it freely open to the storm.

The impetuous fury of the entering gust nearly lifted us from our feet. It was, indeed, a tempestuous, yet sternly beautiful, night, and one wildly singular in its terror and its beauty. A whirlwind had apparently collected its force in our vicinity; for there were frequent and violent alterations in the direction of the wind; and the exceeding density of the clouds (which hung so low as to press upon the turrets of the house) did not prevent our perceiving the life-long velocity with which they flew careering from all points against each other, without passing away into the distance. I say that even their exceeding density did not prevent our perceiving this—yet we had no glimpse of the moon or stars—nor was there any flashing forth of the lightning. But the under surfaces of the huge masses of agitated vapour, as well as all terrestrial objects immediately around us, were glowing in the unnatural light of a faintly luminous and distinctly visible gaseous exhalation which hung about and enshrouded the mansion.

"You must not—you shall not behold this!" said I, shudderingly, to Usher, as I led him, with a gentle violence, from the window to a seat. "These appearances, which bewilder you, are merely electrical phenomena not uncommon —or it may be that they have their ghastly origin in the rank miasma of the tarn. Let us close this casement; the air is chilling and dangerous to your frame. Here is one of your favourite romances. I will read, and you shall listen—and so we will pass away this terrible night together."

The antique volume which I had taken up was the *Mad Trist* of Sir Lancelot Canning; but I had called it a favourite of Usher's more in sad jest than in earnest; for, in truth, there is little in its uncouth and unimaginative prolixity which could have had interest for the lofty and spiritual ideality of my friend. It was, however, the only book immediately at hand; and I indulged a vague hope that the excitement which now agitated the hypochondriac might find relief (for the history of mental disorder is full of similar anomalies) even in the extremeness of the folly which I should read. Could I have judged, indeed, by the wild, overstrained air of vivacity with which he hearkened, or apparently hearkened, to the words of the tale, I might well have congratulated myself upon the success of my design.

I had arrived at that well-known portion of the story where Ethelred, the hero of the Trist, having sought in vain for peaceable admission into the dwelling of the hermit, proceeds to make good an entrance by force. Here, it will be remembered, the words of the narrative run thus:

" And Ethelred, who was by nature of a doughty heart, and who was now mighty withal, on account of the powerfulness of the wine which he had drunken, waited no longer to hold parley with the hermit, who, in sooth, was of an obstinate and maliceful turn, but feeling the rain upon his shoulders, and fearing the rising of the tempest, uplifted his mace outright, and, by blows, made quickly room in the plankings of the door for his gauntleted hand; and now pulling therewith sturdily, he so cracked and ripped, and tore all asunder, that the noise of the dry and hollow-sounding wood alarumed and reverberated throughout the forest."

At the termination of this sentence I started, and, for a moment, paused; for it appeared to me (although I at once concluded that my excited fancy had deceived me)—it appeared to me that, from some very remote portion of the mansion, there came, indistinctly, to my ears, what might have been, in its exact similarity of character, the echo (but a stifled and dull one certainly) of the very cracking and ripping sound which Sir Lancelot had so particularly described. It was, beyond doubt, the coincidence alone which had arrested my attention; for, amid the rattling of the sashes of the casements, and the ordinary commingled noises of the still-increasing storm, the sound, in itself, had nothing, surely, which should have interested or disturbed me. I continued the story :

"But the good champion, Ethelred, now entering within the door, was sore enraged and amazed to perceive no signal of the maliceful hermit ; but, in the stead thereof, a dragon of a scaly and prodigious demeanour, and of a fiery tongue, which sate in guard before a palace of gold, with a floor of silver ; and upon the wall there hung a shield of shining brass with this legend written :

Who entereth herein, a conqueror hath bin ;
Who slayeth the dragon, the shield he shall win :

And Ethelred uplifted his mace, and struck upon the head of the dragon, which fell before him, and gave up his pesty breath, with a shriek so horrid and harsh, and withal so piercing, that Ethelred had fain to close his ears with his hands against the dreadful noise of it, the like whereof was never before heard."

Here, again, I paused abruptly, and now with a feeling of wild amazement—for there could be no doubt whatever that, in this instance, I did actually hear (although from what direction it proceeded I found it impossible to say) a low and apparently distinct, but harsh, protracted, and most unusual screaming or grating sound—the exact counterpart of what my fancy had already conjured up for the dragon's unnatural shriek as described by the romancer.

Oppressed, as I certainly was, upon the occurrence of this second and most extraordinary coincidence, by a thousand conflicting sensations, in which wonder and extreme terror were predominant, I still retained sufficient presence of mind to avoid exciting, by any observation, the sensitive nervousness of my companion. I was by no means certain that he had noticed the sounds in question ; although, assuredly, a strange alteration had, during the last few minutes, taken place in his demeanour. From a position fronting my own, he had gradually brought round his chair, so as to sit with his face to the door of the chamber, and thus I could but partially perceive his features, although I saw that his lips trembled as if he were murmuring inaudibly. His head had dropped upon his breast—yet I knew that he was not asleep, from the wide and rigid opening of the eye as I caught a glance of it in profile.

The motion of his body, too, was at variance with this idea—for he rocked from side to side with a gentle yet constant and uniform sway. Having rapidly taken notice of all this, I resumed the narrative of Sir Lancelot, which thus proceeded :

" And now, the champion, having escaped from the terrible fury of the dragon, bethinking himself of the brazen shield, and of the breaking up of the enchantment which was upon it, removed the carcass from out of the way before him and approached valorously over the silver pavement of the castle to where the shield was upon the wall; which, in sooth, tarried not for his full coming, but fell down at his feet upon the silver floor, with a mighty great and terrible ringing sound."

No sooner had these syllables passed my lips, than—as if a shield of brass had indeed, at the moment, fallen heavily upon a floor of silver—I became aware of a distinct, hollow, metallic, and clangorous, yet apparently muffled reverberation. Completely unnerved, I leaped to my feet; but the measured rocking movement of Usher was undisturbed. I rushed to the chair in which he sat. His eyes were bent fixedly before him, and throughout his whole countenance there reigned a stony rigidity. But, as I placed my hand upon his shoulder, there came a strong shudder over his whole person; a sickly smile quivered about his lips; and I saw that he spoke in a low, hurried, and gibbering murmur, as if unconscious of my presence. Bending closely over him, I at length drank in the hideous import of his words.

" Not hear it ?—yes, I hear it, and *have* heard it. Long—long—long—many minutes, many hours, many days, have I heard it—yet I dared not—oh, pity me, miserable wretch that I am!—I dared not—I *dared* not speak ! *We have put her living in the tomb !* Said I not that my senses were acute ? I *now* tell you that I heard her first feeble movements in the hollow coffin. I heard them—many, many days ago—yet I dared not—*I dared not speak !* And now—to-night—Ethelred—ha ! ha !—the breaking of the hermit's door, and the death-cry of the dragon, and the clangour of the shield !—say, rather, the rending of her coffin, and the grating of the iron hinges of her prison, and her struggles within the coppered archway of the vault ! Oh, whither shall I fly ? Will she not be here anon ? Is she not hurrying to upbraid me for my haste ? Have I not heard her footstep on the stair ? Do I not distinguish that heavy and horrible beating of her heart? Madman!"—here he sprang furiously to his feet, and shrieked out his syllables, as if in the effort he were giving up his soul— "*Madman! I tell you that she now stands without the door!*"

As if in the superhuman energy of his utterance there had been found the potency of a spell, the huge antique panels to which the speaker pointed, threw slowly back upon the instant, their ponderous and ebony jaws. It was the work of the rushing gust—but then without those doors there *did* stand the lofty and enshrouded figure of the lady Madeline of Usher. There was blood upon her white robes, and the evidence of some bitter struggle upon every portion of her emaciated frame. For a moment she remained trembling and reeling to and fro upon the threshold—then, with a low, moaning cry, fell heavily inward upon the person of her brother, and in violent and now final death-agonies, bore him to the floor a corpse, and a victim to the terrors he had anticipated.

From that chamber, and from that mansion, I fled aghast. The storm was still abroad in all its wrath as I found myself crossing the old causeway. Suddenly there shot along the path a wild light, and I turned to see whence a gleam so unusual could have issued; for the vast house and its shadows were alone behind me. The radiance was that of the full, setting, and blood-red moon, which now shone vividly through that once barely discernible fissure, of which I have before spoken as extending from the roof of that building, in a zigzag direction, to the base. While I gazed, this fissure rapidly widened—there came a fierce breath of the whirlwind— the entire orb of the satellite burst at once upon my sight— my brain reeled as I saw the mighty walls rushing asunder— there was a long tumultuous shouting sound like the voice of a thousand waters—and the deep and dank tarn at my feet closed sullenly and silently over the fragments of the "*House of Usher.*"

A WARNING TO THE CURIOUS
M.R. James

THE place on the east coast which the reader is asked to consider is Seaburgh. It is not very different now from what I remember it to have been when I was a child. Marshes intersected by dykes to the south, recalling the early chapters of *Great Expectations* ; flat fields to the north, merging into heath ; heath, fir woods, and, above all, gorse, inland. A long sea-front and a street : behind that a spacious church of flint, with a broad, solid western tower and a peal of six bells. How well I remember their sound on a hot Sunday in August, as our party went slowly up the white, dusty slope of road towards them, for the church stands at the top of a short, steep incline. They rang with a flat clacking sort of sound on those hot days, but when the air was softer they were mellower too. The railway ran down to its little terminus farther along the same road. There was a gay white windmill just before you came to the station, and another down near the shingle at the south end of the town, and yet others on higher ground to the north. There were cottages of bright red brick with slate roofs . . . but why do I encumber you with these commonplace details ? The fact is that they come crowding to the point of the pencil when it begins to write of Seaburgh. I should like to be sure that I had allowed the right ones to get on to the paper. But I forgot. I have not quite done with the word-painting business yet.

Walk away from the sea and the town, pass the station, and turn up the road on the right. It is a sandy road, parallel with the railway, and if you follow it, it climbs to somewhat higher ground. On your left (you are now going northwards) is heath, on your right (the side towards the sea) is a belt of old firs, wind-beaten, thick at the top, with the slope that old seaside trees have ; seen on the skyline from the train they would tell you in an instant, if you did not know it, that you were approaching a windy coast. Well, at the top of my little hill a line of these firs strikes out and runs towards the sea, for there is a ridge that goes that way ; and the ridge ends in a rather well-defined mound commanding the level fields of rough grass, and a little knot of fir trees crowns it. And here you may sit on a hot spring day, very well content to look at blue sea, white windmills, red cottages, bright green grass, church tower, and distant martello tower on the south.

As I have said, I began to know Seaburgh as a child ; but a gap of a good many years separates my early knowledge from that which is more recent. Still, it keeps its place in my affections, and any tales of it that I pick up have an interest for me. One such tale is this : it came to me in a place very remote from Seaburgh, and quite accidentally, from a man whom I had been able to oblige—enough in his opinion to justify his making me his confidant to this extent.

I know all that country more or less (he said). I used to go to Seaburgh pretty regularly for golf in the spring. I generally put up at the "Bear", with a friend—Henry Long it was, you knew him perhaps—("Slightly," I said) and we used to take a sitting-room and be very happy there. Since he died I haven't cared to go there. And I don't know that I should anyhow after the particular thing that happened on our last visit.

It was April 19—, we were there, and by some chance we were almost the only people in the hotel. So the ordinary public rooms were practically empty, and we were the more surprised when, after dinner, our sitting-room door opened and a young man put his head in. We were aware of this young man. He was rather a rabbity, anaemic subject—light hair and light eyes—but not unpleasing. So when he said : "I beg your pardon, is this a private room?" we did not growl and say : "Yes, it is," but Long said, or I did—no matter which : "Please come in." "Oh, may I ?" he said, and seemed relieved. Of course it was obvious that he wanted company ; and as he was a reasonable kind of person—not the sort to bestow his whole family history on you—we urged him to make himself at home. "I dare say you find the other rooms rather bleak," I said. Yes, he did : but it was really too good of us, and so on. That being got over, he made some pretence of reading a book. Long was playing Patience, I was writing.

It became plain to me after a few minutes that this visitor of ours was in rather a state of fidgets or nerves, which communicated itself to me, and so I put away my writing and turned to at engaging him in talk.

After some remarks, which I forget, he became rather confidential. "You'll think it very odd of me" (this was the sort of way he began), "but the fact is I've had something of a shock." Well, I recommended a drink of some cheering kind, and we had it. The waiter coming in made an interruption (and I thought our young man seemed very jumpy when the door opened), but after a while he got back to his woes again. There was nobody he knew in the place, and he did happen to know who we both were (it turned out there was some common acquaintance in Town), and really he did want a word of advice, if we didn't mind. Of course we both said : "By all means", or "Not at all", and Long put away his cards. And we settled down to hear what his difficulty was.

"It began," he said, "more than a week ago, when I bicycled over to Froston, only about five or six miles, to see the church ; I'm very much interested in architecture, and it's got one of those pretty porches with niches and shields. I took a photograph of it, and then an old man who was tidying up in the churchyard came and asked if I'd care to look into the church. I said yes, and he produced a key and let me in. There wasn't much inside, but I told him it was a nice little church and he kept it very clean, 'but,' I said, 'the porch is the best part of it'. We were just outside the porch then, and he said, 'Ah yes, that is a nice porch ; and do you know, sir, what's the meanin' of that coat of arms there ?'

"It was the one with the three crowns, and though I'm not much of a herald, I was able to say yes, I thought it was the old arms of the kingdom of East Anglia.

" 'That's right, sir,' he said, 'and do you know the meanin' of them three crowns that's on it ?'

"I said I'd no doubt it was known, but I couldn't recollect to have heard it myself.

" 'Well, then,' he said, 'for all you're a scholard, I can tell you something you don't know. Them's the three 'oly crowns what was buried in the ground near by the coast to keep the Germans from landing—ah, I can see you don't believe that. But I tell you, if it hadn't have been for one of them 'oly crowns bein' there still, them Germans would a landed here time and again, they would. Landed with their ships, and killed man, woman, and child in their beds. Now then, that's the truth what I'm telling you, that is ; and if you don't believe me, you ast the rector. There he comes : you ast him, I says.'

"I looked round, and there was the rector, a nice-looking old man, coming up the path ; and before I could begin assuring my old man, who was getting quite excited, that I didn't disbelieve him, the rector struck in and said : 'What's all this about, John ? Good day to you, sir. Have you been looking at our little church ?'

"So then there was a little talk which allowed the old man to calm down, and then the rector asked him again what was the matter.

" 'Oh,' he said, 'it warn't nothink, only I was telling this gentleman he'd ought to ast you about them 'oly crowns.'

" 'Ah yes, to be sure,' said the rector, 'that's a very curious matter, isn't it ? But I don't know whether the gentleman is interested in our old stories, eh ?'

" 'Oh, he'll be interested fast enough,' says the old man, 'he'll put his confidence in what you tells him, sir ; why, you known William Ager yourself, father and son too.'

"Then I put in a word to say how much I should like to hear all about it, and before many minutes I was walking up the village street with the rector, who had one or two words to say to parishioners, and then to the rectory, where he took me into his study. He had made out, on the way, that I really was capable of taking an intelligent interest in a piece of folk-lore, and not quite the ordinary tripper. So he was very willing to talk, and it is rather surprising to me that the particular legend he told me has not made its way into print before. His account of it was this : 'There has always been a belief in these parts in the three holy crowns. The old people say they were buried in different places near the coast to keep off the Danes or the French or the Germans. And they say that one of the three was dug up a long time ago, and another has disappeared by the encroaching of the sea, and one's still left doing its work, keeping off invaders. Well, now, if you have read the ordinary guides and histories of this county, you will remember perhaps that in 1687 a crown, which was said to be the crown of Redwald, King of the East Angles, was dug up at Rendlesham, and alas! alas! melted down before it was even properly described or drawn. Well, Rendlesham isn't on the coast, but it isn't so very far inland, and it's on a very important line of access. And I believe that is the crown which the people mean when they say that one has been dug up. Then, on the south, you don't want me to tell you where there was a Saxon royal palace which is now under the sea, eh? Well, there was the second crown, I take it. And up beyond these two, they say, lies the third.'

" 'Do they say where it is?' of course I asked.

"He said, 'Yes, indeed, they do, but they don't tell,' and his manner did not encourage me to put the obvious question. Instead of that I waited a moment, and said : 'What did the old man mean when he said you knew William Ager, as if that had something to do with the crowns?'

" 'To be sure,' he said, 'now that's another curious story. These Agers—it's a very old name in these parts, but I can't find that they were ever people of quality or big owners—these Agers say, or said, that their branch of the family were the guardians of the last crown. A certain old Nathaniel Ager was the first one I knew—I was born and brought up quite near here—and he, I believe, camped out at the place during the whole of the war of 1870. William, his son, did the same, I know, during the South African War. And young William, *his* son, who has only died fairly recently, took lodgings at the cottage nearest the spot, and I've no doubt hastened his end, for he was a consumptive, by exposure and night watching. And he was the last of that branch. It was a dreadful grief to him to think that he was the last, but he could do nothing, the only relations at all near to him were in the colonies. I wrote letters for him to them imploring them to come over on business very important to the family, but there has been no answer. So the last of the holy crowns, if it's there, has no guardian now.'

"That was what the rector told me, and you can fancy how interesting I found it. The only thing I could think of when I left him was how to hit upon the spot where the crown was supposed to be. I wish I'd left it alone.

"But there was a sort of fate in it, for as I bicycled back past the churchyard wall my eye caught a fairly new gravestone, and on it was the name of William Ager. Of course I got off and read it. It said 'of this parish, died at Seaburgh, 19—, aged 28'. There it was, you see. A little judicious questioning in the right place, and I should at least find the cottage nearest the spot. Only I didn't quite know what was the right place to begin my questioning at. Again there was fate : it took me to the curiosity-shop down that way—you know—and I turned over some old books, and, if you please, one was a prayerbook of 1740 odd, in a rather handsome binding—I'll just go and get it, it's in my room."

He left us in a state of some surprise, but we had hardly time to exchange any remarks when he was back, panting, and handed us the book opened at the fly-leaf, on which was, in a straggly hand :

> Nathaniel Ager is my hame and England is my nàtion,
> Seaburgh is my dwelling-place and Christ is my Salvation,
> When I'm dead and in my Grave, and all my bones are rotton,
> I hope the Lord will think on me when I am quite forgotton.

This poem was dated 1754, and there were many more entries of Agers, Nathaniel, Frederick, William, and so on, ending with William, 19—.

"You see," he said, "anybody would call it the greatest bit of luck. *I* did, but I don't now. Of course I asked the shopman about William Ager, and of course he happened to remember that he lodged in a cottage in the North Field and died there. This was just chalking the road for me. I knew which the cottage must be : there is only one sizable one about there. The next thing was to scrape some sort of acquaintance with the people, and I took a walk that way at once.

A dog did the business for me : he made at me so fiercely that they had to run out and beat him off, and then naturally begged my pardon, and we got into talk. I had only to bring up Ager's name, and pretend I knew, or thought I knew, something of him, and then the woman said how sad it was him dying so young, and she was sure it came of him spending the night out of doors in the cold weather. Then I had to say : 'Did he got out on the sea at night ?' and she said : 'Oh no, it was on the hillock yonder with the trees on it.' And there I was.

"I know something about digging in these barrows :

I've opened many of them in the down country. But that was with the owner's leave, and in broad daylight, and with men to help. I had to prospect very carefully here before I put a spade in : I couldn't trench across the mound, and with those old firs growing there I knew there would be awkward tree-roots. Still, the soil was very light and sandy and easy, and there was a rabbit hole or so that might be developed into a sort of tunnel. The going out and coming back at odd hours to the hotel was going to be the awkward part. When I made up my mind about the way to excavate I told the people that I was called away for a night, and I spent it out there. I made my tunnel : I won't bore you with the details of how I supported it and filled it in when I'd done, but the main thing is that I got the crown."

Naturally we both broke out into exclamations of surprise and interest. I for one had long known about the finding of the crown at Rendlesham and had often lamented its fate. No one has ever seen an Anglo-Saxon crown—at least no one had. But our man gazed at us with a rueful eye. "Yes," he said, "and the worst of it is I don't know how to put it back."

"Put it back ?" we cried out. "Why, my dear sir, you've made one of the most exciting finds ever heard of in this country. Of course it ought to go to the Jewel House at the Tower. What's your difficulty ? If you're thinking about the owner of the land, and treasure-trove, and all that, we can certainly help you through. Nobody's going to make a fuss about technicalities in a case of this kind."

Probably more was said, but all he did was to put his face in his hands and mutter : "I don't know how to put it back."

At last Long said : "You'll forgive me, I hope, if I seem impertinent, but are you *quite* sure you've got it ?" I was wanting to ask much the same question myself, for of course the story did seem a lunatic's dream when one thought over it. But I hadn't quite dared to say what might hurt the poor young man's feelings. However, he took it quite calmly —really, with the calm of despair, you might say. He sat up and said : "Oh yes, there's no doubt of that ; I have it here in my room, locked up in my bag. You can come and look at it if you like ; I won't offer to bring it here."

We were not likely to let the chance slip. We went with him ; his room was only a few doors off. The boots was just collecting shoes in the passage : or so we thought : afterwards we were not sure. Our visitor—his name was Paxton—was in a worse state of shivers than before, and went hurriedly into the room and beckoned us after him, turned on the light and shut the door carefully. Then he unlocked his kitbag, and produced a bundle of clean pocket-handkerchiefs in which something was wrapped, laid it on the bed and undid it. I can now say I *have* seen an actual Anglo-Saxon crown. It was of silver—as the Rendlesham one is always said to have been—it was set with some gems, mostly antique intaglios and cameos, and was of rather plain, almost rough, workmanship. In fact, it was like those you see on the coins and in the manuscripts.

I found no reason to think it was later than the ninth century. I was intensely interested, of course, and I wanted to turn it over in my hands, but Paxton prevented me. "Don't *you* touch it," he said, "I'll do that." And with a sigh that was, I declare to you, dreadful to hear, he took it up and turned it about so that we could see every part of it. "Seen enough?" he said at last, and we nodded. He wrapped it up and locked it in his bag, and stood looking at us dumbly. "Come back to our room," Long said, "and tell us what the trouble is." He thanked us and said : "Will you go first and see if—if the coast is clear?" That wasn't very intelligible, for our proceedings hadn't been, after all, very suspicious, and the hotel, as I said, was practically empty.

However, we were beginning to have inklings of—we didn't know what, and anyhow, nerves are infectious. So we did go, first peering out as we opened the door, and fancying (I found we both had the fancy) that a shadow, or more than a shadow—but it made no sound —passed from before us to one side as we came out into the passage. "It's all right," we whispered to Paxton—whispering seemed the proper tone—and we went, with him between us, back to our sitting-room. I was preparing, when we got there, to be ecstatic about the unique interest of what we had seen, but when I looked at Paxton I saw that would be terribly out of place, and I left it to him to begin.

"What *is* to be done?" was his opening. Long thought it right (as he explained to me afterwards) to be obtuse, and said : "Why not find out who the owner of the land is and inform——" "Oh no, no !" Paxton broke in impatiently,

"I beg your pardon ; you've been very kind, but don't you see it's *got* to go back, and I daren't be there at night, and daytime's impossible. Perhaps, though, you don't see ; well, then, the truth is that I've never been alone since I touched it." I was beginning some fairly stupid comment, but Long caught my eye, and I stopped. Long said : "I think I do see, perhaps ; but wouldn't it be a relief to tell us a little more clearly what the situation is ?"

Then it all came out : Paxton looked over his shoulder and beckoned to us to come nearer to him, and began speaking in a low voice. We listened most intently, of course, and compared notes afterwards, and I wrote down our version, so I am confident I have told what he told us almost word for word.

He said : "It began when I was first prospecting, and put me off again and again. There was always somebody—a man —standing by one of the firs. This was in daylight, you know. He was never in front of me. I always saw him with the tail of my eye on the left or the right, and he was never there when I looked straight for him. I would lie down for quite a long time and take careful observations, and make sure there was no one, and then when I got up and began prospecting again, there he was. And he began to give me hints, besides : for wherever I put that prayerbook—short of locking it up, which I did at last—when I came back to my room it was always out on my table open at the fly-leaf where the names are, and one of my razors across it to keep it open. I'm sure he just can't open my bag, or something more would have happened. You see, he's light and weak, but all the same I daren't face him.

Well, then, when I was making the tunnel of course it was worse, and if I hadn't been so keen I should have dropped the whole thing and run. It was like someone scraping at my back all the time : I thought for a long time it was only soil dropping on me, but as I got nearer the—the crown, it was unmistakable. And when I actually laid it bare and got my fingers into the ring of it and pulled it out, there came a sort of cry behind me—oh, I can't tell you how desolate it was ! And horribly threatening too. It spoilt all my pleasure in my find—cut it off that moment. And if I hadn't been the wretched fool I am, I should have put the thing back and left it. But I didn't.

"The rest of the time was just awful. I had hours to get through before I could decently come back to the hotel. First I spent time filling up my tunnel and covering my tracks, and all the while he was there trying to thwart me. Sometimes, you know, you see him, and sometimes you don't, just as he pleases, I think : he's there, but he has some power over your eyes. Well, I wasn't off the spot very long before sunrise, and then I had to get to the junction for Seaburgh, and take a train back. And though it was daylight fairly soon, I don't know if that made it much better.

There were always hedges, or gorse bushes, or park fences along the road—some sort of cover, I mean—and I was never easy for a second. And then when I began to meet people going to work, they always looked behind me very strangely : it might have been that they were surprised at see-ing anyone so early ; but I didn't think it was only that, and I don't know : they didn't look exactly at *me*. And the porter at the train was like that too. And the guard held open the door after I'd got into the carriage—just as he would if there was somebody else coming, you know. Oh, you may be sure it isn't my fancy," he said, with a dull sort of laugh. Then he went on : "And even if I do get it put back, he won't forgive me : I can tell that. And I was so happy a fortnight ago." He dropped into a chair, and I believe he began to cry.

We didn't know what to say, but we felt we must come to the rescue somehow, and so—it really seemed the only thing—we said if he was so set on putting the crown back in its place, we would help him. And I must say that after what we had heard it did seem the right thing. If these horrid consequences had come on this poor man, might there not really be some-thing in the original idea of the crown having some curious power bound up with it, to guard the coast ? At least, that was my feeling, and I think it was Long's too. Our offer was very welcome to Paxton, anyhow. When could we do it ? It was nearing half past ten. Could we contrive to make a late walk plausible to the hotel people that very night ?

We looked out of the window : there was a brilliant full moon—the Paschal moon. Long undertook to tackle the boots and propitiate him. He was to say that we should not be much over the hour, and if we did find it so pleasant that we stopped out a bit longer we would see that he didn't lose by sitting up. Well, we were pretty regular customers of the hotel, and did not give much trouble, and were considered by the servants to be not under the mark in the way of tips ; and so the boots *was* propitiated, and let us out on to the sea-front, and remained, as we heard later, looking after us. Paxton had a large coat over his arm, under which was the wrapped-up crown.

So we were off on this strange errand before we had time to think how very much out of the way it was. I have told this part quite shortly on purpose, for it really does represent the haste with which we settled our plan and took action. "The shortest way is up the hill and through the churchyard," Paxton said, as we stood a moment before the hotel looking up and down the front. There was nobody about—nobody at all. Seaburgh out of the season is an early, quiet place. "We can't go along the dyke by the cottage, because of the dog," Paxton also said, when I pointed to what I thought a shorter way along the front and across two fields. The reason he gave was good enough.

We went up the road to the church, and turned in at the churchyard gate. I confess to having thought that there might be some lying there who might be conscious of our business : but if it was so, they were also conscious that one who was on their side, so to say, had us under surveillance, and we saw no sign of them.

But under observation we felt we were, as I have never felt it at another time. Specially was it so when we passed out of the churchyard into a narrow path with close, high hedges, through which we hurried as Christian did through the Valley ; and so got out into open fields. Then along hedges, though I would sooner have been in the open, where I could see if anyone was visible behind me ; over a gate or two, and then a swerve to the left, taking us up on to the ridge which ended in that mound.

As we neared it, Henry Long felt, and I felt too, that there were what I can only call dim presences waiting for us, as well as a far more actual one attending us. Of Paxton's agitation all this time I can give you no adequate picture : he breathed like a hunted beast, and we could not either of us look at his face. How he would manage when we got to the very place we had not troubled to think : he had seemed so sure that that would not be difficult. Nor was it. I never saw anything like the dash with which he flung himself at a particular spot in the side of the mound, and tore at it, so that in a very few minutes the greater part of his body was out of sight.

We stood holding the coat and that bundle of handkerchiefs, and looking, very fearfully I must admit, about us. There was nothing to be seen : a line of dark firs behind us made one skyline, more trees and the church tower half a mile off on the right, cottages and a windmill on the horizon on the left, calm sea dead in front, faint barking of a dog at a cottage on a gleaming dyke between us and it : full moon making that path we know across the sea : the eternal whisper of the Scotch firs just above us, and of the sea in front. Yet, in all this quiet, an acute, an acrid consciousness of a restrained hostility very near us, like a dog on a leash that might be let go at any moment.

Paxton pulled himself out of the hole and stretched a hand back to us. "Give it to me," he whispered, "unwrapped." We pulled off the handkerchiefs, and he took the crown. The moonlight just fell on it as he snatched it. We had not ourselves touched that bit of metal, and I have thought since that it was just as well. In another moment Paxton was out of the hole again and busy shovelling back the soil with hands that were already bleeding. He would have none of our help, though. It was much the longest part of the job to get the place to look undisturbed ; yet—I don't know how—he made a wonderful success of it. At last he was satisfied, and we turned back.

We were a couple of hundred yards from the hill when Long suddenly said to him : "I say, you've left your coat there. That won't do. See ?" And I certainly did see it —the long dark overcoat lying where the tunnel had been. Paxton had not stopped, however : he only shook his head and held up the coat on his arm. And when we joined him he said, without any excitement, but as if nothing mattered any more : "That wasn't my coat." And, indeed, when we looked back again, that dark thing was not to be seen.

Well, we got out on to the road, and came rapidly back that way. It was well before twelve when we got in, trying to put a good face on it, and saying—Long and I—what a lovely night it was for a walk. The boots was on the look-out for us, and we made remarks like that for his edification as we

entered the hotel. He gave another look up and down the
sea-front before he locked the front door, and said: "You
didn't meet many people about, I s'pose, sir?" "No, indeed,
not a soul," I said; at which I remember Paxton looked oddly
at me. "Only I thought I see someone turn up the station
road after you gentlemen," said the boots. "Still, you was
three together, and I don't suppose he meant mischief." I
didn't know what to say; Long merely said "Good night".
and we went off upstairs, promising to turn out all lights and
go to bed in a few minutes.

Back in our room we did our very best to make Paxton
take a cheerful view. "There's the crown safe back," we
said; "very likely you'd have done better not to touch it"
(and he heavily assented to that), "but no real harm has been
done, and we shall never give this away to anyone who would
be so mad as to go near it. Besides, don't you feel better
yourself? I don't mind confessing," I said, "that on the way
there I was very much inclined to take your view about—
well, about being followed; but coming back, it wasn't at all
the same thing, was it?" No, it wouldn't do: "*You've*
nothing to trouble yourselves about," he said, "but I'm not
forgiven. I've got to pay for that miserable sacrilege still.
I know what you are going to say. The Church might help.
Yes, but it's the body that has to suffer. It's true I'm not feeling that he's waiting outside for me just now. But——"
Then he stopped. Then he turned to thanking us, and we
put him off as soon as we could. And naturally we pressed
him to use our sitting-room next day, and said we should be
glad to go out with him. Or did he play golf, perhaps?
Yes, he did, but he didn't think he should care about that
tomorrow.

Well, we recommended him to get up late and sit in our
room in the morning while we were playing, and we would
have a walk later in the day. He was very submissive and
piano about it all: ready to do just what we thought best,
but clearly quite certain in his own mind that what was
coming could not be averted or palliated.

You'll wonder why we didn't insist on accompanying him
to his home and seeing him safe into the care of brothers or
someone. The fact was he had nobody. He had had a
flat in Town, but lately he had made up his mind to settle for
a time in Sweden, and he had dismantled his flat and shipped

off his belongings, and was whiling away a fortnight or three weeks before he made a start. Anyhow, we didn't see what we could do better than sleep on it—or not sleep very much, as was my case—and see what we felt like tomorrow morning. We felt very different, Long and I, on as beautiful an April morning as you could desire; and Paxton also looked very different when we saw him at breakfast. "The first approach to a decent night I seem ever to have had," was what he said. But he was going to do as we had settled : stay in probably all the morning and come out with us later. We went to the links : we met some other men and played with them in the morning, and had lunch there rather early, so as not to be late back. All the same, the snares of death overtook him.

Whether it could have been prevented, I don't know. I think he would have been got at somehow, do what we might. Anyhow, this is what happened.

We went straight up to our room. Paxton was there, reading quite peaceably. "Ready to come out shortly?" said Long, "say in half an hour's time?" "Certainly," he said : and I said we would change first and perhaps have baths, and went and lay down on my bed and slept for about ten minutes. We came out of our rooms at the same time, and went together to the sitting-room. Paxton wasn't there —only his book. Nor was he in his room, nor in the downstair rooms. We shouted for him. A servant came out and said : "Why, I thought you gentlemen was gone out already, and so did the other gentleman. He heard you a-calling from the path there, and run out in a hurry, and I looked out of the coffee-room window, but I didn't see you. 'Owever, he run off down the beach, that way."

Without a word we ran that way too—it was the opposite direction to that of last night's expedition. It wasn't quite four o'clock, and the day was fair, though not so fair as it had been, so there was really no reason, you'd say, for anxiety : with people about, surely a man couldn't come to much harm.

But something in our look as we ran out must have struck the servant, for she came out on the steps and pointed, and said, "Yes, that's the way he went." We ran on as far as the top of the shingle bank, and there pulled up. There was a choice of ways : past the houses on the sea-front, or along the sand at the bottom of the beach, which, the tide being now out, was fairly broad. Or, of course, we might keep along the shingle between these two tracks and have some view of both of them ; only that was heavy going. We chose the sand, for that was the loneliest, and someone *might* come to harm there without being seen from the public path.

Long said he saw Paxton some distance ahead, running and waving his stick, as if he wanted to signal to people who were on ahead of him. I couldn't be sure : one of those sea-mists was coming up very quickly from the south. There was someone, that's all I could say. And there were tracks on the sand as of someone running who wore shoes ; and there were other tracks made before those—for the shoes sometimes trod in them and interfered with them—of someone not in shoes. Oh, of course, it's only my word you've got to take for all this : Long's dead, we'd no time or means to make sketches or take casts, and the next tide washed everything away. All we could do was to notice these marks as we hurried on. But there they were over and over again, and we had no doubt whatever that what we saw was the track of a bare foot, and one that showed more bones than flesh.

The notion of Paxton running after—after anything like this, and supposing it to be the friends he was looking for, was very dreadful to us. You can guess what we fancied : how the thing he was following might stop suddenly and turn round on him, and what sort of face it would show, half-seen at first in the mist—which all the while was getting thicker and thicker. And as I ran on wondering how the poor wretch could have been lured into mistaking that other thing for us, I remembered his saying, "He has some power over your eyes." And then I wondered what the end would be, for I had no hope now that the end could be averted, and—well, there is no need to tell all the dismal and horrid thoughts that flitted through my head as we ran on into the mist.

It was uncanny, too, that the sun should still be bright in the sky and we could see nothing. We could only tell that we were now past the houses and had reached that gap there is between them and the old martello tower. When you are past the tower, you know, there is nothing but shingle for a long way—not a house, not a human creature, just that spit of land, or, rather, shingle, with the river on your right and the sea on your left.

But just before that, just by the martello tower, you remember there is the old battery, close to the sea. I believe there are only a few blocks of concrete left now : the rest has all been washed away, but at this time there was a lot more, though the place was a ruin. Well, when we got there we clambered to the top as quickly as we could, to take breath and look over the shingle in front if by chance the mist would let us see anything. But a moment's rest we must have. We had run a mile at least. Nothing whatever was visible ahead of us, and we were just turning by common consent to get down and run hopelessly on, when we heard what I can only call a laugh : and if you can understand what I mean by a breathless, a lungless laugh, you have it ; but I don't suppose you can. It came from below, and swerved away into the mist. That was enough. We bent over the wall. Paxton was there at the bottom.

You don't need to be told that he was dead. His tracks showed that he had run along the side of the battery, had turned sharp round the corner of it, and, small doubt of it, must have dashed straight into the open arms of someone who was waiting there. His mouth was full of sand and stones, and his teeth and jaws were broken to bits. I only glanced once at his face.

At the same moment, just as we were scrambling down from the battery to get to the body, we heard a shout, and saw a man running down the bank of the martello tower. He was the caretaker stationed there, and his keen old eyes had managed to descry through the mist that something was wrong. He had seen Paxton fall, and had seen us a moment after, running up—fortunate this, for otherwise we could hardly have escaped suspicion of being concerned in the dreadful business. Had he, we asked, caught sight of anybody attacking our friend ? He could not be sure.

We sent him off for help, and stayed by the dead man till they came with the stretcher. It was then that we traced out how he had come, on the narrow fringe of sand under the battery wall. The rest was shingle, and it was hopelessly impossible to tell whither the other had gone.

What were we to say at the inquest ? It was a duty, we felt, not to give up, there and then, the secret of the crown, to be published in every paper. I don't know how much you would have told; but what we did agree upon was this : to say that we had only made acquaintance with Paxton the day before, and that he had told us he was under some apprehension of danger at the hands of a man called William Ager. Also that we had seen some other tracks besides Paxton's when we followed him along the beach. But, of course, by that time everything was gone from the sands.

No one had any knowledge, fortunately, of any William Ager living in the district. The evidence of the man at the martello tower freed us from all suspicion. All that could be done was to return a verdict of wilful murder by some person or persons unknown.

Paxton was so totally without connections that all the inquiries that were subsequently made ended in a No Thoroughfare. And I have never been at Seaburgh, or even near it, since.

NOBODY'S HOUSE
A. M. Burrage

THEY faced each other across the threshold of the great door in the dimness of two meagre lights. It was just dusk on a windy autumn evening, and Mrs. Park, the caretaker, had brought a candle with her to answer the summons at the door. Behind the stranger the last grey light of the day filtered through veils of dingy, low-flying clouds. Between them the candle flame fluttered in the draught like a yellow pennon, the cavernous darkness of the hall advancing and retreating like some monster at once curious and shy.

The man was tall and broad and seemingly in the early fifties. He wore a grey moustache and beard, both closely trimmed, and his black velour hat was pulled low down over a high forehead. His overcoat was cut to an old-fashioned pattern, having a cape to it and it was perhaps this which lent him an air of—even at his years—having outlived his age.

He was fumbling in an inside pocket when the door was opened, and he said nothing until he had produced an envelope.

"I have an order from Messrs. Flake and Limepenny to see the house." Here he offered Mrs. Park the envelope. "I am afraid I have called at an inopportune time, but I missed one train and the next arrived late. Perhaps, however, you won't mind showing me over?"

He spoke slowly and a little nervously, as if he were repeating a speech which he had previously prepared. His voice was very low and mellowed and gentle. Mrs. Park stood back from the threshold.

"Will you come in, sir?" she said. "I am afraid you won't be seeing the house at its best. I shall have to show you over by candle; there is no gas or electric light."

He stepped inside and scrutinized her. She was a tall,

gaunt, middle-aged woman of the kind which is generally described as "superior". Nature had intended her to become matron of an institute. Fate and widowhood had forced her a rung or two down the ladder. She looked what she was —honest, hard-working, and almost devoid of sympathy.

"I'm afraid," she added in her hard, toneless voice, "you'll find everything just anyhow. I wasn't expecting anybody. Very few people come here nowadays. And a place of this size takes more than one pair of hands to keep it clean."

"It has been empty a long time, then?" he hazarded.

"Ever since——" She checked herself suddenly. "For more than twenty years, I should think." She turned her shoulder upon him, lifting the candle above her head. "This is supposed to be a fine hall, and everybody admires the staircase. If the house doesn't find a tenant or a purchaser soon, I hear they intend removing the staircase and selling it separately. There is a lot of fine oak panelling, too. The library——"

Turning to see if he were listening, she saw him start and shiver and rub his long, thin hands together.

"Excuse me," he said. "I have been a long time in the train and I am very cold. I wonder if it would be troubling you too much to get me a cup of tea."

"Yes, I could do that," she answered. "The kettle is on, for I intended having one myself. Will you come this way? Perhaps you would like a warm by the fire?"

She led the way across the hall and through a baize-covered door at the end. Turning once to see if she were giving him sufficient light, Mrs. Park noticed that he walked with a slight limp.

He followed her down a short passage, through a great kitchen ruddy with firelight, down another passage, and into a small room intended to be used as a housekeeper's parlour. Here there was warmth, even stuffiness. A paraffin lamp stood burning on a flaming red table-cloth.

The room was full of hideous modern cottage furniture, and decorated largely with the portraits of people who ought to have known better than to be photographed. But a fire burned brightly in the grate and a kettle on a brass trivet murmured and rattled its lid. This commonplace room lighted and hot and over-furnished, was at least a relief from the dark passage and the draughty, gloom-ridden hall.

"I'll give you your tea in here, sir, and take mine in the kitchen," the caretaker said.

"Nonsense. Why should you? Besides, I want to talk. Oh, here's the order to view. You see . . . Mr. Stephen Royds—that's my name . . . to view. . . ."

He was running his thumbnail along the sheet of heavily headed office note-paper. Mrs. Park glanced perfunctorily at the typewriting. So far as she was concerned, an order to view was a superfluous formality. She was more interested in this Mr. Royds, who, having removed his hat, disclosed a head of sparse iron-grey hair. He spoke like a gentleman but there was nothing opulent in his appearance. He looked an unlikely purchaser or tenant; but for that matter she had never been able to visualize the sort of person whom the house would suit.

"I'll remove my greatcoat if you don't mind," he said while Mrs. Park went to a cupboard for another cup and saucer. "The room is warm." He laid the coat across the back of a chair. "Do you live here entirely alone?"

"Yes."

"Aren't you—nervous?"

She looked up sharply.

"Nervous? What is there to be nervous about?"

"I didn't know. Some people cannot bear loneliness. Can you tell me why the house has been on the market all these years?"

Mrs. Park smiled grimly.

"That's easy enough," she said. "It's nobody's house."

"What do you mean—nobody's house?"

"People who can afford to keep up a great house like this generally want land along with it. There isn't any land. People who don't want land can't afford to keep up a house like this. The estate was sold to Major Skirting. He's a house of his own. He's let the land and he's been trying to let or sell the house ever since. I've shown hundreds over but nobody's ever thought twice about taking it."

"Strange. It's a good house. But the land . . . yes I quite follow you. Whom used it to belong to?"

Mrs. Park set the cup and saucer down upon the table with a rattle.

"A gentleman named Harboys," she said; and suddenly stood rigid, her head a little on one side, in an attitude of listening.

"Do you hear anything ?" he asked sharply.

"No, I'll make the tea."

"I suppose you sometimes fancy you hear things ?"

She bent over the kettle, giving him no answer. He waited until the teapot was full and then gently repeated the question.

"Hear things ?" she repeated with some show of asperity. "No. Why should I ?"

"I didn't know. These empty old houses. . . ."

"I'm not one of the fanciful sort, sir. . . . Will you help yourself to milk and sugar ?"

She let him see that the talk had veered in a direction contrary to her liking. There was veiled fear in her eyes, and, watching her intently, he could see that she was not impervious to loneliness. Here was a woman who suffered more than she knew. She could bluff her nerves by sheer will-power, but this will-power was steadily losing in the long battle. Mrs. Park was afraid of something, and always, in her inner consciousness, fighting against that fear.

"Thank you," the stranger said, taking the cup and saucer. "Who was this Harboys ? Is he still alive ?"

"I couldn't say."

"Isn't there some story about the house ?"

"I don't know."

"Forgive me. I think you do."

"There are stories. . . . You don't need to listen. . . ."

She spoke jerkily. Once more he remarked that look in her eyes.

"Tell me," he said gently.

"I can't sir. If Major Skirting knew I told people I should lose my job. He'd think I was trying to prevent people from taking the house."

"It wouldn't prevent me. Wasn't this Harboys supposed to have shot——"

"Ah !" She set cup and saucer down with a rattle. "Then you've heard something already, sir !"

"A little. You had better tell me all. It will not affect me as a prospective purchaser."

Mrs. Park passed a hand across her forehead.

"I don't like talking about it, sir. You see, I live here all alone. . . ."

She checked herself suddenly, finding herself about to admit to a second person something which she never confessed even to herself.

"Just so," Royds said sympathetically. "And you some-times hear noises ? What noises ?"

"Oh, it's imagination," she said. "Or the wind. Some-times the wind sounds like footsteps and voices, and sometimes I seem to hear. . . . It may be a loose door somewhere that bangs."

He leaned forward, his eyes shining with the excitement of some strange fascination.

"You mean you hear a shot fired ?" he asked, scarcely above a whisper.

Her one hand resting on the tablecloth contracted nervously.

"I've known it sound like a shot. Oh, I don't believe. . . ."

"They say the house is haunted ?" he asked eagerly.

"They say. . . . Oh, when there's been a tragedy happen in a house people will always——"

"Never mind what people say. What do *you* say ?" The timbre of his voice had changed ; under excitement it had hardened, grown louder. "*Is* the house haunted ?"

There was something compelling in Royds's gaze, in the new tone of his voice. She answered him sullenly, help-lessly.

"I don't know. I've heard things. I tell myself they're nothing." She groped for a handkerchief. "I've *got* to tell myself they're nothing."

"You haven't—*seen* anything ?" he asked, in a low, strained, voice.

"No, thank God ! I never go near the library after dark."

"The library ? So it was there. Tell me."

Mrs. Park gulped some tea and replenished her cup with a shaking hand.

"It must have been about twenty years ago," she said in a low and curiously unwilling tone. "The place belonged to a Mr. Gerald Harboys. He was quite young—not much more than thirty, and very well liked. Some said he was a bit queer, but there was a strain of queerness in all the Harboys. Mad on hunting, he was, and one of the best riders in these parts. You'll be surprised at the size of the stables when you see them. He had them built.

"He'd married a young wife, one of the Miss Greys from

Hornfield Manor, and some say he thought more of her than he did of his horses. She used to ride, too, and the pair of them, and Mr. Peter Marsh from Brinkchurch, were always together.

"Harboys and Marsh had known each other since they were in the cradle. Whether there was really anything between Marsh and Mrs. Harboys I don't know. There's been arguments about that for years, but they're both dead and gone now, and nobody will ever know.

"About one Christmas-time Harboys took a fall in the hunting field and broke his leg and it was during his convalescence that he got into one of his queer moods. I dare say it was being kept out of the hunting field which brought it on. His leg mended slowly, and right at the end of January he could only just get about with a stick.

"Mrs. Harboys followed the hounds every time there was a meet in the neighbourhood, and, with her husband unable to get about, she saw more of Peter Marsh than usual. But nobody seemed to know that Mr. Harboys was jealous or that he suspected anything wrong.

"Well, one day, at the end of January, Mrs. Harboys went out hunting, and her husband brooded all day over the library fire. During the afternoon he amused himself by cleaning a revolver, which he afterwards laid aside on the mantelpiece within reach.

"Mrs. Harboys came in just after dark. Peter Marsh had been piloting her, and she brought him with her. While she was ordering tea and poached eggs to be sent up to the morning-room, she sent Peter Marsh into the library to get himself a whisky, and tell Mr. Harboys about the day's hunting. He had not been in the library a minute, when angry voices were heard and then a shot.

"The butler then burst into the room and found Peter Marsh lying dead, and Mr. Harboys, still in his chair before the fire, staring wildly at the body, with the revolver in his hand."

She paused, and in the silence she heard Royds breathing heavily. His head was bent and his gaze lowered to the near edge of the table, so that she could scarcely see his face.

"Mr. Harboys," she resumed, "pleaded not guilty at the trial and said that his mind was a blank at the time when the shot was fired. He couldn't remember anything that had happened between Marsh coming into the room and then the butler bending over the dead body. His counsel put in a plea for insanity, but the jury would not have it. They found him guilty and added a recommendation to mercy. The death penalty was changed to penal servitude for life."

She broke off and began to muse, knitting her brows.

"That must be twenty years ago. . . . They let them out after twenty years. He's out already, or soon will be, if he's alive."

Slowly Royds lifted his head and turned burning eyes upon her face.

"And do you think Harboys did it ?" he demanded.

The question took Mrs. Park aback.

"Of course ! Why ! How else could it have happened ? There was only those two in the room. It couldn't have happened any other way."

Royds got upon his legs. His pale face shining with little drops of moisture, his eyes aflame with a strange passion.

"I swear to you," he cried, "that I don't believe Harboys did it. I knew the men——"

Mrs. Park's stare intensified and she uttered a smothered exclamation.

"—— I knew him well as child and boy and man. I was at school with Harboys. I tell you he was incapable of murder ! All the circumstantial evidence in the world would not weigh an atom with me against my knowledge of his character. They say he had fits of madness. Another lie ! But mad or sane he couldn't have done it. He loved his wife—and old Peter Marsh. He knew that they were two of God's best and whitest people. I tell you——"

He broke off suddenly and lowered his voice.

"I'm frightening you," he said. "I didn't mean to. Oh, but think ! There's Harboys been rotting in prison these twenty years, remembering nothing of those few dreadful moments. To this day he doesn't know if he's innocent or guilty. Think of it."

Mrs. Park lifted her white face and twitching lips. One hand had stolen to the region of her heart. Each rapid stroke of her pulses seemed to shake her.

"Why have you come here ?" she cried in a voice which rose high and querulous with a nameless dread. "You don't want the house ! You never intended——"

338

"No," said Royds, "I came here to find out."

"What ?"

"They say strange things happen in the library. I have heard stories. You tell me you have heard footfalls, voices, the sound of a shot. Don't you understand, woman ? What happened in the library that evening twenty years ago is known only to God ! The man who lives remembers nothing. If it be true that Peter Marsh returns. . . . Oh, don't you understand ? It is the only way of learning . . . the only way. . . ."

Mrs. Park stood up ; her slim body made a barrier between him and the door.

"I can't let you go to the library," she cried sharply.

"I must. I'm going to spend the night there. I'm going to wait until Peter——"

"I can't let you," she said again.

"But you must. Don't you understand ? This means life or death to a man."

She backed almost to the door.

"It's madness !" she cried. "Nobody has ever endured that room after nightfall."

"I will !"

"I shall be sent away if it is found out."

"It won't be found out. I'll recompense you if it is. Here, I came prepared to pay for the privilege." He tugged a bundle of bank notes roughly out of his breast pocket and flung them on the table. "How much do you want ? Five pounds ? Ten ? Twenty ?"

Mrs. Park's gaze lingered on the roll of notes. She knew the value of money. Besides, she was alone in the great house with a man it might be dangerous to thwart.

"Come," said Royds, "here are five five-pound notes. Take them and act like a sensible woman. Then I shall go to the library, and you will make me a fire. Is there any furniture there ?"

"No," muttered the woman, her gaze still on the roll of bank notes.

"Then, if you will permit me, I will take a chair."

He picked up the notes again and transferred all of them but five to his breast pocket. With these five he advanced and pressed them into the woman's hand. Her fingers closed over them.

"I'm doing wrong," she muttered.

"You're doing right. I'll get the truth to-night if I have to summon the devil himself. Now come and help me make a fire in the library."

She turned heavily away without a word and went to a cupboard, from the bottom of which she took a bundle of firewood and an old sheet of newspaper, which she dropped on top of the contents of the half-filled scuttle. Then she lit a candle in a brass stick and motioned him towards the door. He picked up a chair as he followed her.

The house was very still as they passed through the kitchen and passages leading to the hall. Their footfalls on the uncarpeted floors rang out sonorously through the hollow shell of the house.

To the woman this shattering of a silence which seemed almost sacred was a new weapon put into the hands of Terror. Her overstrained nerves cried out in protest at each of the man's heavy steps. Around her, in the shifting penumbra beyond reach of the candle light, above her in the empty upper chambers of the house, all manner of sleeping horrors, shapeless abominations of the night-world, seemed to waken and listen and draw near. The silent house seemed full of stealthy movement, and each blotch of darkness was an ambush peopled by the lewd phantasms of her mind. The man walking behind her seemed to be without nerves, or he had so stimulated them as to bring them entirely under his control.

Evidently he knew the house, for he passed her in the hall taking the lead in the procession of two, and went straight to the library door, which he flung open and passed on the crest of the following candle light.

The library was a long room in an angle of the house. A long row of windows fronted the hearth, and two more faced the door. The walls were of oak panels stained a mahogany colour, but in that dim light they looked black, as if they were hung with funereal trappings.

The man lingered between the door and the first of the windows, while Mrs. Park, half-closing her eyes, hurried across to the fireplace with the scuttle. He seemed to be searching for something. Presently he found it.

"There's a hole in one of these panels," he announced.

Mrs. Park's heart gave a leap.

"Yes," she stammered. "It's a—a bullet hole. The shot lodged there after—after——"

"Yes," he said, quietly, "I understand." He crossed the room with the chair and set it down at that corner of the hearth which faced the door and the damaged panel. "And that afternoon, over twenty years ago, I was sitting here——"

There was a crash as the scuttle fell from the woman's hands. All her horror and amazement expressed itself in one thin, muffled scream.

"*You* were sitting there ! *You* ! Gerald Harboys ! Gerald Harboys, the murderer !"

He answered quietly : "Gerald Harboys or Stephen Royds— God help me, what does it matter ? Murderer or not—only God knows ! But I shall learn to-night. Light that fire, woman, and leave me."

She left him, and stumbled blindly back to the little vulgar room behind the kitchen. But a fascination stronger than terror drew her back to the outside of the library door, there trembling to wait and to listen. . . .

Harboys, to give him his real name at the last, settled himself on the chair and at first busied himself with the building up of the fire. Then he took a revolver from his coat pocket, and placed it upon the mantelpiece within his reach. This done he looked out across the room with a steady gaze.

The firelight wrought strange patterns among the shadows, but in the swiftly changing measures of this shadow-dance he found nothing of what he sought. Presently he began to speak aloud, quietly but very distinctly, so that the shivering woman outside the door brought her hands to her tightening throat.

"Peter, Peter." The tone was almost wheedling. "Can you hear me ? I'm sitting in just the same place that I sat that evening, with my bad leg resting on a stool. Here am I, and here's that damned revolver. Now, Peter, won't you come ? They say you're always here—that you can't rest because your best friend shot you. Did I shoot you, Peter ? My mind's a blank—a blank ! For twenty years I have been trying to remember. I have not known peace day and night for twenty years, Peter. Oh, come and tell me ! I want to know—to *know*. There's something wrong, Peter. I couldn't have done it. How could I have shot you, boy ?"

He relapsed into silence, his gaze never leaving the space between the door and the first window. After a long minute his voice broke out again, choked and almost tearful.

"Is it because you hate me that you won't show yourself Peter? Was I mad? And did I do it after all? Don't, hate me, Peter. I've suffered! Have pity! One way or another I want to end this agony to-night. Oh, God, make him merciful to me! Peter, we'd been friends so long. School . . . don't you remember Wryvern, and those long talks under the lime-trees in the Close on summer nights? And study teas? And going up to Lords'?"

He babbled on, while kaleidoscopic pictures passed before the eyes of his memory. Cool, dewy morning, and the cricket eleven tumbling out of houses for fielding practice; rows of languid boys in dim classrooms and a scratching of pens; bright sunlight, and white shapes moving on a green sward; crowded touch-lines, and the scrum forming, and goal-posts standing up stark against a grey November sky. In each and all of them he caught a wavering, vanishing glimpse of Peter Marsh.

"Peter!" he cried out again. "Can't you hear me? Won't you come to me? You *do* come back. They all say so. That woman hears you. You—in your scarlet coat, as you came in that evening. I remember . . . when I saw you lying there . . . the blood scarcely showed. I was sitting here waiting for Muriel. I heard you both come up the drive. Muriel was laughing at something. You were both talking to the groom outside. Then I heard you in the hall, and Muriel ordered tea and went upstairs. And I thought: 'She doesn't come in to see me. I'm nothing to her now I'm crocked. It's all Peter, Peter, Peter. By God!' I said, 'I've been blind as well as lame. The things I've seen which they pretended were nothing . . . The things I haven't seen, but heard of in whispers and hints.' All in a moment my brain caught fire. 'Damn you!' I said, 'I'll teach you to make a cuckold of a lame man!' Then . . . you came in."

The trembling woman outside heard him utter a hoarse cry.

"Peter! Peter! Oh, God, I'm beginning to remember! You stood where you're standing now, touching the handle of the door. That's right! And you said—I remember now —'Give us a peg, Jerry. I'm frozen. There's a devil of an

east wind.' Peter! Peter! Don't look like that! I'm
remembering . . . remembering. Oh, God, have mercy
. . . have mercy!"

A hoarse scream echoed through the room, a chair reeled
over with a crash, and then followed a frenzied shouting.

*"I remember . . . I remember . . . damn you! when you turned
your back on me . . . like that. . . ."*

A shot rang out; then another. Then silence enfolded
Nobody's House and its one living inmate, a swooning woman,
who clung to the oak balustrade.

It was half an hour later when Mrs. Park forced herself into
the library. The red glow of the fire was still dancing on the
walls and floor. For a moment one ruddy gleam seemed to
take a fantastic shape—like the prostrate figure of a man in
hunting pink.

Harboys lay crumpled and face downwards across the
hearth, the revolver still in his hand, the ugly wound in his
temple mercifully hidden. To that end had he remembered.

Where there had been a bullet hole in one of the panels the
police next morning found two. They were side by side and
scarcely an inch apart.

THE WEREWOLF
Frederick Marryat

BEFORE noon Philip and Krantz had embarked, and made sail in the peroqua.

They had no difficulty in steering their course; the islands by day, and the clear stars by night, were their compass. It is true that they did not follow the more direct track, but they followed the more secure, working up the smooth waters, and gaining to the northward more than to the west. Many times they were chased by the Malay proas, which infested the islands, but the swiftness of their little peroqua was their security; indeed, the chase was, generally speaking, abandoned as soon as the smallness of the vessel was made out by the pirates, who expected that little or no booty was to be gained.

One morning, as they were sailing between the isles, with less wind than usual, Philip observed:

"Krantz, you said that there were events in your own life, or connected with it, which would corroborate the mysterious tale I confided to you. Will you now tell me to what you referred?"

"Certainly," replied Krantz; "I have often thought of doing so, but one circumstance or another has hitherto prevented me; this is, however, a fitting opportunity. Prepare therefore to listen to a strange story, quite as strange, perhaps, as your own.

"I take it for granted that you have heard people speak of the Hartz Mountains," observed Krantz.

"I have never heard people speak of them, that I can recollect," replied Philip; "but I have read of them in some book, and of the strange things which have occurred there."

"It is indeed a wild region," rejoined Krantz, "and many strange tales are told of it; but strange as they are, I have good reason for believing them to be true.

"My father was not born, or originally a resident, in the Hartz Mountains; he was a serf of an Hungarian nobleman, of great possessions, in Transylvania; but although a serf, he was not by any means a poor or illiterate man. In fact, he was rich, and his intelligence and respectability were such, that he had been raised by his lord to the stewardship; but whoever may happen to be born a serf, a serf must he remain, even though he become a wealthy man : such was the condition of my father. My father had been married for about five years; and by his marriage had three children—my eldest brother Cæsar, myself (Hermann), and a sister named Marcella. You know, Philip, that Latin is still the language spoken in that country; and that will account for our high-sounding names. My mother was a very beautiful woman, unfortunately more beautiful than virtuous : she was seen and admired by the lord of the soil; my father was sent away upon some mission; and during his absence, my mother flattered by the attentions, and won by the assiduities, of this nobleman, yielded to his wishes. It so happened that my father returned very unexpectedly, and discovered the intrigue. The evidence of my mother's shame was positive : he surprised her in the company of her seducer ! Carried away by the impetuosity of his feelings, he watched the opportunity of a meeting taking place between them, and murdered both his wife and her seducer. Conscious that, as a serf, not even the provocation which he had received would be allowed as a justification of his conduct, he hastily collected together what money he could lay his hands upon, and, as we were then in the depth of winter, he put his horses to the sleigh, and taking his children with him, he set off in the middle of the night, and was far away before the tragical circumstance had transpired. Aware that he would be pursued, and that he had no chance of escape if he remained in any portion of his native country (in which the authorities could lay hold of him), he continued his flight without intermission until he had buried himself in the intricacies and seclusions of the Hartz Mountains. Of course, all that I have now told you I learned afterwards. My oldest recollections are knit to a rude, yet comfortable cottage, in which I lived with my father, brother, and sister. It was on the confines of one of those vast forests which cover the northern part of Germany; around it were a few acres of ground, which, during the summer months, my father cultivated, and which, though they yielded a doubtful harvest, were sufficient for our support. In the winter we remained much indoors, for, as my father followed the chase, we were left alone, and the wolves during that season incessantly prowled about. My father had purchased the cottage, and land about it, of one of the rude foresters, who gain their livelihood partly by hunting, and partly by burning charcoal, for the purpose of smelting the ore from the neighbouring mines ; it was distant about two miles from any other habitation. I can call to mind the whole landscape now ; the tall pines which rose up on the mountain above us, and the wide expanse of the forest beneath, on the topmost boughs and heads of whose trees we looked down from our cottage, as the mountain below us rapidly descended into the distant valley. In summer time the prospect was beautiful : but during the severe winter a more desolate scene could not well be imagined.

"I said that, in the winter, my father occupied himself with the chase ; every day he left us, and often would he lock the door, that we might not leave the cottage. He had no one to assist him, or to take care of us—indeed, it was not easy to find a female servant who would live in such a solitude ; but, could he have found one, my father would not have received her, for he had imbibed a horror of the sex, as the difference of his conduct towards us, his two boys and my poor little sister Marcella evidently proved. You may suppose we were sadly neglected ; indeed, we suffered much, for my father, fearful that we might come to some harm, would not allow us fuel when he left the cottage ; and we were obliged, therefore, to creep under the heaps of bears' skins, and there to keep ourselves as warm as we could until he returned in the evening, when a blazing fire was our delight. That my father chose this restless sort of life may appear strange, but the fact was, that he could not remain quiet ; whether from the remorse for having committed murder, or from the misery consequent on his change of situation, or from both combined, he was never happy unless he was in a state of activity. Children, however, when left so much to themselves, acquire a thoughtfulness not common to their age. So it was with us ; and during the short cold days of winter, we would sit silent, longing for the happy hours when the snow would melt and the leaves burst out, and the birds begin their songs, and when we should again be set at liberty.

"Such was our peculiar and savage sort of life until my brother Cæsar was nine, myself seven, and my sister five years old, when the circumstances occurred on which is based the extraordinary narrative which I am about to relate.

"One evening my father returned home rather later than usual; he had been unsuccessful, and as the weather was very severe, and many feet of snow were upon the ground, he was not only very cold, but in a very bad humour. He had brought in wood, and we were all three gladly assisting each other in blowing on the embers to create a blaze, when he caught poor little Marcella by the arm and threw her aside ; the child fell, struck her mouth, and bled very much. My brother ran to raise her up. Accustomed to ill-usage, and afraid of my father, she did not dare to cry, but looked up in his face very piteously. My father drew his stool nearer to the hearth, muttered something in abuse of women, and busied himself with the fire, which both my brother and I had deserted when our sister was so unkindly treated. A cheerful blaze was soon the result of his exertions ; but we did not, as usual, crowd round it. Marcella, still bleeding, retired to a corner, and my brother and I took our seats beside her, while my father hung over the fire gloomily and alone. Such had been our position for about half an hour, when the howl of a wolf, close under the window of the cottage, fell on our ears. My father started up, and seized his gun ; the howl was repeated ; he examined the priming, and then hastily left the cottage, shutting the door after him. We all waited (anxiously listening), for we thought that if he succeeded in shooting the wolf, he would return in a better humour ; and, although he was harsh to all of us, and particularly so to our little sister, still we loved our father, and loved to see him cheerful and happy, for what else had we to look up to ? And I may here observe, that perhaps there never were three children who were fonder of each other ; we did not, like other children, fight and dispute together ; and if, by chance, any disagreement did arise, between my elder brother and me, little Marcella would run to us, and kissing us both, seal, through her entreaties, the peace between us. Marcella was a lovely, amiable child ; I can recall her beautiful features even now. Alas ! poor little Marcella."

"She is dead, then ?" observed Philip.

"Dead! yes, dead! but how did she die?—But I must not anticipate, Philip; let me tell my story.

"We waited for some time, but the report of the gun did not reach us, and my elder brother then said: 'Our father has followed the wolf, and will not be back for some time. Marcella, let us wash the blood from your mouth, and then we will leave this corner and go to the fire to warm ourselves.'

"We did so, and remained there until near midnight, every minute wondering, as it grew later, why our father did not return. We had no idea that he was in any danger, but we thought that he must have chased the wolf for a very long time. 'I will look out and see if father is coming,' said my brother Cæsar, going to the door. 'Take care,' said Marcella, 'the wolves must be about now, and we cannot kill them, brother.' My brother opened the door very cautiously, and but a few inches; he peeped out. 'I see nothing,' said he, after a time, and once more he joined us at the fire. 'We have had no supper,' said I, for my father usually cooked the meat as soon as he came home; and during his absence we had nothing but the fragments of the preceding day.

"'And if our father comes home, after his hunt, Cæsar,' said Marcella, 'he will be pleased to have some supper; let us cook it for him and for ourselves.' Cæsar climbed upon the stool, and reached down some meat—I forget now whether it was venison or bear's meat, but we cut off the usual quantity, and proceeded to dress it, as we used to do under our father's superintendence. We were all busy putting it into the platters before the fire, to await his coming, when we heard the sound of a horn. We listened—there was a noise outside, and a minute afterwards my father entered, ushered in a young female, and a large dark man in a hunter's dress.

"Perhaps I had better now relate what was only known to me many years afterwards. When my father had left the cottage, he perceived a large white wolf about thirty yards from him; as soon as the animal saw my father, it retreated slowly, growling and snarling. My father followed; the animal did not run, but always kept at some distance; and my father did not like to fire until he was pretty certain that his ball would take effect; thus they went on for some time, the wolf now leaving my father far behind, and then stopping and snarling defiance at him, and then, again, on his approach, setting off at speed.

"Anxious to shoot the animal (for the white wolf is very rare), my father continued the pursuit for several hours, during which he continually ascended the mountain.

"You must know, Philip, that there are peculiar spots on those mountains which are supposed, and, as my story will prove, truly supposed, to be inhabited by the evil influences : they are well known to the huntsmen, who invariably avoid them. Now, one of these spots, an open space in the pine forest above us, had been pointed out to my father as dangerous on that account. But whether he disbelieved these wild stories, or whether, in his eager pursuit of the chase, he disregarded them, I know not ; certain, however, it is, that he was decoyed by the white wolf to this open space, when the animal appeared to slacken her speed. My father approached, came close up to her, raised his gun to his shoulder and was about to fire, when the wolf suddenly disappeared. He thought that the snow on the ground must have dazzled his sight, and he let down his gun to look for the beast—but she was gone ; how she could have escaped over the clearance, without his seeing her, was beyond his comprehension. Mortified at the ill-success of his chase, he was about to retrace his steps, when he heard the distant sound of a horn. Astonishment at such a sound—at such an hour—in such a wilderness, made him forget for the moment his disappointment, and he remained riveted to the spot. In a minute the horn was blown a second time, and at no great distance ; my father stood still, and listened ; a third time it was blown. I forget the term used to express it, but it was the signal which, my father well knew, implied that the party was lost in the woods. In a few minutes more my father beheld a man on horseback, with a female seated on the crupper, enter the cleared space, and ride up to him. At first, my father called to mind the strange stories which he had heard of the supernatural beings who were said to frequent these mountains ; but the nearer approach of the parties satisfied him that they were mortals like himself. As soon as they came up to him, the man who guided the horse accosted him. 'Friend hunter, you are out late, the better fortune for us ; we have ridden far, and are in fear of our lives, which are eagerly sought after. These mountains have enabled us to elude our pursuers ; but if we find not shelter and refreshment, that will avail us little, as we must perish from hunger and the inclemency of the night. My daughter, who rides behind me, is now more dead than alive—say, can you assist us in our difficulty ?'

" 'My cottage is some few miles distant,' replied my father, 'but I have little to offer you besides a shelter from the weather ; to the little I have you are welcome. May I ask whence you come ?'

" 'Yes, friend, it is no secret now ; we have escaped from Transylvania, where my daughter's honour and my life were equally in jeopardy !'

"This information was quite enough to raise an interest in my father's heart. He remembered his own escape : he remembered the loss of his wife's honour, and the tragedy by which it was wound up. He immediately, and warmly, offered all the assistance which he could afford them.

" 'There is no time to be lost, then, good sir,' observed the horseman ; 'my daughter is chilled with the frost, and cannot hold out much longer against the severity of the weather.'

" 'Follow me,' replied my father, leading the way towards his home.

" 'I was lured away in pursuit of a large white wolf,' observed my father ; 'it came to the very window of my hut, or I should not have been out at this time of night.'

" 'The creature passed by us just as we came out of the wood,' said the female, in a silvery tone.

" 'I was nearly discharging my piece at it,' observed the hunter ; 'but since it did us such good service, I am glad that I allowed it to escape.'

"In about an hour and a half, during which my father walked at a rapid pace, the party arrived at the cottage, and, as I said before, came in.

" 'We are in good time, apparently,' observed the dark hunter, catching the smell of the roasted meat, as he walked to the fire and surveyed my brother and sister and myself. 'You have young cooks here, Meinheer.' 'I am glad that we shall not have to wait,' replied my father. 'Come, mistress, seat yourself by the fire ; you require warmth after your cold ride.' 'And where can I put up my horse, Meinheer ?' observed the huntsman. 'I will take care of him,' replied my father, going out of the cottage door.

"The female must, however, be particularly described. She was young, and apparently twenty years of age. She was

dressed in a travelling dress, deeply bordered with white fur,
and wore a cap of white ermine on her head. Her features
were very beautiful, at least I thought so, and so my father
has since declared. Her hair was flaxen, glossy, and shining,
and bright as a mirror ; and her mouth, although somewhat
large when it was open, showed the most brilliant teeth I have
ever beheld. But there was something about her eyes, bright
as they were, which made us children afraid ; they were so
restless, so furtive ; I could not at that time tell why, but I
felt as if there was cruelty in her eye ; and when she beckoned
us to come to her, we approached her with fear and trembling.
Still she was beautiful, very beautiful. She spoke kindly to
my brother and myself, patted our heads and caressed us ;
but Marcella would not come near her ; on the contrary, she
slunk away, and hid herself in the bed, and would not wait
for the supper, which half an hour before she had been so
anxious for.

"My father, having put the horse into a close shed, soon
returned, and supper was placed on the table. When it was
over, my father requested the young lady would take possession
of the bed, and he would remain at the fire, and sit up with her
father. After some hesitation on her part, this arrangement
was agreed to, and I and my brother crept into the other bed
with Marcella, for we had as yet always slept together.

"But we could not sleep ; there was something so unusual,
not only in seeing strange people, but in having those people
sleep at the cottage, that we were bewildered. As for poor
little Marcella, she was quiet, but I perceived that she trembled
during the whole night, and sometimes I thought that she was
checking a sob. My father had brought out some spirits,
which he rarely used, and he and the strange hunter remained
drinking and talking before the fire. Our ears were ready to
catch the slightest whisper—so much was our curiosity
excited.

" 'You said you came from Transylvania ?' observed my
father.

" 'Even so, Meinheer,' replied the hunter. 'I was a serf
to the noble house of —— ; my master would insist upon my
surrendering up my fair girl to his wishes ; it ended in my
giving him a few inches of my hunting-knife.'

' 'We are countrymen and brothers in misfortune,' replied
my father, taking the huntsman's hand and pressing it warmly.

" 'Indeed ! Are you then from that country ?'

" 'Yes ; and I too have fled for my life. But mine is a melancholy tale.'

" 'Your name ?' inquired the hunter.

" 'Krantz.'

" 'What ! Krantz of —— ? I have heard your tale ; you need not renew your grief by repeating it now. Welcome, most welcome, Meinheer, and, I may say, my worthy kinsman. I am your second cousin, Wilfred of Barnsdorf,' cried the hunter, rising up and embracing my father.

"They filled their horn-mugs to the brim, and drank to one another after the German fashion. The conversation was then carried on in a low tone ; all that we could collect from it was that our new relative and his daughter were to take up their abode in our cottage, at least for the present. In about an hour they both fell back in their chairs and appeared to sleep.

" 'Marcella, dear, did you hear ?' said my brother, in a low tone.

" 'Yes,' replied Marcella, in a whisper, 'I heard all. Oh ! brother, I cannot bear to look upon that woman—I feel so frightened.'

"My brother made no reply, and shortly afterwards we were all three fast asleep.

"When we awoke the next morning, we found that the hunter's daughter had risen before us. I thought she looked more beautiful than ever. She came up to little Marcella and caressed her ; the child burst into tears, and sobbed as if her heart would break.

"But not to detain you with too long a story, the huntsman and his daughter were accommodated in the cottage. My father and he went out hunting daily, leaving Christina with us. She performed all the household duties ; was very kind to us children ; and gradually the dislike even of little Marcella wore away. But a great change took place in my father ; he appeared to have conquered his aversion to the sex, and was most attentive to Christina. Often, after her father and we were in bed, would he sit up with her, conversing in a low tone by the fire. I ought to have mentioned that my father and the huntsman Wilfred slept in another portion of the cottage, and that the bed which he formerly occupied, and which was in the same room as ours, had been given up to the

354

use of Christina. These visitors had been about three weeks at the cottage, when, one night, after we children had been sent to bed, a consultation was held. My father had asked Christina in marriage, and had obtained both her own consent and that of Wilfred; after this, a conversation took place, which was, as nearly as I can recollect, as follows :

" 'You may take my child, Meinheer Krantz, and my blessing with her, and I shall then leave you and seek some other habitation—it matters little where.'

" 'Why not remain here, Wilfred ?'

" 'No, no, I am called elsewhere; let that suffice, and ask no more questions. You have my child.'

" 'I thank you for her, and will duly value her; but there is one difficulty.'

" 'I know what you would say; there is no priest here in this wild country; true; neither is there any law to bind. Still must some ceremony pass between you, to satisfy a father. Will you consent to marry her after my fashion ? if so, I will marry you directly.'

" 'I will,' replied my father.

" 'Then take her by the hand. Now, Meinheer, swear.'

" 'I swear,' repeated my father.

" 'By all the spirits of the Hartz Mountains——'

" 'Nay, why not by Heaven ?' interrupted my father.

" 'Because it is not my humour,' rejoined Wilfred. 'If I prefer that oath, less binding, perhaps, than another, surely you will not thwart me.'

" 'Well, be it so, then; have your humour. Will you make me swear by that in which I do not believe ?'

" 'Yet many do so, who in outward appearance are Christians,' rejoined Wilfred; 'say, will you be married, or shall I take my daughter away with me ?'

" 'Proceed,' replied my father impatiently.

" 'I swear by all the spirits of the Hartz Mountains, by all their power for good or for evil, that I take Christina for my wedded wife; that I will ever protect her, cherish her, and love her; that my hand shall never be raised against her to harm her.'

"My father repeated the words after Wilfred.

" 'And if I fail in this my vow, may all the vengeance of the spirits fall upon me and upon my children; may they perish by the vulture, by the wolf, or other beasts of the forest; may their flesh be torn from their limbs, and their bones blanch in the wilderness : all this I swear.'

"My father hesitated, as he repeated the last words ; little Marcella could not restrain herself, and as my father repeated the last sentence, she burst into tears. This sudden interruption appeared to discompose the party, particularly my father ; he spoke harshly to the child, who controlled her sobs, burying her face under the bedclothes.

"Such was the second marriage of my father. The next morning, the hunter Wilfred mounted his horse and rode away.

"My father resumed his bed, which was in the same room as ours ; and things went on much as before the marriage, except that our new mother-in-law did not show any kindness towards us ; indeed, during my father's absence, she would often beat us, particularly little Marcella, and her eyes would flash fire, as she looked eagerly upon the fair and lovely child.

"One night my sister awoke me and my brother.

" 'What is the matter ?' said Cæsar.

" 'She has gone out,' whispered Marcella.

" 'Gone out !'

" 'Yes, gone out at the door, in her night-clothes,' replied the child ; 'I saw her get out of bed, look at my father to see if he slept, and then she went out at the door.'

"What could induce her to leave her bed, and all undressed to go out, in such bitter wintry weather, with the snow deep on the ground, was to us incomprehensible ; we lay awake, and in about an hour we heard the growl of a wolf close under the window.

" 'There is a wolf,' said Cæsar. 'She will be torn to pieces.'

" 'Oh, no !' cried Marcella.

"In a few minutes afterwards our mother-in-law appeared ; she was in her night-dress, as Marcella had stated. She let down the latch of the door, so as to make no noise, went to a pail of water, and washed her face and hands, and then slipped into the bed where my father lay.

"We all three trembled—we hardly knew why ; but we resolved to watch the next night. We did so ; and not only on the ensuing night, but on many others, and always at about the same hour, would our mother-in-law rise from her bed and leave the cottage ; and after she was gone we invariably heard the growl of a wolf under our window, and always saw her on her return wash herself before she retired to bed. We observed also that she seldom sat down to meals, and that when she did she appeared to eat with dislike ; but when the meat was taken down to be prepared for dinner, she would often furtively put a raw piece into her mouth.

"My brother Cæsar was a courageous boy ; he did not like to speak to my father until he knew more. He resolved that he would follow her out, and ascertain what she did. Marcella and I endeavoured to dissuade him from the project ; but he would not be controlled ; and the very next night he lay down in his clothes, and as soon as our mother-in-law had left the cottage he jumped up, took down my father's gun, and followed her.

"You may imagine in what a state of suspense Marcella and I remained during his absence. After a few minutes we heard the report of a gun. It did not awaken my father ; and we lay trembling with anxiety. In a minute afterwards we saw our mother-in-law enter the cottage—her dress was bloody. I put my hand to Marcella's mouth to prevent her crying out, although I was myself in great alarm. Our mother-in-law approached my father's bed, looked to see if he was asleep, and then went to the chimney and blew up the embers into a blaze.

" 'Who is there ?' said my father, waking up.

" 'Lie still, dearest,' replied my mother-in-law ; 'it is only me ; I have lighted the fire to warm some water; I am not quite well.'

"My father turned round, and was soon asleep ; but we watched our mother-in-law. She changed her linen, and threw the garments she had worn into the fire ; and we then perceived that her right leg was bleeding profusely, as if from a gun-shot wound. She bandaged it up, and then dressing herself, remained before the fire until the break of day.

"Poor little Marcella, her heart beat quick as she pressed me to her side—so indeed did mine. Where was our brother Cæsar ? How did my mother-in-law receive the wound unless from his gun ? At last my father rose, and then for the first time I spoke, saying : 'Father, where is my brother Cæsar ?'

" 'Your brother ?' exclaimed he ; 'why, where can he be ?'

" 'Merciful Heaven ! I thought as I lay very restless last night,' observed our mother-in-law, 'that I heard somebody open the latch of the door ; and, dear me, husband, what has become of your gun ?'

"My father cast his eyes up above the chimney, and perceived that his gun was missing. For a moment he looked perplexed ; then, seizing a broad axe, he went out of the cottage without saying another word.

"He did not remain away from us long ; in a few minutes he returned, bearing in his arms the mangled body of my poor brother ; he laid it down, and covered up his face.

"My mother-in-law rose up, and looked at the body, while Marcella and I threw ourselves by its side, wailing and sobbing bitterly.

" 'Go to bed again, children,' said she sharply. 'Husband,' continued she, 'your boy must have taken the gun down to shoot a wolf, and the animal has been too powerful for him. Poor boy ! he has paid dearly for his rashness.'

"My father made no reply. I wished to speak—to tell all —but Marcella, who perceived my intention, held me by the arm, and looked at me so imploringly, that I desisted.

"My father, therefore, was left in his error ; but Marcella and I, although we could not comprehend it, were conscious that our mother-in-law was in some way connected with my brother's death.

"That day my father went out and dug a grave ; and when he laid the body in the earth he piled up stones over it, so that the wolves should not be able to dig it up. The shock of this catastrophe was to my poor father very severe ; for several days he never went to the chase, although at times he would utter bitter anathemas and vengeance against the wolves.

"But during this time of mourning on his part, my mother-in-law's nocturnal wanderings continued with the same regularity as before.

"At last my father took down his gun to repair to the forest ; but he soon returned, and appeared much annoyed.

" 'Would you believe it, Christina, that the wolves— perdition to the whole race !—have actually contrived to dig up the body of my poor boy, and now there is nothing left of him but his bones.'

" 'Indeed !' replied my mother-in-law. Marcella looked

at me, and I saw in her intelligent eye all she would have uttered.

"'A wolf growls under our window every night, father,' said I.

"'Ay, indeed! Why did you not tell me, boy? Wake me the next time you hear it.'

"I saw my mother-in-law turn away; her eyes flashed fire, and she gnashed her teeth.

"My father went out again, and covered up with a larger pile of stones the little remains of my poor brother which the wolves had spared. Such was the first act of the tragedy.

"The spring now came on; the snow disappeared, and we were permitted to leave the cottage; but never would I quit for one moment my dear little sister, to whom, since the death of my brother, I was more ardently attached than ever; indeed, I was afraid to leave her alone with my mother-in-law, who appeared to have a particular pleasure in ill-treating the child. My father was now employed upon his little farm, and I was able to render him some assistance.

"Marcella used to sit by us while we were at work, leaving my mother-in-law alone in the cottage. I ought to observe that, as the spring advanced, so did my mother-in-law decrease her nocturnal rambles, and that we never heard the growl of the wolf under the window after I had spoken of it to my father.

"One day, when my father and I were in the field, Marcella being with us, my mother-in-law came out, saying that she was going into the forest to collect some herbs my father wanted, and that Marcella must go to the cottage and watch the dinner. Marcella went; and my mother-in-law soon disappeared in the forest, taking a direction quite contrary to that in which the cottage stood, and leaving my father and me, as it were, between her and Marcella.

"About an hour afterwards we were startled by shrieks from the cottage—evidently the shrieks of little Marcella. 'Marcella has burnt herself, father,' said I, throwing down my spade. My father threw down his, and we both hastened to the cottage. Before we could gain the door, out darted a large white wolf, which fled with the utmost celerity. My father had no weapon; he rushed into the cottage, and there saw poor little Marcella expiring. Her body was dreadfully mangled and the blood pouring from it had formed a large pool on the cottage floor. My father's first intention had been to seize his gun and pursue; but he was checked by this horrid spectacle; he knelt down by his dying child, and burst into tears. Marcella could just look kindly on us for a few seconds, and then her eyes were closed in death.

"My father and I were still hanging over my poor sister's body when my mother-in-law came in. At the dreadful sight she expressed much concern; but she did not appear to recoil from the sight of blood, as most women do.

" 'Poor child!' said she, 'it must have been that great white wolf which passed me just now, and frightened me so. She's quite dead, Krantz.'

" 'I know it!—I know it!' cried my father, in agony.

"I thought my father would never recover from the effects of this second tragedy; he mourned bitterly over the body of his sweet child, and for several days would not consign it to its grave, although frequently requested by my mother-in-law to do so. At last he yielded, and dug a grave for her close by that of my poor brother, and took every precaution that the wolves should not violate her remains.

"I was now really miserable as I lay alone in the bed which I had formerly shared with my brother and sister. I could not help thinking that my mother-in-law was implicated in both their deaths, although I could not account for the manner; but I no longer felt afraid of her; my little heart was full of hatred and revenge.

"The night after my sister had been buried, as I lay awake, I perceived my mother-in-law get up and go out of the cottage. I waited some time, then dressed myself, and looked out through the door, which I half opened. The moon shone bright, and I could see the spot where my brother and my sister had been buried; and what was my horror when I perceived my mother-in-law busily removing the stones from Marcella's grave!

"She was in her white night-dress, and the moon shone full upon her. She was digging with her hands, and throwing away the stones behind her with all the ferocity of a wild beast. It was some time before I could collect my senses and decide what I should do. At last I perceived that she had arrived at the body, and raised it up to the side of the grave. I could bear it no longer: I ran to my father, and awoke him.

" 'Father, father!' cried I, 'dress yourself, and get your gun.'

" 'What!' cried my father, 'the wolves are there, are they?'

"He jumped out of bed, threw on his clothes, and in his anxiety did not appear to perceive the absence of his wife. As soon as he was ready I opened the door, he went out, and I followed him.

"Imagine his horror, when (unprepared as he was for such a sight) he beheld, as he advanced towards the grave, not a wolf, but his wife, in her night-dress, on her hands and knees, crouching by the body of my sister, and tearing off large pieces of the flesh, and devouring them with all the avidity of a wolf. She was too busy to be aware of our approach. My father dropped his gun; his hair stood on end, so did mine; he breathed heavily, and then his breath for a time stopped. I picked up the gun and put it into his hand. Suddenly he appeared as if concentrated rage had restored him to double vigour; he levelled his piece, fired, and with a loud shriek down fell the wretch whom he had fostered in his bosom.

" 'God of heaven!' cried my father, sinking down upon the earth in a swoon, as soon as he had discharged his gun.

"I remained some time by his side before he recovered. 'Where am I?' said he, 'what has happened? Oh!—yes, yes! I recollect now. Heaven forgive me!'

"He rose and we walked up to the grave; what again was our astonishment and horror to find that, instead of the dead body of my mother-in-law, as we expected, there was lying over the remains of my poor sister a large white she-wolf.

" 'The white wolf,' exclaimed my father, 'the white wolf which decoyed me into the forest—I see it all now—I have dealt with the spirits of the Hartz Mountains.'

"For some time my father remained in silence and deep thought. He then carefully lifted up the body of my sister, replaced it in the grave, and covered it over as before, having struck the head of the dead animal with the heel of his boot, and raving like a madman. He walked back to the cottage, shut the door, and threw himself on the bed; I did the same, for I was in a stupor of amazement.

"Early in the morning we were both roused by a loud knocking at the door, and in rushed the hunter Wilfred.

" 'My daughter—man—my daughter!—where is my daughter?' cried he in a rage.

" 'Where the wretch, the fiend should be, I trust,' replied my father, starting up, and displaying equal choler : 'where she should be—in hell ! Leave this cottage, or you may fare worse.'

" 'Ha—ha !' replied the hunter, 'would you harm a potent spirit of the Hartz Mountains ? Poor mortal, who must needs wed a werewolf.'

" 'Out, demon ! I defy thee and thy power.'

" 'Yet shall you feel it ; remember your oath—your solemn oath—never to raise your hand against her to harm her.'

" 'I made no compact with evil spirits.'

" 'You did, and if you failed in your vow, you were to meet the vengeance of the spirits. Your children were to perish by the vulture, the wolf——'

" 'Out, out, demon !'

" 'And their bones blanch in the wilderness. Ha—ha !'

"My father, frantic with rage, seized his axe and raised it over Wilfred's head to strike.

" 'All this I swear,' continued the huntsman mockingly.

"The axe descended ; but it passed through the form of the hunter, and my father lost his balance, and fell heavily on the floor.

" 'Mortal !' said the hunter, striding over my father's body, 'we have power over those only who have committed murder. You have been guilty of a double murder : you shall pay the penalty attached to your marriage vow. Two of your children are gone, the third is yet to follow—and follow them he will, for your oath is registered. Go—it were kindness to kill thee—your punishment is, that you live !'

"With these words the spirit disappeared. My father rose from the floor, embraced me tenderly, and knelt down in prayer.

"The next morning he quitted the cottage for ever. He took me with him, and bent his steps to Holland, where we safely arrived. He had some little money with him ; but he had not been many days in Amsterdam before he was seized with a brain fever, and died raving mad. I was put into the asylum, and afterwards was sent to sea before the mast. You now know all my history. The question is, whether I am to pay the penalty of my father's oath? I am myself perfectly convinced that, in some way or another, I shall."

II

On the twenty-second day the high land of the south of Sumatra was in view: as there were no vessels in sight, they resolved to keep their course through the Straits, and run for Pulo Penang, which they expected, as their vessel lay so close to the wind, to reach in seven or eight days. By constant exposure Philip and Krantz were now so bronzed, that with their long beards and Mussulman dresses, they might easily have passed off for natives. They had steered during the whole of the days exposed to a burning sun; they had lain down and slept in the dew of the night; but their health had not suffered. But for several days, since he had confided the history of his family to Philip, Krantz had become silent and melancholy; his usual flow of spirits had vanished, and Philip had often questioned him as to the cause. As they entered the Straits, Philip talked of what they should do upon their arrival at Goa; when Krantz gravely replied: "For some days, Philip, I have had a presentiment that I shall never see that city."

"You are out of health, Krantz," replied Philip.

"No, I am in sound health, body and mind. I have endeavoured to shake off the presentiment but in vain; there is a warning voice that continually tells me that I shall not be long with you. Philip, will you oblige me by making me content on one point? I have gold about my person which may be useful to you; oblige me by taking it, and securing it on your own."

"What nonsense, Krantz."

"It is no nonsense, Philip. Have you not had your warnings? Why should I not have mine? You know that I have little fear in my composition, and that I care not about death; but I feel the presentiment which I speak of more strongly every hour. . . ."

"These are the imaginings of a disturbed brain, Krantz; why you, young, in full health and vigour, should not pass your days in peace, and live to a good old age, there is no cause for believing. You will be better to-morrow."

"Perhaps so," replied Krantz; "but you still must yield

to my whim, and take the gold. If I am wrong, and we do arrive safe, you know, Philip, you can let me have it back," observed Krantz, with a faint smile—"but you forget, our water is nearly out, and we must look out for a rill on the coast to obtain a fresh supply."

"I was thinking of that when you commenced this unwelcome topic. We had better look out for the water before dark, and as soon as we have replenished our jars, we will make sail again."

At the time that this conversation took place, they were on the eastern side of the Strait, about forty miles to the northward. The interior of the coast was rocky and mountainous, but it slowly descended to low land of alternate forest and jungles, which continued to the beach; the country appeared to be uninhabited. Keeping close in to the shore, they discovered, after two hours' run, a fresh stream which burst in a cascade from the mountains, and swept its devious course through the jungle, until it poured its tribute into the waters of the Strait.

They ran close into the mouth of the stream, lowered the sails, and pulled the peroqua against the current, until they had advanced far enough to assure them that the water was quite fresh. The jars were soon filled, and they were again thinking of pushing off, when enticed by the beauty of the spot, the coolness of the fresh water, and wearied with their long confinement on board of the peroqua, they proposed to bathe—a luxury hardly to be appreciated by those who have not been in a similar situation. They threw off their Mussulman dresses, and plunged into the stream, where they remained for some time. Krantz was the first to get out; he complained of feeling chilled, and he walked on to the banks where their clothes had been laid. Philip also approached nearer to the beach, intending to follow him.

"And now, Philip," said Krantz, "this will be a good opportunity for me to give you the money. I will open my sash and pour it out, and you can put it into your own before you put it on."

Philip was standing in the water, which was about level with his waist.

"Well, Krantz," said he, "I suppose if it must be so, it must; but it appears to me an idea so ridiculous—however, you shall have your own way."

Philip quitted the run, and sat down by Krantz, who was already busy shaking the doubloons out of the folds of his sash; at last he said:

"I believe, Philip, you have got them all now?—I feel satisfied."

"What danger there can be to you, which I am not equally exposed to, I cannot conceive," replied Philip; "however——"

Hardly had he said these words, when there was a tremendous roar—a rush like a mighty wind through the air—a blow which threw him on his back—a loud cry—and a contention. Philip recovered himself, and perceived the naked form of Krantz carried off with the speed of an arrow by an enormous tiger through the jungle. He watched with distended eyeballs; in a few seconds the animal and Krantz had disappeared.

"God of heaven! would that Thou hadst spared me this," cried Philip, throwing himself down in agony on his face. "O Krantz! my friend—my brother—too sure was your presentiment. Merciful God! have pity—but Thy will be done." And Philip burst into a flood of tears.

For more than an hour did he remain fixed upon the spot, careless and indifferent to the danger by which he was surrounded. At last, somewhat recovered, he rose, dressed himself, and then again sat down—his eyes fixed upon the clothes of Krantz, and the gold which still lay on the sand.

"He would give me that gold. He foretold his doom. Yes! yes! it was his destiny, and it has been fulfilled. *His bones will bleach in the wilderness*, and the spirit-hunter and his wolfish daughter are avenged."

THE MYSTERIOUS MANSION
Honoré de Balzac

ABOUT a hundred yards from the town of Vendôme, on the borders of the Loire, there is an old grey house, surmounted by very high gables, and so completely isolated that neither tanyard nor shabby hostelry, such as you may find at the entrance to all small towns, exists in its immediate neighbourhood.

In front of this building, overlooking the river, is a garden, where the once well-trimmed box borders that used to define the walks now grow wild as they list. Several willows that spring from the Loire have grown as rapidly as the hedge that encloses it, and half conceal the house. The rich vegetation of those weeds that we call foul adorns the sloping shore. Fruit trees, neglected for the last ten years, no longer yield their harvest, and their shoots form coppices. The wall-fruit grows like hedges against the walls. Paths once gravelled are overgrown with moss, but, to tell the truth, there is no trace of a path. From the height of the hill, to which cling the ruins of the old castle of the Dukes of Vendôme, the only spot whence the eye can plunge into this enclosure, it strikes you that, at a time not easy to determine, this plot of land was the delight of a country gentleman, who cultivated roses and tulips and horticulture in general, and who was besides a lover of fine fruit. An arbour is still visible, or rather the debris of an arbour, where there is a table that time has not quite destroyed. The aspect of this garden of bygone days suggests the negative joys of peaceful, provincial life, as one might reconstruct the life of a worthy tradesman by reading the epitaph on his tombstone. As if to complete the sweetness and sadness of the ideas that possess one's soul, one of the walls displays a sun-dial decorated with the following commonplace Christian inscription : " Ultimam cogita ! " The roof of this house is horribly dilapidated, the shutters are always closed, the balconies are covered with swallows' nests, the doors are perpetually shut, weeds have drawn green lines in the cracks of the flights of steps, the locks and bolts are rusty. Sun, moon, winter, summer, and snow have worn the panelling, warped the boards, gnawed the paint. The lugubrious silence which reigns there is only broken by birds, cats, martins, rats and mice, free to course to and fro, to fight and to eat each other. Everywhere an invisible hand has graven the word *mystery*.

Should your curiosity lead you to glance at this house from the side that points to the road, you would perceive a great door which the children of the place have riddled with holes. I afterward heard that this door had been closed for the last ten years. Through the holes broken by the boys you would have observed the perfect harmony that existed between the façades of both garden and courtyard. In both the same disorder prevails. Tufts of weed encircle the paving-stones. Enormous cracks furrow the walls, round whose blackened crests twine the thousand garlands of the pellitory. The steps are out of joint, the wire of the bell is rusted, the spouts are cracked. What fire from heaven has fallen here? What tribunal has decreed that salt should be strewn on this dwelling? Has God been blasphemed, has France been here betrayed? These are the questions we ask ourselves, but get no answer from the crawling things that haunt the place. The empty and deserted house is a gigantic enigma, of which the key is lost. In bygone times it was a small fief, and bears the name of the Grande Bretêche.

I inferred that I was not the only person to whom my good landlady had communicated the secret of which I was to be the sole recipient, and I prepared to listen.

"Sir," she said, "when the Emperor sent the Spanish prisoners of war and others here, the Government quartered on me a young Spaniard who had been sent to Vendôme on parole. Parole notwithstanding he went out every day to show himself to the sous-préfet. He was a Spanish grandee! Nothing less! His name ended in os and dia, something like Burgos de Férédia. I have his name on my books; you can read it if you like. Oh! but he was a handsome young man for a Spaniard; they are all said to be ugly. He was only five feet and a few inches high, but he was well grown; he had small hands that he took such care of; ah! you should have seen! He had as many brushes for his hands as a woman for her whole dressing apparatus! He had thick black hair, a fiery eye, his skin was rather bronzed, but I liked the look of it. He wore the finest linen I have ever seen on anyone, although I have had princesses staying here, and, among others, General Bertrand, the Duke and Duchess d'Abrantès, Monsieur Decazes, and the King of Spain. He didn't eat much; but his manners were so polite, so amiable, that one could not owe him a grudge. Oh! I was very fond of him, although he didn't open his lips four times in the day, and it was impossible to keep up a conversation with him. For if you spoke to him, he did not answer. It was a fad, a mania with them all, I heard say. He read his breviary like a priest, he went to Mass and to all the services regularly. Where did he sit? Two steps from the chapel of Madame de Merret. As he took his place there the first time he went to church, nobody suspected him of any intention in so doing. Besides, he never raised his eyes from his prayer-book, poor young man! After that, sir, in the evening he would walk on the mountains, among the castle ruins. It was the poor man's only amusement, it reminded him of his country. They say that Spain is all mountains! From the commencement of his imprisonment he stayed out late. I was anxious when I found that he did not come home before midnight; but we got accustomed to this fancy of his. He took the key of the door, and we left off sitting up for him. He lodged in a house of ours in the Rue des Casernes. After that, one of our stable-men told us that in the evening when he led the horses to the water, he thought he had seen the Spanish grandee swimming far down the river like a live fish. When he returned, I told him to take care of the rushes; he appeared vexed to have been seen in the water. At last, one day, or rather one morning, we did not find him in his room; he had not returned. After searching everywhere, I found some writing in the drawer of a table, where there were fifty gold pieces of Spain that are called doubloons and were worth about five thousand francs; and ten thousand francs' worth of diamonds in a small sealed box. The writing said, that in case he did not return, he left us the money and the diamonds, on condition of paying for Masses to thank God for his escape, and for his salvation. In those days my husband had not been taken from me; he hastened to seek him everywhere.

" And now for the strange part of the story. He brought home the Spaniard's clothes, that he had discovered under a big stone, in a sort of pilework by the river-side near the castle, nearly opposite to the Grande Bretêche. My husband had gone there so early that no one had seen him. After reading the letter, he burned the clothes, and according to Count Férédia's desire we declared that he had escaped. The sous-préfet sent all the gendarmerie in pursuit of him; but brust! they never caught him. Lepas believed that the Spaniard had drowned himself. I, sir, don't think so; I am more inclined to believe that he had something to do with the affair of Madame de Merret, seeing that Rosalie told me that the crucifix that her mistress thought so much of, that she had it buried with her, was of ebony and silver. Now in the beginning of his stay here, Monsieur de Férédia had one in ebony and silver, that I never saw him with later. Now, sir, don't you consider that I need have no scruples about the Spaniard's fifteen thousand francs, and that I have a right to them?"

"Certainly; but you haven't tried to question Rosalie?" I said.

"Oh, yes, indeed, sir; but to no purpose! the girl's like a wall. She knows something, but it is impossible to get her to talk."

After exchanging a few more words with me, my landlady left me a prey to vague and gloomy thoughts, to a romantic curiosity, and a religious terror not unlike the profound impression produced on us when by night, on entering a dark church, we perceive a faint light under high arches; a vague figure glides by—the rustle of a robe or cassock is heard, and we shudder.

Suddenly the Grande Bretêche and its tall weeds, its barred windows, its rusty ironwork, its closed doors, its deserted apartments, appeared like a fantastic apparition before me. I essayed to penetrate the mysterious dwelling, and to find the knot of its dark story—the drama that had killed three persons. In my eyes Rosalie became the most interesting person in Vendôme. As I studied her, I discovered the traces of secret care, despite the radiant health that shone in her plump countenance. There was in her the germ of remorse or hope; her attitude revealed a secret, like the attitude of a bigot who prays to excess, or of the infanticide who ever hears the last cry of her child. Yet her manners were rough and ingenuous—her silly smile was not that of a criminal, and could you but have seen the great kerchief that encompassed her portly bust, framed and laced in by a lilac and blue cotton gown, you would have dubbed her innocent. No, I thought, I will not leave Vendôme without learning the history of the Grande Bretêche. To gain my ends I will strike up a friendship with Rosalie, if needs be.

" Rosalie," said I, one evening.

" Sir ? "

" You are not married ? "

She started slightly.

" Oh, I can find plenty of men, when the fancy takes me to be made miserable," she said, laughing.

She soon recovered from the effects of her emotion, for all women, from the great lady to the maid of the inn, possess a composure that is peculiar to them.

" You are too good-looking and well favoured to be short of lovers. But tell me, Rosalie, why did you take service in an inn after leaving Madame de Merret ? Did she leave you nothing to live on ? "

" Oh, yes ! But, sir, my place is the best in all Vendôme."

The reply was one of those that judges and lawyers would call evasive. Rosalie appeared to me to be situated in this romantic history like the square in the midst of a chessboard. She was at the heart of the truth and chief interest ; she seemed to me to be bound in the very knot of it. The conquest of Rosalie was no longer to be an ordinary siege—in this girl was centred the last chapter of a novel, therefore from this moment Rosalie became the object of my preference.

One morning I said to Rosalie : " Tell me all you know about Madame de Merret."

" Oh ! " she replied in terror, " do not ask that of me, Monsieur Horace."

Her pretty face fell—her clear, bright colour faded—and her eyes lost their innocent brightness.

" Well, then," she said, " if you must have it so, I will tell you about it ; but promise to keep my secret ! "

" Done ! my dear girl, I must keep your secret with the honour of a thief, which is the most loyal in the world."

Were I to transcribe Rosalie's diffuse eloquence faithfully, an entire volume would scarcely contain it ; so I shall abridge.

The room occupied by Madame de Merret at the Bretêche was on the ground-floor. A little closet about four feet deep, built in the thickness of the wall, served as her wardrobe.

Three months before the eventful evening of which I am about to speak, Madame de Merret had been so seriously indisposed that her husband had left her to herself in her own apartment, while he occupied another on the first floor. By one of those chances that it is impossible to foresee, he returned home from the club (where he was accustomed to read the papers and discuss politics with the inhabitants of the place) two hours later than usual. His wife supposed him to be at home, in bed and asleep. But the invasion of France had been the subject of a most animated discussion ; the billiard-match had been exciting, he had lost forty francs, an enormous sum for Vendôme, where every one hoards, and where manners are restricted within the limits of a praiseworthy modesty, which perhaps is the source of the true happiness that no Parisian covets. For some time past Monsieur de Merret had been satisfied to ask Rosalie if his wife had gone to bed ; and on her reply, which was always in the affirmative, had immediately gained his own room with the good temper engendered by habit and confidence. On entering his house, he took it into his head to go and tell his wife of his misadventure, perhaps by way of consolation. At dinner he found Madame de Merret most coquettishly attired. On his way to the club it had occurred to him that his wife was restored to health, and that her convalescence had added to her beauty. He was, as husbands are wont to be, somewhat slow in making this discovery. Instead of calling Rosalie, who was occupied just then in watching the cook and coachman play a difficult hand at brisque, Monsieur de Merret went to his wife's room by the light of a lantern that he deposited on the first step of the staircase. His unmistakable step resounded under the vaulted corridor. At the moment that the Count turned the handle of his wife's door, he fancied he could hear the door of the closet I spoke of close ; but when he entered Madame de Merret was alone before the fire-place. The husband thought ingenuously that Rosalie was in the closet, yet a suspicion that jangled in his ear put him on his guard. He looked at his wife and saw in her eyes I know not what wild and hunted expression.

" You are very late," she said. Her habitually pure, sweet voice seemed changed to him.

Monsieur de Merret did not reply, for at that moment Rosalie entered. It was a thunderbolt for him. He strode about the room, passing from one window to the other, with mechanical motion and folded arms.

" Have you heard bad news, or are you unwell ? " inquired his wife timidly, while Rosalie undressed her.

He kept silent.

" You can leave me," said Madame de Merret to her maid ; " I will put my hair in curl papers myself."

From the expression of her husband's face she foresaw trouble, and wished to be alone with him. When Rosalie had gone, or was supposed to have gone (for she stayed in the corridor for a few minutes), Monsieur de Merret came and stood in front of his wife, and said coldly to her :

" Madame, there is someone in your closet ! " She looked calmly at her husband, and replied simply :

" No, sir."

This answer was heartrending to Monsieur de Merret ; he did not believe in it. Yet his wife had never appeared to him purer or more saintly than at that moment. He rose to open the closet door ; Madame de Merret took his hand, looked at him with an expression of melancholy, and said in a voice that betrayed singular emotion :

" If you find no one there, remember this, all will be over between us ! " The extraordinary dignity of his wife's manner restored the Count's profound esteem for her, and inspired him with one of those resolutions that only lack a vaster stage to become immortal.

" No," said he, " Josephine, I will not go there. In either case it would separate us for ever. Hear me, I know how pure you are at heart, and that your life is a holy one. You would not commit a mortal sin to save your life."

At these words Madame de Merret turned a haggard gaze upon her husband.

" Here, take your crucifix," he added. " Swear to me before God that there is no one in there ; I will believe you, I will never open that door."

Madame de Merret took the crucifix and said :

" I swear."

" Louder," said the husband, " and repeat ' I swear before God that there is no one in that closet.' "

She repeated the sentence calmly.

" That will do," said Monsieur de Merret, coldly.

After a moment of silence :

" I never saw this pretty toy before," he said, examining the ebony crucifix inlaid with silver, and most artistically chiselled.

" I found it at Duvivier's, who bought it of a Spanish monk when the prisoners passed through Vendôme last year."

" Ah ! " said Monsieur de Merret, as he replaced the crucifix on the nail, and he rang. Rosalie did not keep him waiting. Monsieur de Merret went quickly to meet her, led her to the bay window that opened on to the garden and whispered to her :

" Listen ! I know that Gorenflot wishes to marry you, poverty is the only drawback, and you told him that you would be his wife if he found the means to establish himself as a master mason. Well ! go and fetch him, tell him to come here with his trowel and tools. Manage not to awaken anyone in his house but himself ; his fortune will be more than your desires. Above all, leave this room without babbling, other-wise——" He frowned. Rosalie went away, he recalled her.

" Here, take my latchkey," he said. " Jean ! " then cried Monsieur de Merret, in tones of thunder in the corridor. Jean, who was at the same time his coachman and his confidential servant, left his game of cards and came.

" Go to bed, all of you," said his master, signing to him to approach ; and the Count added, under his breath : " When they are all asleep—*asleep*, d'ye hear ?—you will come down and tell me." Monsieur de Merret, who had not lost sight of his wife all the time he was giving his orders, returned quietly to her at the fireside and began to tell her of the game of billiards and the talk of the club. When Rosalie returned she found Monsieur and Madame de Merret conversing very amicably.

The Count had lately had all the ceilings of his reception rooms on the ground floor repaired. Plaster of Paris is difficult to obtain in Vendôme ; the carriage raises its price. The Count had therefore bought a good deal, being well aware that he could find plenty of purchasers for whatever might remain over. This circumstance inspired him with the design he was about to execute.

" Sir, Gorenflot has arrived," said Rosalie in low tones.

" Show him in," replied the Count in loud tones.

Madame de Merret turned rather pale when she saw the mason.

"Gorenflot," said her husband, "go and fetch bricks from the coach-house, and bring sufficient to wall up the door of this closet; you will use the plaster I have over to coat the wall with." Then calling Rosalie and the workman aside:

"Listen, Gorenflot," he said in an undertone, "you will sleep here to-night. But to-morrow you will have a passport to a foreign country, to a town to which I will direct you. I shall give you six thousand francs for your journey. You will stay ten years in that town; if you do not like it, you may establish yourself in another, provided it be in the same country. You will pass through Paris, where you will await me. There I will insure you an additional six thousand francs by contract, which will be paid to you on your return, provided you have fulfilled the conditions of our bargain. This is the price for your absolute silence as to what you are about to do to-night. As to you, Rosalie, I will give you ten thousand francs on the day of your wedding, on condition of your marrying Gorenflot; but if you wish to marry, you must hold your tongues; or—no dowry."

"Rosalie," said Madame de Merret, "do my hair."

The husband walked calmly up and down, watching the door, the mason, and his wife, but without betraying any insulting doubts. Madame de Merret chose a moment when the workman was unloading bricks and her husband was at the other end of the room to say to Rosalie: "A thousand francs a year for you, my child, if you can tell Gorenflot to leave a chink at the bottom." Then out loud, she added coolly:

"Go and help him!"

Monsieur and Madame de Merret were silent all the time that Gorenflot took to brick up the door. This silence, on the part of the husband, who did not choose to furnish his wife with a pretext for saying things of a double meaning, had its purpose; on the part of Madame de Merret it was either pride or prudence. When the wall was about half-way up, the sly workman took advantage of a moment when the Count's back was turned, to strike a blow with his trowel in one of the glass panes of the closet-door. This act informed Madame de Merret that Rosalie had spoken to Gorenflot.

All three then saw a man's face; it was dark and gloomy with black hair and eyes of flame. Before her husband turned, the poor woman had time to make a sign to the stranger that signified : Hope !

At four o'clock, toward dawn, for it was the month of September, the construction was finished. The mason was handed over to the care of Jean, and Monsieur de Merret went to bed in his wife's room.

On rising the following morning, he said carelessly :

"The deuce ! I must go to the Mairie for the passport." He put his hat on his head, advanced three steps toward the door, altered his mind and took the crucifix.

His wife trembled for joy. "He is going to Duvivier," she thought. As soon as the Count had left, Madame de Merret rang for Rosalie ; then in a terrible voice :

"The trowel, the trowel ! " she cried, " and quick to work ! I saw how Gorenflot did it ; we shall have time to make a hole and to mend it again."

In the twinkling of an eye, Rosalie brought a sort of mattock to her mistress, who with unparalleled ardour set about demolishing the wall. She had already knocked out several bricks and was preparing to strike a more decisive blow when she perceived Monsieur de Merret behind her. She fainted.

"Lay Madame on her bed," said the Count coldly. He had foreseen what would happen in his absence and had set a trap for his wife ; he had simply written to the mayor, and had sent for Duvivier. The jeweller arrived just as the room had been put in order.

"Duvivier," inquired the Count, " did you buy crucifixes of the Spaniards who passed through here ? "

"No, sir."

"That will do, thank you," he said, looking at his wife like a tiger. "Jean," he added, " you will see that my meals are served in the Countess's room ; she is ill, and I shall not leave her until she has recovered."

The cruel gentleman stayed with his wife for twenty days. In the beginning, when there were sounds in the walled closet, and Josephine attempted to implore his pity for the dying stranger, he replied, without permitting her to say a word :

"You have sworn on the cross that there is no one there."

NO.1 BRANCH LINE: THE SIGNALMAN
Charles Dickens

"HALLOA! Below there!"

When he heard a voice thus calling to him, he was standing at the door of his box, with a flag in his hand, furled round its short pole. One would have thought, considering the nature of the ground, that he could not have doubted from what quarter the voice came; but, instead of looking up to where I stood on the top of the steep cutting nearly over his head, he turned himself about and looked down the Line. There was something remarkable in his manner of doing so, though I could not have said, for my life, what. But, I know it was remarkable enough to attract my notice.

"Halloa! Below!"

From looking down the Line, he turned himself about again, and, raising his eyes, saw my figure high above him.

"Is there any path by which I can come down and speak to you?"

He looked up at me without replying, and I looked down at him without pressing him too soon with a repetition of my idle question. Just then, there came a vague vibration in the earth and air, quickly changing into a violent pulsation and an oncoming rush that caused me to start back, as though it had force to draw me down. When such vapour as rose to my height from this rapid train had passed me, and was skimming away over the landscape, I looked down again, and saw him re-furling the flag he had shown while the train went by.

I repeated my inquiry. After a pause, during which he seemed to regard me with fixed attention, he motioned with his rolled-up flag towards a point on my level, some two or three hundred yards distant. I called down to him, "All right!" and made for that point. There, by dint of looking closely about me, I found a rough zig-zag descending path.

The cutting was extremely deep, and unusually precipitate. It was made through a clammy stone that became oozier and wetter as I went down.

When I came down low enough upon the zig-zag descent to see him again, I saw that he was standing between the rails on the way by which the train had lately passed, in an attitude as if he were waiting for me to appear.

I resumed my downward way, and, stepping out upon the level of the railroad and drawing nearer to him, saw that he was a dark sallow man, with a dark beard and rather heavy eyebrows. His post was in as solitary and dismal a place as ever I saw. On either side, a dripping-wet wall of jagged stone, excluding all view but a strip of sky; the perspective one way, only a crooked prolongation of this great dungeon; the shorter perspective in the other direction, terminating in a gloomy red light, and the gloomier entrance to a black tunnel, in whose massive architecture there was a barbarous, depressing, and forbidding air.

Before he stirred, I was near enough to him to have touched him. Not even then removing his eyes from mine, he stepped back one step, and lifted his hand.

This was a lonesome post to occupy (I said), and it had riveted my attention when I looked down from up yonder. A visitor was a rarity, I should suppose; not an unwelcome rarity, I hoped? In me, he merely saw a man who had been shut up within narrow limits all his life, and who, being at last set free, had a newly-awakened interest in these great works.

He directed a most curious look towards the red light near the tunnel's mouth, and looked all about it, as if something were missing from it, and then looked at me.

That light was part of his charge? Was it not?

He answered in a low voice: " Don't you know it is?"

The monstrous thought came into my mind as I perused the fixed eyes and the saturnine face that this was a spirit, not a man.

In my turn, I stepped back. But in making the action I detected in his eyes some latent fear of me. This put the monstrous thought to flight.

" You look at me," I said, forcing a smile, " as if you had a dread of me."

"I was doubtful," he returned, "whether I had seen you before."

"Where?"

He pointed to the red light he had looked at.

"There?" I said.

Intently watchful of me, he replied (but without sound), "Yes."

"My good fellow, what should I do there? However, be that as it may, I never was there, you may swear.'

"I think I may," he rejoined. "Yes. I am sure I may.

His manner cleared, like my own. He replied to my remarks with readiness, and in well-chosen words. Had he much to do there? Yes; that was to say, he had enough responsibility to bear; but exactness and watchfulness were what was required of him, and of actual work—manual labour—he had next to none. To change that signal, to trim those lights, and to turn this iron handle now and then, was all he had to do under that head. Regarding those many long and lonely hours of which I seemed to make so much, he could only say that the routine of his life had shaped itself into that form, and he had grown used to it.

Was it necessary for him when on duty always to remain in that channel of damp air, and could he never rise into the sunshine from between these high stone walls? Why, that depended upon times and circumstances. Under some conditions there would be less upon the line than under others, and the same held good as to certain hours of the day and night. In bright weather, he did choose occasions for getting a little above these lower shadows; but, being at all times liable to be called by his electric bell, and at such times listening for it with redoubled anxiety, the relief was less than I would suppose.

He took me into his box, where there was a fire, a desk for an official book in which he had to make certain entries, a telegraphic instrument with its dial face and needles, and the little bell of which he had spoken.

He had been, when young (if I could believe it, sitting in that hut; he scarcely could), a student of natural philosophy, and had attended lectures; but he had run wild, misused his opportunities, gone down and never risen again. He had no complaint to offer about that.

In the discharge of his duties I observed him to be re-

markably exact and vigilant, breaking off his discourse at a
syllable, and remaining silent until what he had to do was
done.

In a word, I should have set this man down as one of the
safest of men to be employed in that capacity, but for the
circumstance that while he was speaking to me he twice broke
off with a fallen colour, turned his face towards the little bell
when it did *not* ring, opened the door of the hut (which was
kept shut to exclude the unhealthy damp), and looked out
towards the red light near the mouth of the tunnel. On
both of those occasions he came back to the fire with the
inexplicable air upon him which I had remarked, without
being able to define, when we were so far asunder.

Said I when I rose to leave him : " You almost make me
think that I have met with a contented man."

" I believe I used to be so," he rejoined, in the low voice
in which he had first spoken ; " but I am troubled, sir, I
am troubled.

" It is very difficult to impart, sir. It is very, very difficult
to speak of. If ever you make me another visit, I will try
to tell you."

" But I expressly intend to make you another visit. Say,
when shall it be ? "

" I go off early in the morning, and I shall be on again at
ten to-morrow night, sir."

" I will come at eleven."

He thanked me, and went out at the door with me. " I'll
show my white light, sir," he said, in his peculiar low voice,
" till you have found the way up. When you have found
it, don't call out ! And when you are at the top, don't call
out ! "

His manner seemed to make the place strike colder to
me, but I said no more than " Very well."

" And when you come down to-morrow night don't call
out ! Let me ask you a parting question. What made you
cry ' Halloa ! Below there ! ' to-night ? "

" Heaven knows," said I. " I cried something to that
effect—— "

" Not to that effect, sir. Those were the very words.
I know them well."

" I admit those were the very words. I said them, no doubt,
because I saw you below."

"For no other reason?"

"What other reason could I possibly have?"

"You had no feeling that they were conveyed to you in any supernatural way?"

"No."

He wished me good-night, and held up his light. I walked by the side of the down line of rails (with a very disagreeable sensation of a train coming behind me), until I found the path. I got back to my inn without any adventure.

Punctual to my appointment, I placed my foot on the first notch of the zig-zag next night, as the distant clocks were striking eleven. He was waiting for me at the bottom, with his white light on. "I have not called out," I said, when we came close together; "may I speak now?" "By all means, sir," "Good-night then, and here's my hand." "Good-night, sir, and here's mine." With that we walked side by side to his box, entered it, closed the door, and sat down by the fire.

"I have made up my mind, sir," he began, bending forward as soon as we were seated, and speaking in a tone but a little above a whisper, "that you shall not have to ask me twice what troubles me. I took you for someone else yesterday evening. That troubles me."

"That mistake?"

"No. That someone else."

"Who is it?"

"I don't know."

"Like me?"

"I don't know. I never saw the face. The left arm is across the face and the right arm is waved. Violently waved. This way."

I followed his action with my eyes, and it was the action of an arm gesticulating with the utmost passion and vehemence : "For God's sake, clear the way!"

"One moonlight night," said the man, "I was sitting here, when I heard a voice cry 'Halloa! Below there!' I started up, looked from that door, and saw this someone else standing by the red light near the tunnel, waving as I just now showed you. The voice seemed hoarse with shouting, and it cried, 'Look out! Look out!' And then again 'Halloa! Below there! Look out!' I caught up my lamp, turned it on red, and ran towards the figure calling

' What's wrong ? What has happened ? Where ? ' It stood just outside the blackness of the tunnel. I advanced so close upon it that I wondered at its keeping the sleeve across its eyes. I ran right up to it, and had my hand stretched out to pull the sleeve away when it was gone."

" Into the tunnel," said I.

" No. I ran on into the tunnel, five hundred yards. I stopped and held my lamp above my head and saw the figures of the measured distance, and saw the wet stains stealing down the walls and trickling through the arch. I ran out again, faster than I had run in (for I had a mortal abhorrence of the place upon me), and I looked all round the red light with my own red light and I went up the iron ladder to the gallery atop of it, and I came down again, and ran back here. I telegraphed both ways : ' An alarm has been given. Is anything wrong ? ' The answer came back, both ways : ' All Well.' "

Resisting the slow touch of a frozen finger tracing out my spine, I showed him how that this figure must be a deception of his sense of sight, and how that figures, originating in disease of the delicate nerves that minister to the functions of the eye, were known to have often troubled patients, some of whom had become conscious of the nature of their affliction, and had even proved it by experiments upon themselves.

That was all very well, he returned, after we had sat listening for a while. But he would beg to remark that he had not finished.

I asked his pardon, and he slowly added these words, touching my arm :

" Within six hours after the Appearance the memorable accident on this Line happened, and within ten hours the dead and wounded were brought along through the tunnel over the spot where the figure had stood."

A disagreeable shudder crept over me, but I did my best against it. It was not to be denied, I rejoined, that this was a remarkable coincidence, calculated deeply to impress his mind. But, it was unquestionable that remarkable coincidences did continually occur, and they must be taken into account in dealing with such a subject.

" This," he said, again laying his hand upon my arm, and glancing over his shoulder with hollow eyes, " was just a year ago. Six or seven months passed, and I had recovered from the surprise and shock, when one morning, as the day was breaking, I, standing at that door, looked towards the red light, and saw the spectre again." He stopped, with a fixed look at me.

" Did it cry out ? "

" No. It was silent."

" Did it wave its arm ? "

" No. It leaned against the shaft of the light, with both hands before the face. Like this."

Once more, I followed his action with my eyes. It was an action of mourning.

" Did you go up to it ? "

" I came in and sat down, partly to collect my thoughts, partly because it had turned me faint. When I went to the door again, daylight was above me, and the ghost was gone."

" But nothing followed ? Nothing came of this ? "

He touched me on the arm with his forefinger twice or thrice, giving a ghastly nod each time :

" That very day, as a train came out of the tunnel, I noticed at a carriage window on my side what looked like a confusion of hands and heads, and something waved. I saw it, just in time to signal the driver Stop ! He shut off, and put his brake on, but the train drifted past here a hundred and fifty yards or more. I ran after it, and, as I went along, heard terrible screams and cries. A beautiful young lady had died instantaneously in one of the compartments, and was brought in here and laid down on this floor between us."

He resumed. " Now, sir, mark this, and judge how my mind is troubled. The spectre came back, a week ago. Ever since it has been there, now and again, by fits and starts."

" At the light ? "

" At the Danger-light."

" What does it seem to do ? "

He repeated, if possible with increased passion and vehemence, that former gesticulation of " For God's sake, clear the way ! "

Then he went on. " I have no peace or rest for it. It calls to me, for many minutes together, in an agonised manner, ' Below there ! Look out ! Look out ! ' It stands waving to me. It rings my little bell—— "

I caught at that. " Did it ring your bell yesterday evening when I was here and you went to the door ? "

" Twice."

" Why, see," said I, " how your imagination misleads you. My eyes were on the bell and my ears were open to the bell, and if I am a living man it did *not* ring at those times. No, nor at any other time, except when it was rung in the natural course of physical things by the station communicating with you."

He shook his head. " I have never made a mistake as to that yet, sir. I have never confused the spectre's ring with the man's. The ghost's ring is a strange vibration in the bell that it derives from nothing else, and I have not asserted that the bell stirs to the eye. I don't wonder that you failed to hear it. But *I* heard it."

" And did the spectre seem to be there when you looked out ? "

" It *was* there."

" Both times ? "

He repeated firmly : " Both times."

" Will you come to the door with me and look for it now ? "

He bit his under-lip as though he were somewhat unwilling, but arose. I opened the door and stood on the step, while he stood in the doorway.

" Do you see it ? " I asked him, taking particular note of his face. His eyes were prominent and strained ; but not very much more so, perhaps, than my own had been when I had directed them earnestly towards the same spot.

" No," he answeréd. " It is not there."

" Agreed," said I.

We went in again, shut the door, and resumed our seats.

" By this time you will fully understand, sir," he said, " that what troubles me so dreadfully is the question, What does the spectre mean ? "

" What is its warning against ? " he said, ruminating, with his eyes on the fire, and only by times turning them on me. " What is the danger ? Where is the danger ? There is danger overhanging, somewhere on the Line. Some dreadful calamity will happen. It is not to be doubted this third time, after what has gone before. But surely this is a cruel haunting of *me*. What can *I* do ? "

He pulled out his handkerchief and wiped the drops from his heated forehead.

" If I telegraphed Danger on either side of me, or on both, I can give no reason for it," he went on, wiping the palms of his hands. " I should get into trouble, and do no good. They would think I was mad. This is the way it would work :—Message : ' Danger ! Take care ! ' Answer : 'What Danger ? Where ? ' Message : ' Don't know. But for God's sake take care ! ' They would displace me. What else could they do ? "

His pain of mind was most pitiable to see.

" When it first stood under the Danger-light," he went on. putting his dark hair back from his head, and drawing his hands outward across and across his temples in an extremity of feverish distress, " why not tell me where that accident was to happen—if it must happen ? Why not tell me how it could be averted—if it could have been averted ? When on its second coming it hid its face, why not tell me instead : ' She is going to die. Let them keep her at home ' ? If it came, on those two occasions, only to show me that its warnings were true, and so to prepare me for the third, why not warn me plainly now ? And I, Lord help me ! A mere poor signalman on this solitary station ! Why not go to somebody with credit to be believed, and power to act ! "

When I saw him in this state I saw that for the poor man's sake, as well as for the public safety, what I had to do for the time was to compose his mind. Therefore, setting aside all question of reality or unreality between us, I represented to him that whoever thoroughly discharged his duty must do well, and that at least it was his comfort that he understood his duty, though he did not understand these confounding Appearances. In this effort I succeeded far better than in the attempt to reason him out of his conviction. He became calm ; the occupations incidental to his post as the night advanced began to make larger demands on his attention ; and I left him at two in the morning.

That I more than once looked back at the red light as I ascended the pathway, that I did not like the red light, and that I should have slept but poorly if my bed had been under it I see no reason to conceal.

But, what ran most in my thoughts was the consideration how ought I to act, having become the recipient of this disclosure ? I had proved the man to be intelligent, vigilant, painstaking, and exact; but how long might he remain so, in his state of mind?

Unable to overcome a feeling that there would be something treacherous in my communicating what he had told me to his superiors in the company, without first being plain with himself and proposing a middle course to him, I ultimately resolved to offer to accompany him (otherwise keeping his secret for the present) to the wisest medical practitioner we could hear of in those parts, and to take his opinion. A change in his time of duty would come round next night, he had apprised me, and he would be off an hour or two after sunrise, and on again soon after sunset. I had appointed to return accordingly.

Next evening was a lovely evening, and I walked out early to enjoy it. The sun was not yet quite down when I traversed the field-path near the top of the deep cutting. I would extend my walk for an hour, I said to myself.

Before pursuing my stroll I stepped to the brink and mechanically looked down, from the point from which I had first seen him. I cannot describe the thrill that seized upon me when, close at the mouth of the tunnel, I saw the appearance of a man, with his left sleeve across his eyes, passionately waving his right arm.

The nameless horror that oppressed me passed in a moment, for in a moment I saw that this appearance of a man was a man indeed, and that there was a little group of other men standing at a short distance, to whom he seemed to be rehearsing the gesture he made. The Danger-light was not yet lighted. Against its shaft, a little low hut, entirely new to me, had been made of some wooden supports and tarpaulin. It looked no bigger than a bed.

With an irresistible sense that something was wrong—with a flashing self-reproachful fear that fatal mischief had come of my leaving the man there, and causing no one to be sent to overlook or correct what he did—I descended the notched path with all the speed I could make.

" What is the matter? " I asked the men.

" Signalman killed this morning, sir "

" Not the man belonging to that box? "

" Yes, sir."

" Not the man I know? "

" You will recognise him, sir, if you knew him," said the

man who spoke for the others, solemnly uncovering his own head and raising an end of the tarpaulin, "for his face is quite composed."

"O! how did this happen, how did this happen?" I asked, turning from one to another as the hut closed in again.

"He was cut down by an engine, sir. No man in England knew his work better. But somehow he was not clear of the outer rail. It was just at broad day. He had struck the light, and had the lamp in his hand. As the engine came out of the tunnel, his back was towards her, and she cut him down. That man drove her and was showing how it happened. Show the gentleman, Tom."

The man, who wore a rough dark dress, stepped back to his former place at the mouth of the tunnel:

"Coming round the curve in the tunnel, sir," he said, "I saw him at the end, like as if I saw him down a perspective-glass. There was no time to check speed, and I knew him to be very careful. As he didn't seem to take heed of the whistle I shut it off when we were running down upon him, and called to him as loud as I could call."

"What did you say?"

"I said, 'Below there! Look out! Look out! For God's sake, clear the way!'"

I started.

"Ah! it was a dreadful time, sir; I never left off calling to him. I put this arm before my eyes, not to see, and I waved this arm to the last; but it was no use."

THE MONKEY'S PAW
W. W. Jacobs

WITHOUT, the night was cold and wet, but in the small parlour of Laburnum Villa the blinds were drawn and the fire burned brightly. Father and son were at chess ; the former, who possessed ideas about the game involving radical changes, putting his king into such sharp and unnecessary perils that it even provoked comment from the white-haired old lady knitting placidly by the fire.

" Hark at the wind," said Mr. White, who, having seen a fatal mistake after it was too late, was amiably desirous of preventing his son from seeing it.

" I'm listening," said the latter, grimly surveying the board as he stretched out his hand. " Check."

" I should hardly think that he'd come to-night," said his father, with his hand poised over the board.

" Mate," replied the son.

" That's the worst of living so far out," bawled Mr. White, with sudden and unlooked-for violence ; " of all the beastly, slushy, out-of-the-way places to live in, this is the worst. Path's a bog, and the road's a torrent. I don't know what people are thinking about. I suppose because only two houses in the road are let, they think it doesn't matter."

" Never mind, dear," said his wife soothingly ; " perhaps you'll win the next one."

Mr. White looked up sharply, just in time to intercept a knowing glance between mother and son. The words died away on his lips, and he hid a guilty grin in his thin grey beard.

" There he is," said Herbert White, as the gate banged to loudly and heavy footsteps came toward the door.

The old man rose with hospitable haste, and opening the door, was heard condoling with the new arrival. The new arrival also condoled with himself, so that Mrs. White said, " Tut, tut ! " and coughed gently as her husband entered the room, followed by a tall, burly man, beady of eye and rubicund of visage.

" Sergeant-Major Morris," he said, introducing him.

The sergeant-major shook hands, and taking the proffered seat by the fire, watched contentedly while his host got out whisky and tumblers and stood a small copper kettle on the fire.

At the third glass his eyes got brighter, and he began to talk, the little family circle regarding with eager interest this visitor from distant parts, as he squared his broad shoulders in the chair, and spoke of wild scenes and doughty deeds ; of wars and plagues, and strange peoples.

" Twenty-one years of it," said Mr. White, nodding at his wife and son. " When he went away he was a slip of a youth in the warehouse. Now look at him."

" He don't look to have taken much harm," said Mrs. White politely.

" I'd like to go to India myself," said the old man, " just to look round a bit, you know."

" Better where you are," said the sergeant-major, shaking his head. He put down the empty glass, and sighing softly, shook it again.

" I should like to see those old temples and fakirs and jugglers," said the old man. " What was that you started telling me the other day about a monkey's paw or something, Morris ? "

" Nothing," said the soldier hastily. " Leastways nothing worth hearing."

" Monkey's paw ? " said Mrs. White curiously.

" Well, it's just a bit of what you might call magic, perhaps," said the sergeant-major off-handedly.

His three listeners leaned forward eagerly. The visitor absent-mindedly put his empty glass to his lips and then set it down again. His host filled it for him.

" To look at," said the sergeant-major, fumbling in his pocket, " it's just an ordinary little paw, dried to a mummy."

He took something out of his pocket and proffered it. Mrs. White drew back with a grimace, but her son, taking it, examined it curiously.

" And what is there special about it ? " inquired Mr. White as he took it from his son, and having examined it, placed it upon the table.

" It had a spell put on it by an old fakir," said the sergeant-major, " a very holy man. He wanted to show that fate ruled people's lives, and that those who interfered with it did so to their sorrow. He put a spell on it so that three separate men could each have three wishes from it."

His manner was so impressive that his hearers were conscious that their light laughter jarred somewhat.

" Well, why don't you have three, sir ? " said Herbert White cleverly.

The soldier regarded him in the way that middle age is wont to regard presumptuous youth. " I have," he said quietly, and his blotchy face whitened.

" And did you really have the three wishes granted ? " asked Mrs. White.

" I did," said the sergeant-major, and his glass tapped against his strong teeth.

" And has anybody else wished ? " persisted the old lady.

" The first man had his three wishes. Yes," was the reply ; " I don't know what the first two were, but the third was for death. That's how I got the paw."

His tones were so grave that a hush fell upon the group.

" If you've had your three wishes, it's no good to you now then, Morris," said the old man at last. " What do you keep it for ? "

The soldier shook his head. " Fancy, I suppose," he said slowly. " I did have some idea of selling it, but I don't think I will. It has caused enough mischief already. Besides, people won't buy. They think it's a fairy tale, some of them ; and those who do think anything of it want to try it first and pay me afterward."

" If you could have another three wishes," said the old man, eyeing him keenly, " would you have them ? "

" I don't know," said the other. " I don't know."

He took the paw, and dangling it between his forefinger and thumb, suddenly threw it upon the fire. White, with a slight cry, stooped down and snatched it off.

" Better let it burn," said the soldier solemnly.

" If you don't want it, Morris," said the other, " give it to me."

" I won't," said his friend doggedly. " I threw it on the

fire. If you keep it, don't blame me for what happens. Pitch
it on the fire again like a sensible man."

The other shook his head and examined his new possession
closely. "How do you do it ? " he inquired.

"Hold it up in your right hand and wish aloud," said the
sergeant-major, "but I warn you of the consequences."

"Sounds like the *Arabian Nights*," said Mrs. White, as
she rose and began to set the supper. "Don't you think you
might wish for four pairs of hands for me ? "

Her husband drew the talisman from his pocket, and then
all three burst into laughter as the sergeant-major, with a look
of alarm on his face, caught him by the arm.

"If you must wish," he said gruffly, "wish for something
sensible."

Mr. White dropped it back in his pocket, and placing
chairs, motioned his friend to the table. In the business of
supper the talisman was partly forgotten, and afterward the
three sat listening in an enthralled fashion to a second instal-
ment of the soldier's adventures in India.

"If the tale about the monkey's paw is not more truthful
than those he has been telling us," said Herbert, as the door
closed behind their guest, just in time to catch the last train,
" we shan't make much out of it."

"Did you give him anything for it, father ? " inquired
Mrs. White, regarding her husband closely.

"A trifle," said he, colouring slightly. "He didn't want
it, but I made him take it. And he pressed me again to throw
it away."

"Likely," said Herbert, with pretended horror. "Why,
we're going to be rich, and famous, and happy. Wish to be
an emperor, father, to begin with ; then you can't be hen-
pecked."

He darted round the table, pursued by the maligned Mrs.
White armed with an antimacassar.

Mr. White took the paw from his pocket and eyed it
dubiously. "I don't know what to wish for, and that's a
fact," he said slowly. "It seems to me I've got all I want."

"If you only cleared the house, you'd be quite happy,
wouldn't you ! " said Herbert, with his hand on his shoulder.
"Well, wish for two hundred pounds, then ; that'll just do
it."

His father, smiling shamefacedly at his own credulity, held
up the talisman, as his son, with a solemn face, somewhat

marred by a wink at his mother, sat down at the piano and struck a few impressive chords.

" I wish for two hundred pounds," said the old man distinctly.

A fine crash from the piano greeted the words, interrupted by a shuddering cry from the old man. His wife and son ran toward him.

" It moved," he cried, with a glance of disgust at the object as it lay on the floor. " As I wished, it twisted in my hand like a snake."

" Well, I don't see the money," said his son, as he picked it up and placed it on the table, " and I bet I never shall."

" It must have been your fancy, father," said his wife, regarding him anxiously.

He shook his head. " Never mind, though ; there's no harm done, but it gave me a shock all the same."

They sat down by the fire again while the two men finished their pipes. Outside, the wind was higher than ever, and the old man started nervously at the sound of a door banging upstairs. A silence unusual and depressing settled upon all three, which lasted until the old couple rose to retire for the night.

" I expect you'll find the cash tied up in a big bag in the middle of your bed," said Herbert, as he bade them good-night, " and something horrible squatting up on top of the wardrobe watching you as you pocket your ill-gotten gains."

He sat alone in the darkness, gazing at the dying fire, and seeing faces in it. The last face was so horrible and so simian that he gazed at it in amazement. It got so vivid that, with a little uneasy laugh, he felt on the table for a glass containing a little water to throw over it. His hand grasped the monkey's paw, and with a little shiver he wiped his hand on his coat and went up to bed.

II

IN the brightness of the wintry sun next morning as it streamed over the breakfast table he laughed at his fears. There was an air of prosaic wholesomeness about the room which it had lacked on the previous night, and the dirty, shrivelled little paw was pitched on the sideboard with a carelessness which betokened no great belief in its virtues.

" I suppose all old soldiers are the same," said Mrs. White. " The idea of our listening to such nonsense ! How could wishes be granted in these days ? And if they could, how could two hundred pounds hurt you, father ? "

" Might drop on his head from the sky," said the frivolous Herbert.

" Morris said the things happened so naturally," said his father, " that you might if you so wished attribute it to coincidence."

" Well, don't break into the money before I come back," said Herbert as he rose from the table. " I'm afraid it'll turn you into a mean, avaricious man, and we shall have to disown you."

His mother laughed, and following him to the door, watched him down the road ; and returning to the breakfast table, was very happy at the expense of her husband's credulity. All of which did not prevent her from scurrying to the door at the postman's knock, nor prevent her from referring somewhat shortly to retired sergeant-majors of bibulous habits when she found that the post brought a tailor's bill.

" Herbert will have some more of his funny remarks I expect, when he comes home," she said, as they sat at dinner.

" I dare say," said Mr. White, pouring himself out some beer ; " but for all that, the thing moved in my hand ; that I'll swear to."

" You thought it did," said the old lady soothingly.

" I say it did," replied the other. " There was no thought about it ; I had just—What's the matter ? "

His wife made no reply. She was watching the mysterious movements of a man outside, who, peering in an undecided fashion at the house, appeared to be trying to make up his mind to enter. In mental connection with the two hundred pounds, she noticed that the stranger was well dressed, and wore a silk hat of glossy newness. Three times he paused at the gate, and then walked on again. The fourth time he stood with his hand upon it, and then with sudden resolution flung it open and walked up the path. Mrs. White at the same moment placed her hands behind her, and hurriedly unfastening the strings of her apron, put that useful article of apparel beneath the cushion of her chair.

She brought the stranger, who seemed ill at ease, into the room. He gazed at her furtively, and listened in a preoccupied fashion as the old lady apologised for the appearance of the room, and her husband's coat, a garment which he usually reserved for the garden. She then waited as patiently as her sex would permit for him to broach his business, but he was at first strangely silent.

" I—was asked to call," he said at last, and stooped and picked a piece of cotton from his trousers. " I come from Maw and Meggins."

The old lady started. " Is anything the matter ? " she asked breathlessly. " Has anything happened to Herbert ? What is it ? What is it ? "

Her husband interposed. " There, there, mother," he said hastily. " Sit down, and don't jump to conclusions. You've not brought bad news, I'm sure, sir " ; and he eyed the other wistfully.

" I'm sorry—— " began the visitor.

" Is he hurt ? " demanded the mother wildly.

The visitor bowed in assent. " Badly hurt," he said quietly, " but he is not in any pain."

" Oh, thank God ! " said the old woman, clasping her hands. " Thank God for that ! Thank—— "

She broke off suddenly as the sinister meaning of the assurance dawned upon her, and she saw the awful confirmation of her fears in the other's averted face. She caught her breath, and turning to her slower-witted husband, laid her trembling old hand upon his. There was a long silence.

" He was caught in the machinery," said the visitor at length in a low voice.

" Caught in the machinery," repeated Mr. White, in a dazed fashion, " yes."

He sat staring blankly out at the window, and taking his wife's hand between his own, pressed it as he had been wont to do in their old courting days nearly forty years before.

" He was the only one left to us," he said, turning gently to the visitor. " It is hard."

The other coughed, and rising, walked slowly to the window.

" The firm wished me to convey their sincere sympathy with you in your great loss," he said, without looking round. " I beg that you will understand I am only their servant and merely obeying orders."

There was no reply ; the old woman's face was white, her eyes staring, and her breath inaudible ; on the husband's face was a look such as his friend the sergeant might have carried into his first action.

"I was to say that Maw and Meggins disclaim all responsibility," continued the other. "They admit no liability at all, but in consideration of your son's services, they wish to present you with a certain sum as compensation."

Mr. White dropped his wife's hand, and rising to his feet, gazed with a look of horror at his visitor. His dry lips shaped the words, "How much?"

"Two hundred pounds," was the answer.

Unconscious of his wife's shriek, the old man smiled faintly, put out his hands like a sightless man, and dropped, a senseless heap, to the floor.

III

IN the huge new cemetery, some two miles distant, the old people buried their dead, and came back to the house steeped in shadow and silence. It was all over so quickly that at first they could hardly realise it, and remained in a state of expectation as though of something else to happen—something else which was to lighten this load, too heavy for old hearts to bear.

But the days passed, and expectation gave place to resignation—the hopeless resignation of the old, sometimes miscalled apathy. Sometimes they hardly exchanged a word, for now they had nothing to talk about, and their days were long to weariness.

It was about a week after, that the old man, waking suddenly in the night, stretched out his hand and found himself alone. The room was in darkness, and the sound of subdued weeping came from the window. He raised himself in bed and listened.

"Come back," he said tenderly. "You will be cold."

"It is colder for my son," said the old woman, and wept afresh.

The sound of her sobs died away on his ears. The bed was warm, and his eyes heavy with sleep. He dozed fitfully, and then slept until a sudden wild cry from his wife awoke him with a start.

"*The paw!*" she cried wildly. "The monkey's paw!"

He started up in alarm. "Where? Where is it? What's the matter?"

She came stumbling across the room toward him. " I want it," she said quietly. " You've not destroyed it ? "

" It's in the parlour, on the bracket," he replied, marvelling. " Why ? "

She cried and laughed together, and bending over, kissed his cheek.

" I only just thought of it," she said hysterically. " Why didn't I think of it before ? Why didn't *you* think of it ? "

" Think of what ? " he questioned.

" The other two wishes," she replied rapidly. " We've only had one."

" Was not that enough ? " he demanded fiercely.

" No," she cried triumphantly ; " we'll have one more. Go down and get it quickly, and wish our boy alive again."

The man sat up in bed and flung the bedclothes from his quaking limbs. " Good God, you are mad ! " he cried, aghast.

" Get it," she panted ; " get it quickly, and wish—— Oh, my boy, my boy ! "

Her husband struck a match and lit the candle. " Get back to bed," he said unsteadily. " You don't know what you are saying."

" We had the first wish granted," said the old woman feverishly ; " why not the second ? "

" A coincidence," stammered the old man.

" Go and get it and wish," cried his wife, quivering with excitement.

The old man turned and regarded her, and his voice shook. " He has been dead ten days, and besides he—I would not tell you else, but—I could only recognize him by his clothing. If he was too terrible for you to see then, how now ? "

" Bring him back," cried the old woman, and dragged him toward the door. " Do you think I fear the child I have nursed ? "

He went down in the darkness and felt his way to the parlour, and then to the mantelpiece. The talisman was in its place, and a horrible fear that the unspoken wish might bring his mutilated son before him ere he could escape from the room seized upon him, and he caught his breath as he found that he had lost the direction of the door. His brow cold with sweat, he felt his way round the table, and groped along the wall until he found himself in the small passage with the unwholesome thing in his hand.

Even his wife's face seemed changed as he entered the room. It was white and expectant, and to his fears seemed to have an unnatural look upon it. He was afraid of her.

" *Wish !* " she cried, in a strong voice.

" It is foolish and wicked," he faltered.

" *Wish !* " repeated his wife.

He raised his hand. " I wish my son alive again."

The talisman fell to the floor, and he regarded it fearfully. Then he sank trembling into a chair as the old woman, with burning eyes, walked to the window and raised the blind.

He sat until he was chilled with the cold, glancing occasionally at the figure of the old woman peering through the window. The candle-end, which had burned below the rim of the china candlestick, was throwing pulsating shadows on the ceiling and walls, until, with a flicker larger than the rest it expired. The old man, with an unspeakable sense of relief at the failure of the talisman, crept back to his bed, and a minute or two afterward the old woman came silently and apathetically beside him.

Neither spoke, but lay silently listening to the ticking of the clock. A stair creaked, and a squeaky mouse scurried noisily through the wall. The darkness was oppressive, and after lying for some time screwing up his courage, he took the box of matches, and striking one, went downstairs for a candle.

At the foot of the stairs the match went out, and he paused to strike another ; and at the same moment a knock, so quiet and stealthy as to be scarcely audible, sounded on the front door.

The matches fell from his hand and spilled in the passage. He stood motionless, his breath suspended until the knock was repeated. Then he turned and fled swiftly back to his room, and closed the door behind him. A third knock sounded through the house.

" *What's that ?* " cried the old woman, starting up.

" A rat," said the old man in shaking tones—" a rat. It passed me on the stairs."

His wife sat up in bed listening. A loud knock resounded through the house.

" It's Herbert ! " she screamed. " It's Herbert ! "

She ran to the door, but her husband was before her, and catching her by the arm, held her tightly.

" What are you going to do ? " he whispered hoarsely.

"It's my boy; it's Herbert!" she cried, struggling mechanically. "I forgot it was two miles away. What are you holding me for? Let go. I must open the door."

"For God's sake don't let it in," cried the old man, trembling.

"You're afraid of your own son," she cried, struggling. "Let me go. I'm coming, Herbert; I'm coming."

There was another knock, and another. The old woman with a sudden wrench broke free and ran from the room. Her husband followed to the landing, and called after her appealingly as she hurried downstairs. He heard the chain rattle back and the bottom bolt drawn slowly and stiffly from the socket. Then the old woman's voice strained and panting.

"The bolt," she cried loudly. "Come down. I can't reach it."

But her husband was on his hands and knees groping wildly on the floor in search of the paw. If he could only find it before the thing outside got in. A perfect fusillade of knocks reverberated through the house, and he heard the scraping of a chair as his wife put it down in the passage against the door. He heard the creaking of the bolt as it came slowly back, and at the same moment he found the monkey's paw, and frantically breathed his third and last wish.

The knocking ceased suddenly, although the echoes of it were still in the house. He heard the chair drawn back, and the door opened. A cold wind rushed up the staircase, and a long loud wail of disappointment and misery from his wife gave him courage to run down to her side, and then to the gate beyond. The street lamp flickering opposite shone on a quiet and deserted road.

THE TURN OF THE SCREW
Henry James

THE story had held us, round the fire, sufficiently breathless, but except the obvious remark that it was gruesome, as on Christmas Eve in an old house a strange tale should essentially be, I remember no comment uttered till somebody happened to note it as the only case he had met in which such a visitation had fallen on a child. The case, I may mention, was that of an apparition in just such an old house as had gathered us for the occasion—an appearance, of a dreadful kind, to a little boy sleeping in the room with his mother and waking her up in the terror of it ; waking her not to dissipate his dread and soothe him to sleep again, but to encounter also herself, before she had succeeded in doing so, the same sight that had shocked him. It was this observation that drew from Douglas—not immediately, but later in the evening—a reply that had the interesting consequence to which I call attention. Some one else told a story not particularly effective, which I saw he was not following. This I took for a sign that he had himself something to produce and that we should only have to wait. We waited in fact till two nights later ; but that same evening, before we scattered, he brought out what was in his mind.

" I quite agree—in regard to Griffin's ghost, or whatever it was—that its appearing first to the little boy, at so tender an age, adds a particular touch. But it's not the first occurrence of its charming kind that I know to have been concerned with a child. If the child gives the effect another turn of the screw, what do you say to *two* children——? "

"We say, of course," somebody exclaimed, "that two children give two turns ! Also that we want to hear about them."

I can see Douglas there before the fire, to which he had
got up to present his back, looking down at this converser with
his hands in his pockets. " Nobody but me, till now, has ever
heard. It's quite too horrible." This was naturally declared
by several voices to give the thing the utmost price, and our
friend, with quiet art, prepared his triumph by turning his
eyes over the rest of us and going on : " It's beyond everything. Nothing at all that I know touches it."

" For sheer terror ? " I remember asking.

He seemed to say it wasn't so simple as that ; to be really
at a loss how to qualify it. He passed his hand over his eyes,
made a little wincing grimace. " For dreadful—dreadful-
ness ! "

" Oh how delicious ! " cried one of the women.

He took no notice of her ; he looked at me, but as if, instead
of me, he saw what he spoke of. " For general uncanny ugliness
and horror and pain."

" Well then," I said, " just sit right down and begin."

He turned round to the fire, gave a kick to a log, watched
it an instant. Then as he faced us again : " I can't begin.
I shall have to send to town." There was a unanimous groan
at this, and much reproach ; after which, in his preoccupied
way, he explained. " The story's written. It's in a locked
drawer—it has not been out for years. I could write to my
man and enclose the key ; he could send down the packet as
he finds it." It was to me in particular that he appeared to
propound this—appeared almost to appeal for aid not to hesitate.
He had broken a thickness of ice, the formation of many a
winter ; had had his reasons for a long silence. The others
resented postponement but it was just his scruples that charmed
me. I adjured him to write by the first post and to agree with
us for an early hearing ; then I asked him if the experience in
question had been his own. To this his answer was prompt.
" Oh thank God, no ! "

" And is the record yours ? You took the thing down ? "

" Nothing but the impression. I took that *here* "—he
tapped his heart. " I've never lost it."

" Then your manuscript——? "

" Is in old faded ink and in the most beautiful hand."
He hung fire again. " A woman's. She has been dead these
twenty years. She sent me the pages in question before she
died." They were all listening now, and of course there was
somebody to be arch, or at any rate to draw the inference.

But if he put the inference by without a smile it was also without irritation. " She was a most charming person, but she was ten years older than I. She was my sister's governess," he quietly said. " She was the most agreeable woman I've ever known in her position ; she would have been worthy of any whatever. It was long ago, and this episode was long before. I was at Trinity, and I found her at home on my coming down the second summer. I was much there that year— It was a beautiful one ; and we had, in her off-hours, some strolls and talks in the garden—talks in which she struck me as awfully clever and nice. Oh yes ; don't grin : I liked her extremely and am glad to this day to think she liked me too. If she hadn't she wouldn't have told me. She had never told anyone. It wasn't simply that she said so, but that I knew she hadn't. I was sure ; I could see. You'll easily judge why when you hear."

" Because the thing had been such a scare ? "

He continued to fix me. " You'll easily judge," he repeated ; " *you* will."

I fixed him too. " I see. She was in love."

He laughed for the first time. " You *are* acute. Yes, she was in love. That is she *had* been. That came out—she couldn't tell her story without its coming out. I saw it, and she saw I saw it ; but neither of us spoke of it. I remember the time and the place—the corner of the lawn, the shade of the great beeches and the long hot summer afternoon. It wasn't a scene for a shudder ; but oh——! " He quitted the fire and dropped back into his chair.

" You'll receive the packet Thursday morning ? " I said.

" Probably not till the second post."

" Well then ; after dinner——"

" You'll all meet me here ? " He looked us round again. " Isn't anybody going ? " It was almost the tone of hope.

" Everybody will stay ! "

" *I* will—and *I* will ! " cried the ladies whose departure had been fixed. Mrs. Griffin, however, expressed the need for a little more light. " Who was it she was in love with ? "

" The story will tell," I took upon myself to reply.

" Oh I can't wait for the story ! "

" The story *won't* tell," said Douglas ; " not in any literal vulgar way."

" More's the pity then. That's the only way I ever understand."

" Won't *you* tell, Douglas ? " somebody else enquired.

He sprang to his feet again. " Yes—to-morrow. Now I must go to bed. Good night." And, quickly catching up a candlestick, he left us slightly bewildered. From our end of the great brown hall we heard his step on the stair ; whereupon Mrs. Griffin spoke. " Well, if I don't know who she was in love with I know who *he* was."

" She was ten years older," said her husband.

" Raison de plus—at that age ! But it's rather nice, his long reticence."

" Forty years ! " Griffin put in.

" With this outbreak at last."

" The outbreak," I returned, " will make a tremendous occasion of Thursday night " ; and every one so agreed with me that in the light of it we lost all attention for everything else. The last story, however incomplete and like the mere opening of a serial, had been told ; we handshook and " candlestuck," as somebody said, and went to bed.

I knew the next day that a letter containing the key had, by the first post, gone off to his London apartments ; but in spite of—or perhaps just on account of—the eventual diffusion of this knowledge we quite let him alone till after dinner, till such an hour of the evening in fact as might best accord with the kind of emotion on which our hopes were fixed. Then he became as communicative as we could desire, and indeed gave us his best reason for being so. We had it from him again before the fire in the hall, as we had had our mild wonders of the previous night. It appeared that the narrative he had promised to read us really required for a proper intelligence a few words of prologue. Let me say here distinctly, to have done with it, that this narrative, from an exact transcript of my own made much later, is what I shall presently give. Poor Douglas, before his death—when it was in sight—committed to me the manuscript that reached him on the third of these days and that, on the same spot, with immense effect, he began to read to our hushed little circle on the night of the fourth. The departing ladies who had said they would stay didn't, of course, thank heaven, stay : they departed, in consequence of arrangements made, in a rage of curiosity, as they professed, produced by the touches with which he had already worked us up. But that only made his little final auditory more compact and select, kept it round the hearth subject to a common thrill.

The first of these touches conveyed that the written statement took up the date at a point after it had, in a manner,
begun. The fact to be in possession of was therefore that his
old friend, the youngest of several daughters of a poor country
parson, had at the age of twenty, on taking service for the
first time in the schoolroom, come up to London, in trepidation,
to answer in person an advertisement that had already placed
her in brief correspondence with the advertiser. This person
proved, on her presenting herself for judgment at a house in
Harley Street that impressed her as vast and imposing—this
prospective patron proved a gentleman, a bachelor in the prime
of life, such a figure as had never risen, save in a dream or an
old novel, before a fluttered anxious girl out of a Hampshire
vicarage. One could easily fix his type ; it never, happily, dies
out. He was handsome and bold and pleasant, off-hand and
gay and kind. He struck her, inevitably, as gallant and splendid.
but what took her most of all and gave her the courage she
afterwards showed was that he put the whole thing to her as a
favour, an obligation he should gratefully incur. She figured
him as rich, but as fearfully extravagant—saw him all in a glow
of high fashion, of good looks, of expensive habits, of charming
ways with women. He had for his town residence a big house
filled with the spoils of travel and the trophies of the chase ;
but it was to his country home, an old family place in Essex,
that he wished her immediately to proceed.

He had been left, by the death of their parents in India,
guardian to a small nephew and a small niece, children of a
younger, a military brother whom he had lost two years before.
These children were, by the strangest of chances for a man in
his position—a lone man without the right sort of experience
or a grain of patience—very heavy on his hands. It had all
been a great worry and, on his own part doubtless, a series of
blunders, but he immensely pitied the poor chicks and had done
all he could ; had in particular sent them down to his other
house, the proper place for them being of course the country,
and kept them there from the first with the best people he
could find to look after them, parting even with his own
servants to wait on them and going down himself, whenever he
might, to see how they were doing. The awkward thing was
that they had practically no other relations and that his own
affairs took up all his time. He had put them in possession of
Bly, which was healthy and secure, and had placed at the head
of their little establishment—but below stairs only—an excellent

woman, Mrs. Grose, whom he was sure his visitor would like
and who had formerly been maid to his mother. She was now
housekeeper and was also acting for the time as superintendent
to the little girl, of whom, without children of her own, she
was by good luck extremely fond. There were plenty of people
to help, but of course the young lady who should go down as
governess would be in supreme authority. She would also
have, in holidays, to look after the small boy, who had been
for a term at school—young as he was to be sent, but what else
could be done ?—and who, as the holidays were about to begin,
would be back from one day to the other. There had been
for the two children at first a young lady whom they had had
the misfortune to lose. She had done for them quite beautifully—she was a most respectable person—till her death, the
great awkwardness of which had, precisely, left no alternative
but the school for little Miles. Mrs. Grose, since then, in
the way of manners and things, had done as she could for
Flora ; and there were further, a cook, a housemaid, a dairy-
woman, an old pony, an old groom and an old gardener, all
likewise thoroughly respectable.

So far had Douglas presented his picture when someone
put a question. " And what did the former governess die of ?
Of so much respectability ? "

Our friend's answer was prompt. " That will come out.
I don't anticipate."

" Pardon me—I thought that was just what you *are*
doing."

" In her successor's place," I suggested, " I should have
wished to learn if the office brought with it——"

" Necessary danger to life ? " Douglas completed my
thought. " She did wish to learn, and she did learn. You
shall hear to-morrow what she learnt. Meanwhile of course the
prospect struck her as slightly grim. She was young, untried,
nervous : it was a vision of serious duties and little company,
of really great loneliness. She hesitated—took a couple of
days to consult and consider. But the salary offered much
exceeded her modest measure, and on a second interview she
faced the music, she engaged." And Douglas, with this, made
a pause that, for the benefit of the company, moved me to
throw in——

" The moral of which was of course the seduction exercised
the splendid young man. She succumbed to it."

He got up and, as he had done the night before, went to the

fire, gave a stir to a log with his foot, then stood a moment with his back to us. " She saw him only twice."

" Yes, but that's just the beauty of her passion."

A little to my surprise, on this, Douglas turned round to me. " It *was* the beauty of it. There were others," he went on, " who hadn't succumbed. He told her frankly all his difficulty —that for several applicants the conditions had been prohibitive. They were somehow simply afraid. It sounded dull —it sounded strange ; and all the more so because of his main condition."

" Which was——? "

" That she should never trouble him—but never, never : neither appeal nor complain nor write about anything ; only meet all questions herself, receive all moneys from his solicitor, take the whole thing over and let him alone. She promised to do this, and she mentioned to me that when, for a moment, disburdened, delighted, he held her hand, thanking her for the sacrifice, she already felt rewarded."

" But was that all her reward ? " one of the ladies asked.

" She never saw him again."

" Oh ! " said the lady ; which, as our friend immediately again left us, was the only other word of importance contributed to the subject till, the next night, by the corner of the hearth, in the best chair, he opened the faded red cover of a thin old-fashioned gilt-edged album. The whole thing took indeed more nights than one, but on the first occasion the same lady put another question. " What's your title ? "

" I haven't one."

" Oh, *I* have ! " I said. But Douglas, without heeding me, had begun to read with a fine clearness that was like a rendering to the ear of the beauty of his author's hand.

I

I REMEMBER the whole beginning as a succession of flights and drops, a little see-saw of the right throbs and the wrong. After rising, in town, to meet his appeal I had at all events a couple of very bad days—found all my doubts bristle again, felt indeed sure I had made a mistake. In this state of mind I spent the long hours of bumping swinging coach that carried me to the stopping-place at which I was to be met by a vehicle from the house. This convenience, I was told, had been ordered, and I found, toward the close of the June afternoon, a commodious fly in waiting for me. Driving at that hour, on a lovely day, through a country the summer sweetness of which served as a friendly welcome, my fortitude revived and, as we turned into the avenue, took a flight that was probably but a proof of the point to which it had sunk. I suppose I had expected, or had dreaded, something so dreary that what greeted me was a good surprise. I remember as a thoroughly pleasant impression the broad clear front, its open windows and fresh curtains and the pair of maids looking out ; I remember the lawn and the bright flowers and the crunch of my wheels on the gravel and the clustered tree-tops over which the rooks circled and cawed in the golden sky. The scene had a greatness that made it a different affair from my own scant home, and there immediately appeared at the door, with a little girl in her hand, a civil person who dropped me as decent a curtsey as if I had been the mistress or a distinguished visitor. I had received in Harley Street a narrower notion of the place, and that, as I recalled it, made me think the proprietor still more of a gentleman, suggested that what I was to enjoy might be a matter beyond his promise.

I had no drop again till the next day, for I was carried triumphantly through the following hours by my introduction to the younger of my pupils. The little girl who accompanied Mrs. Grose affected me on the spot as a creature too charming not to make it a great fortune to have to do with her. She was the most beautiful child I had ever seen, and I afterwards wondered why my employer hadn't made more of a point to me of this. I slept little that night—I was too much excited ; and this astonished me too, I recollect, remained with me, adding to my sense of the liberality with which I was treated. The large impressive room one of the best in the house, the great state bed as I almost felt it, the figured full draperies, the long glasses in which, for the first time, I could see myself from head to foot, all struck me—like the wonderful appeal of my small charge—as so many things thrown in. It was thrown in as well, from the first moment, that I should get on with Mrs. Grose in a relation over which, on my way, in the coach, I fear I had rather brooded. The one appearance indeed that in this early outlook might have made me shrink again was that of her being so inordinately glad to see me. I felt within half an hour that she was so glad—stout simple plain clean wholesome woman—as to be positively on her guard against showing it too much. I wondered even then a little why she

411

should wish *not* to show it, and that, with reflexion, with suspicion, might of course have made me uneasy.

But it was a comfort that there could be no uneasiness in a connexion with anything so beatific as the radiant image of my little girl, the vision of whose angelic beauty had probably more than anything else to do with the restlessness that, before morning, made me several times rise and wander about my room to take in the whole picture and prospect ; to watch from my open window the faint summer dawn, to look at such stretches of the rest of the house as I could catch, and to listen, while in the fading dusk the first birds began to twitter, for the possible recurrence of a sound or two, less natural and not without but within, that I had fancied I heard. There had been a moment when I believed I recognised, faint and far, the cry of a child ; there had been another when I found myself just consciously starting as at the passage, before my door, of a light footstep. But these fancies were not marked enough not to be thrown off, and it is only in the light, or the gloom, I should rather say, of other and subsequent matters that they now come back to me. To watch, teach, " form " little Flora would too evidently be the making of a happy and useful life. It had been agreed between us downstairs that after this first occasion I should have her as a matter of course at night, her small white bed being already arranged, to that end, in my room. What I had undertaken was the whole care of her, and she had remained just this last time with Mrs. Grose only as an effect of our consideration for my inevitable strangeness and her natural timidity. In spite of this timidity— which the child herself, in the oddest way in the world, had been perfectly frank and brave about, allowing it, without a sign of uncomfortable consciousness, with the deep sweet serenity indeed of one of Raphael's holy infants, to be discussed, to be imputed to her and to determine us—I felt quite sure she would presently like me. It was part of what I already liked Mrs. Grose herself for, the pleasure I could see her feel in my admiration and wonder as I sat at supper with four tall candles and with my pupil, in a high chair and a bib, brightly facing me between them over bread and milk. There were naturally things that in Flora's presence could pass between us only as prodigious and gratified looks, obscure and roundabout allusions.

" And the little boy—does he look like her ? Is he too so very remarkable ? "

One wouldn't, it was already conveyed between us, too grossly flatter a child. "Oh Miss, *most* remarkable. If you think well of this one!"—and she stood there with a plate in her hand, beaming at our companion, who looked from one of us to the other with placid heavenly eyes that contained nothing to check us.

"Yes; if I do——?"

"You *will* be carried away by the little gentleman!"

"Well, that, I think, is what I came for—to be carried away. I'm afraid, however," I remember feeling the impulse to add, "I'm rather easily carried away. I was carried away in London!"

I can still see Mrs. Grose's broad face as she took this in. "In Harley Street."

"In Harley Street?"

"Well, Miss, you're not the first—and you won't be the last."

"Oh I've no pretensions," I could laugh, "to being the only one. My other pupil, at any rate, as I understand, comes back to-morrow?"

"Not to-morrow—Friday, Miss. He arrives, as you did, by the coach, under care of the guard, and is to be met by the same carriage."

I forthwith wanted to know if the proper as well as the pleasant and friendly thing wouldn't therefore be that on the arrival of the public conveyance I should await him with his little sister; a proposition to which Mrs. Grose assented so heartily that I somehow took her manner as a kind of comforting pledge—never falsified, thank heaven!—that we should on every question be quite at one. Oh, she was glad I was there!

What I felt the next day was, I suppose, nothing that could be fairly called a reaction from the cheer of my arrival; it was probably at the most only a slight oppression produced by a fuller measure of the scale, as I walked round them, gazed up at them, took them in, of my new circumstances. They had, as it were, an extent and mass for which I had not been prepared and in the presence of which I found myself, freshly, a little scared not less than a little proud. Regular lessons, in this agitation, certainly suffered some wrong; I reflected that my first duty was, by the gentlest arts I could contrive, to win the child into the sense of knowing me. I spent the day with her out of doors; I arranged with her, to her great satisfaction, that it should be she, she only, who might show

me the place. She showed it step by step and room by room
and secret by secret, with droll delightful childish talk about
it and with the result, in half an hour, of our becoming tremendous friends. Young as she was I was struck, throughout
our little tour, with her confidence and courage, with the way,
in empty chambers and dull corridors, on crooked staircases
that made me pause and even on the summit of an old machi-
colated square tower that made me dizzy, her morning music,
her disposition to tell me so many more things than she asked,
rang out and led me on. I have not seen Bly since the day I
left it, and I dare say that to my present older and more informed eyes it would show a very reduced importance. But
as my little conductress, with her hair of gold and her frock of
blue, danced before me round corners and pattered down
passages, I had the view of a castle of romance inhabited by a
rosy sprite, such a place as would somehow, for diversion of
the young idea, take all colour out of story-books and fairy-tales.
Wasn't it just a story-book over which I had fallen a-doze and
a-dream ? No ; it was a big ugly antique but convenient
house, embodying a few features of a building still older, half-
displaced and half-utilised, in which I had the fancy of our being
almost as lost as a handful of passengers in a great drifting ship.
Well, I was strangely at the helm !

II

THIS came home to me when, two days later, I drove over
with Flora to meet, as Mrs. Grose said, the little gentleman ; and all the more for an incident that, presenting itself
the second evening, had deeply disconcerted me. The first
day had been, on the whole, as I have expressed, reassuring ;
but I was to see it wind up to a change of note. The postbag
that evening—it came late—contained a letter for me which,
however, in the hand of my employer, I found to be composed
but of a few words enclosing another, addressed to himself, with
a seal still unbroken. "'This, I recognise, is from the headmaster,
and the headmaster's an awful bore. Read him, please ; deal
with him ; but mind you don't report. Not a word, I'm off!'" I
broke the seal with a great effort—so great a one that I was a long
time coming to it ; took the unopened missive at last up to
my room and only attacked it just before going to bed. I had
better have let it wait till morning, for it gave me a second
sleepless night. With no counsel to take, the next day, I was

414

full of distress ; and it finally got so the better of me that I determined to open myself at least to Mrs. Grose.

" What does it mean ? The child's dismissed his school."

She gave me a look that I remarked at the moment ; then, visibly, with a quick blankness, seemed to try to take it back. " But aren't they all——? "

" Sent home—yes. But only for the holidays. Miles may never go back at all."

Consciously, under my attention, she reddened. " They won't take him ? "

" They absolutely decline."

At this she raised her eyes, which she had turned from me ; I saw them fill with good tears. " What has he done ? "

I cast about ; then I judged best simply to hand her my document—which, however, had the effect of making her, without taking it, simply put her hands behind her. She shook her head sadly. " Such things are not for me, Miss."

My counsellor couldn't read ! I winced at my mistake, which I attenuated as I could, and opened the letter again to repeat it to her ; then, faltering in the act and folding it up once more, I put it back in my pocket. " Is it really *bad* ? "

The tears were still in her eyes. " Do the gentlemen say so ? "

" They go into no particulars. They simply express their regret that it should be impossible to keep him. That can have but one meaning." Mrs. Grose listened with dumb emotion ; she forbore to ask me what this meaning might be ; so that, presently, to put the thing with some coherence and with the mere aid of her presence to my own mind, I went on : " That he's an injury to the others."

At this, with one of the quick turns of simple folk, she suddenly flamed up. " Master Miles !—*him* an injury ? "

There was such a flood of good faith in it that, though I had not yet seen the child, my very fears made me jump to the absurdity of the idea. I found myself, to meet my friend the better, offering it, on the spot, sarcastically. " To his poor little innocent mates ! "

" It's too dreadful," cried Mrs. Grose, " to say such cruel things ! Why he's scarce ten years old."

" Yes, yes ; it would be incredible."

She was evidently grateful for such a profession. " See him, Miss, first. *Then* believe it ! " I felt forthwith a new impatience to see him ; it was the beginning of a curiosity

that, all the next hours, was to deepen almost to pain. Mrs.
Grose was aware, I could judge, of what she had produced in
me, and she followed it up with assurance. ". You might as
well believe it of the little lady. Bless her," she added the
next moment—" *look* at her ! "

I turned and saw that Flora, whom, ten minutes before, I
had established in the schoolroom with a sheet of white paper
a pencil and a copy of nice " round O's," now presented herself
to view at the open door. She expressed in her little way an
extraordinary detachment from disagreeable duties, looking
at me, however, with a great childish light that seemed to offer
it as a mere result of the affection she had conceived for my
person, which had rendered necessary that she should follow
me. I needed nothing more than this to feel the full force
of Mrs. Grose's comparison, and, catching my pupil in my
arms, covered her with kisses in which there was a sob of
atonement.

None the less, the rest of the day, I watched for further
occasion to approach my colleague, especially as, toward
evening, I began to fancy she rather sought to avoid me. I
overtook her, I remember, on the staircase ; we went down
together and at the bottom I detained her, holding her there
with a hand on her arm. " I take what you said to me at noon
as a declaration that *you've* never known him to be bad."

She threw back her head ; she had clearly by this time, and
very honestly, adopted an attitude. " Oh never known him—
I don't pretend *that* ! "

I was upset again. " Then you *have* known him—— ? "

" Yes indeed, Miss, thank God ! "

On reflection I accepted this. " You mean that a boy who
never is—— ? "

" Is no boy for *me* ! "

I held her tighter. " You like them with the spirit to be
naughty ? " Then, keeping pace with her answer, " So do I ! "
I eagerly brought out. " But not to the degree to contaminate——"

" To contaminate ? "—my big word left her at a loss.

I explained it. " To corrupt."

She stared, taking my meaning in ; but it produced in her
an odd laugh. " Are you afraid he'll corrupt *you* ? " She
put the question with such a fine bold humour that with a
laugh, a little silly doubtless, to match her own, I gave way for
the time to the apprehension of ridicule.

But the next day, as the hour for my drive approached, I cropped up in another place. "What was the lady who was here before?"

"The last governess? She was also young and pretty—almost as young and almost as pretty, Miss, even as you."

"Ah then I hope her youth and her beauty helped her!" I recollect throwing off. "He seems to like us young and pretty!"

"Oh he *did*," Mrs. Grose assented: "It was the way he liked every one!" She had no sooner spoken indeed than she caught herself up. "I mean that's *his* way—the master's."

I was struck. "But of whom did you speak first?"

She looked blank, but she coloured. "Why of *him*."

"Of the master?"

"Of who else?"

There was so obviously no one else that the next moment I had lost my impression of her having accidentally said more than she meant; and I merely asked what I wanted to know. "Did *she* see anything in the boy——?"

"That wasn't right? She never told me."

I had a scruple, but I overcame it. "Was she careful—particular?"

Mrs. Grose appeared to try to be conscientious. "About some things—yes."

"But not above all?"

Again she considered. "Well, Miss—she's gone. I won't tell tales."

"I quite understand your feeling," I hastened to reply; but I thought it after an instant not opposed to this concession to pursue: "Did she die here?"

"No—she went off."

I don't know what there was in this brevity of Mrs. Grose's that struck me as ambiguous. "Went off to die?" Mrs. Grose looked straight out of the window, but I felt that, hypothetically, I had a right to know what young persons engaged for Bly were expected to do. "She was taken ill, you mean, and went home?"

"She was not taken ill, so far as appeared, in this house. She left it, at the end of the year, to go home, as she said, for a short holiday, to which the time she had put in had certainly given her a right. We had then a young woman—a nursemaid who had stayed on and who was a good girl and clever; and *she* took the children altogether for the interval. But our young lady never came back, and at the very moment I was expecting her I heard from the master that she was dead."

I turned this over. " But of what ? "

" He never told me ! But please, Miss," said Mrs. Grose, " I must get to my work."

III

HER thus turning her back on me was fortunately not, for my just preoccupations, a snub that could check the growth of our mutual esteem. We met, after I had brought home little Miles, more intimately than ever on the ground of my stupefaction, my general emotion : so monstrous was I then ready to pronounce it that such a child as had now been revealed to me should be under an interdict. I was a little late on the scene of his arrival, and I felt, as he stood wistfully looking out for me before the door of the inn at which the coach had put him down, that I had seen him on the instant, without and within, in the great glow of freshness, the same positive fragrance of purity, in which I had from the first moment seen his little sister. He was incredibly beautiful, and Mrs. Grose had put her finger on it : everything but a sort of passion of tenderness for him was swept away by his presence. What I then and there took him to my heart for was something divine that I have never found to the same degree in any child—his indescribable little air of knowing nothing in the world but love. It would have been impossible to carry a bad name with a greater sweetness of innocence, and by the time I had got back to Bly with him I remained merely bewildered—so far, that is, as I was not outraged—by the sense of the horrible letter locked up in one of the drawers in my room. As soon as I could compass a private word with Mrs. Grose I declared to her that it was grotesque.

She promptly understood me. " You mean the cruel charge——? "

" It doesn't live an instant. My dear woman, *look* at him ! "

She smiled at my pretension to have discovered his charm. " I assure you, Miss, I do nothing else ! What will you say then ? " she immediately added.

" In answer to the letter ? " I had made up my mind. " Nothing at all."

" And to his uncle ? "

I was incisive. " Nothing at all."

" And to the boy himself ? "

I was wonderful. " Nothing at all."

She gave with her apron a great wipe to her mouth. " Then I'll stand by you. We'll see it out."

" We'll see it out ! " I ardently echoed, giving her my hand to make it a vow.

She held me there a moment, then whisked up her apron again with her detached hand. " Would you mind, Miss, if I used the freedom——"

" To kiss me ? No ! " I took the good creature in my arms and after we had embraced like sisters felt still more fortified and indignant.

This at all events was for the time : a time so full that as I recall the way it went it reminds me of all the art I now need to make it a little distinct. What I look back at with amazement is the situation I accepted. I had undertaken, with my companion, to see it out, and I was under a charm apparently that could smooth away the extent and the far and difficult connexions of such an effort. I was lifted aloft on a great wave of infatuation and pity. I found it simple, in my ignorance, my confusion and perhaps my conceit, to assume that I could deal with a boy whose education for the world was all on the point of beginning. I am unable even to remember at this day what proposal I framed for the end of his holidays and the resumption of his studies. Lessons with me indeed, that charming summer, we all had a theory that he was to have ; but I now feel that for weeks the lessons must have been rather my own. I learnt something—at first certainly—that had not been one of the teachings of my small smothered life ; learnt to be amused, and even amusing, and not to think for the morrow. It was the first time, in a manner, that I had known space and air and freedom, all the music of summer and all the mystery of nature. And then there was consideration—and consideration was sweet. Oh it was a trap—not designed but deep—to my imagination, to my delicacy, perhaps to my vanity ; to whatever in me was most excitable. The best way to picture it all is to say that I was off my guard. They gave me so little trouble—they were of a gentleness so extraordinary. I used to speculate—but even this with a dim disconnectedness—as to how the rough future (for all futures are rough !) would handle them and might bruise them. They had the bloom of health and happiness ; and yet, as if I had been in charge of a

419

pair of little grandees, of princes of the blood, for whom every-thing, to be right, would have to be fenced about and ordered and arranged, the only form that in my fancy the after-years could take for them was that of a romantic, a really royal ex-tension of the garden and the park. It may be of course above all what suddenly broke into this gives the previous time a charm of stillness—that hush in which something gathers or crouches. The change was actually like the spring of a beast.

In the first weeks the days were long ; they often, at their finest, gave me what I used to call my own hour, the hour when, for my pupils, tea-time and bed-time having come and gone, I had before my final retirement a small interval alone. Much as I liked my companions this hour was the thing in the day I liked most ; and I liked it best of all when, as the light faded— or rather, I should say, the day lingered and the last calls of the last birds sounded, in a flushed sky, from the old trees— I could take a turn into the grounds and enjoy, almost with a sense of property that amused and flattered me, the beauty and dignity of the place. It was a pleasure at these moments to feel myself tranquil and justified ; doubtless perhaps also to reflect that by my discretion, my quiet good sense and general high propriety, I was giving pleasure—if he ever thought of it ! —to the person to whose pressure I had yielded. What I was doing was what he had earnestly hoped and directly asked of me, and that I *could*, after all, do it proved even a greater joy than I had expected. I dare say I fancied myself, in short, a remarkable young woman and took comfort in the faith that this would more publicly appear. Well, I needed to be remark-able to offer a front to the remarkable things that presently gave their first sign.

It was plump, one afternoon, in the middle of my very hour : the children were tucked away and I had come out for my stroll. One of the thoughts that, as I don't in the least shrink now from noting, used to be with me in these wanderings was that it would be as charming as a charming story suddenly to meet some one. Some one would appear there at the turn of a path and would stand before me and smile and approve. I didn't ask more than that—I only asked that he should *know* ; and the only way to be sure he knew would be to see it, and the kind light of it, in his handsome face. That was exactly present to me—by which I mean the face was—when, on the first of these occasions, at the end of a long June day, I stopped short on emerging from one of the plantations and coming into view of the house. What arrested me on the spot—and with a shock much greater than any vision had allowed for—was the sense that my imagination had, in a flash, turned real. He did stand there !—but high up, beyond the lawn and at the very top of the tower to which, on that first morning, little Flora had conducted me. This tower was one of a pair—square incongruous crenelated structures—that were distinguished, for some reason, though I could see little difference, as the new and the old. They flanked opposite ends of the house and were probably architectural absurdities, redeemed in a measure indeed by not being wholly disengaged nor of a height too pretentious, dating, in their gingerbread antiquity, from a romantic revival that was already a respectable past. I admired them, had fancies about them, for we could all profit in a degree, especially when they loomed through the dusk, by the grandeur of their actual battlements ; yet it was not at such an elevation that the figure I had so often invoked seemed most in place.

It produced in me, this figure, in the clear twilight, I remember, two distinct gasps of emotion, which were, sharply, the shock of my first and that of my second surprise. My second was a violent perception of the mistake of my first : the man who met my eyes was not the person I had precipitately supposed. There came to me thus a bewilderment of vision of which, after these years, there is no living view that I can hope to give. An unknown man in a lonely place is a permitted object of fear to a young woman privately bred ; and the figure that faced me was—a few more seconds assured me—as little any one else I knew as it was the image that had been in my mind. I had not seen it in Harley Street—I had not seen it anywhere. The place, moreover, in the strangest way in the world, had on the instant and by the very fact of its appearance become a solitude. To me at least, making my statement here with a deliberation with which I have never made it, the whole feeling of the moment returns. It was as if, while I took in, what I did take in, all the rest of the scene had been stricken with death. I can hear again, as I write, the intense hush in which the sounds of evening dropped. The rooks stopped cawing in the golden sky and the friendly hour lost for the unspeakable minute all its voice. But there was no other change in nature, unless indeed it were a change that I saw with a stranger sharpness. The gold was still in the sky, the clearness in the air, and the man who looked at me over the battlements was as definite as a picture in a frame. That's how I thought, with extraordinary quickness, of each person he might have been and that he wasn't. We were confronted across our distance quite long enough for me to ask myself with intensity who then he was and to feel, as an effect of my inability to say, a wonder that in a few seconds more became intense.

The great question, or one of these, is afterwards, I know, with regard to certain matters, the question of how long they have lasted. Well, this matter of mine, think what you will of it, lasted while I caught at a dozen possibilities, none of which made a difference for the better, that I could see, in there having been in the house—and for how long, above all?—a person of whom I was in ignorance. It lasted while I just bridled a little with the sense of how my office seemed to require that there should be no such ignorance and no such person. It lasted while this visitant, at all events—and there was a touch of the strange freedom, as I remember, in the sign of familiarity of his wearing no hat—seemed to fix me, from his position, with just the question, just the scrutiny through the fading light, that his own presence provoked. We were too far apart to call to each other, but there was a moment at which, at shorter range, some challenge between us, breaking the hush, would have been the right result of our straight mutual stare. He was in one of the angles, the one away from the house, very erect, as it struck me, and with both hands on the ledge. So I saw him as I see the letters I form on this page; then, exactly, after a minute, as if to add to the spectacle, he slowly changed his place—passed, looking at me hard all the while, to the opposite corner of the platform. Yes, it was intense to me that during this transit he never took his eyes from me, and I can see at this moment the way his hand, as he went, moved from one of the crenelations to the next. He stopped at the other corner, but less long, and even as he turned away still markedly fixed me. He turned away; that was all I knew.

IV

IT was not that I didn't wait, on this occasion, for more, since I was as deeply rooted as shaken. Was there a "secret" at Bly—a mystery of Udolpho or an insane, an unmentionable relative kept in unsuspected confinement? I can't say how long I turned it over, or how long, in a confusion of curiosity and dread, I remained where I had had my collision ; I only recall that when I re-entered the house darkness had quite closed in. Agitation, in the interval, certainly had held me and driven me, for I must, in circling about the place, have walked three miles ; but I was to be later on so much more overwhelmed that this mere dawn of alarm was a comparatively human chill. The most singular part of it in fact—singular as the rest had been—was the part I became, in the hall, aware of in meeting Mrs. Grose. This picture comes back to me in the general train—the impression, as I received it on my return, of the wide white panelled space, bright in the lamplight and with its portraits and red carpets, and of the good surprised look of my friend, which immediately told me she had missed me. It came to me straightway, under her contact, that, with plain heartiness, mere relieved anxiety at my appearance, she knew nothing whatever that could bear upon the incident I had there ready for her. I had not suspected in advance that her comfortable face would pull me up, and I somehow measured the importance of what I had seen by my thus finding myself hesitate to mention it. Scarce anything in the whole history seems to me so odd as this fact that my real beginning of fear was one, as I may say, with the instinct of sparing my companion. On the spot, accordingly, in the pleasant hall and with her eyes on me, I, for a reason that I couldn't then have phrased, achieved an inward revolution —offered a vague pretext for my lateness and, with the idea of the beauty of the night and of the heavy dew and wet feet, went as soon as possible to my room.

Here it was another affair ; here, for many days after, it was a queer affair enough. There were hours, from day to day—or at least there were moments, snatched even from clear duties—when I had to shut myself up to think. It wasn't so much yet that I was more nervous than I could bear to be as that I was remarkably afraid of becoming so ; for the truth I had now to turn over was simply and clearly the truth that I could arrive at no account whatever of the visitor with whom I had been so inexplicably and yet, as it seemed to me, so intimately concerned. It took me little time to see that I might easily sound, without forms of enquiry and without exciting remark, any domestic complication. The shock I had suffered must have sharpened all my senses ; I felt sure, at the end of three days and as the result of mere closer attention, that I had not been practised upon by the servants nor made the object of any " game." Of whatever it was that I knew nothing was known around me. There was but one sane inference : some one had taken a liberty rather monstrous. That was what, repeatedly, I dipped into my room and locked the door to say to myself. We had been, collectively, subject to an intrusion ; some unscrupulous traveller, curious in old houses, had made his way in unobserved, enjoyed the prospect from the best point of view and then stolen out as he came. If he had given me such a bold hard stare, that was but a part of his indiscretion. The good thing, after all, was that we should surely see no more of him.

This was not so good a thing, I admit, as not to leave me to judge that what, essentially, made nothing else much signify was simply my charming work. My charming work was just my life with Miles and Flora, and through nothing could I so like it as through feeling that to throw myself into it was to throw myself out of my trouble. The attraction of my small charges was a constant joy, leading me to wonder afresh at the vanity of my original fears, the distaste I had begun by entertaining for the probable grey prose of my office. There was to be no grey prose, it appeared, and no long grind ; so how could work not be charming that presented itself as daily beauty ? It was all the romance of the nursery and the poetry of the schoolroom. I don't mean by this of course that we studied only fiction and verse ; I mean that I can express no otherwise the sort of interest my companions inspired. How can I describe that except by saying that instead of growing deadly used to them—and it's a marvel for a governess : I call the sisterhood to witness !—I made constant fresh discoveries. There was one direction, assuredly, in which these discoveries stopped : deep obscurity continued to cover the region of the boy's conduct at school. It had been promptly given me, I have noted, to face that mystery without a pang. Perhaps even it would be nearer the truth to say that—without a word—he himself had cleared it up. He had made the whole charge absurd. My conclusion bloomed there with the real rose-flush of his innocence : he was only too fine and fair for the little horrid unclean school-world, and he had paid a price for it. I reflected acutely that the sense of such individual differences, such superiorities of quality, always, on the part of the majority—which could include even stupid sordid head-masters—turns infallibly to the vindictive.

Both the children had a gentleness—it was their only fault, and it never made Miles a muff—that kept them (how shall

I express it ?) almost impersonal and certainly quite unpunish-
able. They were like those cherubs of the anecdote who had
—morally at any rate—nothing to whack ! I remember feeling
with Miles in especial as if he had had, as it were, nothing to
call even an infinitesimal history. We expect of a small child
scant enough " antecedents," but there was in this beautiful
little boy something extraordinarily sensitive, yet extraordinarily
happy, that, more than in any creature of his age I have seen,
struck me as beginning anew each day. He had never for a
second suffered. I took this as a direct disproof of his having
really been chastised. If he had been wicked he would have
" caught " it, and I should have caught it by the rebound—I
should have found the trace, should have felt the wound and
the dishonour. I could reconstitute nothing at all, and he was
therefore an angel. He never spoke of his school, never mentioned a comrade or a master ; and I, for my part, was quite
too much disgusted to allude to them. Of course I was under
the spell, and the wonderful part is that, even at the time, I
perfectly knew I was. But I gave myself up to it ; it was an
antidote to any pain, and I had more pains than one. I was
in receipt in these days of disturbing letters from home, where
things were not going well. But with this joy of my children
what things in the world mattered ? That was the question I
used to put to my scrappy retirements. I was dazzled by their
loveliness.

There was a Sunday—to get on—when it rained with such
force and for so many hours that there could be no procession
to church ; in consequence of which, as the day declined, I
had arranged with Mrs. Grose that, should the evening show
improvement, we would attend together the late service.
The rain happily stopped, and I prepared for our walk, which,
through the park and by the good road to the village, would be
a matter of twenty minutes. Coming downstairs to meet my
colleague in the hall, I remembered a pair of gloves that had
required three stitches and that had received them—with a
publicity perhaps not edifying—while I sat with the children
at their tea, served on Sundays, by exception, in that cold clean
temple of mahogany and brass, the " grown-up " dining-room.
The gloves had been dropped there, and I turned in to recover
them. The day was grey enough, but the afternoon light still
lingered, and it enabled me, on crossing the threshold, not
only to recognise, on a chair near the wide window, then closed,
the articles I wanted, but to become aware of a person on the

other side of the window and looking straight in. One step into the room had sufficed ; my vision was instantaneous ; it was all there. The person looking straight in was the person who had already appeared to me. He appeared thus again with I won't say greater distinctness, for that was impossible, but with a nearness that represented a forward stride in our intercourse and made me, as I met him, catch my breath and turn cold. He was the same—he was the same, and seen, this time, as he had been seen before, from the waist up, the window, though the dining-room was on the ground-floor, not going down to the terrace on which he stood. His face was close to the glass, yet the effect of this better view was, strangely, just to show me how intense the former had been. He remained but a few seconds—long enough to convince me he also saw and recognised ; but it was as if I had been looking at him for years and had known him always. Something, however, happened this time that had not happened before ; his stare into my face, through the glass and across the room, was as deep and hard as then, but it quitted me for a moment during which I could still watch it, see it fix successively several other things. On the spot there came to me the added shock of a certitude that it was not for me he had come. He had come for someone else.

The flash of this knowledge—for it was knowledge in the midst of dread—produced in me the most extraordinary effect, starting, as I stood there, a sudden vibration of duty and courage. I say courage because I was beyond all doubt already far gone. I bounded straight out of the door again, reached that of the house, got in an instant upon the drive and, passing along the terrace as fast as I could rush, turned a corner and came full in sight. But it was in sight of nothing now—my visitor had vanished. I stopped, almost dropped, with the real relief of this ; but I took in the whole scene—I gave him time to reappear. I call it time, but how long was it ? I can't speak to the purpose to-day of the duration of these things. That kind of measure must have left me : they couldn't have lasted as they actually appeared to me to last. The terrace and the whole place, the lawn and the garden beyond it, all I could see of the park, were empty with a great emptiness. There were shrubberies and big trees, but I remember the clear assurance I felt that none of them concealed him. He was there or was not there : not there if I didn't see him. I got hold of this ; then, instinctively, instead of returning as I had come, went to the window. It was confusedly present to me that I ought to place myself where he had stood. I did so ; I applied my face to the pane and looked, as he had looked, into the room. As if, at this moment, to show me exactly what his range had been, Mrs. Grose, as I had done for himself just before, came in from the hall. With this I had the full image of a repetition of what had already occurred. She saw me as I had seen my own visitant ; she pulled up short as I had done ; I gave her something of the shock that I had received. She turned white, and this made me ask myself if I had blanched as much. She stared, in short, and retreated just on *my* lines, and I knew she had then passed out and come round to me and that I should presently meet her. I remained where I was, and while I waited I thought of more things than one. But there's only one I take space to mention. I wondered why *she* should be scared.

V

OH she let me know as soon as, round the corner of the house, she loomed again into view. " What in the name of goodness is the matter——? " She was now flushed and out of breath.

I said nothing till she came quite near. " With me ? " I must have made a wonderful face. " Do I show it ? "

" You're as white as a sheet. You look awful."

I considered ; I could meet on this, without scruple, any degree of innocence. My need to respect the bloom of Mrs. Grose's had dropped, without a rustle, from my shoulders, and if I wavered for the instant it was not with what I kept back. I put out my hand to her and she took it ; I held her hard a little, liking to feel her close to me. There was a kind of support in the shy heave of her surprise. " You came for me for church, of course, but I can't go."

" Has anything happened ? "

" Yes. You must know now. Did I look very queer ? "

" Through this window ? Dreadful ! "

" Well," I said, " I've been frightened." Mrs. Grose's eyes expressed plainly that *she* had no wish to be, yet also that she knew too well her place not to be ready to share with me any marked inconvenience. Oh it was quite settled that she *must* share ! " Just what you saw from the dining-room a minute ago was the effect of that. What *I* saw—just before— was much worse."

Her hand tightened. " What was it ? "

" An extraordinary man. Looking in."

" What extraordinary man ? "

" I haven't the least idea."

Mrs. Grose gazed round us in vain. " Then where is he gone ? "

" I know still less."

" Have you seen him before ? "

" Yes—once. On the old tower."

She could only look at me harder. " Do you mean he's a stranger ? "

" Oh very much ! "

" Yet you didn't tell me ? "

" No—for reasons. But now that you've guessed——"

Mrs. Grose's round eyes encountered this charge. " Ah I haven't guessed ! " she said very simply. " How can I if *you* don't imagine ? "

" I don't in the very least."

" You've seen him nowhere but on the tower ? "

" And on this spot just now."

Mrs. Grose looked round again. " What was he doing on the tower ? "

" Only standing there and looking down at me."

She thought a minute. " Was he a gentleman ? "

I found I had no need to think. " No." She gazed in deeper wonder. " No."

" Then nobody about the place ? Nobody from the village ? "

" Nobody—nobody. I didn't tell you, but I made sure."

She breathed a vague relief : this was, oddly, so much to the good. It only went indeed a little way. " But if he isn't a gentleman——"

" What *is* he ? He's a horror."

" A horror ? "

" He's—God help me if I know *what* he is ! "

Mrs. Grose looked round once more ; she fixed her eyes on the duskier distance and then, pulling herself together, turned to me with full inconsequence. " It's time we should be at church."

" Oh I'm not fit for church ! "

" Won't it do you good ? "

" It won't do *them*——! " I nodded at the house.

" The children ? "

" I can't leave them now."

" You're afraid——? "

I spoke boldly. " I'm afraid of *him*."

Mrs. Grose's large face showed me, at this, for the first time, the far-away faint glimmer of a consciousness more acute : I somehow made out in it the delayed dawn of an idea I myself had not given her and that was as yet quite obscure to me. It comes back to me that I thought instantly of this as something I could get from her ; and I felt it to be connected with the desire she presently showed to know more. " When was it—on the tower ? "

" About the middle of the month. At this same hour."

" Almost at dark," said Mrs. Grose.

" Oh no, not nearly. I saw him as I see you."

" Then how did he get in ? "

" And how did he get out ? " I laughed. " I had no opportunity to ask him ! This evening, you see," I pursued, " he has not been able to get in."

" He only peeps ? "

" I hope it will be confined to that ! " She had now let go my hand ; she turned away a little. I waited an instant ; then I brought out : " Go to church. Good-bye. I must watch."

Slowly she faced me again. " Do you fear for them ? "

We met in another long look. " Don't *you* ? " Instead of answering she came nearer to the window and, for a minute, applied her face to the glass. " You see how he could see," I meanwhile went on.

She didn't move. " How long was he here ? "

" Till I came out. I came to meet him."

Mrs. Grose at last turned round, and there was still more in her face. " *I* couldn't have come out."

" Neither could I ! " I laughed again. " But I did come. I've my duty."

" So have I mine," she replied ; after which she added : " What's he like ? "

" I've been dying to tell you. But he's like nobody."

" Nobody ? " she echoed.

" He has no hat." Then seeing in her face that she already, in this, with a deeper dismay, found a touch of picture, I quickly added stroke to stroke. " He has red hair, very red, close-curling, and a pale face, long in shape, with straight good features and little rather queer whiskers that are as red as his hair.

His eyebrows are somehow darker ; they look particularly arched and as if they might move a good deal. His eyes are sharp, strange—awfully ; but I only know clearly that they're rather small and very fixed. His mouth's wide and his lips are thin, and except for his little whiskers he's quite clean-shaven. He gives me a sort of sense of looking like an actor."

" An actor ! " It was impossible to resemble one less, at least, than Mrs. Grose at that moment.

" I've never seen one, but so I suppose them. He's tall, active, erect," I continued, " but never—no, never !—a gentleman."

My companion's face had blanched as I went on ; her round eyes started and her mild mouth gaped. " A gentleman ? " she gasped, confounded, stupefied : " a gentleman *he* ? "

" You know him then ? "

She visibly tried to hold herself. " But he *is* handsome ? "

I saw the way to help her. " Remarkably ! "

" And dressed——? "

" In somebody's clothes. They're smart, but they're not his own."

She broke into a breathless affirmative groan. " They're the master's ! "

I caught it up. " You *do* know him ? "

She faltered but a second. " Quint ! " she cried.

" Quint ? "

" Peter Quint—his own man, his valet, when he was here ! "

" When the master was ? "

Gaping still, but meeting me, she pieced it all together. " He never wore his hat, but he did wear—well, there were waistcoats missed ! They were both here—last year. Then the master went, and Quint was alone."

I followed, but halting a little. " Alone ? "

" Alone with *us*." Then as from a deeper depth, " In charge," she added.

" And what became of him ? "

She hung fire so long that I was still more mystified. " He went too," she brought out at last.

" Went where ? "

Her expression, at this, became extraordinary. " God knows where ! He died."

" Died ? " I almost shrieked.

She seemed fairly to square herself, plant herself more firmly to express the wonder of it. " Yes, Mr. Quint's dead."

VI

IT took of course more than that particular passage to place us together in presence of what we had now to live with as we could, my dreadful liability to impressions of the order so vividly exemplified, and my companion's knowledge henceforth—a knowledge half consternation and half compassion—of that liability. There had been this evening, after the revelation that left me for an hour so prostrate—there had been for either of us no attendance on any service but a little service of tears and vows, of prayers and promises, a climax to the series of mutual challenges and pledges that had straightway ensued on our retreating together to the schoolroom and shutting ourselves up there to have everything out. The result of our having everything out was simply to reduce our situation to the last rigour of its elements. She herself had seen nothing, not the shadow of a shadow, and nobody in the house but the governess was in the governess's plight ; yet she accepted without directly impugning my sanity the truth as I gave it to her, and ended by showing me on this ground an awestricken tenderness, a deference to my more than questionable privilege, of which the very breath has remained with me as that of the sweetest of human charities.

What was settled between us accordingly that night was that we thought we might bear things together ; and I was not even sure that in spite of her exemption it was she who had the best of the burden. I knew at this hour, I think, as well as I knew later, what I was capable of meeting to shelter my pupils ; but it took me some time to be wholly sure of what my honest comrade was prepared for to keep terms with so stiff an agreement. I was queer company enough—quite as queer as the company I received ; but as I trace over what we went through I see how much common ground we must have found in the one idea that, by good fortune, *could* steady us. It was the idea, the second movement, that led me straight out, as I may say, of the inner chamber of my dread. I could take the air in the court, at least, and there Mrs. Grose could join me. Perfectly can I recall now the particular way strength came to me before we separated for the night. We had gone over and over every feature of what I had seen.

" He was looking for someone else, you say—someone who was not you ? "

"He was looking for little Miles." A portentous clearness now possessed me. "*That's* whom he was looking for."

"But how do you know?"

"I know, I know, I know!" My exaltation grew. "And *you* know, my dear!"

She didn't deny this, but I required, I felt, not even so much telling as that. She took it up again in a moment. "What if *he* should see him?"

"Little Miles? That's what he wants!"

She looked immensely scared again. "The child?"

"Heaven forbid! The man. He wants to appear to *them*." That he might was an awful conception, and yet somehow I could keep it at bay; which moreover, as we lingered there, was what I succeeded in practicaly proving. I had an absolute certainty that I should see again what I had already seen, but something within me said that by offering myself bravely as the sole subject of such experience, by accepting, by inviting, by surmounting it all, I should serve as an expiatory victim and guard the tranquillity of the rest of the household. The children in especial I should thus fence about and absolutely save. I recall one of the last things I said that night to Mrs. Grose.

"It does strike me that my pupils have never mentioned——!"

She looked at me hard as I musingly pulled up. "His having been here and the time they were with him?"

"The time they were with him, and his name, his presence, his history, in any way. They've never alluded to it."

"Oh the little lady doesn't remember. She never heard or knew."

"The circumstances of his death?" I thought with some intensity. "Perhaps not. But Miles would remember— Miles would know."

"Ah don't try him!" broke from Mrs. Grose.

I returned her the look she had given me. "Don't be afraid." I continued to think. "It *is* rather odd."

"That he has never spoken of him?"

"Never by the least reference. And you tell me they were 'great friends'?"

"Oh, it wasn't *him*!" Mrs. Grose with emphasis declared. "It was Quint's own fancy. To play with him, I mean—to spoil him." She paused a moment; then she added: "Quint was much too free."

This gave me, straight from my vision of his face—*such a* face!—a sudden sickness of disgust. "Too free with *my* boy?"

"Too free with every one!"

I forbore for the moment to analyse this description further than by the reflexion that a part of it applied to several of the members of the household, of the half-dozen maids and men who were still of our small colony. But there was everything, for our apprehension, in the lucky fact that no discomfortable legend, no perturbation of scullions, had ever, within any one's memory, attached to the kind old place. It had neither bad name nor ill fame, and Mrs. Grose, most apparently, only desired to cling to me and to quake in silence. I even put her, the very last thing of all, to the test. It was when, at midnight, she had her hand on the schoolroom door to take leave. "I *have* it from you then—for it's of great importance—that he was definitely and admittedly bad?"

"Oh not admittedly. *I* knew it—but the master didn't."

"And you never told him?"

"Well, he didn't like tale-bearing—he hated complaints. He was terribly short with anything of that kind, and if people were all right to *him*——"

"He wouldn't be bothered with more?" This squared well enough with my impression of him: he was not a trouble-loving gentleman, nor so very particular perhaps about some of the company he himself kept. All the same, I pressed my informant. "I promise you I would have told!"

She felt my discrimination. "I dare say I was wrong. But really I was afraid."

"Afraid of what?"

"Of things that man could do. Quint was so clever—he was so deep."

I took this in still more than I probably showed. "You weren't afraid of anything else? Not of his effect——?"

"His effect?" she repeated with a face of anguish and waiting while I faltered.

"On innocent little precious lives. They were in your charge."

"No, they weren't in mine!" she roundly and distressfully returned. "The master believed in him and placed him here because he was supposed not to be quite in health and the country air so good for him. So he had everything to say. Yes"—she let me have it—"even about *them*."

" Them—that creature ? " I had to smother a kind of howl.
" And you could bear it ? "

" No. I couldn't—and I can't now ! " And the poor
woman burst into tears.

A rigid control, from the next day, was, as I have said, to
follow them ; yet how often and how passionately, for a week,
we came back together to the subject ! Much as we had discussed it that Sunday night, I was, in the immediate later
hours in especial—for it may be imagined whether I slept—
still haunted with the shadow of something she had not told
me. I myself had kept back nothing, but there was a word
Mrs. Grose had kept back. I was sure moreover by morning
that this was not from a failure of frankness, but because on
every side there were fears. It seems to me indeed, in raking
it all over, that by the time the morrow's sun was high I had
restlessly read into the facts before us almost all the meaning
they were to receive from subsequent and more cruel occurrences. What they gave me above all was just the sinister
figure of the living man—the dead one would keep a while !—
and of the months he had continuously passed at Bly, which,
added up, made a formidable stretch. The limit of this evil
time had arrived only when, on the dawn of a winter's morning,
Peter Quint was found, by a labourer going to early work, stone
dead on the road from the village : a catastrophe explained—
superficially at least—by a visible wound to his head ; such a
wound as might have been produced (and as, on the final evidence, *had* been) by a fatal slip, in the dark and after leaving the
public-house, on the steepish icy slope, a wrong path altogether,
at the bottom of which he lay. The icy slope, the turn mistaken
at night and in liquor, accounted for much—practically, in the
end, and after the inquest and boundless chatter, for everything ;
but there had been matters in his life—strange passages and
perils, secret disorders, vices more than suspected, that would
have accounted for a good deal more.

I scarce know how to put my story into words that shall
be a credible picture of my state of mind ; but I was in these
days literally able to find a joy in the extraordinary flight of
heroism the occasion demanded of me. I now saw that I had
been asked for a service admirable and difficult ; and there
would be a greatness in letting it be seen—oh in the right
quarter !—that I could succeed where many another girl might
have failed. It was an immense help to me—I confess I rather
applaud myself as I look back !—that I saw my response so

strongly and so simply. I was there to protect and defend the little creatures in the world the most bereaved and the most loveable, the appeal of whose helplessness had suddenly become only too explicit, a deep constant ache of one's own engaged affection. We were cut off, really, together ; we were united in our danger. They had nothing but me, and I —well, I had *them*. It was in short a magnificent chance. This chance presented itself to me in an image richly material. I was a screen—I was to stand before them. The more I saw the less they would. I began to watch them in a stifled suspense, a disguised tension, that might well, had it continued too long, have turned to something like madness. What saved me, as I now see, was that it turned to another matter altogether. It didn't last as suspense—it was superseded by horrible proofs. Proofs, I say, yes—from the moment I really took hold.

This moment dated from an afternoon hour that I happened to spend in the grounds with the younger of my pupils alone. We had left Miles indoors, on the red cushion of a deep window-seat ; he had wished to finish a book, and I had been glad to encourage a purpose so laudable in a young man whose only defect was a certain ingenuity of restlessness. His sister, on the contrary, had been alert to come out, and I strolled with her half an hour, seeking the shade, for the sun was still high and the day exceptionally warm. I was aware afresh with her, as we went, of how, like her brother, she contrived—it was the charming thing in both children—to let me alone without appearing to drop me and to accompany me without appearing to oppress. They were never importunate and yet never listless. My attention to them all really went to seeing them amuse themselves immensely without me : this was a spectacle they seemed actively to prepare and that employed me as an active admirer. I walked in a world of their invention—they had no occasion whatever to draw upon mine ; so that my time was taken only with being for them some remarkable person or thing that the game of the moment required and that was merely, thanks to my superior, my exalted stamp, a happy and highly distinguished sinecure. I forget what I was on the present occasion ; I only remember that I was something very important and very quiet and that Flora was playing very hard. We were on the edge of the lake, and, as we had lately begun geography, the lake was the Sea of Azof.

Suddenly, amid these elements, I became aware that on the other side of the Sea of Azof we had an interested spectator.

The way this knowledge gathered in me was the strangest thing in the world—the strangest, that is, except the very much stranger in which it quickly merged itself. I had sat down with a piece of work—for I was something or other that could sit—on the old stone bench which overlooked the pond ; and in this position I began to take in with certitude and yet without direct vision the presence, a good way off, of a third person. The old trees, the thick shrubbery, made a great and pleasant shade, but it was all suffused with the brightness of the hot still hour. There was no ambiguity in anything ; none whatever at least in the conviction I from one moment to another found myself forming as to what I should see straight before me and across the lake as a consequence of raising my eyes. They were attached at this juncture to the stitching in which I was engaged, and I can feel once more the spasm of my effort not to move them till I should so have steadied myself as to be able to make up my mind what to do. There was an alien object in view—a figure whose right of presence I instantly and passionately questioned. I recollect counting over perfectly the possibilities, reminding myself that nothing was more natural, for instance, than the appearance of one of the men about the place, or even of a messenger, a postman or a tradesman's boy, from the village. That reminder had as little effect on my practical certitude as I was conscious—still even without looking—of its having upon the character and attitude of our visitor. Nothing was more natural than that these things should be the other things they absolutely were not.

Of the positive identity of the apparition I would assure myself as soon as the small clock of my courage should have ticked out the right second ; meanwhile, with an effort that was already sharp enough, I transferred my eyes straight to little Flora, who, at the moment, was about ten yards away. My heart had stood still for an instant with the wonder and terror of the question whether she too would see ; and I held my breath while I waited for what a cry from her, what some sudden innocent sign either of interest or of alarm, would tell me. I waited, but nothing came ; then in the first place—and there is something more dire in this, I feel, than in anything I have to relate—I was determined by a sense that within a minute all spontaneous sounds from her had dropped ; and in the second by the circumstance that also within the minute she had, in her play, turned her back to the water. This was her attitude when I at last looked at her—looked with the confirmed conviction that we were still, together, under direct personal notice. She had picked up a small flat piece of wood which happened to have in it a little hole that had evidently suggested to her the idea of sticking in another fragment that might figure as a mast and make the thing a boat. This second morsel, as I watched her, she was very markedly and intently attempting to tighten in its place. My apprehension of what she was doing sustained me so that after some seconds I felt I was ready for more. Then I again shifted my eyes—I faced what I had to face.

VII

I GOT hold of Mrs. Grose as soon after this as I could ; and I can give no intelligible account of how I fought out the interval. Yet I still hear myself cry as I fairly threw myself into her arms : " They *know*—it's too monstrous : they know, they know ! "

" And what on earth——? " I felt her incredulity as she held me.

" Why all that *we* know—and heaven knows what more besides ! " Then as she released me I made it out to her, made it out perhaps only now with full coherency even to myself. " Two hours ago, in the garden "—I could scarce articulate— " Flora *saw* ! "

Mrs. Grose took it as she might have taken a blow in the stomach. " She has told you ? " she panted.

" Not a word—that's the horror. She kept it to herself ! The child of eight, *that* child ! " Unutterable still for me was the stupefaction of it.

Mrs. Grose of course could only gape the wider. " Then how do you know ? "

" I was there—I saw with my eyes : saw she was perfectly aware."

" Do you mean aware of *him* ? "

" No—of *her*." I was conscious as I spoke that I looked prodigious things, for I got the slow reflection of them in my companion's face. " Another person—this time ; but a figure of quite as unmistakable horror and evil : a woman in black, pale and dreadful—with such an air also, and such a face !—on the other side of the lake. I was there with the child—quiet for the hour ; and in the midst of it she came."

" Came how—from where ? "

"From where they come from! She just appeared and stood there—but not so near."

"And without coming nearer?"

"Oh for the effect and the feeling she might have been as close as you!"

My friend, with an odd impulse, fell back a step. "Was she some one you've never seen?"

"Never. But some one the child has. Some one *you* have." Then to show how I had thought it all out: "My predecessor—the one who died."

"Miss Jessel?"

"Miss Jessel. You don't believe me?" I pressed.

She turned right and left in her distress. "How can you be sure?"

This drew from me, in the state of my nerves, a flash of impatience. "Then ask Flora—*she's* sure!" But I had no sooner spoken than I caught myself up. "No, for God's sake, *don't*. She'll say she isn't—she'll lie!"

Mrs. Grose was not too bewildered instinctively to protest. "Ah how *can* you?"

"Because I'm clear. Flora doesn't want me to know."

"It's only then to spare you."

"No, no—there are depths, depths! The more I go over it the more I see in it, and the more I see in it the more I fear. I don't know what I *don't* see—what I *don't* fear!"

Mrs. Grose tried to keep up with me. "You mean you're afraid of seeing her again?"

"Oh no; that's nothing—now!" Then I explained. "It's of *not* seeing her."

But my companion only looked wan. "I don't understand."

"Why, it's that the child may keep it up—and that the child assuredly *will*—without my knowing it."

At the image of this possibility Mrs. Grose for a moment collapsed, yet presently to pull herself together again as from the positive force of the sense of what, should we yield an inch, there would really be to give way to. "Dear, dear—we must keep our heads! And after all, if she doesn't mind it——!" She even tried a grim joke. "Perhaps she likes it!"

"Like *such* things—a scrap of an infant!"

"Isn't it just a proof of her blest innocence?" my friend bravely enquired.

She brought me, for the instant, almost round. "Oh we

must clutch at *that*—we must cling to it! If it isn't a proof of what you say, it's a proof of—God knows what! For the woman's a horror of horrors."

Mrs. Grose at this, fixed her eyes a minute on the ground; then at last raising them, " Tell me how you know," she said.

" Then you admit it's what she was ? " I cried.

" Tell me how you know," my friend simply repeated.

" Know ? By seeing her ! By the way she looked."

" At you, do you mean—so wickedly ? "

" Dear me, no—I could have borne that. She gave me never a glance. She only fixed the child."

Mrs. Grose tried to see it. " Fixed her ? "

" Ah with such awful eyes ! "

She stared at mine as if they might really have resembled them. " Do you mean of dislike ? "

" God help us, no. Of something much worse."

" Worse than dislike ? "—this left her indeed at a loss.

" With a determination—indescribable. With a kind of fury of intention."

I made her turn pale. " Intention ? "

" To get hold of her." Mrs. Grose—her eyes just lingering on mine—gave a shudder and walked to the window; and while she stood there looking out I completed my statement. " *That's* what Flora knows."

After a little she turned round. " The person was in black, you say ? "

" In mourning—rather poor, almost shabby. But—yes— with extraordinary beauty." I now recognised to what I had at last, stroke by stroke, brought the victim of my confidence, for she quite visibly weighed this. " Oh handsome—very, very," I insisted; " wonderfully handsome. But infamous."

She slowly came back to me. " Miss Jessel—*was* infamous." She once more took my hand in both her own, holding it as tight as if to fortify me against the increase of alarm I might draw from this disclosure. " They were both infamous," she finally said.

So for a little we faced it once more together; and I found absolutely a degree of help in seeing it now so straight. " I appreciate," I said, " the great decency of your not having hitherto spoken; but the time has certainly come to give me the whole thing." She appeared to assent to this, but still only in silence; seeing which I went on : " I must have it now.

Of what did she die ? Come, there was something between them."

" There was everything."

" In spite of the difference——? "

" Oh of their rank, their condition "—she brought it woefully out. " *She* was a lady."

I turned it over ; I again saw. " Yes—she was a lady."

" And he so dreadfully below," said Mrs. Grose.

I felt that I doubtless needn't press too hard, in such company, on the place of a servant in the scale ; but there was nothing to prevent an acceptance of my companion's own measure of my predecessor's abasement. There was a way to deal with that, and I dealt ; the more readily for my full vision —on the evidence—of our employer's late good-looking " own " man ; impudent, assured, spoiled, depraved. " The fellow was a hound."

Mrs. Grose considered as if it were perhaps a little a case for a sense of shades. " I've never seen one like him. He did what he wished."

" With *her* ? "

" With them all."

It was as if now in my friend's own eyes Miss Jessel had again appeared. I seemed at any rate for an instant to trace their evocation of her as distinctly as I had seen her by the pond ; and I brought out with decision : " It must have been also what *she* wished ! "

Mrs. Grose's face signified that it had been indeed, but she said at the same time : " Poor woman—she paid for it ! "

" Then you do know what she died of ? " I asked.

" No—I know nothing. I wanted not to know ; I was glad enough I didn't ; and I thanked heaven she was well out of this ! "

" Yet you had then your idea——"

" Of her real reason for leaving ? Oh yes—as to that. She couldn't have stayed. Fancy it here—for a governess ! And afterwards I imagined—and I still imagine. And what I imagine is dreadful."

" Not so dreadful as what *I* do," I replied ; on which I must have shown her—as I was indeed but too conscious—a front of miserable defeat. It brought out again all her compassion for me, and at the renewed touch of her kindness my power to resist broke down. I burst, as I had the other time made her burst, into tears ; she took me to her motherly breast, and my lamentation overflowed. " I don't do it ! " I sobbed in despair ; " I don't save or shield them ! It's far worse than I dreamed. They're lost ! "

VIII

WHAT I had said to Mrs. Grose was true enough : there were in the matter I had put before her depths and possibilities that I lacked resolution to sound, so that when we met once more in the wonder of it we were of a common mind about the duty of resistance to extravagant fancies. We were to keep our heads if we should keep nothing else—difficult indeed as that might be in the face of all that, in our prodigious experience, seemed least to be questioned. Late that night, while the house slept, we had another talk in my room ; when she went all the way with me as to its being beyond doubt that I had seen exactly what I had seen. I found that to keep her thoroughly in the grip of this I had only to ask her how, if I had " made it up," I came to be able to give, of each of the persons appearing to me, a picture disclosing, to the last detail, their special marks—a portrait on the exhibition of which she had instantly recognised and named them. She wished, of course—small blame to her !—to sink the whole subject ; and I was quick to assure her that my own interest in it had now violently taken the form of a search for the way to escape from it. I closed with her cordially on the article of the likelihood that with recurrence—for recurrence we took for granted—I should get used to my danger ; distinctly professing that my personal exposure had suddenly become the least of my discomforts. It was my new suspicion that was intolerable ; and yet even to this complication the later hours of the day had brought a little ease.

On leaving her, after my first outbreak, I had of course returned to my pupils, associating the right remedy for my dismay with that sense of their charm which I had already recognised as a resource I could positively cultivate and which had never failed me yet. I had simply, in other words, plunged afresh into Flora's special society and there become aware—it was almost a luxury !—that she could put her little conscious hand straight upon the spot that ached. She had looked at me in sweet speculation and then had accused me to my face of having " cried." I had supposed the ugly signs of it brushed away ; but I could literally—for the time at all events—rejoice, under this fathomless charity, that they had not entirely disappeared. To gaze into the depths of blue of the child's eyes and pronounce their loveliness a trick of premature cunning was to be guilty of a cynicism in preference to which I naturally preferred to abjure my judgment and, so far as might be, my agitation. I couldn't abjure for merely wanting to, but I could repeat to Mrs. Grose—as I did there, over and over, in the small hours—that with our small friends' voices in the air, their pressure on one's heart and their fragrant faces against one's cheek, everything fell to the ground but their incapacity and their beauty. It was a pity that, somehow, to settle this once for all, I had equally to re-enumerate the signs of subtlety that, in the afternoon, by the lake, had made a miracle of my show of self-possession. It was a pity to be obliged to reinvestigate the certitude of the moment itself and repeat how it had come to me as a revelation that the inconceivable communion I then surprised must have been for both parties a matter of habit. It was a pity I should have had to quaver out again the reasons for my not having, in my delusion, so much as questioned that the little girl saw our visitant even as I actually saw Mrs. Grose herself, and that she wanted, by just so much as she did thus see, to make me suppose she didn't, and at the same time, without showing anything, arrive at a guess as to whether I myself did ! It was a pity I needed to recapitulate the portentous little activities by which she sought to divert my attention —the perceptible increase of movement, the greater intensity of play, the singing, the gabbling of nonsense and the invitation to romp.

Yet if I had not indulged, to prove there was nothing in it, in this review, I should have missed the two or three dim elements of comfort that still remained to me. I shouldn't for instance have been able to asseverate to my friend that I was certain—which was so much to the good—that I at least had not betrayed myself. I shouldn't have been prompted, by stress of need, by desperation of mind—I scarce know what to call it—to invoke such further aid to intelligence as might spring from pushing my colleague fairly to the wall. She had told me, bit by bit, under pressure, a great deal ; but a small shifty spot on the wrong side of it all still sometimes brushed my brow like the wing of a bat ; and I remember how on this occasion—for the sleeping house and the concentration alike of our danger and our watch seemed to help—I felt the importance of giving the last jerk to the curtain. " I don't believe anything so horrible," I recollect saying ; " no, let us put it definitely, my dear, that I don't. But if I did, you know, there's a thing I should require now, just without sparing you the least bit more—oh not a scrap, come !—to get out of you. What was it you had in mind when, in our distress, before Miles came back, over the letter from his school, you said, under my insistence, that you didn't pretend for him he hadn't literally *ever* been ' bad ' ? He has *not*, truly, ' ever,' in these weeks that I myself have lived with him and so closely watched him ; he has been an imperturbable little prodigy of delightful loveable goodness. Therefore you might perfectly have made the claim for him if you had not, as it happened, seen an exception to take. What was your exception, and to what passage in your personal observation of him did you refer ? "

It was a straight question enough, but levity was not our note, and in any case I had before the grey dawn admonished us to separate got my answer. What my friend had had in mind proved immensely to the purpose. It was neither more nor less than the particular fact that for a period of several months Quint and the boy had been perpetually together. It was indeed the very appropriate item of evidence of her having ventured to criticise the propriety, to hint at the incongruity, of so close an alliance, and even to go so far on the subject as a frank overture to Miss Jessel would take her. Miss Jessel had, with a very high manner about it, requested her to mind her business, and the good woman had on this directly approached little Miles. What she had said to him, since I pressed, was that *she* liked to see young gentlemen not forget their station.

I pressed again, of course, the closer for that. " You reminded him that Quint was only a base menial ? "

" As you might say ! And it was his answer, for one thing, that was bad."

" And for another thing ? " I waited. " He repeated your words to Quint ? "

" No, not that. It's just what he *wouldn't* ! " she could still impress on me. " I was sure, at any rate," she added, " that he didn't. But he denied certain occasions."

" What occasions ? "

" When they had been about together quite as if Quint were his tutor—and a very grand one—and Miss Jessel only for the little lady. When he had gone off with the fellow, I mean, and spent hours with him."

"He then prevaricated about it—he said he hadn't ? "
Her assent was clear enough to cause me to add in a moment :
"I see. He lied."

"Oh !" Mrs. Grose mumbled. This was a suggestion
that it didn't matter ; which indeed she backed up by a further
remark. "You see, after all, Miss Jessel didn't mind. She
didn't forbid him."

I considered. "Did he put that to you as a justification ? "
At this she dropped again. "No, he never spoke of it."

"Never mentioned her in connexion with Quint ? "

She saw, visibly flushing, where I was coming out. "Well,
he didn't show anything. He denied," she repeated ; "he
denied."

Lord, how I pressed her now ! "So that you could see he
knew what was between the two wretches ? "

"I don't know—I don't know !" the poor woman wailed.

"You do know, you dear thing," I replied ; "only you
haven't my dreadful boldness of mind, and you keep back,
out of timidity and modesty and delicacy, even the impression
that in the past, when you had, without my aid, to flounder
about in silence, most of all made you miserable. But I shall
get it out of you yet ! There was something in the boy that
suggested to you," I continued, "his covering and concealing
their relation."

"Oh he couldn't prevent——"

"Your learning the truth ? I dare say ! But, heavens,"
I fell, with vehemence, a-thinking, "what it shows that they
must, to that extent, have succeeded in making of him ! "

"Ah nothing that's not nice *now* !" Mrs. Grose lugubriously
pleaded.

"I don't wonder you looked queer," I persisted, "when I
mentioned to you the letter from his school ! "

"I doubt if I looked as queer as you !" she retorted with
homely force. "And if he was so bad then as that comes to,
how is he such an angel now ? "

"Yes indeed—and if he was a fiend at school ! How,
how, how ? Well," I said in my torment, "you must put it to
me again, though I shall not be able to tell you for some days.
Only put it to me again !" I cried in a way that made my friend
stare. "There are directions in which I mustn't for the
present let myself go." Meanwhile I returned to her first
example—the one to which she had just previously referred—of
the boy's happy capacity for an occasional slip. "If Quint—

on your remonstrance at the time you speak of—was a base menial, one of the things Miles said to you, I find myself guessing, was that you were another." Again her admission was so adequate that I continued : " And you forgave him that ? "

" Wouldn't *you ?* "

" Oh yes ! " And we exchanged there, in the stillness, a sound of the oddest amusement. Then I went on : " At all events, while he was with the man——"

" Miss Flora was with the woman. It suited them all ! "

It suited me too, I felt, only too well ; by which I mean that it suited exactly the particular deadly view I was in the very act of forbidding myself to entertain. But I so far succeeded in checking the expression of this view that I will throw, just here, no further light on it than may be offered by the mention of my final observation to Mrs. Grose. " His having lied and been impudent are, I confess, less engaging specimens than I had hoped to have from you of the outbreak in him of the little natural man. Still," I mused, " they must do, for they make me feel more than ever that I must watch."

It made me blush, the next minute, to see in my friend's face how much more unreservedly she had forgiven him than her anecdote struck me as pointing out to my own tenderness any way to do. This was marked when, at the schoolroom door, she quitted me. " Surely you don't accuse *him*——"

" Of carrying on an intercourse that he conceals from me ? Ah remember that, until further evidence, I now accuse nobody." Then before shutting her out to go by another passage to her own place, " I must just wait," I wound up.

IX

I WAITED and waited, and the days took as they elapsed something from my consternation. A very few of them, in fact, passing, in constant sight of my pupils, without a fresh incident, sufficed to give to grievous fancies and even to odious memories a kind of brush of the sponge. I have spoken of the surrender to their extraordinary childish grace as a thing I could actively promote in myself, and it may be imagined if I neglected now to apply at this source for whatever balm it would yield. Stranger than I can express, certainly, was the effort to struggle against my new lights. It would doubtless have been a greater tension still, however, had it not been so frequently successful. I used to wonder how my little charges could help guessing that I thought strange things about them ; and the circumstance that these things only made them more interesting was not by itself a direct aid to keeping them in the dark. I trembled lest they should see that they *were* so immensely more interesting. Putting things at the worst, at all events, as in meditation I so often did, any clouding of their innocence could only be—blameless and foredoomed as they were—a reason the more for taking risks. There were moments when I knew myself to catch them up by an irresistible impulse and press them to my heart. As soon as I had done so I used to wonder—" What will they think of that ? Doesn't it betray too much ? " It would have been easy to get into a sad wild tangle about how much I might betray ; but the real account, I feel, of the hours of peace I could still enjoy was that the immediate charm of my companions was a beguilement still effective even under the shadow of the possibility that it was studied. For if it occurred to me that I might occasionally excite suspicion by the little outbreaks of my sharper passion for them, so too I remember asking if I mightn't see a queerness in the traceable increase of their own demonstrations.

They were at this period extravagantly and preternaturally fond of me ; which, after all, I could reflect, was no more than a graceful response in children perpetually bowed down over and hugged. The homage of which they were so lavish succeeded in truth for my nerves quite as well as if I never appeared to myself, as I may say, literally to catch them at a purpose in it. They had never, I think, wanted to do so many things for their poor protectress ; I mean—though they got their lessons better and better, which was naturally what would please her most—in the way of diverting, entertaining, surprising her ; reading her passages, telling her stories, acting her charades, pouncing out at her, in disguises, as animals and historical characters, and above all astonishing her by the " pieces " they had secretly got by heart and could interminably recite. I should never get to the bottom—were I to let myself go even now—of the prodigious private commentary, all under still more private correction, with which I in these days overscored their full hours. They had shown me from the first a facility for everything, a general faculty which, taking a fresh start, achieved remarkable flights. They got their little tasks as if they loved them ; they indulged, from the mere exuberance of the gift, in the most unimposed little miracles of memory.

They not only popped out at me as tigers and as Romans, but as Shakespeareans, astronomers and navigators. This was so singularly the case that it had presumably much to do with the fact as to which, at the present day, I am at a loss for a different explanation : I allude to my unnatural composure on the subject of another school for Miles. What I remember is that I was content for the time not to open the question, and that contentment must have sprung from the sense of his perpetually striking show of cleverness. He was too clever for a bad governess, for a parson's daughter, to spoil ; and the strangest if not the brightest thread in the pensive embroidery I just spoke of was the impression I might have got, if I had dared to work it out, that he was under some influence operating in his small intellectual life as a tremendous incitement.

If it was easy to reflect, however, that such a boy could postpone school, it was at least as marked that for such a boy to have been " kicked out " by a schoolmaster was a mystification without end. Let me add that in their company now—and I was careful almost never to be out of it—I could follow no scent very far. We lived in a cloud of music and affection and success and private theatricals. The musical sense in each of the children was of the quickest, but the elder in especial had a marvellous knack of catching and repeating. The schoolroom piano broke into all gruesome fancies ; and when that failed there were confabulations in corners, with a sequel of one of them going out in the highest spirits in order to " come in " as something new. I had had brothers myself, and it was no revelation to me that little girls could be slavish idolators of little boys. What surpassed everything was that there was a little boy in the world who could have for the inferior age, sex and intelligence so fine a consideration. They were extraordinarily at one, and to say that they never either quarrelled or complained is to make the note of praise coarse for their quality of sweetness. Sometimes perhaps indeed (when I dropped into coarseness) I came across traces of little understandings between them by which one of them should keep me occupied while the other slipped away. There is a naïf side, I suppose, in all diplomacy ; but if my pupils practised upon me it was surely with the minimum of grossness. It was all in the other quarter that, after a lull, the grossness broke out.

I find that I really hang back : but I must take my horrid

plunge. In going on with the record of what was hideous at Bly I not only challenge the most liberal faith—for which I little care ; but (and this is another matter) I renew what I myself suffered, I again push my dreadful way through it to the end. There came suddenly an hour after which, as I look back, the business seems to me to have been all pure suffering ; but I have at least reached the heart of it, and the straightest road out is doubtless to advance. One evening—with nothing to lead up or prepare it—I felt the cold touch of the impression that had breathed on me the night of my arrival and which, much lighter then as I have mentioned, I should probably have made little of in memory had my subsequent sojourn been less agitated. I had not gone to bed ; I sat reading by a couple of candles. There was a roomful of old books at Bly— last-century fiction some of it, which, to the extent of a distinctly deprecated renown, but never to so much as that of a stray specimen, had reached the sequestered home and appealed to the unavowed curiosity of my youth. I remember that the book I had in my hand was Fielding's *Amelia* ; also that I was wholly awake. I recall further both a general conviction that it was horribly late and a particular objection to looking at my watch. I figure finally that the white curtain draping, in the fashion of those days, the head of Flora's little bed, shrouded, as I had assured myself long before, the perfection of childish rest. I recollect in short that though I was deeply interested in my author I found myself, at the turn of a page and with his spell all scattered, looking straight up from him and hard at the door of my room. There was a moment during which I listened, reminded of the faint sense I had had, the first night, of there being something undefinably astir in the house, and noted the soft breath of the open casement just move the half-drawn blind. Then, with all the marks of a deliberation that must have seemed magnificent had there been anyone to admire it, I laid down my book, rose to my feet and, taking a candle, went straight out of the room and, from the passage, on which my light made little impression, noiselessly closed and locked the door.

I can say now neither what determined nor what guided me, but I went straight along the lobby, holding my candle high, till I came within sight of the tall window that presided over the great turn of the staircase. At this point I precipitately found myself aware of three things. They were practically simultaneous, yet they had flashes of succession. My candle, under a bold flourish, went out, and I perceived, by the uncovered window, that the yielding dusk of earliest morning rendered it unnecessary. Without it, the next instant, I knew that there was a figure on the stair. I speak of sequences, but I required no lapse of seconds to stiffen myself for a third encounter with Quint. The apparition had reached the landing half-way up and was therefore on the spot nearest the window, where, at sight of me, it stopped short and fixed me exactly as it had fixed me from the tower and from the garden. He knew me as well as I knew him ; and so, in the cold faint twilight, with a glimmer in the high glass and another on the polish of the oak stair below, we faced each other in our common intensity. He was absolutely, on this occasion, a living detestable dangerous presence. But that was not the wonder of wonders ; I reserve this distinction for quite another circumstance : the circumstance that dread had unmistakeably quitted me and that there was nothing in me unable to meet and measure him.

I had plenty of anguish after that extraordinary moment, but I had, thank God, no terror. And he knew I hadn't—I found myself at the end of an instant magnificently aware of this. I felt, in a fierce rigour of confidence, that if I stood my ground a minute I should cease—for the time at least—to have him to reckon with ; and during the minute, accordingly, the thing was as human and hideous as a real interview : hideous just because it *was* human, as human as to have met alone, in the small hours, in a sleeping house, some enemy, some adventurer, some criminal. It was the dead silence of our long gaze at such close quarters that gave the whole horror, huge as it was, its only note of the unnatural. If I had met a murderer in such a place and at such an hour we still at least would have spoken. Something would have passed, in life, between us ; if nothing had passed one of us would have moved. The moment was so prolonged that it would have taken but little more to make me doubt if even I were in life. I can't express what followed it save by saying that the silence itself—which was indeed in a manner an attestation of my strength—became the element into which I saw the figure disappear ; in which I definitely saw it turn, as I might have seen the low wretch to which it had once belonged turn on receipt of an order, and pass, with my eyes on the villainous back that no hunch could have more disfigured, straight down the staircase and into the darkness in which the next bend was lost.

X

I REMAINED a while at the top of the stair, but with the effect presently of understanding that when my visitor had gone, he had gone ; then I returned to my room. The foremost thing I saw there by the light of the candle I had left burning was that Flora's little bed was empty : and on this I caught my breath with all the terror that, five minutes before, I had been able to resist. I dashed at the place in which I had left her lying and over which—for the small silk counterpane and the sheets were disarranged—the white curtains had been deceivingly pulled forward ; then my step, to my unutterable relief, produced an answering sound : I noticed an agitation of the window-blind, and the child, ducking down, emerged rosily from the other side of it. She stood there in so much of her candour and so little of her night-gown, with her pink bare feet and the golden glow of her curls. She looked intensely grave, and I had never had such a sense of losing an advantage acquired (the thrill of which had just been so prodigious) as on my consciousness that she addressed me with a reproach— " You naughty : where *have* you been ? " Instead of challenging her own irregularity I found myself arraigned and explaining. She herself explained, for that matter, with the loveliest eagerest simplicity. She had known suddenly, as she lay there, that I was out of the room, and had jumped up to see what had become of me. I had dropped, with the joy of her reappearance, back into my chair—feeling then, and then only, a little faint ; and she had pattered straight over to me, thrown herself upon my knee, given herself to be held with the flame of the candle full in the wonderful little face that was still flushed with sleep. I remember closing my eyes an instant, yieldingly, consciously, as before the excess of something beautiful that shone out of the blue of her own. " You were looking for me out of the window ? " I said. " You thought I might be walking in the grounds ? "

" Well, you know, I thought someone was "—she never blanched as she smiled out that at me.

Oh how I looked at her now ! " And did you see anyone ? "

" Ah *no* ! " she returned almost (with the full privilege of childish inconsequence) resentfully, though with a long sweetness in her little drawl of the negative.

At that moment, in the state of my nerves, I absolutely believed she lied ; and if I once more closed my eyes it was before the dazzle of the three or four possible ways in which I might take this up. One of these for a moment tempted me with such singular force that, to resist it, I must have gripped my little girl with a spasm that, wonderfully, she submitted to without a cry or a sign of fright. Why not break out at her on the spot and have it all over ?—give it to her straight in her lovely little lighted face ? " You see, you see, you *know* that you do and that you already quite suspect I believe it ; therefore why not frankly confess it to me, so that we may at least live with it together and learn perhaps, in the strangeness of our fate, where we are and what it means ? " This solicitation dropped, alas, as it came : if I could immediately have succumbed to it I might have spared myself—well, you'll see what. Instead of succumbing I sprang again to my feet, looking at her bed and took a helpless middle way. " Why did you pull the curtain over the place to make me think you were still there ? "

Flora luminously considered ; after which, with her little divine smile : " Because I don't like to frighten you ! "

" But if I had, by your idea, gone out——? "

She absolutely declined to be puzzled ; she turned her eyes to the flame of the candle as if the question were as irrelevant, or at any rate as impersonal, as Mrs. Marcet or nine-times-nine. "Oh but you know," she quite adequately answered, " that you might come back, you dear, and that you *have* ! " And after a little, when she had got into bed, I had, for a long time, by almost sitting on her for the retention of her hand, to show how I recognised the pertinence of my return.

You may imagine the general complexion, from that moment of my nights. I repeatedly sat up till I didn't know when ; I selected moments when my room-mate unmistakeably slept, and, stealing out, took noiseless turns in the passage. I even pushed as far as to where I had last met Quint. But I never met him there again, and I may as well say at once that I on no other occasion saw him in the house. I just missed, on the staircase, nevertheless, a different adventure. Looking down it from the top I once recognised the presence of a woman seated on one of the lower steps with her back presented to me, her body half-bowed and her head, in an attitude of woe, in her hands. I had been there but an instant, however, when she vanished without looking round at me. I knew, for all that, exactly what dreadful face she had to show; and I wondered whether, if instead of being above I had been below, I should have had the same nerve for going up that I had lately shown Quint. Well, there continued to be plenty of call for nerve. On the eleventh night after my latest encounter with that gentleman—they were all numbered now—I had an alarm that perilously skirted it and that indeed, from the particular quality of its unexpectedness, proved quite my sharpest shock. It was precisely the first night during this series, that, weary with vigils, I had conceived I might again without laxity lay myself down at my old hour. I slept immediately and, as I afterwards knew, till about one o'clock; but when I woke it was to sit straight up as completely roused as if a hand had shaken me. I had left a light burning, but it was now out, and I felt an instant certainty that Flora had extinguished it. This brought me to my feet and straight, in the darkness, to her bed, which I found she had left. A glance at the window enlightened me further, and the striking of a match completed the picture.

The child had again got up—this time blowing out the taper, and had again, for some purpose of observation or response, squeezed in behind the blind and was peering out into the night. That she now saw—as she had not, I had satisfied myself, the previous time—was proved to me by the fact that she was disturbed neither by my re-illumination nor by the haste I made to get into slippers and into a wrap. Hidden, protected, absorbed, she evidently rested on the sill—the casement opened forward—and gave herself up. There was a great still moon to help her, and this fact had counted in my quick decision. She was face to face with the apparition we had met at the lake, and could now communicate with it as she had not then been able to do. What I, on my side, had to care for was, without disturbing her, to reach, from the corridor, some other window turned to the same quarter. I got to the door without her hearing me; I got out of it, closed it, and listened from the other side for some sound from her. While I stood in the passage I had my eyes on her brother's door, which was but ten steps off and which, indescribably, produced in me a renewal of the strange impulse that I lately spoke of as my temptation. What if I should go straight in and march to *his* window?—what if, by risking to his boyish bewilderment a revelation of my motive, I should throw across the rest of the mystery the long halter of my boldness?

This thought held me sufficiently to make me cross to his threshold and pause again. I preternaturally listened ; I figured to myself what might portentously be ; I wondered if his bed were also empty and he also secretly at watch. It was a deep soundless minute, at the end of which my impulse failed. He was quiet ; he might be innocent ; the risk was hideous ; I turned away. There was a figure in the grounds—a figure prowling for a sight, the visitor with whom Flora was engaged ; but it wasn't the visitor most concerned with my boy. I hesitated afresh, but on other grounds and only a few seconds ; then I had made my choice. There were empty rooms enough at Bly, and it was only a question of choosing the right one. The right one suddenly presented itself to me as the lower one—though high above the gardens—in the solid corner of the house that I have spoken of as the old tower. This was a large square chamber, arranged with some state as a bedroom, the extravagant size of which made it so inconvenient that it had not for years, though kept by Mrs. Grose in exemplary order, been occupied. I had often admired it and I knew my way about in it ; I had only, after just faltering at the first chill gloom of its disuse, to pass across it and unbolt in all quietness one of the shutters. Achieving this transit I uncovered the glass without a sound and, applying my face to the pane, was able, the darkness without being much less than within, to see that I commanded the right direction. Then I saw something more. The moon made the night extraordinarily penetrable and showed me on the lawn a person, diminished by distance, who stood there motionless and as if fascinated, looking up to where I had appeared—looking, that is, not so much straight at me as at something that was apparently above me. There was clearly another person above me—there was a person on the tower ; but the presence on the lawn was not in the least what I had conceived and had confidently hurried to meet. The presence on the lawn—I felt sick as I made it out—was poor little Miles himself.

XI

IT was not till late next day that I spoke to Mrs. Grose ; the rigour with which I kept my pupils in sight making it often difficult to meet her privately ; the more as we each felt the importance of not provoking—on the part of the servants quite as much as on that of the children—any suspicion of a secret flurry or of a discussion of mysteries. I drew a great security in this particular from her mere smooth aspect. There was nothing in her fresh face to pass on to others the least of my horrible confidences. She believed me, I was sure, absolutely : if she hadn't I don't know what would have become of me, for I couldn't have borne the strain alone. But she was a magnificent monument to the blessing of a want of imagination, and if she could see in our little charges nothing but their beauty and amiability, their happiness and cleverness, she had no direct communication with the sources of my trouble. If they had been at all visibly blighted or battered she would doubtless have grown, on tracing it back, haggard enough to match them ; as matters stood, however, I could feel her, when she surveyed them with her large white arms folded and the habit of serenity in all her look, thank the Lord's mercy that if they were ruined the pieces would still serve. Flights of fancy gave place, in her mind, to a steady fireside glow, and I had already begun to perceive how, with the development of the conviction that—as time went on without a public accident—our young things could, after all, look out for themselves, she addressed her greatest solicitude to the sad case presented by their deputy-guardian. That, for myself, was a sound simplification : I could engage that, to the world, my face should tell no tales, but it would have been, in the conditions, an immense added worry to find myself anxious about hers.

At the hour I now speak of she had joined me, under pressure, on the terrace, where, with the lapse of the season, the afternoon sun was now agreeable ; and we sat there together while before us and at a distance, yet within call if we wished, the children strolled to and fro in one of their most manageable moods. They moved slowly, in unison, below us, over the lawn, the boy, as they went, reading aloud from a story-book and passing his arm round his sister to keep her quite in touch. Mrs. Grose watched them with positive placidity ; then I caught the suppressed intellectual creak with which she conscientiously turned to take from me a view of the back of the tapestry. I had made her a receptacle of lurid things, but there was an odd recognition of my superiority—my accomplishments and my function—in her patience under my pain. She offered her mind to my disclosures as, had I wished to mix a witch's broth and proposed it with assurance, she would have held out a large clean saucepan. This had become thoroughly her attitude by the time that, in my recital of the events of the night, I reached the point of what Miles had said to me when, after seeing him, at such a monstrous hour, almost on the very spot where he happened now to be, I had gone down to bring him in ; choosing then, at the window, with a concentrated need of not alarming the house, rather that method than any noisier process. I had left her meanwhile in little doubt of my small hope of representing with success even to her actual sympathy my sense of the real splendour of the little inspiration with which, after I had got him into the house, the boy met my final articulate challenge. As soon as I appeared in the moonlight on the terrace he had come to me as straight as possible ; on which I had taken his hand without a word and led him, through the dark spaces, up the staircase where Quint had so hungrily hovered for him, along the lobby where I had listened and trembled, and so to his forsaken room.

Not a sound, on the way, had passed between us, and I had wondered—oh *how* I had wondered !—if he were groping about in his dreadful little mind for something plausible and not too grotesque. It would tax his invention certainly, and I felt, this time, over his real embarrassment, a curious thrill of triumph. It was a sharp trap for any game hitherto successful. He could play no longer at perfect propriety, nor could he pretend to it ; so how the deuce would he get out of the scrape ? There beat in me indeed, with the passionate throb of this question, an equal dumb appeal as to how the deuce *I* should. I was confronted at last, as never yet, with all the risk attached even now to sounding my own horrid note. I remember in fact that as we pushed into his little chamber, where the bed had not been slept in at all, and the window, uncovered to the moonlight, made the place so clear that there was no need of striking a match—I remember how I suddenly dropped, sank upon the edge of the bed from the force of the idea that he must know how he really, as they say, " had " me. He could do what he liked, with all his cleverness to help him, so long as I should continue to defer to the old tradition of the criminality of those caretakers of the young who minister to superstitions and fears. He " had " me indeed, and in a cleft stick ; for who would ever absolve me, who would consent that I should go unhung, if, by the faintest tremor of an overture, I were the first to introduce into our perfect intercourse an element so dire ? No, no : it was useless to attempt to convey to

Mrs. Grose, just as it is scarcely less so to attempt to suggest here, how, during our short stiff brush there in the dark, he fairly shook me with admiration. I was of course thoroughly kind and merciful; never, never yet had I placed on his small shoulders hands of such tenderness as those with which, while I rested against the bed, I held him there well under fire. I had no alternative but, in form at least, to put it to him.

"You must tell me now—and all the truth. What did you go out for? What were you doing there?"

I can still see his wonderful smile, the whites of his beautiful eyes and the uncovering of his clear teeth, shine to me in the dusk. "If I tell you why, will you understand?" My heart, at this, leaped into my mouth. *Would* he tell me why? I found no sound on my lips to press it, and I was aware of answering only with a vague repeated grimacing nod. He was gentleness itself, and while I wagged my head at him he stood there more than ever a little fairy prince. It was his brightness indeed that gave me a respite. Would it be so great if he were really going to tell me? "Well," he said at last, "just exactly in order that you should do this."

"Do what?"

"Think me—for a change—*bad!*" I shall never forget the sweetness and gaiety with which he brought out the word, nor how, on top of it, he bent forward and kissed me. It was practically the end of everything. I met his kiss and I had to make, while I folded him for a minute in my arms, the most stupendous effort not to cry. He had given exactly the account of himself that permitted least my going behind it, and it was only with the effect of confirming my acceptance of it that, as I presently glanced about the room, I could say—

"Then you didn't undress at all?"

He fairly glittered in the gloom. "Not at all. I sat up and read."

"And when did you go down?"

"At midnight. When I'm bad I *am* bad!"

"I see, I see—it's charming. But how could you be sure I should know it?"

"Oh I arranged that with Flora." His answers rang out with a readiness! "She was to get up and look out."

"Which is what she did do." It was I who fell into the trap!

". So she disturbed you, and, to see what she was looking at, you also looked—you saw."

"While you," I concurred, "caught your death in the night air ! "

He literally bloomed so from this exploit that he could afford radiantly to assent. " How otherwise should I have been bad enough ? " he asked. Then, after another embrace, the incident and our interview closed on my recognition of all the reserves of goodness that, for his joke, he had been able to draw upon.

XII

THE particular impression I had received proved in the morning light, I repeat, not quite successfully presentable to Mrs. Grose, though I re-enforced it with the mention of still another remark that he had made before we separated. " It all lies in half a dozen words," I said to her, " words that really settle the matter. ' Think, you know, what I *might* do ! ' He threw that off to show me how good he is. He knows down to the ground what he ' might do.' That's what he gave them a taste of at school."

" Lord, you do change ! " cried my friend.

" I don't change—I simply make it out. The four, depend upon it, perpetually meet. If on either of these last nights you had been with either child you'd clearly have understood. The more I've watched and waited the more I've felt that if there were nothing else to make it sure it would be made so by the systematic silence of each. *Never*, by a slip of the tongue, have they so much as alluded to either of their old friends, any more than Miles has alluded to his expulsion. Oh yes, we may sit here and look at them, and they may show off to us there to their fill ; but even while they pretend to be lost in their fairy-tale they're steeped in their vision of the dead restored to them. He's not reading to her," I declared ; " they're talking of *them*—they're talking horrors ! I go on, I know, as if I were crazy ; and it's a wonder I'm not. What I've seen would have made *you* so ; but it has only made me more lucid, made me get hold of still other things."

My lucidity must have seemed awful, but the charming creatures who were victims of it, passing and repassing in their interlocked sweetness, gave my colleague something to hold on by ; and I felt how tight she held as, without stirring in the breath of my passion, she covered them still with her eyes. " Of what other things have you got hold ? "

"Why of the very things that have delighted, fascinated and yet, at bottom, as I now so strangely see, mystified and troubled me. Their more than earthly beauty, their absolutely unnatural goodness. It's a game," I went on ; "it's a policy and a fraud ! "

" On the part of little darlings——? "

" As yet mere lovely babies ? Yes, mad as that seems ! " The very act of bringing it out really helped me to trace it—follow it all up and piece it all together. "They haven't been good—they've only been absent. It has been easy to live with them because they're simply leading a life of their own. They're not mine—they're not ours. They're his and they're her's ! "

" Quint's and that woman's ? "

" Quint's and that woman's. They want to get to them." Oh how, at this, poor Mrs. Grose appeared to study them ! " But for what ? "

" For the love of all the evil that, in those dreadful days, the pair put into them. And to ply them with that evil still, to keep up the work of demons, is what brings the others back."

" Laws ! " said my friend under her breath. The exclamation was homely, but it revealed a real acceptance of my further proof of what, in the bad time—for there had been a worse even than this !—must have occurred. There could have been no such justification for me as the plain assent of her experience to whatever depth of depravity I found credible in our brace of scoundrels. It was in obvious submission of memory that she brought out after a moment : " They were rascals ! But what can they now do ? " she pursued.

" Do ? " I echoed so loud that Miles and Flora, as they passed at their distance, paused an instant in their walk and looked at us. " Don't they do enough ? " I demanded in a lower tone, while the children, having smiled and nodded and kissed hands to us, resumed their exhibition. We were held by it a minute ; then I answered : " They can destroy them ! " At this my companion did turn, but the appeal she launched was a silent one, the effect of which was to make me more explicit. " They don't know as yet quite how—but they're trying hard. They're seen only across, as it were, and beyond—in strange places and on high places, the top of towers, the roof of houses, the outside of windows, the further edge of pools ; but there's a deep design on either side, to shorten the distance and overcome the obstacle : so the success of the tempters is only a question of time. They've only to keep to their suggestions of danger."

" For the children to come ? "

" And perish in the attempt ! " Mrs. Grose slowly got up, and I scrupulously added : " Unless, of course, we can prevent ! "

Standing there before me while I kept my seat she visibly turned things over. " Their uncle must do the preventing. He must take them away."

" And who's to make him ? "

She had been scanning the distance, but she now dropped on me a foolish face. " You, Miss."

" By writing to him that his house is poisoned and his nephew and niece mad ? "

" But if they *are*, Miss ? "

" And if I am myself, you mean ? That's charming news to be sent him by a person enjoying his confidence and whose prime undertaking was to give him no worry."

Mrs. Grose considered, following the children again. " Yes, he do hate worry. That was the great reason——"

" Why those fiends took him in so long ? No doubt, though his indifference must have been awful. As I'm not a fiend, at any rate, I shouldn't take him in."

My companion, after an instant and for all answer, sat down again and grasped my arm. " Make him at any rate come to you."

I stared. " To *me* ? " I had a sudden fear of what she might do. " ' Him ' ? "

" He ought to *be* here—he ought to help."

I quickly rose and I think I must have shown her a queerer face than ever yet. " You see me asking him for a visit ? " No, with her eyes on my face she evidently couldn't. Instead of it even—as a woman reads another—she could see what I myself saw : his derision, his amusement, his contempt for the breakdown of my resignation at being left alone and for the fine machinery I had set in motion to attract his attention to my slighted charms. She didn't know—no one knew— how proud I had been to serve him and to stick to our terms ; yet she none the less took the measure, I think, of the warning I now gave her. " If you should so lose your head as to appeal to him for me——"

She was really frightened. " Yes, Miss ? "

" I would leave, on the spot, both him and you."

XIII

IT was all very well to join them, but speaking to them proved quite as much as ever an effort beyond my strength—offered, in close quarters, difficulties as insurmountable as before. This situation continued a month, and with new aggravations and particular notes, the note above all, sharper and sharper, of the small ironic consciousness on the part of my pupils. It was not, I am as sure to-day as I was sure then, my mere infernal imagination : it was absolutely traceable that they were aware of my predicament and that this strange relation made, in a manner, for a long time, the air in which we moved. I don't mean that they had their tongues in their cheeks or did anything vulgar, for that was not one of their dangers : I do mean, on the other hand, that the element of the unnamed and untouched became, between us, greater than any other, and that so much avoidance couldn't have been made successful without a great deal of tacit arrangement. It was as if, at moments, we were perpetually coming into sight of subjects before which we must stop short, turning suddenly out of alleys that we perceived to be blind, closing with a little bang that made us look at each other—for, like all bangs, it was something louder than we had intended—the doors we had indiscreetly opened. All roads lead to Rome, and there were times when it might have struck us that almost every branch of study or subject of conversation skirted forbidden ground. Forbidden ground was the question of the return of the dead in general and of whatever, in especial, might survive, for memory, of the friends little children had lost. There were days when I could have sworn that one of them had, with a small invisible nudge, said to the other : " She thinks she'll do it this time—but she *won't* ! " To " do it " would have been to indulge for instance—and for once in a way—in some direct reference to the lady who had prepared them for my discipline. They had a delightful endless appetite for passages in my own history to which I had again and again treated them ; they were in possession of everything that had ever happened to me, had had, with every circumstance, the story of my smallest adventures and of those of my brothers and sisters and of the cat and the dog at home, as well as many particulars of the whimsical bent of my father, of the furniture and arrangement of our house and of the conversation of the old women of our village. There were things enough, taking one with another, to chatter about, if one went very fast and knew by instinct when to go round. They pulled with an art of their own the strings of my invention and my memory ; and nothing else perhaps, when I thought of such occasions afterwards, gave me so the suspicion of being watched from under cover. It was in any case over *my* life, *my* past and *my* friends alone that we could take anything like our ease ; a state of affairs that lead them sometimes without the least pertinence to break out into sociable reminders. I was invited—with no visible connexion—to repeat afresh Goody Gosling's celebrated mot or to confirm the details already supplied as to the cleverness of the vicarage pony.

It was partly at such junctures as these and partly at quite different ones that, with the turn my matters had now taken, my predicament, as I have called it, grew most sensible. The fact that the days passed for me without another encounter ought, it would have appeared, to have done something toward soothing my nerves. Since the light brush, that second night on the upper landing, of the presence of a woman at the foot of the stair, I had seen nothing, whether in or out of the house, that one had better not have seen. There was many a corner round which I expected to come upon Quint, and many a situation that, in a merely sinister way, would have favoured the appearance of Miss Jessel. The summer had turned, the summer had gone ; the autumn had dropped upon Bly and had blown out half our lights. The place, with its grey sky and withered garlands, its bared spaces and scattered dead leaves, was like a theatre after the performance—all strewn with crumpled playbills. There were exactly states of the air, conditions of sound and of stillness, unspeakable impressions of the *kind* of ministering moment, that brought back to me, long enough to catch it, the feeling of the medium in which, that June evening out of doors, I had had my first sight of Quint, and in which too, at those other instants, I had, after seeing him through the window, looked for him in vain in the circle of shrubbery. I recognized the signs, the portents —I recognised the moment, the spot. But they remained unaccompanied and empty, and I continued unmolested ; if unmolested one could call a young woman whose sensibility had, in the most extraordinary fashion, not declined but deepened. I had said in my talk with Mrs. Grose on that horrid scene of Flora's by the lake—and had perplexed her by so saying—that it would from that moment distress me much more to lose my power than to keep it. I had then expressed what was vividly in my mind : the truth that, whether the children really saw or not—since, that is, it was not yet definitely proved—I greatly preferred, as a safeguard, the fulness of my own exposure. I was ready to know the very worst that was to be known. What I had then had an ugly glimpse of was that my eyes might be sealed just while theirs were most opened. Well, my eyes *were* sealed, it appeared, at present—a consummation for which it seemed blasphemous not to thank God. There was, alas, a difficulty about that : I would have thanked Him with all my soul had I not had in a proportionate measure this conviction of the secret of my pupils.

How can I retrace to-day the strange steps of my obsession ? There were times of our being together when I would have been ready to swear that, literally, in my presence, but with my direct sense of it closed, they had visitors who were known and were welcome. Then it was that, had I not been deterred by the very chance that such an injury might prove greater than the injury to be averted, my exaltation would have broken out. " They're here, they're here, you little wretches," I would have cried, " and you can't deny it now ! " The little wretches denied it with all the added volume of their sociability and their tenderness, just in the crystal depths of which—like the flash of a fish in a stream—the mockery of their advantage peeped up. The shock had in truth sunk into me still deeper than I knew on the night when, looking out either for Quint or for Miss Jessel under the stars, I had seen there the boy over whose rest I watched and who had immediately brought in with him—had straightway there turned on me —the lovely upward look with which, from the battlements above us, the hideous apparition of Quint had played. If it was a question of a scare my discovery on this occasion had scared me more than any other, and it was essentially in the scared state that I drew my actual conclusions. They harassed me so that sometimes, at odd moments, I shut myself up audibly to rehearse—it was at once a fantastic relief and a renewed despair—the manner in which I might come to the point. I approached it from one side and the other while, in my room, I flung myself about, but I always broke down in the monstrous utterances of names. As they died away on my lips I said to myself that I should indeed help them to represent something infamous if by pronouncing them I should violate as rare a little case of instinctive delicacy as any schoolroom probably had ever known. When I said to myself : " *They* have the manners to be silent, and you, trusted as you are, the baseness to speak ! " I felt myself crimson and covered my face with my hands. After these secret scenes I chattered more than ever, going on volubly enough till one of our prodigious palpable hushes occurred—I can call them nothing else—the strange dizzy lift or swim (I try for terms !) into a stillness, a pause of all life, that had nothing to do with the more or less noise we at the moment might be engaged in making and that I could hear through any intensified mirth or quickened recitation or louder strum of the piano. Then it was that the others, the outsiders, were there. Though they were not angels they " passed," as the French say, causing me, while they stayed, to tremble with the fear of their addressing to their younger victims some yet more infernal message or more vivid image than they had thought good enough for myself.

What it was least possible to get rid of was the cruel idea that, whatever I had seen, Miles and Flora saw *more*—things terrible and unguessable and that sprang from dreadful passages of intercourse in the past. Such things naturally left on the surface, for the time, a chill that we vociferously denied we felt ; and we had all three, with repetition, got into such splendid training that we went, each time, to mark the close of the incident, almost automatically through the very same movements. It was striking of the children at all events to kiss me inveterately with a wild irrelevance and never to fail—one or the other—of the precious question that had helped us through many a peril. " When do you think he *will* come ? Don't you think we *ought* to write ? "—there was nothing like that enquiry we found by experience, for carrying off an awkwardness. " He " of course was their uncle in Harley Street ; and we lived in much profusion of theory that he might at any moment arrive to mingle in our circle. It was impossible to have given less encouragement than he had administered to such a doctrine, but if we had not had the doctrine to fall back upon we should have deprived each other of some of our finest exhibitions. He never wrote to them—that may have been selfish, but it was a part of the flattery of his trust of myself ; for the way in which a man pays his highest tribute to a woman is apt to be put by the more festal celebration of one of the sacred laws of his comfort.

So I held that I carried out the spirit of the pledge given not to appeal to him when I let our young friends understand that their own letters were but charming literary exercises. They were too beautiful to be posted ; I kept them myself ; I have them all to this hour. This was a rule indeed which only added to the satiric effect of my being plied with the supposition that he might at any moment be among us. It was exactly as if our young friends knew how almost more awkward than anything else that might be for me. There appears to me moreover as I look back no note in all this more extraordinary than the mere fact that, in spite of my tension and of their triumph, I never lost patience with them. Adorable they must in truth have been, I now feel, since I didn't in these days hate them ! Would exasperation, however, if relief had longer been postponed, finally have betrayed me ? It little matters, for relief arrived. I call it relief though it was only the relief that a snap brings to a strain or the burst of a thunderstorm to a day of suffocation. It was at least change, and it came with a rush.

XIV

WALKING to church a certain Sunday morning, I had little Miles at my side and his sister, in advance of us and at Mrs. Grose's, well in sight. It was a crisp clear day, the first of its order for some time ; the night had brought a touch of frost and the autumn air, bright and sharp, made the church bells almost gay. It was an odd accident of thought that I should have happened at such a moment to be particularly and very gratefully struck with the obedience of my little charges. Why did they never resent my inexorable, my perpetual society ? Something or other had brought nearer home to me that I had all but pinned the boy to my shawl, and that in the way our companions were marshalled before me I might have appeared to provide against some danger of rebellion. I was like a gaoler with an eye to possible surprises and escapes. But all this belonged—I mean their magnificent little surrender —just to the special array of the facts that were most abysmal. Turned out for Sunday by his uncle's tailor, who had had a free hand and a notion of pretty waistcoats and of his grand little air, Miles's whole title to independence, the rights of his sex and situation, were so stamped upon him that if he had suddenly struck for freedom I should have had nothing to say.

I was by the strangest of chances wondering how I should meet him when the revolution unmistakeably occurred. I call it a revolution because I now see how, with the word he spoke, the curtain rose on the last act of my dreadful drama and the catastrophe was precipitated. "Look here, my dear, you know," he charmingly said, "when in the world, please, am I going back to school?"

Transcribed here the speech sounds harmless enough, particularly as uttered in the sweet, high, casual pipe with which, at all interlocutors, but above all at his eternal governess, he threw off intonations as if he were tossing roses. There was something in them that always made one "catch," and I caught at any rate now so effectually that I stopped as short as if one of the trees of the park had fallen across the road. There was something new, on the spot, between us, and he was perfectly aware I recognised it, though to enable me to do so he had no need to look a whit less candid and charming than usual. I could feel in him how he already, from my at first finding nothing to reply, perceived the advantage he had gained. I was so slow to find anything that he had plenty of time, after a minute, to continue with his suggestive but inconclusive smile: "You know, my dear, that for a fellow to be with a lady *always*——!" His "my dear" was constantly on his lips for me, and nothing could have expressed more the exact shade of the sentiment with which I desired to inspire my pupils than its fond familiarity. It was so respectfully easy.

But oh how I felt that at present I must pick my own phrases! I remember that, to gain time I tried to laugh, and I seemed to see in the beautiful face with which he watched me how ugly and queer I looked. "And always with the same lady?" I returned.

He neither blenched nor winked. The whole thing was virtually out between us. "Ah of course she's a jolly 'perfect' lady; but after all I'm a fellow, don't you see? who's—well, getting on."

I lingered there with him an instant ever so kindly. "Yes, you're getting on." Oh but I felt helpless!

I have kept to this day the heartbreaking little idea of how he seemed to know that and to play with it. "And you can't say I've not been awfully good, can you?"

I laid my hand on his shoulder, for though I felt how much better it would have been to walk on I was not yet quite able. "No, I can't say that, Miles."

"Except just that one night, you know——!"

"That one night?" I couldn't look as straight as he.

"Why when I went down—went out of the house."

"Oh yes. But I forget what you did it for."

"You forget?"—he spoke with the sweet extravagance of childish reproach. "Why it was just to show you I could!"

"Oh yes—you could."

"And I can again."

I felt I might perhaps after all succeed in keeping my wits about me. "Certainly. But you won't."

"No, not *that* again. It was nothing."

"It was nothing," I said. "But we must go on."

He resumed our walk with me, passing his hand into my arm. "Then when *am* I going back?"

I wore, in turning it over, my most responsible air. "Were you very happy at school?"

He just considered. "Oh I'm happy enough anywhere!"

"Well then," I quavered, "if you're just as happy here——!"

"Ah, but that isn't everything! Of course *you* know a lot——"

"But you hint that you know almost as much?" I risked as he paused.

"Not half I want to!" Miles honestly professed. "But it isn't so much that."

"What is it then?"

"Well—I want to see more life."

"I see; I see." We had arrived within sight of the church and of various persons, including several of the household of Bly, on their way to it and clustered about the door to see us go in. I quickened our step; I wanted to get there before the question between us opened up much further; I reflected hungrily that he would have for more than an hour to be silent; and I thought with envy of the comparative dusk of the pew and of the almost spiritual help of the hassock on which I might bend my knees. I seemed literally to be running a race with some confusion to which he was about to reduce me, but I felt he had got in first when, before we had entered the churchyard, he threw out—

"I want my own sort!"

It literally made me bound forward. "There aren't many of your own sort, Miles!" I laughed.

"Unless perhaps dear little Flora!"

"You really compare me to a baby girl ? "

This found me singularly weak. " Don't you then *love* our sweet Flora ? "

" If I didn't—and you too ; if I didn't——! " he repeated as if retreating for a jump, yet leaving his thought so unfinished that, after we had come into the gate, another stop, which he imposed on me by the pressure of his arm, had become inevitable. Mrs. Grose and Flora had passed into the church, the other worshippers had followed and we were, for the minute, alone among the old thick graves. We had paused, on the path from the gate, by a low oblong table-like tomb.

" Yes, if you didn't——? "

He looked, while I waited, about at the graves. " Well, you know what ! " But he didn't move, and he presently produced something that made me drop straight down on the stone slab as if suddenly to rest. " Does my uncle think what *you* think ? "

I markedly rested. " How do you know what I think ? "

" Ah well, of course I don't ; for it strikes me you never tell me. But I mean does *he* know ? "

" Know what, Miles ? "

" Why the way I'm going on."

I recognised quickly enough that I could make, to this enquiry, no answer that wouldn't involve something of a sacrifice of my employer. Yet it struck me that we were all, at Bly, sufficiently sacrificed to make than venial. " I don't think your uncle much cares."

Miles, on this, stood looking at me. " Then don't you think he can be made to ? "

" In what way ? "

" Why by his coming down."

" But who'll get him to come down ? "

" *I* will ! " the boy said with extraordinary brightness and emphasis. He gave me another look charged with that expression and then marched off alone into church.

XV

THE business was practically settled from the moment I never followed him. It was a pitiful surrender to agitation, but my being aware of this had somehow no power to restore me. I only sat there on my tomb and read into what our young friend had said to me the fulness of its meaning ; by the time I had grasped the whole of which I had also embraced, for absence, the pretext that I was ashamed to offer my pupils and the rest of the congregation such an example of delay. What I said to myself above all was that Miles had got something out of me and that the gage of it for him would be just this awkward collapse. He had got out of me that there was something I was much afraid of, and that he should probably be able to make use of my fear to gain, for his own purpose, more freedom. My fear was of having to deal with the intolerable question of the grounds of his dismissal from school, since that was really but the question of the horrors gathered behind. That his uncle should arrive to treat with me of these things was a solution that, strictly speaking, I ought now to have desired to bring on ; but I could so little face the ugliness and the pain of it that I simply procrastinated and lived from hand to mouth. The boy, to my deep discomposure, was immensely in the right, was in a position to say to me : " Either you clear up with my guardian the mystery of this interruption of my studies, or you cease to expect me to lead with you a life that's so unnatural for a boy." What was so unnatural for the particular boy I was concerned with was this sudden revelation of a consciousness and a plan.

That was what really overcame me, what prevented my going in. I walked round the church, hesitating, hovering ; I reflected that I had already, with him, hurt myself beyond repair. Therefore I could patch up nothing and it was too extreme an effort to squeeze beside him into the pew : he would be so much more sure than ever to pass his arm into mine and make me sit there for an hour in close silent contact with his commentary on our talk. For the first minute since his arrival I wanted to get away from him. As I paused beneath the high east window and listened to the sounds of worship I was taken with an impulse that might master me, I felt, and completely, should I give it the least encouragement. I might easily put an end to my ordeal by getting away altogether. Here was my chance ; there was no one to stop me ; I could give the whole thing up—turn my back and bolt. It was only a question of hurrying again, for a few preparations, to the house which the attendance at church of so many of the servants would practically have left unoccupied. No one, in short, could blame me if I should just drive desperately off. What was it to get away if I should get away only till dinner ? That would be in a couple of hours, at the end of which—I had the acute prevision—my little pupils would play at innocent wonder about my non-appearance in their train.

" What *did* you do, you naughty bad thing ? Why in the world, to worry us so—and take our thoughts off too, don't you know ?—did you desert us at the very door ? " I couldn't meet such questions nor, as they asked them, their false little lovely eyes ; yet it was all so exactly what I should have to meet that, as the prospect grew sharp to me, I at last let myself go.

I got, so far as the immediate moment was concerned, away ; I came straight out of the churchyard and, thinking hard, retraced my steps through the park. It seemed to me that by the time I reached the house I had made up my mind to cynical flight. The Sunday stillness both of the approaches and of the interior, in which I met no one, fairly stirred me with a sense of opportunity. Were I to get off quickly this way I should get off without a scene, without a word. My quickness would have to be remarkable, however, and the question of a conveyance was the great one to settle. Tormented, in the hall, with difficulties and obstacles, I remember sinking down at the foot of the staircase—suddenly collapsing there on the lowest step and then, with a revulsion, recalling that it was exactly where, more than a month before, in the darkness of night and just so bowed with evil things, I had seen the spectre of the most horrible of women. At this I was able to straighten myself ; I went the rest of the way up ; I made, in my turmoil, for the schoolroom, where there were objects belonging to me that I should have to take. But I opened the door to find again, in a flash, my eyes unsealed. In the presence of what I saw I reeled straight back upon resistance.

Seated at my own table in the clear noonday light I saw a person whom, without my previous experience, I should have taken at the first blush for some housemaid who might have stayed at home to look after the place and who, availing herself of rare relief from observation and of the schoolroom table and my pens, ink and paper, had applied herself to the considerable effort of a letter to her sweetheart. There was an effort in the way that, while her arms rested on the table, her hands, with evident weariness, supported her head ; but at the moment I took this in I had already become aware that, in spite of my entrance, her attitude strangely persisted. Then it was—with the very act of its announcing itself—that her identity flared up in a change of posture. She rose, not as if she had heard me, but with an indescribable grand melancholy of indifference and detachment, and, within a dozen feet of me, stood there as my vile predecessor. Dishonoured and tragic, she was all before me ; but even as I fixed and, for memory, secured it, the awful image passed away. Dark as midnight in her dark dress, her haggard beauty and her unutterable woe, she had looked at me long enough to appear to say that her right to sit at my table was as good as mine to sit at hers. While these instants lasted indeed I had the extraordinary chill of a feeling that it was I who was the intruder. It was as a wild protest against it that, actually addressing her—" You terrible miserable woman ! " —I heard myself break into a sound that, by the open door, rang through the long passage and the empty house. She looked at me as if she heard me, but I had recovered myself and cleared the air. There was nothing in the room the next minute but the sunshine and the sense that I must stay.

XVI

I HAD so perfectly expected the return of the others to be marked by a demonstration that I was freshly upset at having to find them merely dumb and discreet about my desertion. Instead of gaily denouncing and caressing me they made no allusion to my having failed them, and I was left, for the time, on perceiving that she too said nothing, to study Mrs. Grose's odd face. I did this to such purpose that I made sure they had in some way bribed her to silence ; a silence that, however, I would engage to break down on the first private opportunity. This opportunity came before tea : I secured five minutes with her in the housekeeper's room, where, in the twilight, amid a smell of lately-baked bread, but with the place all swept and garnished, I found her sitting in pained placidity before the fire. So I see her still, so I see her best : facing the flame from her straight chair in the dusky shining room, a large clean picture of the " put away "—of drawers closed and locked and rest without a remedy.

" Oh yes, they asked me to say nothing ; and to please them—so long as they were there—of course I promised. But what had happened to you ? "

" I only went with you for the walk," I said. " I had then to come back to meet a friend."

She showed her surprise. " A friend—you ? "

" Oh yes, I've a couple ! " I laughed. " But did the children give you a reason ? "

" For not alluding to your leaving us ? Yes ; they said you'd like it better. *Do* you like it better ? "

My face had made her rueful. " No, I like it worse ! " But after an instant I added : " Did they say why I should like it better ? "

" No ; Master Miles only said ' We must do nothing but what she likes ' ! "

" I wish indeed he would ! And what did Flora say ? "

" Miss Flora was too sweet. She said, ' Oh of course, of course ! '—and I said the same."

I thought a moment. " You were too sweet too—I can hear you all. But none the less, between Miles and me, it's now all out."

" All out ? " My companion stared. " But what, Miss ? "

" Everything. It doesn't matter. I've made up my mind. I came home, my dear," I went on, " for a talk with Miss Jessel."

I had by this time formed the habit of having Mrs. Grose literally well in hand in advance of my sounding that note ; so that even now, as she bravely blinked under the signal of my word, I could keep her comparatively firm. " A talk ! Do you mean she spoke ? "

" It came to that. I found her, on my return, in the schoolroom."

" And what did she say ? " I can hear the good woman still, and the candour of her stupefaction.

" That she suffers the torments——! "

It was this, of a truth, that made her, as she filled out my picture, gape. " Do you mean," she faltered " —of the lost ? "

" Of the lost. Of the damned. And that's why, to share them——" I faltered myself with the horror of it.

But my companion, with less imagination, kept me up. " To share them——? "

" She wants Flora." Mrs. Grose might, as I gave it to her, fairly have fallen away from me had I not been prepared. I still held her there, to show I was. " As I've told you, however, it doesn't matter."

" Because you've made up your mind ? But to what ? "

" To everything."

" And what do you call ' everything ' ? "

" Why to sending for their uncle."

" Oh Miss, in pity do," my friend broke out.

" Ah but I will, I *will !* I see it's the only way. What's

' out,' as I told you, with Miles is that he thinks if I'm afraid
to—and has ideas of what he gains by that—he shall see he's
mistaken. Yes, yes ; his uncle shall have it here from me
on the spot (and before the boy himself if necessary) that if
I'm to be reproached with having done nothing again about
more school——"

" Yes, Miss——" my companion pressed me.

" Well, there's that awful reason."

There were now clearly só many of these for my poor
colleague that she was excusable for being vague. " But—a
—which ? "

" Why the letter from his old place."

" You'll show it to the master ? "

" I ought to have done so on the instant."

" Oh no ! " said Mrs. Grose with decision.

" I'll put it before him," I went on inexorably, " that I
can't undertake to work the question on behalf of a child
who has been expelled——"

" For we've never in the least known what ! " Mrs. Grose
declared.

" For wickedness. For what else—when he's so clever and
beautiful and perfect ? Is he stupid ? Is he untidy ? Is he
infirm ? Is he ill-natured ? He's exquisite—so it can be only
that ; and that would open up the whole thing. After all," I
said, " it's their uncle's fault. If he left here such people——! "

" He didn't really in the least know them. The fault's
mine." She had turned quite pale.

" Well, you shan't suffer," I answered.

" The children shan't ! " she emphatically returned.

I was silent a while ; we looked at each other. " Then
what am I to tell him ? "

" You needn't tell him anything. *I'll* tell him."

I measured this. " Do you mean you'll write——? "
remembering she couldn't, I caught myself up. " How do
you communicate ? "

" I tell the bailiff. *He* writes."

" And should you like him to write our story ? "

My question had a sarcastic force that I had not fully intended, and it made her after a moment inconsequently
break down. The tears were again in her eyes. " Ah Miss,
you write ! "

" Well—to-night," I at last returned ; and on this we
separated.

XVII

I WENT so far, in the evening, as to make a beginning. The weather had changed back, a great wind was abroad, and beneath the lamp, in my room, with Flora at peace beside me, I sat for a long time before a blank sheet of paper and listened to the lash of the rain and the batter of the gusts. Finally I went out, taking a candle ; I crossed the passage and listened a minute at Miles's door. What, under my endless obsession, I had been impelled to listen for was some betrayal of his not being at rest, and I presently caught one, but not in the form I had expected. His voice tinkled out. " I say, you there—come in." It was gaiety in the gloom !

I went in with my light and found him in bed, very wide awake but very much at his ease. " Well, what are *you* up to ? " he asked with a grace of sociability in which it occurred to me that Mrs. Grose, had she been present, might have looked in vain for proof that anything was " out."

I stood over him with my candle. " How did you know I was there ? "

" Why of course I heard you. Did you fancy you made no noise ? You're like a troop of cavalry ! " he beautifully laughed.

" Then you weren't asleep ? "

" Not much ! I lie awake and think."

I had put my candle, designedly, a short way off, and then, as he held out his friendly old hand to me, had sat down on the edge of his bed. " What is it ? " I asked, " that you think of ? "

" What in the world, my dear, but *you* ? "

" Ah the pride I take in your appreciation doesn't insist on that ! I had so far rather you slept."

" Well, I think also, you know, of this queer business of ours."

I marked the coolness of his firm little hand. " Of what queer business, Miles ? "

" Why the way you bring me up. And all the rest ! "

I fairly held my breath a minute, and even from my glimmering taper there was light enough to show how he smiled up at me from his pillow. " What do you mean by all the rest ? "

" Oh you know, you know ! "

I could say nothing for a minute, though I felt as I held his hand and our eyes continued to meet that my silence had all the air of admitting his charge and that nothing in the whole world of reality was perhaps at that moment so fabulous as our actual relation. " Certainly you shall go back to school," I said, " if it be that that troubles you. But not to the old place—we must find another, a better. How could I know it did trouble you, this question, when you never told me so, never spoke of it at all ? " His clear listening face, framed in its smooth whiteness, made him for the minute as appealing as some wistful patient in a children's hospital ; and I would have given, as the resemblance came to me, all I possessed on earth really to be the nurse or the sister of charity who might have helped to cure him. Well, even as it was I perhaps might help ! " Do you know you've never said a word to me about your school—I mean the old one ; never mentioned it in any way ? "

He seemed to wonder ; he smiled with the same loveliness. But he clearly gained time ; he waited, he called for guidance. " Haven't I ? " It wasn't for *me* to help him—it was for the thing I had met !

Something in his tone and the expression of his face, as I got this from him, set my heart aching with such a pang as it had never yet known ; so unutterably touching was it to see his little brain puzzled and his little resources taxed to play, under the spell laid on him, a part of innocence and consistency. " No, never—from the hour you came back. You've never mentioned to me one of your masters, one of your comrades, nor the least little thing that ever happened to you at school. Never, little Miles—no never—have you given me an inkling of anything that *may* have happened there. Therefore you can fancy how much I'm in the dark. Until you came out, that way, this morning, you had since the first hour I saw you scarce even made a reference to anything in your previous life. You seemed so perfectly to accept the present." It was extraordinary how my absolute conviction of his secret precocity—or whatever I might call the poison of an influence that I dared but half-phrase—made him, in spite of the faint breath of his inward trouble, appear as accessible as an older person, forced me to treat him as an intelligent equal. " I thought you wanted to go on as you are."

It struck me that at this he just faintly coloured. He gave, at any rate, like a convalescent slightly fatigued, a languid shake of his head. " I don't—I don't. I want to get away."

" You're tired of Bly ? "

" Oh no, I like Bly."

" Well then——? "

" Oh *you* know what a boy wants ! "

I felt I didn't know so well as Miles, and I took temporary refuge. " You want to go to your uncle ? "

Again, at this, with his sweet ironic face, he made a movement on the pillow. " Ah you can't get off with that ! "

I was silent a little, and it was I now, I think, who changed colour. " My dear, I don't want to get off ! "

" You can't even if you do. You can't, you can't ! "—he lay beautifully staring. " My uncle must come down and you must completely settle things."

" If we do," I returned with some spirit, " **you** may be sure it will be to take you quite away."

" Well, don't you understand that that's exactly what I'm working for ? You'll have to *tell* him—about the way you've let it all drop : you'll have to tell him a tremendous lot ! "

The exultation with which he uttered this helped me somehow for the instant to meet him rather more. " And how much will *you*, Miles, have to tell him ? There are things he'll ask you ! "

He turned it over. " Very likely. But what things ? "

" The things you've never told me. To make up his mind what to do with you. He can't send you back——"

" I don't want to go back ! " he broke in. " I want a new field."

He said it with admirable serenity, with positive unimpeachable gaiety ; and doubtless it was that very note that most evoked for me the poignancy, the unnatural childish tragedy, of his probable reappearance at the end of three months with all this bravado and still more dishonour. It overwhelmed me now that I should never be able to bear that, and it made me let myself go. I threw myself upon him and in the tenderness of my pity I embraced him. " Dear little Miles, dear little Miles——! "

My face was close to his, and he let me kiss him, simply taking it with indulgent good-humour. " Well, old lady ? "

" Is there nothing—nothing at all that you want to tell me ? "

He turned off a little, facing round toward the wall and holding up his hand to look at as one had seen sick children look. " I've told you—I told you this morning."

Oh, I was sorry for him ! " That you just want me not to worry you ? "

He looked round at me now as if in recognition of my understanding him ; then ever so gently, " To let me alone," he replied.

There was even a strange little dignity in it, something that made me release him, yet, when I had slowly risen, linger beside him. God knows *I* never wished to harass him, but I felt that merely, at this, to turn my back on him was to abandon or, to put it more truly, to lose him. " I've just begun a letter to your uncle," I said.

" Well then, finish it ! "

I waited a minute. " What happened before ? "

He gazed up at me again. " Before what ? "

" Before you came back. And before you went away."

For some time he was silent, but he continued to meet my eyes. " What happened ? "

It made me, the sound of the words, in which it seemed to me I caught for the very first time a small faint quaver of consenting consciousness—it made me drop to my knees beside the bed and seize once more the chance of possessing him. " Dear little Miles, dear little Miles, if you *knew* how I want to help you ! It's only that, it's nothing but that, and I'd rather die than give you a pain or do you a wrong —I'd rather die than hurt a hair of you. Dear little Miles " —oh I brought it out now even if I *should* go too far—" I just want you to help me to save you ! " But I knew in a moment after this that I had gone too far. The answer to my appeal was instantaneous, but it came in the form of an extraordinary blast and chill, a gust of frozen air and a shake of the room as great as if, in the wild wind, the casement had crashed in. The boy gave a loud high shriek which, lost in the rest of the shock of sound, might have seemed, indistinctly, though I was close to him, a note either of jubilation or of terror. I jumped to my feet again and was conscious of darkness. So for a moment we remained, while I stared about me and saw the drawn curtains unstirred and the window tight. " Why, the candle's out ! " I then cried.

" It was I who blew it, dear ! " said Miles.

XVIII

THE next day, after lessons, Mrs. Grose found a moment to say to me quietly : " Have you written, Miss ? "

" Yes—I've written." But I didn't add—for the hour—that my letter, sealed and directed, was still in my pocket. There would be time enough to send it before the messenger should go to the village. Meanwhile there had been on the part of my pupils no more brilliant, more exemplary morning. It was exactly as if they had both had at heart to gloss over any recent little friction. They performed the dizziest feats of arithmetic, soaring quite out of *my* feeble range, and per-petrated, in higher spirits than ever, geographical and historical jokes. It was conspicuous of course in Miles in particular that he appeared to wish to show how easily he could let me down. This child, to my memory, really lives in a setting of beauty and misery that no words can translate ; there was a distinction all his own in every impulse he revealed ; never was a small natural creature, to the uninformed eye all frank-ness and freedom, a more ingenious, a more extraordinary little gentleman. I had perpetually to guard against the wonder of contemplation into which my initiated view betrayed me ; to check the irrelevant gaze and discouraged sigh in which I con-stantly both attacked and renounced the enigma of what such a little gentleman could have done that deserved a penalty. Say that, by the dark prodigy I knew, the imagination of all evil *had* been opened up to him : all the justice within me ached for the proof that it could ever have flowered into an act.

He had never at any rate been such a little gentleman as when, after our early dinner on this dreadful day, he came round to me and asked if I shouldn't like him for half an hour to play to me. David playing to Saul could never have shown a finer sense of the occasion. It was literally a charming exhibi-tion of tact, of magnanimity, and quite tantamount to his saying outright : " The true knights we love to read about never push an advantage too far. I know what you mean now : you mean that—to be let alone yourself and not followed up—you'll cease to worry and spy upon me, won't keep me so close to you, will let me go and come. Well, I ' come,' you see—but I don't go ! There'll be plenty of time for that. I do really delight in your society and I only want to show you that I contended for a principle." It may be imagined whether I resisted this appeal or failed to accompany him again, hand in hand, to the schoolroom. He sat down at the old piano and played as he had never played ; and if there are those who think he had better have been kicking a football I can only say that I wholly agree with them. For at the end of a time that under his influence I had quite ceased to measure I started up with a strange sense of having literally slept at my post. It was after luncheon, and by the schoolroom fire, and yet I hadn't really in the least slept ; I had only done something much worse—I had forgotten. Where all this time was Flora ? When I put the question to Miles he played on a minute before answering, and then could only say : " Why, my dear, how do _I_ know ? "—breaking moreover into a happy laugh which immediately after, as if it were a vocal accompaniment, he prolonged into incoherent extravagant song.

I went straight to my room, but his sister was not there ; then, before going downstairs, I looked into several others. As she was nowhere about she would surely be with Mrs. Grose, whom in the comfort of that theory I accordingly proceeded in quest of. I found her where I had found her the evening before, but she met my quick challenge with blank scared ignorance. She had only supposed that, after the repast, I had carried off both the children ; as to which she was quite in her right, for it was the very first time I had allowed the little girl out of my sight without some special provision. Of course now indeed she might be with the maids, so that the immediate thing was to look for her without an air of alarm. This we promptly arranged between us ; but when, ten minutes later and in pursuance of our arrangement we met in the hall, it was only to report on either side that after guarded enquiries we had altogether failed to trace her. For a minute there, apart from observation, we exchanged mute alarms, and I could feel with what high interest my friend returned me all those I had from the first given her.

" She'll be above," she presently said—" in one of the rooms you haven't searched."

" No ; she's at a distance." I had made up my mind. " She has gone out."

Mrs. Grose stared. " Without a hat ! "

I naturally also looked volumes. " Isn't that woman always without one ? "

" She's with _her_ ? "

" She's with _her_ ! " I declared. " We must find them."

My hand was on my friend's arm, but she failed for the moment, confronted with such an account of the matter, to respond to my pressure. She communed, on the contrary, where she stood, with her uneasiness. " And where's Master Miles ? "

" Oh *he's* with Quint. They'll be in the schoolroom."

" Lord, Miss ! " My view, I was myself aware—and therefore I suppose my tone—had never yet reached so calm an assurance.

" The trick's played," I went on ; " they've successfully worked their plan. He found the most divine little way to keep me quiet while she went off."

" ' Divine ' ? " Mrs. Grose bewilderedly echoed.

" Infernal then ! " I almost cheerfully rejoined. " He has provided for himself as well. But come ! "

She had helplessly gloomed at the upper regions. " You leave him——? "

" So long with Quint ? Yes—I don't mind that now."

She always ended at these moments by getting possession of my hand, and in this manner she could at present still stay me. But after gasping an instant at my sudden resignation, " Because of your letter ? " she eagerly brought out.

I quickly, by way of answer, felt for my letter, drew it forth, held it up, and then, freeing myself, went and laid it on the great hall-table. " Luke will take it," I said as I came back. I reached the house-door and opened it ; I was already on the steps.

My companion still demurred : the storm of the night and the early morning had dropped, but the afternoon was damp and grey. I came down to the drive while she stood in the doorway. " You go with nothing on ? "

" What do I care when the child has nothing ? I can't wait to dress," I cried, " and if you must do so I leave you. Try meanwhile yourself upstairs."

" With *them* ? " Oh on this the poor woman promptly joined me !

XIX

WE went straight to the lake, as it was called at Bly, and I dare say rightly called, though it may have been a sheet of water less remarkable than my untravelled eyes supposed it. My acquaintance with sheets of water was small, and the pool of Bly, at all events on the few occasions of my consenting, under the protection of my pupils, to affront its surface in the old flat-bottomed boat moored there for our use, had impressed me both with its extent and its agitation. The usual place of embarkation was half a mile from the house, but I had an intimate conviction that, wherever Flora might be, she was not near home. She had not given me the slip for any small adventure, and, since the day of the very great one that I had shared with her by the pond, I had been aware, in our walks, of the quarter to which she most inclined. This was why I had now given to Mrs. Grose's steps so marked a direction —a direction making her, when she perceived it, oppose a resistance that showed me she was freshly mystified. " You're going to the water, Miss ?——you think she's *in*——? "

" She may be, though the depth is, I believe, nowhere very great. But what I judge most likely is that she's on the spot from which, the other day, we saw together what I told you."

" When she pretended not to see——? "

" With that astounding self-possession ! I've always been sure she wanted to go back alone. And now her brother has managed it for her."

Mrs. Grose still stood where she had stopped. " You suppose they really *talk* of them ? "

I could meet this with an assurance ! " They say things that, if we heard them, would simply appal us."

" And if she *is* there——? "

" Yes ? "

" Then Miss Jessel is ? "

" Beyond a doubt. You shall see."

" Oh thank you ! " my friend cried, planted so firm that, taking it in, I went straight on without her. By the time I reached the pool, however, she was close behind me, and I knew that, whatever, to her apprehension, might befall me, the exposure of sticking to me struck her as her least danger. She exhaled a moan of relief as we at last came in sight of the greater part of the water without a sight of the child. There was no trace of Flora on that nearer side of the bank where my observation of her had been most startling, and none on the opposite edge, where, save for a margin of some twenty yards, a thick copse came down to the water. This expanse, oblong in shape, was so narrow compared to its length that, with its ends out of view, it might have been taken for a scant river. We looked at the empty stretch, and then I felt the suggestion in my friend's eyes. I knew what she meant and I replied with a negative headshake.

" No, no ; wait ! She has taken the boat."

My companion stared at the vacant mooring-place and then again across the lake. " Then where is it ? "

" Our not seeing it is the strongest of proofs. She has used it to go over, and then has managed to hide it."

" All alone—that child ? "

" She's not alone, and at such times she's not a child : she's an old, old woman." I scanned all the visible shore while Mrs. Grose took again, into the queer element I offered her, one of her plunges of submission ; then I pointed out that the boat might perfectly be in a small refuge formed by one of the recesses of the pool, an indentation masked, for the hither side, by a projection of the bank and by a clump of trees growing close to the water.

" But if the boat's there, where on earth's *she* ? " my colleague anxiously asked.

" That's exactly what we must learn." And I started to walk farther.

" By going all the way round ? "

" Certainly, far as it is. It will take us but ten minutes, yet it's far enough to have made the child prefer not to walk. She went straight over."

" Laws ! " cried my friend again ; the chain of my logic was ever too strong for her. It dragged her at my heels even now, and when we had got half-way round—a devious tiresome process, on ground much broken and by a path choked with overgrowth—I paused to give her breath. I sustained her with a grateful arm, assuring her that she might hugely help me ; and this started us afresh, so that in the course of but few minutes more we reached a point from which we found the boat to be where I had supposed it. It had been intentionally left as much as possible out of sight and was tied to one of the stakes of a fence that came, just there, down to the brink and that had been an assistance to disembarking. I recognised, as I looked at the pair of short thick oars, quite safely drawn up, the prodigious character of the feat for a little girl ; but I had by this time lived too long among wonders and had panted to too many livelier measures. There was a gate in the fence, through which we passed, and that brought us after a trifling interval more into the open. Then " There she is ! " we both exclaimed at once.

481

Flora, a short way off, stood before us on the grass and smiled as if her performance had now become complete. The next thing she did, however, was to stoop straight down and pluck—quite as if it were all she was there for—a big ugly spray of withered fern. I at once felt sure she had just come out of the copse. She waited for us, not herself taking a step, and I was conscious of the rare solemnity with which we presently approached her. She smiled and smiled, and we met ; but it was all done in a silence by this time flagrantly ominous. Mrs. Grose was the first to break the spell : she threw herself on her knees and, drawing the child to her breast, clasped in a long embrace the little tender yielding body. While this dumb convulsion lasted I could only watch it—which I did the more intently when I saw Flora's face peep at me over our companion's shoulder. It was serious now—the flicker had left it ; but it strengthened the pang with which I at that moment envied Mrs. Grose the simplicity of *her* relation. Still, all this while, nothing more passed between us save that Flora had let her foolish fern again drop to the ground. What she and I had virtually said to each other was that pretexts were useless now. When Mrs. Grose finally got up she kept the child's hand, so that the two were still before me ; and the singular reticence of our communion was even more marked in the frank look she addressed me. " I'll be hanged," it said, " if *I'll* speak ! "

It was Flora who, gazing all over me in candid wonder, was the first. She was struck with our bare-headed aspect. " Why where are your things ? "

" Where yours are, my dear ! " I promptly returned.

She had already got back her gaiety and appeared to take this as an answer quite sufficient. " And where's Miles ? " she went on.

There was something in the small valour of it that quite finished me : these three words from her were in a flash like the glitter of a drawn blade, the jostle of the cup that my hand for weeks and weeks had held high and full to the brim and that now, even before speaking, I felt overflow in a deluge. " I'll tell you if you'll tell *me*——" I heard myself say, then heard the tremor in which it broke.

" Well, what ? "

Mrs. Grose's suspense blazed at me, but it was too late now, and I brought the thing out handsomely. " Where, my pet, is Miss Jessel ? "

XX

JUST as in the churchyard with Miles, the whole thing was upon us. Much as I had made of the fact that this name had never once, between us, been sounded, the quick smitten glare with which the child's face now received it fairly likened my breach of the silence to the smash of a pane of glass. It added to the interposing cry, as if to stay the blow, that Mrs. Grose at the same instant uttered over my violence—the shriek of a creature scared, or rather wounded, which, in turn, within a few seconds, was completed by a gasp of my own. I seized my colleague's arm. " She's there, she's there ! "

Miss Jessel stood before us on the opposite bank exactly as she had stood the other time, and I remember, strangely, as the first feeling now produced in me, my thrill of joy at having brought on a proof. She was there, so I was justified ; she was there, so I was neither cruel nor mad. She was there for poor scared Mrs. Grose, but she was there most for Flora ; and no moment of my monstrous time was perhaps so extraordinary as that in which I consciously threw out to her—with the sense that, pale and ravenous demon as she was, she would catch and understand it—an inarticulate message of gratitude. She rose erect on the spot my friend and I had lately quitted, and there wasn't in all the long reach of her desire an inch of her evil that fell short. This first vividness of vision and emotion were things of a few seconds, during which Mrs. Grose's dazed blink across to where I pointed struck me as showing that she too at last saw, just as it carried my own eyes precipitately to the child. The revelation then of the manner in which Flora was affected startled me in truth far more than it would have done to find her also merely agitated, for direct dismay was of course not what I had expected. Prepared and on her guard as our pursuit had actually made her, she would repress every betrayal ; and I was therefore at once shaken by my first glimpse of the particular one for which I had not allowed. To see her, without a convulsion of her small pink face, not even feign to glance in the direction of the prodigy I announced, but only, instead of that, turn at *me* an expression of hard still gravity, an expression absolutely new and unprecedented and that appeared to read and accuse and judge me—this was a stroke that somehow converted the little girl herself into a figure portentous. I gaped at her coolness even though my certitude of her thoroughly seeing was never greater than at that instant, and then, in the immediate need to defend myself, I called her passionately to witness. " She's there, you little unhappy thing—there, there, *there*, and you know it as well as you know me ! " I had said shortly before to Mrs. Grose that she was not at these times a child, but an old, old woman, and my description of her couldn't have been more strikingly confirmed than in the way in which, for all notice of this, she simply showed me, without an expressional concession or admission, a countenance of deeper and deeper, of indeed suddenly quite fixed reprobation. I was by this time—if I can put the whole thing at all together—more appalled at what I may properly call her manner than at anything else, though it was quite simultaneously that I became aware of having Mrs. Grose also, and very formidably, to reckon with. My elder companion, the next moment, at any rate, blotted out everything but her own flushed face and her loud shocked protest, a burst of high disapproval. " What a dreadful turn, to be sure, Miss ! Where on earth do you see anything ? "

I could only grasp her more quickly yet, for even while she spoke the hideous plain presence stood undimmed and un-daunted. It had already lasted a minute, and it lasted while I continued, seizing my colleague, quite thrusting her at it and presenting her to it, to insist with my pointing hand. " You don't see her exactly as *we* see ?—you mean to say you don't now—*now* ? She's as big as a blazing fire ! Only look, dearest woman, *look*——! " She looked, just as I did, and gave me, with her deep groan of negation, repulsion, compassion—the mixture with her pity of her relief at her exemption—a sense, touching to me even then, that she would have backed me up if she had been able. I might well have needed that, for with this hard blow of the proof that her eyes were hopelessly sealed I felt my own situation horribly crumble, I felt—I *saw*—my livid predecessor press, from her position, on my defeat, and I took the measure, more than all, of what I should have from this instant to deal with in the astounding little attitude of Flora. Into this attitude Mrs. Grose immediately and violently entered, breaking, even while there pierced through my sense of ruin a prodigious private triumph, into breathless reassurance.

" She isn't there, little lady, and nobody's there—and you never see nothing, my sweet ! How can poor Miss Jessel— when poor Miss Jessel's dead and buried ? *We* know, don't we, love ? "—and she appealed, blundering in, to the child. " It's all a mere mistake and a worry and a joke—and we'll go home as fast as we can ! "

Our companion, on this, had responded with a strange quick primness of propriety, and they were again, with Mrs. Grose on her feet, united, as it were, in shocked opposition to me. Flora continued to fix me with her small mask of disaffection, and even at that minute I prayed God to forgive me for seeming to see that, as she stood there holding tight to our friend's dress, her incomparable childish beauty had suddenly failed, had quite vanished. I've said it already—she was literally, she was hideously hard ; she had turned common and almost ugly. " I don't know what you mean. I see nobody. I see nothing. I never *have*. I think you're cruel. I don't like you ! " Then, after this deliverance, which might have been that of a vulgarly pert little girl in the street, she hugged Mrs. Grose more closely and buried in her skirts the dreadful little face. In this position she launched an almost furious wail. " Take me away, take me away—oh take me away from *her* ! "

" From *me* ? " I panted.

" From you—from you ! " she cried.

Even Mrs. Grose looked across at me dismayed ; while I had nothing to do but communicate again with the figure that, on the opposite bank, without a movement, as rigidly still as if catching, beyond the interval, our voices, was as vividly there for my disaster as it was not there for my service. The wretched child had spoken exactly as if she had got from some outside source each of her stabbing little words, and I could therefore, in the full despair of all I had to accept, but sadly shake my head at her. " If I had ever doubted all my doubt would at present have gone. I've been living with the miserable truth, and now it has only too much closed round me. Of course I've lost you : I've interfered, and you've seen, under *her* dictation " —with which I faced, over the pool again, our infernal witness— " the easy and perfect way to meet it. I've done my best, but I've lost you. Good-bye." For Mrs. Grose I had an imperative, an almost frantic " Go, go ! " before which, in infinite distress, but mutely possessed of the little girl and clearly convinced, in spite of her blindness that something awful had occurred and some collapse engulfed us, she retreated, by the way we had come, as fast as she could move.

Of what first happened when I was left alone I had no subsequent memory. I only knew that at the end of, I suppose, a quarter of an hour, an odorous dampness and roughness,

chilling and piercing my trouble, had made me understand
that I must have thrown myself, on my face, to the ground and
given way to a wildness of grief. I must have lain there long
and cried and wailed, for when I raised my head the day was
almost done. I got up and looked a moment, through the
twilight, at the grey pool and its black haunted edge, and then
I took, back to the house, my dreary and difficult course. When
I reached the gate in the fence the boat, to my surprise, was
gone, so that I had a fresh reflexion to make on Flora's extraordinary command of the situation. She passed that night, by
the most tacit and, I should add, were not the word so grotesque
a false note, the happiest of arrangements, with Mrs. Grose.
I saw neither of them on my return, but on the other hand I
saw, as by an ambiguous compensation, a great deal of Miles.
I saw—I can use no other phrase—so much of him that it fairly
measured more than it had ever measured. No evening I had
passed at Bly was to have had the portentous quality of this
one ; in spite of which—and in spite also of the deeper depths
of consternation that had opened beneath my feet—there was
literally, in the ebbing actual, an extraordinarily sweet sadness.
On reaching the house I had never so much as looked for the
boy ; I had simply gone straight to my room to change what I
was wearing and to take in, at a glance, much material testimony
to Flora's rupture. Her little belongings had all been removed.
When later, by the schoolroom fire, I was served with tea by
the usual maid, I indulged, on the article of my other pupil, in
no enquiry whatever. He had his freedom now—he might
have it to the end ! Well, he did have it ; and it consisted—in
part at least—of his coming in at about eight o'clock and sitting
down with me in silence. On the removal of the tea-things I
had blown out the candles and drawn my chair closer : I was
conscious of a mortal coldness and felt as if I should never again
be warm. So when he appeared I was sitting in the glow with
my thoughts. He paused a moment by the door as if to look
at me ; then—as if to share them—came to the other side of
the hearth and sank into a chair. We sat there in absolute stillness ; yet he wanted, I felt, to be with me.

XXI

BEFORE a new day, in my room, had fully broken, my
eyes opened to Mrs. Grose, who had come to my bedside with worse news. Flora was so markedly feverish that

an illness was perhaps at hand ; she had passed a night of
extreme unrest, a night agitated above all by fears that had
for their subject not in the least her former but wholly her
present governess. It was not against the possible re-entrance
of Miss Jessel on the scene that she protested—it was con-
spicuously and passionately against mine. I was at once on
my feet, and with an immense deal to ask ; the more that my
friend had discernibly now girded her loins to meet me afresh.
This I felt as soon as I had put to her the question of her sense
of the child's sincerity as against my own. " She persists in
denying to you that she saw, or has ever seen, anything ? "

My visitor's trouble truly was great. " Ah Miss, it isn't
a matter on which I can push her. Yet it isn't either, I must
say, as if I much needed to. It has made her, every inch of
her, quite old."

" Oh I see her perfectly from here. She resents, for all
the world like some high little personage, the imputation on
her truthfulness and, as it were, her respectability. ' Miss
Jessel indeed—she ! ' Ah she's ' respectable,' the chit ! The
impression she gave me there yesterday was, I assure you,
the very strangest of all ; it was quite beyond any of the others.
I *did* put my foot in it ! She'll never speak to me again."

Hideous and obscure as it all was, it held Mrs. Grose briefly
silent ; then she granted my point with a frankness which,
I made sure, had more behind it. " I think indeed, Miss,
she never will. She do have a grand manner about it ! "

" And that manner "—I summed it up—" is practically
what's the matter with her now."

Of that matter, I could see in my visitor's face, and not a
little else besides ! " She asks me every three minutes if I
think you're coming in."

" I see—I see." I too, on my side, had so much more
than worked it out. " Has she said to you since yesterday
—except to repudiate her familiarity with anything so dreadful
—a single other word about Miss Jessel ? "

" Not one, Miss. And of course, you know," my friend
added, " I took it from her by the lake that just then and there
at least there *was* nobody."

" Rather ! And naturally you take it from her still."

" I don't contradict her. What else can I do ? "

" Nothing in the world ! You've the cleverest little person
to deal with. They've made them—their two friends, I mean
—still cleverer even than Nature did ; for it was wondrous

487

material to play on ! Flora has now her grievance, and she'll work it to the end."

" Yes, Miss ; but to *what* end ? "

" Why that of dealing with me to her uncle. She'll make me out to him the lowest creature——! "

I winced at the fair show of the scene in Mrs. Grose's face ; she looked for a minute as if she sharply saw them together. " And him who thinks so well of you ! "

" He has an odd way—it comes over me now," I laughed, "—of proving it ! But that doesn't matter. What Flora wants of course is to get rid of me."

My companion bravely concurred. " Never again to so much as look at you."

" So that what you've come to me now for," I asked, " is to speed me on my way ? " Before she had time to reply, however, I had her in check. " I've a better idea—the result of my reflexions. My going *would* seem the right thing, and on Sunday I was terribly near it. Yet that won't do. It's *you* who must go. You must take Flora."

My visitor, at this, did speculate. " But where in the world——? "

" Away from here. Away from *them*. Away, even most of all, now, from me. Straight to her uncle."

" Only to tell on you——? "

" No, not ' only ' ! To leave me, in addition, with my remedy."

She was still vague. " And what *is* your remedy ? "

" Your loyalty, to begin with. And then Miles's."

She looked at me hard. " Do you think he——? "

" Won't, if he has the chance, turn on me ? Yes, I venture still to think it. At all events I want to try. Get off with his sister as soon as possible and leave me with him alone." I was amazed, myself, at the spirit I had still in reserve, and therefore perhaps a trifle the more disconcerted at the way in which, in spite of this fine example of it, she hesitated. " There's one thing, of course," I went on : " they mustn't, before she goes, see each other for three seconds." Then it came over me that, in spite of Flora's presumable sequestration from the instant of her return from the pool, it might already be too late. " Do you mean," I anxiously asked, " that they *have* met ? "

At this she quite flushed. " Ah, Miss, I'm not such a fool as that ! If I've been obliged to leave her three or four times, it has been each time with one of the maids, and at present, though she's alone, she's locked in safe. And yet—and yet!" There were too many things.

"And yet what?"

"Well, are you so sure of the little gentleman?"

"I'm not sure of anything but *you*. But I have, since last evening, a new hope. I think he wants to give me an opening. I do believe that—poor little exquisite wretch!— he wants to speak. Last evening, in the firelight and the silence, he sat with me for two hours as if it were just coming."

Mrs. Grose looked hard through the window at the grey gathering day. "And did it come?"

"No, though I waited and waited I confess it didn't and it was without a breach of the silence, or so much as a faint allusion to his sister's condition and absence, that we at last kissed for good night. All the same," I continued, "I can't, if her uncle sees her, consent to his seeing her brother without my having given the boy—and most of all because things have got so bad—a little more time."

My friend appeared on this ground more reluctant than I could quite understand. "What do you mean by more time?"

"Well, a day or two—really to bring it out. He'll then be on *my* side—of which you see the importance. If nothing comes I shall only fail, and you at the worst have helped me by doing on your arrival in town whatever you may have found possible." So I put it before her, but she continued for a little so lost in other reasons that I came again to her aid. Unless indeed," I wound up, " you really want *not* to go."

I could see it, in her face, at last clear itself; she put out her hand to me as a pledge. "I'll go—I'll go. I'll go this morning."

I wanted to be very just. "If you *should* wish still to wait I'll engage she shouldn't see me."

"No, no: it's the place itself. She must leave it." She held me a moment with heavy eyes, then brought out the rest. "Your idea's the right one. I myself, Miss——"

"Well?"

"I can't stay."

The look she gave me with it made me jump at possibilities. "You mean that, since yesterday you *have* seen——?"

She shook her head with dignity. "I've *heard*——!"

"Heard?"

"From that child—horrors! There!" she sighed with

tragic relief. " On my honour Miss, she says things——! "
But at this evocation she broke down ; she dropped with a
sudden cry upon my sofa and, as I had seen her do before,
gave way to all the anguish of it.

It was in quite another manner that I for my part let myself
go. " Oh thank God ! "

She sprang up again at this, drying her eyes with a groan.
" ' Thank God ' ? "

" It so justifies me ! "

" It does that, Miss ! "

I couldn't have desired more emphasis, but I just waited.
" She's so horrible ? "

I saw my colleague scarce knew how to put it. " Really
shocking."

" And about me ? "

" About you, Miss—since you must have it. It's beyond
everything, for a young lady ; and I can't think wherever
she must have picked up——"

" The appalling language she applies to me ? I can
then ! " I broke in with a laugh that was doubtless significant enough.

It only in truth left my friend still more grave. " Well,
perhaps I ought to also—since I've heard some of it before !
Yet I can't bear it," the poor woman went on while with the
same movement she glanced on my dressing-table, at the face
of my watch. " But I must go back."

I kept her, however. " Ah if you can't bear it——! "

" How can I stop with her, you mean ? Why just *for*
that : to get her away. Far from this," she pursued, " far
from *them*——"

" She may be different ? she may be free ? " I seized her
almost with joy. " Then in spite of yesterday you *believe*——"

" In such doings ? " Her simple description of them
required, in the light of her expression, to be carried no further,
and she gave me the whole thing as she had never done.
" I believe."

Yes, it was a joy, and we were still shoulder to shoulder :
if I might continue sure of that I should care but little what
else happened. My support in the presence of disaster
would be the same as it had been in my early need of confidence, and if my friend would answer for my honesty I would
answer for all the rest. On the point of taking leave of her,

none the less, I was to some extent embarrassed. "There's one thing of course—it occurs to me—to remember. My letter, giving the alarm, will have reached town before you."

I now felt still more how she had been beating about the bush and how weary at last it had made her. "Your letter won't have got there. Your letter never went."

"What then became of it?"

"Goodness knows! Master Miles——"

"Do you mean *he* took it?" I gasped.

She hung fire, but she overcame her reluctance. "I mean that I saw yesterday, when I came back with Miss Flora, that it wasn't where you had put it. Later in the evening I had the chance to question Luke, and he declared that he had neither noticed nor touched it." We could only exchange, on this, one of our deeper mutual soundings, and it was Mrs. Grose who first brought up the plumb with an almost elate "You see!"

"Yes, I see that if Miles took it instead he probably will have read it and destroyed it."

"And don't you see anything else?"

I faced her a moment with a sad smile. "It strikes me that by this time your eyes are open even wider than mine."

They proved to be so indeed, but she could still almost blush to show it. "I make out now what he must have done at school." And she gave, in her simple sharpness, an almost droll disillusioned nod. "He stole!"

I turned it over—I tried to be more judicial. "Well—perhaps."

She looked as if she found me unexpectedly calm. "He stole *letters*!"

She couldn't know my reasons for a calmness after all pretty shallow; so I showed them off as I might. "I hope then it was to more purpose than in this case! The note, at all events, that I put on the table yesterday," I pursued, "will have given him so scant an advantage—for it contained only the bare demand for an interview—that he's already much ashamed of having gone so far for so little, and that what he had on his mind last evening was precisely the need of confession." I seemed to myself for the instant to have mastered it, to see it all. "Leave us, leave us"—I was already, at the door, hurrying her off. "I'll get it out of him. He'll meet me. He'll confess. If he confesses he's saved. And if he's saved——"

" Then *you* are ? " The dear woman kissed me on this, and I took her farewell. " I'll save you without him ! " she cried as she went.

XXII

YET it was when she had got off — and I missed her on the spot—that the great pinch really came. If I had counted on what it would give me to find myself alone with Miles I quickly recognised that it would give me at least a measure. No hour of my stay in fact was so assailed with apprehensions as that of my coming down to learn that the carriage containing Mrs. Grose and my younger pupil had already rolled out of the gates. Now I *was*, I said to myself, face to face with the elements, and for much of the rest of the day, while I fought my weakness, I could consider that I had been supremely rash. It was a tighter place still than I had yet turned round in ; all the more that, for the first time, I could see in the aspect of others a confused reflexion of the crisis. What had happened naturally caused them all to stare ; there was too little of the explained, throw out whatever we might, in the suddenness of my colleague's act. The maids and the men looked blank ; the effect of which on my nerves was an aggravation until I saw the necessity of making it a positive aid. It was in short by just clutching the helm that I avoided total wreck ; and I dare say that, to bear up at all, I became that morning very grand and very dry. I welcomed the consciousness that I was charged with much to do, and I caused it to be known as well that, left thus to myself, I was quite remarkably firm. I wandered with that manner for the next hour or two, all over the place and looked, I have no doubt, as if I were ready for any onset. So, for the benefit of whom it may concern, I paraded with a sick heart.

The person it appeared least to concern proved to be, till dinner, little Miles himself. My perambulations had given me meantime no glimpse of him, but they had tended to make more public the change taking place in our relation as a consequence of his having at the piano, the day before, kept me, in Flora's interest, so beguiled and befooled. The stamp of publicity had of course been fully given by her confinement and departure, and the change itself was now ushered in by our non-observance of the regular custom of the schoolroom. He had already disappeared when, on my way down, I pushed open his door, and I learned below that he had breakfasted—in the presence of a couple of the maids —with Mrs. Grose and his sister. He had then gone out, as he said, for a stroll ; than which nothing, I reflected, could better have expressed his frank view of the abrupt transformation of my office. What he would now permit this office to consist of was yet to be settled : there was at the least a queer relief—I mean for myself in especial—in the renouncement of one pretension. If so much had sprung to the surface I scarce put it too strongly in saying that what had perhaps sprung highest was the absurdity of our prolonging the fiction that I had anything more to teach him. It sufficiently stuck out that, by tacit little tricks in which even more than myself he carried out the care for my dignity. I had had to appeal to him to let me off straining to meet him on the ground of his true capacity. He had at any rate his freedom now ; I was never to touch it again ; as I had amply shown, moreover, when, on his joining me in the schoolroom the previous night, I uttered, in reference to the interval just concluded, neither challenge nor hint. I had too much, from this moment, my other ideas. Yet when he at last arrived the difficulty of applying them, the accumulations of my problem were brought straight home to me, by the beautiful little presence on which what had occurred had as yet, for the eye, dropped neither stain nor shadow.

To mark, for the house, the high state I cultivated I decreed that my meals with the boy should be served, as we called it, downstairs ; so that I had been awaiting him in the ponderous pomp of the room outside the window of which I had had from Mrs. Grose, that first scared Sunday, my flash of something it would scarce have done to call light. Here at present I felt afresh—for I had felt it again and again—how my equilibrium depended on the success of my rigid will, the will to shut my eyes as tight as possible to the truth that what I had to deal with was, revoltingly, against nature. I could only get on at all by taking " nature " into my confidence and my account, by treating my monstrous ordeal as a push in a direction unusual, of course, and unpleasant, but demanding after all, for a fair front, only another turn of the screw of ordinary human virtue. No attempt, none the less, could well require more tact than just this attempt to supply, one's self, *all* the virtue. How could I put even a little of that article into a suppression of reference to what had occurred ? How on the other hand could I make a reference without a new plunge into the hideous obscure ? Well, a sort of answer, after a time, had come to me, and it was so far confirmed as that I was met, incontestably, by the quickened vision of what was rare in my little companion. It was indeed as if he had found even now—as he had so often found at lessons—still some other delicate way to ease me off. Wasn't there light in the fact which, as we shared our solitude, broke out with a specious glitter it had never yet quite worn ?—the fact that (opportunity aiding, precious opportunity which had now come) it would be preposterous, with a child so endowed, to forego the help one might wrest from absolute intelligence ? What had his intelligence been given him for but to save him ? Mightn't one, to reach his mind, risk the stretch of a stiff arm across his character ? It was as if, when we were face to face in the dining-room, he had literally shown me the way. The roast mutton was on the table, and I had dispensed with attendance. Miles, before he sat down, stood a moment with his hands in his pockets and looked at the joint, on which he seemed on the point of passing some humorous judgment. But what he presently produced was : " I say, my dear, is she really very awfully ill ? "

" Little Flora ? Not so bad but that she'll presently be better. London will set her up. Bly had ceased to agree with her. Come here and take your mutton."

He alertly obeyed me, carried the plate carefully to his seat and, when he was established, went on. " Did Bly disagree with her so terribly all at once ? "

" Not so suddenly as you might think. One had seen it coming on."

" Then why didn't you get her off before ? "

" Before what ? "

" Before she became too ill to travel."

I found myself prompt. " She's *not* too ill to travel : she only might have become so if she had stayed. This was just the moment to seize. The journey will dissipate the influence "—oh I was grand !—" and carry it off."

" I see, I see "—Miles, for that matter, was grand too. He settled to this repast with the charming little " table manner " that, from the day of his arrival, had relieved me of all grossness of admonition. Whatever he had been expelled from school for, it wasn't for ugly feeding. He was irreproachable, as always, to-day ; but was unmistakably more conscious

He was discernibly trying to take for granted more things than
he found, without assistance, quite easy ; and he dropped
into peaceful silence while he felt his situation. Our meal
was of the briefest—mine a vain pretence, and I had the things
immediately removed. While this was done Miles stood again
with his hands in his little pockets and his back to me—stood
and looked out of the wide window through which, that other
day, I had seen what pulled me up. We continued silent
while the maid was with us—as silent, it whimsically occurred
to me, as some young couple who, on their wedding-journey,
at the inn, feel shy in the presence of the waiter. He turned
round only when the waiter had left us. " Well—so we're
alone ! "

XXIII

" OH more or less." I imagine my smile was pale. " Not
absolutely. We shouldn't like that ! " I went on.
" No—I suppose we shouldn't. Of course we've the
others."
" We've the others—we've indeed the others," I concurred.
" Yet even though we have them," he returned, still with
his hands in his pockets and planted there in front of me,
" they don't much count, do they ? "
I made the best of it, but I felt wan. " It depends on
what you call ' much ' ! "
" Yes "—with all accommodation—" everything depends ! "
On this, however, he faced to the window again and presently
reached it with his vague restless cogitating step. He remained
there a while with his forehead against the glass, in contemplation of the stupid shrubs I knew and the dull things of
November. I had always my hypocrisy of " work," behind
which I now gained the sofa. Steadying myself with it there
as I had repeatedly done at those moments of torment that I
have described as the moments of my knowing the children
to be given to something from which I was barred, I sufficiently
obeyed my habit of being prepared for the worst. But an
extraordinary impression dropped on me as I extracted a
meaning from the boy's embarrassed back—none other than
the impression that I was not barred now. This inference
grew in a few minutes to sharp intensity and seemed bound
up with the direct perception that it was positively *he* who
was. The frames and squares of the great window were a

kind of image, for him, of a kind of failure. I felt that I saw him, in any case, shut in or shut out. He was admirable but not comfortable : I took it in with a throb of hope. Wasn't he looking through the haunted pane for something he couldn't see ?—and wasn't it the first time in the whole business that he had known such a lapse ? The first, the very first : I found it a splendid portent. It made him anxious, though he watched himself ; he had been anxious all day and, even while in his usual sweet little manner he sat at table, had needed all his small strange genius to give it a gloss. When he at last turned round to meet me it was almost as if this genius had succumbed. " Well, I think I'm glad Bly agrees with me ! "

" You'd certainly seem to have seen, these twenty-four hours, a good deal more of it than for some time before. I hope," I went on bravely, " that you've been enjoying yourself."

" Oh yes, I've been ever so far ; all round about—miles and miles away. I've never been so free."

He had really a manner of his own, and I could only try to keep up with him. " Well, do you like it ? "

He stood there smiling ; then at last he put into two words —" Do *you* ? "—more discrimination than I had ever heard two words contain. Before I had time to deal with that, however, he continued as if with the sense that this was an impertinence to be softened. " Nothing could be more charming than the way you take it, for of course if we're alone together now it's you that are alone most. But I hope," he threw in, " you don't particularly mind ! "

" Having to do with you ? " I asked. " My dear child, how can I help minding ? Though I've renounced all claim to your company—you're so beyond me—I at least greatly enjoy it. What else should I stay on for ? "

He looked at me more directly, and the expression of his face, graver now, struck me as the most beautiful I had ever found in it. " You stay on just for *that* ? "

" Certainly. I stay on as your friend and from the tremendous interest I take in you till something can be done for you that may be worth more your while. That needn't surprise you." My voice trembled so that I felt it impossible to suppress the shake. " Don't you remember how I told you, when I came and sat on your bed the night of the storm, that there was nothing in the world I wouldn't do for you ? "

"Yes, yes!" He, on his side, more and more visibly nervous, had a tone to master; but he was so much more successful than I that, laughing out through his gravity, he could pretend we were pleasantly jesting. "Only that, I think, was to get me to do something for *you*!"

"It was partly to get you to do something," I conceded. "But, you know, you didn't do it."

"Oh yes," he said with the brightest superficial eagerness, "you wanted me to tell you something."

"That's it. Out, straight out. What you have on your mind, you know."

"Ah then is *that* what you've stayed over for?"

He spoke with a gaiety through which I could still catch the finest little quiver of resentful passion; but I can't begin to express the effect upon me of an implication of surrender even so faint. It was as if what I had yearned for had come at last only to astonish me. "Well, yes—I may as well make a clean breast of it. It was precisely for that."

He waited so long that I supposed it for the purpose of repudiating the assumption on which my action had been founded; but what he finally said: "Do you mean now—here?"

"There couldn't be a better place or time." He looked round him uneasily, and I had the rare—oh the queer!—impression of the very first symptom I had seen in him of the approach of immediate fear. It was as if he were suddenly afraid of me—which struck me indeed as perhaps the best thing to make him. Yet in the very pang of the effort I felt it vain to try sternness, and I heard myself the next instant so gentle as to be almost grotesque. "You want so to go out again?"

"Awfully!" He smiled at me heroically, and the touching little bravery of it was enhanced by his actually flushing with pain. He had picked up his hat, which he had brought in, and stood twirling it in a way that gave me, even as I was just nearly reaching port, a perverse horror of what I was doing. To do it in *any* way was an act of violence, for what did it consist of but the obtrusion of the idea of grossness and guilt on a small helpless creature who had been for me a revelation of the possibilities of beautiful intercourse? Wasn't it base to create for a being so exquisite a mere alien awkwardness? I suppose I now read into our situation a clearness it couldn't have had at the time, for I seem to see our poor eyes already lighted with some spark of a prevision of the anguish that was to come. So we circled about with terrors and scruples, fighters not daring to close. But it was for each other we feared! That kept us a little longer suspended and unbruised. "I'll tell you everything," Miles said—"I mean I'll tell you anything you like. You'll stay on with me, and we shall both be all right, and I *will* tell you—I *will*. But not now."

"Why not now?"

My resistance turned him from me and kept him once more at his window in a silence during which, between us, you might have heard a pin drop. Then he was before me again with the air of a person for whom, outside, some one who frankly to be reckoned with was waiting. "I have to see Luke."

I had not yet reduced him to quite so vulgar a lie, and I felt proportionately ashamed. But, horrible as it was, his lies made up my truth. I achieved thoughtfully a few loops of my knitting. "Well then go to Luke, and I'll wait for what you promise. Only in return for that satisfy, before you leave me, one very much smaller request."

He looked as if he felt he had succeeded enough to be able still a little to bargain. "Very much smaller——?"

"Yes, a mere fraction of the whole. Tell me"—oh my work preoccupied me, and I was offhand!—"if, yesterday afternoon, from the table in the hall, you took, you know, my letter."

XXIV

My grasp of how he received this suffered for a minute from something that I can describe only as a fierce split of my attention—a stroke that at first, as I sprang straight up, reduced me to the mere blind movement of getting hold of him, drawing him close, and, while I just fell for support against the nearest piece of furniture, instinctively keeping him with his back to the window. The appearance was full upon us that I had already had to deal with here : Peter Quint had come into view like a sentinel before a prison. The next thing I saw was that, from outside, he had reached the window, and then I knew that, close to the glass and glaring in through it, he offered once more to the room his white face of damnation. It represents but grossly what took place within me at the sight to say that on the second my decision was made ; yet I believe that no woman so overwhelmed ever in so short a time recovered her command of the *act*. It came to me in the very horror of the immediate presence that the act would be, seeing and facing what I saw and faced, to keep the boy himself unaware. The inspiration—I can call it by no other name—was that I felt how voluntarily, how transcendently, I *might*. It was like fighting with a demon for a human soul, and when I had fairly so appraised it I saw how the human soul—held out, in the tremor of my hands, at arms' length—had a perfect dew of sweat on a lovely childish forehead. The face that was close to mine was as white as the face against the glass, and out of it presently came a sound, not low nor weak, but as if from much farther away, that I drank like a waft of fragrance.

" Yes—I took it."

At this, with a moan of joy, I enfolded, I drew him close ; and while I held him to my breast, where I could feel in the sudden fever of his little body the tremendous pulse of his little heart, I kept my eyes on the thing at the window and saw it move and shift its posture. I have likened it to a sentinel, but its slow wheel, for a moment, was rather the prowl of a baffled beast. My present quickened courage, however, was such that, not too much to let it through, I had to shade, as it were, my flame. Meanwhile the glare of the face was again at the window, the scoundrel fixed as if to watch and wait. It was the very confidence that I might now defy him, as well as the positive certitude, by this time, of the child's unconsciousness, that made me go on. " What did you take it for ? "

" To see what you said about me."

" You opened the letter ? "

" I opened it."

My eyes were now, as I held him off a little again, on Miles's own face, in which the collapse of mockery showed me how complete was the ravage of uneasiness. What was prodigious was that at last, by my success, his sense was sealed and his communication stopped : he knew that he was in presence, but knew not of what, and knew still less that I also was and that I did know. And what did this strain of trouble matter when my eyes went back to the window only to see that the air was clear again and—by my personal triumph—the influence quenched ? There was nothing there. I felt that the cause was mine and that I should surely get *all*. " And you found nothing ! "—I let my elation out.

He gave me the most mournful, thoughtful little headshake. " Nothing."

" Nothing, nothing ! " I almost shouted in my joy.

" Nothing, nothing," he sadly repeated.

I kissed his forehead ; it was drenched. " So what have
you done with it ? "

" I've burnt it."

" Burnt it ? " It was now or never. " Is that what you
did at school ? "

Oh what this brought up ! " At school ? "

" Did you take letters ?—or other things ? "

" Other things ? " He appeared now to be thinking of
something far off and that reached him only through the
pressure of his anxiety. Yet it did reach him. " Did I *steal* ? "

I felt myself redden to the roots of my hair as well as wonder
if it were more strange to put to a gentleman such a question
or to see him take it with allowances that gave the very distance
of his fall in the world. " Was it for that you mightn't go
back ? "

The only thing he felt was rather a dreary little surprise.
" Did you know I mightn't go back ? "

" I know everything."

He gave me at this the longest and strangest look. " Everything ? "

" Everything. Therefore *did* you——? " But I couldn't
say it again.

Miles could, very simply. " No. I didn't steal."

My face must have shown him I believed him utterly ; yet
my hands—but it was for pure tenderness—shook him as if
to ask him why, if it was all for nothing, he had condemned me
to months of torment. " What then did you do ? "

He looked in vague pain all round the top of the room and
drew his breath, two or three times over, as if with difficulty.
He might have been standing at the bottom of the sea and
raising his eyes to some faint green twilight. " Well—I said
things."

" Only that ? "

" They thought it was enough ! "

" To turn you out for ? "

Never, truly, had a person " turned out " shown so little
to explain it as this little person ! He appeared to weigh my
question, but in a manner quite detached and almost helpless.
" Well, I suppose I oughtn't."

" But to whom did you say them ? "

He evidently tried to remember, but it dropped—he had
lost it. " I don't know ! "

He almost smiled at me in the desolation of his surrender, which was indeed practically, by this time, so complete that I ought to have left it there. But I was infatuated—I was blind with victory, though even then the very effect that was to have brought him so much nearer was already that of added separation. "Was it to every one?" I asked.

"No; it was only to——" But he gave a sick little head-shake. "I don't remember their names."

"Were they then so many?"

"No—only a few. Those I liked."

Those he liked? I seemed to float not into clearness, but into a darker obscure, and within a minute there had come to me out of my very pity the appalling alarm of his being perhaps innocent. It was for the instant confounding and bottomless, for if he *were* innocent what then on earth was *I*? Paralysed, while it lasted, by the mere brush of the question, I let him go a little, so that, with a deep-drawn sigh, he turned away from me again; which, as he faced toward the clear window, I suffered, feeling that I had nothing now there to keep him from. "And did they repeat what you said?" I went on after a moment.

He was soon at some distance from me, still breathing hard and again with the air, though now without anger for it, of being confined against his will. Once more, as he had done before, he looked up at the dim day as if, of what had hitherto sustained him, nothing was left but an unspeakable anxiety. "Oh yes," he nevertheless replied—"they must have repeated them. To those *they* liked," he added.

There was somehow less of it than I had expected; but I turned it over. "And these things came round——?"

"To the masters? Oh yes!" he answered very simply. "But I didn't know they'd tell."

"The masters? They didn't—they've never told. That's why I ask you."

He turned to me again his little beautiful fevered face. "Yes, it was too bad."

"Too bad?"

"What I suppose I sometimes said. To write home."

I can't name the exquisite pathos of the contradiction given to such a speech by such a speaker; I only know that the next instant I heard myself throw off with homely force: "Stuff and nonsense!" But the next after that I must have sounded stern enough. "What *were* these things?"

My sternness was all for his judge, his executioner; yet it made him avert himself again, and that movement made *me*, with a single bound and an irrepressible cry, spring straight upon him. For there again, against the glass, as if to blight his confession and stay his answer, was the hideous author of our woe—the white face of damnation. I felt a sick swim at the drop of my victory and all the return of my battle. so that the wildness of my veritable leap only served as a great betrayal. I saw him, from the midst of my act, meet it with a divination, and on the perception that even now he only guessed, and that the window was still to his own eyes free, I let the impulse flame up to convert the climax of his dismay into the very proof of his liberation. " No more, no more, no more ! " I shrieked to my visitant as I tried to press him against me.

" Is she *here* ? " Miles panted as he caught with his sealed eyes the direction of my words. Then as his strange " she " staggered me and, with a gasp, I echoed it, " Miss Jessel, Miss Jessel ! " he with sudden fury gave me back.

I seized, stupefied, his supposition—some sequel to what we had done to Flora, but this made me only want to show him that it was better still than that. " It's not Miss Jessel ! But it's at the window—straight before us. It's *there*—the coward horror, there for the last time ! "

At this, after a second in which his head made the movement of a baffled dog's on a scent and then gave a frantic little shake for air and light, he was at me in a white rage, bewildered, glaring vainly over the place and missing wholly, though it now, to my sense, filled the room like the taste of poison, the wide overwhelming presence. " It's *he* ? "

I was so determined to have all my proof that I dashed into ice to challenge him. " Whom do you mean by ' he ' ? "

" Peter Quint—you devil ! " His face gave again, round the room, its convulsed supplication. " *Where* ? "

They are in my ears still, his supreme surrender of the name and his tribute to my devotion. " What does he matter now, my own ?—what will he *ever* matter ? *I* have you," I launched at the beast, " but he has lost you for ever ! " Then, for the demonstration of my work, " There, *there* ! " I said to Miles.

But he had already jerked straight round, stared, glared again, and seen but the quiet day. With the stroke of the loss I was so proud of he uttered the cry of a creature hurled over an abyss, and the grasp with which I recovered him might have been that of catching him in his fall. I caught him, yes, I held him—it may be imagined with what a passion ; but at the end of a minute I began to feel what it truly was that I held. We were alone with the quiet day, and his little heart, dispossessed, had stopped.

WANDERING WILLIE'S TALE
Sir Walter Scott

Ye maun have heard of Sir Robert Redgauntlet of that Ilk, who lived in these parts before the dear years. The country will lang mind him; and our fathers used to draw breath thick if ever they heard him named. He was out wi' the Hielandmen in Montrose's time; and again he was in the hills wi' Glencairn in the saxteen hundred and fifty-twa; and sae when King Charles the Second came in, wha was in sic favour as the Laird of Redgauntlet? He was knighted at Lonon court, wi' the king's ain sword; and being a redhot prelatist, he came down here, rampauging like a lion, with commissions of lieutenancy (and of lunacy, for what I ken) to put down a' the Whigs and Covenanters in the country. Wild wark they made of it; for the Whigs were as dour as the Cavaliers were fierce, and it was which should first tire the other. Redgauntlet was ay for the strong hand; and his name is kend as wide in the country as Claverhouse's or Tam Dalyell's. Glen, nor dargle, nor mountain, nor cave, could hide the puir hill-folk when Redgauntlet was out with bugle and bloodhound after them, as if they had been sae mony deer. And troth when they fand them they didna mak muckle mair ceremony than a Hielandman wi' a roebuck —it was just, "Will ye tak the test?"—if not, "Make ready —present—fire!"—and there lay the recusant.

Far and wide was Sir Robert hated and feared. Men thought he had a direct compact with Satan—that he was proof against steel—and that bullets happed aff his buff-coat like hailstanes from a hearth—that he had a mear that would turn a hare on the side of Carrifra-gawns [1]—and

---

[1] A precipitous side of a mountain in Moffatdale.

muckle to the same purpose, of whilk mair anon. The best blessing they wared on him was, "Deil scowp wi' Redgauntlet!" He wasna a bad master to his ain folk, though, and was weel aneugh liked by his tenants; and as for the lackies and troopers that raid out wi' him to the persecutions, as the Whigs caa'd those killing times, they wad hae drunken themsells blind to his health at ony time.

Now you are to ken that my gudesire lived on Redgauntlet's grund—they ca' the place Primrose Knowe. We had lived on the grund, and under the Redgauntlets, since the riding days, and lang before. It was a pleasant bit; and I think the air is callerer and fresher there than onywhere else in the country. It's a' deserted now; and I sat on the broken door-cheek three days since, and was glad I couldna see the plight the place was in; but that's a' wide o' the mark. There dwelt my gudesire, Steenie Steenson, a rambling, rattling chiel' he had been in his young days, and could play weel on the pipes; he was famous at "Hoopers and Girders"—a' Cumberland couldna touch him at "Jockie Lattin"—and he had the finest finger for the backlilt between Berwick and Carlisle. The like o' Steenie wasna the sort that they made Whigs o'. And so he became a Tory, as they ca' it, which we now ca' Jacobites, just out of a kind of needcessity, that he might belang to some side or other. He had nae ill will to the Whig bodies, and liked little to see the blude rin, though, being obliged to follow Sir Robert in hunting and hoisting, watching and warding, he saw muckle mischief, and maybe did some, that he couldna avoid.

Now Steenie was a kind of favourite with his master, and kend a' the folks about the castle, and was often sent for to play the pipes when they were at their merriment. Auld Dougal MacCallum, the butler, that had followed Sir Robert through gude and ill, thick and thin, pool and stream, was specially fond of the pipes, and ay gae my gudesire his gude word wi' the laird; for Dougal could turn his master round his finger.

Weel, round came the Revolution, and it had like to have broken the hearts baith of Dougal and his master. But the change was not a'thegether sae great as they feared, and other folk thought for. The Whigs made an unco crawing what they wad do with their auld enemies, and in special wi' Sir Robert Redgauntlet. But there were ower mony great folks dipped in the same doings, to mak a spick and span new warld.

So Parliament passed it a' ower easy ; and Sir Robert, bating
that he was held to hunting foxes instead of Covenanters,
remained just the man he was.[1] His revel was as loud, and his
hall as weel lighted, as ever it had been, though maybe he
lacked the fines of the nonconformists, that used to come to
stock his larder and cellar ; for it is certain he began to be
keener about the rents than his tenants used to find him before,
and they behoved to be prompt to the rent-day, or else the
laird wasna pleased. And he was sic an awsome body, that
naebody cared to anger him ; for the oaths he swore, and the
rage that he used to get into, and the looks that he put on,
made men sometimes think him a devil incarnate.

Weel, my gudesire was nae manager—no that he was a
very great misguider—but he hadna the saving gift, and he
got twa terms' rent in arrear. He got the first brash at Whit-
sunday put ower wi' fair word and piping ; but when Martin-
mas came, there was a summons from the grund-officer to
come wi' the rent on a day preceese, or else Steenie behoved
to flit. Sair wark he had to get the siller ; but he was weel-
freended, and at last he got the haill scraped thegither—a
thousand merks—the maist of it was from a neighbour they
ca'd Laurie Lapraik—a sly tod. Laurie had walth o' gear—
could hunt wi' the hound and rin wi' the hare—and be Whig
or Torry, saunt or sinner, as the wind stood. He was a
professor in this Revolution warld, but he liked an orra
sough of this warld, and a tune on the pipes weel aneugh at
a bytime ; and abune a', he thought he had gude security
for the siller he lent my gudesire ower the stocking at
Primrose Knowe.

Away trots my gudesire to Redgauntlet Castle wi' a heavy
purse and a light heart, glad to be out of the laird's danger.
Weel, the first thing he learned at the castle was, that Sir
Robert had fretted himsell into a fit of the gout, because he
did not appear before twelve o'clock. It wasna a'thegether
for sake of the money, Dougal thought ; but because he didna
like to part wi' my gudesire aff the grund. Dougal was glad
to see Steenie, and brought him into the great oak parlour,

---

[1] The caution and moderation of King William III., and his principles of
unlimited toleration, deprived the Cameronians of the opportunity they
ardently desired, to retaliate the injuries which they had received during the
reign of prelacy, and purify the land, as they called it, from the pollution of
blood. They esteemed the Revolution, therefore, only a half measure,
which neither comprehended the rebuilding of the Kirk in its full splendour,
nor the revenge of the death of the Saints on their persecutors.

and there sat the laird his leesome lane, excepting that he had beside him a great, ill-favoured jackanape, that was a special pet of his ; a cankered beast it was, and mony an ill-natured trick it played—ill to please it was, and easily angered—ran about the haill castle, chattering and yowling, and pinching, and biting folk, specially before ill weather, or disturbances in the state. Sir Robert caa'd it Major Weir, after the warlock that was burnt ; [1] and few folk liked either the name or the conditions of the creature—they thought there was something in it by ordinar—and my gudesire was not just easy in mind when the door shut on him, and he saw himself in the room wi' naebody but the laird, Dougal MacCallum, and the major, a thing that hadna chanced to him before.

Sir Robert sat, or, I should say, lay, in a great armed chair, wi' his grand velvet gown, and his feet on a cradle ; for he had baith gout and gravel, and his face looked as gash and ghastly as Satan's. Major Weir sat opposite to him, in a red laced coat, and the laird's wig on his head ; and ay as Sir Robert girned wi' pain, the jackanape girned too, like a sheep's-head between a pair of tangs—an ill-faur'd, fearsome couple they were. The laird's buff-coat was hung on a pin behind him, and his broadsword and his pistols within reach ; for he keepit up the auld fashion of having the weapons ready, and a horse saddled day and night, just as he used to do when he was able to loup on horseback, and away after ony of the hill-folk he could get speerings of. Some said it was for fear of the Whigs taking vengeance, but I judge it was just his auld custom—he wasna gien to fear onything. The rental-book, wi' its black cover and brass clasps, was lying beside him ; and a book of sculduddry sangs was put betwixt the leaves, to keep it open at the place where it bore evidence against the Goodman of Primrose Knowe, as behind the hand with his mails and duties. Sir Robert gave my gudesire a look, as if he would have withered his heart in his bosom. Ye maun ken he had a way of bending his brows, that men saw the visible mark of a horseshoe in his forehead, deep dinted, as if it had been stamped there.

" Are ye come light-handed, ye son of a toom whistle ? " said Sir Robert. " Zounds ! if you are———"

My gudesire, with as gude a countenance as he could put on, made a leg, and placed the bag of money on the table wi'

[1] A celebrated wizard, executed at Edinburgh for sorcery and other crimes.

a dash, like a man that does something clever. The laird drew it to him hastily—" Is it all here, Steenie, man ? "

" Your honour will find it right," said my gudesire.

" Here, Dougal," said the laird, " gie Steenie a tass of brandy downstairs, till I count the siller and write the receipt."

But they werena weel out of the room, when Sir Robert gied a yelloch that garr'd the castle rock. Back ran Dougal —in flew the livery-men—yell on yell gied the laird, ilk ane mair awfu' than the ither. My gudesire knew not whether to stand or flee, but he ventured back into the parlour, where a' was gaun hirdy-girdie—naebody to say " come in," or " gae out." Terribly the laird roared for cauld water to his feet, and wine to cool his throat; and Hell, hell, hell, and its flames, was ay the word in his mouth. They brought him water, and when they plunged his swollen feet into the tub, he cried out it was burning ; and folk say that it *did* bubble and sparkle like a seething cauldron. He flung the cup at Dougal's head, and said he had given him blood instead of burgundy ; and, sure eneugh, the lass washed clotted blood aff the carpet the neist day. The jackanape they caa'd Major Weir, it jibbered and cried as if it was mocking its master ; my gudesire's head was like to turn—he forgot baith siller and receipt, and downstairs he banged ; but as he ran, the shrieks came faint and fainter ; there was a deep-drawn shivering groan, and word gaed through the castle that the laird was dead.

Weel, away came my gudesire, wi' his finger in his mouth, and his best hope was that Dougal had seen the money-bag, and heard the laird speak of writing the receipt. The young laird, now Sir John, came from Edinburgh, to see things put to rights. Sir John and his father never gree'd weel. Sir John had been bred an advocate, and afterwards sat in the last Scots Parliament and voted for the Union, having gotten, it was thought, a rug of the compensations—if his father could have come out of his grave, he would have brained him for it on his awn hearthstane. Some thought it was easier counting with the auld rough knight than the fairspoken young ane— but mair of that anon.

Dougal MacCallum, poor body, neither grat nor grained, but gaed about the house looking like a corpse, but directing, as was his duty, a' the order of the grand funeral. Now, Dougal looked ay waur and waur when night was coming, and was ay the last to gang to his bed, whilk was in a little round just opposite the chamber of dais, whilk his master occupied while he was living, and where he now lay in state, as they caa'd it, weel-a-day! The night before the funeral, Dougal could keep his awn counsel nae langer; he came doun with his proud spirit, and fairly asked auld Hutcheon to sit in his room with him for an hour. When they were in the round, Dougal took ae tass of brandy to himsell, and gave another to Hutcheon, and wished him all health and lang life, and said that, for himsell, he wasna lang for this world; for that, every night since Sir Robert's death, his silver call had sounded from the state chamber, just as it used to do at nights in his lifetime, to call Dougal to help to turn him in his bed. Dougal said that being alone with the dead on that floor of the tower (for naebody cared to wake Sir Robert Redgauntlet like another corpse) he had never daured to answer the call, but that now his conscience checked him for neglecting his duty; for "though death breaks service," said MacCallum, "it shall never break my service to Sir Robert; and I will answer his next whistle, so be you will stand by me, Hutcheon."

Hutcheon had nae will to the wark, but he had stood by Dougal in battle and broil, and he wad not fail him at this pinch; so down the carles sat ower a stoup of brandy, and Hutcheon, who was something of a clerk, would have read a chapter of the Bible; but Dougal would hear naething but a blaud of Davie Lindsay, whilk was the waur preparation.

When midnight came, and the house was quiet as the grave, sure enough the silver whistle sounded as sharp and shrill as if Sir Robert was blowing it, and up got the two auld serving-men, and tottered into the room where the dead man lay. Hutcheon saw aneugh at the first glance; for there were torches in the room, which showed him the foul fiend, in his ain shape, sitting on the laird's coffin! Ower he cowped as if he had been dead. He could not tell how lang he lay in a trance at the door, but when he gathered himself, he cried on his neighbour, and getting nae answer, raised the house, when Dougal was found lying dead within twa steps of the bed where his master's coffin was placed. As for the whistle, it was gaen anes and ay; but mony a time was it heard at the top of the house on the bartizan, and amang the auld chimneys and turrets where the howlets have their rests. Sir John hushed the matter up, and the funeral passed over without mair bogle-wark.

But when a' was ower, and the laird was beginning to settle his affairs, every tenant was called up for his arrears, and my gudesire for the full sum that stood against him in the rental-book. Weel, away he trots to the castle, to tell his story, and there he is introduced to Sir John, sitting in his father's chair, in deep mourning, with weepers and hanging cravat, and a small walking rapier by his side, instead of the auld broadsword that had a hundredweight of steel about it, what with blade, chape, and basket-hilt. I have heard their communing so often tauld ower, that I almost think I was there myself, though I couldna be born at the time. (In fact, Alan, my companion mimicked, with a good deal of humour, the flattering, conciliating tone of the tenant's address, and the hypocritical melancholy of the laird's reply. His grand-father, he said, had, while he spoke, his eye fixed on the rental-book, as if it were a mastiff-dog that he was afraid would spring up and bite him.)

" I wuss ye joy, sir, of the head seat, and the white loaf, and the braid lairdship. Your father was a kind man to friends and followers ; muckle grace to you, Sir John, to fill his shoon—his boots, I suld say, for he seldom wore shoon, unless it were muils when he had the gout."

"Aye, Steenie," quoth the laird, sighing deeply, and putting his napkin to his een, "his was a sudden call, and he will be missed in the country ; no time to set his house in order—weel prepared Godward, no doubt, which is the root of the matter—but left us behind a tangled hesp to wind, Steenie.—Hem ! hem ! We maun go to business, Steenie ; much to do, and little time to do it in."

Here he opened the fatal volume. I have heard of a thing they call Doomsday Book—I am clear it has been a rental of back-ganging tenants.

"Stephen," said Sir John, still in the same soft, sleekit tone of voice—" Stephen Stevenson, or Steenson, ye are down here for a year's rent behind the hand—due at last term."

Stephen. " Please your honour, Sir John, I paid it to your father."

Sir John. " Ye took a receipt, then, doubtless, Stephen ; and can produce it ? "

Stephen. " Indeed I hadna time, an it like your honour ; for nae sooner had I set doun the siller, and just as his honour, Sir Robert, that's gaen, drew it till him to count it, and write out the receipt, he was ta'en wi' the pains that removed him."

512

"That was unlucky," said Sir John, after a pause. "But ye maybe paid it in the presence of somebody. I want but a *talis qualis* evidence, Stephen. I would go ower strictly to work with no poor man."

Stephen. "Troth, Sir John, there was naebody in the room but Dougal MacCallum the butler. But, as your honour kens, he has e'en followed his auld master."

"Very unlucky again, Stephen," said Sir John, without altering his voice a single note. "The man to whom ye paid the money is dead—and the man who witnessed the payment is dead too—and the siller, which should have been to the fore, is neither seen nor heard tell of in the repositories. How am I to believe a' this?"

Stephen. "I dinna ken, your honour; but there is a bit memorandum note of the very coins, for, God help me! I had to borrow out of twenty purses; and I am sure that ilka man there set down will take his grit oath for what purpose I borrowed the money."

Sir John. "I have little doubt ye *borrowed* the money, Steenie. It is the *payment* to my father that I want to have some proof of."

Stephen. "The siller maun be about the house, Sir John. And since your honour never got it, and his honour that was canna have ta'en it wi' him, maybe some of the family may have seen it."

Sir John. "We will examine the servants, Stephen; that is but reasonable."

But lackey and lass, and page and groom, all denied stoutly that they had ever seen such a bag of money as my gudesire described. What was waur, he had unluckily not mentioned to any living soul of them his purpose of paying his rent. Ae quean had noticed something under his arm, but she took it for the pipes.

Sir John Redgauntlet ordered the servants out of the room, and then said to my gudesire, "Now, Steenie, ye see ye have fair play; and, as I have little doubt ye ken better where to find the siller than ony other body, I beg, in fair terms, and for your own sake, that you will end this fasherie; for, Stephen, ye maun pay or fly."

"The Lord forgie your opinion," said Stephen, driven almost to his wit's end—"I am an honest man."

"So am I, Stephen," said his honour; "and so are all the folks in the house, I hope. But if there be a knave amongst us, it must be he that tells the story he cannot prove." He paused, and then added, mair sternly, " If I understand your trick, sir, you want to take advantage of some malicious reports concerning things in this family, and particularly respecting my father's sudden death, thereby to cheat me out of the money, and perhaps take away my character, by insinuating that I have received the rent I am demanding. Where do you suppose this money to be ? I insist upon knowing."

My gudesire saw everything look so muckle against him, that he grew nearly desperate—however, he shifted from one foot to another, looked to every corner of the room, and made no answer.

" Speak out, sirrah," said the laird, assuming a look of his father's, a very particular ane, which he had when he was angry—it seemed as if the wrinkles of his frown made that selfsame fearful shape of a horse's shoe in the middle of his brow ;—" Speak out, sir ! I *will* know your thoughts ;— do you suppose that I have this money ? "

" Far be it frae me to say so," said Stephen.

" Do you charge any of my people with having taken it ? "

" I wad be laith to charge them that may be innocent," said my gudesire ; " and if there be any one that is guilty, I have nae proof."

" Somewhere the money must be, if there is a word of truth in your story," said Sir John ; " I ask where you think it is—and demand a correct answer ? "

" In hell, if you *will* have my thoughts of it," said my gudesire, driven to extremity, " in hell ! with your father, his jackanape, and his silver whistle."

Down the stairs he ran (for the parlour was nae place for him after such a word) and he heard the laird swearing blood and wounds behind him, as fast as ever did Sir Robert, and roaring for the bailie and the baron-officer.

Away rode my gudesire to his chief creditor (him they ca'd Laurie Lapraik) to try if he could make onything out of him ; but when he tauld his story, he got but the worst word in his wame—thief, beggar, and dyvour, were the saftest terms ; and to the boot of these hard terms, Laurie brought up the auld story of his dipping his hand in the blood of God's saunts, just as if a tenant could have helped riding with the laird, and that a laird like Sir Robert Redgauntlet. My gudesire was, by this time, far beyond the bounds of patience, and, while he and Laurie were at deil speed the liars, he was wanchancie aneugh to abuse Lapraik's doctrine as weel as the man, and said things that garr'd folks' flesh grue that heard them ;— he wasna just himsell, and he had lived wi' a wild set in his day.

At last they parted, and my gudesire was to ride hame through the wood of Pitmurkie, that is a' fou of black firs, as they say.—I ken the wood, but the firs may be black or white for what I can tell.—At the entry of the wood there is a wild common, and on the edge of the common, a little lonely change-house, that was keepit then by an ostler-wife, they suld hae caa'd her Tibbie Faw, and there puir Steenie cried for a mutchkin of brandy, for he had had no refreshment the haill day. Tibbie was earnest wi' him to take a bite of meat, but he couldna think o't, nor would he take his foot out of the stirrup, and took off the brandy wholely at twa draughts, and named a toast at each :—the first was the memory of Sir Robert Red-gauntlet, and might he never lie quiet in his grave till he had righted his poor bond-tenant ; and the second was a health to Man's Enemy if he would but get him back the pock of siller or tell him what came o't, for he saw the haill world was like to regard him as a thief and a cheat, and he took that waur than even the ruin of his house and hauld.

On he rode, little caring where. It was a dark night turned, and the trees made it yet darker, and he let the beast take its ain road through the wood ; when all of a sudden from tired and wearied that it was before, the nag began to spring and flee, and stend, that my gudesire could hardly keep the saddle. Upon the whilk, a horseman, suddenly riding up beside him, said, "That's a mettle beast of yours, freend ; will you sell him ? " So saying, he touched the horse's neck with his riding-wand, and it fell into its auld heigh-ho of a stumbling trot. "But his spunk's soon out of him, I think," continued the stranger, " and that is like mony a man's courage, that thinks he wad do great things till he come to the proof."

My gudesire scarce listened to this, but spurred his horse, with " Gude e'en to you, freend."

But it's like the stranger was ane that doesna lightly yield his point ; for, ride as Steenie liked, he was ay beside him at the selfsame pace. At last my gudesire, Steenie Steenson, grew half angry, and, to say the truth, half feared.

"What is it that ye want with me, freend ? " he said. " If ye be a robber, I have nae money ; if ye be a leal man, wanting company, I have nae heart to mirth or speaking ; and if ye want to ken the road, I scarce ken it mysell."

515

" If you will tell me your grief," said the stranger, " I am one that, though I have been sair miscaa'd in the world, am the only hand for helping my freends."

So my gudesire, to ease his ain heart, mair than from any hope of help, told him the story from beginning to end.

" It's a hard pinch," said the stranger ; " but I think I can help you."

" If you could lend the money, sir, and take a lang day— I ken nae other help on earth," said my gudesire.

" But there may be some under the earth," said the stranger. " Come, I'll be frank wi' you ; I could lend you the money on bond, but you would maybe scruple my terms. Now, I can tell you, that your ald laird is disturbed in his grave by your curses, and the wailing of your family, and if ye daur venture to go to see him, he will give you the receipt."

My gudesire's hair stood on end at this proposal, but he thought his companion might be some humoursome chield that was trying to frighten him, and might end with lending him the money. Besides, he was bauld wi' brandy, and desperate wi' distress ; and he said he had courage to go to the gate of hell, and a step farther, for that receipt. The stranger laughed.

Weel, they rode on through the thickest of the wood, when, all of a sudden, the horse stopped at the door of a great house ; and, but that he knew the place was ten miles off, my father would have thought he was at Redgauntlet Castle. They rode into the outer courtyard, through the muckle faulding yetts and aneath the auld portcullis ; and the whole front of the house was lighted, and there were pipes and fiddles, and as much dancing and deray within as used to be at Sir Robert's house at Pace and Yule, and such high seasons. They lap off, and my gudesire, as seemed to him, fastened his horse to the very ring he had tied him to that morning, when he gaed to wait on the young Sir John.

" God ! " said my gudesire, " if Sir Robert's death be but a dream ! "

He knocked at the ha' door just as he was wont, and his auld acquaintance, Dougal MacCallum—just after his wont, too,—came to open the door, and said, " Piper Steenie, are ye there, lad ? Sir Robert has been crying for you."

My gudesire was like a man in a dream—he looked for the stranger, but he was gane for the time. At last he just tried to say, " Ha ! Dougal Driveower, are ye living ? I thought ye had been dead."

" Never fash yoursell wi' me," said Dougal, " but look to yoursell ; and see ye tak naething frae ony body here, neither meat, drink, nor siller, except just the receipt that is your ain."

So saying, he led the way out through halls and trances that were weel kend to my gudesire, and into the auld oak parlour ; and there was as much singing of profane sangs, and birling of red wine, and speaking blasphemy and sculduddry, as had ever been in Redgauntlet Castle when it was at the blithest.

But, Lord take us in keeping, what a set of ghastly revellers they were that sat around that table ! My gudesire kend mony that had long before gane to their place, for often had he piped to the most part in the hall of Redgauntlet. There was the fierce Middleton, and the dissolute Rothes and the crafty Lauderdale ; and Dalyell, with his bald head and a beard to his girdle ; and Earlshall, with Cameron's blude on his hand ; and wild Bonshaw, that tied blessed Mr. Cargill's limbs till the blude sprung ; and Dunbarton Douglas, the twice-turned traitor baith to country and king. There was the Bluidy Advocate MacKenyie, who, for his worldly wit and wisdom had been to the rest as a god. And there was Claverhouse, as beautiful as when he lived, with his long, dark, curled locks streaming down over his laced buff-coat, and his left hand always on his right spule-blade, to hide the wound that the silver bullet had made. He sat apart from them all, and looked at them with a melancholy, haughty countenance ; while the rest hallooed, and sang, and laughed, that the room rang. But their smiles were fearfully contorted from time to time ; and their laugh passed into such wild sounds as made my gudesire's very nails grow blue, and chilled the marrow in his banes.

They that waited at the table were just the wicked servingmen and troopers, that had done their work and cruel bidding on earth. There was the Lang Lad of the Nethertown, that helped to take Argyle ; and the bishop's summoner, that they called the Deil's Rattle-bag ; and the wicked guardsmen in their laced coats ; and the savage Highland Amorites, that shed blood like water ; and many a proud serving-man, haughty of heart and bloody of hand, cringing to the rich, and making them wickeder than they would be ; grinding the poor to powder, when the rich had broken them to fragments. And mony, mony mair were coming and ganging, a' as busy in their vocation as if they had been alive.

Sir Robert Redgauntlet, in the midst of a' this fearful riot, cried, wi' a voice like thunder, on Steenie Piper to come to the board-head where he was sitting ; his legs stretched out before him, and swathed up with flannel, with his holster pistols aside him, while the great broadsword rested against his chair, just as my gudesire had seen him the last time upon earth—the very cushion for the jackanape was close to him, but the creature itself was not there—it wasna its hour, it's likely ; for he heard them say as he came forward, " Is not the major come yet ? " And another answered, " The jackanape will be here betimes the morn." And when my gudesire came forward, Sir Robert, or his ghaist, or the deevil in his likeness, said, " Weel, piper, hae ye settled wi' my son for the year's rent ? "

With much ado my father gat breath to say that Sir John would not settle without his honour's receipt.

" Ye shall hae that for a tune of the pipes, Steenie," said the appearance of Sir Robert—" Play us up ' Weel hoddled, Luckie.' "

Now this was a tune my gudesire learned frae a warlock, that heard it when they were worshipping Satan at their meetings, and my gudesire had sometimes played it at the ranting suppers in Redgauntlet Castle, but never very willingly ; and now he grew cauld at the very name of it, and said, for excuse, he hadna his pipes wi' him.

" MacCallum, ye limb of Belzebub," said the fearfu' Sir Robert, " bring Steenie the pipes that I am keeping for him ! "

MacCallum brought a pair of pipes might have served the piper of Donald of the Isles. But he gave my gudesire a nudge as he offered them ; and looking secretly and closely, Steenie saw that the chanter was of steel, and heated to a white heat ; so he had fair warning not to trust his fingers with it. So he excused himself again, and said he was faint and frightened, and had not wind aneugh to fill the bag.

" Then ye maun eat and drink, Steenie," said the figure ; " for we do little else here ; and it's ill speaking between a fou man and a fasting."

Now these were the very words that the bloody Earl of Douglas said to keep the king's messenger in hand while he cut the head off MacLellan of Bombie, at the Threave Castle, and that put Steenie mair and mair on his guard. So he spoke up like a man, and said he came neither to eat, nor drink, nor make minstrelsy; but simply for his ain—to ken what was come o' the money he had paid, and to get a discharge for it; and he was so stout-hearted by this time that he charged Sir Robert for conscience-sake (he had no power to say the holy name) and as he hoped for peace and rest, to spread no snares for him, but just to give him his ain.

The appearance gnashed its teeth and laughed, but it took from a large pocket-book the receipt, and handed it to Steenie. "There is your receipt, ye pitiful cur; and for the money, my dog-whelp of a son may go look for it in the Cat's Cradle."

My gudesire uttered mony thanks, and was about to retire when Sir Robert roared aloud, "Stop, though, thou sack-doudling son of a whore! I am not done with thee. HERE we do nothing for nothing; and you must return on this very day twelvemonth, to pay your master the homage that you owe me for my protection."

My father's tongue was loosed of a suddenty, and he said aloud, "I refer mysell to God's pleasure, and not to yours."

He had no sooner uttered the word than all was dark around him; and he sank on the earth with such a sudden shock, that he lost both breath and sense.

How lang Steenie lay there, he could not tell; but when he came to himsell, he was lying in the auld kirkyard of Red-gauntlet parochine just at the door of the family aisle, and the scutcheon of the auld knight, Sir Robert, hanging over his head. There was a deep morning fog on grass and grave-stane around him, and his horse was feeding quietly beside the minister's twa cows. Steenie would have thought the whole was a dream, but he had the receipt in his hand, fairly written and signed by the auld laird; only the last letters of his name were a little disorderly, written like one seized with sudden pain.

Sorely troubled in his mind, he left that dreary place, rode through the mist to Redgauntlet Castle, and with much ado he got speech of the laird.

"Well, you dyvour bankrupt," was the first word, "have you brought me my rent?"

"No," answered my gudesire, "I have not; but I have brought your honour Sir Robert's receipt for it."

"How, sirrah? Sir Robert's receipt! You told me he had not given you one."

" Will your honour please to see if that bit line is right ? "

Sir John looked at every line, and at every letter, with much attention ; and at last, at the date, which my gudesire had not observed,—" *From my appointed place,*" he read, " *this twenty-fifth of November.*"—" What !—That is yesterday !—Villain, thou must have gone to hell for this ! "

" I got it from your honour's father—whether he be in heaven or hell, I know not," said Steenie.

" I will delate you for a warlock to the Privy Council ! " said Sir John. " I will send you to your master, the devil, with the help of a tar-barrel and a torch ! "

" I intend to delate mysell to the Presbytery," said Steenie, " and tell them all I have seen last night, whilk are things fitter for them to judge of than a borrel man like me."

Sir John paused, composed himsell, and desired to hear the full history ; and my gudesire told it him from point to point, as I have told it you—word for word, neither more nor less.

Sir John was silent again for a long time, and at last he said, very composedly, " Steenie, this story of yours concerns the honour of many a noble family besides mine ; and if it be a leasing-making, to keep yourself out of my danger, the least you can expect is to have a red-hot iron driven through your tongue, and that will be as bad as scauding your fingers wi' a redhot chanter. But yet it may be true, Steenie ; and if the money cast up, I shall not know what to think of it. But where shall we find the Cat's Cradle ? There are cats enough about the old house, but I think they kitten without the ceremony of bed or cradle."

" We were best ask Hutcheon," said my gudesire ; " he kens a' the odd corners about as weel as—another serving-man that is now gane, and that I wad not like to name."

Aweel, Hutcheon, when he was asked, told them, that a ruinous turret, lang disused, next to the clock-house, only accessible by a ladder, for the opening was on the outside, and far above the battlements, was called of old the Cat's Cradle.

" There will I go immediately," said Sir John ; and he took (with what purpose, Heaven kens) one of his father's pistols from the hall-table, where they had lain since the night he died, and hastened to the battlements.

It was a dangerous place to climb, for the ladder was auld and frail, and wanted ane or twa rounds. However, up got

Sir John, and entered at the turret-door, where his body stopped the only little light that was in the bit turret. Something flees at him wi' a vengeance, maist dang him back ower— bang gaed the knight's pistol, and Hutcheon, that held the ladder, and my gudesire that stood beside him, hears a loud skelloch. A minute after, Sir John flings the body of the jackanape down to them, and cries that the siller is fund, and that they should come up and help him. And there was the bag of siller sure aneugh, and mony orra thing besides, that had been missing for mony a day. And Sir John, when he had riped the turret weel, led my gudesire into the dining-parlour, and took him by the hand and spoke kindly to him, and said he was sorry he should have doubted his word and that he would here-after be a good master to him to make amends.

"And now, Steenie," said Sir John, "although this vision of yours tend, on the whole, to my father's credit, as an honest man, that he should, even after his death, desire to see justice done to a poor man like you, yet you are sensible that ill-dispositioned men might make bad constructions upon it, concerning his soul's health. So, I think, we had better lay the haill dirdum on that ill-deedie creature, Major Weir, and say naething about your dream in the wood of Pitmurkie. You had taken ower muckle brandy to be very certain about onything; and, Steenie, this receipt " (his hand shook while he held it out),—" it's but a queer kind of document, and we will do best, I think, to put it quietly in the fire."

"Od, but for as queer as it is, it's a' the voucher I have for my rent," said my gudesire, who was afraid, it may be, of losing the benefit of Sir Robert's discharge.

"I will bear the contents to your credit in the rental-book, and give you a discharge under my own hand," said Sir John, "and that on the spot. And, Steenie, if you can hold your tongue about this matter, you shall sit, from this term downward, at an easier rent."

"Mony thanks to your honour," said Steenie, who saw easily in what corner the wind was ; "doubtless I will be conformable to all your honour's commands ; only I would willingly speak wi' some powerful minister on the subject, for I do not like the sort of soumons of appointment whilk your honour's father "——

"Do not call the phantom my father !" said Sir John, interrupting him.

"Weel, then, the thing that was so like him," said my

gudesire ; " he spoke of my coming back to see him this time twelvemonth, and it's a weight on my conscience."

"Aweel, then," said Sir John, " if you be so much distressed in mind, you may speak to our minister of the parish ; he is a douce man, regards the honour of our family, and the mair that he may look for some patronage from me."

Wi' that, my father readily agreed that the receipt should be burnt, and the laird threw it into the chimney with his ain hand. Burn it would not for them, though ; but away it flew up the lum, wi' a lang train of sparks at its tail, and a hissing noise like a squib.

My gudesire gaed down to the Manse, and the minister, when he had heard the story, said it was his real opinion that though my gudesire had gaen very far in tampering with dangerous matters, yet, as he had refused the devil's arles (for such was the offer of meat and drink) and had refused to do homage by piping at his bidding, he hoped, that if he held a circumspect walk hereafter, Satan could take little advantage by what was come and gane. And, indeed, my gudesire of his ain accord, lang foreswore baith the pipes and the brandy— it was not even till the year was out, and the fatal day past, that he would so much as take the fiddle, or drink usquebaugh or tippeny.

Sir John made up his story about the jackanape as he liked himsell ; and some believe till this day there was no more in the matter than the filching nature of the brute. Indeed, ye'll no hinder some to threap that it was nane o' the auld Enemy that Dougal and my gudesire saw in the laird's room, but only that wanchancy creature, the major, capering on the coffin ; and that, as to the blawing on the laird's whistle that was heard after he was dead, the filthy brute could do that as weel as the laird himsell, if no better. But Heaven kens the truth, whilk first came out by the minister's wife, after Sir John and her ain gudeman were baith in the moulds. And then my gudesire, wha was failed in his limbs, but not in his judgment or memory —at least nothing to speak of—was obliged to tell the real narrative to his friends, for the credit of his good name. He might else have been charged for a warlock.

The shades of evening were growing thicker around us as my conductor finished his long narrative with this moral— " Ye see, birkie, it is nae chancy thing to tak a stranger traveller for a guide, when you are in an uncouth land."

" I should not have made that inference," said I. " Your

grandfather's adventure was fortune for himself whom it saved from ruin and distress ; and fortunate for his landlord also, whom it prevented from committing a gross act of injustice."

" Aye, but they had baith to sup the sauce o't sooner or later," said Wandering Willie—" what was fristed wasna forgiven. Sir John died before he was much over three-score ; and it was just like of a moment's illness. And for my gudesire, though he departed in fullness of life, yet there was my father, a yauld man of forty-five, fell down betwixt the stilts of his pleugh, and rase never again, and left nae bairn but me, a puir sightless, fatherless, motherless creature, could neither work nor want. Things gaed weel aneugh at first ; for Sir Redwald Redgauntlet, the only son of Sir John, and the oye of auld Sir Robert, and, waes me ! the last of the honourable house, took the farm aff our hands, and brought me into his household to have care of me. He liked music, and I had the best teachers baith England and Scotland could gie me. Mony a merry year was I wi' him ; but waes me ! he gaed out with other pretty men in the 'Forty-five—I'll say nae mair about it—My head never settled weel since I lost him ; and if I say another word about it, deil a bar will I have the heart to play the night.— Look out, my gentle chap," he resumed in a different tone, " ye should see the lights at Brokenburn Glen by this time."

THE HORLA

Guy de Maupassant

8th May.—What a wonderful day! I spent the whole morning stretched out on the grass in front of my house under the huge plane-tree that covers and shelters and overshadows it entirely.

I love this country and I love to live here because I have my roots here, those profound and delicate roots that bind a man to the land where his ancestors were born and died, which endear him to ways of thinking and eating, to customs as well as actual food, to local turns of speech, to the accent of the country folk, to the smell of the earth, of the villages, and of the air itself.

I love my house where I have grown up. From my windows I see the Seine that flows beside my garden behind the road, almost at my doorstep, the great broad Seine that goes from Rouen to Havre, covered with passing boats. Far away to the left lies Rouen, the vast city of blue roofs, under a bristling multitude of Gothic spires. They are innumerable, slight or heavy, dominated by the iron tower of the Cathedral, and filled with bells that chime in the clear air of sunny mornings, sending me a sweet and distant clangour, their brazen song brought to me by the breeze, sometimes louder and sometimes softer as it freshens or dies away.

How fine it was this morning!

About eleven o'clock a long line of boats passed by my gate drawn by a tug like a great fly that choked with anxiety as it coughed up a thick cloud of smoke.

After two English yachts whose red flags billowed against the sky came a superb Brazilian three-master, all white, wonderfully clean and shining. I waved to it, I don't know why, this boat that gave me such pleasure to see.

12th May.—I have been slightly feverish for some days ; I feel ill, or rather, I feel unhappy.

Whence come these mysterious influences that transform our happiness into distress, our confidence into discouragement ? It is as if the air, the invisible air, is full of unrecognisable Powers whose mysterious proximity one must endure. I awaken full of joy, feeling like bursting into song. Why ? I go down to the water's edge ; and suddenly, after a short walk, I return home wretched, as if some misfortune awaited me. Why ? Can it be that a cold shudder, lightly touching my skin, has jangled my nerves and clouded my soul ? Can it be that the shapes of the clouds or the colour of the day, that all-too-changeable colour of things, has glided through my vision to trouble my thoughts ? Who can say ? Everything that surrounds us, everything that we see without looking at, everything that we brush by unknowingly, everything that we come across without noticing it, has on us, on our senses and, through them, on our thoughts, on our very hearts, rapid surprising and unexplainable effects.

How deep it is, this mystery of the Invisible ! We are unable to fathom it with our poor senses, with eyes that can perceive neither the too small nor the too large, neither the too near nor the too distant, neither the inhabitants of a star nor the dwellers within a drop of water . . . with our ears that deceive us, since they transmit to us vibrations of the air as deep-toned sounds. They are fairies who perform this miracle of transforming movement into sound and by this change give birth to music, who give a voice to the dumb tumult of Nature . . . with our sense of smell, more feeble than that of a dog . . . with our taste that is scarce able to discern the age of a wine !

Ah ! had we but other senses with which to work different miracles in our favour, what further things could we discover round about us !

16th May.—I am ill, definitely ! I was so well last month! I have a fever, a terrible fever that inflames my mind as much as my body. I feel persistently this awful sense of threatening danger, this apprehension of approaching danger or death, this presentiment that is doubtless the symptom of an unforeseen malady germinating in my blood and flesh.

18th May.—I have just been to see my doctor, as I was unable to sleep. He found my pulse rapid, my eyes dilated, my

nerves on edge, but not one other alarming indication. I have
to have douches and drink potassium bromide.

25th May.—No change. My condition is really odd. As
evening falls a strange uneasiness comes over me, as if the
night time would disclose some terrible menace. I dine quickly,
then I try to read ; but I cannot understand the words ; I
can scarcely distinguish the letters. Then I walk up and down
in my room, oppressed by a vague yet irresistible fear, fear of
my bed and of going to sleep.

About two o'clock I go to my bedroom. As soon as I am
inside I lock the door and fasten the bolts. I am afraid . . . of
what ? I never dreaded anything till now. . . . I open the cupboards, I look under the bed, I listen . . . listen . . . for what ?
. . . Is it not strange that a simple ailment, something to do
with the circulation, perhaps, the irritation of a nerve or a slight
congestion, the smallest interference in the action of our living
machine that is so faulty and so frail, can sadden the happiest
of men and make a coward out of a hero ? Next, I lie down and
I wait for sleep as for an executioner. I wait with terror for
its approach, my heart throbs, my limbs tremble and my entire
body shudders in the warmth of the bedclothes until the
moment comes when I fall asleep as into a stagnant pool, to
drown. I can no longer feel it approaching, this treacherous
sleep that lurks behind me, spying on me, ready to grasp me
by the head, to close my eyes and overwhelm me.

I sleep—for a long time—two or three hours—then a dream
—no—a nightmare seizes me. I am aware that I am in bed and
asleep . . . I feel it and I know it . . . and I know now that
someone is beside me, is looking at me, touching me, climbs
on my bed, kneels on my chest, grips my throat with his hands
and squeezes . . . squeezes . . . with all his strength to throttle
me.

I writhe and struggle, held by that fearful powerlessness that
paralyses us in dreams ; I try to call—I cannot ; I try to move—
I cannot ; gasping, I try with desperate efforts to turn, to throw
off this being who strangles and stifles me—I cannot !

And suddenly I awake, terrified and drenched in sweat.
I light a candle. I am alone.

After this attack which comes on every night, I at length
get to sleep again and slumber calmly till the dawn.

2nd June.—My condition has become worse. What is the
matter with me ? Bromides are useless, and so are douches.
Once, in order to tire my already exhausted body, I took a

walk in the forest of Roumare. I thought at first that the clear, fresh, mild air full of the scent of grass and leaves would put new blood into my veins, new energy into my heart. I went down a broad glade, then I turned towards La Bouille along a narrow path between two rows of immeasurably high trees that formed a thick, green, almost black roof between the sky and me.

All at once a shudder ran through me, not a shudder of cold but a strange trembling of anguish.

I hurried on, anxious at being alone in the wood, frightened without reason, stupified, through the profound solitude. Suddenly I felt that I was being followed, that someone was walking close behind me, near enough to touch me.

I turned sharply. I was alone. I saw behind me only the straight broad glade, empty, vast—undeniably empty ; and in front of me, too, it stretched out as far as the eye could see, just the same, terrifying.

I closed my eyes. Why ? And I started to turn round on my heels like a top. I almost fell ; I opened my eyes ; the trees danced, the earth swam ; I had to sit down. Then, ah ! then I could not tell which way I had come ! A queer thing, that ! Queer, queer thing ! I knew no more. I kept to the right and found myself back in the avenue that had led me into the heart of the forest.

3rd June.—Last night was terrible. I am going to go away for a few weeks. A short journey will no doubt put me right again.

2nd July.—I have come back. I am cured. And moreover, I have had a delightful holiday. I went to Mont-St.-Michel, which I had not seen before.

What a view one gets on arriving at Avranches, as I did, in the evening ! The town is on a hill and I was shown the public garden at the end of the city. I exclaimed with astonishment. A huge bay lay in front of me as far as the eye could see between two distant headlands that vanished in the far-off mists ; and in the middle of this great yellow bay, under a clear and golden sky, rose a strange hill, dark and pointed, amidst the sand. The sun had just set, and against the still-flaming horizon was sketched the outline of this fantastic rock that bore on its summit a fantastic monument.

At dawn I went over to it. The tide was out, as on the previous evening, and I watched the astonishing abbey rise up in front of me as I approached it. After walking for several hours I reached the tremendous heap of stones that bears the little city dominated by the great church. After climbing the steep and narrow street I entered the most wonderful Gothic dwelling for God ever built on earth, as vast as a town, full of low rooms hollowed out under the vaults and high galleries sustained by slender columns. I penetrated this gigantic piece of granite jewellery, as fine as a bit of lace, covered with towers and airy belfries reached by twisting stairways that are linked one to the other by thin, carved and ornamented arches, and pierce the blue sky of the day and the black sky of the night with their strange heads bristling with gargoyles, devils, fantastic beasts and monstrous flowers.

When I was at the top I said to the monk who accompanied me : " How contented you must be here, Father."

He answered : " It's a windy place." And we began to talk as we watched the rising tide that ran over the sand and covered it with a breastplate of steel.

And the monk told me stories, all the old stories of the place—legends, and more legends.

One of them struck me particularly. The people in these parts, they who dwell on the Mount, declare that they hear voices on the sands at night, followed by the bleating of two goats, one with a powerful voice, the other weak. Sceptics affirm that this is due to the cries of the sea-birds, sometimes resembling bleating and sometimes human wailing ; but belated fishermen swear that they have met, between the tides, an old shepherd wandering over the dunes round the little town set down so far from the rest of the world. No one ever sees his head, which is covered by his cloak ; and he leads, walking in front of them, a goat with the face of a man and a she-goat with a woman's face, both with long white hair and ceaselessly talking, quarrelling in an unknown tongue, then stopping suddenly to bleat with all their might.

I said to the monk : " Do you believe it ? "

" I do not know," he murmured.

I continued : " If other beings than ourselves exist on earth, how have we never known about them, long ago ? How is it that you have never seen them ? How is it that I have never seen them myself ? "

" Do we see the hundred-thousandth part of what exists ? " he replied. " Take the wind, for instance, the greatest force in nature, which throws men down, shatters buildings, uproots trees, piles up the sea into billowing mountains, destroys cliffs, and flings great ships upon the coast, the wind that kills, that whistles, that whines, that roars—have you seen it ? Can you see it ? Nevertheless, it exists."

I was silent before this simple logic. This man was either very wise or a fool. I should not have liked to say which ; but I kept quiet. What he had said, I had often thought.

3rd July.—I slept badly. There is definitely some feverish influence in the air, for my coachman is suffering from the same illness as myself. I noticed his extraordinary pallor yesterday, as I was coming home.

" What's the matter with you, Jean ? " I asked.

" It's just that I can't sleep, sir. My night's rest is broken into. Since you went away, sir, it's as if I was bewitched."

The other servants are all right, however, but I am very much afraid of being caught again.

4th July.—It has really got me again. My former nightmares have come back. Last night I felt someone crouching on me, drinking my life from my lips, his mouth to mine. Yes, he sucked it from my throat like a leech ! Then he arose, replete, and I awoke so bruised and shattered and exhausted that I was unable to stir. If this continues for any length of time I shall certainly go away again.

5th July.—Am I going mad ? What happened last night is so strange that my head reels at the very thought of it !

I had locked my door, as I now do every evening, then, being thirsty, I drank half a glass of water, and I happened to notice that my carafe was full right up to its crystal stopper.

I lay down afterwards and fell into one of my dreadful slumbers out of which I was jerked, when about two hours had passed, by a still more dreadful shock.

Imagine a sleeping man who is murdered and wakes with the knife in his lungs, in the last throes, covered with blood, unable to breathe, on the point of death and understanding nothing—that was my dream ! Having at length recovered my reason I felt thirsty again. I lit a candle and went to the table where my carafe lay. I lifted it and tipped it over my glass ; not a drop ran out. It was empty ! It was completely empty ! At first I did not understand, then, suddenly, I was overcome by an emotion so terrible that I had to sit down—or rather, fall down upon a chair ! Immediately I started up again to stare about me, then I sat down again transfixed with astonishment and fear in front of the transparent crystal. I gazed at it fixedly trying to guess the riddle. My hands trembled.

Someone had drunk the water. Who? Myself? Myself obviously. There could be nobody else. Then I must be a somnambulist. I was living without knowing it that mysterious double life that makes us wonder whether there are not two selves within us, or whether some exterior being, unknown, invisible, animates us at moments when our spirit lies unconscious, the captive body obedient to it as to ourselves—more obedient than to ourselves.

Ah, who will be able to understand my fearful agony? Who will be able to understand the feelings of a sane, healthy, wide-awake man staring through the glass of a carafe whence the water has disappeared while he slept! I stayed where I was till daybreak, not daring to return to bed.

6th July.—I am going mad. Once more someone emptied my carafe last night—or rather, I emptied it!

But is it I? Is it I? Who else could it be? Who? Oh, my God! I am going mad! Who will save me?

10th July.—I have just made some astonishing tests.

Oh, I must be mad!

On the sixth of July before going to bed I placed on my table some wine, milk, water, bread and strawberries.

Someone drank—I drank—all the water and a little of the milk. Neither the wine nor the strawberries were touched.

On the seventh of July I tried the same experiment, with the same result.

On the eighth I had no water or milk. Nothing was touched.

Finally on the ninth of July I left only water and milk on the table, carefully wrapping the carafes in white muslin cloths, and tying down the stoppers. Then I rubbed my lips, beard and hands with black-lead, and went to bed.

The same invincible sleep overpowered me, followed shortly by the fearful awakening. I had not stirred : my bedclothes themselves bore no traces. I rushed to the table. The cloths wrapped round the bottles remained spotless. I untied the string, trembling with fear. Someone had drunk all the water. Someone had drunk all the milk. Oh, my God! . . . I am leaving for Paris at once.

13th July. Paris. I must have lost my head these last few days. I must have been at the mercy of my disordered imagination, unless I really am a somnambulist, or have fallen into the power of one of those indubitable but hitherto inexplicable influences we call suggestions. Whatever it was, my malady was akin to madness, and twenty-four hours of Paris have been sufficient to make me once more myself.

Yesterday, after calls and visits that put new life into me, I finished the evening at the Théâtre Francais. They were doing a play by the younger Dumas, and his alert and powerful mind put the finishing touches to my cure. Solitude is undoubtedly dangerous for active minds. We must have about us men who think and speak. When we are alone for any length of time we people the void with phantasms.

I went back to the hotel by the boulevards, feeling very gay. Amid the thronging crowds I thought, not without irony, of my terrors, of my hallucinations of the previous week when I believed—yes, I really did believe—that an invisible being had come to share the same roof with me. How weak and bewildered and scattered our wits become when we are up against the smallest unexplainable fact !

Instead of concluding with the simple words : " I do not understand because I cannot trace the cause," we immediately imagine terrifying mysteries and supernatural powers.

14th July. Fête de la République.—I walked through the streets. The rockets and flags amused me as if I had been a child. It is, however, rather silly to be joyful on a certain date by government order. The people are a foolish mob, at one time brutishly patient, at another fiercely in revolt. They are told to " Enjoy yourselves," and they proceed to enjoy themselves. They are told to " Go and fight your neighbour," and off they go. They are told to " Vote for the Emperor," and they vote for the Emperor. Then someone says " Vote for the Republic," and they vote for the Republic.

Those in command are also stupid ; but instead of obeying men they obey principles that can only be cracked, false and sterile since they are principles, that is to say ideas reputed to be exact and unchanging in this world where nothing is certain since light and sound are both illusions.

16th July.—I witnessed things yesterday that have made me most uneasy.

I dined with my cousin, Mme. Sablé, whose husband commands the 76th Chasseurs at Limoges. I met two young women, one of whom is married to a Dr. Parent, who specialises in nervous diseases and those extraordinary manifestations that are the result of recent experiments in hypnotism and suggestion.

He told us at length about the amazing results obtained

by English scientists and doctors of the school at Nancy. The facts he brought forward struck me as very odd and I confessed myself utterly incredulous.

"We are," he affirmed, "on the point of discovering one of the most important secrets of nature, I mean one of the most important secrets of this earth, for there are, of course, others as important far beyond, in the stars. Since man began to think, since he first learned to speak and to write down his thoughts, he has sensed the presence of a mystery impenetrable by his clumsy and imperfect senses, and he has tried to supplement his organism's lack of power by the effort of his intelligence. While this intelligence was still in a rudimentary state, the haunting sense of invisible phenomena has taken crudely terrifying forms. From this was born the more popular beliefs in the supernatural. Legends of wandering spirits, fairies, gnomes, ghosts, I will say even the legend of God, for our conceptions of the artificer-creator, to whatever religion they belong, are really the most ordinary, the most stupid, the least acceptable inventions that ever emerged from the fear-ridden brain of man. Nothing is truer than that saying of Voltaire's: 'God made man in his own image, but man has certainly returned the compliment.'

"But for a little over a century we have begun to sense something new. Mesmer and others have set our feet on an untrodden path and, especially during the last four or five years, we have arrived at really remarkable results."

My cousin, who was also incredulous, smiled. Dr. Parent said to her: "Would you like me to try to put you to sleep, Madame?"

"Yes, do."

She sat in an arm-chair and he began by gazing fixedly at her as if to fascinate her. I felt suddenly uneasy, my heart throbbed, my throat contracted. I saw Mme. Sablé's eyes grow heavy, her mouth twitch, her bosom heave.

At the end of ten minutes she was asleep.

"Get behind her," said the doctor.

I seated myself behind her. He put a visiting card in her hand and said:

"This is a mirror; what can you see?"

She replied:

"I see my cousin."

"What is he doing?"

"He is twisting his moustache."

534

" And now ? "

" He is taking a photograph out of his pocket."

" Whose photograph is it ? "

" His own."

It was true ! And this photograph had only just been delivered to me at my hotel that same evening.

" What is his position in the portrait ? "

" He is standing with his hat in his hand."

She was able to see into this card, this white pasteboard, as into a mirror. The young women, terrified, cried : " Stop ! Enough ! Enough ! "

But the doctor said to her impressively : " You will get up to-morrow at eight o'clock ; you will then go to your cousin at his hotel and you will ask him to lend you five thousand francs that your husband has asked you to get, and that he will demand on his next leave."

Then he wakened her.

On my way back to the hotel I thought about this curious séance, and doubts assailed me—not of the absolutely unimpeachable good faith of my cousin, whom I had known like a sister since childhood, but of possible trickery on the part of the doctor. Might he not have concealed a mirror in his hand that he gave to the sleeping woman at the same time as the card ? Professional conjurers can do things just as strange.

I reached the hotel and went to bed.

Now, this morning about half-past eight I was wakened by my man, who said :

" Mme. Sablé wishes to see you, sir, at once."

I dressed hastily and had her shown up. She sat down without raising her veil and said very agitatedly with her eyes lowered :

" I have a great favour to ask you, my dear cousin."

" What is it, my dear ? "

" It upsets me terribly to have to ask you, but I must. I have simply got to have five thousand francs."

" What ! You ! "

" Yes—or rather my husband, who has asked me to get it for him."

I was so surprised that I stammered in reply. I wondered whether she and Dr. Parent were not having a joke at my expense, whether it were a little jest prepared beforehand and very well acted.

But as I watched her closely all my doubts vanished. The whole thing was so painful to her that she was trembling with anguish, and I realised that she was restraining her tears with difficulty.

I knew that she was quite wealthy so I went on :

" Do you mean to tell me that your husband can't put his hands on five thousand francs ? Think it over. Are you quite sure he told you to ask me ? "

" Yes . . . yes . . . I am sure."

" Has he written to you ? "

She hesitated again, reflecting. I guessed at the tortured workings of her mind. She did not know. She only knew that she had to borrow five thousand francs for her husband. She ventured a lie.

" Yes, he wrote to me."

" When ? You said nothing about it yesterday."

" It only came this morning."

" Can you show it to me ? "

" No . . . no . . . no . . . it is very intimate . . . too personal. . . . I—I've burned it ! "

" Is it because your husband is in debt ? "

She hesitated again, then she murmured : " I don't know."

I told her abruptly : " I just can't get hold of five thousand francs at the moment, my dear."

She gave a kind of agonised wail. " Oh, I beg you, I beg you to get it for me."

She became desperately worked up, clasping her hands as if she would have prayed to me. I heard the tone of her voice change. She wept and stammered, agonised, driven on by the irresistible order she had received.

" Oh, I implore you . . . if you knew what I am suffering. . . . I must have it to-day."

I took pity on her. " You shall have it soon, I promise you."

" Thank you ! Thank you ! " she cried. " How good you are ! "

I continued: " Do you remember what happened yesterday at your house ? "

" Yes."

" Do you remember that Dr. Parent put you to sleep ? "

" Yes."

" Well, then ! He commanded you to come to me this morning to borrow five thousand francs, and you are now obeying his suggestion."

She reflected for a moment, then replied : " Because my husband wants it."

For an hour I tried to convince her but all to no purpose.

When she had gone, I hurried to the doctor's house. He was just going out and he listened to me with a smile. Then he said :

" Now, do you believe ? "

" I must ! "

" Let us go and see your cousin."

She was already half-asleep on a couch, overcome with fatigue. The doctor felt her pulse, and gazed at her for some time, one hand raised towards her eyes that slowly closed under the irresistible compulsion of his magnetic power.

When she was fast asleep : " Your husband no longer needs the five thousand francs. You will, therefore, forget that you have begged your cousin to lend you the money ; and if he mentions it to you you will not understand."

Then he awakened her. I drew a note-case from my pocket. " Here is what you asked me for this morning, my dear."

She was so surprised that I did not dare to press the matter. I tried, all the same, to restore her memory, but she denied it hotly, thought that I was making fun of her, and finally began to get annoyed.

.   .   .   .

I have just got back to the hotel. The experience has upset me so much that I could not take my lunch.

19*th July*.—I told this story to quite a lot of people. They laughed at me. I don't know what to think. The wise man says " Perhaps ? "

21*st July*.—I dined at Bougival, then I passed the evening at the rowing-club dance. It is evidently all a question of places and surroundings. To believe in the supernatural on the island of Grenouillère would be the height of folly . . . but at the top of Mont-Saint-Michel ? . . . or in the Indies ? We are terribly influenced by our surroundings. I shall return home next week.

30*th July*.—I have been home since yesterday. All is well.

2*nd August*.—Nothing new. The weather is magnificent. I spend my days watching the Seine flow past.

4*th August*.—Quarrels among the servants. They say that someone breaks the glasses in the cupboards at night. My man blames the cook, who blames the housemaid, who blames the other two. Who is the culprit? It would take a clever man to say.

6th August.—This time I am not mad. I have seen . . . I have seen . . . I have seen . . . I can no longer doubt . . . I have seen . . . I am still frozen all over, still chilled to the marrow . . . I have seen !

At two o'clock I was walking in the broad sunlight in my rose garden . . . through the autumn roses that have just begun to flower.

Just as I stopped to look at a Géant des Batailles which bore three magnificent blooms, I saw, I distinctly saw the stem of one of these roses bend just beside me, as if an invisible hand had twisted it, then break, as if the hand had plucked it. Then the flower rose, following a curve that an arm would have made in carrying it to a mouth, and it hung suspended in the clear air, motionless, solitary, a terrifying scarlet splash three feet away from my eyes.

I lost my head and plunged forward to seize it. I found nothing. It had disappeared. Then I became furiously angry with myself : it isn't done for a reasonable, serious man to have such hallucinations !

But was it really a hallucination ? I turned round to look for the flower and I found it immediately under the bush, still fresh, between the two remaining roses on the branch.

I went back to the house, my senses reeling, for I am now sure, as sure as I am that day follows night, that there exists near to me an invisible being who lives on milk and water, who can touch things, take them and move them about, endowed therefore with a material nature although imperceptible to our senses—and who shares my roof. . . .

7th August.—I slept calmly. He drank the water in my carafe but he did not disturb my sleep.

I wonder if I am mad ? As I walk along the river bank in the bright sunlight, I am filled with doubts of my sanity, no longer vague, as hitherto, but precise uncompromising doubts. I have seen madmen, I have known those who were intelligent, lucid and discerning on every subject in life except one. They spoke with clarity, profundity and ease till suddenly their mind struck the reef of their madness and was torn in pieces, scattered and sunk in that terrifying and furious ocean of surging waves, fogs, squalls that we call " insanity."

I should certainly think I was mad, absolutely mad, if I

were not conscious, if I did not realise my condition; if I were not able to examine and analyse it with such complete lucidity. I can only be a sane man troubled with hallucination. An unknown malady must be afflicting my brain, one of those maladies that modern physiologists are trying to observe and define, and this malady must have opened a vast gulf in my mind, in the order and logic of my thoughts. Similar phenomena take place in a dream that takes us through the most unlikely phantasmagoria without our being surprised because the mechanism of judgment, the centre of intellectual reaction, is asleep, while the imaginative faculty is awake and hard at work. Can it be that one note on the invisible keyboard of my mind no longer sounds? Some men, as the result of an accident, lose their power to remember proper names, or verbs or figures. The localisation of the various divisions of thought is proved to-day. Is it therefore surprising that my faculty for controlling the unreality of certain hallucinations is temporarily out of order?

I thought of all this as I followed the course of the water. The sun had shed its glory on the river and intensified the beauty of the earth, saturating my being with love—of life, of the swallows whose graceful flight is a delight to the eye, and for the grasses by the water's edge whose whispering falls soothingly on my ears.

Gradually, however, an inexplicable uneasiness overcame me. It seemed as if some occult force was paralysing my movements, halting me, preventing me from going further, calling me back. I experienced an uncomfortable impulse to return, as when a loved one has been left ill at home, and a foreboding clouds the mind that the illness has taken a turn for the worse.

So, in spite of myself, I returned, sure that I should find bad news awaiting me at the house, a letter or a telegram. There was nothing, and I became more surprised and disquieted than if I had had yet another fantastic vision.

8th August.—I had an awful night. He did not manifest himself, but I feel him near me, spying on me, watching me, entering into me, and more redoubtable when he hides himself thus than if he indicated his invisible and constant presence by supernatural phenomena.

I managed to sleep, however.

9th August.—Nothing, but I am afraid.

10th August.—Nothing; what will happen to-morrow?

11th August.—Still nothing. I can no longer remain at

home with this fear and these thoughts engraved on my mind :
I shall go away.

12*th August.*—Ten o'clock in the evening. All day I wanted
to go away ; I have not been able to. I have tried to accomplish
this simple, easy act of liberty—to go out—to get into my
carriage and go to Rouen—I cannot. Why ?

13*th August.*—When one is attacked by certain maladies,
all the resources of one's physical being seem dried up, all
one's energy exhausted, muscles become relaxed, bones
go soft as flesh, and that flesh liquid as water. In a strange
and desolate way I experience this in my spiritual being. I
have no longer strength or courage. I am no longer master of
myself. I have not even power to exercise my will. I can
no longer will ; but someone wills for me—and I obey.

14*th August.*—I am lost. Someone has taken possession of
my soul and is master of it. Someone has taken possession
of my soul and is master of it ! Someone directs all my actions,
all my movements, all my thoughts. I am no longer anything
in myself, nothing but a spectator, enslaved and terrified of
everything that I do. I wish to go out. I cannot ! He does not
wish it ; and I remain, lost, trembling, in the chair where he
holds me seated. I desire only to get up, to raise myself, that
I may believe I am still my own master. I cannot ! I am
riveted to my seat ; and my seat is fast to the earth in such
a way that no force could ever shift us.

Then, suddenly, I must, I must, I must—must go to the
end of the garden to pick strawberries and eat them. And
I go. I pick strawberries and I eat them ! Oh, my God ! My
God ! My God ! Is there a God ? If there is one, deliver me,
save me, succour me ! Pardon me ! Have pity upon me !
Have mercy upon me ! Save me ! Oh, what suffering ! What
torture ! What horror !

15*th August.*—This is how my poor cousin was possessed
and dominated when she came to borrow five thousand francs
from me. She allowed an alien will to enter into her, like
another soul, a parasitic, tyrannical soul. Is the world coming
to an end ?

What is this thing that governs me, what is it, this invisible,
unrecognisable wanderer from a supernatural race ?

And so the unseen ones do exist ! Then why is it that,
since the world began, they have never manifested themselves
distinctly as they do to me now ? I have never read of anything that resembles what is happening in my house. Oh, if

I could only leave it, if I could only go away, fly away and never return ! I should be saved, but I cannot.

16*th August*.—I was able to escape for two hours to-day, like a prisoner who finds the door of his dungeon left open by chance. I suddenly felt that I was free and that he was far away. I ordered the carriage quickly and I reached Rouen. Oh, what joy it was to be able to say to a man : " Go to Rouen!" and be obeyed.

I stopped at the library and I begged them to lend me the long treatise by Dr. Herman Herestauss on the unseen inhabitants of the ancient and modern world.

Then, just as I was getting into my carriage, I wanted to say " To the station ! " and I shouted—I did not say the words, I shouted—in a voice so strong that the passers-by turned round—" Home ! " and I fell back, overwhelmed with anguish, on the cushions of my carriage. He had found me once more and taken command again.

17*th August*.—Oh, what a night ! What a night ! All the same, it seems I must congratulate myself. I read till one o'clock in the morning. Hermann Herestauss, doctor of philosophy and theogony, has set down the history and the manifestations of all those invisible beings that wander among men or are imagined by them. He describes their origins, their habitat, their powers. But none of them resembles the being who haunts me. It is as if man, since he began to think, has foreseen and feared a new type of being, stronger than himself, his successor in this world ; in whose image, feeling himself near to, and being unable to anticipate the nature of, this master, he has created in his terror all the grotesque inhabitants of the other world, dim phantoms born of fear.

Now, having read until one o'clock in the morning, I went and sat near my open window to cool my brow and my thoughts in the peaceful breath of the darkness.

It was fine and mild. How I should formerly have loved such a night !

There was no moon. The stars shimmered and gleamed in the depths of the black sky. Who dwells in those worlds ? What forms, what living things, what animals, what plants do they have ? What more can the sentient beings of those distant worlds know, than we do ? What more *can* they ? What do they see that we shall never be aware of ? One of them, perhaps, travelling through the void, will appear upon our earth to conquer it, as, in former days, the Normans crossed the sea to enslave weaker races than themselves. We are so weak, so defenceless, so ignorant, so minute, on this speck of dust that spins, dissolving, in a drop of water. And dreaming thus, I drowsed in the fresh evening air.

Having slept for about forty minutes, I opened my eyes without moving, awakened by I know not what vague, confused emotions. At first I saw nothing, then suddenly it seemed to me that a page of a book lying open on my table had turned over by itself. No draught had entered through my window. I was surprised and I waited. At the end of about four minutes I saw—yes, I saw with my own eyes—another page rise and turn over on to the preceding one, as if a finger had folded it back. My arm-chair was empty, or seemed empty, but I realised that he was there, himself, seated in my place, and that he was reading. With a furious leap, like a maddened beast that turns to rend its trainer, I crossed my room to seize him, to strangle him, to kill him. . . . But before I had reached it, my chair was overturned, as if he had fled in front of me. . . . My table rocked, my lamp fell and was extinguished, my window shut, as if a malefactor caught red-handed had flung himself into the night, slamming the shutters behind him.

So he had escaped. He was afraid, afraid of me ! Then . . . then . . . to-morrow . . . or the day after . . . or some day . . . I would be able to hold him in my grasp and crush him against the ground ! Even dogs sometimes will turn to bite and fly at their master's throat !

18th August.—I have thought about it all day. Oh yes, I shall obey him, submit to his compulsion, humble myself, meek, servile. He is the stronger. But an hour will come . . .

19th August.—I understand . . . I understand . . . I understand it all ! I have just read the following in the *Revue du Monde Scientifique*. "A somewhat curious item of news comes to us from Rio de Janeiro. Madness, an epidemic of madness comparable to the contagious manias which used to attack the people of Europe in the Middle Ages, is now raging in the province of San Paulo. The distracted inhabitants are leaving their houses, deserting their villages, abandoning their fields, believing themselves to be pursued, possessed and governed like a human herd by invisible though tangible beings, vampires of some kind, who feed on their vitality during sleep, and who drink water and milk as well, without appearing to touch any other kind of food or nourishment.

" Professor Don Pedro Henriquez, accompanied by several

medical authorities, has left for the province of San Paulo, to study on the spot the origin and symptoms of this surprising madness, and to suggest to the Emperor such measures as he considers most likely to restore the delirious inhabitants to sanity."

Ah ! Ah ! I remember, I remember now the lovely Brazilian three-master that sailed up the Seine past my windows on the 8th of May last ! I thought she was so pretty, so white, so gay ! The Being was on board, coming from over there, the birthplace of his race ! And he has seen me. He saw my white house too, and he has jumped from the vessel to the shore. Oh, my God !

In this hour I am aware, I have guessed it: the reign of man is at an end.

He has come, that One foreshadowed in the dawning terrors of primitive peoples. He who was exorcised by troubled priests, evoked in the darkness of night by warlocks without their ever seeing him materialise, to whom the prevision of the temporary masters of this world gave all the monstrous or gracious shapes of gnomes, spirits, jinns, fairies and hobgoblins. After the crude conceptions of primitive dismay, more en-lightened men have seen him with clearer vision. Mesmer guessed at his existence, and for ten years now doctors have divined exactly the nature of his power before he himself had exercised it. They have played with this weapon of the new god, the domination of a mysterious will over the enslaved soul of humanity. They have called it magnetism, hypnotism, suggestion—what you will. I have seen them amusing them-selves with this horrible power like foolish children. Woe to us ! Woe to mankind ! He is here, the . . . the . . . what is his name . . . the . . . it seems to me that he calls out his name and I cannot hear it . . . the . . . yes . . . he is shout-ing it . . . I am listening . . . I cannot hear . . . again . . . the . . . Horla . . . I heard . . . the Horla . . . it is he . . . the Horla . . . he is here ! . . .

Ah, the vulture has eaten the dove, the wolf has eaten the lamb ; the lion has devoured the sharp-horned buffalo ; man has killed the lion with arrow, spear and gun ; but the Horla will make of man what we have made of the horse and the cow : his thing, his servant, and his food, by the mere force of his will. Woe to us !

Sometimes, however, the beast rebels and kills his tamer. . . . I also would like . . . I might be able . . . but I must know him, touch him, see him ! Scientists say that the eye of an

animal is different from ours, and does not see as ours does . . .
and my eye cannot show me the newcomer who oppresses me.

Why ? Oh ! I remember now the words of the monk at
Mont-Saint-Michel : " Do we see the hundred-thousandth
part of what exists ? Take the wind, for instance, the greatest
force in nature, which throws men down, shatters buildings,
uproots trees, piles up the sea into billowing mountains, destroys cliffs and flings great ships upon the coast, the wind that
kills, that whistles, that whines, that roars—have you seen it,
can you see it ? Nevertheless, it exists."

And I considered further : my eye so weak, so imperfect,
that it does not even distinguish solid bodies if they are transparent, like glass . . . if a mirror without backing bars my
way I throw myself against it as a bird in a room shatters itself
upon the window pane. A thousand other things besides
deceive and mislead it. Is it, therefore, surprising that it cannot
see a new substance through which the light can pass.

A new being ! Why not ? He must assuredly come. Why
should we be the last ? Unlike all created beings before us,
he is invisible to us. It is because his nature is more perfect,
his body finer and more finished than ours—ours so feeble, so
clumsily conceived, encumbered with organs always tired,
always strained, like too-complex springs, which lives like a
plant or a beast, drawing its nourishment with difficulty from
the air, from green things, and from flesh. Living machine,
a prey to illness, deformity and corruption, short-winded, ill-
regulated, childish and fantastic, ingeniously ill-made, clumsy
and insecure, a rough sketch of a being who might become
intelligent and noble !

We are one of a very few types that have appeared in the
world from the bivalve to man. Why not one more, once the
period is ended that separates each successive appearance of a
new type ?

Why not one more ? Why not also new kinds of trees with
huge and blazing flowers perfuming the air for miles around ?
Why not other elements than fire, air, earth, and water ?—
they are four, nothing but four, these foster-fathers of our
being. What a pity ! Why not forty, four hundred, four thousand ! How poor, mean, and wretched is life ! Grudgingly
given, poorly conceived, heavily executed ! Consider the grace of
the elephant and the hippopotamus ! The elegance of the camel !

But, you say, look at the butterfly ! A winged flower ! I
can imagine one vast as a hundred worlds, with wings, shape,

beauty, colour and movement I cannot find words to describe. But I can visualise it . . . it flits from star to star, refreshing and perfuming them with the soft, gracious wind of its passing. And the inhabitants of the upper air watch it pass in an ecstasy of joy !

. . . .

What is the matter with me ? It is he, he, the Horla, who is haunting me, who makes me imagine these fantasies. He is in me, he is becoming my very soul . . . I will kill him !

19*th August*.—I will kill him. I have seen him ! I was sitting yesterday evening at my table, and I pretended to be absorbed in my writing. I knew well that he would come prowling round near me, so close that I might perhaps be able to touch him, to seize him ? And then ! . . . Then I should have the courage of desperation ; I should use my hands, my knees, my breast, my head, my teeth, to strangle him, crush him, tear him, rend him . . .

With every nerve tensed and alert, I watched for him. I had lit both my lamps and the eight candles on my mantelpiece, as if I might be able to see him better in this brightness.

In front of me was my bed, an old oak fourposter ; to the right, the mantelpiece; to the left, my door, carefully closed after I had left it open for a long time to attract him ; behind me, a very tall wardrobe with a mirror that I used every day to shave and dress by, and in which I had the habit of looking at myself from head to foot each time I passed.

Well, I pretended to write to deceive him, for he was spying on me too ; and suddenly I felt I was certain that he was there, that he was reading over my shoulder, almost brushing my ear.

I stood up, my hands outstretched, turning so quickly that I almost fell, and do you know . . . though it was as bright as day, I could not see myself in the glass ! . . . It was blank, transparent, deep, filled with light ! I was not reflected in it . . . and I was standing in front of it ! I could see the wide, clear glass from top to bottom, and I stared at it with starting eyes. I dared not advance, I dared not make a movement, knowing well, however, that he was there, whose impalpable body had devoured my reflection, but that he would escape me still.

How frightened I was ! Then suddenly I began to see myself in a mist at the bottom of the mirror, as if seen through a sheet of water, and it seemed to me as if this water flowed from left to right, slowly, leaving my image to become more distinct each moment. It was like the passing of an eclipse. Whatever was hiding me did not appear to have a sharply defined outline but a kind of opaque transparency that gradually cleared.

At last I could see myself distinctly, just as I saw myself every day.

I had seen him ! The horror of it is with me still, and makes me shudder.

20th August.—Kill him, but how—since I cannot touch him ? Poison ? But he would see me put it in the water ; and perhaps our poisons would not affect an immaterial body. No . . . no . . . they undoubtedly would not. . . . Then how . . . how . . .

21st August.—I sent for a locksmith from Rouen and have ordered iron shutters for my room as they have in Paris on the ground floor of certain hotels for fear of thieves. He is to make me a similar kind of door as well. Everyone thinks me a coward, but I don't care ! . . .

.   .   .   .

10th September.—*Rouen, Hôtel Continental.*—It is done . . . it is done . . . but is he dead ? My brain reels with what I have seen.

Yesterday, after the locksmith had put up my shutters and my iron door, I left everything open until midnight, although it began to get cold.

All at once I felt that he was there, and I was filled with a mad joy. I got up slowly and I walked up and down for a long time, so that he would suspect nothing : then I took off my boots and carelessly drew on my slippers ; next I closed my iron shutters and, sauntering towards the door, I locked it too. Going then to the window, I secured it with a padlock, putting the key in my pocket.

Suddenly I realised that he was prowling anxiously round me, that he was afraid in his turn, that he was commanding me to open the door. I almost yielded ; I did not yield, but with my back to the door, I set it ajar, just wide enough for me to slip out backwards, and as I am very tall, my head touched the lintel. I was sure that he could not have escaped me, and I shut him in, all alone, all alone. I had him at last ! Then I ran downstairs ; I took two lamps in my drawing-room which is beneath my bedroom and emptied all the oil on the carpet, the furniture, everywhere ; then I lit it, and escaped, after having double locked the main door.

And I went and hid myself at the bottom of the garden, in a clump of laurels. How long it took, how long ! Everything was black, silent, motionless ; not a breath of air, not a star, with mountains of unseen clouds that weighed heavily, so heavily, on my spirits.

I watched my house and I waited. How long it took ! I began to think that the fire had gone out by itself, or that He had put it out, when one of the lower windows collapsed under the blast of the fire, and a flame, a huge red and yellow flame, a long, curling, caressing flame, leapt up the white wall, to lick the roof itself. A glow of light appeared in the trees, in the branches and the leaves, and a shadow, a shadow of fear ran through them ! The birds awakened, a dog howled ; I thought daybreak was near. Soon two other windows burst, and I saw that the whole of the lower half of my house was one terrifying furnace. But a cry, a horrible, piercing, agonised cry, a woman's cry, stabbed the darkness, and two skylights opened. I had forgotten my servants ! I saw their distraught faces and their waving arms. . . .

Then, frantic with horror, I started to run towards the village, screaming " Help ! Help ! Fire ! Fire ! " I met some people already on their way, and I turned back with them to watch.

The house was now nothing more than a horrible and magnificent funeral pyre, a monstrous pyre lighting the entire earth, a pyre that was consuming men and consuming Him, Him, my prisoner, the new Being, the new Master, the Horla !

Suddenly the whole roof fell in and a volcano of flames rushed heavenwards.

Through all the windows open on the furnace I watched the fire, and I reflected that he was there, in that oven, dead. . . .

Dead ? Perhaps ? . . . His body ? Perhaps his body, through which light passed, could not be destroyed by the means that kill our bodies.

Suppose he was not dead. . . . Only time, perhaps, has power over the Invisible and Dreadful One. Why should this transparent, unrecognisable body, this body of the spirit, fear sickness, wounds, disease, premature destruction ?

Premature destruction ? The source of all human terror ! After man, the Horla—after man who can die any day, any hour, any moment, by every kind of accident, comes the Horla who can only die on his appointed day, hour, minute, then only because he has reached the limit of his existence !

No . . . no . . . there's no doubt about it, no doubt about it . . . he is not dead . . . and so . . . so . . . I must kill myself, *myself*. . . .

THE HAUNTED AND THE HAUNTERS
E. Bulwer Lytton

A FRIEND of mine, who is a man of letters and a philosopher, said to me one day, as if between jest and earnest—"Fancy! since we last met, I have discovered a haunted house in the midst of London."

"Really haunted?—and by what?—ghosts?"

"Well, I can't answer these questions—all I know is this—six weeks ago I and my wife were in search of a furnished apartment. Passing a quiet street, we saw on the window of one of the houses a bill, 'Apartments Furnished.' The situation suited us : we entered the house—liked the rooms—engaged them by the week—and left them the fourth day. No power on earth could have reconciled my wife to stay longer, and I don't wonder at it."

"What did you see?"

"Excuse me—I have no desire to be ridiculed as a superstitious dreamer—nor, on the other hand, could I ask you to accept on my affirmation what you would hold to be incredible without the evidence of your own senses. Let me only say this, it was not so much what we saw or heard (in which you might fairly suppose that we were the dupes of our own excited fancy, or the victims of imposture in others) that drove us away, as it was an undefinable terror which seized both of us whenever we passed by the door of a certain unfurnished room, in which we neither saw nor heard anything. And the strangest marvel of all was, that for once in my life I agreed with my wife—silly woman though she be—and allowed, after the third night, that it was impossible to stay a fourth in that house. Accordingly, on the fourth morning, I summoned the woman who kept the house and attended on us, and told her that the rooms did not quite suit us, and we would not stay out our week. She said, dryly : ' I know why ; you have stayed longer than any other lodger ; few ever stayed a second night ; none, before you, a third. But I take it they have been very kind to you.'

" ' They—who ? ' I asked, affecting a smile.

" ' Why, they who haunt the house, whoever they are. I don't mind them ; I remember them many years ago, when I lived in this house, not as a servant ; but I know they will be the death of me some day. I don't care—I'm old, and must die soon, anyhow ; and then I shall be with them, and in this house still.' The woman spoke with so dreary a calmness, that really it was a sort of awe that prevented my conversing with her further. I paid for my week, and too happy were I and my wife to get off so cheaply."

" You excite my curiosity," said I ; " nothing I should like better than to sleep in a haunted house. Pray give me the address of the one which you left so ignominiously."

My friend gave me the address ; and when we parted, I walked straight towards the house thus indicated.

It is situated on the north side of Oxford Street, in a dull but respectable thoroughfare. I found the house shut up— no bill at the window, and no response to my knock. As I was turning away, a beer-boy, collecting pewter pots at the neighbouring areas, said to me, " Do you want any one in that house, sir ? "

" Yes, I heard it was to let."

" Let !—why, the woman who kept it is dead—has been dead these three weeks, and no one can be found to stay there, though Mr. J—— offered ever so much. He offered mother, who chars for him, £1 a week just to open and shut the windows, and she would not."

" Would not !—and why ? "

" The house is haunted ; and the old woman who kept it was found dead in her bed, with her eyes wide open. They say the devil strangled her."

" Pooh !—you speak of Mr. J——. Is he the owner of the house ? "

" Yes."

" Where does he live ? "

" In G—— Street, No. —."

" What is he ?—in any business ? "

" No, sir—nothing particular ; a single gentleman."

I gave the pot-boy the gratuity earned by his liberal information, and proceeded to Mr. J——, in G—— Street, which was close by the street that boasted the haunted house. I was lucky enough to find Mr. J—— at home—an elderly man, with intelligent countenance and prepossessing manners.

I communicated my name and my business frankly. I said I heard the house was considered to be haunted—that I had a strong desire to examine a house with so equivocal a reputation—that I should be greatly obliged if he would allow me to hire it, though only for a night. I was willing to pay for that privilege whatever he might be inclined to ask.

" Sir," said Mr. J——, with great courtesy, " the house is at your service, for as short or as long a time as you please. Rent is out of the question—the obligation will be on my side should you be able to discover the cause of the strange phenomena which at present deprive it of all value. I cannot let it, for I cannot even get a servant to keep it in order or answer the door. Unluckily, the house is haunted, if I may use that expression, not only by night, but by day ; though at night the disturbances are of a more unpleasant and sometimes of a more alarming character.

" The poor old woman who died in it three weeks ago was a pauper whom I took out of a workhouse, for in her childhood she had been known to some of my family, and had once been in such good circumstances that she had rented that house of my uncle. She was a woman of superior education and strong mind, and was the only person I could ever induce to remain in the house. Indeed, since her death, which was sudden, and the coroner's inquest, which gave it a notoriety in the neighbourhood, I have so despaired of finding any person to take charge of it, much more a tenant, that I would willingly let it rent-free for a year to any one who would pay its rates and taxes."

" How long is it since the house acquired this sinister character ? "

" That I can scarcely tell you, but very many years since. The old woman I spoke of said it was haunted when she rented it between thirty and forty years ago. The fact is that my life has been spent in the East Indies and in the civil service of the Company. I returned to England last year on inheriting the fortune of an uncle, amongst whose possessions was the house in question. I found it shut up and uninhabited. I was told that it was haunted, that no one would inhabit it.

I smiled at what seemed to me so idle a story. I spent some money in repainting and roofing it—added to its old-fashioned furniture a few modern articles—advertised it, and obtained a lodger for a year. He was a colonel retired on half-pay. He came in with his family, a son and a daughter, and four or five servants : they all left the house the next day, and although they deponed that they had all seen something different, that something was equally terrible to all. I really could not in conscience sue, or even blame, the colonel for breach of agreement.

"Then I put in the old woman I have spoken of ; and she was empowered to let the house in apartments. I never had one lodger who stayed more than three days. I do not tell you their stories—to no two lodgers have there been exactly the same phenomena repeated. It is better that you should judge for yourself, than enter the house with an imagination influenced by previous narratives ; only be prepared to see and to hear something or other, and take whatever precautions you yourself please."

"Have you never had a curiosity yourself to pass a night in that house ? "

"Yes. I passed not a night, but three hours in broad daylight alone in that house. My curiosity is not satisfied, but it is quenched. I have no desire to renew the experiment. You cannot complain, you see, sir, that I am not sufficiently candid ; and unless your interest be exceedingly eager and your nerves unusually strong, I honestly add that I advise you *not* to pass a night in that house."

"My interest *is* exceedingly keen," said I, "and though only a coward will boast of his nerves in situations wholly unfamiliar to him, yet my nerves have been seasoned in such variety of danger that I have the right to rely on them—even in a haunted house."

Mr. J—— said very little more ; he took the keys of the house out of his bureau, gave them to me—and thanking him cordially for his frankness, and his urbane concession to my wish, I carried off my prize.

Impatient for the experiment, as soon as I reached home I summoned my confidential servant,—a young man of gay spirits, fearless temper, and as free from superstitious prejudice as any one I could think of.

"F——," said I, "you remember in Germany how disappointed we were at not finding a ghost in that old castle, which was said to be haunted by a headless apparition ? Well, I have heard of a house in London which, I have reason to hope, is decidedly haunted. I mean to sleep there to-night. From what I hear, there is no doubt that something will allow itself to be seen or to be heard—something, perhaps, excessively horrible. Do you think, if I take you with me, I may rely on your presence of mind, whatever may happen ? "

" Oh, sir ! pray trust me," answered F——, grinning with delight.

" Very well—then here are the keys of the house—this is the address. Go now—select for me any bedroom you please ; and since the house has not been inhabited for weeks, make up a good fire—air the bed well—see, of course, that there are candles as well as fuel. Take with you my revolver and my dagger—so much for my weapons—arm yourself equally well ; and if we are not a match for a dozen ghosts, we shall be but a sorry couple of Englishmen."

I was engaged for the rest of the day on business so urgent that I had not leisure to think much on the nocturnal adventure to which I had plighted my honour. I dined alone, and very late, and while dining, read, as is my habit. The volume I selected was one of Macaulay's *Essays*. I thought to myself that I would take the book with me ; there was so much of healthfulness in the style, and practical life in the subjects, that it would serve as an antidote against the influences of superstitious fancy.

Accordingly, about half-past nine, I put the book into my pocket, and strolled leisurely towards the haunted house. I took with me a favourite dog—an exceedingly sharp, bold, and vigilant bull-terrier—a dog fond of prowling about strange ghostly corners and passages at night in search of rats—a dog of dogs for a ghost.

It was a summer night, but chilly, the sky somewhat gloomy and overcast. Still, there was a moon—faint and sickly, but still a moon—and if the clouds permitted, after midnight it would be brighter.

I reached the house, knocked, and my servant opened with a cheerful smile.

" All right, sir, and very comfortable."

" Oh ! " said I, rather disappointed ; " have you not seen nor heard anything remarkable ? "

" Well, sir, I must own I have heard something queer."

" What ?—what ? "

" The sound of feet pattering behind me ; and once or twice small noises like whispers close at my ear—nothing more."

" You are not at all frightened ? "

" I I not a bit of it, sir " ; and the man's bold look re-assured me on one point—viz. that, happen what might, he would not desert me.

We were in the hall, the street-door closed, and my attention was now drawn to my dog. He had at first run in eagerly enough, but had sneaked back to the door, and was scratching and whining to get out. After patting him on the head, and encouraging him gently, the dog seemed to reconcile himself to the situation and followed me and F—— through the house, but keeping close at my heels instead of hurrying in-quisitively in advance, which was his usual and normal habit in all strange places. We first visited the subterranean apart-ments, the kitchen and other offices, and especially the cellars, in which last there were two or three bottles of wine still left in a bin, covered with cobwebs, and evidently, by their appear-ance, undisturbed for many years. It was clear that the ghosts were not wine-bibbers.

For the rest we discovered nothing of interest. There was a gloomy little backyard, with very high walls. The stones of this yard were very damp—and what with the damp, and what with the dust and smoke-grime on the pavement, our feet left a slight impression where we passed. And now appeared the first strange phenomenon witnessed by myself in this strange abode. I saw, just before me, the print of a foot suddenly form itself, as it were. I stopped, caught hold of my servant, and pointed to it. In advance of that footprint as suddenly dropped another. We both saw it. I advanced quickly to the place ; the footprint kept advancing before me, a small footprint—the foot of a child : the impression was too faint thoroughly to distinguish the shape, but it seemed to us both that it was the print of a naked foot. This phenomenon ceased when we arrived at the opposite wall, nor did it repeat itself on returning.

We remounted the stairs, and entered the rooms on the ground floor, a dining parlour, a small back-parlour, and a still smaller third room that had been probably appropriated to a footman—as still as death. We then visited the drawing-rooms, which seemed fresh and new. In the front room I seated myself in an armchair. F—— placed on 'he table the candlestick with which he had lighted us. I told him to shut the door. As he turned to do so, a chair opposite to me moved from the wall quickly and noiselessly, and dropped itself about a yard from my own chair, immediately fronting it.

"Why, this is better than the turning-tables," said I, with a half-laugh—and as I laughed, my dog put back his head and howled.

F——, coming back, had not observed the movement of the chair. He employed himself now in stilling the dog. I continued to gaze on the chair, and fancied I saw on it a pale blue misty outline of a human figure, but an outline so indistinct that I could only distrust my own vision. The dog now was quiet. " Put back that chair opposite to me," said I to F—— ; " put it back to the wall."

F—— obeyed. " Was that you, sir ? " said he, turning abruptly.

" I—what ? "

" Why, something struck me. I felt it sharply on the shoulder—just here."

" No," said I. " But we have jugglers present, and though we may not discover their tricks, we shall catch *them* before they frighten *us*."

We did not stay long in the drawing-rooms—in fact, they felt so damp and so chilly that I was glad to get to the fire upstairs. We locked the doors of the drawing-rooms—a precaution which, I should observe, we had taken with all the rooms we had searched below. The bedroom my servant had selected for me was the best on the floor—a large one, with two windows fronting the street. The four-posted bed, which took up no inconsiderable space, was opposite to the fire, which burned clear and bright ; a door in the wall to the left, between the bed and the window, communicated with the room which my servant appropriated to himself.

This last was a small room with a sofa-bed, and had no communication with the landing-place, no other door but that which conducted to the bedroom I was to occupy. On either side of my fireplace was a cupboard, without locks, flushed with the wall, and covered with the same dull-brown paper. We examined these cupboards—only hooks to suspend female dresses—nothing else ; we sounded the walls—evidently solid—the outer walls of the building. Having finished the survey of these apartments, warmed myself a few moments, and lighted my cigar, I then, still accompanied by F——, went forth to complete my reconnoitre. In the landing-place there was another door; it was closed firmly. "Sir," said my servant in surprise, "I unlocked this door with all the others when I first came; it cannot have got locked from the inside, for it is a——"

Before he had finished his sentence the door, which neither of us then was touching, opened quietly of itself. We looked at each other a single instant. The same thought seized both —some human agency might be detected here. I rushed in first, my servant followed. A small blank dreary room without furniture—a few empty boxes and hampers in a corner—a small window—the shutters closed—not even a fire place—no other door but that by which we had entered—no carpet on the floor, and the floor seemed very old, uneven, worm-eaten, mended here and there, as was shown by the whiter patches on the wood; but no living being, and no visible place in which a living being could have hidden. As we stood gazing around, the door by which we had entered closed as quietly as it had before opened : we were imprisoned.

For the first time I felt a creep of undefinable horror. Not so my servant. "Why, they don't think to trap us, sir; I could break that trumpery door with a kick of my boot."

"Try first if it will open to your hand," said I, shaking off the vague apprehension that had seized me, "while I open the shutters and see what is without."

I unbarred the shutters—the window looked on the little backyard I have before described; there was no ledge without —nothing but sheer descent. No man getting out of that window would have found any footing till he had fallen on the stones below.

F——, meanwhile, was vainly attempting to open the door. He now turned round to me, and asked my permission to use force. And I should here state, in justice to the servant, that, far from evincing any superstitious terrors, his nerve, composure, and even gaiety amidst circumstances so extraordinary compelled my admiration, and made me congratulate myself on having secured a companion in every way fitted to the occasion. I willingly gave him the permission he required. But though he was a remarkably strong man, his force was as idle as his milder efforts; the door did not even shake to his stoutest kick. Breathless and panting, he desisted. I then tried the door myself, equally in vain.

As I ceased from the effort, again that creep of horror

came over me ; but this time it was more cold and stubborn.
I felt as if some strange and ghastly exhalation were rising
up from the chinks of that rugged floor, and filling the atmosphere with a venomous influence hostile to human life. The
door now very slowly and quietly opened as of its own accord.
We preciptated ourselves into the landing-place. We both
saw a large pale light—as large as the human figure, but shapeless and unsubstantial—move before us, and ascend the stairs
that led from the landing into the attics. I followed the light,
and my servant followed me. It entered, to the right of the
landing, a small garret, of which the door stood open. I entered
in the same instant. The light then collapsed into a small
globule, exceedingly brilliant and vivid ; rested a moment on
a bed in the corner, quivered, and vanished. We approached
the bed and examined it—a half-tester, such as is commonly
found in attics devoted to servants. On the drawers that stood
near it we perceived an old faded silk kerchief, with the needle
still left in a rent half repaired. The kerchief was covered with
dust ; probably it had belonged to the old woman who had last
died in that house, and this might have been her sleeping-room.

I had sufficient curiosity to open the drawers ; there were
a few odds and ends of female dress, and two letters tied
round with a narrow ribbon of faded yellow. I took the
liberty to possess myself of the letters. We found nothing
else in the room worth noticing—nor did the light reappear ;
but we distinctly heard, as we turned to go, a pattering footfall
on the floor—just before us. We went through the other
attics (in all, four), the footfall still preceding us. Nothing to
be seen—nothing but the footfall heard. I had the letters in
my hand ; just as I was descending the stairs I distinctly felt
my wrist seized, and a faint, soft effort made to draw the letters
from my clasp. I only held them the more tightly, and the
effort ceased.

We regained the bed-chamber appropriated to myself,
and I then remarked that my dog had not followed us when
we had left it. He was thrusting himself close to the fire,
and trembling. I was impatient to examine the letters ; and
while I read them, my servant opened a little box in which
he had deposited the weapons I had ordered him to bring,
took them out, placed them on a table close at my bed-head,
and then occupied himself in soothing the dog, who, however,
seemed to heed him very little.

The letters were short—they were dated ; the dates

exactly thirty-five years ago. They were evidently from a lover to his mistress, or a husband to some young wife. Not only the terms of expression, but a distinct reference to a former voyage indicated the writer to have been a seafarer. The spelling and handwriting were those of a man imperfectly educated, but still the language itself was forcible. In the expressions of endearment there was a kind of rough wild love ; but here and there were dark unintelligible hints at some secret not of love—some secret that seemed of crime. "We ought to love each other," was one of the sentences I remember, "for how every one else would execrate us if all was know." Again : "Don't let anyone be in the same room with you at night—you talk in your sleep." And again : "What's done can't be undone ; and I tell you there's nothing against us unless the dead could come to life." Here there was underlined in a better handwriting (a female's), "They do !" At the end of the letter latest in date the same female hand had written these words : "Lost at sea the 4th of June, the same day as——"

I put down the letters, and began to muse over their contents.

Fearing, however, that the train of thought into which I fell might unsteady my nerves I fully determined to keep my mind in a fit state to cope with whatever of marvellous the advancing night might bring forth. I roused myself—laid the letters on the table—stirred up the fire, which was still bright and cheering—and opened my volume of Macaulay. I read quietly enough till about half-past eleven. I then threw myself dressed upon the bed, and told my servant he might retire to his own room, but must keep himself awake. I bade him leave open the door between the two rooms. Thus alone, I kept two candles burning on the table by my bed-head. I placed my watch beside the weapons, and calmly resumed my Macaulay.

Opposite to me the fire burned clear ; and on the hearth-rug, seemingly asleep, lay the dog. In about twenty minutes I felt an exceedingly cold air pass by my cheek, like a sudden draught. I fanced the door to my right, communicating with the landing-place, must have got open ; but no—it was closed. I then turned my glance to my left, and saw the flame of the candles violently swayed as by a wind. At the same moment the watch beside the revolver softly slid from the table—softly, softly—no visible hand—it was gone. I sprang up, seizing the revolver with the one hand, the dagger with the other ; I was not willing that my weapons should share the fate of the watch. Thus armed, I looked round the floor—no sign of the watch. Three slow, loud, distinct knocks were now heard at the bed-head ; my servant called out, " Is that you, sir ? "

" No ; be on your guard."

The dog now roused himself and sat on his haunches, his ears moving quickly backwards and forwards. He kept his eyes fixed on me with a look so strange that he concentrated all my attention on himself. Slowly he rose up, all his hair bristling, and stood perfectly rigid, and with the same wild stare. I had no time, however, to examine the dog. Presently my servant emerged from his room ; and if ever I saw horror in the human face, it was then. I should not have recognised him had we met in the streets, so altered was every lineament. He passed by me quickly, saying in a whisper that seemed scarcely to come from his lips, " Run—run ! ' it is after me." He gained the door to the landing, pulled it open, and rushed forth. I followed him into the landing involuntarily, calling him to stop ; but, without heeding me, he bounded down the stairs, clinging to the balusters, and taking several steps at a time. I heard, where I stood, the street-door open—heard it again clap to. I was left alone in the haunted house.

It was but for a moment that I remained undecided whether or not to follow my servant ; pride and curiosity alike forbade so dastardly a flight. I re-entered my room, closing the door after me, and proceeded cautiously into the interior chamber. I encountered nothing to justify my servant's terror. I again carefully examined the walls, to see if there were any concealed door. I could find no trace of one—not even a seam in the dull-brown paper with which the room was hung. How, then, had the Thing, whatever it was, which had so scared him, obtained ingress except through my own chamber ?

I returned to my room, shut and locked the door that opened upon the interior one, and stood on the hearth, expectant and prepared. I now perceived that the dog had slunk into an angle of the wall, and was pressing himself close against it, as if literally trying to force his way into it. I approached the animal and spoke to it ; the poor brute was evidently beside itself with terror. It showed all its teeth, the slaver dropping from its jaws, and would certainly have bitten me if I had touched it. It did not seem to recognise me. Whoever has seen at the Zoological Gardens a rabbit fascinated by a serpent, cowering in a corner, may form some idea of the anguish which the dog exhibited. Finding all efforts to soothe the animal in vain, and fearing that his bite might be as venomous in that state as if in the madness of hydrophobia, I left him alone, placed my weapons on the table beside the fire, seated myself, and recommenced my Macaulay.

Perhaps in order not to appear seeking credit for a courage, or rather a coolness, which the reader may conceive I exaggerate, I may be pardoned if I pause to indulge in one or two egotistical remarks.

As I hold presence of mind, or what is called courage, to be precisely proportioned to familiarity with the circumstances that lead to it, so I should say that I had been long sufficiently familiar with all experiments that appertain to the Marvellous. I had witnessed many very extraordinary phenomena in various parts of the world—phenomena that would be either totally disbelieved if I stated them, or ascribed to supernatural agencies. Now, my theory is that the Supernatural is the Impossible, and that what is called supernatural is only a something in the laws of nature of which we have been hitherto ignorant. Therefore, if a ghost rise before me, I have not the right to say, " So, then, the supernatural is possible," but rather, " So, then, the apparition of a ghost is, contrary to received opinion, within the laws of nature—*i.e.* not supernatural."

Now, in all that I had hitherto witnessed, and indeed in all the wonders which the amateurs of mystery in our age record as facts, a material living agency is always required. On the Continent you will find still magicians who assert that they can raise spirits. Assume for the moment that they assert truly, still the living material form of the magician is present ; and he is the material agency by which from some constitutional peculiarities, certain strange phenomena are represented to your natural senses.

Accept again, as truthful, the tales of Spirit Manifestation in America—musical or other sounds—writings on paper, produced by no discernible hand—articles of furniture moved about without apparent human agency—or the actual sight and touch of hands, to which no bodies seem to belong—still there must be found the *medium* or living being, with constitutional peculiarities capable of obtaining these signs. In fine, in all such marvels, supposing even that there is no imposture, there must be a human being like ourselves, by whom, or through whom, the effects presented to human beings are produced. It is so with the now familiar phenomena of mesmerism or electro-biology ; the mind of the person operated on is affected through a material living agent. Nor, supposing it true that a mesmerised patient can respond to the will or passes of a mesmeriser a hundred miles distant, is the response less occasioned by a material being ; it may be through a material fluid—call it Electric, call it Odic, call it what you will—which has the power of traversing space and passing obstacles, that the material effect is communicated from one to the other.

Hence all that I had hitherto witnessed, or expected to witness, in this strange house, I believed to be occasioned through some agency or medium as mortal as myself ; and this idea necessarily prevented the awe with which those who regard as supernatural things that are not within the ordinary operations of nature, might have been impressed by the adventures of that memorable night.

As, then, it was my conjecture that all that was presented, or would be presented, to my senses, must originate in some human being gifted by constitution with the power so to present them, and having some motive so to do, I felt an interest in my theory which, in its way, was rather philosophical than superstitious. And I can sincerely say that I was in as tranquil a temper for observation as any practical experimentalist could be in awaiting the effects of some rare though perhaps perilous chemical combination. Of course, the more I kept my mind detached from fancy, the more the temper fitted for observation would be obtained ; and I therefore riveted eye and thought on the strong daylight sense in the page of my Macaulay.

I now became aware that something interposed between the page and the light—the page was over-shadowed ; I looked up, and I saw what I shall find it very difficult, perhaps impossible, to describe.

It was a Darkness shaping itself out of the air in very undefined outline. I cannot say it was of a human form, and yet it had more resemblance to a human form, or rather shadow, than anything else. As it stood, wholly apart and distinct from the air and the light around it, its dimensions seemed gigantic, the summit nearly touching the ceiling. While I gazed, a feeling of intense cold seized me. An iceberg before me could not more have chilled me ; nor could the cold of an iceberg have been more purely physical. I feel convinced that it was not the cold caused by fear. As I continued to gaze, I thought—but this I cannot say with precision —that I distinguished two eyes looking down on me from the height. One moment I seemed to distinguish them clearly, the next they seemed gone ; but still two rays of a pale-blue light frequently shot through the darkness, as from the height on which I half-believed, half-doubted, that I had encountered the eyes.

I strove to speak—my voice utterly failed me ; I could only think to myself, " Is this fear ? it is *not* fear ! " I strove to rise—in vain ; I felt as if weighed down by an irresistible force. Indeed, my impression was that of an immense and overwhelming Power opposed to my volition ; that sense of utter inadequacy to cope with a force beyond men's, which one may feel *physically* in a storm at sea, in a conflagration, or when confronting some terrible wild beast, or rather, perhaps, the shark of the ocean, I felt *morally*. Opposed to my will was another will, as far superior to its strength as storm, fire, and shark are superior in material force to the force of men.

And now, as this impression grew on me, now came, at last, horror—horror to a degree that no words can convey. Still I retained pride, if not courage ; and in my own mind I said, " This is horror, but it is not fear ; unless I fear, I cannot be harmed ; my reason rejects this thing ; it is an illusion—I do not fear." With a violent effort I succeeded at last in stretching out my hand towards the weapon on the table ; as I did so, on the arm and shoulder I received a strange shock, and my arm fell to my side powerless. And now, to add to my horror, the light began slowly to wane from the candles—they were not, as it were, extinguished, but their flame seemed very gradually withdrawn ; it was the same with the fire—the light was extracted from the fuel ; in a few minutes the room was in utter darkness.

The dread that came over me, to be thus in the dark with that dark Thing, whose power was so intensely felt, brought a reaction of nerve. In fact, terror had reached that climax, that either my senses must have deserted me, or I must have burst through the spell. I did burst through it. I found voice, though the voice was a shriek. I remember that I broke forth with words like these—" I do not fear, my soul does not fear " ; and at the same time I found the strength to rise.

Still in that profound gloom I rushed to one of the windows—tore aside the curtain—flung open the shutters; my first thought was—LIGHT. And when I saw the moon high, clear, and calm, I felt a joy that almost compensated for the previous terror. There was the moon, there was also the light from the gas-lamps in the deserted, slumberous street. I turned to look back into the room; the moon penetrated its shadow very palely and partially—but still there was light. The dark Thing, whatever it might be, was gone—except that I could yet see a dim shadow which seemed the shadow of that shade, against the opposite wall.

My eye now rested on the table, and from under the table (which was without cloth or cover—an old mahogany round table) there rose a hand, visible as far as the wrist. It was a hand, seemingly, as much of flesh and blood as my own, but the hand of an aged person—lean, wrinkled, small too—a woman's hand.

That hand very softly closed on the two letters that lay on the table : hand and letters both vanished. There then came the same three loud measured knocks I had heard at the bed-head before this extraordinary drama had commenced.

As those sounds slowly ceased, I felt the whole room vibrate sensibly ; and at the far end there rose, as from the floor, sparks or globules like bubbles of light, many-coloured—green, yellow, fire-red, azure. Up and down, to and fro, hither, thither, as tiny will-o'-the-wisps, the sparks moved, slow or swift, each at its own caprice. A chair (as in the drawing-room below) was now advanced from the wall without apparent agency, and placed at the opposite side of the table. Suddenly, as forth from the chair, there grew a shape—a woman's shape. It was distinct as a shape of life—ghastly as a shape of death. The face was that of youth, with a strange mournful beauty ; the throat and shoulders were bare, the rest of the form in a loose robe of cloudy white. It began sleeking its long yellow hair, which fell over its shoulders ; its eyes were not turned towards me, but to the door ; it seemed listening, watching, waiting. The shadow of the shade in the background grew darker ; and again I thought I beheld the eyes gleaming out from the summit of the shadow—eyes fixed upon that shape.

As if from the door, though it did not open, there grew out another shape equally distinct, equally ghastly—a man's shape—a young man's. It was in the dress of the last century,

or rather in a likeness of such dress ; for both the male shape
and the female, though defined, were evidently unsubstantial,
impalpable—simulacra—phantasms ; and there was something incongruous, grotesque, yet fearful, in the contrast
between the elaborate finery, the courtly precision of that old-
fashioned garb, with its ruffles and lace and buckles, and the
corpse-like aspect and ghost-like stillness of the flitting wearer.
Just as the male shape approached the female, the dark Shadow
started from the wall, all three for a moment wrapped in
darkness. When the pale light returned, the two phantoms
were as if in the grasp of the Shadow that towered between
them ; and there was a bloodstain on the breast of the female ;
and the phantom-male was leaning on its phantom-sword, and
blood seemed trickling fast from the ruffles, from the lace ; and
the darkness of the intermediate Shadow swallowed them up
—they were gone. And again the bubbles of light shot, and
sailed, and undulated, growing thicker and thicker and more
wildly confused in their movements.

The closet-door to the right of the fireplace now opened,
and from the aperture there came the form of a woman, aged.
In her hand she held letters—the very letters over which I
had seen *the* Hand close ; and behind her I heard a footstep.
She turned round as if to listen, then she opened the letters
and seemed to read ; and over her shoulder I saw a livid face,
the face as of a man long drowned—bloated, bleached—sea-
weed tangled in its dripping hair ; and at her feet lay a form
as of a corpse and beside the corpse there cowered a child, a
miserable, squalid child, with famine in its cheeks and fear
in its eyes. And as I looked in the old woman's face, the
wrinkles and lines vanished, and it became a face of youth—
hard-eyed, stony, but still youth ; and the Shadow darted
forth and darkened over these phantoms as it had darkened
over the last.

Nothing now was left but the Shadow, and on that my
eyes were intently fixed, till again eyes grew out of the Shadow
—malignant, serpent eyes. And the bubbles of light again
rose and fell, and in their disordered, irregular, turbulent
maze, mingled with the wan moonlight. And now from these
globules themselves as from the shell of an egg, monstrous
things burst out ; the air grew filled with them ; larvæ so
bloodless and so hideous that I can in no way describe them
except to remind the reader of the swarming life which the
solar microscope brings before his eyes in a drop of water—

things transparent, supple, agile, chasing each other, devouring each other—forms like nought ever beheld by the naked eye. As the shapes were without symmetry, so their movements were without order. In their very vagrancies there was no sport ; they came round me and round, thicker and faster and swifter swarming over my head, crawling over my right arm, which was outstretched in involuntary command against all evil beings.

Sometimes I felt myself touched, but not by them ; invisible hands touched me. Once I felt the clutch as of cold soft fingers at my throat. I was still equally conscious that if I gave way to fear I should be in bodily peril ; and I concentrated all my faculties in the single focus of resisting, stubborn will. And I turned my sight from the Shadow—above all, from those strange serpent eyes—eyes that had now become distinctly visible. For there, though in nought else around me, I was aware that there was a *will*, and a will of ir tense, creative, working evil, which might crush down my own.

The pale atmosphere in the room began now to redden as if in the air of some near conflagration. The larvæ grew lurid as things that live in fire. Again the room vibrated ; again were heard the three measured knocks ; and again all things were swallowed up in the darkness of the dark Shadow, as if out of that darkness all had come, into that darkness all returned.

As the gloom receded, the Shadow was wholly gone. Slowly as it had been withdrawn, the flame grew again into the candles on the table, again into the fuel in the grate. The whole room came once more calmly, healthfully into sight.

The two doors were still closed, the door communicating with the servants' room still locked. In the corner of the wall, into which he had so convulsively niched himself, lay the dog. I called to him—no movement ; I approached—the animal was dead ; his eyes protruded ; his tongue out of his mouth ; the froth gathered round his jaws. I took him in my arms ; I brought him to the fire ; I felt acute grief for the loss of my poor favourite—acute self-reproach ; I accused myself of his death ; I imagined he had died of fright. But what was my surprise on finding that his neck was actually broken—actually twisted out of the vertebræ. Had this been done in the dark ?—must it not have been by a hand human as mine ?—must there not have been a human agency all the while in that room ? Good cause to suspect it. I cannot tell. I cannot do more than state the fact fairly ; the reader may draw his own inference.

Another surprising circumstance—my watch was restored to the table from which it had been so mysteriously withdrawn ; but it had stopped at the very moment it was so withdrawn ; nor, despite all the skill of the watchmaker, has it ever gone since—that is, it will go in a strange erratic way for a few hours, and then comes to a dead stop—it is worthless.

Nothing more chanced for the rest of the night. Nor, indeed, had I long to wait before the dawn broke. Not till it was broad daylight did I quit the haunted house. Before I did so, I revisited the little blind room in which my servant and myself had been for a time imprisoned. I had a strong impression—for which I could not account—that from that room had originated the mechanism of the phenomena—if I may use the term—which had been experienced in my chamber. And though I entered it now in the clear day, with the sun peering through the filmy window, I still felt, as I stood on its floor, the creep of the horror which I had first there experienced the night before, and which had been so aggravated by what had passed in my own chamber. I could not, indeed, bear to stay more than half a minute within those walls. I descended the stairs, and again I heard the footfall before me ; and when I opened the street door, I thought I could distinguish a very low laugh. I gained my own home, expecting to find my runaway servant there. But he had not presented himself ; nor did I hear more of him for three days, when I received a letter from him, dated from Liverpool, to this effect :—

" HONOURED SIR,—I humbly entreat your pardon, though I can scarcely hope that you will think I deserve it, unless— which Heaven forbid !—you saw what I did. I feel that it will be years before I can recover myself ; and as to being fit for service, it is out of the question. I am therefore going to my brother-in-law at Melbourne. The ship sails to-morrow. Perhaps the long voyage may set me up. I do nothing but start and tremble, and fancy It is behind me. I humbly beg you, honoured sir, to order my clothes, and whatever wages are due to me, to be sent to my mother's, at Walworth—John knows her address."

The letter ended with additional apologies, somewhat incoherent, and explanatory details as to effects that had been under the writer's charge.

This flight may perhaps warrant a suspicion that the man

wished to go to Australia, and had been somehow or other
fraudulently mixed up with the events of the night. I say
nothing in refutation of that conjecture ; rather, I suggest it
as one that would seem to many persons the most probable
solution of improbable occurrences. My own theory remained
unshaken. I returned in the evening to the house, to bring
away in a hack-cab the things I had left there, with my poor
dog's body. In this task I was not disturbed, nor did any incident worth note befall me, except that still, on ascending
and descending the stairs I heard the same footfall in advance.
On leaving the house, I went to Mr. J——'s. He was at
home. I returned him the keys, told him that my curiosity
was sufficiently gratified, and was about to relate quickly
what had passed, when he stopped me, and said, though
with much politeness, that he had no longer any interest in a
mystery which none had ever solved.

I determined at least to tell him of the two letters I had
read, as well as of the extraordinary manner in which they
had disappeared, and I then inquired if he thought they had
been addressed to the woman who had died in the house,
and if there were anything in her early history which could
possibly confirm the dark suspicions to which the letters
gave rise. Mr. J—— seemed startled, and, after musing a few
moments, answered, " I know but little of the woman's earlier
history, except, as I before told you, that her family were
known to mine. But you revive some vague reminiscences
to her prejudice. I will make inquiries, and inform you of
their result. Still, even if we could admit the popular superstition that a person who had been either the perpetrator or
the victim of dark crimes in life could revisit, as a restless
spirit, the scene in which those crimes had been committed,
I should observe that the house was infested by strange sights
and sounds before the old woman died—you smile—what
would you say ? "

" I would say this, that I am convinced, if we could get
to the bottom of these mysteries, we should find a living human
agency."

" What ! you believe it is all an imposture ? For what
object ? "

" Not an imposture in the ordinary sense of the word.
If suddenly I were to sink into a deep sleep, from which
you could not awake me, but in that sleep could answer
questions with an accuracy which I could not pretend to

when awake—tell you what money you had in your pocket —nay, describe your very thoughts—it is not necessarily an imposture, any more than it is necessarily supernatural. I should be, unconsciously to myself, under a mesmeric influence, conveyed to me from a distance by a human being who had acquired power over me by previous *rapport*."

" Granting mesmerism, so far carried, to be a fact, you are right. And you would infer from this that a mesmeriser might produce the extraordinary effects you and others have witnessed over inanimate objects—fill the air with sights and sounds ? "

" Or impress our senses with the belief in them—we never having been *en rapport* with the person acting on us ? No. What is commonly called mesmerism could not do this ; but there may be a power akin to mesmerism, and superior to it—the power that in the old days was called Magic. That such a power may extend to all inanimate objects of matter, I do not say ; but if so, it would not be against nature, only a rare power in nature which might be given to constitutions with certain peculiarities, and cultivated by practice to an extraordinary degree. That such a power might extend over the dead—that is, over certain thoughts and memories that the dead may still retain—and compel, not that which ought properly to be called the *soul*, and which is far beyond human reach, but rather a phantom of what has been most earth-stained on earth, to make itself apparent to our senses—is a very ancient though obsolete theory, upon which I will hazard no opinion. But I do not conceive the power would be supernatural.

" Let me illustrate what I mean from an experiment which Paracelsus describes as not difficult, and which the author of the *Curiosities of Literature* cites as credible : A flower perishes ; you burn it. Whatever were the elements of that flower while it lived are gone, dispersed, you know not whither ; you can never discover nor re-collect them. But you can, by chemistry, out of the burnt dust of that flower, raise a spectrum of the flower, just as it seemed in life. It may be the same with the human being. The soul has so much escaped you as the essence or elements of the flower. Still you may make a spectrum of it. And this phantom, though in the popular superstition it is held to be the soul of the departed, must not be confounded with the true soul ; it is but the eidolon of the dead form.

" Hence, like the best-attested stories of ghosts or spirits, the thing that most strikes us is the absence of what we hold to be soul—that is, of superior emancipated intelligence. They come for little or no object—they seldom speak, if they do come ; they utter no ideas above that of an ordinary person on earth. These American spirit-seers have published volumes of communications in prose and verse, which they assert to be given in the names of the most illustrious dead—Shakespeare, Bacon—heaven knows whom. Those communications, taking the best, are certainly not a whit of higher order than would be communications from living persons of fair talent and education ; they are wondrously inferior to what Bacon, Shakespeare and Plato said and wrote when on earth.

" Nor, what is more notable, do they ever contain an idea that was not on the earth before. Wonderful, therefore, as such phenomena may be (granting them to be truthful), I see much that philosophy may question, nothing that it is incumbent on philosophy to deny—viz. nothing supernatural. They are but ideas conveyed somehow or other (we have not yet discovered the means) from one mortal brain to another. Whether, in so doing, tables walk of their own accord, or fiend-like shapes appear in a magic circle, or bodiless hands rise and remove material objects, or a Thing of Darkness, such as presented itself to me, freeze our blood—still I am persuaded that these are but agencies conveyed, as by electric wires, to my own brain from the brain of another. In some constitutions there is a natural chemistry, and those may produce chemic wonders—in others a natural fluid, call it electricity, and these produce electric wonders. But they differ in this from Normal Science—they are alike objectless, purposeless, puerile, frivolous. They lead on to no grand results ; and therefore the world does not heed, and true sages have not cultivated them. But sure I am, that of all I saw or heard, a man, human as myself, was the remote originator ; and I believe unconsciously to himself as to the exact effects produced, for this reason : no two persons, you say, have ever told you that they experienced exactly the same thing. Well, observe, no two persons ever experience exactly the same dream. If this were an ordinary imposture, the machinery would be arranged for results that would but little vary ; if it were a supernatural agency permitted by the Almighty, it would surely be for some definite end.

" These phenomena belong to neither class ; my persuasion is, that they originate in some brain now far distant ; that that brain had no distinct volition in anything that occurred ; that what does occur reflects but its devious, motley, ever-shifting, half-formed thoughts ; in short, that it has been but the dreams of such a brain put into action and invested with a semi-substance. That this brain is of immense power, that it can set matter into movement, that it is malignant and destructive, I believe : some material force must have killed my dog ; it might, for aught I know, have sufficed to kill myself, had I been as subjugated by terror as the dog—had my intellect or my spirit given me no countervailing resistance in my will."

" It killed your dog ! that is fearful ! indeed, it is strange that no animal can be induced to stay in that house ; not even a cat. Rats and mice are never found in it."

" The instincts of the brute creation detect influences deadly to their existence. Man's reason has a sense less subtle, because it has a resisting power more supreme. But enough ; do you comprehend my theory ? "

" Yes, though imperfectly—and I accept any crotchet (pardon the word), however odd, rather than embrace at once the notion of ghosts and hobgoblins we imbibed in our nurseries. Still, to my unfortunate house the evil is the same. What on earth can I do with the house ? "

" I will tell you what I would do. I am convinced from my own internal feelings that the small unfurnished room at right angles to the door of the bedroom which I occupied, forms a starting-point or receptacle for the influences which haunt the house ; and I strongly advise you to have the walls opened, the floor removed—nay, the whole room pulled down. I observe that it is detached from the body of the house, built over the small back-yard, and could be removed without injury to the rest of the building."

" And you think, if I did that——"

" You would cut off the telegraph wires. Try it. I am so persuaded that I am right, that I will pay half the expense if you will allow me to direct the operations."

" Nay, I am well able to afford the cost ; for the rest, allow me to write to you."

About ten days afterwards I received a letter from Mr. J——, telling me that he had visited the house since I had seen him ; that he had found the two letters I had described replaced in the drawer from which I had taken them ; that he had read them with misgivings like my own ; that he had instituted a cautious inquiry about the woman to whom I rightly conjectured they had been written. It seemed that thirty-six years ago (a year before the date of the letters), she had married, against the wish of her relatives, an American of very suspicious character ; in fact, he was generally believed to have been a pirate. She herself was the daughter of very respectable tradespeople, and had served in the capacity of a nursery governess before her marriage. She had a brother, a widower, who was considered wealthy, and who had one child of about six years old. A month after the marriage, the body of this brother was found in the Thames, near London Bridge ; there seemed some marks of violence about his throat, but they were not deemed sufficient to warrant the inquest in any verdict other than that of " found drowned."

The American and his wife took charge of the little boy, the deceased brother having by his will left his sister the guardian of his only child—and in the event of the child's death, the sister inherited. The child died about six months afterwards—it was supposed to have been neglected and ill-treated. The neighbours deposed to have heard it shriek at night. The surgeon who had examined it after death, said that it was emaciated as if from want of nourishment, and the body was covered with livid bruises. It seemed that one winter night the child had sought to escape—crept out into the back-yard, tried to scale the wall—fallen back exhausted, and been found at morning on the stones in a dying state. But though there was some evidence of cruelty, there was none of murder ; and the aunt and her husband had sought to palliate cruelty by alleging the exceeding stubborness and perversity of the child, who was declared to be half-witted. Be that as it may, at the orphan's death the aunt inherited her brother's fortune.

Before the first wedded year was out, the American quitted England abruptly, and never returned to it. He obtained a cruising vessel, which was lost in the Atlantic two years after-wards. The widow was left in affluence ; but reverses of various kinds had befallen her ; a bank broke—an investment failed—she went into a small business and became insolvent —then she entered into service, sinking lower and lower, from housekeeper down to maid-of-all-work—never long retaining a place, though nothing peculiar against her character was ever alleged. She was considered sober, honest, and peculiarly quiet in her ways ; still nothing prospered with her. And so she had dropped into the workhouse, from which Mr. J—— had taken her, to be placed in charge of the very house which she had rented as mistress in the first year of her wedded life.

Mr. J—— added that he had passed an hour alone in the unfurnished room which I had urged him to destroy, and that his impressions of dread while there were so great, though he had neither heard nor seen anything, that he was eager to have the walls bared and the floors removed as I had suggested. He had engaged persons for the work, and would commence any day I would name.

The day was accordingly fixed. I repaired to the haunted house—we went into the blind dreary room, took up the skirting, and then the floor. Under the rafters, covered with rubbish, was found a trap-door, quite large enough to admit a man. It was closely nailed down, with clamps and rivets of iron. On removing these we descended into a room below, the existence of which had never been suspected. In this room there had been a window and a flue, but they had been bricked over, evidently for many years. By the help of candles we examined this place : it still retained some mouldering furniture—three chairs, an oak settee, a table—all of the fashion of about eighty years ago. There was a chest-of-drawers against the wall, in which we found, half-rotted away, old-fashioned articles of a man's dress, such as might have been worn eighty or a hundred years ago by a gentleman of some rank—costly steel buckles and buttons, like those yet worn in court dresses—a handsome court sword—in a waistcoat which had once been rich with gold lace, but which was now blackened and foul with damp, we found five guineas, a few silver coins, and an ivory ticket, probably for some place of entertainment long since passed away. But our main discovery was in a kind of iron safe fixed to the wall, the lock of which it cost us much trouble to get picked.

In this safe were three shelves and two small drawers. Ranged on the shelves were several small bottles of crystal, hermetically stopped. They contained colourless volatile essences, of what nature I shall say no more than that they were not poisons—phosphor and ammonia entered into some of them. There were also some very curious glass tubes, and a small pointed rod of iron, with a large lump of rock-crystal, and another of amber—also a loadstone of great power.

In one of the drawers we found a miniature portrait set in gold and retaining the freshness of its colours most remarkably, considering the length of time it had probably been there. The portrait was that of a man who might be somewhat advanced in middle life, perhaps forty-seven or forty-eight.

It was a most peculiar face—a most impressive face. If you could fancy some mighty serpent transformed into man, preserving in the human lineaments the old serpent type, you would have a better idea of that countenance than long descriptions can convey : the width and flatness of frontal— the tapering elegance of contour disguising the strength of the deadly jaw—the long, large, terrible eye, glittering and green as the emerald—and withal a certain ruthless calm, as if from the consciousness of an immense power. The strange thing was this—the instant I saw the miniature I recognised a startling likeness to one of the rarest portraits in the world— the portrait of a man of a rank only below that of royalty, who in his own day had made a considerable noise. History says little or nothing of him ; but search the correspondence of his contemporaries, and you find reference to his wild daring, his bold profligacy, his restless spirit, his taste for the occult sciences. While still in the meridian of life he died and was buried, so say the chronicles, in a foreign land. He died in time to escape the grasp of the law, for he was accused of crimes which would have given him to the headsman.

After his death, the portraits of him, which had been numerous, for he had been a munificent encourager of art, were bought up and destroyed—it was supposed by his heirs, who might have been glad could they have razed his very name from their splendid line. He had enjoyed a vast wealth ; a large portion of this was believed to have been embezzled by a favourite astrologer or soothsayer—at all events, it had unaccountably vanished at the time of his death. One portrait alone of him was supposed to have escaped the general destruction ; I had seen it in the house of a collector some months before. It had made on me a wonderful impression, as it does on all who behold it—a face never to be forgotten ; and there was that face in the miniature that lay within my hand. True, that in the miniature the man was a few years older than in the portrait I had seen, or than the original was even at the time of his death. But a few years !—why, between the date in which flourished that direful noble, and the date in which the miniature was evidently painted, there was an interval of more than two centuries. While I was thus gazing, silent and wondering, Mr. J—— said :

"But is it possible ? I have known this man."

" How—where ? " I cried.

" In India. He was high in the confidence of the Rajah of ——, and wellnigh drew him into a revolt which would have lost the Rajah his dominions. The man was a Frenchman— his name de V——, clever, bold, lawless. We insisted on his dismissal and banishment : it must be the same man—no two faces like his—yet this miniature seems nearly a hundred years old."

Mechanically I turned round the miniature to examine the back of it, and on the back was engraved a pentacle ; in the middle of the pentacle a ladder, and the third step of the ladder was formed by the date 1765. Examining still more minutely, I detected a spring ; this, on being pressed, opened the back of the miniature as a lid. Withinside the lid was engraved " Mariana to thee—Be faithful in life and in death to——" Here follows a name that I will not mention, but it was not unfamiliar to me. I had heard it spoken of by old men in my childhood as the same borne by a dazzling charlatan, who made a great sensation in London for a year or so, and had fled the country on the charge of a double murder within his own house—that of his mistress and his rival. I said nothing of this to Mr. J——, to whom reluctantly I resigned the miniature.

We had found no difficulty in opening the first drawer within the iron safe ; we found great difficulty in opening the second : it was not locked, but it resisted all efforts till we inserted in the chinks the edge of a chisel. When we had thus drawn it forth, we found a very singular apparatus in the nicest order. Upon a small thin book, or rather tablet, was placed a saucer of crystal ; this saucer was filled with a clear liquid—on that liquid floated a kind of compass, with a needle shifting rapidly round, but instead of the usual points of a compass were seven strange characters, not very unlike those used by astrologers to denote the planets. A very peculiar, but not strong nor displeasing odour came from this drawer, which was lined with a wood that we afterwards discovered to be hazel. Whatever the cause of this odour, it produced a material effect on the nerves. We all felt it, even the two workmen who were in the room—a creeping tingling sensation from the tips of the fingers to the roots of the hair. Impatient to examine the tablet, I removed the saucer. As I did so the needle of the compass went round and round with exceeding swiftness, and I felt a shock that ran through my whole frame, so that I dropped the saucer on the floor. The liquid was spilt —the saucer was broken—the compass rolled to the end of the room—and at that instant the walls shook to and fro, as if a giant had swayed and rocked them.

The two workmen were so frightened that they ran up the ladder by which we had descended from the trap-door ; but seeing that nothing more happened, they were easily induced to return.

Meanwhile I had opened the tablet : it was bound in a plain red leather, with a silver clasp ; it contained but one sheet of thick vellum, and on that sheet were inscribed, within a double pentacle, words in old monkish Latin, which are literally to be translated thus :—" On all that it can reach within these walls—sentient or inanimate, living or dead—as moves the needle, so work my will ! Accursed be the house, and restless be the dwellers therein."

We found no more. Mr. J—— burnt the tablet and its anathema. He razed to the foundations the part of the building containing the secret room with the chamber over it. He had then the courage to inhabit the house himself for a month, and a quieter, better-conditioned house could not be found in all London. Subsequently he let it to advantage, and his tenant has made no complaints. But my story is not yet done. A few days after Mr. J—— had removed into the house, I paid him a visit. We were standing by the open window and conversing. A van containing some articles of furniture which he was moving from his former house was at the door. I had just urged on him my theory that all those phenomena regarded as super-mundane had emanated from a human brain : adducing the charm, or rather curse, we had found and destroyed in support of my philosophy. Mr. J—— was observing in reply, " That even if mesmerism, or whatever analogous power it might be called, could really thus work in the absence of the operator, and produce effects so extra-ordinary, still could those effects continue when the operator himself was dead ? and if the spell had been wrought, and, indeed, the room walled up, more than seventy years ago, the probability was, that the operator had long since departed this life " ; Mr. J——, I say, was thus answering, when I caught hold of his arm and pointed to the street below.

A well-dressed man had crossed from the opposite side, and was accosting the carrier in charge of the van. His face, as he stood, was exactly fronting our window. It was the face of the miniature we had discovered ; it was the face of the portrait of the noble three centuries ago.

" Good Heavens ! " cried Mr. J——, " that is the face of de V——, and scarcely a day older than when I saw it in the Rajah's court in my youth ! "

Seized by the same thought, we both hastened downstairs. I was first in the street ; but the man had already gone. I caught sight of him, however, not many yards in advance, and in another moment I was by his side.

I had resolved to speak to him, but when I looked into his face I felt as if it were impossible to do so. That eye— the eye of the serpent—fixed and held me spellbound. And withal, about the man's whole person was a dignity, there an air of pride and station and superiority, that would have made any one, habituated to the usages of the world, hesitate long before venturing upon a liberty or impertinence. And what could I say ? what was it I would ask ? Thus ashamed of my first impulse, I fell a few paces back, still, however, following the stranger, undecided what else to do. Meanwhile he turned the corner of the street ; a plain carriage was in waiting, with a servant out of livery, dressed like a *valet-de-place*, at the carriage door. In another moment he had stepped into the carriage, and it drove off. I returned to the house. Mr. J—— was still at the street door. He had asked the carrier what the stranger had said to him.

" Merely asked whom that house now belonged to."

The same evening I happened to go with a friend to a place in town called the Cosmopolitan Club, a place open to men of all countries, all opinions, all degrees. One orders one's coffee, smokes one's cigar. One is always sure to meet agreeable, sometimes remarkable persons.

I had not been two minutes in the room before I beheld at a table, conversing with an acquaintance of mine, whom I will designate by the initial G——, the man—the Original of the Miniature. He was now without his hat, and the likeness was yet more startling, only I observed that while he was conversing there was less severity in the countenance ; there was even a smile, though a very quiet and very cold one. The dignity of mien I had acknowledged in the street was also more striking ; a dignity akin to that which invests some prince of the East—conveying the idea of supreme indifference and habitual, indisputable, indolent, but resistless power.

G—— soon after left the stranger, who then took up a scientific journal, which seemed to absorb his attention.

I drew G—— aside. "Who and what is that gentleman?"

"That? Oh, a very remarkable man indeed. I met him last year amidst the caves of Petra,—the scriptural Edom. He is the best Oriental scholar I know. We joined company, had an adventure with robbers, in which he showed a coolness that saved our lives; afterwards he invited me to spend a day with him in a house he had bought at Damascus—a house buried amongst almond blossoms and roses—the most beautiful thing! He had lived there for some years, quite as an Oriental, in grand style. I half suspect he is a renegade, immensely rich, very odd; by the by, a great mesmeriser. I have seen him with my own eyes produce an effect on inanimate things. If you take a letter from your pocket and throw it to the other end of the room, he will order it to come to his feet, and you will see the letter wriggle itself along the floor till it has obeyed his command. 'Pon my honour, 'tis true: I have seen him affect even the weather, disperse or collect clouds, by means of a glass tube or wand. But he does not like talking of these matters to strangers. He has only just arrived in England; says he has not been for a great many years; let me introduce him to you."

"Certainly! He is English, then? What is his name?"

"Oh!—a very homely one—Richards."

"And what is his birth—his family?"

"How do I know? What does it signify!—no doubt some parvenu, but rich—so infernally rich!"

G—— drew me up to the stranger, and the introduction was effected. The manners of Mr. Richards were not those of an adventurous traveller. Travellers are in general constitutionally gifted with high animal spirits: they are talkative, eager, imperious. Mr. Richards was calm and subdued in tone, with manners which were made distant by the loftiness of punctilious courtesy—the manners of a former age. I observed that the English he spoke was not exactly of our day. I should even have said that the accent was slightly foreign. But then Mr. Richards remarked that he had been little in the habit for many years of speaking in his native tongue. The conversation fell upon the changes in the aspect of London since he had last visited our metropolis. G——

then glanced off to the moral changes—literary, social, political —the great men who were removed from the stage within the last twenty years—the new great men who were coming on. In all this Mr. Richards evinced no interest. He had evidently read none of our living authors, and seemed scarcely acquainted by name with our younger statesmen. Once and only once he laughed ; it was when G—— asked him whether he had any thought of getting into Parliament. And the laugh was inward—sarcastic—sinister—a sneer raised into a laugh. After a few minutes G—— left us to talk to some other acquaint-ances who had just lounged into the room and I then said quietly :

" I have seen a miniature of you, Mr. Richards, in the house you once inhabited, and perhaps built, if not wholly, at least in part, in —— Street. You passed by that house this morning."

Not till I had finished did I raise my eyes to his, and then he fixed my gaze so steadfastly that I could not withdraw it— those fascinating serpent eyes. But involuntarily, and as if the words that translated my thought were dragged from me, I added in a low whisper, " I have been a student in the mys-teries of life and nature ; of those mysteries I have known the occult professors. I have the right to speak to you thus." And I uttered a certain pass-word.

" Well," said he, dryly, " I concede the right—what would you ask ? "

" To what extent human will in certain temperaments can extend ? "

" To what extent can thought extend ? Think, and before you draw breath you are in China."

" True. But my thought has no power in China."

" Give it expression, and it may have : you may write down a thought which, sooner or later, may alter the whole condition of China. What is a law but a thought ? Therefore thought is infinite—therefore thought has power ; not in proportion to its value—a bad thought may make a bad law as potent as a good thought can make a good one."

" Yes : what you say confirms my own theory. Through invisible currents one human brain may transmit its ideas to other human brains with the same rapidity as a thought pro-mulgated by visible means. And as thought is imperishable— as it leaves its stamp behind it in the natural world even when the thinker has passed out of this world—so the thought of the living may have power to rouse up and revive the thoughts of the dead—such as those thoughts *were in life*—though the thought of the living cannot reach the thoughts which the dead *now* may entertain. Is it not so ? "

" I decline to answer, if, in my judgment, thought has the limit you would fix to it ; but proceed. You have a special question you wish to put."

" Intense malignity in an intense will, engendered in a peculiar temperament, and aided by natural means within the reach of science, may produce effects like those ascribed of old to evil magic. It might thus haunt the walls of a human habitation with spectral revivals of all guilty thoughts and guilty deeds once conceived and done within those walls ; all, in short, with which the evil will claims *rapport* and affinity —imperfect, incoherent, fragmentary snatches at the old dramas acted therein years ago. Thoughts thus crossing each other haphazard, as in the nightmare of a vision, growing up into phantom sights and sounds, and all serving to create horror, not because those sights and sounds all really visitations from a world without, but that they are ghastly monstrous renewals of what have been in this world itself, set into malignant play by a malignant mortal.

" And it is through the material agency of that human brain that these things would acquire even a human power— would strike as with the shock of electricity, and might kill, if the thought of the person assailed did not rise superior to the dignity of the original assailer—might kill the most powerful animal if unnerved by fear, but not injure the feeblest man, if, while his flesh crept, his mind stood out fearless. Thus, when in old stories we read of a magician rent to pieces by the fiends he had evoked—or still more, in Eastern legends, that one magician succeeds by arts in destroying another—there may be so far truth, that a material being has clothed, from its own evil propensities, certain elements and fluids, usually quiescent or harmless, with awful shape and terrific force— just as the lightning that had lain hidden and innocent in the cloud becomes by natural law suddenly visible, takes a distinct shape to the eye, and can strike destruction to the object to which it is attracted."

" You are not without glimpses of a very mighty secret," said Mr. Richards, composedly. " According to your view, could a mortal obtain the power you speak of, he would necessarily be a malignant and evil being."

" If the power were exercised as I have said, most malignant and most evil—though I believe in the ancient traditions that he could not injure the good. His will could only injure those with whom it has established an affinity, or over whom it forces unresisted sway. I will now imagine an example that may be within the laws of nature, yet seem wild as the fables of a bewildered monk.

" You will remember that Albertus Magnus, after describing minutely the process by which spirits may be invoked and commanded, adds emphatically that the process will instruct and avail only to the few—that a *man must be born a magician !*—that is, born with a peculiar physical temperament, as a man is born a poet. Rarely are men in whose constitution lurks this occult power of the highest order of intellect ;— usually in the intellect there is some twist, perversity, or disease. But, on the other hand, they must possess, to an astonishing degree, the faculty to concentrate thought on a single object —the energetic faculty that we call *will*. Therefore, though their intellect be not sound, it is exceedingly forcible for the attainment of what it desires. I will imagine such a person, pre-eminently gifted with this constitution and its concomitant forces. I will place him in the loftier grades of society. I will suppose his desires emphatically those of the sensualist—he has, therefore, a strong love of life. He is an absolute egotist —his will is concentrated in himself—he has fierce passions— he knows no enduring, no holy affections, but he can covet eagerly what for the moment he desires—he can hate implac- ably what opposes itself to his objects—he can commit fearful crimes, yet feel small remorse—he resorts rather to curses upon others, than to penitence for his misdeeds. Circum- stances, to which his constitution guides him, lead him to a rare knowledge of the natural secrets which may serve his egotism. He is a close observer where his passions encourage observation, he is a minute calculator, not from love of truth, but where love of self sharpens his faculties—therefore he can be a man of science.

" I suppose such a being, having by experience learned the power of his arts over others, trying what may be the power of will over his own frame, and studying all that in natural philosophy may increase that power. He loves life, he dreads death ; he *wills to live on*. He cannot restore himself to youth, he cannot entirely stay the progress of death, he cannot make himself immortal in the flesh and blood ; but he may arrest for a time so prolonged as to appear incredible, if I said it—that hardening of the parts which constitutes old age. A year may age him no more than an hour ages another. His intense will, scientifically trained into system, operates, in short, over the wear and tear of his own frame. He lives on. That he may not seem a portent and a miracle, he *dies* from time to time, seemingly, to certain persons. Having schemed the transfer of a wealth that suffices to his wants, he disappears from one corner of the world, and contrives that his obsequies shall be celebrated. He reappears at another corner of the world, where he resides undetected, and does not revisit the scenes of his former career till all who could remember his features are no more. He would be profoundly miserable if he had affections—he has none but for himself. No good man would accept his longevity, and to no men, good or bad, would he or could he communicate its true secret. Such a man might exist ; such a man as I have described I see now before me !—Duke of ——, in the court of ——, dividing time between lust and brawl, alchemists and wizards ;—again, in the last century, charlatan and criminal, with name less noble, domiciled in the house at which you gazed to-day, and flying from the law you had outraged, none knew whither ; traveller once more revisiting London, with the same earthly passions which filled your heart when races now no more walked through yonder streets ; outlaw from the school of all the nobler and diviner mystics ; execrable Image of Life in Death and Death in Life, I warn you back from the cities and homes of healthful men ; back to the ruins of departed empires ; back to the deserts of nature unredeemed ! "

There answered me a whisper so musical, so potently musical, that it seemed to enter into my whole being, and subdue me despite myself. Thus it said :

" I have sought one like you for the last hundred years. Now I have found you, we part not till I know what I desire. The vision that sees through the Past, and cleaves through the veil of the Future, is in you at this hour ; never before, never to come again. The vision of no puling fantastic girl, of no sick-bed somnambule, but of a strong man, with a vigorous brain. Soar and look forth ! "

As he spoke I felt as if I rose out of myself upon eagle wings. All the weight seemed gone from air—roofless the room, roofless the dome of space. I was not in the body— where I knew not—but aloft over time, over earth.

Again I heard the melodious whisper,—" You say right.
I have mastered great secrets by the power of Will; true, by
Will and by Science I can retard the process of years: but
death comes not by age alone. Can I frustrate the accidents
which bring death upon the young ? "

" No ; every accident is a providence. Before a providence
snaps every human will."

" Shall I die at last, ages and ages hence, by the slow,
though inevitable, growth of time, or by the cause that I call
accident ? "

" By a cause you call accident."

" Is not the end still remote ? " asked the whisper with a
slight tremor.

" Regarded as my life regards time, it is still remote."

" And shall I, before then, mix with the world of men
as I did ere I learned these secrets, resume eager interest in
their strife and their trouble—battle with ambition, and use
the power of the sage to win the power that belongs to
kings ? "

" You will yet play a part on the earth that will fill earth
with commotion and amaze. For wondrous designs have you,
a wonder yourself, been permitted to live on through the
centuries. All the secrets you have stored will then have their
uses—all that now makes you a stranger amidst the generations
will contribute then to make you their lord. As the trees and
the straws are drawn into a whirlpool—as they spin round, are
sucked to the deep, and again tossed aloft by the eddies, so
shall races and thrones be plucked into the charm of your
vortex. Awful Destroyer—but in destroying, made, against
your own will, a Constructor ! "

" And that date, too, is far off ? "

" Far off ; when it comes, think your end in this world is
at hand ! "

" How and what is the end ? Look east, west, south, and
north."

" In the north, where you never yet trod, towards the
point whence your instincts have warned you, there a spectre
will seize you. 'Tis Death ! I see a ship—it is haunted—
'tis chased—it sails on. Baffled navies sail after that ship.
It enters the regions of ice. It passes a sky red with meteors.
Two moons stand on high, over ice-reefs. I see the ship
locked between white defiles—they are ice-rocks. I see the
dead strew the decks—stark and livid, green mould on their

limbs. All are dead, but one man—it is you ! But years, though so slowly they come, have then scathed you. There is the coming of age on your brow, and the will is relaxed in the cells of the brain. Still that will, though enfeebled, exceeds all that man knew before you, though the will you live on, gnawed with famine ; and nature no longer obeys you in that death-spreading region ; the sky is a sky of iron, and the air has iron clamps, and the ice-rocks wedge in the ship. Hark how it cracks and groans. Ice will imbed it as amber imbeds a straw. And a man has gone forth, living yet, from the ship and its dead ; and he has clambered up the spikes of an iceberg, and the two moons gaze down on his form. That man is yourself ; and terror is on you—terror ; and terror has swallowed your will. And I see swarming up the steep ice-rock, grey grisly things. The bears of the north have scented their quarry—they come near you and nearer, shambling and rolling their bulk. And in that day every moment shall seem to you longer than the centuries through which you have passed. And heed this—after life, moments continued make the bliss or the hell of eternity."

" Hush," said the whisper ; " but the day, you assure me, is far off—very far ! I go back to the almond and rose of Damascus !—sleep ! "

The room swam before my eyes. I became insensible. When I recovered, I found G—— holding my hand and smiling. He said, " You who have always declared yourself proof against mesmerism have succumbed at last to my friend Richards."

" Where is Mr. Richards ? "

" Gone, when you passed into a trance—saying quietly to me, ' Your friend will not wake for an hour.' "

I asked, as collectedly as I could, where Mr. Richards lodged.

" At the Trafalgar Hotel."

" Give me your arm," said I to G—— ; " let us call on him ; I have something to say."

When we arrived at the hotel, we were told that Mr. Richards had returned twenty minutes before, paid his bill, left directions with his servant (a Greek) to pack his effects and proceed to Malta by the steamer that should leave Southampton the next day. Mr. Richards had merely said of his own movements that he had visits to pay in the neighbourhood of London, and it was uncertain whether he should be able to reach Southampton in time for that steamer ; if not, he should follow in the next one.

The waiter asked me my name. On my informing him, he gave me a note that Mr. Richards had left for me, in case I called.

The note was as follows : " I wished you to utter what was in your mind. You obeyed. I have therefore established power over you. For three months from this day you can communicate to no living man what has passed between us— you cannot even show this note to the friend by your side During three months, silence complete as to me and mine. Do you doubt my power to lay on you this command ?—try to disobey me. At the end of the third month, the spell is raised. For the rest I spare you. I shall visit your grave a year and a day after it has received you."

So ends this strange story, which I ask no one to believe. I write it down exactly three months after I received the above note. I could not write it before, nor could I show to G——, in spite of his urgent request, the note which I read under the gas-lamp by his side.

CARMILLA
Sheridan Le Fanu

UPON a paper attached to the Narrative which follows, Doctor Hesselius has written a rather elaborate note, which he accompanies with a reference to his Essay on the strange subject which the MS. illuminates.

This mysterious subject he treats, in that Essay, with his usual learning and acumen, and with remarkable directness and condensation. It will form but a one volume of the series of that extraordinary man's collected papers.

As I publish the case, in this volume, simply to interest the "laity," I shall forestall the intelligent lady, who relates it, in nothing ; and, after due consideration, I have determined, therefore, to abstain from presenting any *précis* of the learned Doctor's reasoning, or extract from his statement on a subject which he describes as "involving, not improbably, some of the profoundest arcana of our dual existence, and its intermediates."

I was anxious, on discovering this paper, to reopen the correspondence commenced by Doctor Hesselius, so many years before, with a person so clever and careful as his informant seems to have been.   Much to my regret, however, I found that she had died in the interval.

She, probably, could have added little to the Narrative which she communicates in the following pages, with, so far as I can pronounce, such a conscientious particularity.

I

AN EARLY FRIGHT

IN Styria, we, though by no means magnificent people, inhabit a castle, or schloss.   A small income, in that part of the world, goes a great way. Eight or nine hundred a year does wonders.   Scantily enough ours would have answered among wealthy people at home.   My father is English, and I bear an English name, although I never saw England. But here, in this lonely and primitive place, where everything is so marvellously cheap, I really don't see how ever so much more money would at all materially add to our comforts, or even luxuries.

My father was in the Austrian service, and retired upon a pension and his patrimony, and purchased this feudal residence, and the small estate on which it stands, a bargain.

Nothing can be more picturesque or solitary.   It stands on a slight eminence in a forest.   The road, very old and narrow, passes in front of its drawbridge, never raised in my time, and its moat, stocked with perch, and sailed over by many swans, and floating on its surface white fleets of water-lilies.

Over all this the schloss shows its many-windowed front ; its towers, and its Gothic chapel.

The forest opens in an irregular and very picturesque glade before its gate, and at the right a steep Gothic bridge carries the road over a stream that winds in deep shadow through the wood.

I have said that this is a very lonely place. Judge whether I say truth. Looking from the hall door towards the road, the forest in which our castle stands extends fifteen miles to the right, and twelve to the left. The nearest inhabited village is about seven of your English miles to the left. The nearest inhabited schloss of any historic associations, is that of old General Spielsdorf, nearly twenty miles away to the right.

I have said " the nearest *inhabited* village," because there is, only three miles westward, that is to say in the direction of General Spielsdorf's schloss, a ruined village, with its quaint little church, now roofless, in the aisle of which are the mouldering tombs of the proud family of Karnstein, now extinct, who once owned the equally-desolate château which, in the thick of the forest, overlooks the silent ruins of the town.

Respecting the cause of the desertion of this striking and melancholy spot, there is a legend which I shall relate to you another time.

I must tell you now, how very small is the party who constitute the inhabitants of our castle. I don't include servants, or those dependants who occupy rooms in the buildings attached to the schloss. Listen, and wonder ! My father, who is the kindest man on earth, but growing old ; and I, at the date of my story, only nineteen. Eight years have passed since then. I and my father constituted the family at the schloss. My mother, a Styrian lady, died in my infancy, but I had a good-natured governess, who had been with me from, I might almost say, my infancy. I could not remember the time when her fat, benignant face was not a familiar picture in my memory. This was Madame Perrodon, a native of Berne, whose care and good nature in part supplied to me the loss of my mother, whom I do not even remember, so early I lost her. She made a third at our little dinner party. There was a fourth, Mademoiselle De Lafontaine, a lady such as you term, I believe, a " finishing governess." She spoke French and German, Madame Perrodon French and broken English, to which my father and I added English, which, partly to prevent its becoming a lost language among us, and partly from patriotic motives, we spoke every day. The consequence was a Babel, at which strangers used to laugh, and which I shall make no attempt to reproduce in this narrative. And there were two or three young lady friends besides, pretty nearly of my own age, who were occasional visitors, for longer or shorter terms ; and these visits I sometimes returned.

These were our regular social resources ; but of course there were chance visits from " neighbours " of only five or six leagues' distance. My life was, notwithstanding, rather a solitary one, I can assure you.

My gouvernantes had just so much control over me as you might conjecture such sage persons would have in the case of a rather spoiled girl, whose only parent allowed her pretty nearly her own way in everything.

The first occurrence in my existence, which produced a terrible impression upon my mind, which, in fact, never has been effaced, was one of the very earliest incidents of my life which I can recollect. Some people will think it so trifling that it should not be recorded here. You will see, however, by-and-by, why I mention it. The nursery, as it was called, though I had it all to myself, was a large room in the upper story of the castle, with a steep oak roof. I can't have been more than six years old, when one night I awoke, and looking round the room from my bed, failed to see the nursery-maid. Neither was my nurse there ; and I thought myself alone. I was not frightened, for I was one of those happy children who are studiously kept in ignorance of ghost stories, of fairy tales, and of all such lore as makes us cover up our heads when the door creaks suddenly, or the flicker of an expiring candle makes the shadow of a bed-post dance upon the wall, nearer to our faces. I was vexed and insulted at finding myself, as I conceived, neglected, and I began to whimper, preparatory to a hearty bout of roaring ; when to my surprise, I saw a solemn, but very pretty face looking at me from the side of the bed. It was that of a young lady who was kneeling, with her hands under the coverlet. I looked at her with a kind of pleased wonder, and ceased whimpering. She caressed me with her hands, and lay down beside me on the bed, and drew me towards her, smiling ; I felt immediately delightfully soothed, and fell asleep again. I was wakened by a sensation as if two needles ran into my breast very deep at the same moment, and I cried loudly. The lady started back, with her eyes fixed on me, and then slipped down upon the floor, and, as I thought, hid herself under the bed.

I was now for the first time frightened, and I yelled with all my might and main. Nurse, nurserymaid, housekeeper, all came running in, and hearing my story, they made light of it, soothing me all they could meanwhile. But, child as I was, I could perceive that their faces were pale with an unwonted look of anxiety, and I saw them look under the bed, and about the room, and peep under tables and pluck open cupboards ; and the housekeeper whispered to the nurse : " Lay your hand along that hollow in the bed ; some one *did* lie there, so sure as you did not ; the place is still warm."

I remember the nursery-maid petting me, and all three examining my chest, where I told them I felt the puncture, and pronouncing that there was no sign visible that any such thing had happened to me.

The housekeeper and the two other servants who were in charge of the nursery, remained sitting up all night ; and from that time a servant always sat up in the nursery until I was about fourteen.

I was very nervous for a long time after this. A doctor was called in, he was pallid and elderly. How well I remember his long saturnine face, slightly pitted with small-pox, and his chestnut wig. For a good while, every second day, he came and gave me medicine, which of course I hated.

The morning after I saw this apparition I was in a state of terror, and could not bear to be left alone, daylight though it was, for a moment.

I remember my father coming up and standing at the bedside, and talking cheerfully, and asking the nurse a number of questions, and laughing very heartily at one of the answers ; and patting me on the shoulder, and kissing me, and telling me not to be frightened, that it was nothing but a dream and could not hurt me.

But I was not comforted, for I knew the visit of the strange woman was *not* a dream ; and I was *awfully* frightened.

I was a little consoled by the nursery-maid's assuring me that it was she who had come and looked at me, and lain down beside me in the bed and that I must have been half-dreaming not to have known her face. But this, though supported by the nurse, did not quite satisfy me.

I remember, in the course of that day, a venerable old man, in a black cassock, coming into the room with the nurse and housekeeper, and talking a little to them, and very kindly to me ; his face was very sweet and gentle, and he told me they were going to pray, and joined my hands together, and desired me to say, softly, while they were praying, "Lord, hear all good prayers for us, for Jesus' sake." I think these were the very words, for I often repeated them to myself, and my nurse used for years to make me say them in my prayers.

I remember so well the thoughtful sweet face of that white-haired old man, in his black cassock, as he stood in that rude, lofty, brown room, with the clumsy furniture of a fashion three hundred years old, about him, and the scanty light entering its shadowy atmosphere through the small lattice. He kneeled, and the three women with him, and he prayed aloud with an earnest quavering voice for, what appeared to me, a long time. I forget all my life preceding that event, and for some time after it is all obscure also ; but the scenes I have just described stand out vivid as the isolated pictures of the phantas-magoria surrounded by darkness.

II

A Guest

I AM now going to tell you something so strange that it will require all your faith in my veracity to believe my story. It is not only true, nevertheless, but truth of which I have been an eye-witness.

It was a sweet summer evening, and my father asked me, as he some-times did, to take a little ramble with him along that beautiful forest vista which I have mentioned as lying in front of the schloss.

"General Spielsdorf cannot come to us so soon as I had hoped," said my father, as we pursued our walk.

He was to have paid us a visit of some weeks, and we had expected his arrival next day. He was to have brought with him a young lady, his niece and ward, Mademoiselle Rheinfeldt, whom I had never seen, but whom I had heard described as a very charming girl, and in whose society I had promised myself many happy days. I was more disappointed than a young lady living in a town, or a bustling neighbourhood can possibly imagine. This visit, and the new acquaintance it promised, had furnished my day dream for many weeks.

"And how soon does he come ? " I asked.

"Not till autumn. Not for two months, I dare say," he answered. "And I am very glad now, dear, that you never knew Mademoiselle Rheinfeldt."

"And why ? " I asked, both mortified and curious.

"Because the poor young lady is dead," he replied. "I quite forgot I had not told you, but you were not in the room when I received the General's letter this evening."

I was very much shocked. General Spielsdorf had mentioned in his first letter, six or seven weeks before, that she was not so well as he would wish her, but there was nothing to suggest the remotest suspicion of danger.

"Here is the General's letter," he said, handing it to me. "I am afraid he is in great affliction ; the letter appears to me to have been written very nearly in distraction."

We sat down on a rude bench, under a group of magnificent lime trees. The sun was setting with all its melancholy splendour behind the sylvan horizon, and the stream that flows beside our home, and passes under the steep old bridge I have mentioned, wound through many a group of noble trees, almost at our feet, reflecting in its current the fading crimson of the sky. General Spielsdorf's letter was so extraordinary, so vehement, and in some places so self-contradictory, that I read it twice over—the second time aloud to my father—and was still unable to account for it, except by supposing that grief had unsettled his mind.

It said, "I have lost my darling daughter, for as such I loved her. During the last days of dear Bertha's illness I was not able to write to you. Before then I had no idea of her danger. I have lost her, and now learn *all*, too late. She died in the peace of innocence, and in the glorious hope of a blessed futurity. The fiend who betrayed our infatutated hospitality has done it all. I thought I was receiving into my house innocence, gaiety, a charming companion for my lost Bertha. Heavens ! what a fool have I been ! I thank God my child died without a suspicion of the cause of her sufferings. She is gone without so much as conjecturing the nature of her illness, and the accursed passion of the agent of all this misery. I devote my remaining days to tracking and extinguishing a monster. I am told I may hope to accomplish my righteous and merciful purpose. At present there is scarcely a gleam of light to guide me. I curse my conceited incredulity, my despicable affectation of superiority, my blindness, my obstinacy—all

—too late. I cannot write or talk collectedly now. I am distracted. So soon as I shall have a little recovered, I mean to devote myself for a time to enquiry, which may possibly lead me as far as Vienna. Some time in the autumn, two months hence, or earlier if I live, I will see you—that is, if you permit me ; I will then tell you all that I scarce dare put upon paper now. Farewell. Pray for me, dear friend."

In these terms ended this strange letter. Though I had never seen Bertha Rheinfeldt, my eyes filled with tears at the sudden intelligence ; I was startled, as well as profoundly disappointed.

The sun had now set, and it was twilight by the time I had returned the General's letter to my father.

It was a soft clear evening, and we loitered, speculating upon the possible meanings of the violent and incoherent sentences which I had just been reading. We had nearly a mile to walk before reaching the road that passes the schloss in front, and by that time the moon was shining brilliantly. At the drawbridge we met Madame Perrodon and Mademoiselle De Lafontaine, who had come out, without their bonnets, to enjoy the exquisite moonlight.

We heard their voices gabbling in animated dialogue as we approached. We joined them at the drawbridge, and turned about to admire with them the beautiful scene.

The glade through which we had just walked lay before us. At our left the narrow road wound away under clumps of lordly trees, and was lost to sight amid the thickening forest. At the right the same road crosses the steep and picturesque bridge, near which stands a ruined tower, which once guarded that pass ; and beyond the bridge an abrupt eminence rises, covered with trees, and showing in the shadow some grey ivy-clustered rocks.

Over the sward and low grounds, a thin film of mist was stealing, like moke, marking the distances with a transparent veil ; and here and there we could see the river faintly flashing in the moonlight.

No softer, sweeter scene could be imagined. The news I had just heard made it melancholy ; but nothing could disturb its character of profound serenity, and the enchanted glory and vagueness of the prospect.

My father, who enjoyed the picturesque, and I, stood looking in silence over the expanse beneath us. The two good governesses, standing a little way behind us, discoursed upon the scene, and were eloquent upon the moon.

Madame Perrodon was fat, middle-aged, and romantic, and talked and sighed poetically. Mademoiselle De Lafontaine—in right of her father, who was a German, assumed to be psychological, metaphysical, and something of a mystic—now declared that when the moon shone with a light so intense it was well known that it indicated a special spiritual activity. The effect of the full moon in such a state of brilliancy was manifold. It acted on dreams, it acted on lunacy, it acted on nervous people ; it had marvellous physical influences connected with life. Mademoiselle related that her cousin, who was mate of a merchant ship, having taken a nap on deck on such a night, lying on his back, with his face full in the light of the moon, had wakened, after a dream of an old woman clawing him by the cheek, with his features horribly drawn to one side ; and his countenance had never quite recovered its equilibrium.

" The moon, this night," she said, " is full of odylic and magnetic influence—and see, when you look behind you at the front of the schloss, how all its windows flash and twinkle with that silvery splendour, as if unseen hands had lighted up the rooms to receive fairy guests."

There are indolent states of the spirits in which, indisposed to talk ourselves, the talk of others is pleasant to our listless ears ; and I gazed on, pleased with the tinkle of the ladies' conversation.

" I have got into one of my moping moods to-night," said my father, after a silence, and quoting Shakespeare, whom, by way of keeping up our English, he used to read aloud, he said :—

> " ' In truth I know not why I am so sad :
> It wearies me ; you say it wearies you ;
> But how I got it—came by it.'

" I forget the rest. But I feel as if some great misfortune were hanging over us. I suppose the poor General's afflicted letter has had something to do with it."

At this moment the unwonted sound of carriage wheels and many hoofs upon the road, arrested our attention.

They seemed to be approaching from the high ground overlooking the bridge, and very soon the equipage emerged from that point. Two horsemen first crossed the bridge, then came a carriage drawn by four horses, and two men rode behind.

It seemed to be travelling carriage of a person of rank ; and we were all immediately absorbed in watching that very unusual spectacle. It became, in a few moments, greatly more interesting, for just as the carriage had passed the summit of the steep bridge, one of the leaders, taking fright, communicated his panic to the rest, and, after a plunge or two, the whole team broke into a wild gallop together, and dashing between the horsemen who rode in front, came thundering along the road towards us with the speed of a hurricane.

The excitement of the scene was made more painful by the clear, long-drawn screams of a female voice from the carriage window.

We all advanced in curiosity and horror ; my father in silence, the rest with various ejaculations of terror.

Our suspense did not last long. Just before you reach the castle drawbridge, on the route they were coming, there stands by the road-side a magnificent lime tree, on the other stands an ancient stone cross, at sight of which the horses, now going at a pace that was perfectly frightful, swerved so as to bring the wheel over the projecting roots of the tree.

I knew what was coming. I covered my eyes, unable to see it out, and turned my head away; at the same moment I heard a cry from my lady-friends, who had gone on a little.

Curiosity opened my eyes, and I saw a scene of utter confusion. Two of the horses were on the ground, the carriage lay upon its side, with two wheels in the air; the men were busy removing the traces, and a lady, with a commanding air and figure had got out, and stood with clasped hands, raising the handkerchief that was in them every now and then to her eyes. Through the carriage door was now lifted a young lady, who appeared to be lifeless. My dear old father was already beside the elder lady, with his hat in his hand, evidently tendering his aid and the resources of his schloss. The lady did not appear to hear him, or to have eyes for anything but the slender girl who was being placed against the slope of the bank.

I approached; the young lady was apparently stunned, but she was certainly not dead. My father, who piqued himself on being something of a physician, had just had his fingers to her wrist and assured the lady, who declared herself her mother, that her pulse, though faint and irregular, was undoubtedly still distinguishable. The lady clasped her hands and looked upward, as if in a momentary transport of gratitude; but immediately she broke out again in that theatrical way which is, I believe, natural to some people.

She was what is called a fine-looking woman for her time of life, and must have been handsome; she was tall, but not thin, and dressed in black velvet, and looked rather pale, but with a proud and commanding countenance, though now agitated strangely.

" Was ever being so born to calamity ? " I heard her say, with clasped hands, as I came up. " Here am I, on a journey of life and death, in prosecuting which to lose an hour is possibly to lose all. My child will not have recovered sufficiently to resume her route for who can say how long. I must leave her; I cannot, dare not, delay. How far on, sir, can you tell, is the nearest village ? I must leave her there; and shall not see my darling, or even hear of her till my return, three months hence."

I plucked my father by the coat, and whispered earnestly in his ear, " Oh ! papa, pray ask her to let her stay with us—it would be so delightful. Do, pray."

" If Madame will entrust her child to the care of my daughter, and of her good gouvernante, Madame Perrodon, and permit her to remain as our guest, under my charge, until her return, it will confer a distinction and an obligation upon us, and we shall treat her with all the care and devotion which so sacred a trust deserves."

" I cannot do that, sir, it would be to task your kindness and chivalry too cruelly," said the lady, distractedly.

" It would, on the contrary, be to confer on us a very great kindness at the moment when we most need it. My daughter has just been disappointed by a cruel misfortune, in a visit from which she had long anticipated a great deal of happiness. If you confide this young lady to our care it will be her best consolation. The nearest village on your route is distant, and affords no such inn as you think of placing your daughter at; you cannot allow her to continue her journey for any considerable distance without danger. If, as you say, you cannot suspend your journey, you must part with her to-night, and nowhere could you do so with more honest assurances of care and tenderness than here."

There was something in this lady's air and appearance so distinguished, and even imposing, and in her manner so engaging, as to impress one, quite apart from the dignity of her equipage, with a conviction that she was a person of consequence.

By this time the carriage was replaced in its upright position, and the horses, quite tractable, in the traces again.

The lady threw on her daughter a glance which I fancied was not quite so affectionate as one might have anticipated from the beginning of the scene; then she beckoned slightly to my father, and withdrew two or three steps with him out of hearing; and talked to him with a fixed and stern countenance, not at all like that with which she had hitherto spoken.

I was filled with wonder that my father did not seem to perceive the change, and also unspeakably curious to learn what it could be that she was speaking, almost in his ear, with so much earnestness and rapidity.

Two or three minutes at most, I think, she remained thus employed, then she turned, and a few steps brought her to where her daughter lay, supported by Madame Perrodon. She kneeled beside her for a moment and whispered, as Madame supposed, a little benediction in her ear; then hastily kissing her, she stepped into her carriage, the door was closed, the footmen in stately liveries jumped up behind, the outriders spurred on, the postilions cracked their whips, the horses plunged and broke suddenly into a furious canter that threatened soon again to become a gallop, and the carriage whirled away, followed at the same rapid pace by the two horsemen in the rear.

III

We Compare Notes

We followed the *cortége* with our eyes until it was swiftly lost to sight in the misty wood; and the very sound of the hoofs and wheels died away in the silent night air.

Nothing remained to assure us that the adventure had not been an illusion of a moment but the young lady, who just at that moment opened her eyes. I could not see, for her face was turned from me, but she raised her head, evidently looking about her, and I heard a very sweet voice ask complainingly, " Where is mamma ? "

Our good Madame Perrodon answered tenderly, and added some comfortable assurances.

I then heard her ask :

" Where am I ?   What is this place ? " and after that she said, " I don't see the carriage ; and Matska, where is she ? "

Madame answered all her questions in so far as she understood them ; and gradually the young lady remembered how the misadventure came about, and was glad to hear that no one in, or in attendance on, the carriage was hurt ; and on learning that her mamma had left her here, till her return in about three months, she wept.

I was going to add my consolations to those of Madame Perrodon when Mademoiselle De Lafontaine placed her hand upon my arm, saying :

" Don't approach, one at a time is as much as she can at present converse with ; a very little excitement would possibly overpower her now."

As soon as she is comfortably in bed, I thought, I will run up to her room and see her.

My father in the meantime had sent a servant on horseback for the physician, who lived about two leagues away ; and a bedroom was being prepared for the young lady's reception.

The stranger now rose, and leaning on Madame's arm, walked slowly over the drawbridge and into the castle gate.

In the hall, servants waited to receive her, and she was conducted forthwith to her room.

The room we usually sat in as our drawing-room is long, having four windows, that looked over the moat and drawbridge, upon the forest scene I have just described.

It is furnished in old carved oak, with large carved cabinets, and the chairs are cushioned with crimson Utrecht velvet. The walls are covered with tapestry, and surrounded with great gold frames, the figures being as large as life, in ancient and very curious costume, and the subjects represented are hunting, hawking and generally festive. It is not too stately to be extremely comfortable ; and here we had our tea, for with his usual patriotic leanings he insisted that the national beverage should make its appearance regularly with our coffee and chocolate.

We sat here this night, and with candles lighted, were talking over the adventure of the evening.

Madame Perrodon and Mademoiselle De Lafontaine were both of our party.   The young stranger had hardly lain down in her bed when she sank into a deep sleep ; and those ladies had left her in the care of a servant.

" How do you like our guest ? " I asked, as soon as Madame entered. " Tell me all about her ? "

" I like her extremely," answered Madame, " she is, I almost think the prettiest creature I ever saw ; about your age, and so gentle and nice."

" She is absolutely beautiful," threw in Mademoiselle, who had peeped for a moment into the stranger's room.

" And such a sweet voice ! " added Madame Perrodon.

" Did you remark a woman in the carriage, after it was set up again, who did not get out," inquired Mademoiselle, " but only looked from the window ? "

No, we had not seen her.

Then she described a hideous black woman, with a sort of coloured turban on her head, who was gazing all the time from the carriage window, nodding and grinning derisively towards the ladies, with gleaming eyes and large white eye-balls, and her teeth set as if in fury.

" Did you remark what an ill-looking pack of men the servants were ?" asked Madame.

" Yes," said my father, who had just come in, " ugly, hang-dog looking fellows, as ever I beheld in my life. I hope they mayn't rob the poor lady in the forest. They are clever rogues, however ; they got everything to rights in a minute."

" I dare say they are worn out with too long travelling," said Madame. " Besides looking wicked, their faces were so strangely lean, and dark, and sullen. I am very curious, I own ; but I dare say the young lady will tell us all about it to-morrow, if she is sufficiently recovered."

" I don't think she will," said my father, with a mysterious smile, and a little nod of his head, as if he knew more about it than he cared to tell us.

This made me all the more inquisitive as to what had passed between him and the lady in the black velvet, in the brief but earnest interview that had immediately preceded her departure.

We were scarcely alone, when I entreated him to tell me. He did not need much pressing.

" There is no particular reason why I should not tell you. She expressed a reluctance to trouble us with the care of her daughter, saying she was in delicate health, and nervous, but not subject to any kind of seizure—she volunteered that—nor to any illusion ; being, in fact, perfectly sane."

" How very odd to say all that ! " I interpolated. " It was so unnecessary."

" At all events it *was* said," he laughed, " and as you wish to know all that passed, which was indeed very little, I tell you. She then said, ' I am making a long journey of *vital* importance '—she emphasized the word—' rapid and secret ; I shall return for my child in three months ; in the meantime, she will be silent as to who we are, whence we come, and whither we are travelling.' That is all she said. She spoke very pure French. When she said the word ' secret,' she paused for a few seconds, looking sternly, her eyes fixed on mine. I fancy she makes a great point of that. You saw how quickly she was gone. I hope I have not done a very foolish thing, in taking charge of the young lady."

For my part, I was delighted. I was longing to see and talk to her ; and only waiting till the doctor should give me leave. You, who live in towns, can have no idea how great an event the introduction of a new friend is, in such a solitude as surrounded us.

The doctor did not arrive till nearly one o'clock; but I could no more have gone to my bed and slept, than I could have overtaken, on foot, the carriage in which the princess in black velvet had driven away.

When the physician came down to the drawing-room, it was to report very favourably upon his patient. She was now sitting up, her pulse quite regular, apparently perfectly well. She had sustained no injury, and the little shock to her nerves had passed away quite harm-lessly. There could be no harm certainly in my seeing her, if we both wished it; and, with this permission, I sent, forthwith, to know whether she would allow me to visit her for a few minutes in her room.

The servant returned immediately to say that she desired nothing more.

You may be sure I was not long in availing myself of this permission.

Our visitor lay in one of the handsomest rooms in the schloss. It was, perhaps a little stately. There was a sombre piece of tapestry opposite the foot of the bed, representing Cleopatra with the asps to her bosom; and other solemn classic scenes were displayed, a little faded, upon the other walls. But there was gold carving, and rich and varied colour enough in the other decorations of the room, to more than redeem the gloom of the old tapestry.

There were candles at the bed side. She was sitting up; her slender pretty figure enveloped in the soft silk dressing-gown, embroidered with flowers, and lined with thick quilted silk, which her mother had thrown over her feet as she lay upon the ground.

What was it that, as I reached the bed side and had just begun my little greeting, struck me dumb in a moment, and made me recoil a step or two from before her? I will tell you.

I saw the very face which had visited me in my childhood at night, which remained so fixed in my memory, and on which I had for so many years so often ruminated with horror, when no one suspected of what I was thinking.

It was pretty, even beautiful; and when I first beheld it, wore the same melancholy expression.

But this almost instantly lighted into a strange fixed smile of recognition.

There was a silence of fully a minute, and then at length *she* spoke; *I* could not.

"How wonderful!" she exclaimed. "Twelve years ago, I saw your face in a dream, and it has haunted me ever since."

"Wonderful indeed!" I repeated, overcoming with an effort the horror that had for a time suspended my utterances. "Twelve years ago, in vision or reality, *I* certainly saw you. I could not forget your face. It has remained before my eyes ever since."

Her smile had softened. Whatever I had fancied strange in it, was gone, and it and her dimpling cheeks were now delightfully pretty and intelligent.

I felt reassured, and continued more in the vein which hospitality indicated, to bid her welcome, and to tell her how much pleasure her accidental arrival had given us all, and especially what a happiness it was to me.

I took her hand as I spoke. I was a little shy, as lonely people are, but the situation made me eloquent, and even bold. She pressed my hand, she laid hers upon it, and her eyes glowed, as, looking hastily into mine, she smiled again, and blushed.

She answered my welcome very prettily. I sat down beside her, still wondering; and she said:

" I must tell you my vision about you; it is so very strange that you and I should have had, each of the other so vivid a dream, that each should have seen, I you and you me, looking as we do now, when of course we both were mere children. I was a child, about six years old, and I awoke from a confused and troubled dream, and found myself in a room, unlike my nursery, wainscoted clumsily in some dark wood, and with cupboards and bedsteads, and chairs, and benches placed about it. The beds were, I thought, all empty, and the room itself without any one but myself in it; and I, after looking about me for some time, and admiring especially an iron candlestick, with two branches, which I should certainly know again, crept under one of the beds to reach the window; but as I got from under the bed, I heard some one crying; and looking up, while I was still upon my knees, I saw *you*—most assuredly you—as I see you now; a beautiful young lady, with golden hair and large blue eyes, and lips—your lips—you, as you are here. Your looks won me; I climbed on the bed and put my arms about you, and I think we both fell asleep. I was aroused by a scream; you were sitting up screaming. I was frightened, and slipped down upon the ground, and, it seemed to me, lost consciousness for a moment; and when I came to myself, I was again in my nursery at home. Your face I have never forgotten since. I could not be misled by mere resemblance. You *are* the lady whom I then saw."

It was now my turn to relate my corresponding vision, which I did, to the undisguised wonder of my new acquaintance.

" I don't know which should be most afraid of the other," she said, again smiling. " If you were less pretty I think I should be very much afraid of you, but being as you are, and you and I both so young, I feel only that I have made your acquaintance twelve years ago, and have already a right to your intimacy; at all events, it does seem as if we were destined, from our earliest childhood, to be friends. I wonder whether you feel as strangely drawn towards me as I do to you; I have never had a friend—shall I find one now?" She sighed, and her fine dark eyes gazed passionately on me.

Now the truth is, I felt rather unaccountably towards the beautiful stranger. I did feel, as she said, " drawn towards her," but there was also something of repulsion. In this ambiguous feeling, however, the sense of attraction immensely prevailed. She interested and won me ; she was so beautiful and so indescribably engaging.

I perceived now something of languor and exhaustion stealing over her, and hastened to bid her good-night.

" The doctor thinks," I added, " that you ought to have a maid to sit up with you to-night ; one of ours is waiting, and you will find her a very useful and quiet creature."

" How kind of you, but I could not sleep, I never could with an attendant in the room. I shan't require any assistance—and, shall I confess my weakness, I am haunted with a terror of robbers. Our house was robbed once, and two servants murdered, so I always lock my door. It has become a habit—and you look so kind I know you will forgive me. I see there is a key in the lock."

She held me close in her pretty arms for a moment and whispered in my ear, " Good-night, darling, it is very hard to part with you, but good-night ; to-morrow, but not early, I shall see you again."

She sank back on the pillow with a sigh, and her fine eyes followed me with a fond and melancholy gaze, and she murmured again " Good-night, dear friend."

Young people like, and even love, on impulse. I was flattered by the evident, though as yet undeserved, fondness she showed me. I liked the confidence with which she at once received me. She was determined that we should be very dear friends.

Next day came and we met again. I was delighted with my companion ; that is to say, in many respects.

Her looks lost nothing in daylight—she was certainly the most beautiful creature I had ever seen, and the unpleasant remembrance of the face presented in my early dream, had lost the effect of the first unexpected recognition.

She confessed that she had experienced a similar shock on seeing me, and precisely the same faint antipathy that had mingled with my admiration of her. We now laughed together over our momentary horrors.

IV

Her Habits—A Saunter

I TOLD you that I was charmed with her in most particulars.

There were some that did not please me so well.

She was above the middle height of women. I shall begin by describing her. She was slender, and wonderfully graceful. Except that her movements were languid—*very* languid—indeed, there was nothing in her appearance to indicate an invalid. Her complexion was rich and brilliant ; her features were small and beautifully formed ; her eyes large, dark, and lustrous ; her hair was quite wonderful, I never saw hair so magnificently thick and long when it was down about her shoulders ; I have often placed my hands under it, and laughed with wonder at its weight. It was exquisitely fine and soft, and in colour a rich very dark brown, with something of gold. I loved to let it down, tumbling with its own weight, as, in her room, she lay back in her chair talking in her sweet low voice, I used to fold and braid it, and spread it out and play with it. Heavens! If I had but known all!

I said there were particulars which did not please me. I have told you that her confidence won me the first night I saw her; but I found that she exercised with respect to herself, her mother, her history, everything in fact connected with her life, plans, and people, an ever-wakeful reserve. I dare say I was unreasonable, perhaps I was wrong; I dare say I ought to have respected the solemn injunction laid upon my father by the stately lady in black velvet. But curiosity is a restless and unscrupulous passion, and no one girl can endure, with patience, that her's should be baffled by another. What harm could it do anyone to tell me what I so ardently desired to know? Had she no trust in my good sense or honour? Why would she not believe me when I assured her, so solemnly, that I would not divulge one syllable of what she told me to any mortal breathing.

There was a coldness, it seemed to me, beyond her years, in her smiling melancholy persistent refusal to afford me the least ray of light.

I cannot say we quarrelled upon this point, for she would not quarrel upon any. It was, of course, very unfair of me to press her, very ill-bred, but I really could not help it; and I might just as well have let it alone.

What she did tell me amounted, in my unconscionable estimation—to nothing.

It was all summed up in three very vague disclosures:

First.—Her name was Carmilla.

Second.—Her family was very ancient and noble.

Third.—Her home lay in the direction of the west.

She would not tell me the name of her family, nor their armorial bearings, nor the name of their estate, nor even that of the country they lived in.

You are not to suppose that I worried her incessantly on these subjects. I watched opportunity, and rather insinuated than urged my inquiries. Once or twice, indeed, I did attack her more directly. But no matter what my tactics, utter failure was invariably the result. Reproaches and caresses were all lost upon her. But I must add this, that her evasion was conducted with so pretty a melancholy and de-precation, with so many, and even passionate declarations of her liking for me, and trust in my honour, and with so many promises that I should at last know all, that I could not find it in my heart long to be offended with her.

She used to place her pretty arms about my neck, draw me to her, and laying her cheek to mine, murmur with her lips near my ear, " Dearest, your little heart is wounded; think me not cruel because I obey the irresistible law of my strength and weakness; if your dear heart is wounded, my wild heart bleeds with yours. In the rapture of my enormous humiliation I live in your warm life, and you shall die—die, sweetly die—into mine. I cannot help it ; as I draw near to you, you, in your turn, will draw near to others, and learn the rapture of that cruelty, which yet is love ; so, for a while, seek to know no more of me and mine, but trust me with all your loving spirit."

And when she had spoken such a rhapsody, she would press me more closely in her trembling embrace, and her lips in soft kisses gently glow upon my cheek.

Her agitations and her language were unintelligible to me.

From these foolish embraces, which were not of very frequent occurrence, I must allow, I used to wish to extricate myself ; but my energies seemed to fail me. Her murmured words sounded like a lullaby in my ear, and soothed my resistance into a trance, from which I only seemed to recover myself when she withdrew her arms.

In these mysterious moods I did not like her. I experienced a strange tumultuous excitement that was pleasurable, ever and anon, mingled with a vague sense of fear and disgust. I had no distinct thoughts about her while such scenes lasted, but I was conscious of a love growing into adoration, and also of abhorrence. This I know is paradox, but I can make no other attempt to explain the feeling.

I now write, after an interval of more than ten years, with a trembling hand, with a confused and horrible recollection of certain occurrences and situations, in the ordeal through which I was unconsciously passing ; though with a vivid and very sharp remembrance of the main current of my story. But, I suspect, in all lives there are certain emotional scenes, those in which our passions have been most wildly and terribly roused, that are of all others the most vaguely and dimly remembered.

Sometimes after an hour of apathy, my strange and beautiful companion would take my hand and hold it with a fond pressure, renewed again and again ; blushing softly, gazing in my face with languid and burning eyes, and breathing so fast that her dress rose and fell with the tumultuous respiration. It was like the ardour of a lover; it embarrassed me ; it was hateful and yet overpowering ; and with gloating eyes she drew me to her, and her hot lips travelled along my cheek in kisses ; and she would whisper, almost in sobs, " You are mine, you *shall* be mine, and you and I are one for ever." Then she has thrown herself back in her chair, with her small hands over her eyes, leaving me trembling.

" Are we related," I used to ask ; " what can you mean by all this ? I remind you perhaps of some one whom you love ; but you must not, I hate it ; I don't know you—I don't know myself when you look so and talk so."

She used to sigh at my vehemence, then turn away and drop my hand.

Respecting these very extraordinary manifestations I strove in vain to form any satisfactory theory—I could not refer them to affectation or trick. It was unmistakably the momentary breaking out of suppressed instinct and emotion. Was she, notwithstanding her mother's volunteered denial, subject to brief visitations of insanity ; or was there here a disguise and a romance ? I had read in old story books of such things. What if a boyish lover had found his way into the house, and sought to prosecute his suit in masquerade, with the assistance of a clever old adventuress. But there were many things against this hypothesis, highly interesting as it was to my vanity.

I could boast of no little attentions such as masculine gallantry delights to offer. Between these passionate moments there were long intervals of common-place, of gaiety, of brooding melancholy, during which, except that I detected her eyes so full of melancholy fire, following me, at times I might have been as nothing to her. Except in these brief periods of mysterious excitement her ways were girlish ; and there was always a languor about her, quite incompatible with a masculine system in a state of health.

In some respects her habits were odd. Perhaps not so singular in the opinion of a town lady like you, as they appeared to us rustic people. She used to come down very late, generally not till one o'clock, she would then take a cup of chocolate, but eat nothing ; we then went out for a walk, which was a mere saunter, and she seemed, almost immediately, exhausted, and either returned to the schloss or sat on one of the benches that were placed, here and there, among the trees. This was a bodily languor in which her mind did not sympathise. She was always an animated talker, and very intelligent.

She sometimes alluded for a moment to her own home, or mentioned an adventure or situation, or an early recollection, which indicated a people of strange manners, and described customs of which we knew nothing. I gathered from these chance hints that her native country was much more remote than I had at first fancied.

As we sat thus one afternoon under the trees a funeral passed us by. It was that of a pretty young girl, whom I had often seen, the daughter of one of the rangers of the forest. The poor man was walking behind the coffin of his darling ; she was his only child, and he looked quite heartbroken. Peasants walking two-and-two came behind, they were singing a funeral hymn.

I rose to mark my respect as they passed, and joined in the hymn they were very sweetly singing.

My companion shook me a little roughly, and I turned surprised.

She said brusquely, " Don't you perceive how discordant that is ? "

" I think it very sweet, on the contrary," I answered, vexed at the interruption, and very uncomfortable, lest the people who composed the little procession should observe and resent what was passing.

I resumed, therefore, instantly, and was again interrupted. " You pierce my ears," said Carmilla, almost angrily, and stopping her ears with her tiny fingers. " Besides, how can you tell that your religion and mine are the same; your forms wound me, and I hate funerals. What a fuss! Why, *you* must die—*everyone* must die; and all are happier when they do. Come home."

" My father has gone on with the clergyman to the churchyard. I thought you knew she was to be buried to-day."

" *She?* I don't trouble my head about peasants. I don't know who she is," answered Carmilla, with a flash from her fine eyes.

" She is the poor girl who fancied she saw a ghost a fortnight ago, and has been dying ever since, till yesterday, when she expired."

" Tell me nothing about ghosts. I shan't sleep to-night if you do."

" I hope there is no plague or fever coming; all this looks very like it," I continued. " The swineherd's young wife died only a week ago, and she thought something seized her by the throat as she lay in her bed, and nearly strangled her. Papa says such horrible fancies do accompany some forms of fever. She was quite well the day before. She sank afterwards, and died before a week."

" Well, *her* funeral is over, I hope, and *her* hymn sung; and our ears shan't be tortured with that discord and jargon. It has made me nervous. Sit down here, beside me; sit close; hold my hand; press it hard—hard—harder."

We had moved a little back, and had come to another seat.

She sat down. Her face underwent a change that alarmed and even terrified me for a moment. It darkened, and became horribly livid; her teeth and hands were clenched, and she frowned and compressed her lips, while she stared down upon the ground at her feet, and trembled all over with a continued shudder as irrespressible as ague. All her energies seemed strained to suppress a fit, with which she was then breathlessly tugging; and at length a low convulsive cry of suffering broke from her, and gradually the hysteria subsided. "There! That comes of strangling people with hymns! " she said at last. "Hold me, hold me still. It is passing away."

And so gradually it did; and perhaps to dissipate the sombre impression which the spectacle had left upon me, she became unusually animated and chatty; and so we got home.

This was the first time I had seen her exhibit any definable symptoms of that delicacy of health which her mother had spoken of. It was the first time, also, I had seen her exhibit anything like temper.

Both passed away like a summer cloud; and never but once afterwards did I witness on her part a momentary sign of anger. I will tell you how it happened.

She and I were looking out of one of the long drawing-room windows, when there entered the court-yard, over the drawbridge, a figure of a wanderer whom I knew very well. He used to visit the schloss generally twice a year.

It was the figure of a hunchback, with the sharp lean features that generally accompany deformity. He wore a pointed black beard, and he was smiling from ear to ear, showing his white fangs. He was dressed in buff, black, and scarlet, and crossed with more straps and belts than I could count, from which hung all manner of things. Behind, he carried a magic-lantern, and two boxes, which I well knew, in one of which was a salamander, and in the other a mandrake. These monsters used to make my father laugh. They were compounded of parts of monkeys, parrots, squirrels, fish, and hedgehogs, dried and stitched together with great neatness and startling effect. He had a fiddle, a box of conjuring apparatus, a pair of foils and masks attached to his belt, several other mysterious cases dangling about him, and a black staff with copper ferrules in his hand. His companion was a rough spare dog, that followed at his heels, but stopped short, suspiciously at the drawbridge, and in a little while began to howl dismally.

In the meantime, the mountebank, standing in the midst of the courtyard, raised his grotesque hat, and made us a very ceremonious bow, paying his compliments very volubly in execrable French, and German not much better. Then, disengaging his fiddle, he began to scrape a lively air, to which he sang with a merry discord, dancing with ludicrous airs and activity, that made me laugh, in spite of the dog's howling.

Then he advanced to the window with many smiles and salutations, and his hat in his left hand, his fiddle under his arm, and with a fluency that never took breath, he grabbed a long advertisement of all his accomplishments, and the resources of the various arts which he placed at our service, and the curiosities and entertainments which it was in his power, at our bidding to display.

"Will your ladyships be pleased to buy an amulet against the oupire, which is going like the wolf, I hear, through these woods," he said, dropping his hat on the pavement. "They are dying of it right and left, and here is a charm that never fails; only pinned to the pillow, and you may laugh in his face."

These charms consisted of oblong slips of vellum, with cabalistic ciphers and diagrams upon them.

Carmilla instantly purchased one, and so did I.

He was looking up, and we were smiling down upon him, amused; at least, I can answer for myself. His piercing black eye, as he looked up in our faces, seemed to detect something that fixed for a moment his curiosity.

In an instant he unrolled a leather case, full of all manner of odd little steel instruments.

"See here, my lady," he said, displaying it, and addressing me, "I profess, among other things less useful, the art of dentistry. Plague take the dog!" he interpolated. "Silence, beast! He howls so that your ladyships can scarcely hear a word. Your noble friend, the young lady at your right, has the sharpest tooth—long, thin, pointed, like an awl, like a needle; ha, ha! With my sharp and long sight, as I look up, I have seen it distinctly; now if it happens to hurt the young lady, and I think it must, here am I, here are my file, my punch, my nippers; I will make it round and blunt, if her ladyship pleases; no longer the tooth of a fish, but of a beautiful young lady as she is. Hey? Is the young lady displeased? Have I been too bold? Have I offended her?"

The young lady, indeed, looked very angry as she drew back from the window.

" How dares that mountebank insult us so? Where is your father? I shall demand redress from him. My father would have had the wretch tied up to the pump, and flogged with a cart-whip, and burnt to the bones with the castle brand! "

She retired from the window a step or two, and sat down, and had hardly lost sight of the offender, when her wrath subsided as suddenly as it had risen, and she gradually recovered her usual tone, and seemed to forget the little hunchback and his follies.

My father was out of spirits that evening. On coming in he told us that there had been another case very similar to the two fatal ones which had lately occurred. The sister of a young peasant on his estate, only a mile away, was very ill, had been, as she described it, attacked very nearly in the same way, and was now slowly but steadily sinking.

" All this," said my father, " is strictly referable to natural causes. These poor people infect one another with their superstitions, and so repeat in imagination the images of terror that have infested their neighbours."

" But that very circumstance frightens one horribly," said Carmilla.

" How so? " inquired my father.

" I am so afraid of fancying I see such things; I think it would be as bad as reality."

" We are in God's hands; nothing can happen without His permission, and all will end well for those who love Him. He is our faithful creator; He has made us all, and will take care of us."

" Creator! *Nature!* " said the young lady in answer to my gentle father. " And this disease that invades the country is natural. Nature. All things spring from Nature—don't they? All things in the heaven, in the earth, and under the earth, act and live as Nature ordains? I think so."

" The doctor said he would come here to-day," said my father, after a silence. " I want to know what he thinks about it, and what he thinks we had better do."

" Doctors never did me any good," said Carmilla.

" Then you have been ill? " I asked.

" More ill than ever you were," she answered.

" Long ago? "

" Yes, a long time. I suffered from this very illness; but I forget all but my pain and weakness, and they were not so bad as are suffered in other diseases."

" You were very young then? "

" I dare say; let us talk no more of it. You would not wound a friend ? " She looked languidly in my eyes, and passed her arm round my waist lovingly, and led me out of the room. My father was busy over some papers near the window.

" Why does your papa like to frighten us ? " said the pretty girl, with a sigh and a little shudder.

" He doesn't, dear Carmilla, it is the very furthest thing from his mind."

" Are you afraid, dearest ? "

" I should be very much if I fancied there was any real danger of my being attacked as those poor people were."

" You are afraid to die ? "

" Yes, every one is."

" But to die as lovers may—to die together, so that they may live together. Girls are caterpillars while they live in the world, to be finally butterflies when the summer comes ; but in the meantime there are grubs and larvæ, don't you see—each with their peculiar propensities, necessities and structure. So says Monsieur Buffon, in his big book, in the next room."

Later in the day the doctor came, and was closeted with papa for some time. He was a skilful man, of sixty and upwards, he wore powder, and shaved his pale face as smooth as a pumpkin. He and papa emerged from the room together, and I heard papa laugh, and say as they came out :

" Well, I do wonder at a wise man like you. What do you say to hippogriffs and dragons ? "

The doctor was smiling, and made answer, shaking his head—

" Nevertheless, life and death are mysterious states, and we know little of the resources of either."

And so they walked on, and I heard no more. I did not then know what the doctor had been broaching, but I think I guess it now.

V

A WONDERFUL LIKENESS

THIS evening there arrived from Gratz the grave, dark-faced son of the picture-cleaner, with a horse and cart laden with two large packing-cases, having many pictures in each. It was a journey of ten leagues, and whenever a messenger arrived at the schloss from our little capital of Gratz, we used to crowd about him in the hall, to hear the news.

This arrival created in our secluded quarters quite a sensation. The cases remained in the hall, and the messenger was taken charge of by the servants till he had eaten his supper. Then with assistants, and armed with hammer, ripping chisel, and turnscrew, he met us in the hall, where we had assembled to witness the unpacking of the cases.

Carmilla sat looking listlessly on, while one after the other the old pictures, nearly all portraits, which had undergone the process of renovation, were brought to light. My mother was of an old Hungarian family, and most of these pictures, which were about to be restored to their places, had come to us through her.

My father had a list in his hand, from which he read, as the artist rummaged out the corresponding numbers. I don't know that the pictures were very good, but they were, undoubtedly very old, and some of them very curious also. They had, for the most part, the merit of being now seen by me, I may say, for the first time; for the smoke and dust of time had all but obliterated them.

" There is a picture that I have not seen yet," said my father. " In one corner, at the top of it, is the name, as well as I could read, 'Marcia Karnstein,' and the date ' 1698 ; ' and I am curious to see how it has turned out."

I remembered it ; it was a small picture, about a foot and a half high, and nearly square, without a frame ; but it was so blackened by age that I could not make it out.

The artist now produced it, with evident pride. It was quite beautiful ; it was startling ; it seemed to live. It was the effigy of Carmilla !

" Carmilla, dear, here is an absolute miracle. Here you are, living, smiling, ready to speak, in this picture. Isn't it beautiful, papa ? And see, even the little mole on her throat."

My father laughed, and said " Certainly it is a wonderful likeness," but he looked away, and to my surprise seemed but little struck by it, went on talking to the picture-cleaner, who was also something of an artist, and discoursed with intelligence about the portraits or other works, which his art had just brought into light and colour, while *I* was more and more lost in wonder the more I looked at the picture.

" Will you let me hang this picture in my room, papa ? " I asked.

" Certainly, dear," said he, smiling, " I'm very glad you think it so like. It must be prettier even than I thought it, if it is."

The young lady did not acknowledge this pretty speech, did not seem to hear it. She was leaning back in her seat, her fine eyes under their long lashes gazing on me in contemplation, and she smiled in a kind of rapture.

" And now you can read quite plainly the name that is written in the corner. It is not Marcia ; it looks as if it was done in gold. The name is Mircalla, Countess Karnstein, and this is a little coronet over it, and underneath A.D. 1698. I am descended from the Karnsteins ; that is, mamma was."

" Ah ! " said the lady, languidly, " so am I, I think, a very long descent, very ancient. Are there any Karnsteins living now ? "

" None who bear the name, I believe. The family were ruined, I believe, in some civil wars, long ago, but the ruins of the castle are only about three miles away."

" How interesting ! " she said, languidly. " But see what beautiful moonlight ! " She glanced through the hall door, which stood a little open. " Suppose you take a little ramble round the court, and look down at the road and river."

" It is so like the night you came to us," I said.

She sighed, smiling.

She rose, and each with her arm about the other's waist, we walked out upon the pavement.

In silence, slowly we walked down to the draw-bridge, where the beautiful landscape opened before us.

" And so you were thinking of the night I came here ? " she almost whispered. " Are you glad I came ? "

" Delighted, dear Carmilla," I answered.

" And you ask for the picture you think like me, to hang in your room," she murmured with a sigh, as she drew her arm closer about my waist, and let her pretty head sink upon my shoulder.

" How romantic you are, Carmilla," I said. " Whenever you tell me your story, it will be made up chiefly of some one great romance."

She kissed me silently.

" I am sure, Carmilla, you have been in love ; that there is, at this moment, an affair of the heart going on."

" I have been in love with no one, and never shall," she whispered, " unless it should be with you."

How beautiful she looked in the moonlight !

Shy and strange was the look with which she quickly hid her face in my neck and hair, with tumultuous sighs, that seemed almost to sob, and pressed in mine a hand that trembled.

Her soft cheek was glowing against mine. " Darling, darling," she murmured, " I live in you ; and you would die for me, I love you so."

I started from her.

She was gazing on me with eyes from which all fire, all meaning had flown, and a face colourless and apathetic.

" Is there a chill in the air, dear ? " she said drowsily. " I almost shiver ; have I been dreaming ? Let us come in. Come, come ; come in."

" You look ill, Carmilla ; a little faint. You certainly must take some wine," I said.

" Yes, I will. I'm better now. I shall be quite well in a few minutes. Yes, do give me a little wine," answered Carmilla, as we approached the door. " Let us look again for a moment ; it is the last time, perhaps, I shall see the moonlight with you."

" How do you feel now, dear Carmilla ? Are you really better ? " I asked.

I was beginning to take alarm, lest she should have been stricken with the strange epidemic that they said had invaded the country about us.

" Papa would be grieved beyond measure," I added, " if he thought you were ever so little ill, without immediately letting us know. We have a very skilful doctor near this, the physician who was with papa to-day."

" I'm sure he is. I know how kind you all are ; but, dear child, I am quite well again. There is nothing ever wrong with me, but a little weakness. People say I am languid ; I am incapable of exertion ; I can scarcely walk as far as a child of three years old ; and every now and then the little strength I have falters, and I become as you have just seen me. But after all I am very easily set up again ; in a moment I am perfectly myself. See how I have recovered."

So, indeed, she had ; and she and I talked a great deal, and very animated she was ; and the remainder of that evening passed without any recurrence of what I called her infatuations. I mean her crazy talk and looks, which embarrassed, and even frightened me.

But there occurred that night an event which gave my thoughts quite a new turn, and seemed to startle even Carmilla's languid nature into momentary energy.

VI

A Very Strange Agony

WHEN we got into the drawing-room, and had sat down to our coffee and chocolate, although Carmilla did not take any, she seemed quite herself again and Madame, and Mademoiselle De Lafontaine, joined us, and made a little card party, in the course of which papa came in for what he called his " dish of tea."

When the game was over he sat down beside Carmilla on the sofa, and asked her, a little anxiously, whether she had heard from her mother since her arrival.

She answered " No."

He then asked her whether she knew where a letter would reach her at present.

" I cannot tell," she answered, ambiguously, " but I have been thinking of leaving you ; you have been already too hospitable and too kind to me. I have given you an infinity of trouble, and I should wish to take a carriage to-morrow, and post in pursuit of her ; I know where I shall ultimately find her, although I dare not tell you."

" But you must not dream of any such thing," exclaimed my father, to my great relief. " We can't afford to lose you so, and I won't con- sent to your leaving us, except under the care of your mother, who was so good as to consent to your remaining with us till she should herself return. I should be quite happy if I knew that you heard from her ; but this evening the accounts of the progress of the mysterious disease that has invaded our neighbourhood, grow even more alarming ; and my beautiful guest, I do feel the responsibility, unaided by advice from your mother, very much. But I shall do my best ; and one thing is certain, that you must not think of leaving us without her distinct direction to that effect. We should suffer too much in parting from you to consent to it easily."

" Thank you, sir, a thousand times for your hospitality," she answered, smiling bashfully. " You have all been too kind to me ; I have seldom been so happy in all my life before, as in your beautiful château, under your care, and in the society of your dear daughter."

So he gallantly, in his old-fashioned way, kissed her hand, smiling, and pleased at her little speech.

I accompanied Carmilla as usual to her room, and sat and chatted with her while she was preparing for bed.

" Do you think," I said, at length, " that you will ever confide fully in me ? "

She turned round smiling, but made no answer, only continued to smile on me.

" You won't answer that ? " I said. " You can't answer pleasantly ; I ought not to have asked you."

" You were quite right to ask me that, or anything. You do not know how dear you are to me, or you could not think any confidence too great to look for. But I am under vows, no nun half so awfully, and I dare not tell my story yet, even to you. The time is very near when you shall know everything. You will think me cruel, very selfish, but love is always selfish ; the more ardent the more selfish. How jealous I am you cannot know. You must come with me, loving me, to death ; or else hate me, and still come with me, and *hating* me through death and after. There is no such word as indifference in my apathetic nature."

" Now, Carmilla, you are going to talk your wild nonsense again," I said hastily.

" Not I, silly little fool as I am, and full of whims and fancies ; for your sake I'll talk like a sage. Were you ever at a ball ? "

" No ; how you do run on. What is it like ? How charming it must be."

" I almost forget, it is years ago."

I laughed.

" You are not so old. Your first ball can hardly be forgotten yet."

" I remember everything about it—with an effort. I see it all, as divers see what is going on above them, through a medium, dense, rippling, but transparent. There occurred that night what has confused the picture, and made its colours faint. I was all but assassinated in my bed, wounded *here*," she touched her breast, " and never was the same since."

" Were you near dying ? "

" Yes, very—a cruel love—strange love, that would have taken my life. Love will have its sacrifices. No sacrifice without blood. Let us go to sleep now ; I feel so lazy. How can I get up just now and lock my door ? "

She was lying with her tiny hands buried in her rich wavy hair, under her cheek, her little head upon the pillow, and her glittering eyes followed me wherever I moved, with a kind of shy smile that I could not decipher.

I bid her good-night, and crept from the room with an uncomfortable sensation.

I often wondered whether our pretty guest ever said her prayers. *I* certainly had never seen her upon her knees. In the morning she never came down until long after our family prayers were over, and at night she never left the drawing-room to attend our brief evening prayers in the hall.

If it had not been that it had casually come out in one of our careless talks that she had been baptised, I should have doubted her being a Christian. Religion was a subject on which I had never heard her speak a word. If I had known the world better, this particular neglect or antipathy would not have so much surprised me.

The precautions of nervous people are infectious, and persons of a like temperament are pretty sure, after a time, to imitate them. I had adopted Carmilla's habit of locking her bed-room door, having taken into my head all her whimsical alarms about midnight invaders, and prowling assassins. I had also adopted her precaution of making a brief search through her room, to satisfy herself that no lurking assassin or robber was " ensconced."

These wise measures taken, I got into my bed and fell asleep. A light was burning in my room. This was an old habit, of very early date, and which nothing could have tempted me to dispense with.

Thus fortified I might take my rest in peace. But dreams come through stone walls, light up dark rooms, or darken light ones, and their persons make their exits and their entrances as they please, and laugh at locksmiths.

I had a dream that night that was the beginning of a very strange agony.

I cannot call it a nightmare, for I was quite conscious of being asleep. But I was equally conscious of being in my room, and lying in bed, precisely as I actually was. I saw, or fancied I saw, the room and its furniture just as I had seen it last, except that it was very dark, and I saw something moving round the foot of the bed, which at first I could not accurately distinguish. But I soon saw that it was a sooty-black animal that resembled a monstrous cat. It appeared to me about four or five feet long, for it measured fully the length of the hearth-rug as it passed over it; and it continued to-ing and fro-ing with the lithe sinister restlessness of a beast in a cage. I could not cry out, although as you may suppose, I was terrified. Its pace was growing faster, and the room rapidly darker and darker, and at length so dark that I could no longer see anything of it but its eyes. I felt it spring lightly on the bed. The two broad eyes approached my face, and suddenly I felt a stinging pain as if two large needles darted, an inch or two apart, deep into my breast. I waked with a scream. The room was lighted by the candle that burnt there all through the night, and I saw a female figure standing at the foot of the bed, a little at the right side. It was in a dark loose dress, and its hair was down and covered its shoulders. A block of stone could not have been more still. There was not the slightest stir of respiration. As I stared at it, the figure appeared to have changed its place, and was now nearer the door; then, close to it, the door opened, and it passed out.

I was now relieved, and able to breathe and move. My first thought was that Carmilla had been playing me a trick, and that I had forgotten to secure my door. I hastened to it, and found it locked as usual on the inside. I was afraid to open it—I was horrified. I sprang into my bed and covered my head up in the bed-clothes, and lay there more dead than alive till morning.

VII

DESCENDING

IT would be vain my attempting to tell you the horror with which, even now, I recall the occurrence of that night. It was no such transitory terror as a dream leaves behind it. It seemed to deepen by time, and communicated itself to the room and the very furniture that had encompassed the apparition.

I could not bear next day to be alone for a moment. I should have told papa, but for two opposite reasons. At one time I thought he would laugh at my story, and I could not bear its being treated as a jest; and at another, I thought he might fancy that I had been attacked by the mysterious complaint which had invaded our neighbourhood. I had myself no misgivings of the kind, and as he had been rather an invalid for some time, I was afraid of alarming him.

I was comfortable enough with my good-natured companions, Madame Perrodon, and the vivacious Mademoiselle Lafontaine. They both perceived that I was out of spirits and nervous, and at length I told them what lay so heavy at my heart.

Mademoiselle laughed, but I fancied that Madame Perrodon looked anxious.

" By-the-by," said Mademoiselle, laughing, " the long lime tree walk, behind Carmilla's bedroom window, is haunted ! "

" Nonsense ! " exclaimed Madame, who probably thought the theme rather inopportune, " and who tells that story, my dear ? "

" Martin says that he came up twice, when the old yard-gate was being repaired before sunrise, and twice saw the same female figure walking down the lime tree avenue."

" So he well might, as long as there are cows to milk in the river fields," said Madame.

" I daresay; but Martin chooses to be frightened, and never did I see fool *more* frightened."

" You must not say a word about it to Carmilla, because she can see down that walk from her room window," I interposed, " and she is, if possible, a greater coward than I."

Carmilla came down rather later than usual that day.

" I was so frightened last night," she said, so soon as we were together, " and I am sure I should have seen something dreadful if it had not been for that charm I bought from the poor little hunchback whom I called such hard names. I had a dream of something black coming round my bed, and I awoke in a perfect horror, and I really thought, for some seconds, I saw a dark figure near the chimney piece, but I felt under my pillow for my charm, and the moment my fingers touched it, the figure disappeared, and I felt quite certain, only that I had it by me, that something frightful would have made its appearance, and, perhaps, throttled me, as it did those poor people we heard of."

" Well, listen to me," I began, and recounted my adventure, at the recital of which she appeared horrified.

" And had you the charm near you ? " she asked earnestly.

" No, I had dropped it into a china vase in the drawing-room, but I shall certainly take it with me to-night, as you have so much faith in it."

At this distance of time I cannot tell you, or even understand, how I overcame my horror so effectually as to lie alone in my room that night. I remember distinctly that I pinned the charm to my pillow. I fell asleep almost immediately, and slept even more soundly than usual all night.

Next night I passed as well. My sleep was delightfully deep and dreamless. But I wakened with a sense of lassitude and melancholy, which, however, did not exceed a degree that was almost luxurious.

" Well, I told you so," said Carmilla, when I described my quiet sleep, " I had such delightful sleep myself last night ; I pinned the charm to the breast of my nightdress. It was too far away the night before. I am quite sure it was all fancy, except the dreams. I used to think that evil spirits made dreams, but our doctor told me it is no such thing. Only a fever passing by, or some other malady, as they often do, he said, knocks at the door, and not being able to get in, passes on, with that alarm."

" And what do you think the charm is ? " said I.

" It has been fumigated or immersed in some drug, and is an antidote against the malaria," she answered.

" Then it acts only on the body ? "

" Certainly ; you don't suppose that evil spirits are frightened by bits of ribbon, or the perfumes of a druggist's shop ? No, these complaints, wandering in the air, begin by trying the nerves, and so infect the brain ; but before they can seize upon you, the antidote repels them. That I am sure is what the charm has done for us. It is nothing magical, it is simply natural."

I should have been happier if I could quite have agreed with Carmilla, but I did my best, and the impression was a little losing its force.

For some nights I slept profoundly ; but still every morning I felt the same lassitude, and a languor weighed upon me all day. I felt myself a changed girl. A strange melancholy was stealing over me, a melancholy that I would not have interrupted. Dim thoughts of death began to open, and an idea that I was slowly sinking took gentle, and, some-how, not unwelcome possession of me. If it was sad, the tone of mind which this induced was also sweet. Whatever it might be, my soul acquiesced in it.

I would not admit that I was ill, I would not consent to tell my papa, or to have the doctor sent for.

Carmilla became more devoted to me than ever, and her strange paroxysms of languid adoration more frequent. She used to gloat on me with increasing ardour the more my strength and spirits waned. This always shocked me like a momentary glare of insanity.

Without knowing it, I was now in a pretty advanced stage of the strangest illness under which mortal ever suffered. There was an unaccountable fascination in its earlier symptoms that more than reconciled me to the incapacitating effect of that stage of the malady. This fascination increased for a time, until it reached a certain point, when gradually a sense of the horrible mingled itself with it, deepening as you shall hear, until it discoloured and perverted the whole state of my life.

The first change I experienced was rather agreeable. It was very near the turning point from which began the descent of Avernus.

Certain vague and strange sensations visited me in my sleep. The prevailing one was of that pleasant, peculiar cold thrill which we feel in bathing, when we move against the current of a river. This was soon accompanied by dreams that seemed interminable, and were so vague that I could never recollect their scenery and persons, or any one con-nected portion of their action. But they left an awful impression, and a sense of exhaustion, as if I had passed through a long period of great mental exertion and danger. After all these dreams there remained on waking a remembrance of having been in a place very nearly dark, and of having spoken to people whom I could not see ; and especially of one clear voice, of a female's, very deep, that spoke as if at a distance, slowly, and producing always the same sensa-tion of indescribable solemnity and fear. Sometimes there came a sensation as if a hand was drawn softly along my cheek and neck. Sometimes it was as if warm lips kissed me, and longer and more lovingly as they reached my throat, but there the caress fixed itself. My heart beat faster, my breathing rose and fell rapidly and full drawn; a sobbing, that rose into a sense of strangulation, supervened, and turned into a dreadful convulsion, in which my senses left me, and I became unconscious.

It was now three weeks since the commencement of this unaccount-able state. My sufferings had, during the last week, told upon my appearance. I had grown pale, my eyes were dilated and darkened underneath, and the languor which I had long felt began to display itself in my countenance.

My father asked me often whether I was ill ; but, with an obstinacy which now seems to me unaccountable, I persisted in assuring him that I was quite well.

In a sense this was true. I had no pain, I could complain of no bodily derangement. My complaint seemed to be one of the imagination, or the nerves, and, horrible as my sufferings were, I kept them, with a morbid reserve, very nearly to myself.

It could not be that terrible complaint which the peasants call the oupire, for I had now been suffering for three weeks, and they were seldom ill for much more than three days, when death put an end to their miseries.

Carmilla complained of dreams and feverish sensations, but by no means of so alarming a kind as mine. I say that mine were extremely alarming. Had I been capable of comprehending my condition, I would have invoked aid and advice on my knees. The narcotic of an unsuspected influence was acting upon me, and my perceptions were benumbed.

I am going to tell you now of a dream that led immediately to an odd discovery.

One night, instead of the voice I was accustomed to hear in the dark, I heard one, sweet and tender, and at the same time terrible, which said, " Your mother warns you to beware of the assassin." At the same time a light unexpectedly sprang up, and I saw Carmilla, standing near the foot of my bed, in her white nightdress, bathed, from her chin to her feet, in one great stain of blood.

I wakened with a shriek, possessed with the one idea that Carmilla was being murdered. I remember springing from my bed, and my next recollection is that of standing on the lobby, crying for help.

Madame and Mademoiselle came scurrying out of their rooms in alarm ; a lamp burned always on the lobby, and seeing me, they soon learned the cause of my terror.

I insisted on our knocking at Carmilla's door. Our knocking was unanswered. It soon became a pounding and an uproar. We shrieked her name, but all was vain.

We all grew frightened, for the door was locked. We hurried back, in panic, to my room. There we rang the bell long and furiously. If my father's room had been at that side of the house, we would have called him up at once to our aid. But, alas ! he was quite out of hearing, and to reach him involved an excursion for which we none of us had courage.

Servants, however, soon came running up the stairs ; I had got on my dressing-gown and slippers meanwhile, and my companions were already similarly furnished. Recognizing the voices of the servants on the lobby, we sallied out together ; and having renewed, as fruitlessly, our summons at Carmilla's door, I ordered the men to force the lock. They did so, and we stood, holding our lights aloft, in the doorway, and so stared into the room.

We called her by name ; but there was still no reply. We looked round the room. Everything was undisturbed. It was exactly in the state in which I left it on bidding her good night. But Carmilla was gone.

VIII

Search

AT sight of the room, perfectly undisturbed except for our violent entrance, we began to cool a little, and soon recovered our senses sufficiently to dismiss the men. It had struck Mademoiselle that possibly Carmilla had been wakened by the uproar at her door, and in her first panic had jumped from her bed, and hid herself in a press, or behind a curtain, from which she could not, of course, emerge until the majordomo and his myrmidons had withdrawn. We now recommenced our search, and began to call her by name again.

It was all to no purpose. Our perplexity and agitation increased. We examined the windows, but they were secured. I implored of Carmilla, if she had concealed herself, to play this cruel trick no longer —to come out, and to end our anxieties. It was all useless. I was by this time convinced that she was not in the room, nor in the dressing-room, the door of which was still locked on this side. She could not have passed it. I was utterly puzzled. Had Carmilla discovered one of those secret passages which the old housekeeper said were known to exist in the schloss, although the tradition of their exact situation had been lost. A little time would, no doubt, explain all—utterly perplexed as, for the present, we were.

It was past four o'clock, and I preferred passing the remaining hours of darkness in Madame's room. Daylight brought no solution of the difficulty.

The whole household, with my father at its head, was in a state of agitation next morning. Every part of the château was searched. The grounds were explored. Not a trace of the missing lady could be discovered. The stream was about to be dragged; my father was in distraction; what a tale to have to tell the poor girl's mother on her return. I, too, was almost beside myself, though my grief was quite of a different kind.

The morning was passed in alarm and excitement. It was now one o'clock, and still no tidings. I ran up to Carmilla's room, and found her standing at her dressing-table. I was astounded. I could not believe my eyes. She beckoned me to her with her pretty finger, in silence. Her face expressed extreme fear.

I ran to her in an ecstasy of joy; I kissed and embraced her again and again. I ran to the bell and rang it vehemently, to bring others to the spot, who might at once relieve my father's anxiety.

" Dear Carmilla, what has become of you all this time ? We have been in agonies of anxiety about you," I exclaimed. " Where have you been ? How did you come back ? "

" Last night has been a night of wonders," she said.

" For mercy's sake, explain all you can."

" It was past two last night," she said, " when I went to sleep as usual in my bed, with my doors locked, that of the dressing-room, and that opening upon the gallery. My sleep was uninterrupted, and, so far as I know, dreamless; but I awoke just now on the sofa in the dressing-room there, and I found the door between the rooms open, and the other door forced. How could all this have happened without my being wakened? It must have been accompanied with a great deal of noise, and I am particularly easily wakened; and how could I have been carried out of my bed without my sleep having been interrupted, I whom the slightest stir startles?"

By this time, Madame, Mademoiselle, my father, and a number of the servants were in the room. Carmilla was, of course, overwhelmed with inquiries, congratulations, and welcomes. She had but one story to tell, and seemed the least able of all the party to suggest any way of accounting for what had happened.

My father took a turn up and down the room, thinking. I saw Carmilla's eye follow him for a moment with a sly, dark glance.

When my father had sent the servants away, Mademoiselle having gone in search of a little bottle of valerian and sal-volatile, and there being no one now in the room with Carmilla except my father, Madame, and myself, he came to her thoughtfully, took her hand very kindly, led her to the sofa, and sat down beside her.

"Will you forgive me, my dear, if I risk a conjecture, and ask a question?"

"Who can have a better right?" she said. "Ask what you please, and I will tell you everything. But my story is simply one of bewilderment and darkness. I know absolutely nothing. Put any question you please. But you know, of course, the limitations mamma has placed me under."

"Perfectly, my dear child. I need not approach the topics on which she desires our silence. Now, the marvel of last night consists in your having been removed from your bed and your room without being wakened, and this removal having occurred apparently while the windows were still secured, and the two doors locked upon the inside. I will tell you my theory, and first ask you a question."

Carmilla was leaning on her hand dejectedly; Madame and I were listening breathlessly.

"Now, my question is this. Have you ever been suspected of walking in your sleep?"

"Never since I was very young indeed."

"But you did walk in your sleep when you were young?"

"Yes; I know I did. I have been told so often by my old nurse."

My father smiled and nodded.

"Well, what has happened is this. You got up in your sleep, unlocked the door, not leaving the key, as usual, in the lock, but taking it out and locking it on the outside; you again took the key out, and carried it away with you to some one of the five-and-twenty rooms on this floor, or perhaps upstairs or downstairs. There are so many rooms and closets, so much heavy furniture, and such accumulations of

CARMILLA

lumber, that it would require a week to search this old house thoroughly. Do you see, now, what I mean ? "

" I do, but not all," she answered.

" And how, papa, do you account for her finding herself on the sofa in the dressing-room, which we had searched so carefully ? "

" She came there after you had searched it, still in her sleep, and at last awoke spontaneously, and was as much surprised to find herself where she was as any one else. I wish all mysteries were as easily and innocently explained as yours, Carmilla," he said, laughing. " And so we may congratulate ourselves on the certainty that the most natural explanation of the occurrence is one that involves no drugging, no tampering with locks, no burglars, or poisoners, or witches—nothing that need alarm Carmilla, or any one else, for our safety."

Carmilla was looking charmingly. Nothing could be more beautiful than her tints. Her beauty was, I think, enhanced by that graceful languor that was peculiar to her. I think my father was silently contrasting her looks with mine, for he said :—

" I wish my poor Laura was looking more like herself," and he sighed.

So our alarms were happily ended, and Carmilla restored to her friends.

IX

THE DOCTOR

As Carmilla would not hear of an attendant sleeping in her room, my father arranged that a servant should sleep outside her door, so that she could not attempt to make another such excursion without being arrested at her own door.

That night passed quietly; and next morning early, the doctor, whom my father had sent for without telling me a word about it, arrived to see me.

Madame accompanied me to the library; and there the grave little doctor, with white hair and spectacles, whom I mentioned before, was waiting to receive me.

I told him my story, and as I proceeded he grew graver and graver.

We were standing, he and I, in the recess of one of the windows, facing one another. When my statement was over, he leaned with his shoulders against the wall, and with his eyes fixed on me earnestly, with an interest in which was a dash of horror.

After a minute's reflection, he asked Madame if he could see my father.

He was sent for accordingly, and as he entered, smiling, he said :

" I dare say, doctor, you are going to tell me that I am an old fool for having brought you here; I hope I am."

But his smile faded into shadow as the doctor, with a very grave face, beckoned him to him.

He and the doctor talked for some time in the same recess where I had just conferred with the physician. It seemed an earnest and argumentative conversation. The room is very large, and I and Madame stood together, burning with curiosity, at the further end. Not a word could we hear, however, for they spoke in a very low tone, and the deep recess of the window quite concealed the doctor from view, and very nearly my father, whose foot, arm, and shoulder only could we see; and the voices were, I suppose, all the less audible for the sort of closet which the thick wall and window formed.

After a time my father's face looked into the room; it was pale, thoughtful, and, I fancied, agitated.

"Laura, dear, come here for a moment. Madame, we shan't trouble you, the doctor says, at present."

Accordingly I approached, for the first time a little alarmed; for, although I felt very weak, I did not feel ill; and strength, one always fancies, is a thing that may be picked up when we please.

My father held out his hand to me as I drew near, but he was looking at the doctor, and he said:

"It certainly *is* very odd; I don't understand it quite. Laura, come here, dear; now attend to Doctor Spielsberg, and recollect yourself."

"You mentioned a sensation like that of two needles piercing the skin, somewhere about your neck, on the night when you experienced your first horrible dream. Is there still any soreness?"

"None at all," I answered.

"Can you indicate with your finger about the point at which you think this occurred?"

"Very little below my throat—*here*," I answered.

I wore a morning dress, which covered the place I pointed to.

"Now you can satisfy yourself," said the doctor. "You won't mind your papa's lowering your dress a very little. It is necessary, to detect a symptom of the complaint under which you have been suffering."

I acquiesced. It was only an inch or two below the edge of my collar.

"God bless me!—so it is," exclaimed my father, growing pale.

"You see it now with your own eyes," said the doctor, with a gloomy triumph.

"What is it?" I exclaimed, beginning to be frightened.

"Nothing, my dear young lady, but a small blue spot, about the size of the tip of your little finger; and now," he continued, turning to papa, "the question is what is best to be done?"

"Is there any danger?" I urged, in great trepidation.

"I trust not, my dear," answered the doctor. "I don't see why you should not recover. I don't see why you should not begin *immediately* to get better. That is the point at which the sense of strangulation begins?"

" Yes," I answered.

" And—recollect as well as you can—the same point was a kind of centre of that thrill which you described just now, like the current of a cold stream running against you ? "

" It may have been ; I think it was."

" Ay, you see ? " he added, turning to my father. " Shall I say a word to Madame ? "

" Certainly," said my father.

He called Madame to him, and said :

" I find my young friend here far from well. It won't be of any great consequence, I hope ; but it will be necessary that some steps be taken, which I will explain by-and-by ; but in the meantime, Madame, you will be so good as not to let Miss Laura be alone for one moment. That is the only direction I need give for the present. It is indispensable."

" We may rely upon your kindness, Madame, I know," added my father.

Madame satisfied him eagerly.

" And you, dear Laura, I know you will observe the doctor's direction."

" I shall have to ask your opinion upon another patient, whose symptoms slightly resemble those of my daughter, that have just been detailed to you—very much milder in degree, but I believe quite of the same sort. She is a young lady—our guest ; but as you say you will be passing this way again this evening, you can't do better than take your supper here, and you can then see her. She does not come down till the afternoon."

" I thank you," said the doctor. " I shall be with you, then, at about seven this evening."

And then they repeated their directions to me and to Madame, and with this parting charge my father left us, and walked out with the doctor ; and I saw them pacing together up and down between the road and the moat, on the grassy platform in front of the castle, evidently absorbed in earnest conversation.

The doctor did not return. I saw him mount his horse there, take his leave, and ride away eastward through the forest. Nearly at the same time I saw the man arrive from Dranfeld with the letters, and dismount and hand the bag to my father.

In the meantime, Madame and I were both busy, lost in conjecture as to the reasons of the singular and earnest direction which the doctor and my father had concurred in imposing. Madame, as she afterwards told me, was afraid the doctor apprehended a sudden seizure, and that, without prompt assistance, I might either lose my life in a fit, or at least be seriously hurt.

This interpretation did not strike me ; and I fancied, perhaps luckily for my nerves, that the arrangement was prescribed simply to secure a companion, who would prevent my taking too much exercise, or eating unripe fruit, or doing any of the fifty foolish things to which young people are supposed to be prone.

About half-an-hour after my father came in—he had a letter in his hand—and said :

" This letter had been delayed ; it is from General Spielsdorf. He might have been here yesterday, he may not come till to-morrow, or he may be here to-day."

He put the open letter into my hand ; but he did not look pleased, as he used when a guest, especially one so much loved as the General, was coming. On the contrary, he looked as if he wished him at the bottom of the Red Sea. There was plainly something on his mind which he did not choose to divulge.

" Papa, darling, will you tell me this ? " said I, suddenly laying my hand on his arm, and looking, I am sure, imploringly in his face.

" Perhaps," he answered, smoothing my hair caressingly over my eyes.

" Does the doctor think me very ill ? "

" No, dear ; he thinks, if right steps are taken, you will be quite well again, at least on the high road to a complete recovery, in a day or two," he answered, a little drily. " I wish our good friend, the General, had chosen any other time ; that is, I wish you had been perfectly well to receive him."

" But do tell me, papa," I insisted, " *what* does he think is the matter with me ? "

" Nothing ; you must not plague me with questions," he answered, with more irritation than I ever remember him to have displayed before ; and seeing that I looked wounded, I suppose, he kissed me, and added, " You shall know all about it in a day or two ; that is, all that *I* know. In the meantime, you are not to trouble your head about it."

He turned and left the room, but came back before I had done wondering and puzzling over the oddity of all this ; it was merely to say that he was going to Karnstein, and had ordered the carriage to be ready at twelve, and that I and Madame should accompany him ; he was going to see the priest who lived near those picturesque grounds upon business, and as Carmilla had never seen them, she could follow, when she came down, with Mademoiselle, who would bring materials for what you call a pic-nic, which might be laid for us in the ruined castle.

At twelve o'clock, accordingly, I was ready, and not long after, my father, Madame and I set out upon our projected drive. Passing the drawbridge we turn to the right, and follow the road over the steep Gothic bridge, westward, to reach the deserted village and ruined castle of Karnstein.

No sylvan drive can be fancied prettier. The ground breaks into gentle hills and hollows, all clothed with beautiful wood, totally destitute of the comparative formality which artificial planting and early culture and pruning impart.

The irregularities of the ground often lead the road out of its course, and cause it to wind beautifully round the sides of broken hollows and the steeper sides of the hills, among varieties of ground almost inexhaustible.

Turning one of these points, we suddenly encountered our old friend, the General, riding towards us, attended by a mounted servant. His portmanteaus were following in a hired waggon, such as we term a cart.

The General dismounted as we pulled up, and, after the usual greetings, was easily persuaded to accept the vacant seat in the carriage, and send his horse on with his servant to the schloss.

X

BEREAVED

IT was about ten months since we had last seen him ; but that time had sufficed to make an alteration of years in his appearance. He had grown thinner ; something of gloom and anxiety had taken the place of that cordial serenity which used to characterise his features. His dark blue eyes, always penetrating, now gleamed with a sterner light from under his shaggy grey eyebrows. It was not such a change as grief alone usually induces, and angrier passions seemed to have had their share in bringing it about.

We had not long resumed our drive, when the General began to talk, with his usual soldierly directness, of the bereavement, as he termed it, which he had sustained in the death of his beloved niece and ward ; and he then broke out in a tone of intense bitterness and fury, inveighing against the " hellish arts " to which she had fallen a victim, and expressing, with more exasperation than piety, his wonder that Heaven should tolerate so monstrous an indulgence of the lusts and malignity of hell.

My father, who saw at once that something very extraordinary had befallen, asked him, if not too painful to him, to retail the circumstances which he thought justified the strong terms in which he expressed himself.

" I should tell you all with pleasure," said the General, " but you would not believe me."

" Why should I not ? " he asked.

" Because," he answered testily, " you believe in nothing but what consists with your own prejudices and illusions. I remember when I was like you, but I have learned better."

" Try me," said my father ; " I am not such a dogmatist as you suppose. Besides which, I very well know that you generally require proof for what you believe, and am, therefore, very strongly predisposed to respect your conclusions."

" You are right in supposing that I have not been led lightly into a belief in the marvellous—for what I have experienced *is* marvellous—and I have been forced by extraordinary evidence to credit that which ran counter, diametrically, to all my theories. I have been made the dupe of a preternatural conspiracy."

Notwithstanding his professions of confidence in the General's penetration, I saw my father, at this point, glance at the General, with, as I thought, a marked suspicion of his sanity.

The General did not see it, luckily. He was looking gloomily and curiously into the glades and vistas of the woods that were opening before us.

" You are going to the Ruins of Karnstein ? " he said. " Yes, it is a lucky coincidence ; do you know I was going to ask you to bring me there to inspect them. I have a special object in exploring. There is a ruined chapel, ain't there, with a great many tombs of that extinct family ? "

" So there are—highly interesting," said my father. " I hope you are thinking of claiming the title and estates ? "

My father said this gaily, but the General did not recollect the laugh, or even the smile, which courtesy exacts for a friend's joke ; on the contrary, he looked grave and even fierce, ruminating on a matter that stirred his anger and horror.

" Something very different," he said, gruffly. " I mean to unearth some of those fine people. I hope, by God's blessing, to accomplish a pious sacrilege here, which will relieve our earth of certain monsters, and enable honest people to sleep in their beds without being assailed by murderers. I have strange things to tell you, my dear friend, such as I myself would have scouted as incredible a few months since."

My father looked at him again, but this time not with a glance of suspicion—with an eye, rather, of keen intelligence and alarm.

" The house of Karnstein," he said, " has been long extinct : a hundred years at least. My dear wife was maternally descended from the Karnsteins. But the name and title have long ceased to exist. The castle is a ruin ; the very village is deserted ; it is fifty years since the smoke of a chimney was seen there ; not a roof left."

" Quite true. I have heard a great deal about that since I last saw you ; a great deal that will astonish you. But I had better relate everything in the order in which it occurred," said the General. " You saw my dear ward—my child, I may call her. No creature could have been more beautiful, and only three months ago none more blooming."

" Yes, poor thing ! when I saw her last she certainly was quite lovely," said my father. " I was grieved and shocked more than I can tell you, my dear friend ; I knew what a blow it was to you."

He took the General's hand, and they exchanged a kind pressure. Tears gathered in the old soldier's eyes. He did not seek to conceal them. He said :

" We have been very old friends ; I knew you would feel for me, childless as I am. She had become an object of very dear interest to me, and repaid my care by an affection that cheered my home and made my life happy. That is all gone. The years that remain to me on earth may not be very long ; but by God's mercy I hope to accomplish a service to mankind before I die, and to subserve the vengeance of Heaven upon the fiends who have murdered my poor child in the spring of her hopes and beauty ! "

" You said, just now, that you intended relating everything as it occurred," said my father. " Pray do ; I assure you that it is not mere curiosity that prompts me."

By this time we had reached the point at which the Drunstall road, by which the General had come, diverges from the road which we were travelling to Karnstein.

" How far is it to the ruins ? " inquired the General, looking anxiously forward.

" About half a league," answered my father. " Pray let us hear the story you were so good as to promise."

XI
THE STORY

" WITH all my heart," said the General, with an effort ; and after a short pause in which to arrange his subject, he commenced one of the strangest narratives I ever heard.

" My dear child was looking forward with great pleasure to the visit you had been so good as to arrange for her to your charming daughter." Here he made me a gallant but melancholy bow. " In the meantime we had an invitation to my old friend the Count Carlsfeld, whose schloss is about six leagues to the other side of Karnstein. It was to attend the series of fêtes which, you remember, were given by him in honour of his illustrious visitor, the Grand Duke Charles."

" Yes ; and very splendid, I believe, they were," said my father.

" Princely ! But then his hospitalities are quite regal. He has Aladdin's lamp. The night from which my sorrow dates was devoted to a magnificent masquerade. The grounds were thrown open, the trees hung with coloured lamps. There was such a display of fireworks as Paris itself had never witnessed. And such music—music, you know, is my weakness—such ravishing music ! The finest instrumental band, perhaps, in the world, and the finest singers who could be collected from all the great operas in Europe. As you wandered through these fantastically illuminated grounds, the moon-lighted château throwing a rosy light from its long rows of windows, you would suddenly hear these ravishing voices stealing from the silence of some grove, or rising from boats upon the lake. I felt myself, as I looked and listened, carried back into the romance and poetry of my early youth.

" When the fireworks were ended, and the ball beginning, we returned to the noble suite of rooms that were thrown open to the dancers.

A masked ball, you know, is a beautiful sight; but so brilliant a spectacle of the kind I never saw before.

" It was a very aristocratic assembly. I was myself almost the only ' nobody ' present.

" My dear child was looking quite beautiful. She wore no mask. Her excitement and delight added an unspeakable charm to her features, always lovely. I remarked a young lady, dressed magnificently, but wearing a mask, who appeared to me to be observing my ward with extraordinary interest. I had seen her, earlier in the evening, in the great hall, and again, for a few minutes, walking near us, on the terrace under the castle windows, similarly employed. A lady, also masked, richly and gravely dressed, and with a stately air, like a person of rank, accompanied her as a chaperon. Had the young lady not worn a mask, I could, of course, have been much more certain upon the question whether she was really watching my poor darling. I am now well assured that she was.

" We were now in one of the *salons*. My poor dear child had been dancing, and was resting a little in one of the chairs near the door ; I was standing near. The two ladies I have mentioned had approached, and the younger took the chair next my ward ; while her companion stood beside me, and for a little time addressed herself, in a low tone, to her charge.

" Availing herself of the privilege of her mask, she turned to me, and in the tone of an old friend, and calling me by my name, opened a conversation with me, which piqued my curiosity a good deal. She referred to many scenes where she had met me—at Court, and at distinguished houses. She alluded to little incidents which I had long ceased to think of, but which, I found, had only lain in abeyance in my memory, for they instantly started into life at her touch.

" I became more and more curious to ascertain who she was, every moment. She parried my attempts to discover very adroitly and pleasantly. The knowledge she showed of many passages in my life seemed to me all but unaccountable ; and she appeared to take a not unnatural pleasure in foiling my curiosity, and in seeing me flounder in my eager perplexity, from one conjecture to another.

" In the meantime the young lady, whom her mother called by the odd name of Millarca, when she once or twice addressed her, had, with the same ease and grace, got into conversation with my ward.

" She introduced herself by saying that her mother was a very old acquaintance of mine. She spoke of the agreeable audacity which a mask rendered practicable ; she talked like a friend ; she admired her dress, and insinuated very prettily her admiration of her beauty. She amused her with laughing criticisms upon the people who crowded the ballroom, and laughed at my poor child's fun. She was very witty and lively when she pleased, and after a time they had grown very good friends, and the young stranger lowered her mask, displaying a remarkably beautiful face. I had never seen it before, neither had my dear child. But though it was new to us, the features were so engaging, as well as lovely, that it was impossible not to feel the attraction powerfully. My poor girl did so. I never saw anyone more taken with another at first sight, unless, indeed, it was the stranger herself, who seemed quite to have lost her heart to her.

" In the meantime, availing myself of the licence of a masquerade, I put not a few questions to the elder lady.

" ' You have puzzled me utterly,' I said, laughing. ' Is that not enough ? won't you, now, consent to stand on equal terms, and do me the kindness to remove your mask ? '

" ' Can any request be more unreasonable ? ' she replied. ' Ask a lady to yield an advantage ! Beside, how do you know you should recognize me ? Years make changes.'

" ' As you see,' I said, with a bow, and, I suppose, a rather melancholy little laugh.

" ' As philosophers tell us,' she said ; ' and how do you know that a sight of my face would help you ? '

" ' I should take chance for that,' I answered. ' It is vain trying to make yourself out an old woman ; your figure betrays you.'

" ' Years, nevertheless, have passed since I saw you, rather since you saw me, for that is what I am considering. Millarca, there, is my daughter ; I cannot then be young, even in the opinion of people whom time has taught to be indulgent, and I may not like to be compared with what you remember me. You have no mask to remove. You can offer me nothing in exchange.'

" ' My petition is to your pity, to remove it.'

" ' And mine to yours, to let it stay where it is,' she replied.

" ' Well, then, at least you will tell me whether you are French or German ; you speak both languages so perfectly.'

" ' I don't think I shall tell you that, General ; you intend a surprise, and are meditating the particular point of attack.'

" ' At all events, you won't deny this,' I said, ' that being honoured by your permission to converse, I ought to know how to address you. Shall I say Madame la Comtesse ? '

" She laughed, and she would, no doubt, have met me with another evasion—if, indeed, I can treat any occurrence in an interview every circumstance of which was pre-arranged, as I now believe, with the profoundest cunning, as liable to be modified by accident.

" ' As to that,' she began ; but she was interrupted, almost as she opened her lips, by a gentleman, dressed in black, who looked particularly elegant and distinguished, with this drawback, that his face was the most deadly pale I ever saw, except in death. He was in no masquerade—in the plain evening dress of a gentleman ; and he said without a smile, but with a courtly and unusually low bow :—

" ' Will Madame la Comtesse permit me to say a very few words which may interest her ? '

" The lady turned quickly to him, and touched her lip in token of silence ; she then said to me, ' Keep my place for me, General ; I shall return when I have said a few words.'

" And with this injunction, playfully given, she walked a little aside with the gentleman in black, and talked for some minutes, apparently very earnestly. They then walked away slowly together in the crowd, and I lost them for some minutes.

" I spent the interval in cudgelling my brains for conjecture as to the identity of the lady who seemed to remember me so kindly, and I was thinking of turning about and joining in the conversation between my pretty ward and the Countess's daughter, and trying whether, by the time she returned, I might not have a surprise in store for her, by having her name, title, chateau, and estates at my fingers' ends. But at this moment she returned, accompanied by the pale man in black, who said :

" ' I shall return and inform Madame la Comtesse when her carriage is at the door.'

" He withdrew with a bow."

XII

A Petition

" ' Then we are to lose Madame la Comtesse, but I hope only for a few hours,' I said, with a low bow.

" ' It may be that only, or it may be a few weeks. It was very unlucky his speaking to me just now as he did. Do you now know me ? '

" I assured her I did not.

" ' You shall know me,' she said, ' but not at present. We are older and better friends than, perhaps, you suspect. I cannot yet declare myself. I shall in three weeks pass your beautiful schloss about which I have been making enquiries. I shall then look in upon you for an hour or two, and renew a friendship which I never think of without a thousand pleasant recollections. This moment a piece of news has reached me like a thunderbolt. I must set out now, and travel by a devious route, nearly a hundred miles, with all the dispatch I can possibly make. My perplexities multiply. I am only deterred by the compulsory reserve I practise as to my name from making a very singular request of you. My poor child has not quite recovered her strength. Her horse fell with her, at a hunt which she had ridden out to witness, her nerves have not yet recovered the shock, and our physician says that she must on no account exert herself for some time to come. We came here, in consequence, by very easy stages—hardly six leagues a day. I must now travel day and night, on a mission of life and death—a mission the critical and momentous nature of which I shall be able to explain to you when we meet, as I hope we shall, in a few weeks, without the necessity of any concealment.'

" She went on to make her petition, and it was in the tone of a person from whom such a request amounted to conferring, rather than seeking a favour. This was only in manner, and, as it seemed, quite unconsciously. Than the terms in which it was expressed, nothing could be more deprecatory. It was simply that I would consent to take charge of her daughter during her absence.

" This was, all things considered, a strange, not to say, an audacious request. She in some sort disarmed me, by stating and admitting everything that could be urged against it, and throwing herself entirely upon my chivalry. At the same moment, by a fatality that seems to have predetermined all that happened, my poor child came to my side, and, in an undertone, besought me to invite her new friend, Millarca, to pay us a visit. She had just been sounding her, and thought, if her mamma would allow her, she would like it extremely.

" At another time I should have told her to wait a little, until, at least, we knew who they were. But I had not a moment to think in. The two ladies assailed me together, and I must confess the refined and beautiful face of the young lady, about which there was something extremely engaging, as well as the elegance and fire of high birth, determined me ; and quite overpowered, I submitted, and undertook too easily, the care of the young lady, whom her mother called Millarca.

" The Countess beckoned to her daughter, who listened with grave attention while she told her, in general terms, how suddenly and peremptorily she had been summoned, and also of the arrangement she had made for her under my care, adding that I was one of her earliest and most valued friends.

" I made, of course, such speeches as the case seemed to call for, and found myself, on reflection, in a position which I did not half like.

" The gentleman in black returned, and very ceremoniously conducted the lady from the room.

" The demeanour of this gentleman was such as to impress me with the conviction that the Countess was a lady of very much more importance than her modest title alone might have led me to assume.

" Her last charge to me was that no attempt was to be made to learn more about her than I might have already guessed, until her return. Our distinguished host, whose guest she was, knew her reasons.

" ' But here,' she said, ' neither I nor my daughter could safely remain for more than a day. I removed my mask imprudently for a moment, about an hour ago, and, too late, I fancied you saw me. So I resolved to seek an opportunity of talking a little to you. Had I found that you *had* seen me, I should have thrown myself on your high sense of honour to keep my secret for some weeks. As it is, I am satisfied that you did not see me ; but if you now *suspect*, or, on reflection, *should* suspect, who I am, I commit myself, in like manner, entirely to your honour. My daughter will observe the same secrecy, and I well know that you will, from time to time, remind her, lest she should thoughtlessly disclose it.'

" She whispered a few words to her daughter, kissed her hurriedly twice, and went away, accompanied by the pale gentleman in black, and disappeared in the crowd.

" ' In the next room,' said Millarca, ' there is a window that looks upon the hall door. I should like to see the last of mamma, and to kiss my hand to her.'

" We assented, of course, and accompanied her to the window. We looked out, and saw a handsome old-fashioned carriage, with a troop of couriers and footmen. We saw the slim figure of the pale gentleman in black, as he held a thick velvet cloak, and placed it about her shoulders and threw the hood over her head. She nodded to him, and just touched his hand with hers. He bowed low repeatedly as the door closed, and the carriage began to move.

" ' She is gone,' said Millarca, with a sigh.

" ' She is gone,' I repeated to myself, for the first time—in the hurried moments that had elapsed since my consent—reflecting upon the folly of my act.

" ' She did not look up,' said the young lady, plaintively.

" ' The Countess had taken off her mask, perhaps, and did not care to show her face,' I said ; ' and she could not know that you were in the window.'

" She sighed and looked in my face. She was so beautiful that I relented. I was sorry I had for a moment repented of my hospitality, and I determined to make her amends for the unavowed churlishness of my reception.

" The young lady, replacing her mask, joined my ward in persuading me to return to the grounds, where the concert was soon to be re-newed. We did so, and walked up and down the terrace that lies under the castle windows. Millarca became very intimate with us, and amused us with lively descriptions and stories of most of the great people whom we saw upon the terrace. I liked her more and more every minute. Her gossip, without being ill-natured, was extremely diverting to me, who had been so long out of the great world. I thought what life she would give to our sometimes lonely evenings at home.

" This ball was not over until the morning sun had almost reached the horizon. It pleased the Grand Duke to dance till then, so loyal people could not go away, or think of bed.

" We had just got through a crowded saloon, when my ward asked me what had become of Millarca. I thought she had been by her side, and she fancied she was by mine. The fact was, we had lost her.

" All my efforts to find her were vain. I feared that she had mis-taken, in the confusion of a momentary separation from us, other people for her new friends, and had, possibly, pursued and lost them in the extensive grounds which were thrown open to us.

" Now, in its full force, I recognized a new folly in my having under-taken the charge of a young lady without so much as knowing her name; and fettered as I was by promises, of the reasons for imposing which I knew nothing, I could not even point my inquiries by saying that the missing young lady was the daughter of the Countess who had taken her departure a few hours before.

" Morning broke. It was clear daylight before I gave up my search. It was not till near two o'clock next day that we heard anything of my missing charge.

" At about that time a servant knocked at my niece's door, to say that he had been earnestly requested by a young lady, who appeared to be in great distress, to make out where she could find the General Baron Spielsdorf and the young lady, his daughter, in whose charge she had been left by her mother.

" There could be no doubt, notwithstanding the slight inaccuracy, that our young friend had turned up; and so she had. Would to Heaven we had lost her !

" She told my poor child a story to account for her having failed to recover us for so long. Very late, she said, she had got into the housekeeper's bedroom in despair of finding us, and had then fallen into a deep sleep which, long as it was, had hardly sufficed to recruit her strength after the fatigues of the ball.

" That day Millarca came home with us. I was only too happy, after all, to have secured so charming a companion for my dear girl.

XIII
THE WOOD-MAN

" THERE soon, however, appeared some drawbacks. In the first place, Millarca complained of extreme languor—the weakness that remained after her late illness—and she never emerged from her room till the afternoon was pretty far advanced. In the next place, it was accidentally discovered, although she always locked her door on the inside, and never disturbed the key from its place, till she admitted the maid to assist at her toilet, that she was undoubtedly sometimes absent from her room in the very early morning, and at various times later in the day, before she wished it to be understood that she was stirring. She was repeatedly seen from the windows of the schloss, in the first faint grey of the morning, walking through the trees, in an easterly direction, and looking like a person in a trance. This convinced me that she walked in her sleep. But this hypothesis did not solve the puzzle. How did she pass out from her room, leaving the door locked on the inside. How did she escape from the house without unbarring door or window ?

" In the midst of my perplexities, an anxiety of a far more urgent kind presented itself.

" My dear child began to lose her looks and health, and that in a manner so mysterious, and even horrible, that I became thoroughly frightened.

" She was at first visited by appalling dreams ; then, as she fancied, by a spectre, sometimes resembling Millarca, sometimes in the shape of a beast, indistinctly seen, walking round the foot of her bed, from side to side. Lastly came sensations. One, not unpleasant, but very peculiar, she said, resembled the flow of an icy stream against her breast. At a later time, she felt something like a pair of large needles pierce her, a little below the throat, with a very sharp pain. A few nights after, followed a gradual and convulsive sense of strangulation ; then came unconsciousness."

I could hear distinctly every word the kind old General was saying, because by this time we were driving upon the short grass that spreads on either side of the road as you approach the roofless village which had not shown the smoke of a chimney for more than half a century.

You may guess how strangely I felt as I heard my own symptoms so exactly described in those which had been experienced by the poor girl who, but for the catastrophe which followed, would have been at that moment a visitor at my father's chateau. You may suppose, also, how I felt as I heard him detail habits and mysterious peculiarities which were, in fact, those of our beautiful guest, Carmilla !

A vista opened in the forest ; we were on a sudden under the chimneys and gables of the ruined village, and the towers and battlements of the dismantled castle, round which gigantic trees are grouped, overhung us from a slight eminence.

In a frightened dream I got down from the carriage, and in silence, for we had each abundant matter for thinking ; we soon mounted the ascent, and were among the spacious chambers, winding stairs, and dark corridors of the castle.

" And this was once the palatial residence of the Karnsteins ! " said the old General at length, as from a great window he looked out across the village, and saw the wide, undulating expanse of forest. " It was a bad family, and here its blood-stained annals were written," he continued. " It is hard that they should, after death, continue to plague the human race with their atrocious lusts. That is the chapel of the Karnsteins, down there."

He pointed down to the grey walls of the Gothic building, partly visible through the foliage, a little way down the steep. " And I hear the axe of a woodman," he added, " busy among the trees that surround it ; he possibly may give us the information of which I am in search, and point out the grave of Mircalla, Countess of Karnstein. These rustics preserve the local traditions of great families, whose stories die out among the rich and titled so soon as the families themselves become extinct."

" We have a portrait, at home, of Mircalla, the Countess Karnstein ; should you like to see it ? " asked my father.

" Time enough, dear friend," replied the General. " I believe that

I have seen the original ; and one motive which has led me to you earlier than I at first intended, was to explore the chapel which we are now approaching."

" What ! see the Countess Mircalla," exclaimed my father ; " why, she has been dead more than a century ! "

" Not so dead as you fancy, I am told," answered the General.

" I confess, General, you puzzle me utterly," replied my father, looking at him, I fancied, for a moment with a return of the suspicion I detected before. But although there was anger and detestation, at times, in the old General's manner, there was nothing flighty.

" There remains to me," he said, as we passed under the heavy arch of the Gothic church—for its dimensions would have justified its being so styled—" but one object which can interest me during the few years that remain to me on earth, and that is to wreak on her the vengeance which, I thank God, may still be accomplished by a mortal arm."

" What vengeance can you mean ? " asked my father, in increasing amazement.

" I mean, to decapitate the monster," he answered, with a fierce flush, and a stamp that echoed mournfully through the hollow ruin, and his clenched hand was at the same moment raised, as if it grasped the handle of an axe, while he shook it ferociously in the air.

" What ! " exclaimed my father, more than ever bewildered.

" To strike her head off."

" Cut her head off ? "

" Aye, with a hatchet, with a spade, or with anything that can cleave through her murderous throat. You shall hear," he answered, trembling with rage. And hurrying forward he said :

" That beam will answer for a seat ; your dear child is fatigued ; let her be seated, and I will, in a few sentences, close my dreadful story."

The squared block of wood, which lay on the grass-grown pavement of the chapel, formed a bench on which I was very glad to seat myself, and in the meantime the General called to the woodman, who had been removing some boughs which leaned upon the old walls ; and, axe in hand, the hardy old fellow stood before us.

He could not tell us anything of these monuments ; but there was an old man, he said, a ranger of this forest, at present sojourning in the house of the priest, about two miles away, who could point out every monument of the old Karnstein family ; and, for a trifle, he undertook to bring him back with him, if we would lend him one of our horses, in little more than half-an-hour.

" Have you been long employed about this forest ? " asked my father of the old man.

" I have been a woodman here," he answered in his *patois*, " under the forester, all my days ; so has my father before me, and so on, as many generations as I can count up. I could show you the very house in the village here, in which my ancestors lived."

"How came the village to be deserted?" asked the General.

"It was troubled by *revenants*, sir; several were tracked to their graves, there detected by the usual tests, and extinguished in the usual way, by decapitation, by the stake, and by burning; but not until many of the villagers were killed.

"But after all these proceedings according to law," he continued—"so many graves opened, and so many vampires deprived of their horrible animation—the village was not relieved. But a Moravian nobleman, who happened to be travelling this way, heard how matters were, and being skilled—as many people are in his country—in such affairs, he offered to deliver the village from its tormentor. He did so thus: There being a bright moon that night, he ascended, shortly after sunset, the tower of the chapel here, from whence he could distinctly see the churchyard beneath him; you can see it from that window. From this point he watched until he saw the vampire come out of his grave, and place near it the linen clothes in which he had been folded, and glide away towards the village to plague its inhabitants.

"The stranger, having seen all this, came down from the steeple, took the linen wrappings of the vampire, and carried them up to the top of the tower, which he again mounted. When the vampire returned from his prowlings and missed his clothes, he cried furiously to the Moravian, whom he saw at the summit of the tower, and who, in reply, beckoned him to ascend and take them. Whereupon the vampire, accepting his invitation, began to climb the steeple, and so soon as he had reached the battlements, the Moravian, with a stroke of his sword, clove his skull in twain, hurling him down to the churchyard, whither, descending by the winding stairs, the stranger followed and cut his head off, and next day delivered it and the body to the villagers, who duly impaled and burnt them.

"This Moravian nobleman had authority from the then head of the family to remove the tomb of Mircalla, Countess Karnstein, which he did effectually, so that in a little while its site was quite forgotten."

"Can you point out where it stood?" asked the General, eagerly.

The forester shook his head and smiled.

"Not a soul living could tell you that now," he said; "besides, they say her body was removed; but no one is sure of that either."

Having thus spoken, as time pressed, he dropped his axe and departed, leaving us to hear the remainder of the General's strange story.

XIV

THE MEETING

"My beloved child," he resumed, "was now growing rapidly worse. The physician who attended her had failed to produce the slightest impression upon her disease, for such I then supposed it to be. He saw my alarm, and suggested a consultation. I called in an abler physician, from Gratz. Several days elapsed before he arrived. He was a good and pious, as well as a learned man. Having seen my poor ward together, they withdrew to my library to confer and discuss. I, from the adjoining room, where I waited their summons, heard these two gentlemen's voices raised in something sharper than a strictly philosophical discussion. I knocked at the door and entered. I found the old physician from Gratz maintaining his theory. His rival was combating it with undisguised ridicule, accompanied with bursts of laughter. This unseemly manifestation subsided and the altercation ended on my entrance.

" ' Sir,' said my first physician, ' my learned brother seems to think that you want a conjuror, and not a doctor.'

" ' Pardon me,' said the old physician from Gratz, looking displeased, ' I shall state my own view of the case in my own way another time. I grieve, Monsieur le General, that by my skill and science I can be of no use. Before I go I shall do myself the honour to suggest something to you.'

" He seemed thoughtful, and sat down at a table, and began to write. Profoundly disappointed, I made my bow, and as I turned to go, the other doctor pointed over his shoulder to his companion who was writing, and then, with a shrug, significantly touched his forehead.

" This consultation, then, left me precisely where I was. I walked out into the grounds, all but distracted. The doctor from Gratz, in ten or fifteen minutes, overtook me. He apologised for having followed me, but said that he could not conscientiously take his leave without a few words more. He told me that he could not be mistaken; no natural disease exhibited the same symptoms; and that death was already very near. There remained, however, a day, or possibly two, of life. If the fatal seizure were at once arrested, with great care and skill her strength might possibly return. But all hung now upon the confines of the irrevocable. One more assault might extinguish the last spark of vitality which is, every moment, ready to die.

" ' And what is the nature of the seizure you speak of ? ' I entreated.

" ' I have stated all fully in this note, which I place in your hands, upon the distinct condition that you send for the nearest clergyman, and open my letter in his presence, and on no account read it till he is with you; you would despise it else, and it is a matter of life and death. Should the priest fail you, then, indeed, you may read it.'

" He asked me, before taking his leave finally, whether I would wish to see a man curiously learned upon the very subject, which, after I had read his letter, would probably interest me above all others, and he urged me earnestly to invite him to visit him there; and so took his leave.

" The ecclesiastic was absent, and I read the letter by myself. At another time, or in another case, it might have excited my ridicule. But into what quackeries will not people rush for a last chance, where all accustomed means have failed, and the life of a beloved object is at stake ?

" Nothing, you will say, could be more absurd than the learned man's letter. It was monstrous enough to have consigned him to a madhouse. He said that the patient was suffering from the visits of a vampire! The punctures which she described as having occurred near the throat were, he insisted, the insertion of those two long, thin, and sharp teeth which, it is well known, are peculiar to vampires; and there could be no doubt, he added, as to the well-defined presence of the small livid mark which all concurred in describing as that induced by the demon's lips, and every symptom described by the sufferer was in exact conformity with those recorded in every case of a similar visitation.

" Being myself wholly sceptical as to the existence of any such portent as the vampire, the supernatural theory of the good doctor furnished, in my opinion, but another instance of learning and intelligence oddly associated with some one hallucination. I was so miserable, however, that, rather than try nothing, I acted upon the instructions of the letter.

" I concealed myself in the dark dressing-room, that opened upon the poor patient's room, in which a candle was burning, and watched there till she was fast asleep. I stood at the door, peeping through the small crevice, my sword laid on the table beside me, as my directions prescribed, until, a little after one, I saw a large black object, very ill-defined, crawl, as it seemed to me, over the foot of the bed, and swiftly spread itself up to the poor girl's throat, where it swelled, in a moment, into a great, palpitating mass.

" For a few moments I had stood petrified. I now sprang forward, with my sword in my hand. The black creature suddenly contracted toward the foot of the bed, glided over it, and, standing on the floor about a yard below the foot of the bed, with a glare of skulking ferocity and horror fixed on me, I saw Millarca. Speculating I know not what, I struck at her instantly with my sword; but I saw her standing near the door, unscathed. Horrified, I pursued, and struck again. She was gone! and my sword flew to shivers against the door.

" I can't describe to you all that passed on that horrible night. The whole house was up and stirring. The spectre Millarca was gone. But her victim was sinking fast, and before the morning dawned, she died."

The old General was agitated. We did not speak to him. My father walked to some little distance, and began reading the inscriptions on the tombstones; and thus occupied, he strolled into the door of a side chapel to prosecute his researches. The General leaned against the wall, dried his eyes, and sighed heavily. I was relieved on hearing the voices of Carmilla and Madame, who were at that moment approaching. The voices died away.

In this solitude, having just listened to so strange a story, connected, as it was, with the great and titled dead, whose monuments were mouldering among the dust and ivy round us, and every incident of which bore so awfully upon my own mysterious case—in this haunted spot, darkened by the towering foliage that rose on every side, dense and high above its noiseless walls—a horror began to steal over me, and my heart sank as I thought that my friends were, after all, not about to enter and disturb this triste and ominous scene.

The old General's eyes were fixed on the ground, as he leaned with his hand upon the basement of a shattered monument.

Under a narrow, arched doorway, surmounted by one of those demoniacal grotesques in which the cynical and ghastly fancy of old Gothic carving delights, I saw very gladly the beautiful face and figure of Carmilla enter the shadowy chapel.

I was just about to rise and speak, and nodded smiling, in answer to her peculiarly engaging smile; when with a cry, the old man by my side caught up the woodman's hatchet, and started forward. On seeing him a brutalised change came over her features. It was an instantaneous and horrible transformation, as she made a crouching step backwards. Before I could utter a scream, he struck at her with all his force, but she dived under his blow, and unscathed, caught him in her tiny grasp by the wrist. He struggled for a moment to release his arm, but his hand opened, the axe fell to the ground, and the girl was gone.

He staggered against the wall. His grey hair stood upon his head, a moisture shone over his face, as if he were at the point of death.

The frightful scene had passed in a moment. The first thing I recollect after, is Madame standing before me, and impatiently repeating again and again, the question, " Where is Mademoiselle Carmilla ? "

I answered at length, " I don't know—I can't tell—she went there," and I pointed to the door through which Madame had just entered ; " only a minute or two since."

" But I have been standing there, in the passage, ever since Mademoiselle Carmilla entered ; and she did not return."

She then began to call " Carmilla " through every door and passage and from the windows, but no answer came.

" She called herself Carmilla ? " asked the General, still agitated.

" Carmilla, yes," I answered.

" Aye," he said ; " that is Millarca. That is the same person who long ago was called Mircalla, Countess Karnstein. Depart from this accursed ground, my poor child, as quickly as you can. Drive to the clergyman's house, and stay there till we come. Begone ! May you never behold Carmilla more ; you will not find her here."

XV

ORDEAL AND EXECUTION

As he spoke one of the strangest-looking men I ever beheld, entered the chapel at the door through which Carmilla had made her entrance and her exit. He was tall, narrow-chested, stooping, with high shoulders, and dressed in black. His face was brown and dried in with deep furrows; he wore an oddly-shaped hat with a broad leaf. His hair, long and grizzled, hung on his shoulders. He wore a pair of gold spectacles, and walked slowly, with an odd shambling gait, with his face sometimes turned up to the sky, and sometimes bowed down toward the ground, seemed to wear a perpetual smile; his long thin arms were swinging, and his lank hands, in old black gloves ever so much too wide for them, waving and gesticulating in utter abstraction.

"The very man!" exclaimed the General, advancing with manifest delight. "My dear Baron, how happy I am to see you, I had no hope of meeting you so soon." He signed to my father, who had by this time returned, and leading the fantastic old gentleman, whom he called the Baron, to meet him. He introduced him formally, and they at once entered into earnest conversation. The stranger took a roll of paper from his pocket, and spread it on the worn surface of a tomb that stood by. He had a pencil case in his fingers, with which he traced imaginary lines from point to point on the paper, which from their often glancing from it, together, at certain points of the building, I concluded to be a plan of the chapel. He accompanied, what I may term his lecture, with occasional readings from a dirty little book, whose yellow leaves were closely written over.

They sauntered together down the side aisle, opposite to the spot where I was standing, conversing as they went; then they begun measuring distances by paces, and finally they all stood together, facing a piece of the side-wall, which they began to examine with great minuteness; pulling off the ivy that clung over it, and rapping the plaster with the ends of their sticks, scraping here, and knocking there. At length they ascertained the existence of a broad marble tablet, with letters carved in relief upon it.

With the assistance of the woodman, who soon returned, a monumental inscription, and carved escutcheon, were disclosed. They proved to be those of the long lost monument of Mircella, Countess Karnstein.

The old General, though not I fear given to the praying mood, raised his hands and eyes to heaven, in mute thanksgiving for some moments.

"To-morrow," I heard him say; "the commissioner will be here, and the Inquisition will be held according to law."

Then turning to the old man with the gold spectacles, whom I have described, he shook him warmly by both hands and said:

"Baron, how can I thank you? How can we all thank you? You will have delivered this region from a plague that has scourged its inhabitants for more than a century. The horrible enemy, thank God, is at last tracked."

My father led the stranger aside, and the General followed. I knew that he had led them out of hearing, that he might relate my case, and I saw them glance often quickly at me, as the discussion proceeded.

My father came to me, kissed me again and again, and leading me from the chapel, said :

" It is time to return, but before we go home, we must add to our party the good priest, who lives but a little way from this ; and persuade him to accompany us to the schloss."

In this quest we were successful : and I was glad, being unspeakably fatigued when we reached home. But my satisfaction was changed to dismay, on discovering that there were no tidings of Carmilla. Of the scene that had occurred in the ruined chapel, no explanation was offered to me, and it was clear that it was a secret which my father for the present determined to keep from me.

The sinister absence of Carmilla made the remembrance of the scene more horrible to me. The arrangements for that night were singular. Two servants and Madame were to sit up in my room that night ; and the ecclesiastic with my father kept watch in the adjoining dressing-room.

The priest had performed certain solemn rites that night, the purport of which I did not understand any more than I comprehended the reason of this extraordinary precaution taken for my safety during sleep.

I saw all clearly a few days later.

The disappearance of Carmilla was followed by the discontinuance of my nightly sufferings.

You have heard, no doubt, of the appalling superstition that prevails in Upper and Lower Styria, in Moravia, Silesia, in Turkish Servia, in Poland, even in Russia ; the superstition, so we must call it, of the vampire.

If human testimony, taken with every care and solemnity, judicially, before commissions innumerable, each consisting of many members, all chosen for integrity and intelligence, and constituting reports more voluminous perhaps than exist upon any one other class of cases, is worth anything, it is difficult to deny, or even to doubt the existence of such a phenomenon as the vampire.

For my part I have heard no theory by which to explain what I myself have witnessed and experienced, other than that supplied by the ancient and well-attested belief of the country.

The next day the formal proceedings took place in the Chapel of Karnstein. The grave of the Countess Mircalla was opened ; and the General and my father recognized each his perfidious and beautiful guest, in the face now disclosed to view. The features, though a hundred and fifty years had passed since her funeral, were tinted with the warmth of life. Her eyes were open ; no cadaverous smell exhaled from the coffin. The two medical men, one officially present, the other on the part of the promotor of the inquiry, attested the marvellous fact, that there was a faint but appreciable respiration, and a corresponding action of the heart. The limbs were perfectly flexible, the flesh elastic ; and the leaden coffin floated with blood, in which to a depth of seven inches, the body lay immersed. Here then, were all the admitted signs and proofs of vampirism. The body, therefore, in accordance with the ancient practice, was raised, and a sharp stake driven through the heart of the vampire, who uttered a piercing shriek at the moment, in all respects such as might escape from a living person in the last agony. Then the head was struck off, and a torrent of blood flowed from the severed neck. The body and head were next placed on a pile of wood, and reduced to ashes, which were thrown upon the river and borne away, and that territory has never since been plagued by the visits of a vampire.

My father has a copy of the report of the Imperial Commission, with the signatures of all who were present at these proceedings, attached in verification of the statement. It is from this official paper that I have summarized my account of this last shocking scene.

XVI

CONCLUSION

I WRITE all this you suppose with composure. But far from it; I cannot think of it without agitation. Nothing but your earnest desire so repeatedly expressed, could have induced me to sit down to a task that has unstrung my nerves for months to come, and reinduced a shadow of the unspeakable horror which years after my deliverance continued to make my days and nights dreadful, and solitude insupportably terrific.

Let me add a word or two about that quaint Baron Vordenburg, to whose curious lore we were indebted for the discovery of the Countess Mircalla's grave.

He had taken up his abode in Gratz, where, living upon a mere pittance, which was all that remained to him of the once princely estates of his family, in Upper Styria, he devoted himself to the minute and laborious investigation of the marvellously authenticated tradition of vampirism. He had at his fingers' ends all the great and little works upon the subject. " Magia Posthuma," " Phlegon de Mirabilibus," " Augustinus de curâ pro Mortuis," " Philosophicæ et Christianæ Cogitationes de Vampiris," by John Christofer Herenberg; and a thousand others, among which I remember only a few of those which he lent to my father. He had a voluminous digest of all the judicial cases, from which he had extracted a system of principles that appear to govern—some always, and others occasionally only—the condition of the vampire. I may mention, in passing, that the deadly pallor attributed to that sort of *revenants*, is a mere melodramatic fiction. They present, in the grave, and when they show themselves in human society, the appearance of healthy life. When disclosed to light in their coffins, they exhibit all the symptoms that are enumerated as those which proved the vampire-life of the long-dead Countess Karnstein.

How they escape from their graves and return to them for certain hours every day, without displacing the clay or leaving any trace of disturbance in the state of the coffin or the cerements, has always been admitted to be utterly inexplicable. The amphibious existence of the vampire is sustained by daily renewed slumber in the grave. Its horrible lust for living blood supplies the vigour of its waking existence. The vampire is prone to be fascinated with an engrossing vehemence, resembling the passion of love, by particular persons. In pursuit of these it will exercise inexhaustible patience and stratagem, for access to a particular object may be obstructed in a hundred ways. It will never desist until it has satiated its passion, and drained the very life of its coveted victim. But it will, in these cases, husband and protract its murderous enjoyment with the refinement of an epicure, and heighten it by the gradual approaches of an artful courtship. In these cases it seems to yearn for something like sympathy and consent. In ordinary ones it goes direct to its object, overpowers with violence, and strangles and exhausts often at a single feast.

The vampire is, apparently, subject, in certain situations, to special conditions. In the particular instance of which I have given you a relation, Mircalla seemed to be limited to a name which, if not her real one, should at least reproduce, without the omission or addition of a single letter, those, as we say, anagrammatically, which compose it. *Carmilla* did this ; so did *Millarca.*

My father related to the Baron Vordenburg, who remained with us for two or three weeks after the expulsion of Carmilla, the story about the Moravian nobleman and the vampire at Karnstein churchyard, and then he asked the Baron how he had discovered the exact position of the long-concealed tomb of the Countess Millarca? The Baron's grotesque features puckered up into a mysterious smile ; he looked down, still smiling on his worn spectacle-case and fumbled with it. Then looking up, he said :

" I have many journals, and other papers, written by that remarkable man ; the most curious among them is one treating of the visit of which you speak, to Karnstein. The tradition, of course, discolours and distorts a little. He might have been termed a Moravian nobleman, for he had changed his abode to that territory, and was, beside, a noble. But he was, in truth, a native of Upper Styria. It is enough to say that in very early youth he had been a passionate and favoured lover of the beautiful Mircalla, Countess Karnstein. Her early death plunged him into inconsolable grief. It is the nature of vampires to increase and multiply, but according to an ascertained and ghostly law.

" Assume, at starting, a territory perfectly free from that pest. How does it begin, and how does it multiply itself? I will tell you. A person, more or less wicked, puts an end to himself. A suicide, under certain circumstances, becomes a vampire. That spectre visits living people in their slumbers ; *they* die, and almost invariably, in the grave, develop into vampires. This happened in the case of the beautiful Mircalla, who was haunted by one of those demons. My ancestor, Vordenburg, whose title I still bear, soon discovered this, and in the course of the studies to which he devoted himself, learned a great deal more.

" Among other things, he concluded that suspicion of vampirism would probably fall, sooner or later, upon the dead Countess, who in life had been his idol. He conceived a horror, be she what she might, of her remains being profaned by the outrage of a posthumous execution. He has left a curious paper to prove that the vampire, on its expulsion from its amphibious existence, is projected into a far more horrible life ; and he resolved to save his once beloved Mircalla from this.

" He adopted the stratagem of a journey here, a pretended removal of her remains, and a real obliteration of her monument. When age had stolen upon him, and from the vale of years he looked back on the scenes he was leaving, he considered, in a different spirit, what he had done, and a horror took possession of him. He made the tracings and notes which have guided me to the very spot, and drew up a confession of the deception that he had practised. If he had intended any further action in this matter, death prevented him ; and the hand of a remote descendant has, too late for many, directed the pursuit to the lair of the beast."

We talked a little more, and among other things he said was this :

" One sign of the vampire is the power of the hand. The slender hand of Mircalla closed like a vice of steel on the General's wrist when he raised the hatchet to strike. But its power is not confined to its grasp ; it leaves a numbness in the limb it seizes, which is slowly, if ever, recovered from."

The following Spring my father took me a tour through Italy. We remained away for more than a year. It was long before the terror of recent events subsided ; and to this hour the image of Carmilla returns to memory with ambigious alternations—sometimes the playful, languid, beautiful girl ; sometimes the writhing fiend I saw in the ruined church ; and often from a reverie I have started, fancying I heard the light step of Carmilla at the drawing-room door.

DR. JEKYLL AND MR. HYDE
Robert Louis Stevenson

MR. UTTERSON the lawyer was a man of a rugged countenance, that was never lighted by a smile; cold, scanty and embarrassed in discourse; backward in sentiment; lean, long, dusty, dreary, and yet somehow lovable. At friendly meetings, and when the wine was to his taste, something eminently human beaconed from his eye; something indeed which never found its way into his talk, but which spoke not only in these silent symbols of the after-dinner face, but more often and loudly in the acts of his life. He was austere with himself; drank gin when he was alone, to mortify a taste for vintages; and though he enjoyed the theatre, had not crossed the doors of one for twenty years. But he had an approved tolerance for others; sometimes wondering, almost with envy, at the high pressure of spirits involved in their misdeeds; and in any extremity inclined to help rather than to reprove. " I incline to Cain's heresy," he used to say quaintly : " I let my brother go to the devil in his own way." In this character, it was frequently his fortune to be the last reputable acquaintance and the last good influence in the lives of down-going men. And to such as these, so long as they came about his chambers, he never marked a shade of change in his demeanour.

No doubt the feat was easy to Mr. Utterson; for he was undemonstrative at the best, and even his friendship seemed to be founded in a similar catholicity of good-nature. It is the mark of a modest man to accept his friendly circle ready made from the hands of opportunity; and that was the lawyer's way. His friends were those of his own blood, or those whom he had known the longest; his affections, like ivy, were the growth of time, they implied no aptness in the object. Hence, no doubt, the bond that united him to Mr. Richard Enfield, his distant kinsman, the well-known man about town. It was a nut to crack for many, what these two could see in each other, or what subject they could find in common. It was reported by those who encountered them in their Sunday walks, that they said nothing, looked singularly dull, and would hail with obvious relief the appearance of a friend. For all that, the two men put the greatest store by these excursions, counted them the chief jewel of each week, and not only set aside occasions of pleasure, but even resisted the calls of business, that they might enjoy them uninterrupted.

It chanced on one of these rambles that their way led them down a by-street in a busy quarter of London. The street was small and what is called quiet, but it drove a thriving trade on the week-days. The inhabitants were all doing well, it seemed, and all emulously hoping to do better still, and laying out the surplus of their gains in coquetry; so that the shop fronts stood along that thoroughfare with an air of invitation, like rows of smiling saleswomen. Even on Sunday, when it veiled its more florid charms and lay comparatively empty of passage, the streets shone out in contrast to its dingy neighbourhood, like a fire in a forest; and with its freshly painted shutters, well-polished brasses, and general cleanliness and gaiety of note, instantly caught and pleased the eye of the passenger.

Two doors from one corner, on the left hand going east, the line was broken by the entry of a court; and just at that point, a certain sinister block of building thrust forward its gable on the street. It was two storeys high; showed no window, nothing but a door on the lower storey and a blind forehead of discoloured wall on the upper; and bore in every feature the marks of prolonged and sordid negligence. The door, which was equipped with neither bell nor knocker, was blistered and distained. Tramps slouched into the recess and struck matches on the panels; children kept shop upon the steps; the schoolboy had tried his knife on the mouldings; and for close on a generation, no one had appeared to drive away these random visitors or to repair their ravages.

Mr. Enfield and the lawyer were on the other side of the by-street; but when they came abreast of the entry, the former lifted up his cane and pointed.

" Did you ever remark that door ? " he asked; and when his companion had replied in the affirmative, " It is connected in my mind," added he, " with a very odd story."

" Indeed ! " said Mr. Utterson, with a slight change of voice, " and what was that ? "

" Well, it was this way," returned Mr. Enfield: " I was coming home from some place at the end of the world, about three o'clock of a black winter morning, and my way lay through a part of town where there was literally nothing to be seen but lamps. Street after street, and all the folks asleep—street after street, all lighted up as if for a procession, and all as empty as a church—till at last I got into that state of mind when a man listens and listens and begins to long for the sight of a policeman. All at once, I saw two figures: one a little man who was stumping along eastward at a good walk, and the other a girl of maybe eight or ten who was running as hard as she was able down a cross street. Well, sir, the two ran into one another naturally enough at the corner; and then came the horrible part of the thing; for the man trampled calmly over the child's body and left her screaming on the ground. It sounds nothing to hear, but it was hellish to see. It wasn't like a man; it was like some damned Juggernaut. I gave a view halloa, took to my heels, collared my gentleman, and brought him back to where there was already quite a group about the screaming child. He was perfectly cool and made no resistance, but gave me one look, so ugly that it brought out the sweat on me like running.

The people who had turned out were the girl's own family ; and pretty soon the doctor, for whom she had been sent, put in his appearance. Well, the child was not much the worse, more frightened, according to the Sawbones ; and there you might have supposed would be an end to it. But there was one curious circumstance. I had taken a loathing to my gentleman at first sight. So had the child's family, which was only natural. But the doctor's case was what struck me. He was the usual cut and dry apothecary, of no particular age and colour, with a strong Edinburgh accent, and about as emotional as a bagpipe. Well, sir, he was like the rest of us ; every time he looked at my prisoner, I saw that Sawbones turned sick and white with the desire to kill him. I knew what was in his mind, just as he knew what was in mine ; and killing being out of the question, we did the next best. We told the man we could and would make such a scandal out of this, as should make his name stink from one end of London to the other. If he had any friends or any credit, we undertook that he should lose them. And all the time, as we were pitching it in red hot, we were keeping the women off him as best we could, for they were as wild as harpies. I never saw a circle of such hateful faces ; and there was the man in the middle, with a kind of black, sneering coolness—frightened too, I could see that—but carrying it off, sir, really like Satan. ' If you choose to make capital out of this accident,' said he, ' I am naturally helpless. No gentleman but wishes to avoid a scene,' says he. ' Name your figure.' Well, we screwed him up to a hundred pounds for the child's family ; he would have clearly liked to stick out ; but there was something about the lot of us that meant mischief, and at last he struck. The next thing was to get the money ; and where do you think he carried us but to that place with the door ?—whipped out a key, went in, and presently came back with the matter of ten pounds in gold and a cheque for the balance on Coutts's, drawn payable to bearer, and signed with a name that I can't mention, though it's one of the points of my story, but it was a name at least very well known and often printed. The figure was stiff ; but the signature was good for more than that, if it was only genuine. I took the liberty of pointing out to my gentleman that the whole business looked apocryphal ; and that a man does not, in real life, walk into a cellar door at four in the morning and come out of it with another man's cheque for close upon a hundred pounds. But he was quite easy and sneering. ' Set your mind at rest,' says he ; ' I will stay with you till the banks open, and cash the cheque myself.' So we all set off, the doctor, and the child's father, and our friend and myself, and passed the rest of the night in my chambers ; and next day, when we had breakfasted, went in a body to the bank. I gave in the cheque myself, and said I had every reason to believe it was a forgery. Not a bit of it. The cheque was genuine."

" Tut-tut ! " said Mr. Utterson.

" I see you feel as I do," said Mr. Enfield. " Yes, it's a bad story. my man was a fellow that nobody could have to do with, a really damnable man ; and the person that drew the cheque is the very pink of the proprieties, celebrated too, and (what makes it worse) one of your fellows who do what they call good. Blackmail, I suppose ; an honest man paying through the nose for some of the capers of his youth. Black Mail House is what I call that place with the door, in consequence. Though even that, you know, is far from explaining all," he added ; and with the words fell into a vein of musing.

From this he was recalled by Mr. Utterson asking rather suddenly : " And you don't know if the drawer of the cheque lives there ? "

" A likely place, isn't it ? " returned Mr. Enfield. " But I happen to have noticed his address ; he lives in some square or other."

" And you never asked about—the place with the door ? " said Mr. Utterson.

" No, sir : I had a delicacy," was the reply. " I feel very strongly about putting questions ; it partakes too much of the style of the day of judgment. You start a question, and it's like starting a stone. You sit quietly on the top of a hill ; and away the stone goes, starting others ; and presently some bland old bird (the last you would have thought of) is knocked on the head in his own back garden, and the family have to change their name. No, sir, I make it a rule of mine : the more it looks like Queer Street, the less I ask."

" A very good rule, too," said the lawyer.

" But I have studied the place for myself," continued Mr. Enfield. " It seems scarcely a house. There is no other door, and nobody goes in or out of that one, but, once in a great while, the gentleman of my adventure. There are three windows looking on the court on the first floor ; none below ; the windows are always shut, but they're clean. And then there is a chimney, which is generally smoking ; so somebody must live there. And yet it's not so sure ; for the buildings are so packed together about that court, that it's hard to say where one ends and another begins."

The pair walked on again for a while in silence ; and then— " Enfield," said Mr. Utterson, " that's a good rule of yours."

" Yes, I think it is," returned Enfield.

" But for all that," continued the lawyer, " there's one point I want to ask : I want to ask the name of that man who walked over the child."

" Well," said Mr. Enfield, " I can't see what harm it would do. It was a man of the name of Hyde."

" H'm," said Mr. Utterson. " What sort of a man is he to see ? "

" He is not easy to describe. There is something wrong with his appearance ; something displeasing, something downright detestable. I never saw a man I so disliked, and yet I scarce know why. He must be deformed somewhere ; he gives a strong feeling of deformity, although I couldn't specify the point. He's an extraordinary-looking man, and yet I really can name nothing out of the way. No, sir ; I can make no hand of it ; I can't describe him. And it's not want of memory ; for I declare I can see him this moment."

Mr. Utterson again walked some way in silence, and obviously under a weight of consideration. " You are sure he used a key," he inquired at last.

" My dear sir . . ." began Enfield, surprised out of himself.

" Yes, I know," said Utterson ; " I know it must seem strange. The fact is, if I do not ask you the name of the other party, it is because I know it already. You see, Richard, your tale has gone home. If you have been inexact in any point, you had better correct it."

" I think you might have warned me," returned the other, with a touch of sullenness. " But I have been pedantically exact, as you call it. The fellow had a key ; and, what's more, he has it still. I saw him use it not a week ago."

Mr. Utterson sighed deeply, but said never a word ; and the young man presently resumed. " Here is another lesson to say nothing," said he. " I am ashamed of my long tongue. Let us make a bargain never to refer to this again."

" With all my heart," said the lawyer. " I shake hands on that, Richard."

SEARCH FOR MR. HYDE

THAT evening Mr. Utterson came home to his bachelor house in sombre spirits, and sat down to dinner without relish. It was his custom of a Sunday, when this meal was over, to sit close by the fire, a volume of some dry divinity on his reading desk, until the clock of the neighbouring church rang out the hour of twelve, when he would go soberly and gratefully to bed. On this night, however, as soon as the cloth was taken away, he took up a candle and went into his business room. There he opened his safe, took from the most private part of it a document endorsed on the envelope as Dr. Jekyll's Will, and sat down with a clouded brow to study its contents. The will was holograph ; for Mr. Utterson, though he took charge of it now that it was made, had refused to lend the least assistance in the making of it ; it provided not only that, in case of the decease of Henry Jekyll, M.D., D.C.L., LL.D., F.R.S., etc., all his possessions were to pass into the hands of his " friend and benefactor Edward Hyde " ; but that in case of Dr. Jekyll's " disappearance or unexplained absence for any period exceeding three calendar months," the said Edward Hyde should step into the said Henry Jekyll's shoes without further delay, and free from any burthen or obligation, beyond the payment of a few small sums to the members of the doctor's household. This document had long been the lawyer's eyesore. It offended him both as a lawyer and as a lover of the sane and customary sides of life, to whom the fanciful was the immodest. And hitherto it was his ignorance of Mr. Hyde that had swelled his indignation ; now, by a sudden turn, it was his knowledge. It was already bad enough when the name was but a name of which he could learn no more. It was worse when it began to be clothed upon with detestable attributes ; and out of the shifting, insubstantial mists that had so long baffled his eye, there leaped up the sudden, definite presentment of a fiend.

" I thought it was madness," he said, as he replaced the obnoxious paper in the safe ; " and now I begin to fear it is disgrace."

With that he blew out his candle, put on a greatcoat, and set forth in the direction of Cavendish Square, that citadel of medicine, where his friend, the great Dr. Lanyon, had his house and received his crowding patients. " If any one knows, it will be Lanyon," he had thought.

The solemn butler knew and welcomed him ; he was subjected to no stage of delay, but ushered direct from the door to the dining-room, where Dr. Lanyon sat alone over his wine. This was a hearty, healthy, dapper, red-faced gentleman, with a shock of hair prematurely white, and a boisterous and decided manner. At sight of Mr. Utterson, he sprang up from his chair and welcomed him with both hands. The geniality, as was the way of the man, was somewhat theatrical to the eye ; but it reposed on genuine feeling. For these two were old friends, old mates both at school and college, both thorough respecters of themselves and of each other, and, what does not always follow, men who thoroughly enjoyed each other's company.

After a little rambling talk, the lawyer led up to the subject which so disagreeably preoccupied his mind.

" I suppose, Lanyon," said he, " you and I must be the two oldest friends that Henry Jekyll has ? "

" I wish the friends were younger," chuckled Dr. Lanyon. " But I suppose we are. And what of that ? I see little of him now."

" Indeed ! " said Utterson. " I thought you had a bond of common interest."

" We had," was the reply. " But it is more than ten years since Henry Jekyll became too fanciful for me. He began to go wrong, wrong in mind ; and though, of course, I continue to take an interest in him for old sake's sake as they say, I see and I have seen devilish little of the man. Such unscientific balderdash," added the doctor, flushing suddenly purple, " would have estranged Damon and Pythias."

This little spirt of temper was somewhat of a relief to Mr. Utterson. " They have only differed on some point of science," he thought ; and being a man of no scientific passions (except in the matter of conveyancing) he even added : " It is nothing worse than that ! " He gave his friend a few seconds to recover his composure, and then approached the question he had come to put.

" Did you ever come across a *protégé* of his—one Hyde ? " he asked.

" Hyde ? " repeated Lanyon. " No. Never heard of him. Since my time."

That was the amount of information that the lawyer carried back with him to the great, dark bed on which he tossed to and fro, until the small hours of the morning began to grow large. It was a night of little ease to his toiling mind, toiling in mere darkness and besieged by questions.

Six o'clock struck on the bells of the church that was so conveniently near to Mr. Utterson's dwelling, and still he was digging at the problem. Hitherto it had touched him on the intellectual side alone ; but now his imagination also was engaged, or rather enslaved ; and as he lay and tossed in the gross darkness of the night and the curtained room, Mr. Enfield's tale went by before his mind in a scroll of lighted pictures. He would be aware of the great field of lamps of a nocturnal city ; then of the figure of a man walking swiftly ; then of a child running from the doctor's ; and then these met, and that human Juggernaut trod the child down and passed on regardless of her screams. Or else he would see a room in a rich house, where his friend lay asleep, dreaming and smiling at his dreams ; and then the door of that room would be opened, the curtains of the bed plucked apart, the sleeper recalled, and, lo ! there would stand by his side a figure to whom power was given, and even at that dead hour, he must rise and do its bidding. The figure in these two phases haunted the lawyer all night ; and if at any time he dozed over, it was but to see it glide more stealthily through sleeping houses, or move the more swiftly and still the more swiftly, even to dizziness, through wider labyrinths of lamp-lighted city, and at every street corner crush a child and leave her screaming. And still the figure had no face by which he might know it ; even in his dreams, it had no face, or one that baffled him and melted before his eyes ; and thus it was that there sprang up and grew apace in the lawyer's mind a singularly strong, almost an inordinate, curiosity to behold the features of the real Mr. Hyde. If he could but once set eyes on him, he thought the mystery would lighten and perhaps roll altogether away, as was the habit of mysterious things when well examined. He might see a reason for his friend's strange preference or bondage (call it which you please), and even for the startling clauses of the will. And at least it would be a face worth seeing : the face of a man who was without bowels of mercy : a face which had but to show itself to raise up, in the mind of the unimpressionable Enfield, a spirit of enduring hatred.

From that time forward, Mr. Utterson began to haunt the door in the by-street of shops. In the morning before office hours, at noon when business was plenty and time scarce, at night under the face of the fogged city moon, by all lights and at all hours of solitude or concourse, the lawyer was to be found on his chosen post.

"If he be Mr. Hyde," he had thought, " I shall be Mr. Seek."

And at last his patience was rewarded. It was a fine dry night ; frost in the air ; the streets as clean as a ball-room floor ; the lamps, unshaken by any wind, drawing a regular pattern of light and shadow. By ten o'clock, when the shops were closed, the by-street was very solitary, and, in spite of the low growl of London from all round, very silent. Small sounds carried far ; domestic sounds out of the houses were clearly audible on either side of the roadway ; and the rumour of the approach of any passenger preceded him by a long time. Mr. Utterson had been some minutes at his post when he was aware of an odd, light footstep drawing near. In the course of his nightly patrols he had long grown accustomed to the quaint effect with which the footfalls of a single person, while he is still a great way off, suddenly spring out distinct from the vast hum and clatter of the city. Yet his attention had never before been so sharply and decisively arrested; and it was with a strong, superstitious prevision of success that he withdrew into the entry of the court.

The steps drew swiftly nearer, and swelled out suddenly louder as they turned the end of the street. The lawyer, looking forth from the entry, could soon see what manner of man he had to deal with. He was small, and very plainly dressed; and the look of him, even at that distance, went somehow strongly against the watcher's inclination. But he made straight for the door, crossing the roadway to save time; and as he came, he drew a key from his pocket, like one approaching home.

Mr. Utterson stepped out and touched him on the shoulder as he passed. "Mr. Hyde, I think?"

Mr. Hyde shrank back with a hissing intake of the breath. But his fear was only momentary; and though he did not look the lawyer in the face, he answered coolly enough: "That is my name. What do you want?"

"I see you are going in," returned the lawyer. "I am an old friend of Dr. Jekyll's—Mr. Utterson, of Gaunt Street—you must have heard my name; and meeting you so conveniently, I thought you might admit me."

"You will not find Dr. Jekyll; he is from home," replied Mr. Hyde, blowing in the key. And then suddenly, but still without looking up, "How did you know me?" he asked.

"On your side," said Mr. Utterson, "will you do me a favour?"

"With pleasure," replied the other. "What shall it be?"

"Will you let me see your face?" asked the lawyer.

Mr. Hyde appeared to hesitate; and then, as if upon some sudden reflection, fronted about with an air of defiance; and the pair stared at each other pretty fixedly for a few seconds. "Now I shall know you again," said Mr. Utterson. "It may be useful."

"Yes," returned Mr. Hyde, "it is as well we have met; and *à propos*, you should have my address." And he gave a number of a street in Soho.

"Good God!" thought Mr. Utterson, "can he too have been thinking of the will?" But he kept his feelings to himself, and only grunted in acknowledgment of the address.

"And now," said the other, "how did you know me?"

"By description," was the reply.

"Whose description?"

"We have common friends," said Mr. Utterson.

"Common friends!" echoed Mr. Hyde, a little hoarsely. "Who are they?"

" Jekyll, for instance," said the lawyer.

" He never told you," cried Mr. Hyde, with a flush of anger. " I did not think you would have lied."

" Come," said Mr. Utterson, " that is not fitting language."

The other snarled aloud into a savage laugh ; and the next moment, with extraordinary quickness, he had unlocked the door and disappeared into the house.

The lawyer stood awhile when Mr. Hyde had left him, the picture of disquietude. Then he began slowly to mount the street, pausing every step or two, and putting his hand to his brow like a man in mental perplexity. The problem he was thus debating as he walked was one of a class that is rarely solved. Mr. Hyde was pale and dwarfish ; he gave an impression of deformity without any nameable malformation, he had a displeasing smile, he had borne himself to the lawyer with a sort of murderous mixture of timidity and boldness, and he spoke with a husky, whispering and somewhat broken voice,—all these were points against him ; but not all of these together could explain the hitherto unknown disgust, loathing and fear with which Mr. Utterson regarded him. " There must be something else," said the perplexed gentleman. " There *is* something more, if I could find a name for it. God bless me, the man seems hardly human ! Something troglodytic, shall we say ? or can it be the old story of Dr. Fell ? or is it the mere radiance of a foul soul that thus transpires through, and transfigures, its clay continent ? The last, I think ; for, O my poor old Harry Jekyll, if ever I read Satan's signature upon a face, it is on that of your new friend."

Round the corner from the by-street there was a square of ancient, handsome houses, now for the most part decayed from their high estate, and let in flats and chambers, to all sorts and conditions of men : map-engravers, architects, shady lawyers, and the agents of obscure enterprises. One house, however, second from the corner, was still occupied entire ; and at the door of this, which wore a great air of wealth and comfort, though it was now plunged in darkness except for the fanlight, Mr. Utterson stopped and knocked. A well-dressed, elderly servant opened the door.

" Is Dr. Jekyll at home, Poole ? " asked the lawyer.

" I will see, Mr. Utterson," said Poole, admitting the visitor as he spoke, into a large, low-roofed, comfortable hall, paved with flags, warmed (after the fashion of a country house) by a bright, open fire, and furnished with costly cabinets of oak. " Will you wait here by the fire, sir ? or shall I give you a light in the dining-room ? "

" Here, thank you," said the lawyer ; and he drew near and leaned on the tall fender. This hall, in which he was now left alone, was a pet fancy of his friend the doctor's ; and Utterson himself was wont to speak of it as the pleasantest room in London. But to-night there was a shudder in his blood ; the face of Hyde sat heavy on his memory ; he felt (what was rare with him) a nausea and distaste of life ; and in the gloom of his spirits, he seemed to read a menace in the flickering of the firelight on the polished cabinets and the uneasy starting of the shadow on the roof. He was ashamed of his relief, when Poole presently returned to announce that Dr. Jekyll was gone out.

" I saw Mr. Hyde go in by the old dissecting room door, Poole," he said. " Is that right, when Dr. Jekyll is from home ? "

" Quite right, Mr. Utterson, sir," replied the servant. " Mr. Hyde has a key."

" Your master seems to repose a great deal of trust in that young man, Poole," resumed the other, musingly.

" Yes, sir, he do, indeed," said Poole. " We have all orders to obey him."

" I do not think I ever met Mr. Hyde ? " asked Utterson.

" O dear no, sir. He never *dines* here," replied the butler. " Indeed, we see very little of him on this side of the house ; he mostly comes and goes by the laboratory."

" Well, good-night, Poole."

" Good-night, Mr. Utterson."

And the lawyer set out homeward with a very heavy heart. " Poor Harry Jekyll," he thought, " my mind misgives me he is in deep waters ! He was wild when he was young ; a long while ago, to be sure ; but in the law of God, there is no statute of limitations. Ah, it must be that ; the ghost of some old sin, the cancer of some concealed disgrace ; punishment coming, *pede claudo*, years after memory has forgotten and self-love condoned the fault." And the lawyer, scared by the thought, brooded awhile on his own past, groping in all the corners of memory, lest by chance some Jack-in-the-Box of an old iniquity should leap to light there. His past was fairly blameless ; few men could read the rolls of their life with less apprehension ; yet he was humbled to the dust by the many ill things he had done, and raised up again into a sober and fearful gratitude by the many that he had come so near to doing, yet avoided. And then by a return on his former subject, he conceived a spark of hope. " This Master Hyde, if he were studied," thought he, " must have secrets of his own : black secrets, by the look of him ; secrets compared to which poor Jekyll's worst would be like sunshine. Things cannot continue as they are. It turns me cold to think of this creature stealing like a thief to Harry's bedside ; poor Harry, what a wakening ! And the danger of it ! for if this Hyde suspects the existence of the will, he may grow impatient to inherit. Ah, I must put my shoulder to the wheel—if Jekyll will but let me," he added, " if Jekyll will only let me." For once more he saw before his mind's eye, as clear as a transparency, the strange clauses of the will.

DR. JEKYLL WAS QUITE AT EASE

A FORTNIGHT later, by excellent good fortune, the doctor gave one of his pleasant dinners to some five or six old cronies, all intelligent reputable men, and all judges of good wine ; and Mr. Utterson so contrived that he remained behind after the others had departed. This was no new arrangement, but a thing that had befallen many scores of times. Where Utterson was liked, he was liked well. Hosts loved to detain the dry lawyer, when the light-hearted and the loose-tongued had already their foot on the threshold ; they liked to sit awhile in his unobtrusive company, practising for solitude, sobering their minds in the man's rich silence, after the expense and strain of gaiety. To this rule, Dr. Jekyll was no exception ; and as he now sat on the opposite side of the fire—a large, well-made, smooth-faced man of fifty, with something of a slyish cast perhaps, but every mark of capacity and kindness—you could see by his looks that he cherished for Mr. Utterson a sincere and warm affection.

"I have been wanting to speak to you, Jekyll," began the latter. "You know that will of yours ? "

A close observer might have gathered that the topic was distasteful ; but the doctor carried it off gaily. "My poor Utterson," said he, "you are unfortunate in such a client. I never saw a man so distressed as you were by my will ; unless it were that hide-bound pedant, Lanyon, at what he called my scientific heresies. O, I know he's a good fellow—you needn't frown—an excellent fellow, and I always mean to see more of him ; but a hide-hound pedant for all that ; an ignorant, blatant pedant. I was never more disappointed in any man than Lanyon."

"You know I never approved of it," pursued Utterson, ruthlessly disregarding the fresh topic.

"My will ? Yes, certainly, I know that," said the doctor, a trifle sharply. "You have told me so."

"Well, I tell you so again," continued the lawyer. "I have been learning something of young Hyde."

The large handsome face of Dr. Jekyll grew pale to the very lips, and there came a blackness about his eyes. "I do not care to hear more," said he. "This is a matter I thought we had agreed to drop."

"What I heard was abominable," said Utterson.

"It can make no change. You do not understand my position," returned the doctor, with a certain incoherency of manner. "I am painfully situated, Utterson ; my position is a very strange one—a very strange one. It is one of those affairs that cannot be mended by talking."

"Jekyll," said Utterson, "you know me : I am a man to be trusted. Make a clean breast of this in confidence ; and I make no doubt I can get you out of it."

"My good Utterson," said the doctor, "this is very good of you, this is downright good of you, and I cannot find words to thank you in. I believe you fully ; I would trust you before any man alive, ay, before myself, if I could make the choice ; but indeed it isn't what you fancy ; it is not so bad as that ; and just to put your good heart at rest, I will tell you one thing : the moment I choose, I can be rid of Mr. Hyde. I give you my hand upon that ; and I thank you again and again ; and I will just add one little word, Utterson, that I'm sure you'll take in good part : this is a private matter, and I beg of you to let it sleep."

Utterson reflected a little, looking in the fire.

" I have no doubt you are perfectly right," he said at last, getting to his feet.

" Well, but since we have touched upon this business, and for the last time I hope," continued the doctor, " there is one point I should like you to understand. I have really a very great interest in poor Hyde. I know you have seen him ; he told me so ; and I fear he was rude. But I do sincerely take a great, a very great interest in that young man ; and if I am taken away, Utterson, I wish you to promise me that you will bear with him and get his rights for him. I think you would, if you knew all ; and it would be a weight off my mind if you would promise."

" I can't pretend that I shall ever like him," said the lawyer.

" I don't ask that," pleaded Jekyll, laying his hand upon the other's arm ; " I only ask for justice ; I only ask you to help him for my sake, when I am no longer here."

Utterson heaved an irrepressible sigh. " Well," said he, " I promise."

The Carew Murder Case

NEARLY a year later, in the month of October 18——, London was startled by a crime of singular ferocity, and rendered all the more notable by the high position of the victim. The details were few and startling. A maid-servant living alone in a house not far from the river, had gone upstairs to bed about eleven. Although a fog rolled over the city in the small hours, the early part of the night was cloudless, and the lane, which the maid's window overlooked, was brilliantly lit by the full moon. It seems she was romantically given ; for she sat down upon her box, which stood immediately under the window, and fell into a dream of musing. Never (she used to say, with streaming tears, when she narrated that experience), never had she felt more at peace with all men or thought more kindly of the world. And as she so sat she became aware of an aged and beautiful gentleman with white hair, drawing near along the lane ; and advancing to meet him, another and very small gentleman, to whom at first she paid less attention. When they had come within speech (which was just under the maid's eyes) the older man bowed and accosted the other with a very pretty manner of politeness. It did not seem as if the subject of his address were of great importance ; indeed, from his pointing, it sometimes appeared as if he were only inquiring his way ; but the moon shone on his face as he spoke, and the girl was pleased to watch it, it seemed to breathe such an innocent and old-world kindness of disposition, yet with something high too, as of a well-founded self-content. Presently her eye wandered to the other, and she was surprised to recognise in him a certain Mr. Hyde, who had once visited her master, and for whom she had conceived a dislike. He had in his hand a heavy cane, with which he was trifling; but he answered never a word, and seemed to listen with an ill-contained impatience. And then all of a sudden he broke out in a great flame of anger, stamping with his foot, brandishing the cane, and carrying on (as the maid described it) like a madman. The old gentleman took a step back, with the air of one very much surprised and a trifle hurt; and at that Mr. Hyde broke out of all bounds, and clubbed him to the earth. And next moment with ape-like fury, he was trampling his victim under foot, and hailing down a storm of blows, under which the bones were audibly shattered and the body jumped upon the roadway. At the horror of these sights and sounds, the maid fainted.

It was two o'clock when she came to herself and called for the police. The murderer was gone long ago; but there lay his victim in the middle of the lane, incredibly mangled. The stick with which the deed had been done, although it was of some rare and very tough and heavy wood, had broken in the middle under the stress of this insensate cruelty; and one splinted half had rolled in the neighbouring gutter—the other, without doubt, had been carried away by the murderer. A purse and a gold watch were found upon the victim; but no cards or papers, except a sealed and stamped envelope, which he had been probably carrying to the post, and which bore the name and address of Mr. Utterson.

This was brought to the lawyer the next morning, before he was out of bed; and he had no sooner seen it, and been told the circumstances, than he shot out a solemn lip. " I shall say nothing till I have seen the body," said he; " this may be very serious. Have the kindness to wait while I dress." And with the same grave countenance he hurried through his breakfast and drove to the police station, whither the body had been carried. As soon as he came into the cell, he nodded.

" Yes," said he, " I recognise him. I am sorry to say that this is Sir Danvers Carew."

" Good God, sir," exclaimed the officer, " is it possible ? " And the next moment his eye lighted up with professional ambition. " This will make a deal of noise," he said. " And perhaps you can help us to the man." And he briefly narrated what the maid had seen, and showed the broken stick.

Mr. Utterson had already quailed at the name of Hyde; but when the stick was laid before him, he could doubt no longer: broken and battered as it was, he recognised it for one that he had himself presented many years before to Henry Jekyll.

" Is this Mr. Hyde a person of small stature ? " he inquired.

" Particularly small and particularly wicked-looking, is what the maid calls him," said the officer.

Mr. Utterson reflected; and then, raising his head, "If you will come with me in my cab," he said, "I think I can take you to his house."

It was by this time about nine in the morning, and the first fog of the season. A great chocolate-coloured pall lowered over heaven, but the wind was continually charging and routing these embattled vapours; so that as the cab crawled from street to street, Mr. Utterson beheld a marvellous number of degrees and hues of twilight; for here it would be dark like the backend of evening; and there would be a glow of a rich, lurid brown, like the light of some strange conflagration; and here, for a moment, the fog would be quite broken up, and a haggard shaft of daylight would glance in between the swirling wreaths. The dismal quarter of Soho seen under these changing glimpses, with its muddy ways, and slatternly passengers, and its lamps, which had never been extinguished or had been kindled afresh to combat this mournful reinvasion of darkness, seemed, in the lawyer's eyes, like a district of some city in a nightmare. The thoughts of his mind, besides, were of the gloomiest dye; and when he glanced at the companion of his drive, he was conscious of some touch of that terror of the law and the law's officers, which may at times assail the most honest.

As the cab drew up before the address indicated, the fog lifted a little and showed him a dingy street, a gin palace, a low French eating-house, a shop for the retail of penny numbers and two-penny salads, many ragged children huddled in the doorways, and many woman of many different nationalities passing out, key in hand, to have a morning glass; and the next moment the fog settled down again upon that part, as brown as umber, and cut him off from his blackguardly surroundings. This was the home of Henry Jekyll's favourite; of a man who was heir to a quarter of a million sterling.

An ivory-faced and silvery-haired old woman opened the door. She had an evil face, smoothed by hypocrisy; but her manners were excellent. Yes, she said, this was Mr. Hyde's, but he was not at home; he had been in that night very late, but had gone away again in less than an hour: there was nothing strange in that; his habits were very irregular, and he was often absent; for instance, it was nearly two months since she had seen him till yesterday.

"Very well then, we wish to see his rooms," said the lawyer; and when the woman began to declare it was impossible, "I had better tell you who this person is," he added. "This is Inspector Newcomen, of Scotland Yard."

A flash of odious joy appeared on the woman's face. "Ah!" said she, "he is in trouble! What has he done?"

Mr. Utterson and the inspector exchanged glances. "He don't seem a very popular character," observed the latter. "And now, my good woman, just let me and this gentleman have a look about us."

In the whole extent of the house, which but for the old woman remained otherwise empty, Mr. Hyde had only used a couple of rooms; but these were furnished with luxury and good taste. A closet was filled with wine; the plate was of silver, the napery elegant; a good picture hung upon the walls, a gift (as Utterson supposed) from Henry Jekyll, who was much of a connoisseur; and the carpets were of many piles and agreeable in colour. At this moment, however, the rooms bore every mark of having been recently and hurriedly ransacked; clothes lay about the floor, with their pockets inside out; lockfast drawers stood open; and on the hearth there lay a pile of grey ashes, as though many papers had been burned. From these embers the inspector disinterred the butt end of a green cheque book, which had resisted the action of the fire; the other half of the stick was found behind the door; and as this clinched his suspicions, the officer declared himself delighted. A visit to the bank, where several thousand pounds were found to be lying to the murderer's credit, completed his gratification.

"You may depend upon it, sir," he told Mr. Utterson: "I have him in my hand. He must have lost his head, or he never would have left the stick, or, above all, burned the cheque book. Why, money's ife to the man. We have nothing to do but wait for him at the bank, and get out the handbills."

This last, however, was not so easy of accomplishment; for the master of the servant-maid had only seen him twice; his family could nowhere be traced; he had never been photographed; and the few who could describe him differed widely, as common observers will. Only on one point were they agreed; and that was the haunting sense of unexpressed deformity with which the fugitive impressed his beholders.

Incident of the Letter

It was late in the afternoon, when Mr. Utterson found his way to Dr. Jekyll's door, where he was at once admitted by Poole, and carried down by the kitchen offices and across a yard which had once been a garden, to the building which was indifferently known as the laboratory or the dissecting rooms. The doctor had bought the house from the heirs of a celebrated surgeon; and his own tastes being rather chemical than anatomical, had changed the destination of the block at the bottom of the garden. It was the first time that the lawyer had been received in that part of his friend's quarters; and he eyed the dingy windowless structure with curiosity, and gazed round with a distasteful sense of strangeness as he crossed the theatre, once crowded with eager students and now lying gaunt and silent, the tables laden with chemical apparatus, the floor strewn with crates and littered with packing straw, and the light falling dimly through the foggy cupola. At the farther end, a flight of stairs mounted to a door covered with red baize; and through this, Mr. Utterson was at last received into the doctor's cabinet. It was a large room, fitted round with glass presses, furnished, among other things, with a cheval-glass and a business table, and looking out upon the court by three dusty windows barred with iron. The fire burned in the grate ; a lamp was set lighted on the chimney-shelf, for even in the houses the fog began to lie thickly ; and there, close up to the warmth, sat Dr. Jekyll, looking deadly sick. He did not rise to meet his visitor, but held out a cold hand, and bade him welcome in a changed voice.

"And now," said Mr. Utterson, as soon as Poole had left them, "you have heard the news ? "

The doctor shuddered. " They were crying it in the square," he said. " I heard them in my dining-room."

" One word," said the lawyer. " Carew was my client, but so are you ; and I want to know what I am doing. You have not been mad enough to hide this fellow ? "

" Utterson, I swear to God," cried the doctor, " I swear to God I will never set eyes on him again. I bind my honour to you that I am done with him in this world. It is all at an end. And indeed he does not want my help ; you do not know him as I do ; he is safe, he is quite safe ; mark my words, he will never more be heard of."

The lawyer listened gloomily ; he did not like his friend's feverish manner. " You seem pretty sure of him," said he ; " and for your sake, I hope you may be right. If it came to a trial, your name might appear."

" I am quite sure of him," replied Jekyll ; " I have grounds for certainty that I cannot share with any one. But there is one thing on which you may advise me. I have—I have received a letter ; and I am at a loss whether I should show it to the police. I should like to leave it in your hands, Utterson ; you would judge wisely, I am sure ; I have so great a trust in you."

" You fear, I suppose, that it might lead to his detection ? " asked the lawyer.

" No," said the other. " I cannot say that I care what becomes of Hyde ; I am quite done with him. I was thinking of my own character, which this hateful business has rather exposed."

Utterson ruminated awhile ; he was surprised at his friend's selfishness, and yet relieved by it. " Well," said he, at last, " let me see the letter."

The letter was written in an odd, upright hand, and signed " Edward Hyde " : and it signified, briefly enough, that the writer's benefactor, Dr. Jekyll, whom he had long so unworthily repaid for a thousand generosities, need labour under no alarm for his safety, as he had means of escape on which he placed a sure dependence. The lawyer liked this letter well enough : it put a better colour on the intimacy than he had looked for ; and he blamed himself for some of his past suspicions.

" Have you the envelope ? " he asked.

" I burned it," replied Jekyll, " before I thought what I was about. But it bore no postmark. The note was handed in."

" Shall I keep this and sleep upon it ? " asked Utterson.

" I wish you to judge for me entirely," was the reply. " I have lost confidence in myself."

" Well, I shall consider," returned the lawyer. " And now one word more : it was Hyde who dictated the terms in your will about that disappearance ? "

The doctor seemed seized with a qualm of faintness ; he shut his mouth tight and nodded.

" I knew it," said Utterson. " He meant to murder you. You have had a fine escape."

" I have had what is far more to the purpose," returned the doctor solemnly : " I have had a lesson—O God, Utterson, what a lesson I have had ! " And he covered his face for a moment with his hands.

On his way out, the lawyer stopped and had a word or two with Poole. " By the by," said he, " there was a letter handed in to-day : what was the messenger like ? " But Poole was positive nothing had come except by post ; " and only circulars by that," he added.

This news sent off the visitor with his fears renewed. Plainly the letter had come by the laboratory door ; possibly, indeed, it had been written in the cabinet ; and, if that were so, it must be differently judged, and handled with the more caution. The news-boys, as he went, were crying themselves hoarse along the footways : " Special edition. Shocking murder of an M.P." That was the funeral oration of one friend and client ; and he could not help a certain apprehension lest the good name of another should be sucked down in the eddy of the scandal. It was, at least, a ticklish decision that he had to make ; and, self-reliant as he was by habit, he began to cherish a longing for advice. It was not to be had directly ; but perhaps, he thought, it might be fished for.

Presently after, he sat on one side of his own hearth, with Mr. Guest, his head clerk, upon the other, and midway between, at a nicely calculated distance from the fire, a bottle of particular old wine that had long dwelt unsunned in the foundations of his house. The fog still slept on the wing above the drowned city, where the lamps glimmered like carbuncles ; and through the muffle and smother of these fallen clouds, the procession of the town's life was still rolling in through the great arteries with a sound as of a mighty wind. But the room was gay with firelight. In the bottle the acids were long ago resolved ; the imperial dye had softened with time, as the colour grows richer in stained windows ; and the glow of hot autumn afternoons on hillside vineyards was ready to be set free and to disperse the fogs of London. Insensibly the lawyer melted. There was no man from whom he kept fewer secrets than Mr. Guest ; and he was not always sure that he kept as many as he meant. Guest had often been on business to the doctors : he knew Poole ; he could scarce have failed to hear of Mr. Hyde's familiarity about the house ; he might draw conclusions : was it not as well, then, that he should see a letter which put that mystery to rights ? and, above all, since Guest, being a great student and critic of handwriting, would consider the step natural and obliging ? The clerk, besides, was a man of counsel; he would scarce read so strange a document without dropping a remark; and by that remark Mr. Utterson might shape his future course.

"This is a sad business about Sir Danvers," he said.

"Yes, sir, indeed. It has elicited a great deal of public feeling," returned Guest. "The man, of course, was mad."

"I should like to hear your views on that," replied Utterson. "I have a document here in his handwriting; it is between ourselves, for I scarce know what to do about it; it is an ugly business at the best. But there it is; quite in your way: a murderer's autograph."

Guest's eyes brightened, and he sat down at once and studied it with passion. "No, sir," he said; "not mad; but it is an odd hand."

"And by all accounts a very odd writer," added the lawyer.

Just then the servant entered with a note.

"Is that from Dr. Jekyll, sir ? " inquired the clerk. "I thought I knew the writing. Anything private, Mr. Utterson ? "

"Only an invitation to dinner. Why ? Do you want to see it ? "

"One moment. I thank you, sir ; " and the clerk laid the two sheets of paper alongside and sedulously compared their contents. "Thank you, sir, he said at last, returning both; "it's a very interesting autograph."

There was a pause during which Mr. Utterson struggled with himself. "Why did you compare them, Guest?" he inquired suddenly.

"Well, sir," returned the clerk, "there's a rather singular resemblance; the two hands are in many points identical: only differently sloped."

"Rather quaint," said Utterson.

"It is, as you say, rather quaint," returned Guest.

"I wouldn't speak of this note, you know," said the master.

"No, sir," said the clerk. "I understand."

But no sooner was Mr. Utterson alone that night, then he locked the note into his safe, where it reposed from that time forward. "What ! " he thought. "Henry Jekyll forge for a murderer ! " And his blood ran cold in his veins.

REMARKABLE INCIDENT OF DR. LANYON

TIME ran on; thousands of pounds were offered in reward, for the death of Sir Danvers was resented as a public injury; but Mr. Hyde had disappeared out of the ken of the police as though he had never existed. Much of his past was unearthed, indeed, and all disreputable: tales came out of the man's cruelty, at once so callous and violent, of his vile life, of his strange associates, of the hatred that seemed to have surrounded his career; but of his present whereabouts, not a whisper. From the time he had left the house in Soho on the morning of the murder, he was simply blotted out; and gradually, as time drew on, Mr. Utterson began to recover from the hotness of his alarm, and to grow more at quiet with himself. The death of Sir Danvers was, to his way of thinking, more than paid for by the disappearance of Mr. Hyde. Now that that evil influence had been withdrawn, a new life began for Dr. Jekyll. He came out of his seclusion, renewed relations with his friends, became once more their familiar guest and entertainer; and whilst he had always been known for charities, he was now no less distinguished for religion. He was busy, he was much in the open air, he did good; his face seemed to open and brighten, as if with an inward consciousness of service; and for more than two months, the doctor was at peace.

On the 8th of January Utterson had dined at the doctor's with a small party; Lanyon had been there; and the face of the host had looked from one to the other as in the old days when the trio were inseparable friends. On the 12th, and again on the 14th, the door was shut against the lawyer. "The doctor was confined to the house," Poole said, "and saw no one." On the 15th, he tried again, and was again refused; and having now been used for the last two months to see his friend almost daily, he found this return of solitude to weigh upon his spirits. The fifth night, he had in Guest to dine with him; and the sixth he betook himself to Dr. Lanyon's.

There at least he was not denied admittance; but when he came in, he was shocked at the change which had taken place in the doctor's appearance. He had his death-warrant written legibly upon his face. The rosy man had grown pale; his flesh had fallen away; he was visibly balder and older; and yet it was not so much these tokens of a swift physical decay that arrested the lawyer's notice, as a look in the eye and quality of manner that seemed to testify to some deep-seated terror of the mind. It was unlikely that the doctor should fear death; and yet that was what Utterson was tempted to suspect. "Yes," he thought; "he is a doctor, he must know his own state and that his days are counted; and the knowledge is more than he can bear." And yet when Utterson remarked on his ill looks, it was with an air of great firmness that Lanyon declared himself a doomed man.

"I have had a shock," he said, "and I shall never recover. It is a question of weeks. Well, life has been pleasant; I liked it; yes, sir, I used to like it. I sometimes think if we knew all, we should be more glad to get away."

"Jekyll is ill, too," observed Utterson. "Have you seen him?"

But Lanyon's face changed, and he held up a trembling hand. "I wish to see or hear no more of Dr. Jekyll," he said, in a loud, unsteady voice. "I am quite done with that person; and I beg that you will spare me any allusion to one whom I regard as dead."

"Tut, tut!" said Mr. Utterson; and then, after a considerable pause, "Can't I do anything?" he inquired. "We are three very old friends, Lanyon; we shall not live to make others."

"Nothing can be done," returned Lanyon; "ask himself."

"He will not see me," said the lawyer.

"I am not surprised at that," was the reply. "Some day, Utterson, after I am dead, you may perhaps come to learn the right and wrong of this. I cannot tell you. And in the meantime, if you can sit and talk with me of other things, for God's sake, stay and do so; but if you cannot keep clear of this accursed topic, then, in God's name, go, for I cannot bear it."

As soon as he got home, Utterson sat down and wrote to Jekyll, complaining of his exclusion from the house, and asking the cause of this unhappy break with Lanyon; and the next day brought him a long answer, often very pathetically worded, and sometimes darkly mysterious in drift. The quarrel with Lanyon was incurable. "I do not blame our old friend," Jekyll wrote, "but I share his view that we must never meet. I mean from henceforth to lead a life of extreme seclusion; you must not be surprised, nor must you doubt my friendship, if my door is often shut even to you. You must suffer me to go my own dark way. I have brought on myself a punishment and a danger that I cannot name. If I am the chief of sinners, I am the chief of sufferers also. I could not think that this earth contained a place for sufferings and terrors so unmanning; and you can do but one thing, Utterson, to lighten this destiny, and that is to respect my silence." Utterson was amazed; the dark influence of Hyde had been withdrawn, the doctor had returned to his old tasks and amities; a week ago, the prospect had smiled with every promise of a cheerful and an honoured age; and now in a moment, friendship and peace of mind and the whole tenor of his life were wrecked. So great and unprepared a change pointed to madness; but in view of Lanyon's manner and words, there must lie for it some deeper ground.

A week afterwards Dr. Lanyon took to his bed, and in something less than a fortnight he was dead. The night after the funeral, at which he had been sadly affected, Utterson locked the door of his business room, and sitting there by the light of a melancholy candle, drew out and set before him an envelope addressed by the hand and sealed with the seal of his dead friend. "PRIVATE: for the hands of J. G. Utterson ALONE, and in case of his predecease *to be destroyed unread*," so it was emphatically superscribed; and the lawyer dreaded to behold the contents. "I have buried one friend to-day," he thought: "what if this should cost me another?" And then he condemned the fear as a disloyalty, and broke the seal. Within there was another enclosure, likewise sealed, and marked upon the cover as "not to be opened till the death or disappearance of Dr. Henry Jekyll." Utterson could not trust his eyes. Yes, it was disappearance; here again, as in the mad will, which he had long ago restored to its author, here again were the idea of a disappearance and the name of Henry Jekyll bracketed. But in the will, that idea had sprung from the sinister suggestion of the man Hyde; it was set there with a purpose all too plain and horrible.

Written by the hand of Lanyon, what should it mean? A great curiosity came to the trustee, to disregard the prohibition, and dive at once to the bottom of these mysteries; but professional honour and faith to his dead friend were stringent obligations; and the packet slept in the inmost corner of his private safe.

It is one thing to mortify curiosity, another to conquer it; and it may be doubted if, from that day forth, Utterson desired the society of his surviving friend with the same eagerness. He thought of him kindly; but his thoughts were disquieted and fearful. He went to call indeed; but he was perhaps relieved to be denied admittance; perhaps, in his heart, he preferred to speak with Poole upon the doorstep, and surrounded by the air and sounds of the open city, rather than to be admitted into that house of voluntary bondage, and to sit and speak with its inscrutable recluse. Poole had, indeed, no very pleasant news to communicate. The doctor, it appeared, now more than ever confined himself to the cabinet over the laboratory, where he would sometimes even sleep: he was out of spirits, he had grown very silent, he did not read; it seemed as if he had something on his mind. Utterson became so used to the unvarying character of these reports, that he fell off little by little in the frequency of his visits.

INCIDENT AT THE WINDOW

IT chanced on Sunday, when Mr. Utterson was on his usual walk with Mr. Enfield, that their way lay once again through the by-street; and that when they came in front of the door, both stopped to gaze on it.

"Well," said Enfield, "that story's at an end, at least. We shall never see more of Mr. Hyde."

"I hope not," said Utterson. "Did I ever tell you that I once saw him, and shared your feeling of repulsion?"

"It was impossible to do the one without the other," returned Enfield. "And, by the way, what an ass you must have thought me, not to know that this was a back way to Dr. Jekyll's! It was partly your own fault that I found it out, even when I did."

"So you found it out, did you?" said Utterson. "But if that be so, we may step into the court and take a look at the windows. To tell you the truth, I am uneasy about poor Jekyll; and even outside, I feel as if the presence of a friend might do him good."

The court was very cool and a little damp, and full of premature twilight, although the sky, high up overhead, was still bright with sunset. The middle one of the three windows was half-way open; and sitting close beside it, taking the air with an infinite sadness of mien, like some disconsolate prisoner, Utterson saw Dr. Jekyll.

"What! Jekyll!" he cried. "I trust you are better."

"I am very low, Utterson," replied the doctor drearily; "very low. It will not last long, thank God."

"You stay too much indoors," said the lawyer. "You should be out, whipping up the circulation, like Mr. Enfield and me. (This is my cousin—Mr. Enfield—Dr. Jekyll.) Come now ; get your hat, and take a quick turn with us."

" You are very good," sighed the other. " I should like to very much ; but no, no, no ; it is quite impossible ; I dare not. But indeed, Utterson, I am very glad to see you ; this is really a great pleasure. I would ask you and Mr. Enfield up, but the place is really not fit."

" Why then," said the lawyer, good-naturedly, " the best thing we can do is to stay down here, and speak with you from where we are."

" That is just what I was about to venture to propose," returned the doctor, with a smile. But the words were hardly uttered, before the smile was struck out of his face and succeeded by an expression of such abject terror and despair, as froze the very blood of the two gentlemen below. They saw it but for a glimpse, for the window was instantly thrust down ; but that glimpse had been sufficient, and they turned and left the court without a word. In silence, too, they traversed the by-street ; and it was not until they had come into a neighbouring thoroughfare, where even upon a Sunday there were still some stirrings of life, that Mr. Utterson at last turned and looked at his companion. They were both pale ; and there was an answering horror in their eyes.

" God forgive us ! God forgive us ! " said Mr. Utterson.

But Mr. Enfield only nodded his head very seriously, and walked on once more in silence.

The Last Night

MR. UTTERSON was sitting by his fireside one evening after dinner, when he was surprised to receive a visit from Poole.

" Bless me, Poole, what brings you here ? " he cried ; and then, taking a second look at him, " What ails you ? " he added ; " is the doctor ill ? "

" Mr. Utterson," said the man, " there is something wrong."

" Take a seat, and here is a glass of wine for you," said the lawyer. " Now, take your time, and tell me plainly what you want."

" You know the doctor's ways, sir," replied Poole, " and how he shuts himself up. Well, he's shut up again in the cabinet ; and I don't like it, sir—I wish I may die if I like it. Mr. Utterson, sir, I'm afraid."

" Now, my good man," said the lawyer, " be explicit. What are you afraid of ? "

" I've been afraid for about a week," returned Poole, doggedly disregarding the question ; " and I can bear it no more."

The man's appearance amply bore out his words ; his manner was altered for the worse : and except for the moment when he had first announced his terror, he had not once looked the lawyer in the face. Even now, he sat with the glass of wine untasted on his knee, and his eyes directed to a corner of the floor. " I can bear it no more," he repeated.

"Come," said the lawyer, "I see you have some good reason, Poole; I see there is something seriously amiss. Try to tell me what it is."

"I think there's been foul play," said Poole, hoarsely.

"Foul play!" cried the lawyer, a good deal frightened, and rather inclined to be irritated in consequence. "What foul play? What does the man mean?"

"I daren't say, sir," was the answer; "but will you come along with me and see for yourself?"

Mr. Utterson's only answer was to rise and get his hat and great-coat; but he observed with wonder the greatness of the relief that appeared upon the butler's face, and perhaps with no less, that the wine was still untasted when he set it down to follow.

It was a wild, cold, seasonable night of March, with a pale moon, lying on her back as though the wind had tilted her, and a flying wrack of the most diaphanous and lawny texture. The wind made talking difficult, and flecked the blood into the face. It seemed to have swept the streets unusually bare of passengers, besides; for Mr. Utterson thought he had never seen that part of London so deserted. He could have wished it otherwise; never in his life had he been conscious of so sharp a wish to see and touch his fellow-creatures; for, struggle as he might, there was borne in upon his mind a crushing anticipation of calamity. The square, when they got there, was all full of wind and dust, and the thin trees in the garden were lashing themselves along the railing. Poole, who had kept all the way a pace or two ahead, now pulled up in the middle of the pavement, and in spite of the biting weather, took off his hat and mopped his brow with a red pocket-handkerchief. But for all the hurry of his coming, these were not the dews of exertion that he wiped away, but the moisture of some strangling anguish; for his face was white, and his voice, when he spoke, harsh and broken.

"Well, sir," he said, "here we are, and God grant there be nothing wrong."

"Amen, Poole," said the lawyer.

Thereupon the servant knocked in a very guarded manner; the door was opened on the chain; and a voice asked from within, "Is that you, Poole?"

"It's all right," said Poole. "Open the door."

The hall, when they entered it, was brightly lighted up; the fire was built high; and about the hearth the whole of the servants, men and women, stood huddled together like a flock of sheep. At the sight of Mr. Utterson, the housemaid broke into hysterical whimpering; and the cook, crying out, "Bless God! it's Mr. Utterson," ran forward as if to take him in her arms.

"What, what? Are you all here?" said the lawyer, peevishly. "Very irregular, very unseemly; your master would be far from pleased."

" They're all afraid," said Poole.

Blank silence followed, no one protesting ; only the maid lifted up her voice, and now wept loudly.

" Hold your tongue ! " Poole said to her, with a ferocity of accent that testified to his own jangled nerves ; and indeed when the girl had so suddenly raised the note of her lamentation, they had all started and turned towards the inner door with faces of dreadful expectation. " And now," continued the butler, addressing the knife-boy, " reach me a candle, and we'll get this through hands at once." And then he begged Mr. Utterson to follow him, and led the way to the back garden.

" Now, sir," said he, " you come as gently as you can. I want you to hear, and I don't want you to be heard. And see here, sir, if by any chance he was to ask you in, don't go."

Mr. Utterson's nerves, at this unlooked for termination, gave a jerk that nearly threw him from his balance ; but he re-collected his courage, and followed the butler into the laboratory building and through the surgical theatre, with its lumber of crates and bottles, to the foot of the stair. Here Poole motioned him to stand on one side and listen ; while he himself, setting down the candle and making a great and obvious call on his resolution, mounted the steps, and knocked with a somewhat uncertain hand on the red baize of the cabinet door.

" Mr. Utterson, sir, asking to see you," he called ; and even as he did so, once more violently signed to the lawyer to give ear.

A voice answered from within : " Tell him I cannot see anyone," it said, complainingly.

" Thank you, sir," said Poole, with a note of something like triumph in his voice ; and taking up his candle, he led Mr. Utterson back across the yard and into the great kitchen, where the fire was out and the beetles were leaping on the floor.

" Sir," he said, looking Mr. Utterson in the eyes, " was that my master's voice ? "

" It seems much changed," replied the lawyer, very pale, but giving look for look.

" Changed ? Well, yes, I think so," said the butler. " Have I been twenty years in this man's house, to be deceived about his voice ? No, sir ; master's made away with ; he was made away with, eight days ago, when we heard him cry out upon the name of God ; and *who's* in there instead of him, and *why* it stays there, is a thing that cries to Heaven, Mr. Utterson ! "

" This is a very strange tale, Poole ; this is rather a wild tale, my man," said Mr. Utterson, biting his finger. " Suppose it were as you suppose, supposing Dr. Jekyll to have been—well, murdered, what could induce the murderer to stay ? That won't hold water ; it doesn't commend itself to reason."

" Well, Mr. Utterson, you are a hard man to satisfy, but I'll do it yet," said Poole. " All this last week (you must know) him, or it, or whatever it is that lives in that cabinet, has been crying night and day

for some sort of medicine and cannot get it to his mind. It was sometimes his way—the master's, that is—to write his orders on a sheet of
paper and throw it on the stair. We've had nothing else this week
back; nothing but papers, and a closed door, and the very meals left
there to be smuggled in when nobody was looking. Well, sir, every
day, ay, and twice and thrice in the same day, there have been orders
and complaints, and I have been sent flying to all the wholesale chemists
in town. Every time I brought the stuff back, there would be another
paper telling me to return it, because it was not pure, and another order
to a different firm. This drug is wanted bitter bad, sir, whatever for."

" Have you any of these papers ? " asked Mr. Utterson.

Poole felt in his pocket and handed out a crumpled note, which the
lawyer, bending nearer to the candle, carefully examined. Its contents ran thus : " Dr. Jekyll presents his compliments to Messrs. Maw.
He assures them that their last sample is impure and quite useless for
his present purpose. In the year 18——, Dr. J. purchased a somewhat large quantity from Messrs. M. He now begs them to search
with the most sedulous care, and should any of the same quality be left,
to forward it to him at once. Expense is no consideration. The importance of this to Dr. J. can hardly be exaggerated." So far the letter
had run composedly enough ; but here, with a sudden splutter of the
pen, the writer's emotion had broken loose. " For God's sake," he
had added, " find me some of the old."

" This is a strange note," said Mr. Utterson ; and then, sharply,
" How do you come to have it open ? "

" The man at Maw's was main angry, sir, and he threw it back to me
like so much dirt," returned Poole.

" This is unquestionably the doctor's hand, do you know ? " resumed the lawyer.

" I thought it looked like it," said the servant, rather sulkily ; and
then, with another voice, " But what matters hand of write ? " he said.
" I've seen him ! "

" Seen him ? " repeated Mr. Utterson. " Well ? "

" That's it ! " said Poole. " It was this way. I came suddenly
into the theatre from the garden. It seems he had slipped out to look
for this drug, or whatever it is ; for the cabinet door was open, and there
he was at the far end of the room, digging among the crates. He
looked up when I came in, gave a kind of cry, and whipped upstairs
into the cabinet. It was but for one minute that I saw him, but the
hair stood upon my head like quills. Sir, if that was my master, why
had he a mask upon his face ? If it was my master, why did he cry out
like a rat, and run from me ? I have served him long enough. And
then . . ." the man paused, and passed his hand over his face.

" These are all very strange circumstances," said Mr. Utterson, " but
I think I begin to see daylight. Your master, Poole, is plainly seized
with one of those maladies that both torture and deform the sufferer ;
hence, for aught I know, the alteration of his voice ; hence the mask

and his avoidance of his friends ; hence his eagerness to find this drug, by means of which the poor soul retains some hope of ultimate recovery —God grant that he be not deceived ! There is my explanation ; it is sad enough, Poole, ay, and appalling to consider ; but it is plain and natural, hangs well together, and delivers us from all exorbitant alarms."

" Sir," said the butler, turning to a sort of mottled pallor, " that thing was not my master, and there's the truth. My master "—here he looked round him, and began to whisper—" is a tall fine build of a man, and this was more of a dwarf." Utterson attempted to protest. " O, sir," cried Poole, " do you think I do not know my master after twenty years ? do you think I do not know where his head comes to in the cabinet door, where I saw him every morning of my life ? No, sir, that thing in the mask was never Dr. Jekyll—God knows what it was, but it was never Dr. Jekyll ; and it is the belief of my heart that there was murder done."

" Poole," replied the lawyer, " if you say that, it will become my duty to make certain. Much as I desire to spare your master's feelings, much as I am puzzled by this note, which seems to prove him to be still alive, I shall consider it my duty to break in at that door."

" Ah, Mr. Utterson, that's talking ! " cried the butler.

" And now comes the second question," resumed Utterson : " Who is going to do it ? "

" Why, you and me, sir," was the undaunted reply.

" That is very well said," returned the lawyer ; " and whatever comes of it, I shall make it my business to see you are no loser."

" There is an axe in the theatre," continued Poole ; " and you might take the kitchen poker for yourself."

The lawyer took that rude but weighty instrument into his hand, and balanced it. " Do you know, Poole," he said, looking up, " that you and I are about to place ourselves in a position of some peril ? "

" You may say so, sir, indeed," returned the butler.

" It is well, then, that we should be frank," said the other. " We both think more than we have said ; let us make a clean breast. This masked figure that you saw, did you recognise it ? "

" Well, sir, it went so quick, and the creature was so doubled up, that I could hardly swear to that," was the answer. " But if you mean, was it Mr. Hyde ?—why, yes, I think it was ! You see, it was much of the same bigness ; and it had the same quick light way with it ; and then who else could have got in by the laboratory door ? You have not forgot, sir, that at the time of the murder he had still the key with him ? But that's not all. I don't know, Mr. Utterson, if ever you met this Mr. Hyde ? "

" Yes," said the lawyer, " I once spoke with him."

" Then you must know, as well as the rest of us, that there was something queer about that gentleman—something that gave a man a turn—I don't know rightly how to say it, sir, beyond this : that you felt it in your marrow—kind of cold and thin."

" I own I felt something of what you describe," said Mr. Utterson.

" Quite so, sir," returned Poole. " Well, when that masked thing like a monkey jumped from among the chemicals and whipped into the cabinet, it went down my spine like ice. O, I know it's not evidence, Mr. Utterson ; I'm book-learned enough for that ; but a man has his feelings ; and I give you my Bible-word it was Mr. Hyde ! "

" Ay, ay," said the lawyer. " My fears incline to the same point. Evil, I fear, founded—evil was sure to come—of that connection. Ay, truly, I believe you ; I believe poor Harry is killed ; and I believe his murderer (for what purpose, God alone can tell) is still lurking in his victim's room. Well, let our name be vengeance. Call Bradshaw."

The footman came at the summons, very white and nervous.

" Pull yourself together, Bradshaw," said the lawyer. " This suspense, I know, is telling upon all of you ; but it is now our intention to make an end of it. Poole, here, and I are going to force our way into the cabinet. If all is well, my shoulders are broad enough to bear the blame. Meanwhile, lest anything should really be amiss, or any male-factor seek to escape by the back, you and the boy must go round the corner with a pair of good sticks, and take your post at the laboratory door. We give you ten minutes to get to your stations."

As Bradshaw left, the lawyer looked at his watch. " And now, Poole, let us get to ours," he said ; and taking the poker under his arm, he led the way into the yard. The scud had banked over the moon, and it was now quite dark. The wind, which only broke in puffs and draughts into that deep well of building, tossed the light of the candle to and fro about their steps, until they came into the shelter of the theatre, where they sat down silently to wait. London hummed solemnly all around ; but nearer at hand, the stillness was only broken by the sound of a footfall moving to and fro along the cabinet floor.

" So it will walk all day, sir," whispered Poole ; " ay, and the better part of the night. Only when a new sample comes from the chemist, there's a bit of a break. Ah, it's an ill conscience that's such an enemy to rest ! Ah, sir, there's blood foully shed in every step of it ! But hark again, a little closer—put your heart in your ears, Mr. Utterson, and tell me, is that the doctor's foot ? "

The steps fell lightly and oddly, with a certain swing, for all they went so slowly ; it was different indeed from the heavy creaking tread of Henry Jekyll. Utterson sighed. " Is there never anything else ? " he asked.

Poole nodded. " Once," he said. " Once I heard it weeping ! "

" Weeping ? how that ? " said the lawyer, conscious of a sudden chill of horror.

" Weeping like a woman or a lost soul," said the butler. " I came away with that upon my heart, that I could have wept too."

But now the ten minutes drew to an end. Poole disinterred the axe from under a stack of packing straw ; the candle was set upon the nearest table to light them to the attack ; and they drew near with bated breath to where that patient foot was still going up and down in the quiet of the night.

"Jekyll," cried Utterson, with a loud voice, "I demand to see you," He paused a moment, but there came no reply. "I give you fair warning, our suspicions are aroused, and I must and shall see you," he resumed; "if not by fair means, then by foul—if not of your consent, then by brute force!"

"Utterson," said the voice, "for God's sake have mercy!"

"Ah, that's not Jekyll's voice—it's Hyde's!" cried Utterson. "Down with the door, Poole!"

Poole swung the axe over his shoulder; the blow shook the building, and the red baize door leaped against the lock and hinges. A dismal screech, as of mere animal terror, rang from the cabinet. Up went the axe again, and again the panels crashed and the frame bounded; four times the blow fell; but the wood was tough and the fittings were of excellent workmanship; and it was not until the fifth, that the lock burst in sunder, and the wreck of the door fell inwards on the carpet.

The beseigers, appalled by their own riot and the stillness that had succeeded, stood back a little and peered in. There lay the cabinet before their eyes in the quiet lamplight, a good fire glowing and chattering on the hearth, the kettle singing its thin strain, a drawer or two open, papers neatly set forth on the business table, and nearer the fire, the things laid out for tea : the quietest room, you would have said, and, but for the glazed presses full of chemicals, the most commonplace that night in London.

Right in the midst there lay the body of a man sorely contorted and still twitching. They drew near on tiptoe, turned it on his back, and beheld the face of Edward Hyde. He was dressed in clothes far too large for him, clothes of the doctor's bigness; the cords of his face still moved with a semblance of life, but life was quite gone; and by the crushed phial in the hand and the strong smell of kernels that hung upon the air, Utterson knew that he was looking on the body of a self-destroyer.

"We have come too late," he said sternly, "whether to save or punish. Hyde is gone to his account; and it only remains for us to find the body of your master."

The far greater proportion of the building was occupied by the theatre, which filled almost the whole ground storey, and was lighted from above, and by the cabinet, which formed an upper storey at one end and looked upon the court. A corridor joined the theatre to the door on the by-street; and with this, the cabinet communicated separately by a second flight of stairs. There were besides a few dark closets and a spacious cellar. All these they now thoroughly examined. Each closet needed but a glance, for all were empty, and all, by the dust that fell from their doors, had stood long unopened. The cellar, indeed, was filled with crazy lumber, mostly dating from the times of the surgeon who was Jekyll's predecessor; but even as they opened the door, they were advertised of the uselessness of further search, by the fall of a perfect mat of cobweb which had for years sealed up the entrance. Nowhere was there any trace of Henry Jekyll, dead or alive.

Poole stamped on the flags of the corridor. " He must be buried here," he said, hearkening to the sound.

" Or he may have fled," said Utterson, and he turned to examine the door in the by-street. It was locked ; and lying near by on the flags, they found the key, already stained with rust.

" This does not look like use," observed the lawyer.

" Use ! " echoed Poole. " Do you not see, sir, it is broken ? much as if a man had stamped on it."

" Ah," continued Utterson, " and the fractures, too, are rusty." The two men looked at each other with a scare. " This is beyond me, Poole," said the lawyer. " Let us go back to the cabinet."

They mounted the stair in silence, and still, with an occasional awe-struck glance at the dead body, proceeded more thoroughly to examine the contents of the cabinet. At one table, there were traces of chemical work, various measured heaps of some white salt being laid on glass saucers, as though for an experiment in which the unhappy man had been prevented.

" That is the same drug that I was always bringing him," said Poole ; and even as he spoke, the kettle with a startling noise boiled over.

This brought them to the fireside, where the easy-chair was drawn cosily up, and the tea things stood ready to the sitter's elbow, the very sugar in the cup. There were several books on a shelf ; one lay beside the tea things open, and Utterson was amazed to find it a copy of a pious work, for which Jekyll had several times expressed a great esteem, annotated, in his own hand, with startling blasphemies.

Next, in the course of their review of the chamber, the searchers came to the cheval-glass, into whose depth they looked with an in-voluntary horror. But it was so turned as to show them nothing but the rosy glow playing on the roof, the fire sparkling in a hundred repetitions along the glazed front of the presses, and their own pale and fearful countenances stooping to look in.

" This glass has seen some strange things, sir," whispered Poole.

" And surely none stranger than itself," echoed the lawyer, in the same tone. " For what did Jekyll "—he caught himself up at the word with a start, and then conquering the weakness : " what could Jekyll want with it ? " he said.

" You may say that ! " said Poole.

Next they turned to the business table. On the desk among the neat array of papers, a large envelope was uppermost, and bore, in the doctor's hand, the name of Mr. Utterson. The lawyer unsealed it, and several enclosures fell to the floor. The first was a will, drawn in the same eccentric terms as the one which he had returned six months before, to serve as a testament in case of death and as a deed of gift in case of disappearance; but in place of the name of Edward Hyde, the lawyer, with indescribable amazement, read the name of Gabriel John Utterson. He looked at Poole, and then back at the papers, and last of all at the dead malefactor stretched upon the carpet.

"My head goes round," he said. "He has been all these days in possession ; he had no cause to like me ; he must have raged to see himself displaced ; and he has not destroyed this document."

He caught the next paper ; it was a brief note in the doctor's hand, and dated at the top. "O Poole!" the lawyer cried, "he was alive and here this day. He cannot have been disposed of in so short a space ; he must be still alive, he must have fled ! And then, why fled ? and how ? and in that case can we venture to declare this suicide ? O, we must be careful. I foresee that we may yet involve your master in some dire catastrophe."

"Why don't you read it, sir ?" asked Poole.

"Because I fear," replied the lawyer, solemnly. "God grant I have no cause for it !" And with that he brought the paper to his eyes, and read as follows :—

"My dear Utterson,—When this shall fall into your hands, I shall have disappeared, under what circumstances I have not the penetration to foresee ; but my instincts and all the circumstances of my nameless situation tell me that the end is sure and must be early. Go then, and first read the narrative which Lanyon warned me he was to place in your hands ; and if you care to hear more, turn to the confession of

"Your unworthy and unhappy friend,

"HENRY JEKYLL."

"There was a third enclosure ?" asked Utterson.

"Here, sir," said Poole, and gave into his hands a considerable packet sealed in several places.

The lawyer put it in his pocket. "I would say nothing of this paper. If your master has fled or is dead, we may at least save his credit. It is now ten ; I must go home and read these documents in quiet ; but I shall be back before midnight, when we shall send for the police."

They went out, locking the door of the theatre behind them ; and Utterson, once more leaving the servants gathered about the fire in the hall, trudged back to his office to read the two narratives in which this mystery was now to be explained.

DR. LANYON'S NARRATIVE

ON the ninth of January, now four days ago, I received by the evening delivery a registered envelope, addressed in the hand of my colleague and old school-companion, Henry Jekyll. I was a good deal surprised by this ; for we were by no means in the habit of correspondence ; I had seen the man, dined with him, indeed, the night before ; and I could imagine nothing in our intercourse that should justify the formality of registration. The contents increased my wonder ; for this is how the letter ran :—

"*10th December*, 18—

" Dear Lanyon—You are one of my oldest friends ; and although we may have differed at times on scientific questions, I cannot remember, at least on my side, any break in our affection. There was never a day when, if you had said to me, ' Jekyll, my life, my honour, my reason, depend upon you,' I would not have sacrificed my fortune or my left hand to help you. Lanyon, my life, my honour, my reason, are all at your mercy ; if you fail me to-night, I am lost. You might suppose, after this preface, that I am going to ask you for something dishonourable to grant. Judge for yourself.

" I want you to postpone all other engagements for to-night—ay, even if you were summoned to the bedside of an emperor ; to take a cab, unless your carriage should be actually at the door ; and, with this letter in your hand for consultation, to drive straight to my house. Poole, my butler, has his orders ; you will find him waiting your arrival with a locksmith. The door of my cabinet is then to be forced ; and you are to go in alone ; to open the glazed press (letter E) on the left hand, breaking the lock if it be shut ; and to draw out, *with all its contents as they stand*, the fourth drawer from the top or (which is the same thing) the third from the bottom. In my extreme distress of mind, I have a morbid fear of misdirecting you ; but even if I am in error, you may know the right drawer by its contents : some powders, a phial, and a paper book. This drawer I beg of you to carry back with you to Cavendish Square exactly as it stands.

" That is the first part of the service : now for the second. You should be back, if you set out at once on the receipt of this, long before midnight ; but I will leave you that amount of margin, not only in the fear of one of those obstacles that can neither be prevented nor foreseen, but because an hour when your servants are in bed is to be preferred for what will then remain to do. At midnight, then, I have to ask you to be alone in your consulting room, to admit with your own hand into the house a man who will present himself in my name, and to place in his hands the drawer that you will have brought with you from my cabinet. Then you will have played your part, and earned my gratitude completely. Five minutes afterwards, if you insist upon an explanation, you will have understood that these arrangements are of capital importance ; and that by the neglect of one of them, fantastic as they must appear, you might have charged your conscience with my death or the shipwreck of my reason.

" Confident as I am that you will not trifle with this appeal, my heart sinks and my hand trembles at the bare thought of such a possibility. Think of me at this hour, in a strange place, labouring under a blackness of distress that no fancy can exaggerate, and yet well aware that, if you will but punctually serve me, my troubles will roll away like a story that is told. Serve me, my dear Lanyon, and save

" Your friend,

" H.J.

" P.S.—I had already sealed this up when a fresh terror struck upon my soul. It is possible that the post office may fail me, and this letter not come into your hands until to-morrow morning. In that case, dear Lanyon, do my errand when it shall be most convenient for you in the course of the day ; and once more expect my messenger at midnight. It may then already be too late ; and if that night passes without event, you will know that you have seen the last of Henry Jekyll."

Upon the reading of this letter, I made sure my colleague was insane ; but till that was proved beyond the possibility of doubt, I felt bound to do as he requested. The less I understood of this farrago, the less I was in a position to judge of its importance ; and an appeal so worded could not be set aside without a grave responsibility. I rose accordingly from table, got into a hansom, and drove straight to Jekyll's house. The butler was awaiting my arrival ; he had received by the same post as mine a registered letter of instruction, and had sent at once for a locksmith and a carpenter. The tradesmen came while we were yet speaking ; and we moved in a body to old Dr. Denman's surgical theatre, from which (as you are doubtless aware) Jekyll's private cabinet is most conveniently entered. The door was very strong, the lock excellent ; the carpenter avowed he would have great trouble, and have to do much damage, if force were to be used ; and the locksmith was near despair. But this last was a handy fellow, and after two hours' work, the door stood open. The press marked E was unlocked ; and I took out the drawer, had it filled up with straw and tied in a sheet, and returned with it to Cavendish Square.

Here I proceeded to examine its contents. The powders were neatly enough made up, but not with the nicety of the dispensing chemist ; so that it was plain they were of Jekyll's private manufacture ; and when I opened one of the wrappers, I found what seemed to me a simple crystalline salt of a white colour. The phial, to which I next turned my attention, might have been about half full of a blood-red liquor, which was highly pungent to the sense of smell, and seemed to me to contain phosphorus and some volatile ether. At the other ingredients I could make no guess. The book was an ordinary version book, and contained little but a series of dates. These covered a period of many years ; but I observed that the entries ceased nearly a year ago, and quite abruptly. Here and there a brief remark was appended to a date, usually no more than a single word : " double " occurring perhaps six times in a total of several hundred entries ; and once very early in the list, and followed by several marks of exclamation, " total failure ! ! ! " All this, though it whetted my curiosity, told me little that was definite. Here were a phial of some tincture, a paper of some salt, and the record of a series of experiments that had led (like too many of Jekyll's investigations) to no end of practical usefulness. How could the presence of these articles in my house affect either the honour, the sanity, or the life of my flighty colleague ? If his messenger could go to one place, why could he not go to another ? And even granting some impediment, why was this gentleman to be received by me in secret ? The more I reflected, the more convinced I grew that I was dealing with a case of cerebral disease ; and though I dismissed my servants to bed, I loaded an old revolver, that I might be found in some posture of self-defence.

Twelve o'clock had scarce rung out over London, ere the knocker sounded very gently on the door. I went myself at the summons, and found a small man crouching against the pillars of the portico.

" Are you come from Dr. Jekyll ? " I asked.

He told me " yes " by a constrained gesture ; and when I had bidden him enter, he did not obey me without a searching backward glance into the darkness of the square. There was a policeman not far off, advancing with his bull's-eye open ; and at the sight, I thought my visitor started and made greater haste.

These particulars struck me, I confess, disagreeably; and as I followed him into the bright light of the consulting room, I kept my hand ready on my weapon. Here, at last, I had a chance of clearly seeing him. I had never set eyes on him before, so much was certain. He was small, I have said ; I was struck besides with the shocking expression of his face, with his remarkable combination of great muscular activity and great apparent debility of constitution, and—last but not least—with the odd, subjective disturbance caused by his neighbourhood. This bore some resemblance to incipient rigor, and was accompanied by a marked sinking of the pulse. At the time, I set it down to some idiosyncratic, personal distaste, and merely wondered at the acuteness of the symptoms ; but I have since had reason to believe the cause to lie much deeper in the nature of man, and to turn on some nobler hinge than the principle of hatred.

This person (who had thus, from the first moment of his entrance, struck in me what I can only describe as a disgustful curiosity) was dressed in a fashion that would have made an ordinary person laughable ; his clothes, that is to say, although they were of rich and sober fabric, were enormously too large for him in every measurement—the trousers hanging on his legs and rolled up to keep them from the ground, the waist of the coat below his haunches, and the collar sprawling wide upon his shoulders. Strange to relate, this ludicrous accoutrement was far from moving me to laughter. Rather, as there was something abnormal and misbegotten in the very essence of the creature that now faced me—something seizing, surprising and revolting—this fresh disparity seemed but to fit in with and to reinforce it ; so that to my interest in the man's nature and character, there was added a curiosity as to his origin, his life, his fortune and status in the world.

These observations, though they have taken so great a space to be set down in, were yet the work of a few seconds. My visitor, was indeed, on fire with sombre excitement.

" Have you got it ? " he cried. " Have you got it ? " and so lively was his impatience that he even laid his hand upon my arm and sought to shake me.

I put him back, conscious at his touch of a certain icy pang along my blood. " Come, sir," said I. " You forget that I have not yet the pleasure of your acquaintance. Be seated, if you please." And I showed him an example, and sat down myself in my customary seat and with as fair an imitation of my ordinary manner to a patient, as the lateness of the hour, the nature of my preoccupations, and the horror I had of my visitor, would suffer me to muster.

" I beg your pardon, Dr. Lanyon," he replied, civilly enough. " What you say is very well founded ; and my impatience has shown its heels to my politeness. I come here at the instance of your colleague, Dr. Henry Jekyll, on a piece of business of some moment ; and I understood . . ." he paused and put his hand to his throat, and I could see, in spite of his collected manner, that he was wrestling against the approaches of the hysteria—" I understood, a drawer. . . ."

But here I took pity on my visitor's suspense, and some perhaps on my own growing curiosity.

" There it is, sir," said I, pointing to the drawer, where it lay on the floor behind a table, and still covered with the sheet.

He sprang to it, and then paused, and laid his hand upon his heart ; I could hear his teeth grate with the convulsive action of his jaws ; and his face was so ghastly to see that I grew alarmed both for his life and reason.

" Compose yourself," said I.

He turned a dreadful smile to me, and, as if with the decision of despair, plucked away the sheet. At sight of the contents, he uttered one loud sob of such immense relief that I sat petrified. And the next moment, in a voice that was already fairly well under control, " Have you a graduated glass ? " he asked.

I rose from my place with something of an effort, and gave him what he asked.

He thanked me with a smiling nod, measured out a few minims of the red tincture and added one of the powders. The mixture, which was at first of a reddish hue, began, in proportion as the crystals melted, to brighten in colour, to effervesce audibly, and to throw off small fumes of vapour. Suddenly, and at the same moment, the ebullition ceased, and the compound changed to a dark purple, which faded again more slowly to a watery green. My visitor, who had watched these metamorphoses with a keen eye, smiled, set down the glass upon the table, and then turned and looked upon me with an air of scrutiny.

" And now," said he, " to settle what remains. Will you be wise ? will you be guided ? will you suffer me to take this glass in my hand, and to go forth from your house without further parley ? or has the greed of curiosity too much command of you ? Think before you answer, for it shall be done as you decide. As you decide, you shall be left as you were before, and neither richer nor wiser, unless the sense of service rendered to a man in mortal distress may be counted as a kind of riches of the soul. Or, if you shall so prefer to choose, a new province of knowledge and new avenues to fame and power shall be laid open to you, here, in this room, upon the instant ; and your sight shall be blasted by a prodigy to stagger the unbelief of Satan."

" Sir," said I, affecting a coolness that I was far from truly possessing, " you speak enigmas, and you will perhaps not wonder that I hear you with no very strong impression of belief. But I have gone too far in the way of inexplicable services to pause before I see the end."

" It is well," replied my visitor. " Lanyon, you remember your vows : what follows is under the seal of our profession. And now, you who have so long been bound to the most narrow and material views, you who have denied the virtue of transcendental medicine, you who have derided your superiors—behold ! "

He put the glass to his lips, and drank at one gulp. A cry followed ; he reeled, staggered, clutched at the table and held on, staring with injected eyes, gasping with open mouth ; and as I looked, there came, I thought, a change—he seemed to swell—his face became suddenly black, and the features seemed to melt and alter—and the next moment I had sprung to my feet and leaped back against the wall, my arm raised to shield me from that prodigy, my mind submerged in terror.

" O God ! " I screamed, and " O God ! " again and again ; for there before my eyes—pale and shaken, and half-fainting, and groping before him with his hands, like a man restored from death—there stood Henry Jekyll !

What he told me in the next hour I cannot bring my mind to set on paper. I saw what I saw, I heard what I heard, and my soul sickened at it ; and yet, now when that sight has faded from my eyes I ask myself if I believe it, and I cannot answer. My life is shaken to its roots ; sleep has left me ; the deadliest terror sits by me at all hours of the day and night ; I feel that my days are numbered, and that I must die ; and yet I shall die incredulous. As for the moral turpitude that man unveiled to me, even with tears of penitence, I cannot, even in memory, dwell on it without a start of horror. I will say but one thing, Utterson, and that (if you can bring your mind to credit it) will be more than enough. The creature who crept into my house that night was, on Jekyll's own confession, known by the name of Hyde and hunted for in every corner of the land as the murderer of Carew.

HASTIE LANYON.

HENRY JEKYLL'S FULL STATEMENT OF THE CASE

I WAS born in the year 18—— to a large fortune, endowed besides with excellent parts, inclined by nature to industry, fond of the respect of the wise and good among my fellow-men, and thus, as might have been supposed, with every guarantee of an honourable and distinguished future. And indeed, the worst of my faults was a certain impatient gaiety of disposition, such as has made the happiness of many, but such as I found it hard to reconcile with my imperious desire to carry my head high, and wear a more than commonly grave countenance before the public. Hence it came about that I concealed my pleasures ; and that when I reached years of reflection, and began to look round me, and take stock of my progress and position in the world, I stood already committed to a profound duplicity of life. Many a man would have even blazoned such irregularities as I was guilty of ; but from the high views that I had set before me, I regarded and hid them with an almost morbid sense of shame. It was thus rather the exacting nature of my aspirations, than any particular degradation in my faults, that made me what I was, and, with even a deeper trench than in the majority of men, severed in me those provinces of good and ill which divide and compound man's dual nature. In this case, I was driven to reflect deeply and inveterately on that hard law of life, which lies at the root of religion, and is one of the most plentiful springs of distress. Though so profound a double-dealer, I was in no sense a hypocrite ; both sides of me were in dead earnest ; I was no more myself when I laid aside restraint and plunged in shame, than when I laboured, in the eye of day, at the furtherance of knowledge or the relief of sorrow and suffering. And it chanced that the direction of my scientific studies, which led wholly towards the mystic and the transcendental, reacted and shed a strong light on this consciousness of the perennial war among my members. With every day, and from both sides of my intelligence, the moral and the intellectual, I thus drew steadily nearer to that truth, by whose partial discovery I have been doomed to such a dreadful shipwreck : that man is not truly one, but truly two. I say two, because the state of my own knowledge does not pass beyond that point. Others will follow, others will outstrip me on the same lines ; and hazard the guess that man will be ultimately known for a mere polity of multifarious, incongruous and independent denizens. I, for my part, from the nature of my life, advanced infallibly in one direction, and in one direction only. It was on the moral side, and in my own person, that I learned to recognise the thorough and primitive duality of man; I saw that, of the two natures that contended in the field of my consciousness, even if I could rightly be said to be either, it was only because I was radically both; and from an early date, even before the course of my scientific discoveries had begun to suggest the most naked possibility of such a miracle, I had learned to dwell with pleasure, as a beloved daydream, on the thought of the separation of these elements. If each, I told myself, could but be housed in separate identities, life would be relieved of all that was unbearable; the unjust might go his way, delivered from the aspirations and remorse of his more upright twin; and the just could walk steadfastly and securely on his upward path, doing the good things in which he found his pleasure, and no longer exposed to disgrace and penitence by the hands of this extraneous evil. It was the curse of mankind that these incongruous faggots were thus bound together—that in the agonised womb of consciousness, these polar twins should be continuously struggling. How, then, were they dissociated?

I was so far in my reflections, when, as I have said, a sidelight began to shine upon the subject from the laboratory table. I began to perceive more deeply than it has ever yet been stated, the trembling immateriality, the mist-like transcience, of this seemingly so solid body in which we walk attired. Certain agents I found to have the power to shake and to pluck back that fleshly vestment, even as a wind might toss the curtains of a pavilion. For two good reasons, I will not enter deeply into this scientific branch of my confession. First, because I have been made to learn that the doom and burthen of our life is bound for ever on man's shoulders; and when the attempt is made to cast it off, it but returns upon us with more unfamiliar and more awful pressure. Second, because, as my narrative will make, alas! too evident, my discoveries were incomplete. Enough, then, that I not only recognised my natural body from the mere aura and effulgence of certain of the powers that made up my spirit, but managed to compound a drug by which these powers should be dethroned from their supremacy, and a second form and countenance substituted, none the less natural to me because they were the expression, and bore the stamp, of lower elements in my soul.

I hesitated long before I put this theory to the test of practice. I knew well that I risked death; for any drug that so potently controlled and shook the very fortress of identity, might by the least scruple of an overdose or at the least inopportunity in the moment of exhibition, utterly blot out that immaterial tabernacle which I looked to it to change. But the temptation of a discovery so singular and profound, at last overcame the suggestions of alarm. I had long since prepared my tincture; I purchased at once, from a firm of wholesale chemists, a large quantity of a particular salt, which I knew, from my experiments, to be the last ingredient required; and, late one accursed night, I compounded the elements, watched them boil and smoke together in the glass, and when the ebullition had subsided, with a strong glow of courage, drank off the potion.

The most racking pangs succeeded : a grinding in the bones, deadly nausea, and a horror of the spirit that cannot be exceeded at the hour of birth or death. Then these agonies began swiftly to subside, and I came to myself as if out of a great sickness. There was something strange in my sensations, something indescribably new, and, from its very novelty, incredibly sweet. I felt younger, lighter, happier in body ; within I was conscious of a heady recklessness, a current of disordered sensual images running like a mill-race in my fancy, a solution of the bonds of obligation, an unknown but not an innocent freedom of the soul. I knew myself, at the first breath of this new life, to be more wicked, tenfold more wicked, sold a slave to my original evil ; and the thought, in that moment, braced and delighted me like wine. I stretched out my hands, exulting in the freshness of these sensations ; and in the act, I was suddenly aware that I had lost in stature.

There was no mirror, at that date, in my room ; that which stands beside me as I write was brought there later on, and for the very purpose of those transformations. The night, however, was far gone into the morning—the morning, black as it was, was nearly ripe for the conception of the day—the inmates of my house were locked in the most rigorous hours of slumber ; and I determined, flushed, as I was with hope and trumph, to venture in my new shape as far as to my bedroom. I crossed the yard, wherein the constellations looked down upon me, I could have thought, with wonder, the first creature of that sort that their unsleeping vigilance had yet disclosed to them ; I stole through the corridors, a stranger in my own house ; and coming to my room, I saw for the first time the appearance of Edward Hyde.

I must here speak by theory alone, saying not that which I know, but that which I suppose to be most probable. The evil side of my nature, to which I had now transferred the stamping efficacy, was less robust and less developed than the good which I had just deposed. Again, in the course of my life, which had been, after all, nine-tenths a life of effort, virtue and control, it had been much less exercised and much less exhausted. And hence, as I think, it came about that Edward Hyde was so much smaller, slighter, and younger than Henry Jekyll. Even as good shone upon the countenance of the one, evil was written broadly and plainly on the face of the other. Evil besides (which I must still believe to be the lethal side of man) had left on that body an imprint of deformity and decay. And yet when I looked upon that ugly idol in the glass, I was conscious of no repugnance, rather of a leap of welcome. This, too, was myself. It seemed natural and human. In my eyes it bore a livelier image of the spirit, it seemed more express and single, than the imperfect and divided countenance I had been hitherto accustomed to call mine. And in so far I was doubtless right. I have observed that when I wore the semblance of Edward

Hyde, none could come near to me at first without a visible misgiving of the flesh. This, as I take it, was because all human beings, as we meet them, are commingled out of good and evil : and Edward Hyde, alone, in the ranks of mankind, was pure evil.

I lingered but a moment at the mirror : the second and conclusive experiment had yet to be attempted ; it yet remained to be seen if I had lost my identity beyond redemption and must flee before daylight from a house that was no longer mine : and hurrying back to my cabinet, I once more prepared and drank the cup, once more suffered the pangs of dissolution, and came to myself once more with the character, the stature, and the face of Henry Jekyll.

That night I had come to the fatal cross-roads. Had I approached my discovery in a more noble spirit, had I risked the experiment while under the empire of generous or pious aspirations, all must have been otherwise, and from these agonies of death and birth I had come forth an angel instead of a fiend. The drug had no discriminating action ; it was neither diabolical nor divine ; it but shook the doors of the prison-house of my disposition ; and, like the captives of Philippi, that which stood within ran forth. At that time my virtue slumbered ; my evil, kept awake by ambition, was alert and swift to seize the occasion ; and the thing that was projected was Edward Hyde. Hence, although I had now two characters as well as two appearances, one was wholly evil, and the other was still the old Henry Jekyll, that incongruous compound of whose reformation and improvement I had already learned to despair. The movement was thus wholly toward the worse.

Even at that time, I had not yet conquered my aversion to the dryness of a life of study. I would still be merrily disposed at times ; and as my pleasures were (to say the least) undignified, and I was not only well known and highly considered, but growing towards the elderly man, this incoherency of my life was daily growing more unwelcome. It was on this side that my new power tempted me until I fell in slavery. I had but to drink the cup, to doff at once the body of the noted professor, and to assume, like a thick cloak, that of Edward Hyde. I smiled at the notion ; it seemed to me at the time to be humorous ; and I made my preparations with the most studious care. I took and furnished that house in Soho, to which Hyde was tracked by the police ; and engaged as housekeeper a creature whom I well knew to be silent and unscrupulous. On the other side, I announced to my servants that a Mr. Hyde (whom I described) was to have full liberty and power about my house in the square ; and, to parry mishaps, I even called and made myself a familiar object, in my second character. I next drew up that will to which you so much objected ; so that if anything befell me in the person of Dr. Jekyll, I could enter on that of Edward Hyde without pecuniary loss. And thus fortified, as I supposed, on every side, I began to profit by the strange immunities of my position.

Men have before hired bravos to transact their crimes, while their own person and reputation sat under shelter. I was the first that ever did so for his pleasures. I was the first that could thus plod in the public eyes with a load of genial respectability, and in a moment, like a schoolboy, strip off these lendings and spring headlong into the sea of liberty. But for me, in my impenetrable mantle, the safety was complete. Think of it—I did not even exist! Let me but escape into my laboratory door, give me but a second or two to mix and swallow the draught that I had always standing ready; and, whatever he had done, Edward Hyde would pass away like the stain of breath upon a mirror; and there in his stead, quietly at home, trimming the midnight lamp in his study, a man who could afford to laugh at suspicion, would be Henry Jekyll.

The pleasures which I made haste to seek in my disguise were, as I have said, undignified; I would scarce use a harder term. But in the hands of Edward Hyde, they soon began to turn towards the monstrous. When I would come back from these excursions, I was often plunged into a kind of wonder at my vicarious depravity. This familiar that I called out of my own soul, and sent forth alone to do his good pleasure, was a being inherently malign and villainous; his every act and thought centred on self; drinking pleasure with bestial avidity from any degree of torture to another; relentless like a man of stone. Henry Jekyll stood at times aghast before the acts of Edward Hyde; but the situation was apart from ordinary laws, and insidiously relaxed the grasp of conscience. It was Hyde, after all, and Hyde alone, that was guilty. Jekyll was no worse; he woke again to his good qualities seemingly unimpaired; he would even make haste, where it was possible, to undo the evil done by Hyde. And thus his conscience slumbered.

Into the details of the infamy at which I thus connived (for even now I can scarce grant that I committed it) I have no design of entering; I mean but to point out the warnings and the successive steps with which my chastisement approached. I met with one accident which, as it brought on no consequence, I shall no more than mention. An act of cruelty to a child aroused against me the anger of a passer-by, whom I recognised the other day in the person of your kinsman; the doctor and the child's family joined him; there were moments when I feared for my life; and at last, in order to pacify their too just resentment, Edward Hyde had to bring them to the door, and pay them in a cheque drawn in the name of Henry Jekyll. But this danger was easily eliminated from the future, by opening an account at another bank in the name of Edward Hyde himself; and when, by sloping my own hand backwards, I had supplied my doubt with a signature, I thought I sat beyond the reach of fate.

Some two months before the murder of Sir Danvers, I had been out for one of my adventures, had returned at a late hour, and woke the next day in bed with somewhat odd sensations. It was in vain I looked about me; in vain I saw the decent furniture and tall proportions of my room in the square; in vain that I recognised the pattern of the bed curtains and the design of the mahogany frame; something still kept insisting that I was not where I was, that I had not wakened where I seemed to be, but in the little room in Soho where I was accustomed to sleep in the body of Edward Hyde. I smiled to myself, and, in my psychological way, began lazily to inquire into the elements of this illusion, occasionally, even as I did so, dropping back into a comfortable morning doze. I was still so engaged when, in one of my more wakeful moments, my eyes fell upon my hand. Now, the hand of Henry Jekyll (as you have often remarked) was professional in shape and size ; it was large, firm, white and comely. But the hand which I now saw, clearly enough, in the yellow light of a mid-London morning, lying half shut on the bedclothes, was lean, corded, knuckly, of a dusky pallor, and thickly shaded with a swart growth of hair. It was the hand of Edward Hyde.

I must have stared upon it for near half a minute, sunk as I was in the mere stupidity of wonder, before terror woke up in my breast as sudden and startling as the crash of cymbals ; and bounding from my bed, I rushed to the mirror. At the sight that met my eyes, my blood was changed into something exquisitely thin and icy. Yes, I had gone to bed Henry Jekyll, I had awakened Edward Hyde. How was this to be explained ? I asked myself ; and then, with another bound of terror—how was it to be remedied ? It was well on in the morning ; the servants were up ; all my drugs were in the cabinet—a long journey down two pair of stairs, through the back passage, across the open court and through the anatomical theatre, from where I was then standing horror-struck. It might indeed be possible to cover my face; but of what use was that, when I was unable to conceal the alteration in my stature ? And then, with an overpowering sweetness of relief, it came back upon my mind that the servants were already used to the coming and going of my second self. I had soon dressed, as well as I was able, in clothes of my own size : had soon passed through the house, where Bradshaw stared and drew back at seeing Mr. Hyde at such an hour and in such a strange array ; and ten minutes later, Dr. Jekyll had returned to his own shape, and was sitting down, with a darkened brow, to make a feint of breakfasting.

Small indeed was my appetite. This inexplicable incident, this reversal of my previous experience, seemed, like the Babylonian finger on the wall, to be spelling out the letters of my judgment ; and I began to reflect more seriously than ever before on the issues and possibilities of my double existence. That part of me which I had the power of projecting had lately been much exercised and nourished ; it had seemed to me of late as though the body of Edward Hyde had grown in stature, as though (when I wore that form) I were conscious of a more generous tide of blood ; and I began to spy a danger that, if this were much prolonged, the balance of my nature might be permanently overthrown, the power of voluntary change be forfeited, and the character of Edward Hyde become irrevocably mine. The power of the drug had not been always equally displayed. Once, very early in my career, it had totally failed me ; since then I had been obliged on more than one occasion to double, and once, with infinite risk of death, to treble the amount ; and these rare uncertainties had cast hitherto the sole shadow on my contentment. Now, however, and in the light of that morning's accident, I was led to remark that whereas, in the beginning, the difficulty had been to throw off the body of Jekyll, it had of late gradually but decidedly transferred itself to the other side. All things therefore seemed to point to this : that I was slowly losing hold of my original and better self, and becoming slowly incorporated with my second and worse.

Between these two, I now felt I had to choose. My two natures had memory in common, but all other faculties were most unequally shared between them. Jekyll (who was composite) now with the most sensitive apprehensions, now with a greedy gusto, projected and shared in the pleasures and adventures of Hyde ; but Hyde was indifferent to Jekyll, or but remembered him as the mountain bandit remembers the cavern in which he conceals himself from pursuit. Jekyll had more than a father's interest ; Hyde had more than a son's indifference. To cast in my lot with Jekyll was to die to those appetites which I had long secretly indulged and had of late begun to pamper. To cast it in with Hyde was to die to a thousand interests and aspirations, and to become, at a blow and for ever, despised and friendless. The bargain might appear unequal ; but there was still another consideration in the scales ; for while Jekyll would suffer smartingly in the fires of abstinence, Hyde would be not even conscious of all that he had lost. Strange as my circumstances were, the terms of this debate are as old and commonplace as man ; much the same inducements and alarms cast the die for any tempted and trembling sinner ; and it fell out with me, as it falls with so vast a majority of my fellows, that I chose the better part, and was found wanting in the strength to keep to it.

Yes, I preferred the elderly and discontented doctor, surrounded by friends, and cherishing honest hopes ; and bade a resolute farewell to the liberty, the comparative youth, the light step, leaping pulses and secret pleasures, that I had enjoyed in the disguise of Hyde. I made this choice perhaps with some unconscious reservation, for I neither gave up the house in Soho, nor destroyed the clothes of Edward Hyde, which still lay ready in my cabinet. For two months, however, I was true to my determination ; for two months I led a life of such severity as I had never before attained to, and enjoyed the compensations of an approving conscience. But time began at last to obliterate the freshness of my alarm ; the praises of conscience began to grow into a thing of course ; I began to be tortured with throes and longings, as of Hyde struggling after freedom ; and at last, in an hour of moral weakness, I once again compounded and swallowed the transforming draught.

I do not suppose that when a drunkard reasons with himself upon his vice, he is once out of five hundred times affected by the dangers that he runs through his brutish physical insensibility ; neither had I, long as I had considered my position, made enough allowance for the complete moral insensibility and insensate readiness to evil, which were the leading characters of Edward Hyde. Yet it was by these that I was punished. My devil had been long caged, he came out roaring. I was conscious, even when I took the draught, of a more unbridled, a more furious propensity to ill. It must have been this, I suppose, that stirred in my soul that tempest of impatience with which I listened to the civilities of my unhappy victim ; I declare at least, before God, no man morally sane could have been guilty of that crime upon so pitiful a provocation ; and that I struck in no more reasonable spirit than that in which a sick child may break a plaything. But I had voluntarily stripped myself of all those balancing instincts by which even the worst of us continues to walk with some degree of steadiness among temptations ; and in my case, to be tempted, however slightly, was to fall.

Instantly the spirit of hell awoke in me and raged. With a transport of glee, I mauled the unresisting body, tasting delight from every blow ; and it was not till weariness had begun to succeed that I was suddenly, in the top fit of my delirium, struck through the heart by a cold thrill of terror. A mist dispersed ; I saw my life to be forfeit ; and fled from the scene of these excesses, at once glorying and trembling, my lust of evil gratified and stimulated, my love of life screwed to the topmost peg. I ran to the house in Soho, and (to make assurance doubly sure) destroyed my papers ; thence I set out through the lamplit streets, in the same divided ecstasy of mind, gloating on my crime, light-headedly devising others in the future, and yet still hastening and still hearkening in my wake for the steps of the avenger. Hyde had a song upon his lips as he compounded the draught, and as he drank it pledged the dead man. The pangs of transformation had not done tearing him, before Henry Jekyll, with streaming tears of gratitude and remorse, had fallen upon his knees and lifted his clasped hands to God. The veil of self-indulgence was rent from head to foot. I saw my life as a whole : I followed it up from the days of childhood, when I had walked with my father's hand, and through the self-denying toils of my professional life, to arrive again and again, with the same sense of unreality, at the damned horrors of the evening. I could have screamed aloud ; I sought with tears and prayers to smother down the crowd of hideous images and sounds with which my memory swarmed against me ; and still, between the petitions, the ugly face of my iniquity stared into my soul. As the acuteness of this remorse began to die away, it was succeeded by a sense of joy. The problem of my conduct was solved. Hyde was thenceforth impossible ; whether I would or not, I was now confined to the better part of my existence ; and, oh, how I rejoiced to think it ! with what willing humility I embraced anew the restrictions of natural life ! with what sincere renunciation I locked the door by which I had so often gone and come, and ground the key under my heel !

The next day came the news that the murder had been overlooked, that the guilt of Hyde was patent to the world, and that the victim was a man high in public estimation. It was not only a crime, it had been a tragic folly. I think I was glad to know it ; I think I was glad to have my better impulses thus buttressed and guarded by the terrors of the scaffold. Jekyll was now my city of refuge ; let but Hyde peep out an instant, and the hands of all men would be raised to take and slay him.

I resolved in my future conduct to redeem the past ; and I can say with honesty that my resolve was fruitful of some good. You know yourself how earnestly in the last months of last year I laboured to relieve suffering ; you know that much was done for others, and that the days passed quietly, almost happily for myself. Nor can I truly say that I wearied of this beneficent and innocent life ; I think instead that I daily enjoyed it more completely ; but I was still cursed with my duality of purpose ; and as the first edge of my penitence wore off, the lower side of me, so long indulged, so recently chained down, began to growl for licence. Not that I dreamed of resuscitating Hyde ; the bare idea of that would startle me to frenzy ; no, it was in my own person that I was once more tempted to trifle with my conscience ; and it was as an ordinary secret sinner that I at last fell before the assaults of temptation.

There comes an end to all things ; the most capacious measure is filled at last ; and this brief condescension to my evil finally destroyed the balance of my soul. And yet I was not alarmed ; the fall seemed natural, like a return to the old days before I had made my discovery. It was a fine, clear January day, wet under foot where the frost had melted, but cloudless overhead ; and the Regent's Park was full of winter chirrupings and sweet with spring odours. I sat in the sun on a bench ; the animal within me licking the chops of memory ; the spiritual side a little drowsed, promising subsequent penitence, but not yet moved to begin. After all, I reflected I was like my neighbours; and then I smiled, comparing myself with other men, comparing my active goodwill with the lazy cruelty of their neglect. And at the very moment of that vainglorious thought, a qualm came over me, a horrid nausea and the most deadly shuddering. These passed away, and left me faint ; and then as in its turn the faintness subsided, I began to be aware of a change in the temper of my thoughts, a greater boldness, a contempt of danger, a solution of the bonds of obligation. I looked down ; my clothes hung formlessly on my shrunken limbs ; the hand that lay on my knee was corded and hairy. I was once more Edward Hyde. A moment before I had been safe of all men's respect, wealthy, beloved—the cloth laying for me in the dining-room at home ; and now I was the common quarry of mankind, hunted, houseless, a known murderer, thrall to the gallows.

My reason wavered, but it did not fail me utterly. I have more than once observed that, in my second character, my faculties seemed sharpened to a point and my spirits more tensely elastic ; thus it came about that, where Jekyll perhaps might have succumbed, Hyde rose to the importance of the moment. My drugs were in one of the presses of my cabinet : how was I to reach them ? That was the problem that (crushing my temples in my hands) I set myself to solve. The laboratory door I had closed. If I sought to enter by the house, my own servants would consign me to the gallows. I saw I must employ another hand, and thought of Lanyon. How was he to be reached ? how persuaded ? Supposing that I escaped capture in the streets, how was I to make my way into his presence ? and how should I, an unknown and displeasing visitor, prevail on the famous physician to rifle the study of his colleague, Dr. Jekyll ? Then I remembered that of my original character, one part remained to me : I could write my own hand ; and once I had conceived that kindling spark, the way that I must follow became lighted up from end to end.

Thereupon, I arranged my clothes as best I could, and summoning a passing hansom, drove to an hotel in Portland Street, the name of which I chanced to remember. At my appearance (which was indeed comical enough, however tragic a fate these garments covered) the driver could not conceal his mirth. I gnashed my teeth upon him with a gust of devilish fury ; and the smile withered from his face —happily for him—yet more happily for myself, for in another instant I had certainly dragged him from his perch. At the inn, as I entered, I looked about me with so black a countenance as made the attendants tremble ; not a look did they exchange in my presence ; but obsequiously took my orders, led me to a private room, and brought me wherewithal to write. Hyde in danger of his life was a creature new to me : shaken with inordinate anger, strung to the pitch of murder, lusting to inflict pain. Yet the creature was astute ; mastered his fury with a great effort of the will ; composed his two important letters, one to Lanyon and one to Poole ; and, that he might receive actual evidence of their being posted, sent them out with directions that they should be registered.

Thenceforward, he sat all day over the fire in the private room, gnawing his nails ; there he dined, sitting alone with his fears, the waiter visibly quailing before his eye ; and thence, when the night was fully come, he set forth in the corner of a closed cab, and was driven to and fro about the streets of the city. He, I say—I cannot say, I. That child of Hell had nothing human ; nothing lived in him but fear and hatred. And when at last, thinking the driver had began to grow suspicious, he discharged the cab and ventured on foot, attired in his misfitting clothes, an object marked out for observation, into the midst of the nocturnal passengers, these two base passions raged within him like a tempest. He walked fast, hunted by his fears, chattering to himself, skulking through the less frequented thoroughfares, counting the minutes that still divided him from midnight. Once a woman spoke to him, offering, I think, a box of lights. He smote her in the face, and she fled.

When I came to myself at Lanyon's, the horror of my old friend perhaps affected me somewhat : I do not know ; it was at least but a drop in the sea to the abhorrence with which I looked back upon these hours. A changed had come over me. It was no longer the fear of the gallows, it was the horror of being Hyde that racked me. I received Lanyon's condemnation partly in a dream ; it was partly in a dream that I came home to my own house and got into bed. I slept after the prostration of the day, with a stringent and profound slumber which not even the nightmares that wrung me could avail to break. I awoke in the morning shaken, weakened, but refreshed. I still hated and feared the thought of the brute that slept within me, and I had not of course forgotten the appalling dangers of the day before ; but I was once more at home, in my own house and close to my drugs ; and gratitude for my escape shone so strong in my soul that it almost rivalled the brightness of hope.

I was stepping leisurely across the court after breakfast, drinking the chill of the air with pleasure, when I was seized again with those indescribable sensations that heralded the change ; and I had but the time to gain the shelter of my cabinet, before I was once again raging and freezing with the passions of Hyde. It took on this occasion a double dose to recall me to myself ; and, alas ! six hours after, as I sat looking sadly in the fire, the pangs returned, and the drug had to be readministered. In short, from that day forth it seemed only by a great effort as of gymnastics, and only under the immediate stimulation of the drug, that I was able to wear the countenance of Jekyll. At all hours of the day and night I would be taken with the premonitory shudder ; above all, if I slept, or even dozed for a moment in my chair, it was always as Hyde that I awakened. Under the strain of this continually impending doom and by the sleeplessness to which I now condemned myself, ay, even beyond what I had thought possible to man, I became, in my own person, a creature eaten up and emptied by fever, languidly weak both in mind and body, and solely occupied by one thought : the horror of my other self. But when I slept, or when the virtue of the medicine wore off, I would leap almost without transition (for the pangs of transformation grew daily less marked) into the possession of a fancy brimming with images of terror, a soul boiling with causeless hatreds, and a body that seemed not strong enough to contain the raging energies of life. The powers of Hyde seemed to have grown with the sickliness of Jekyll. And certainly the hate that now divided them was equal on each side. With Jekyll, it was a thing of vital instinct. He had now seen the full deformity of that creature that shared with him some of the phenomena of consciousness, and was co-heir with him to death : and beyond these links of community, which in themselves made the most poignant part of his distress, he thought of Hyde, for all his energy of life, as of something not only hellish but inorganic. This was the shocking thing ; that the slime of the pit seemed to utter cries and voices ; that the amorphous dust gesticulated and sinned ; that what was dead, and had no shape, should usurp the offices of life. And this again, that that insurgent horror was knit to him closer than a wife, closer than an eye ; lay caged in his flesh, where he heard it mutter and felt it struggle to be born ; and at every hour of weakness, and in the confidence of slumber, pre-vailed against him, and deposited him out of life. The hatred of Hyde for Jekyll was of a different order. His terror of the gallows drove him continually to commit temporary suicide, and return to his subordinate station of a part instead of a person ; but he loathed the necessity, he loathed the despondency into which Jekyll was now fallen, and he resented the dislike with which he was himself regarded. Hence the ape-like tricks that he would play me, scrawling in my own hand blasphemies on the pages of my books, burning the letters and destroying the portrait of my father ; and indeed, had it not been for his fear of death, he would long ago have ruined himself in order to involve me in the ruin. But his love of life is wonderful ; I go further : I, who sicken and freeze at the mere thought of him, when I recall the abjection and passion of this attachment, and when I know how he fears my power to cut him off by suicide, I find it in my heart to pity him.

It is useless, and the time awfully fails me, to prolong this description; no one has ever suffered such torments, let that suffice ; and yet even to these, habit brought—no, not alleviation—but a certain callousness of soul, a certain acquiescence of despair ; and my punishment might have gone on for years, but for the last calamity which has now fallen, and which has finally severed me from my own face and nature. My provision of the salt, which had never been renewed since the date of the first experiment, began to run low. I sent out for a fresh supply, and mixed the draught ; the ebullition followed, and the first change of colour, not the second ; I drank it, and it was without efficiency. You will learn from Poole how I have had London ransacked ; it was in vain ; and I am now persuaded that my first supply was impure, and that it was that unknown impurity which lent efficacy to the draught.

About a week has passed, and I am now finishing this statement under the influence of the last of the old powders. This, then, is the last time, short of a miracle, that Henry Jekyll can think his own thoughts or see his own face (now how sadly altered !) in the glass. Nor must I delay too long to bring my writing to an end ; for if my narrative has hitherto escaped destruction, it has been by a combination of great prudence and great good luck. Should the throes of change take me in the act of writing it, Hyde will tear it in pieces ; but if some time shall have elapsed after I have laid it by, his wonderful selfishness and circum-scription to the moment will probably save it once again from the action of his ape-like spite. And indeed the doom that is closing on us both has already changed and crushed him. Half an hour from now, when I shall again and for ever reindue that hated personality, I know how I shall sit shuddering and weeping in my chair, or continue, with the most strained and fearstruck ecstasy of listening, to pace up and down this room (my last earthly refuge) and give ear to every sound of menace. Will Hyde die upon the scaffold ? or will he find the courage to release himself at the last moment ? God knows ; I am careless ; this is my true hour of death, and what is to follow concerns another than myself. Here, then, as I lay down the pen, and proceed to seal up my confession, I bring the life of that unhappy Henry Jekyll to an end.

THE MAMMOTH BOOK OF

SHORT

FANTASY

NOVELS

Presented by Isaac Asimov

Complete and Unabridged

13 novels – authors include
Poul Anderson, Suzy McKee Charnas,
Sir H. Rider Haggard, John Jakes and Fritz Leiber

A fantasy reader's delight, 13 short novels featuring a fabulous world of spells, magic, curses, heroic battles, strange happenings, superhuman acts and supernatural powers.

These complete and unabridged works include Fritz Leiber's Nebula Award winner *Ill Met in Lankhmar*, *Unicorn Tapestry* by Suzy McKee Charnas, *Thieves's World Tales* by Poul Anderson and Janet Morris, H. Rider Haggard's classic of African magic *Black Heart and White Heart*, Michael Moorcock's *The Lands Beyond the World* and eight more masterpieces for the fantasy fan.

£4.95 paperback

THE MAMMOTH BOOK OF

SHORT

CRIME

NOVELS

Complete and Unabridged

12 masterpieces – authors include
Ed McBain, Daphne du Maurier, Leslie Charteris, Cornell
Woolrich, John D. MacDonald, Erle Stanley Gardner, Ross
Macdonald and Rex Stout.

Murder, sabotage, psychological terror, theft, double cross-
ings and much more cram the pages of this action-packed
omnibus. The collection includes Ed McBain's *Storm*, Ross
Mcdonald's *Bearded Lady*, Rex Stout's *The Zero Clue*, Daphne
du Maurier's *Don't Look Now*, John D. MacDonald's *Death's
Eye View*, Erle Stanley Gardner's *Death Rides A Boxcar* and
Cornell Woolrich's *Nightmare* amongst others.

£4.95 paperback

THE MAMMOTH BOOK OF

SHORT **SPY** NOVELS

Complete and Unabridged

13 masterpieces — authors include
Ian Fleming, Leslie Charteris, John D. MacDonald,
W. Somerset Maugham, Erle Stanley Gardner, Sir Arthur
Conan Doyle and Cornell Woolrich.

A great collection of short novels of international intrigue,
conspiracy, plots and counterplots from the masters of the
espionage novel, including Ian Fleming, W. Somerset
Maugham, Sir Arthur Conan Doyle, Erle Stanley Gardner,
Peter O'Donnell and Cornell Woolrich.

The 544 pages of this omnibus are packed with famous
secret agents of fiction from James Bond, Simon Templar
and Ashenden to Modesty Blaise and Willie Garvin.

A bargain for all lovers of mystery and suspense.

£4.95 paperback

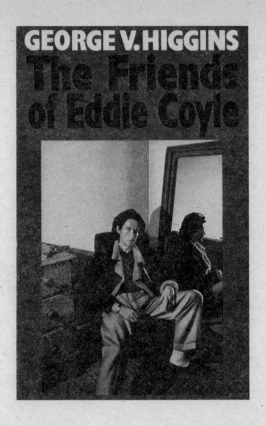

GEORGE V. HIGGINS
The Friends of Eddie Coyle

Eddie 'Fingers' Coyle got his nickname when some men he knew put his hand in a drawer, in a friendly fashion – and kicked it shut: Eddie had sold a man a gun that was traced. Now Eddie is back in business, and taking more care.

This highly praised, bestselling novel was made into a film of the same title starring Robert Mitchum.

£2.95 paperback

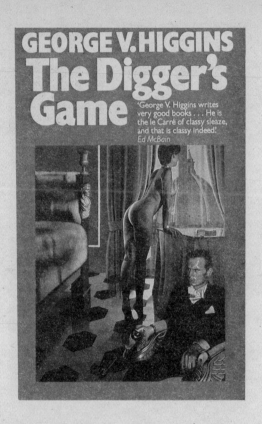

GEORGE V. HIGGINS
The Digger's Game

'George V. Higgins writes very good books . . . He is the le Carré of classy sleaze, and that is classy indeed.'
Ed McBain

The Digger, a Boston bar-owner, takes a package trip to Las Vegas at the invitation of the Regent Sportsmen's Club Inc. – which is curious. He wakes up with a savage hangover and a large debt to a person or persons unknown – which is worrying. He discovers he is in debt to the Greek – which is terrifying.

The Greek's interest rates are brutal and his debt-recovery techniques uncomfortably old-fashioned.

£2.95 paperback

GEORGE V. HIGGINS
**The Judgment
of Deke Hunter**

In this tough, tense novel Higgins turns his attention from
Boston's sleazy underworld to take a hard look at the law-
enforcers themselves. Deke Hunter is a Corporal in the
Massachusetts State Troopers and his story is one of
murder and corruption. This may be the 'respectable side
of crime' but the game is just as dirty.

£3.95 paperback

GEORGE V. HIGGINS
The Patriot Game

'George V. Higgins writes very good books . . . He is the le Carré of classy sleaze, and that is classy indeed.'
Ed McBain

Peter Riordan's a Federal Agent with a simple assignment. There's a man from Ireland somewhere in the US looking for arms. No one knows his name or his face, so they ask Riodan to do the looking.

He starts with Paul Doherty, the Digger's ecclesiastical brother and now a bishop, and 'Seats' Lobianco at the State House. Soon it begins to look like the friends of Mikey-mike Magro might be the men to help, preferably before Magro gets out of the slammer and kills the Digger.

£2.95 paperback

JOHN D. MACDONALD

TRAVIS McGEE

3 COMPLETE NOVELS
THE QUICK RED FOX
A DEADLY SHADE OF GOLD
BRIGHT ORANGE FOR THE SHROUD

His stories not only knock you out; they rabbit-punch you while you're on the floor.

Time Magazine

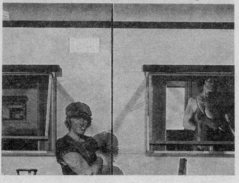

The Quick Red Fox, A Deadly Shade of Gold, and *Bright Orange for the Shroud* – three fast-moving thrillers featuring John D. MacDonald's modern knight-errant and master of wise-cracks in one bargain-price omnibus volume.

£3.50 paperback

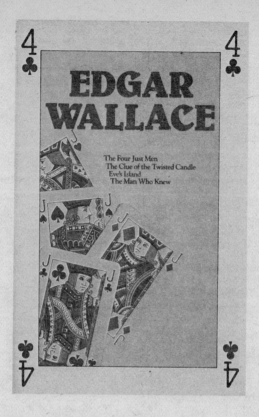

The most successful detective story writer who ever lived, Edgar Wallace, wrote more than 170 books with sales running into tens of millions. This value-for-money omnibus includes four of the best of his output, including his first and most famous, the classic *The Four Just Men*, and *Eve's Island*, *The Clue of the Twisted Candle* and *The Man Who Knew*.

£3.50 paperback

ORDER FORM

If you cannot find these titles in your bookshop, they can be obtained directly from the publisher. Please indicate the number of copies required and fill in the form overleaf in block letters.

The Mammoth Book of Short Fantasy Novels
___ Presented by Isaac Asimov   £4.95

The Mammoth Book of Short Crime Novels
___ Edited by Bill Pronzini and Martin H. Greenberg   £4.95

The Mammoth Book of Short Spy Novels
___ Edited by Bill Pronzini and Martin H. Greenberg   £4.95

The Friends of Eddie Coyle
___ by George V. Higgins   £2.95

The Digger's Game
___ by George V. Higgins   £2.95

The Judgement of Deke Hunter
___ by George V. Higgins   £3.95

The Patriot Game
___ by George V. Higgins   £2.95

Jack's Return Home
___ by Ted Lewis   £2.95

John D. MacDonald –
___ **3 Complete Novels**   £3.50

Edgar Wallace –
___ **4 Complete Novels**   £3.50

Please fill in the form below in block letters:

NAME_____

ADDRESS_____

_____

_____

_____

Send to Robinson Publishing Cash Sales,
P.O. Box 11, Falmouth, Cornwall TR10 9EN

Please enclose cheque or postal order to the value of the
cover price plus:

In UK only – 55p for the first book, 22p for the second
book, and 14p for each additional book to a maximum
£1.75.

BFPO and Eire – 55p for the first book, 22p for the second
book, and 14p for the next seven books and 8p for each
book thereafter.

Overseas – £1.25 for the first book, 31p per copy for each
additional book.

Whilst every effort is made to keep prices low, it is
sometimes necessary to increase prices at short notice.
Robinson Publishing reserve the right to show on covers,
and charge, new retail prices which may differ from those
advertised in text or elsewhere.